RADEK

RADEK

A Novel

Stefan Heym

Translated by Alexander Locascio

MONTHLY REVIEW PRESS

New York

Originally published in German as *Radek: Roman*
by C. Bertelsmann Verlag.

Library of Congress Cataloging-in-Publication Data
available from the publisher

ISBN paper: 978-158367-955-5
ISBN cloth: 978-1-58367-956-2

Typeset in Bulmer Monotype

MONTHLY REVIEW PRESS, NEW YORK
monthlyreview.org

5 4 3 2 1

TABLE OF CONTENTS

INTRODUCTION

Victor Grossman

THE LIVES OF STEFAN HEYM and of Karl Radek were conglomerates of countless contradictions, with definite personal similarities and both wholly shaped by events in a bloody century over full of huge victories and giant defeats, events still quarreled over by those who regard its final decade as a victory over totalitarianism while others, greatly diminished in number, stubbornly mourn a tragic, possibly permanent defeat.

How, at different times in that century, did Heym fit in, how did Radek? Neither ever really "fit in." Since the readers of these words probably have Radek's story ahead of them, with all of its suspense, I will concentrate on Heym, the author of this book, whose successes in the United States have long since been forgotten. I knew him personally.

BORN APRIL 10, 1913, INTO a well-off family in the industrial city of Chemnitz, the boy born as Helmut Flieg was bullied in school for being interested in poetry and also for being Jewish, this at a time when Nazi gangs were gathering for the kill. A poem, published when he was eighteen, caused him to get badly beaten and expelled from high school. It includes the following lines:

> Generals, majors!
> Like hyenas on corpse-fields, roaming about.
> One war for us they went and lost,
> But they're still hungry to fight—
> They gnaw at peace at others' cost!
> From Germany comes the light![1]

He was forced to escape to Berlin, where he mixed in left-wing intellectual circles until the catastrophic winter of 1933. In January Hitler became chancellor, in February the Nazis set fire to the Reichstag building, blaming it on the Communists, whose party they outlawed. In March the Enabling Law gave the Nazi Party total power and the first concentration camps filled up with leftist anti-fascists. Helmut Flieg changed his name to Stefan Heym, fled across the snow-bound mountain border, and landed in the German-exile colony of Prague.

In 1935 he won a rare scholarship to the University of Chicago and, with the help of dishwashing and other odd jobs, achieved both a B.A. and Master's degree (with research on his beloved poet Heinrich Heine). After two years as founder and editor of the *Deutsches Volksecho,* closely connected with the Communist Party, he took a daring risk: writing a novel in English. *Hostages* (Putnam, 1942), based on his two years in Prague, was lauded by *New York Times* critic Orville Prescott as "the best novel I have seen about life under the Nazis, the undying revolt of the supposedly conquered peoples and the methods by which the Nazis strive to rule. . . . *Hostages* is vastly superior, tense, tautly constructed, swift and terrible." A star-studded film based on the book with Oscar-winner Paul Lukas, double Oscar-winner Luise Rainer, and Greek star Katina Paxinou premiered in 1943.

In uniform, as a sergeant, then lieutenant, he was with U.S.

---

1. Peter Hutchinson, *Stefan Heym: The Perpetual Dissident* (Cambridge: Cambridge University Press, 1992), 9–10. The translation of the Heym poem is by Hutchinson.

Army troops from Normandy to the Battle of the Bulge. Using his language skills, his task was trying to reach German soldiers with broadcasts and leaflets urging them to give up in their increasingly hopeless war. After victory he became an editor of the U.S. Army–sponsored newspaper *Die Neue Zeitung* in Munich until his markedly leftist views cost him the job, upon which he left the army, returned to his new American homeland and turned again to fiction, again in English.

The Crusaders (Little, Brown, 1948) is the story of the American war against Germany, seen through the eyes of a uniformed German refugee. It tells of people fighting for a better world but also of greedy, "reformed" Nazis angling for good niches in the U.S. Zone and of egoistic, brutally oppressive American officers seeking personal glory as a ladder to wealthy postwar careers. Reviewer Malcolm Cowley wrote, in *The New Republic*: "It also has a thesis, and a sound one, namely, that the war was fought against evils, some of which exist in our own Army and nation." Again on the best-seller list, translated into German and twenty other languages, with sales in seven digits, it was Heym's all-time biggest success.

But the world was rapidly changing. Little, Brown risked only one more book by Heym, *The Eyes of Reason* (1951), about three Czech brothers meeting again after the war, soon to face the dramatic events of February 1948, when a takeover attempt by pro-Western leaders was met by huge demonstrations leading to full rule by the Communists.

The weapons race following the Armageddon-like destruction of Hiroshima and Nagasaki became the Cold War, hyped by the events in Prague, giant successes of the Communists in China and, most tellingly, the "Berlin Air-lift," when the Western occupying powers suddenly installed a new currency, threatening East Germany with a fatally suffocating flood of older paper. The resulting, predictable shut-off of West Berlin by the Soviets led to the dramatic Air Force supply of West Berlin and a total propaganda victory for the West.

Such events helped wreck the attempt by Henry Wallace and his Progressive Party to save the remnants of 1930s left-wing opposition. The massive stone-throwing attacks following an open-air concert with the great leftist Black singer and actor Paul Robeson in Peekskill, New York, in September 1949, attacks organized with the New York State Police but blamed on Robeson, symbolized the tight reign of the HUAC and Joseph McCarthy at home and Allen Dulles and George C. Marshall abroad.

After 1949 almost every Communist leader was sent to prison. The writer Howard Fast was jailed for three months, the "Hollywood Ten"—screenwriters, a director, a producer— were sent to penitentiaries for a year, and thousands were fired, blacklisted, barred from any work in their fields. The jingoistic hysteria accompanying the Korean War after June 1950 was overwhelming. Heym, having witnessed rabid anti-Communism in Germany, wanted no closer encounters, so he recrossed the Atlantic and, after some hunting around, joined other leftists such as Bertolt Brecht and composers Hanns Eisler and Paul Dessau in the (East) German Democratic Republic. With him was his American wife, Gertrude Gelbin, a skilled editor-publisher who was certainly of great assistance in editing his English.

In April 1953, after settling in East Berlin, he sent a protest letter to President Eisenhower about U.S. war making, and included with it his officer's reserve commission and his Bronze Star, received for participation in the Battle of the Bulge in 1944.

But very soon Heym and Gertrude were confronted by the "workers' uprising" of June 17, 1953, a major event marked for years in the West by a holiday and still lending its awkward name to a major thoroughfare, Strasse der 17th Juni 1953. It requires explanation—still controversial.

When the Red Army fought its way into eastern Germany in 1945, Nazi bigwigs fled west as fast as they could. Their genocidal brutality had meant death for over 25 million Soviet citizens, mostly women and children, and included over three million prisoners of war purposefully starved to death.

Among those moving out were the big landowners, often nobles, known as Junkers. Under the Soviet aegis, German farmers divided up all estates over 100 hectares (about 250 acres) among farm laborers, poor farmers, and the huge numbers of Germans expelled from enlarged Poland, from East Prussia, Czechoslovakia, and Hungary.

Even more important, armament factories, whole or ruined, were also confiscated, as agreed upon by Truman, Stalin, and Attlee at Potsdam. On June 30, 1946, in Saxony, East Germany's leading industrial state, a referendum asked voters: "Are you in favor of the law transferring corporations owned by war criminals and Nazi criminals into ownership by the people?" Much of the population was cynical, bitter about defeat, wrestling with the ideology leading to it, with deeply ingrained anti-socialist ideas and mixed reactions to Soviet occupation, including both its "everything for the children" and, in the early weeks, widespread rape. And yet an impressive 77.6 percent voted "Ja." New legislatures in the other eastern provinces adopted the decision while a similar "Ja" vote in western Hesse was vetoed by U.S. officials.

Krupp, Siemens, Messerschmitt, Agfa, Daimler-Benz—companies that fattened on the First World War, built up Hitler, and made billions with weapons production and slave labor during the Second World War—were gone from the East, and with them the huge banks and insurance companies that had done the financing.

It did not take those companies long to reestablish in West Germany. All but the most infamous industrialists were certified as "clean" or, if sentenced, were soon amnestied and back on top of the heap. All had a devouring obsession for a comeback in the East, a goal they shared with their American overseers, who soon supported a rebuilt Germany—West, and as soon as possible East—as a base against their newly rediscovered old enemy, the USSR. Together they built up their secret networks and waited for opportunities.

They soon found one. Stalin's unification offer in March 1952 for an all-German, freely elected government, but unarmed, and, like Austria and Finland, in no pacts, was rejected by Washington and West German Chancellor Adenauer, who preferred NATO membership and expansion. The GDR was thus faced by a need to go it alone. This meant announcing its aim to build socialism but also meant building up its own coke, steel, and other heavy industry, despite few natural resources and while still paying reparations to the USSR.

The result was a tightening up: no more price cuts or commuter subsidies, higher taxes on small business, tougher treatment of dissidents and, most important, 10 percent higher quotas in the factories to increase productivity.

Puzzlement turned to dissatisfaction; the new leaders in Moscow (after Stalin's death) saw trouble coming and dictated the New Course, full of promise and reversing hardships, but keeping one decisive item: the increased production quotas. Six days later construction workers on the Stalin Allee went on strike and demonstrated, soon joined by young gangs from West Berlin, who went on a wreckage and arson spree until Soviet tanks moved in, with strict orders: "No shooting." Their strict curfew, affecting rebels in many towns and cities, ended the uprising.

Putting aside his novel, Heym began a biweekly newspaper column, "*Offen gesagt*" (Speaking Frankly). He wrote:

> Difficult as it may be for Germans after the war, Hitlerism and American propaganda, they must come to terms with the problem of the Soviet Union.... That is necessary, first of all, because whatever occurs in the Soviet Union decisively influences the world and Germany. It is also necessary because the attitude toward the Soviet Union of every German, especially every German worker, determines their view towards the world and all political events. It is not possible to want progress, democracy, socialism, everything noble and decent and good and at the same time be against the Soviet Union ... which points the path to the future. Every other path leads to atomic war, with the absolute and final destruction of all Germany.

He also wrote:

> There are different kinds of freedom, and one must sharply decide which to support. For example, there is the democratic right of workers to demand fair wages and decent working conditions; that is a freedom which should not be denied them and which every thinking person will defend. There is the freedom of public and private criticism, the freedom to pound on the desks of people in office armchairs who don't want to hear it, and, when necessary, to pull those chairs out from under their backsides—and this freedom must be used. . . . And then there is the freedom of big capitalists to grab back the publicly owned factories, mines and steel mills in the GDR—that is the freedom, basically, which people shouted for on June 17th, and that is a freedom which must not be granted those gentlemen, nor the freedom to start another war, an atomic war.

These themes concerned Heym all his life. His appraisal of the official media: "The cliché-ridden language, well-meant but so often repetitive, with the same constant word connections in the press and radio, are not likely to win people to read or listen and understand them."

The GDR population was composed of a changing amalgam of people, pro and con, some fanatical on returning eastward (always called "re-settlers" in the GDR, never refugees), some warily secretive pro-fascists, many pro-capitalists, far too many two-faced careerists, but perhaps a majority interested above all in building their own normal lives. And then there were those old Communists and Social Democrats, plus many young people, who believed in socialism as a goal and supported the GDR. Such growing acceptance and often enthusiasm, increasing after June 17, was due in no small measure to the immediate East German ousting of the Nazified teachers' staffs in all schools, replacing them with "new teachers," briefly trained, without experience, but anti-fascist. The same was done in the courts, the entire judicial system, the police, and administration at all levels—the exact opposite of West German practice. These radical measures did not make things easier, yet were crucial!

Combining with growing approval, however, there was anguish at the early blunders, anger at the methods of some universal bully types, and above all discontent with the leaders' lack of rapport with the majority, a result of that undigestible language in the daily press and news.

Such progressives (like many of my co-students at the journalism school in Leipzig) waited eagerly every two weeks for Heym's "Speaking Frankly," which dealt with so many of our questions, seeking and expressing the truth while skillfully avoiding stultifying "Marxist-Leninist" jargon.

The New Course, which followed June 17, brought big improvements: no more sudden power breakdowns; big semi-annual price cuts instead of price increases; a reversal of tax and other nasty measures; a switch from house repair to housing construction, its start and symbol again the Stalin Allee—and a sharp decrease in repressive methods against dissenters, a clear result of Stalin's death and Khrushchev's rule in Moscow.

It was also a good period for Stefan Heym. In 1953 his critical American novel *Goldsborough,* about striking miners in Pennsylvania was released, in East German Leipzig but in his original English. Gertrude had organized a publishing venture after moving to Berlin titled Seven Seas Books. It played a remarkable role for left-wing writers in the United States whose books could not get printed or, if they were, were sold only in the few remaining leftist bookshops in big cities. Thus, authors like Ring Lardner, Jr., Howard Fast, Albert Maltz, Alvah Bessie, all of whom had spent time behind bars, and many others, from Britain, Australia, Canada, South Africa, and India, could earn some needed income, much of it from sales in the Eastern Bloc and a new best sales area, India.

Goldsborough and *Crusaders*, translated into German, made Heym one of the most popular GDR authors, admired and honored at every turn. On top levels his choice of the GDR was naturally welcome propaganda, on readers' level his books were not just very good reading but his columns and speeches still contained the frank criticism and clear language that accompanied his total support of the GDR, the USSR, and socialism. But in the GDR, almost suddenly, tides could turn or, to change metaphors, the roller-coaster could take a new, steep dip. Nikita Khrushchev's far from "secret speech" in February 1956, describing the terrible crimes of the Stalin era, led to a brief uprising and leadership change in Poland, followed by revolt in Hungary, unleashed by students and other intellectuals and leading to the deployment of Soviet tanks with over 700 Red Army and 2,500 Hungarian deaths, including the hanging or other execution by anti-Communists of over two hundred Party supporters or security men.

The GDR leaders wanted no replica; their homes were moved well out of the city, and the loosened intellectual screws were tightened. This inevitably hit Heym, who had written a novel based on the events of June 17, 1953, describing both the blunders leading up to it and varying responses, contrasting the courageous efforts of a factory union leader with a lack of them by the same plant's Party leader. At the same time, he pulled no punches in denouncing what he called a brash Western attempt to turn the crisis into regime change—or GDR downfall—and stressing the role of the United States.

Indeed, the CIA-sponsored Radio in the American Sector (RIAS) later boasted that, though it had not originally planned or directed it, its broadcasts had acted "as the catalyst of the uprising. . . . Without RIAS the uprising would never have taken place in this form." In fact, it was RIAS that raised the call for a general strike. And Heym made this very clear.

That was not sufficient for the GDR leadership, however. They regarded every criticism of their Socialist Unity Party as a dangerous hole in the dike, and the book could not be printed.

This quarrel, at the start of Heym's conflict with the authorities, became a sort of game of chess played on the roller-coaster.

It was played against men most of whose Utopian goals were basically similar to his, but whose earlier lives had been shaped by life-and-death struggles against Nazis, imprisoned, in a perilous underground, or fighting in Spain—but often also by petty-bourgeois cultural schooling and, significantly, Stalin's iron-clad style and methods.

This shaky game was played precisely along a delicate Berlin borderline between two world systems, where changes in either one, or between the two, affected every move in the match. For GDR leaders, not without overwhelming evidence, that Berlin border was a barrier against an adversary dominated by the same forces they had feared and fought in the barricades of Madrid, partisan hideouts in the Cevennes, or the defense of Stalingrad.

But these men also had their secrets, especially after the Khrushchev revelations, which touched on a few GDR leaders. And they had some new secrets as well. The press openness demanded by Heym seemed impossible in light of the killings in Hungary or, in 1973, Salvador Allende's attempt to build a socialist society while permitting a free press and freedom of organization—ending in a pool of blood for himself and thousands of others.

Heym kept writing and speaking, always in support of socialism and always provocatively against censorship or anything restricting open criticism. In 1959 he was awarded a National Prize but in 1969 his critical yet sympathetic biography of Ferdinand Lassalle (1825-1864), a major founder of the Social Democratic Party leading Germany today, was vetoed by those in charge (never called censors!) because of critical passages about Marx and Engels. So he published the book in 1969 in West Germany—and paid a small fine for violating regulations.

In 1961, the rulers of West Germany found a second giant opportunity. Increasing fears for the future and their consumer enticements for the present motivated growing waves to "go west," visibly wrecking the GDR economy. The Wall was built as a countermeasure. Heym, though greatly troubled, stuck with the GDR, as he later described it in the *New York Times* (March 23, 1975):

> To an extent, [the GDR] is catching up—strangely enough, with the aid of the Wall, which was both an act of desperation and a new beginning. The Wall set an end to the westward stampede of people. Ugly though it was (and is), it gave visible evidence of the decision that the experiment called socialism would not be given up in that one-third of Germany called the German Democratic Republic.

(President Kennedy allegedly remarked: "It's not a very nice solution, but a wall is a hell of a lot better than a war!")

But the chess game between an inherently stubborn Stefan Heym and adamant GDR leaders continued its shaky course. After Leonid Brezhnev replaced the ousted, more open-minded Khrushchev in 1964, ambitious young Erich Honecker, with strong ties in Moscow, derailed the promising economic reforms of his boss, Walter Ulbricht, at the notorious, numbing Eleventh Plenum of the Socialist Unity Party (SED) with an attack against demoralizing, decadent cultural waves from the West, especially the United States, specifically and threateningly including Heym. When Honecker succeeded in ousting the aging Ulbricht in 1971, however, he surprised all intellectuals by greatly easing pressures: as long as it is pro-socialist (an elastic term) there would be "no taboos." Heym's sixtieth birthday in April 1973 was marked by surprisingly friendly articles in the Party press. Some of his books were now getting published, like the Lassalle novel, though in many fewer thousands than in demand. Readers hunted them out like gems.

GDR bookshops were always crowded. Customers took hand baskets and filled them up. They were often on the lookout for books by Western authors, including Americans like Joseph Heller, John Updike, James Baldwin, and J. D. Salinger. And for books on domestic matters by GDR authors. How openly critical were they, was sharper criticism embedded in the text, perhaps disguised? Did their criticism aim at improving the GDR—or abandoning it? The most debatable and the best written were often "stoop-ware" (*Bückware*), reserved unseen behind the counter for relatives and favored customers. Library waiting lists for such books were often very long.

Whereas theater plays and especially films were treated more strictly because of their far broader audiences (in the nasty year of the Eleventh Plenum a dozen often very good but too sharply critical films were shelved), books, which were ultra-cheap, had it rather easier. A result was a continuing number of thought-provoking, nuanced, well-written books. The authors were totally ignored in the West, a taboo, basically censorship, that also affected GDR films, including some true masterpieces. But this did not apply to those seen as potential pro-Western "dissenters," who were invited to give tours, were wined and dined, honored, and if possible "won over." After the Wall in 1961 their number was reduced; if permitted to visit the West they were wooed, if not, calls for freedom were amplified.

With Stefan Heym such literary-political managers were uncertain; he never approved the West German government or system. But his sparring with GDR authorities sufficed in one way; if they rejected his books he could get them published, in German or English, in West Germany, England, or Switzerland. And they sold! His name popularity and his background story gave him certain advantages, or privileges, including travel.

So Heym kept writing, though sometimes paying a fine because of financial misdemeanors. His books jumped from century to century. One, based on the Old Testament, was about King David. Another centered on Daniel Defoe's (painfully punished) defiance of Queen Anne. A third turned to the armed resistance to Prussia after the 1848 Revolution; the book on Ferdinand Lassalle analyzed the start of Germany's political union movement. In *Ahasver* (English title: *The Wandering Jew*), Heym starts with Lucifer, moves to Christ in Jerusalem, to

Germany in the Martin Luther era, then to the GDR, then back again. Common to them all is a vision of Utopia; harsh, barely disguised criticism of GDR party bureaucrats; and, aside from Defoe, Jewish central figures, reflecting not only Heym's lifelong interest in Jewishness but also a criticism of the strong tendency among party leaders, even Jewish ones, to avoid discussion of anything related to the "Jewish question," especially when Arab-Israel conflicts sharpened.

Most of his novels did finally get printed in the GDR after 1974, in small editions, until 1976 and a new sharp break with Honecker, who had fallen into what was certainly a well-planned Western trap laid by talented, foxy poet and singer Wolf Biermann. After a hugely popular concert in Cologne, and attacking GDR leaders repeatedly on West German television, Biermann, a westerner who had moved to the GDR, was barred from returning. The resulting pressures to approve Honecker's decision led to the estrangement of a troubling number of actors, writers, and intellectuals, including Heym, who, a longtime friend of Biermann, immediately joined the protest.

But in a visit to London he made clear to an interviewer that he still discerned two sides:

> To the writer, the gulf between the imperfections of socialism and the promise it holds poses a question of ethics: does he do more harm than good by a full reflection in his work of the new and often cruel and crude contradictions? Will the public understand and draw the proper conclusions, or will his critique, his presentation of the mistakes and frailties of the new system give aid and comfort to the enemy—his enemy as well as of those he criticized?. . . The purpose of revolution is to create freedom. The danger of too much freedom in a revolutionary society is that it gives the enemies of the revolution freedom to destroy it. For that reason the revolution, which is made for freedom, must therefore limit it in order to maintain itself. . . . This immediately raises the question of who is to limit freedom and how far to limit

it. History, in coming up with a Bonaparte or a Stalin, has not always answered that question in a satisfactory manner.

This question remained basic for Heym. But the conflict with GDR leaders sharpened. In response to unrelenting surveillance by the state security agents, the "Stasi," he published *Collin* in London in 1980, representing, in its attack on a fictionalized security boss, very open defiance. With it the situation on that roller-coaster reached such a low point that in 1979 Heym, along with eight others, was expelled from the GDR Writers Association.

In the mid-1980s the GDR was confronted with severe problems: immensely costly attempts not to fall even further behind West Germany in modern armaments; the need to develop, alone, without Sony, IBM, or even Soviet help, indispensable industrial electronics; and fulfilling Honecker`s promise to provide all citizens with modern, easily affordable housing by 1990. The unqualified leadership, clearly unable to maintain a stable economy without raising prices or rents, thus further troubled the citizenry.

By 1989, while Gorbachev and West German leaders secretly conferred behind the scenes, complaints grew ever louder, protesting crowds ever bigger. Honecker was thrown out; Party control was rapidly waning. On November 4, at a giant mass meeting on Berlin's central Alexanderplatz, over twenty personalities offered varying messages. Heym won loud applause from the critical, sarcastic, but almost triumphant, often jolly, crowd for his words:

> It is as if a window was pushed open after all the years of stagnation, years of mental, economic, political dullness and fog of stupid clichés and bureaucratic arbitrariness, of blind and deaf officialdom. What a change! . . . Today, with you, who have gathered voluntarily for freedom and democracy and for a socialism which is worth the name.

Five days later the Wall was opened, to the joy of millions, but swelling the chances for another major attack against the GDR, this time successful.

Within three weeks even leading "dissident" Heym could not ignore the direction of the rapidly changing events. With an imposing number of other GDR critics he framed a petition, "For Our Country," which, after again castigating the Stalinist past, offered a choice:

> EITHER we insist on the independence of the GDR and attempt to develop a society based on solidarity, guaranteeing peace and social justice, freedom for the individual, free travel for everyone and the preservation of the environment, OR ELSE we must accept that . . . with unrealizable conditions for their aid to the GDR, dictated by influential economic and political forces in the Federal Republic, a sellout of our material and moral values will begin and, sooner or later, the GDR will be incorporated into the Federal Republic. Let us take the first path. . . . We can still reclaim the anti-fascist and humanitarian ideals with which we once began.

The petition quickly received a record number of over a million signatures. But within four months it was obsolete.

In the GDR of 1989, even in its death throes, everyone still had jobs, there was inexpensive food and a home for all, one could still go, at dirt-cheap prices, to theaters, concerts, the best of opera, great films. (Ironically, *Coming Out*, the first GDR film based on gay equality and gay rights, a fine film, premiered the same evening the Wall opened, and was completely upstaged.)

In the end consumerism proved too strong. The commodity assortment, latest fashions, deluxe goods, Mercedeses, tropical imports like bananas, travel to Pisa or the Golden Gate, a promise to quickly switch to the idolized West Mark currency, tipped the scales even for millions who, like Heym, eagerly sought GDR improvements but had not bargained for its burial.

In March the votes were counted, the die was cast. On October 3 crowds watched the fireworks, heard welcoming speeches, and sang their new-old anthem, "Deutschland über alles." I don't imagine that Heym joined in.

He did join in, literally, by running in 1994 as non-party candidate for the explicitly anti-Stalinist Party of Democratic Socialism, follow-up of the old SED (and predecessor of today's Die Linke). A mass-media smear tying Heym to the Stasi was disproven. He won East Berlin's most prestigious seat and, as the oldest member of the Bundestag, was entitled to make the new session's opening speech. It was beautifully written, humorous, never hostile, but it included words otherwise taboo:

> The efficiency of the West, its democratic forms and other qualities of life which the Easterners can take up, are obvious. But on the other hand? Is there no experience from life in the late GDR which might be useful if adopted for Germany's common future? Perhaps the guaranteed job? The guaranteed access to one's learned trade? The security of a roof over one's head?. . . Please do not underestimate a human way-of-living in which, despite all restrictions, money was not the decisive element but rather the right to an equal job for man and woman, an affordable apartment. Where the most important body part was not a sharp elbow.

For the first time the Christian Democratic delegates chattered or read newspapers during his speech in the Bundestag and refused to applaud at the end.

Stocky old Heym, his leonine head now more bowed than ever, took part in vain attempts to maintain some more fairness in the merciless annexation—colonization—of the ex-GDR, then turned to writing two jolly, unpolitical books, in German with a Yiddish inflection. He died of heart failure during a symposium in Israel dealing with his lifelong favorite, Heinrich Heine, another Jewish intellectual, well acquainted with exile and rebellious in many directions. Heym is buried in the enormous Jewish cemetery in Weissensee, East Berlin.

SIX YEARS EARLIER, IN 1995, Stefan Heym published the long novel you are holding. It was another of his books about a brainy, witty writer, as in most cases, Jewish, just like Heym. But he is not Heym, who shows him much sympathy but keeps a critical distance. Like the author, Radek has trouble with the powers that be. In Radek's USSR, however, that was far more dangerous than in the proto-McCarthy United States or the GDR of Ulbricht or Honecker.

When Joseph Stalin died in 1953, Heym wrote a sorrowing eulogy, not idolatrous, but indeed based on praise. After Nikita Khrushchev's detailed account of crimes committed under Stalin's rule in 1956, Heym joined most remaining leftists in burying such sympathy.

Some "ultra-leftists" still demonstrate under banners showing Marx, Lenin, sometimes Mao, but also Stalin. Such views are isolated; yet how can anyone cherish the memory of a man responsible for the imprisonment and execution of so frightening a number? (For me, this is also a personal matter: I knew well some who survived and some whose relatives did not.)

Yet despite the broad scythe of his killing, a completely total repudiation of every facet in his life is, for anyone interested in history, simplistic. Heym has related Stalin to Napoleon, an emperor who blanketed Europe with corpses—but also led in ending feudalism and official anti-Semitism. But with Stalin, can an objective examination find any positive factors?

I would stress one point: the negative meaning of the term "Stalinism," so frequent in political discourse, is constantly extended beyond a description of his one-man, murderous command style to act as a verbal condemnation of all the USSR represented, from start to finish—its tragedies, its achievements, and its sacrifices, including its bitter, costly but final triumph over Hitler fascism. And, beyond that, the term is used to discredit the whole idea of socialism, with anyone advocating socialism running the risk of being condemned as a "Stalinist." *Radek* centers its attack against Stalin, justified in so many ways. But in this I find that something is missing. There must have been something in those years to evoke a more rounded picture of the USSR, even praise, sometimes enthusiastic praise. As with the GDR, some visitors did alter their views, but they often saw what they wanted to see, positive or negative. The great French writer André Gide was greatly soured by what he saw or "was shown." The great writer Lion Feuchtwanger (like Heym a German-Jewish refugee in the United States, though one who stayed) visited the USSR a year later, in 1937, and refuted Gide.

Feuchtwanger attended four days of the "purge trials," including that of Radek. He analyzed what he saw, summarized his conclusions, and decided the trials were genuine. Heym, a half-century later, was able to read the records. His conclusions are certainly closer to the truth.

But what of the broader picture? Heym, concentrating on Radek and the trial, is so scornful of Stalin that he writes almost nothing of the changing Soviet scene except for his own bad housing—and a few remarks like the following:

> . . . his analysis made it clear that the Soviet Union was facing economic bankruptcy, more likely tomorrow than the day after.
> . . . the breakdowns and collapses of Stalin's Five-Year Plans
> . . . Everyone can see that the successes ascribed to our Josif Vissarionovich, examined even cursorily, are anything but that
> . . .

Feuchtwanger, though always cautious and not reticent about shortages and problems (which he raised in a discussion with Stalin), became enthusiastic. Of course he knew nothing of Gulags, and the waves of arrests had hardly begun. But here are some quotations from his book:

I was at first surprised and dubious when I found that all the people with whom I came into contact in the Soviet Union, and this includes casual and obviously spontaneous conversations, were at one with the general scheme of things, even if they were sometimes critical of minor points. Indeed, everywhere in that great city of Moscow there was an atmosphere of harmony and contentment, even of happiness. . . . True, the years of hunger are over. In the many shops food of all kinds can be obtained in great variety and at prices well within the reach of the average citizen. . . . It is only recently that his larder has become so well stocked. In two years, from 1934 to 1936, food consumption per head in Moscow increased by 28.8 percent. . . . Moreover, anyone who knew the earlier Moscow would be astounded by the improvement in clothing. The Soviet people have endured many long years of the worst forms of privation; and the times when light and water were becoming increasingly scarce, and they lined up outside the shops for bread and herrings, are still fresh in their memories. Their economic planning has vindicated itself and has got rid of these gravest miseries. . . . The citizens of Moscow joke about . . . minor inconveniences, usually, if not always, with complete good-humor, but they never think of allowing these shortcomings to blind them to the big things which life in the Soviet Union alone can offer. It is the peasants who are most deeply conscious of the difference. . . . Now these people have food in plenty. They carry on their farming intelligently and with increasing success. They have clothes, movies, radio, theatres, and newspapers. They have learned to read and write, and their children can follow the occupations to which they are attracted. The individual's feeling of complete security, his comfortable certainty that the state is really there for him and not he for the state, goes far to explain the naive pride with which the Moscow citizens speak of "our factories," "our agriculture," "our buildings," "our theatres," and "our army."[2]

---

2. Lion Feuchtwanger, *Moscow 1937: My Visit Described for My Friends,* trans. Irene Josephy (New York: Viking Press, 1937).

Whom should one believe? We have learned to be very skeptical, but was all this just a Potemkin village staging? Many reacted like Gide. Others not, like W. E. B. Du Bois, the Fabian author H. G. Wells, the great Black singer and actor Paul Robeson.

Or perhaps a mix of both reactions? But can one really overlook the accomplishments of those years—a huge new iron, steel, and machine industry, the Dneprostroi Dam, Europe's biggest, literacy, medical care, the fabled Moscow subway, all constructed by millions, not Stalin, though under his rule. And certainly most impressive of all, the resultant ability to withstand and defeat the giant Hitler-led attack.

And though deploring one-man dictatorship—its uncontrolled power, self-righteousness as alone correct (and approved by toadies and careerists), its frequent brutality—one cannot ignore the fact that masses often favor a single leader, good or evil, who can speak to them in their own language, provide answers to their questions, offer hope and, perhaps, carry out promises. This does not apply only to people unacquainted with democracy but to Hitler and Ho Chi Minh, Mao and Mandela, Roosevelt, elected four times, and Trump, elected just once, I hope. It also applies to Stalin, especially during the war, when for millions he was a symbol of their homes and homeland. Heym, writing in 1994, seems to ignore such complications.

But does the repudiation of Stalin in *Radek* also abandon visions of a future Utopia, free of hunger, insecurity, military destruction? Is the downfall of the USSR, some early causes of which were indicated by Heym, truly proof that it is a useless dream to strive for a socialist world that is no longer built on profits and moneymaking? Or of the GDR?

I wonder, on the contrary, whether they are not urgently necessary. Several immense catastrophes now threaten the world. One is the destruction of the environment, with the floods, drowning coastlines, fires, hurricanes, and droughts that we are increasingly witnessing.

Another problem is joblessness, on the one hand, extreme

exploitation on the other. If pittance-paid textile workers in Asia, harvesters of tea, coffee, cocoa, bananas, and palm oil in the South, diggers of coltan in Congo, and fruit-pickers in California were to join in struggle with former industry workers in the North, this could make gains, maybe even succeed—or be met by urgent countermeasures leading straight to fascism.

The biggest threat, for some the most remunerative one, is war, ever more war, ever closer to use of the Armageddon weapons that could end all other problems for the human species.

As I see it, all these problems are caused, basically, by a circle of millionaires and billionaires who have only contempt for the needs and lives of the more than 90 percent they have overtaken with their swollen, ever more astronomic fortunes. And these people seek world hegemony!

The only genuine solution I can imagine is a total abolition of their positions, possessions, and their wealth, as soon as it is possible. Would Stefan Heym, would Karl Radek, have agreed?

RADEK

For Inge
and in memoriam to Heinar Kipphardt
who also followed the traces

of Karl Radek

BOOK ONE

Between the door and doorpost
I will prophesy unto you:
the statue of liberty
has not yet been cast.
The furnace is red hot.
We may yet burn our fingers.
—GEORG BÜCHNER, *Danton's Death*

1

The eternal Polish Jew . . .

No, he had not misheard, even if he had only stood in the entrance doorway to the hall, since they hadn't let him into the hall itself: not you, Comrade Radek, the marshal grinned, not you.

He had heard right, Radek assured himself again; the evil word had been spoken too loudly and clearly for it to have been otherwise; by whom, he hadn't been able to determine, although the voice sounded familiar to him. Besides, that wasn't important; what was important was the laughter that had gloatingly followed, from more than one party convention delegate, and the self-satisfied expression on the face of Comrade Ebert, who sat next to the old, occasionally dozing Bebel at the board table. Now they had what they had been seeking for a long time during their inter-fractional conflicts: an enemy that they could call by its name, and which they could bash together.

He couldn't help the fact that he was a Jew, and from Lemberg at that. A Jew, his blessed mother had said, has to be twice as capable as the others, and one of his uncles—already he couldn't remember which of the two—added in all seriousness: remember that, Lolek. He hadn't even wanted to be a Jew, but rather a true Pole, his language the melodious Polish, reminiscent of French, his ideal the great Mickiewicz, poet and revolutionary. But at home, they spoke German; German was the language of culture, and culture, they firmly believed—Mama and his uncles; Papa had been dead for a long time—was the most necessary thing for enlightened Jews. And it was the language of lords in Galicia and in all countries that the emperor ruled from Vienna, and the Jews always held fast to the lords who, if at all, were the most likely to provide protection.

He, Lolek Sobelsohn, who had found himself in opposition since he was able to think, did not believe in the old wisdom. He believed in freedom, and the rights of the oppressed, and the most fiery warriors for freedom and the rights of the oppressed were the Poles, and he decided to lend them his word and his pen.

And now, he stood here, outside, in front of the door to the hall in which the convention of the great Social Democratic Party of Germany dealt exhaustively and down to the most absurd detail with his person, at a time when the clouds of war were rising darkly on the horizon and there were more important things for the delegates to consider, and they calculated how many pennies had been contributed to the party coffers of which local groups on payment days, and whether he could be considered a member in good standing at all, he who had little sense for such order, and had perhaps just been broke because he had spent his last few pennies on pipe tobacco and was urgently waiting for the next money transfer to arrive from Bremen or Leipzig from the comrade editors for one of his articles, and who therefore had to sign a new application for membership where he had just settled: Radek, Karl, the eternally wandering Polish Jew…

But the Poles also bore a good measure of guilt for this hounding of him; more precisely, Comrade Jogiches, or Tyszka as he called himself in Warsaw, who now, here in the German Empire—the Revolution of 1905 was long over—with the support of dear Rosa, Rosa Luxemburg, ruled his little exile group of the Social Democratic Party of the Kingdom of Poland and Lithuania with an iron fist, while the comrades in Warsaw, due to their work in the underground struggle, conducted their own politics and received their thrashings at the hands of the tsarist Okhrana, and he, Radek, who sought to support the poor comrades in Warsaw with his journalism, was in return expelled by Leo Jogiches and Rosa Luxemburg from the SDKPiL.

★

Later, during an evening beer with Henke, he learned that things were a little different than he had believed regarding the eternal Polish Jew.

Henke from Bremen, whose delegate mandate they hadn't been able to take away—as his had been taken away from him—was a friend, to the extent that friendship could last under the pressure of almost the entire party apparatus, and Henke reported that young Liebknecht, by no means an anti-Semite, was the one who had tossed the phrase into the debate, not in order to deride Radek, but rather to defend him against the party executive, whose speaker, Comrade Müller, with spiteful insinuation, had painted a picture of such a type—nowhere settled and therefore suspicious—for the delegates: expelled for dishonorable actions from the ranks of the Social Democratic Party of the Kingdom of Poland and Lithuania, according to Müller, this person was now moving across Europe in order to register in the respective party of Germany, Austria, Belgium, Switzerland, or whatever country, thus keeping the whole International on tenterhooks with his case for years to come. And he had added that of course nobody would make such a fuss about an ordinary worker; but a man of letters, and especially such an arrogant one: please!... And he had also asked, sanctimoniously, whether for example the German party should reopen a case that a brother party had already conducted, and pay the travel expenses for witnesses from Warsaw, Paris, Petersburg, and Bern, and again conduct interrogations as to whether the man sentenced to expulsion by a special court of the Polish Central Committee had in fact embezzled trade union funds and had carried books that were not his property to the pawnshop, and had refused to pay back borrowed sums of money to comrades, with the cheeky justification that his social democratic Marxist worldview forbade him from paying back debts, and how he had rewarded a youth comrade in Krakow who had welcomed him hospitably and hosted him by shitting in his bed. The money of the German working class was truly too dear for such a pursuit of justice, and as for the rest, Comrade Ebert had explained conclusively enough the irresponsible manner in which the person spoken of here, precisely this Karl Radek, interfered in the affairs of the party, without ever having felt—in contrast to his wife, who at least occasionally paid her dues—the obligation of belonging to the party as a paying member.

According to Henke.

Radek saw the uncertainly flickering look and the tormented expression around the man's mouth and sensed that he was not yet completely finished, however well-considered and well-structured his report had been—ultimately, Henke, editor-in-chief of the Bremen party newspaper, knew how to deal with the construction of a piece of journalistic prose.

Henke pulled out the cardboard coaster from under his beer glass and, under the pressure of his finger, let it rotate slowly. "In the near future," he said, "the *Bürgerzeitung* won't be able to print anything by you."

Radek nodded. He had expected something like that. "You are of course aware, Comrade Henke," he said calmly, "that all the banal talk this afternoon and the accusations against me, all of them unproven, represent only a particularly crude form of the fight against the Left which the party executive has been waging for so long. We've been giving them hell, from your newspaper in Bremen and from Göppingen and Leipzig, and now they're striking back, and although they're taking it out on Radek, you're the target. As for me, I'll know how to defend myself. Who are this Ebert and Müller? Bureaucratic souls, uncreative. And who is Jogiches? A party tyrant, who gets all his thoughts from

Luxemburg, who clings to him with every fiber of her being in the permanent fear that he could leave her alone in her cold bed."

Radek broke off; Henke's eyes had widened in fright; how could somebody speak in such a way about this woman, who was regarded almost as a saint, above all by the party left. And it *was* a mistake, Radek admitted to himself, to talk about Rosa that way; what did he gain from that, from Henke or anyone else? But that's how he was: your tongue, Lolek, runs faster than your reason—who had said that, Mama? Or the other Rosa, his wife?—your tongue will be your doom.

"Fine," he said, "then don't publish me anymore, Comrade Henke, in the *Bremer Bürgerzeitung*. I will continue to write, even if nobody publishes me anymore, like the silkworm spins. But you, who in spite of all difficulties are trying to preserve something of old Marx's spirit within this social democracy: if you give in now, you'll be beaten for all time."

She had come from Leipzig, his good wife, had taken a leave of absence from the hospital she worked at, in order to be with him during these difficult nights and to warm him with the warmth of her body. The others always believed that he didn't mind the attacks and defamations, because he had a way of shrugging off the agitation against him with a couple of witty remarks and a strong wink of the eyes behind his glasses. Only she, his Rosa, knew—although the other Rosa, Luxemburg, should have also known, since she had known him long enough—how much the slander, like the Shirt of Nessus, got under his skin.

"Oh, my poor man," she said, and slipped her arm under his neck and nestled against him, "but you're made of tough stuff; you'll survive it."

He had always survived, until now; starting already with the mockery of his classmates in Lemberg, who noisily followed him—the smallest and slightest of them, with thick glasses that always slipped down—on his way home, until his mother came up to them and chased them away and picked up the books he had dropped, because he always carried books with him and read, in a way building an ideal world around him, which he then tried to turn into reality by the power of his speech alone. For this reason, and also due to terrorist agitation, as stated in the verdict, the faculty expelled him from the grammar school, and he had to move to Tarnow with Mama, to two hideous tenement houses, in order to continue his studies there, and to finally take the *Abitur* examination in another school; oh, he had learned early on what bourgeois freedoms were like.

But his real school was a different one, its earliest teacher a homeless man from the countryside he—half a child—met at night on a park bench, and who told him about the revolt of the peasants, the Polish, in the heroic year 1846; and then the journeymen hatters who held their union meetings in Jitzchak Apfelblüth's bakery, and whom he was allowed to translate and read to from the writings the old man had been sent by the party from Vienna: the Erfurt Program, explained by Kautsky; *Woman and Socialism*, which Bebel had written in his better days; Lassalle's speeches, and Mehring's history of German Social Democracy.

Then, suddenly, he sensed the presence of his Rosa and thought, how dumb can a man be, dumb, deaf, and without feeling, and he turned to her, and then he lay and enjoyed her arousal, and his, which increased more and more, and thought: to hell with theories, left, right, and center; how often does a human being live? Just once; come here, woman.

*

Usually afterward he soon fell asleep, relaxed and happy, a man with solid nerves and simple needs.

Not this time. His head was spinning again, and there was restlessness in his heart. No, they wouldn't dare. The motion was too crude and too transparent: to amend the statutes—ret-roactively, even—in order to be able to apply them against him, Radek, to the effect that anyone who had been expelled from a fraternal party, for whatever reason, could not be admitted to the German party without the express consent of that party. The young Liebknecht had spoken against it; well, he was a leftist and accordingly unpopular with the majority; but the delegate Kurt Rosenfeld as well, doctor of law and widely known and feared as a lawyer, had—"Retroactive! Retroactive!"—had pointed out with all severity that not even in the bourgeoisie were such viola-tions of the most fundamental principles of law tolerated... They won't dare, he thought—but Büchner's Danton had said that, and they had dared to, and it had eneded with the guillotine for Danton. Why was it that they had all conspired against him, the German party as well as the SDKPiL, of which he had been such a proud member for so long?

He was too full of himself and his own opinions; he had been told that by more than one person who meant him well; Lensch in Leipzig, for example, who edited the *Volkszeitung*, or Zeitkin, or Comrade Mehring; and he had too little generosity and not a trace of respect for others and their political experience.

But hadn't what he said and wrote always proved to be true? And had not those who opposed him always been the fools in the end, the fools or, worse still, the traitors? Haecker in Krakow, from the newspaper *Naprzod*, since Radek had turned away from him and opposed him because of his Polish chauvinism, was the first to spread the rumor that he had embezzled books from the editorial library; in fact, he had picked up a few penny dreadfuls from the wastepaper basket and taken them to the secondhand dealer in order to—in spite of Haecker's fees—be able to pay for coffee at the café in the evening. And Luxemburg, on whose lips he hung as if on those of a prophetess, and who, now that he thought about it, he had probably also loved, chaste and with-out hope of ever even being touched by her fingertips, and who then came to him in the midst of the Warsaw turmoil in 1905 and smiled at him when he spoke in front of a few thousand workers in a factory building, and hired him for Tyszka's party newspaper, because Tyszka—in Warsaw he was suddenly no longer called Jogiches—was tactically adept and an organizer par excellence, especially in the underground—he thought and felt so illegally, according to the legend, that he wouldn't have been able to say his own address—only writing: Tyszka couldn't write.

And she had been his angel, with whom he held spiritual discussions in the gloom of the Pawiak prison for six months, in German and Polish and then also in Russian, which a fellow prisoner taught him in the gray, musty cell. And she was still an angel when the Okhrana imprisoned him a second time, this time in the infamous Tenth Pavilion of the Warsaw Citadel. Only when they met again in Terijoki in Finland, a small group of emigrants after the lost revolution, did his respect for Luxemburg fade over the question of whether the party, isolated and broken up as it was in Poland, should ally itself with the trade unions or even with the left wing of Pilsudski's Polish socialists—he, Radek, pleaded for this in agreement with the comrades who stayed in Warsaw and continued the struggle there. But Jogiches, and Luxemburg with him, had nothing else in mind but purity, ideological purity, their doctrine and their party, which meant the five or six men who sat with them in exile and still obeyed Tyszka's orders.

When he woke up, with his Rosa next to him, in the shabby hotel room that the leadership of the party congress had told him to stay in—he couldn't have slept for a long time—there were still fragments in his brain of the dream he'd had. The other Rosa, Luxemburg, had leaned toward him and whispered a few words, tender ones, Lolek, my clever one, my world-changer, my little one, and then an animal had come with callused skin, Tyszka, he thought, Jogiches-Tyszka, sure, and had snatched her away from him, and he had wanted to cry out, but no cry came out of his throat, and besides, the logic of the whole dream wasn't right, because of course it had been Luxemburg who had given Jogiches the means to expel him from the party; namely, the idea of using as accusatory material against him before the party court, the Polish court, her Lolek's youthful sins, which he himself had told her about while merry from wine, even though it was all piddling stuff and unproven and long since past the statute of limitations, and then use the whole thing, including the prefabricated judgment, to play into the hands of the German party when the fellows around Ebert, for reasons of a completely different sort, intended to rob him, Radek, of his base among the comrades.

"You're already awake?" Rosa asked.

"They won't dare," he said. "Or do you think they would?"

2

They found him personally repellent. They tried to hide their feelings; they kept their distance from him and conducted themselves with emphatic correctness, and yet he felt their aversion almost physically. Regardless of what he did or said, publicly and privately, it seemed like a state of nature; they could not, as the German saying went, smell him, like horses that shunned the strange smell of an animal from another stable; but he washed and bathed as much as possible, and used, if he had money left over, a discreet eau de cologne, and the comrades from the party executive, he assumed, took no less care of their skin.

And politically, he was just as repellent to them. This was due to the difference in their thinking, theirs and his, which was not only evident in the basic principles, but also in the phrases and tone of speech; and he knew all too well how the inner balance of the comrades above was disturbed by every one of his speeches, articles, and appeals; he was tempted all the more strongly to expose them again and again to the very heresies to which they reacted most sensitively.

How could they believe that they, who extolled themselves to the workers as disciples of Marx or even of Lassalle and as the ones who would continue their great works—slightly revised, certainly—that they, comfortably reclining in their armchairs, only had to wait until enough votes had been collected so that they could glide into socialism, without the disturbing shocks, without the barricades that had long since gone out of fashion, like the well-endowed virgin in her marital bed. Yet, unlike the other terror to the bourgeoisie, dear Rosa Luxemburg, he was not so overly obsessed with the political mass strike; he had quite different ideas, based on his experience of the Warsaw Revolution, about which he, every word in its own time, only spoke now only in veiled language; but for the philistine behavior of the party executive and its philistine terminology he had only scorn—unabashed, loudly crowed scorn. No wonder that the members of the Executive Committee, deeply moved in their sluggish hearts, angrily persecuted him and tried to shut him up.

Ah, Göppingen!

He was attracted by opposites, and what could be more opposite to his errant nature and his untidy appearance than this small Württemberg town, which looked as if every morning made by God, one of his angels flew down there, brush and paint pot in hand, to touch up the house paint.

And what ingenuous, trusting people! Comrade Thalheimer, August, editor of the local party newspaper, the *Freie Volks-zeitung*: what a wonderful, peaceful life he could have led there with a few quarters of the evening's wine and good conversations with good citizens. Instead, however, he proclaimed in his newspaper that the revolution was approaching, and preached, where the opportunity arose, the most diverse left-wing radical theories, including his own, Radek's, and, together with two or three like-minded people on the local executive committee in Göppingen, incited the workers to oppose the policies of the Berlin party leaders. Moreover, Thalheimer in his hubris induced the comrades of the local party group to borrow money, on their personal word, a total of 30,000 marks, as initial capital for their own newspaper, including their own printing shop, for the very same *Freie Volkszeitung*, so that the Swabian working class would no longer have to read the ridiculous promises of a distant socialism of a tomorrow that never comes in the Stuttgarter *Neckar-Echo*, in thrall to the Berlin headquarters, or the equally revisionist Ulmer *Donauwacht*.

And of course such a paper could not flourish commercially, and the bailiff threatened, and the workers and small craftsmen who had raised the 30,000 marks feared for their money, and all that remained left was a cry for help to the very party committee against whose policies Thalheimer, and Radek as his freelancer, had mounted a great many attacks in the columns of the *Volkszeitung*.

A Gogol, Radek thought, could have made a comedy out of it, the characters acting against the backdrop of the small Göppingen houses and alleyways; Berlin had sent Comrade Ebert as an auditor, with instructions to rescue the investments of the Göppingen workers by simply taking over the paper. Poor Thalheimer, unable to cope with such pressure, asked him, Radek, imploringly, to manage the editorial office while he was on vacation for health reasons; and thus things led to big confrontations, big, that is, within the tiny relations of the southern German province, he, Radek, against Ebert, who had arrived specially from the imperial capital.

And yet, he thought, didn't the whole thing conceal the great conflict of that time? The contradictions between the great empires, Germany, England, France, Russia, plus America, which—as anyone who wanted to see it saw—and he himself had written about it a dozen times before—were arming for the struggle to redistribute the resources of the globe and its markets. And this war would be merciless and murderous and would end—like the Russo-Japanese War did with the revolution in St. Petersburg—with an even greater, even bloodier revolution, a true world revolution, for which the social democracy had to prepare itself and the entire working class, on pain of its own downfall.

And he confronted Comrade Ebert with this in the smoke-filled meeting room of the Göppingen editorial board; the latter sat opposite him at the other end of the table, massaging his fleshy chin with his thumb, and asked whether he, Radek, really believed he could raise money for the further publication of the Göppingen *Freie Volkszeitung* with such arguments.

"The workers of Göppingen"—Radek remembered how he, a true tribune of the people, hurled out his reply—"have a right to their own paper and to demand help from the party executive in Berlin for that purpose!"

Ebert remained unmoved. "We also don't want," he said, "for the workers of Göppingen to lose their newspaper, and with it their money. That is precisely why we are proposing that the Ulm people print their newspaper, the *Donauwacht*, in Göppingen; that would save costs and guarantee the existence of the Göppingen *Zeitung*, especially if you'd work with molds and adapted the political parts of the Ulm and Göppingen newspapers to each other . . ."

"With an editorial board in Ulm?" Radek asked.

Ebert lowered his heavy lids, "With an editorial board in Ulm."

Radek still remembered now, almost a year later, the astonished expressions on the mouths of the participants in that meeting, when he jumped from the table and stepped around the furniture toward Comrade Ebert and pointed his index finger at his chest like a pistol. "That's right!" he had scoffed. "And the people in Ulm print whatever you in Berlin hand them!"

Ebert remained silent.

"But the workers of Göppingen, Comrade Ebert," he exclaimed triumphantly, "have the right to read things in their newspaper that the party executive doesn't approve of!"

Ebert, convinced of his own importance, wore a smile that made Radek's head hot and his voice shrill. "And even," he had threatened, "even if the party leadership, Comrade Ebert, manages to swallow this little paper in this little town, it will only be a Pyrrhic victory for you! The truth will nevertheless prevail, and workers will recognize the methods of the party executive and its aims; and you won't silence me, anyway, Comrade Ebert!"

Radek had known that the man was his enemy from that moment on; and now, at the party congress here, he proved his enmity.

★

The hands were raised; some hesitantly, but nonetheless.

"That's the majority," declared Ebert, looking over the long rows of red delegate cards dutifully raised. A party congress was a matter of sacrosanct seriousness to him, and now that the exclusion of the insolent one was happily behind them, the Plenum could finally turn back to actual business.

Luxemburg rose from her seat in the presidium, but Radek was nowhere to be seen: either he had foreseen the result of the vote—no wonder, given the irrefutable register of sins that Jogiches had compiled against him with the diligence of a bookkeeper—and had preferred not to attend the meeting at all, or, more likely, the stewards had denied him access. Comrade Ebert did not like a rowdy in the hall on solemn occasions.

Someone tapped her on the shoulder. Luxemburg turned around, startled, "Karl!"

Liebknecht smiled. "You don't really believe, Rosa," he said half-quietly, "that the party really got him off its back that way."

"That remains to be seen!"

"A success, maybe, for you Poles," said Liebknecht, and immediately sensed how deeply he hurt her by counting her among the foreign party at this very moment. "But Radek was too often right in his arguments, and to condemn him just because he wouldn't submit to you and Jogiches . . . "

"Please!" Anger reddened her brow. "Radek's expulsion from the German party is now a done deal, and party decisions apply to you, too."

Liebknecht scratched his prickly beard. How relentless she

was! He didn't like relentless women; they placed men in pre-
dicaments; and besides, with these Polish and Russian groups
that were constantly splitting, one never knew what direction
they were headed, fixated as they were on the doctrines of their
own sect. "But Rosa, don't you sense," he tried the amicable
way, "what a strange position you've put yourself in: you, the
most left of the left in German social democracy, suddenly
hand-in-hand with the most right wing of the right, Ebert, just
in order to push Radek out of the way, who you actually should
have supported."

"Does he support us? He supports the splitters in Warsaw."

"Quiet!" somebody hissed.

Luxemburg noted the attention being attracted by her heated
dialogue with Liebknecht here on the platform, and restrained
her tone. "He supports the splitters in Warsaw against the Polish
leadership."

"Against Jogiches, you mean."

She controlled her temper. "Leo is not vindictive. And neither
am I. Go to Radek, tell him that, if you can bring yourself to do
it, to share a table with the charlatan, the vain, two-faced man."

"I'll tell him," said Liebknecht, leaving open what he would
tell Radek: the insult or the offer, or both.

★

"You're just like my blessed mama, Rosa," said Radek. "My
mama also always tried to protect me. But my uncle told me, as I
climbed the big chair in the living room and fell down and got a
bloody nose, 'a boy,' he said, 'has to have his own experiences.'"

Liebknecht looked at the woman who, as Radek had said,
blissfully sought, in the manner of his mama, to always protect
him; blonde with a delicate white complexion, her figure well
proportioned, she sat there on the cheap sofa in the cheap hotel
room, between her fingers the glass with the red wine that Radek
had ordered in honor of his guest. With the open look of her

gray eyes and her well-considered words, she seemed to be one of those women—Liebknecht understood that much about the opposite sex—who could give a man peace and security.

"He will get justice," she said. "Lenin has intervened."

"How's that?" Liebknecht asked, surprised.

"I have," said Radek, "after the scandalous treatment inflicted upon me by Ebert and his people at the party congress, written a small pamphlet, titled 'My Reckoning,' which reduces all the charges against me, including the financial ones, to absurdity— I'll give you a copy, Comrade Liebknecht,—and sent the pamphlet to Lunacharsky in Paris."

"And Lunacharsky presented it to Lenin," Rosa added, "and at Lenin's initiative, a commission met in Paris, Russian and Polish comrades, but none of Tyszka's and Luxemburg's adherents among them, and they will investigate again all of the bizarre things brought up against Radek, point by point, and nothing will remain of the accusations against him, and the German party will have discredited itself in front of the entire world."

She was also passionate, thought Liebknecht, and she obviously loved Radek. A physician by trade, she worked at a hospital in Leipzig; there, it was said, she and Radek had met for the first time; she opened an ulcer in his rectum; Radek, when talking about this not very promising beginning of their love affair, would say that he had not intended to enchant her with the help of his bottom.

"Although he's printed a few of his articles," Liebknecht doubted Rosa's hopeful view, "Lenin was never really particularly a friend of your husband."

Radek grinned. "Lenin isn't known for deciding political questions according to his personal sympathies. To Lenin, I'm nothing but a pawn on the chessboard; he wants to get his hands on the secret fund the International has raised to support party work in Poland and Russia, and which is administered by the German party executive; but Luxemburg and her Tyska are already sitting on the pot, denying Lenin access to the money. So you can see,

Liebknecht, what noble aims the leaders of the socialist movement are pursuing, and by what means they sometimes pursue
them."

"You're a cynic, Radek." Liebknecht laughed. "But I'll confess
this much: if I had known about the secret fund, I would have
briefed the delegates about the background of your affair."

"Cynic?" said Rosa. "If you only knew how vulnerable he is.
He only shows his hard shell to the outside world."

Radek did not regard his inner life as a valid topic of conversation, even when his wife discussed it, and so he returned to political
matters. "What are these party jackasses thinking!" he said angrily.
"Did you sense at the meeting, Liebknecht, you and at least a few
of the delegates in the hall, that the dispute about me was only one
aspect of a power struggle about completely different questions?
The world, my dear, is even larger than even the largest German
party in terms of numbers, and the farce that they conducted in the
hall today around poor Comrade Sobelsohn reflected more than
one of the contradictions that the world is teeming with."

Liebknecht had become uncertain. "The executive had to
make clear, in front of the party members and itself, who the boss
of the Social Democratic house is."

"Exactly." Radek seemed to be speaking less to his guest than
to his wife, who had raised her eyes from her hands, which were
strong and delicate at the same time, and looked at him expectantly. "But why did the executive have to make this clear," he
continued, "and why at this very moment? Because of a few
rubles and the question of who is allowed to dispose of them,
Lenin and his Bolsheviks or Jogiches and his Luxemburg, or
any other equally ambitious group?—Liebknecht, dear friend,
there's a war coming, and who can say what will happen at the
end of this war? You? Me?"

"The party will prevent the war! The party and," Liebknecht
repeated, emphasizing the "*and*," "the International! And I swear
to you, Radek, the old saying will come true again: all the wheels
will stop turning, if your strong arm wants them to."

"All the wheels . . . ," Radek smirked. "Are you hearing this, Rosa?—an illusionist!" And to Liebknecht: "Whose arm? The arm of this party executive? This Reichstag fraction? These union leaders with embroidered doilies on the backs of their chairs? Didn't you just see these people again at their party conference?"

"What was up for debate at this party congress was Comrade Radek, not the war, not the imperial fleet, and not the budget."

"Exactly. God willing, if only someone had put this on the agenda: the war, the fleet, the budget."

"What for? Everything has long since been agreed upon and our principles sealed with our comrades in Paris and London and Brussels and even in St. Petersburg—not a single man or penny for this system!"

"It's the system, if I may remind you, that the comrades live off of, and not badly. And what kind of German Social Democrat will want—when they call him out with cheers and trumpets, Comrade Liebknecht, and put a rifle in his hand for the Fatherland, the dear Fatherland—to be a worse patriot than his neighbor? And will things be much more different with the French? With the English? And what will happen in the heart of the German worker when the first enemy sets foot over the border at the Rhine or the Memel? What then will count for more in his heart: the class to which the man stalking his fellow worker with a gun in his hand belongs, or the nation that sends him onto the bloody battlefield?"

"And they'll even believe that they're protecting home and hearth and wife and child from the Cossacks," Rosa added.

Liebknecht turned away from her—she always said what her husband wanted to hear. "I understand, Radek: You're playing devil's advocate with me."

"I'm not playing. I'm putting myself into the mind of an average functionary of our party."

Liebknecht considered it. What if Radek was right? What if, on the day things got serious, the party made the huge turn, right turn, march, off to war? But that couldn't be. . . . Well, there were all types in the party, and the right wing controlled the apparatus. But there were also rules that were not to be violated, and principles, confirmed many times by history, to which a social democrat adhered.

"War, imperialist war," he postulated, "is not in the interest of the proletariat, and the workers know it."

"We've preached that to them long enough," countered Radek. "But who knows what constellation of circumstances will trigger the catastrophe? And I've lived in Germany long enough to be able to recognize what has changed here since 1870, when your late father, my dear Liebknecht, hand in hand with Comrade Bebel, refused to give his lone vote for war credits to Herr von Bismarck. But at the time, the party wasn't much more than a sect, and a sect could afford to deviate from the mainstream of popular sentiment, and the International, the Socialist International, was a small club of idealists at the time."

"But now there are four million social democratic voters in Germany alone!" protested Liebknecht. "Four million who say no to war! And who will bring about the overthrow of the existing state through their revolutionary deeds!"

"Why do you refuse to follow natural logic?"

"Your logic, you mean."

"My logic, if you please!" Radek stroked his jaw, on which dark curls had sprouted since he had started working in Göppingen. "But there is no other logic—due to the realities in this party, which has long since ceased to consist of the few hundred havenots who had nothing to lose but their chains. The party has become a saturated institution, possessing respectable bank accounts and land and print shops and clubhouses and whatnot, and which has a well-founded interest in the myriad governmental perks that are the most effective means of corrupting the workers. The whole thing is a textbook example of Hegel's quantity that has made the leap to a new quality, and I'm telling you, Liebknecht, on the day that war breaks out, all the old proletarian vows will be forgotten; quite different feelings will fill people's hearts, and no one will talk anymore of international solidarity and brothers joining hands; instead, the German workers' choirs will sing in beautiful harmony of the call roaring like thunder; and first and foremost the leaders of the party will wave the patriotic flags, and will furthermore develop a political theory to justify their betrayal. The proletarians, they will say, must help the Fatherland to victory, for it is not from the ruins of defeat on the battlefield, but only on the basis of an economy emerging strengthened from the war, that a proper socialism can be built after the revolution."

Radek's forehead had reddened. Rosa noticed it with concern; whenever he got excited in this way, his blood pressure rose and his heartbeat became irregular, an illness which, he had tried to reassure her, was endemic among Jewish men, especially from Lithuania and Galicia. At the same time, however, she admired him: to put himself so completely into the mindset of his opponents, so that his own thoughts almost appeared questionable to him: who else but him was capable of that? He was able to write two completely contrary answers to the same question: one in which he believed deeply, and the other which he only advanced in order to push it with all his powers of persuasion to the point of absurdity. This gave him a superiority, both politically and journalistically, that was often envied, but whose Socratic tricks deeply annoyed such single-minded thinkers as Jogiches in a very personal way; and here, opposite Liebknecht, he had played this mental double-cross with such intensity that at the end, his words almost sounded as if, if war came, he would himself advocate for a German victory.

Suddenly, Radek laughed out loud. "You almost believed that I believed all that, didn't you, Liebknecht? No, don't worry— I've only developed for you the train of thought of our comrades in the party executive, to the extent that they even have thoughts about things like war and peace; me, I'm on your side, completely, and hope to the old Jewish God that he will fulfill your pious wishes!"

Liebknecht gave a tormented smile. Rosa stood up, approached him, and gave him, as a sort of sign of reconciliation, a motherly kiss on the cheek.

She was really angry, Radek thought, Rosa—not his, Luxemburg—since, as expected, Lenin's commission in Paris had scattered to the winds the entire charge so carefully constructed by Jogiches out of the alleged theft of an old coat, a few tattered books, 300 union rubles, and a shit in somebody else's bed. He could imagine the secret pleasure with which Lunacharsky, who chaired the commission, took apart the details that had given the German congress so much to talk about: Lunacharsky, like himself, was known for his vicious wit. And he, Radek, had sent him his thick pamphlet, "My Settling of Accounts," which listed in perfect detail every error in thinking, every contradiction that Tyszka had made in his accusations.

And now Luxemburg, in a formal declaration on behalf of the Executive Board of the Social Democratic Party of Russian-Poland and Lithuania—that is, on behalf of herself and Leo Jogiches—wrote that the entire Parisian Commission of Inquiry and its public announcement that it had rehabilitated Comrade Radek—thus removing all obstacles to his rejoining the ranks of the German party—was nothing more than a clumsy exercise that best demonstrated by what means a certain clique was conducting the Radek affair.

She emphasized that according to a resolution of the German party congress—see page 559 of the minutes—the admission to the German Social Democratic Party of persons excluded from the party elsewhere was subject to the consent of the party that had carried out the expulsion; in the case of Radek, the Social Democratic Party of Russian-Poland and Lithuania.

And she concluded, with fine indignation, "But what does the Paris Commission have to do with this party? Not the slightest thing! With the same right, four Portuguese, Argentinian, Bulgarian and other socialists could form a Radek investigative commission in Paris or even in San Francisco. And just as this Paris Commission revised the judgment of the Polish party in the case of Radek, it could revise, with the same right and the same success, the American customs tariff."

Luxemburg's biblical wrath, Radek thought, even lent her a touch of irony. Lenin, however, had little sense for such nuances and cursed loudly and relentlessly about the disgusting way in which the so-called Polish party leadership proceeded in the Radek matter. This leadership—he revealed in his response article, intended for the German *Vorwärts* but rejected by it and then distributed by Krupskaya as a manuscript—no longer had any party behind it; it was only supported by a fictitious small group in Warsaw. And this fact, he sneered, was what our illustrious Rosa was trying to chatter away; she and her so-called party leadership were leading a campaign against the best members of the real Polish party, and their methods became increasingly criminal. And hence the peculiar trial against Radek—because of alleged offenses from the year 1906!...

Radek put both—Luxemburg's publication and Lenin's manuscript—into an envelope and wrote on it: *Keep safe!* Then he thought: how old am I now? Almost twenty-nine. And thought: to be able to experience, at the age of twenty-nine, how two people of such stature were at loggerheads in all seriousness over someone like him—a formidable achievement on the part of little Sobelsohn.

But would blessed Mama also have seen it that way?

3

How does a prophet feel who is forced to experience that his prophecy is reality?

Radek felt terror rather than satisfaction. Who could he have told: look how right I was? His Rosa? His comrades in Bremen, the only ones in the German party who still maintained ties to him? But they too were already in the process of joining the defenders of the fatherland. . . . And ultimately he still hoped, against his better judgment, that the fulfillment of his dark prophecy could be prevented by something unforeseen, a revolt somewhere, a sudden demonstration, a rousing manifesto, perhaps—even though in all the capitals of Europe the trade unions had already voluntarily given up the only weapon they had against the war, the general strike, and had declared a truce with their respective governments. It could not be the case that all the promises of the party leaders had been empty words, and not all the proletarians could have forgotten yesterday's oaths; and so, up to the last minute, he had resisted his own bitter insights, and refused to silently accept them, and had, until the Kaiser's censor had intervened, beat the drum in the last journal still open to him and shouted "*What should we bleed for!*"—and pointed an accusing finger at the small fraternity that was deciding in mysterious darkness over the lives and well-being of hundreds of millions, and he was indignant that not only the toilers of Russia, the empire of absolutism, but also the working class of civilized Germany and republican France should tolerate that a handful of blinkered diplomats and military men determined the fate of the popular masses. And he had warned the workers that if they did not succeed, in the few days remaining for the fight against the war, to avert the danger, they would soon have to obey the mobilization order.

Then he had gone to Berlin.

He did not have a plan; he, in whose head plans usually always formed, sharply drawn and mathematically precise, like patterns of light in a kaleidoscope. The city didn't look much different than on earlier midsummer days: the same dust in the same flickering air, the beer haze from the open doors of the pubs, the tired nags in front of the cabs waiting at the corner; but one saw every-where the black, white, and red splashes of color from flags and cockades.

And there was a new tension in the air, which appeared threat-ening to him; occasionally, troops of men passed on the road, some already in uniform, some still in civilian clothes, and the sergeant at the lead counted loudly, left two three, and then they sang, not exactly melodiously. The second page of the newspaper he carried in his coat pocket announced that Jaurès had been mur-dered, Jaurès, Jean, the apostle of peace of the International. He had just announced in Paris that the harsh tone of the Germans should not be overestimated; they, too, basically only wanted to reach an understanding with the other nations; now he had paid the price.

Radek felt lonely, which was rare enough given his lively tem-perament, which was open to any suggestion that was halfway hopeful. Was this still his world—this crowd, carried by the expectation of great things, *jeder Schuß ein Ruß, jeder Stoß ein Franzos*,[1] these women carrying market baskets on their elbows, their children clinging to their apron strings, cheering on the bystanders to ever renewed enthusiasm and expecting him—fol-lowing the example of all these guys with tattered pant seats and greasy hat brims—to burst into cheers for his majesty the Kaiser and good old Franz Joseph in Vienna, his brave ally, whom we rushed to aid against the insolent Serbs and whose subject Radek was by law, he now remembered, as a native Galician.

As inconspicuously as possible, he retired from the sweaty mob into the shadow of a house entrance, took a deep breath, and consulted the little book from the pocket of his vest, contain-ing his Berlin addresses. Names, names, many of them sonorous. And yet how few of them about which he could allow himself to assume that those to whom they belonged could give him encouragement and support. If they had not themselves jumped

---

1. "A Russian for every shot, a Frenchman for every thrust."

onto the patriotic merry-go-round, they would sit at the kitchen table as if anesthetized, helpless between the doctrines of yesterday and the praxis of today . . . And him: did he have a program?

He stood on the streetcar platform, and swayed with the swaying of the car at every curve, at every bump in the track. And yet, this movement was pleasant to him; the jerky back-and-forth, without rhythm or system that his body had to balance, gave him the illusion that he was doing something of importance; and now, as he reached the western part of the city, where the people were more sedate and the hustle and bustle less hectic, and the cheers of "Hurrah!" sounded a bit more civilized, he had become more at ease, and the decision he was pursuing, which had cost him so much overcoming of the self, even seemed logical to him.

He only feared the encounter with Tyszka physically. Tyszka was tall and broad-shouldered, a muscle-bound giant, whereas he was rather dainty, with arms that could barely carry the packages of books and newspapers he carried around on normal days. Did Tyszka even still live with her? Hadn't they already been living separately from each other for a long time? But it could be that he was with her at this moment, she must have just returned from Brussels, maybe a few hours ago, from the last, futile meeting of the International, and Tyszka might have come to comfort her and embrace her like once before.

So his steps became increasingly hesitant as he ascended the stairs of the multistory apartment building, and on the floor below hers, he even stopped and considered whether it would be better to turn back. What, she would say in her most cutting voice, you, Radek? And now, of all times! And he would answer, yes, now, Rosa, and it wasn't easy for me, believe me, but world history, at least I think so, comes before party quarrels.

He rang the bell. For a while, nothing happened. Then, the chain behind the frosted glass of the apartment door was slid aside, the door opened by a crack, and a young, pale girl with a scarred harelip on her face appeared and answered, in response to his question, no, Frau Luxemburg was not at home, she wasn't yet in Berlin at all, but she had telephoned; there had been various difficulties with the trains from Belgium, the military was everywhere, and cannons were being transported instead of people.

Liebknecht as well, it turned out, couldn't be found at home; his wife, a bit frightened by Radek's hasty insistence, said he was in the Reichstag; wouldn't Comrade Radek like to come in and sit down for a cup of coffee? Her Karl would never forgive her if she let Comrade Radek leave without at least a little hospitality, and she doubted whether her husband would be available to speak to Radek there in the Reichstag, so why not wait for him at the apartment, he'd have to come home sometime, although, sometimes, she didn't hear his key in the lock until long past midnight, and now, where there's one meeting after another...

Radek accepted the coffee, but couldn't find any calm, and after a short while apologized, that he had to leave and continue on, although the day's heat and his fatigue tormented him. He was already standing in front of the Reichstag, the high dome of which appeared to him like a Prussian *Pickelhaube* made specially for the building, before he realized that the country was at war, after all, and that he might have difficulties getting into the building where the highest representative body of the people was meeting in the presence of the ministry, the members of which were gentlemen who, especially after the assassination of the successor to the imperial and royal Austro-Hungarian throne, must have been worried about their precious lives and taken appropriate measures. And indeed, directly under the solemn pillars of the entrance, a guard called out to him, "Hey there, you, where to?" But it was enough to take out his little book from his pocket, hold it in front of the man like an official ID, and rasp "Press!" Heels clicked, and there he was, inside the great temple of the people, from whose tribune Bismarck once steered the fate of Germany.

Not that he was particularly impressed by the solid woods, the elaborate capitals, the resounding echo; but he found pleasant the marble coolness and the refracted light that fell through the glass of the upper windows in a subdued way into high corridors. A strange calm prevailed; he encountered no more than half a dozen people, walking with measured steps; here, a system, long established and unassailable, appeared, despite the excited times, to enter into decline, resting with self-satisfaction. But then, the large door to the assembly hall burst open, press people rushed out, swinging notepads, and after them, no less hurriedly, the first small groups of parliamentarians, speaking fiercely to each other, as well as several military men with rattling swords.

And there he was, alone and lost in thought: Liebknecht.

★

Radek walked up to him.

Liebknecht flinched, but immediately pulled himself together and began defending himself. "What could we do? Didn't they all fall like dominoes, our parties, in Paris, in London, wherever? And our leftists here, whom I still counted on, Ledebour, Zetkin, Mehring, what did they do? I spoke to them; they too, they said, felt uncomfortable with this decision, but an individual, they said, cannot step out of line when the majority makes a turn; the situation, they said, requires party discipline; or did we want to, now of all times, split the party?"

"So you too," Radek said.

"Yes, me too," said Liebknecht. "I voted for war credits. Together with all of them."

"Each," Radek said, "according to his conscience."

And he knew, already at the moment of saying that, how deeply he had just wounded the man there, whose conscience had demanded of him something completely different, something unfulfillable.

They left the Reichstag together, in silence. It was only just in front of the Hotel Adlon, whose splendor sparkled with its early lights, that Liebknecht asked, "And what will you do now, Radek?"

"I'm an imperial and royal subject," Radek replied.

"And in times like these, a man is drawn to his fatherland. Is that what you're trying to tell me?"

Radek laughed scornfully. "I don't feel drawn to Vienna, and certainly not to Lemberg. But I'm afraid the next police patrol that I attract the unpleasant attention of will turn me over to the Austrian consulate, to serve my emperor. And I doubt that I'll cut a good figure as a recruit of the imperial and royal army."

Liebknecht put his arm around his shoulder. "Let's have some wine at the Adlon. To console ourselves."

But the hall of the Adlon was full of noisy officers and their entourages, making it difficult for them to establish the human intimacy they both desired to feel.

4

It had been a farewell like no other before, reserved despite the confusion of feelings in his chest. "Rosa," he had said, and held her by the shoulders and kissed her on the cheek—"just don't show too much feeling, farewells were taking place all over Europe these days—you'll follow me, Rosa, as soon as possible; I'll write to you from Bern."

It would be Bern, no question; he had known Bern from the period of time before he had known Rosa, the period after the failed uprisings in Warsaw, after his withering away in prisons there, which he made more bearable by studying languages, how long ago that was, my God, almost ten years already; he had been a young man then, with dark curly hair, his head full of dreams, although they constantly clashed with reality, he knew how to protect himself behind a protective shield of arrogance, which the philistine world found so reprehensible about him, and Bern lay there between the mountains, solid, clean, with pointed roofs above the narrow streets, a protective wall against the storm, which by right was his element. But she, Rosa, told him—when they hastily discussed the questions of where and when in his

Berlin hotel room—and she told him in a way that made it clear that she had considered it thoroughly—that she would have to stay a while in Germany, because what would happen to him otherwise. She was—she didn't need to mention it at all, but it resonated in their life together—the breadwinner, even though the amount she brought home as assistant doctor was very modest. Sometimes, when he felt the crisp banknote she shoved into his pocket, he felt like he was taking advantage of her in a vile way. But she allowed herself to be taken advantage of, with a gentle smile and without for her part making any demands; was that a sign of her love now, he wondered, or, as she darned his socks, simply the normal case in the marriage of a German woman aware of her obligations to a genius from a foreign land?

And then she stood, very composed, on the platform of the train station, and he stuck his head out of the compartment window, and she waved at him as the train rolled on, an everyday scene, but suddenly tears came to his eyes, and he only saw her as if through a veil, his Rosa.

He tried to get his depressive mood under control.

He told himself that sudden exile might be even more difficult for others than it was for him, who had basically spent his entire political life on the run, or on the advance, depending on how one looked at it; his rootlessness, the constant changes of place were simply part of it; the months he had spent in quiet succession in a single place were easily counted. Balabanoff as well, in her dark, heavy Italian silk, acted as if in mourning; yet Italy, her adopted country, wasn't at war yet, and the party there, along with the Swiss and one or two Balkan ones, was the only one in which it was still possible to risk a word against the social-patriotic prattle of the majority of functionaries.

She was a beautiful woman, daughter of a Russian father and an Italian mother; her temperament had already singed

the wings of more than one of the disciples of the revolutionary movement buzzing around her. From a wealthy Petersburg
home, a branch of which settled somewhere in Romagna, she
lodged, always furnished with money, and despite her academic
degrees and the grande bourgeois way of life originally inherent
to her, wherever possible in the quarters of the dispossessed, her
kind of sympathy for the members of the lower classes, to whom
she devoted her heart; in her appearances there she created a
dramatic costume, part of it the beautifully wavy dark hair and
the smoky voice, respectful silence, in which she announced her
theses to everyone and everything, These, Radek soon found,
didn't sound so bad, especially not to the ears of one who had
only recently arrived from a country where the word "peace"
was only a fading echo.

She had recognized him, he noticed; she broke away from the
circle of her admirers at the large, oilcloth-covered table in the
dining room of the Bern *Volkshaus* and called out, with an opulent gesture of welcome, "Radek!"—approaching him, who was
sitting in the corner, the same cup of coffee in front of him for the
last quarter of an hour, and sighed in greeting. "Oh, Comrade
Radek, what has happened to us! What has become of our proud
German party!"

She dropped into the chair in front of him and looked at him
with one of her long, soulful looks, which did not quite fit in at
this time of day in a working-class locale with a sour smell.

"The proud German party," Radek answered, "has to be completely remade from scratch." He drank the rest of his coffee,
which had turned cold, "and the whole damned International,
too," and pondered, seeing Balabanoff's sensual mouth and the
strand of hair that fell tantalizingly across her arched forehead,
no, not this one, rather not this one, we'll keep our hands off
this one; she's only fixated on herself, and her main preoccupa-
tion is self-realization, which was fine during the day, but would
prove annoying at night; and besides, his wife, Rosa, was there
in her humble Leipzig apartment, waiting for the hour when she

could come to him, or he to her. He tried to remember where Balabanoff knew him from, and where he knew her, Angelica, the dark angel of the steadfast left, which had so pitifully melted away; oh yes, Hanecki had told him about her and her appearances at the International Socialist Bureau; and Hanecki, the faithful one, who had kept the Polish group in Warsaw in touch with Lenin, possessed a truly literary talent for describing people; and as for him, Radek, their sudden joyful greeting today was not further surprising; particularly since the affair at the German Party Congress he had become known as a colorful personality among comrades, even foreign ones.

He wished she would offer to buy him an apple strudel, the kind the Swiss baked so appetizingly, even if it was with vanilla sauce; he suddenly had this hunger for apple strudel. But she wasn't thinking of his physical needs, Balabanoff always only saw the intellectual; she sat down firmly, making it known in such a way that she intended to engage him in conversation for a long time. Well, he didn't have anything better to do at the moment, and maybe he would be able to receive from her, in addition to an exposé of her opinions on the situation and her analysis of it, a few practical tips about the internal conditions in Bern, where it was best to stay, and who was who in the political emigration here, which must have changed considerably since the last time he had stayed in the city, after the suppression of the Russian Revolution of 1905.

Then she ordered fresh coffee and apple strudel, only a single portion, then thought better of it and ordered the same for him. Then she began, in a peculiar tone of lament, "Do you know, Radek, what Plekhanov said to me when he summoned me to Geneva, the great Plekhanov, in whom Russian seriousness and German rigor are united with French spirit, the master Marxist from whom we all learned and who means infinitely much to me personally?"

"I can guess," Radek said soberly.

"No, you can't," she countered.

"He shouted at me, What, you're against the war? Is that your love for Russia, your solidarity with poor Belgium?... Everything in me was shaking, that's a fact, Comrade Radek, and I could hardly form the words when I answered him, but didn't you, Georgy Valentinovich, teach us to see capitalism as the cause of all wars, and now you want me to distinguish between attackers and attacked, between barbaric Germany and noble France?"

Radek attacked his strudel.

"And he, the old man, regretted that he was no longer able to go into battle himself against the Central Powers."

"In Germany, they say even worse things," Radek said with a full mouth.

"And you don't see any hope at all?" Balabanoff's lips trembled. "The international proletariat . . ."

"The international proletariat," he replied, "has gone very eagerly to war and therefore has to undergo its own experiences. At most, we can provide it with commentary on the latter."

"Ha!," she protested, "and you're content to just do that? I want to declare war on war! Preferably today rather than tomorrow! And I won't rest until this war"—the *this* said with raised fist—"has ended victoriously. And I won't stand alone; our word will echo across the globe, and will be heard everywhere!"

He knew what was coming now.

"You'll stand with us, won't you, Comrade Radek? With your pen; your spirit—?"

What did she know about his pen, his spirit? What did she know at all about his thoughts, after this defeat, which demanded a completely new way of thinking, in new categories. How did she know whether he wouldn't tell her, spare me your clichés, Comrade Balabanoff, which, since the days of August of this year, had proved to be just as ineffectual as the entire International Socialist Bureau.

But he didn't say it. He was happy to have someone sitting in front of him who intimated that he could be of use somehow.

"Stand with us," he repeated. "Who is *us*? A *pluralis majestatis*?"

She was visibly piqued. Maybe, Radek thought, among the prominent people of the International, there really wasn't anyone other than this broad with her semi-hysterical posturing who was ready to be engaged so extensively in opposition to the war—other than Lenin, of course, who was also based recently in Switzerland, but who didn't speak this grandiose language. Or, she just didn't like it when somebody dared to doubt one of her pronouncements.

Radek let the last morsel of his strudel melt on his tongue. She named a few Italian names that he hardly knew: Morgari, Modigliani, Mussolini. And then: "Have you spoken with Robert Grimm yet?"

Robert Grimm was the editor-in-chief of the *Berner Tagwacht*, and a man of influence within Swiss social democracy; Radek had long wanted to visit, but had postponed his visit until a day when he could offer him more than the few notes in his breast pocket.

"Grimm," she said, "is like a general in reserve."

"And his army?"

"He'll have an army," said Balabanoff, as if she had been inducted into the man's secret plans.

As Radek knew from history, the warhorses among the Swiss had mostly served abroad; those who had stayed in the country were rather dilettantes when it came to military matters; but this Grimm, since Balabanoff was so impressed by him, might be capable of thinking strategically, provided he took advice from the right people.

"And Lenin?" asked Balabanoff.

Lenin's attitude after the collapse of the International wasn't in doubt; Lenin had even presupposed the matter and, in keeping with his reputation, would probably already have a program up his sleeve, a very unpopular one, of course; and if he, Radek, hesitated to go to him, it was because he feared being co-opted by the man and confronted with decisions that he possibly wasn't ready for yet.

"Lenin," he said, "is a special case."

"He's the boss of the majority group in the Russian party," she reminded him.

Radek remembered the help that Lenin had bestowed upon him. And said: "Lenin's majority also consists of only a handful of people."

"That fact is known to me," she said, and then, with a touch of self-irony that surprised him, "but I am anxious to nourish my hope for better political times, and for that purpose, I scrape together every crumb I can find anywhere."

I could also use some hope, he thought, and said in a comforting tone, "in the near future, one can probably count on not much more than a handful here, a handful there."

She was grateful to him for at least this assurance and asked, "Another strudel?"

He declined with gratitude. He would have accepted a schnitzel.

★

Robert Grimm received him at night in the print shop of the *Berner Tagwacht*, in a crudely thrown together hovel whose primitive furnishings—a couple of boards placed over two trestles, two stools—trembled every time one of the big machines started up. Grimm checked the page proofs that the typesetter brought him before the molds with the leaden columns were closed and adjusted and placed on the press: the last chance to make any changes to tomorrow's edition of his paper.

Radek appreciated the trust the man showed him by involving him in his work from the very first meeting, and the smell of hot lead and printer's ink and sweat that he knew so well created an atmosphere in which he felt, for the first time since Bremen and Göppingen, at home. Grimm scribbled his initials on the bottom of the pages, pressed them into the typesetter's hands, and straightened up. Radek saw the muscular shoulders that threatened to burst the seams of the faded work jacket, shoulders made to carry a crossbow, and said to himself, be careful—what is he aiming at right now, and how sure is his eye?

"Cigar?" offered Grimm.

Radek nodded, and for a while both gazed at the smoke that rose to the ceiling in the yellowish glow of the lamp.

Then Radek asked, "Can you use me?"

"Yeah, would you," Grimm asked back, "write on my terms?"

Radek considered. What other papers were there in the social democratic movement that he could work for? Nevertheless, "The only terms I write on are mine."

Grimm laughed. "Good, good." And then, his gutturals more articulate, "I wouldn't have expected anything else from you. Incidentally, your thinking and mine probably overlap on many points."

"I'm not a pacifist."

Grimm looked at him with amusement. "Who do you want to wage war against—You . . ."

With his limbs, Radek was aware, or on the terrain of military virtues, he could not compete with Grimm. And he responded, "Against the gentlemen of the bourgeoisie, and their collaborators."

"So against all." Again Grimm laughed, "Radek—against all. And Lenin—also against all. And Balabanoff—the same. A bunch of lonely heroes, indeed!" He stubbed out his cigar, stood up, and stretched, his belly bulging over his waistband. "One has to combine forces. Let Comrade Grimm do it—here from this hovel, alongside my new Swiss printing machines. Go over there, Radek, and see how they sparkle." He drew a deep breath. "And you'll help me in my task; but not as Karl Radek; your name is no good anymore, since the German party clowns in association with Madame Luxemburg have pissed all over it. Find yourself a pseudonym."

War, thought Radek, war for peace; if you want peace, prepare a war for peace; if you want peace, prepare for war, *si vis pacem para bellum*. "Parabellum," he said.

A printer brought Grimm the first copy of the printed newspaper. Grimm unfolded the sheet, nodded, and held it out to Radek. "Looks good, doesn't it?" and then, "Parabellum. Okay, Parabellum for all I care. When can I have the first article?"

★

On the horizon, there rose the peak of the Rothorn, not an especially threatening-looking mountain.

He had come from Lucerne in a stagecoach. He felt as if he had been transported to another century; people were calmly eating their cheese with bread on the way and drinking from bulbous bottles; he let trees and meadows and the thick-necked cows pass him by and thought, he has it nice here, Lenin; where does he, under this sky, get the poison that he sprays at his opponents, the real ones as well as the presumed ones?

And who did he not count among his opponents: the Social Revolutionaries, the Mensheviks, the anarchists, the syndicalists, Trotsky, Axelrod, Martov, Parvus, a never-ending list, on which the tsar and his generals appeared least frequently; their present role and future fate did not require any more arguments on the part of Comrade Lenin.

The village was called Sörenberg and was so much a part of its lovely surroundings that one would have hardly noticed it if the driver had not reined in the horses with a "Hoah! Hoah!" and loudly called out its name.

Radek got out. After a while, without even having to ask directions, he found the little house that had already been described to him in Bern, with the overhanging roof and the door painted green and the flowers in front of tiny window panes, in which the afternoon sun was reflected. Lenin was sitting in the garden, with him were two women serving him his snack, one the tea, the other the bread. Lenin looked up: "You've come at just the right time, Radek," and then with a wave of his hand, "Comrade Krupskaya . . ." and a second such gesture, ". . . Comrade Inessa Armand."

Both comrades nodded. Comrade Armand pushed an additional chair to the table and waited until Radek sat down.

"Did you have a good trip?" Lenin asked.

"I would have gone a bit further," Radek assured him, "and sat on an even harder bench in order to see you."

Lenin's cheekbones seemed more prominent, since he was squinting; whether against the already angular rays or against Radek remained unclear. "In any case, I'm pleased," he said, "that you've found your way to me. I have—even though my German is less fluent than yours—been able to follow your publications from a distance, and have agreed with you, except for a few points, such as the national question."

Radek reached for one of the croissants in a basket on the table and spread butter lightly on it. Lenin apparently loved to get straight to the point without wasting time on chitchat; but Radek, always interested in personal idiosyncrasies, not to say gossip, would have loved to know more about the peculiar ménage à trois that the leader of the Bolshevik faction—otherwise known as an ascetic—had set up for himself in this idyllic village.

"And you know indeed," Lenin cunningly continued, "that you're regurgitating nothing but the errors of Rosa Luxemburg, who seriously thinks that in her socialist cloud-cuckoo land that just because industrial development knows no borders, the workers also must automatically become internationalists. Just look at the picture at the beginning of this war, Radek: it reveals how fiercely even the proletarians were drawn to their respective flags and ancestral ruling houses. How much work we'll have to do to once again convince people that there's a difference between fatherland and bourgeoisie, and between nation and imperialist state, and that they've received guns in order to turn around and aim them accordingly."

Armand hung on Lenin's every word, while Krupskaya, apparently more used to her husband's table speeches than the other, sweetened her tea with an ample amount of sugar. Radek decided to continue to assume that, especially among the workers, the war would soon trigger feelings stronger than the nationalist fluke that had gripped so many of them since August. Besides, he thought, neither he nor Lenin were in a position at this time to implement even a single one of their theories in reality; they were therefore engaged in nothing but intellectual games.

Lenin, however, was dead serious, as always. He spoke as if he were the head of a committee deciding the fate of peoples. "Do you want, Comrade Radek, the revolution? Yes?"

Radek reached for a second croissant.

"Then one means to this end, and an extremely formidable one, is the liberation of the oppressed peoples, Russia's in particular. We say to the Finns, the Ukrainians, the Georgians, whoever: break out of the tsar's prison of peoples—and thus weaken the regime at a decisive spot through the new front that will open up there."

"And then, as soon as we have power, will these peoples also be released from the Greater Russian Empire?"

Lenin sensed the guile in the question. "Do you think, Comrade Radek, that I lack consistency?"

"I mean"—Radek shook his head imperceptibly—"we should first cross that bridge when we get to it."

"But one must consider everything, and in advance. What's the use, I ask you, of all the talk of peace at which the émigrés in Switzerland excel, if none of these fellows can say specifically how this peace can be established?"

"Do you know?"

"Through the transformation of the war," Lenin proclaimed, "into a civil war. In Russia and every other country."

Comrade Armand sweezed a slice of lemon in her tea glass. "Read Ilyich's theses."

Krupskaya coughed and reached for her tissue.

Radek turned to Lenin again. "Liebknecht has also, I hear, after initially voting in favor of the Kaiser's war credits, called for a civil war instead of a truce, albeit in a subdued voice for the time being. But that would mean handing victory to whichever government keeps its citizens in line the longest. In the case of unrest in Russia, even revolutionary unrest, this would mean the German general staff, with its Social Democrats trained for defense of the fatherland. Do we want that? Or can you, Comrade Lenin, imagine Comrade Ebert as a civil war hero?"

"I know," Lenin laughed mirthlessly, "about your strained relationship with Comrade Ebert, Comrade Radek. Perhaps, then, with your connections in Germany, you would be willing to help get rid of the man—politically, of course, not physically."

"You notice, Karl Bernhardovich"—Krupskaya smiled amiably—"the subtle difference."

Radek smiled as well. "Sometimes I would've liked to see a little murder and manslaughter in the placid ranks of German social democracy, but it too, although last among the parties, will radicalize as soon as the consequences of the war begin to noticeably bite."

"Radicalize!" Lenin exclaimed. "I want more than that. We cannot do without Germany, it's a very special country, with its industry, its highly developed agriculture. A revolution elsewhere, among us in Russia, for instance, would be unfeasible in the long run without the aid of the German proletariat, that is, without a German revolution."

Radek was fascinated: So Lenin already thought that far ahead, such a short time after the outbreak of this war.

"But you don't believe in the Germans?" asked Lenin.

"It's difficult for me."

"Of course. That's why you left the country. But I tell myself every morning, when the sun rises above the Lucerne Alps: and yet it moves!"

"Yes, it moves!" repeated Armand with bright eyes; maybe, thought Radek, Lenin's sudden poetic vein was a result of his relationship with her.

★

And now he let Parabellum write for Comrade Grimm, mostly on the topic of Germany, and gathered all the material he could, oral, correspondence, as well as the press, and pondered how to make it possible to bring his Rosa to him.

Then Grimm handed him a little letter, addressed to Herr Parabellum, care of *Tagwacht*, a little letter on discreetly perfumed purple handmade paper, from a certain Yekaterina Groman: She urgently wished to speak to him on a matter concerning his future; he should let her know, *poste restante*, when and where she could meet him.

"That's what I call conspiratorial," Grimm opined, sniffing at the envelope. "You know the lady?"

Radek shook his head. "You?"

"According to the rumor," Grimm said, "this Groman works for Parvus." And after a brief pause, "You're not going to turn down such a rendezvous, are you?"

Parvus, thought Radek. As chance would have it, he had just heard a few days ago that the Parvus in question, real name Dr. Alexander Helphand, once number two next to comrade Trotsky in the Petersburg Soviet of 1905, had appeared in Berlin, furnished with all the signs of prosperity, and had been seen entering the foreign ministry and leaving it only after several hours, his whole face beaming, and got into a car.

"No," he said, "I won't turn down such a rendezvous. I am far too conscientious of my duty to your paper, dear Grimm."

Then, on the way to the coffeehouse—an inconspicuously bourgeois one where he and Groman had arranged to meet— and even before, he had been thinking about Comrade Parvus. Although he had met him and his alter ego, Dr. Helphand from Odessa, always only briefly, and they therefore could hardly have had any influence upon each other, it had been suggested to him several times both within and outside of party circles that there were shared affinities between them; not physical ones, due to Parvus's girth, but intellectual affinities, as well as affinities of character; whether it was the shady, dazzling quality of the man, which many also claimed to recognize in Radek; or the fact that they had both rushed to help advance the revolution against the tsar in 1905, Radek to Warsaw and Parvus to St. Petersburg, where the fat man had even taken over the leadership of the Soviet for a few days, substituting for Trotsky, and, after the defeat of the revolution, ending up at the Peter and Paul Fortress, while Radek was taken to the Warsaw citadel; or whether it was the parallels between certain thoughts of theirs, thoughts concerning the necessity and chances for a new revolution, a world revolution, which they expressed in their articles.

After that, however, the parallel course of their destinies changed: Whereas he, Radek, remained a poor wretch, Parvus, after escaping from Russia, seemed to have decided to also make practical use of his Marxist knowledge of the inner mechanisms of capitalism, primarily for his own enrichment: The initial capital allegedly came from brokerage fees on arms shipments to Balkan countries and Turkey, and from bribes paid to some pashas, and Parvus, once a poor newspaper writer and bankrupt, who did not have an intact pair of boots to his name, and who had been expelled from Prussia and the other German kingdoms and duchies for his revolutionary pamphlets, which even Luxemburg and her Jogiches found insufferable, was now basking in the glory of what was said to be multiple bank accounts in several countries.

Who could blame him? Wasn't the great Engels, who was able to study his Marx from the source, also a wealthy businessman in England?

They sat across from each other, he, as usual, dressed in a careless bohemian manner, his coat pockets full of newspapers, while she, Yekaterina Andreyevna Groman, in modest yet solid costume, a Russian face like a thousand others—the handmade paper had evidently been camouflage.

"So, Comrade Radek," she began, right after having placed her leather pouch next to her and ordered two coffees and cognac, "So, Comrade Radek—"

"Just a moment, please," he interrupted, "how do you know Madame Groman, that Parabellum, to whom you addressed your letter, is Radek, and vice versa?"

She laughed. "Dr. Helphand, who sent me to you, carried out a stylistic analysis: the same cryptic wit with Parabellum as with Radek, the same figures of speech, the same—not always impeccable—Marxist ideas, and finally, in the case of both authors, the same lengths when they get excited—people know each other in the business."

"Well, it seems like Comrade Parvus is doing better now, in terms of business, than me."

"That's because, these days, he writes less for the public than for private individuals who better reward his reports and opinions."

"And you're supposed to hire me as a supplier for his opinions and reports, I assume. Didn't he already run an agency once—and go bankrupt?"

"Still, he managed the copyrights to Gorky's literary works in Germany, and earned tens of thousands on *The Lower Depths* alone."

"And then squandered the money. Including the share he was supposed to pay to Gorky—and the Russian party."

"And you're, with all due respect, the appropriate judge there." Groman appeared to be amused. "With your list of sins, which German Social Democracy has unfolded before the astonished world. Cheers, my dear."

He toasted with her. "Touché."

"So now that we understand each other," she said, "the following proposition: Dr. Helphand, for whom I have the pleasure of working, would also like for you to occasionally be at his disposal."

"For what? And in what manner?"

She smiled in a friendly way. "That cannot be determined in advance. But I assume he wishes to use your journalistic talents. In any case, he'll pay you decently, and has authorized me, provided you agree to his proposal, to pay you an advance"—she drew a thick, brownish envelope from her leather pouch—"of two thousand Swiss francs."

Two thousand francs, he thought—that was a cushion that hardly any of the émigrés had; with it, he could, with a clear conscience, bring Rosa from her hospital in Leipzig to Bern. But . . . to sell oneself, he thought, completely, and to Parvus of all people . . . then he might as well go straight to the German or Turkish embassy.

Groman slipped the envelope back into her leather pouch. "Non olet," she said, "they don't smell, the Swiss francs, and if you had taken them, you would have been obliged to nothing more than what you intend to do anyway: make revolution."

"Against who?" he asked.

"Against who is Comrade Lenin planning his revolution?"

Radek tried to consider things.

"Okay, fine," she said, "I can understand that you don't make that kind of deal through an intermediary you just met an hour ago. But after a discussion with Dr. Helphand himself, you'd take one step closer to the matter, wouldn't you?"

Radek continued to remain silent.

"Dr. Helphand invites you. In a few days, he'll arrive in Zurich and stay at the Baur-a-Lac. He'll cover your travel costs, of course."

"I'll come. You can tell him that much, Yekaterina Andreyevna."

"It should be worth it in every way, Karl Bernhardovich," she said. "Dr. Helphand is a very brilliant man."

★

The Baur-a-Lac had a terrace behind glass, with a view of the lake, which shimmered silver. Radek had arrived before the agreed-upon time; that almost never happened to him; he was probably more nervous than he thought. Then he saw the spread wings of the golden bird on the bow of the elegant automobile that drove up slowly, saw the chauffeur in gray uniform open the door wide, and finally Parvus, who, followed by three equally corpulent, bejeweled blondes, stepped out of the car; an impressive appearance, past the saluting porter and into the glassy silence interrupted only here and there by the whisper of a waiter.

Parvus noticed him immediately. Radek saw how he shooed the three blondes through the revolving door into the hotel's lobby with a quick wave of the cigar between his fingers, then approached him with strange, paddling arm movements.

"So, we finally get to know each other properly!" Parvus called out in a husky voice, sinking with a groan into the white wicker armchair, vis-à-vis Radek. "We have always only met like ships passing in the night; one sees the lights from a distance, one knows the other's name, but doesn't know its destination."

"My goal is obvious in what I write."

"Oh, Radek," Parvus sighed. "Who reveals his innermost self! You? Lenin?"

"At least with regard to the workers," Radek responded, "clear language is advisable."

"Sometimes," Parvus said, "sometimes," and scrutinized Radek with wide-open, astute dark eyes.

Radek decided to meet Parvus's scrutinizing gaze with one of his own. The picture that presented itself to him was indeed impressive: the large skull which, as Radek believed, stored the knowledge of a scholar alongside that of a stockbroker, the well-shaped nose above the narrow mouth and the bearded chin, which merged directly into the neck, under which, again without appreciable transition, began the belly, which would have done honor to a Falstaff.

"Champagne," Parvus ordered the approaching waiter, "Veuve Cliquot." And, as soon as his guest and himself were served, pensively contemplating the rising bubbles in the glass, "Groman told me you hesitated?"

"With me," Radek said, "you have to put your cards on the table."

"Counter-question: you have a conception, Radek?"

"Only an extremely vague one."

"I, however"—with a meaningful glance—"have one."

"And that would be?"

"I've lived through it all, Radek, and participated in it myself: the turmoil in St. Petersburg after the tsar's defeat in the Japanese war, the mass strikes reproduced across the country, the revolution, the soviets."

"History doesn't repeat itself, or at least, not so rapidly."

"One can help it along."

"How do you imagine that?"

"We, dear comrade, are back at the problem with the chicken and the egg. In our time, no revolution without a previous defeat, but also no defeat without a previous revolution."

"And how, Dr. Helphand, do you set the priorities?"

Parvus drank the rest of his champagne in a single gulp and waved to the waiter. "One has to work on both at the same time."

That sounded close enough to Lenin's thoughts. But at least Lenin had his party, a party of a new type, as he called it, small but professional, and sworn to him and subordinate to his instructions. And what did Parvus have? the Germans? "I asked you," said Radek, "cards on the table."

"I plan"—Parvus hesitated, then his speech flowed—"to build a network, a dual one: one in the cities of Russia, among the proletarians, the other reaching into the governorates, where the nationalities are concentrated, long since weary of tsarist rule; a network of, let's say, commercial agents—trade is, as you know, unsuspicious and sustains itself, and commodities can always be procured—and the connections to the groups of the discontented run through these agents, as do the publications that we bring to be distributed, and our instructions. No, we won't run such a large enterprise from Switzerland; there are too many unreliables here for me, even and especially among the comrades; and I want to get closer to what is happening in Scandinavia, I think, in Copenhagen or Stockholm. I'll found an institute there, a scholarly one, for Eastern studies or something like that, and assemble the best minds among the *émigrés,* the Russians as well as the Polish, and in thinking of minds, you'll surely understand, Radek, I thought of yours first."

"And you're paying for the project. Out of your pocket. How many millions do you have, then?"

Parvus drew his cigar case out of his pocket and laid it, open, on the small marble table—thick, aromatic Havanas. "Let the finances be my concern, please."

Radek helped himself. "And what does Lenin say? I assume you've spoken with Lenin, since he lives in Zurich now and is easy enough to find?"

"You're Lenin's man?"

"I'm nobody's man. And I intend to stay that way."

Parvus twisted his face into a smile. "I ate lunch with Comrade Groman in the old city, at Yerusalimsky's; you know the place, the borscht is excellent. And there, I saw Lenin, also having lunch, with Krupskaya and Inessa Armand, and I walked up to him and told him that I wished to speak to him about an important matter, and he invited me, without Groman, to accompany him to his home on Distelweg. Have you been to his place yet, Radek?"

"Not the one on Distelweg."

"Books, books, books. And he started to argue immediately. Sometime, in 1910 I think, I wrote about the problems we'd have after the revolution in constructing socialism, and I claimed that the nationalization of the banks and the means of production would fundamentally only modify the appearance of the domination of the proletariat exercised by the bourgeoisie; in essence, after the expropriation of the expropriators, the powers of the state and its bureaucracy will increase, and the citizen will be even more defenseless against the power of the state apparatus than before, and will require special social organs to defend its

individual rights—soviets, for example, or trade unions or arbi-
tration courts, or other, similar institutions—"

He interrupted himself and asked, "It's true, is it not?"

Radek, who followed Parvus's logic with more than mere interest, admitted, "There's something to the idea."

Parvus nodded, satisfied. "I had long since forgotten that; whoever writes on a daily basis doesn't regard every single sentence as
a gift bestowed upon humanity; but Lenin has the memory of an
elephant, and immediately started an argument over this matter
that I had long since forgotten. The post-revolutionary state, he
explained, would be a completely different one than the previous
bourgeois-feudal state, which would be thoroughly smashed; it
would be a state of the formerly oppressed and exploited class,
and would represent this class and act in its name; and did I really
believe that he, Lenin, would be the type of man to place himself
at the head of a new oppressive state, or even tolerate one?"

Radek imagined the scene: the ladies in the background;
Parvus, surprised by Lenin's sudden zeal; and Lenin, his face
red, disgusted by his guest's obtuseness or conscious refusal to
understand the obvious.

"Vladimir Ilyich," Parvus confided, "seemed not to have
noticed that he had betrayed his own ambition to me at the same
time as his political theory. I also left that point aside; I hadn't
come to him to wander so far into the future; I simply wanted to
know if he would be willing to work with me under certain circumstances. And in order to make this palatable to him, I tried
to explain to him why there would be no revolution in Germany
as long as the war lasted; in wartime, I said, a revolution would
only be possible in Russia, and only as a consequence of decisive
German victories, which in turn could be had all the sooner the
more broadly and thoroughly we, him with his people and myself,
undermined the cohesion of the tsarist empire, by word-of-mouth
propaganda and illegally circulated newspapers and polemical
pamphlets, up to strikes and mass demonstrations and uprisings."

"And Vladimir Ilyich?"

Parvus, thinking back to this part of the conversation with Lenin, changed his tone, which up to now had been rather narrative. "The man just isn't capable of listening to anybody at all. He blathered about a journal he would publish, with the aid of which he would lead the European proletariat out of the trenches and instantly into the international revolution. And then apparently he caught the fear that I, by means of my money and ideas, might wish to oust him from his leading position with the Bolsheviks, and exclaimed, German victory, ha, I'm familiar with that line! —and by the way, everyone in all the socialist parties knew that Parvus was a German social-chauvinist and Dr. Helphand an agent of Ebert and Scheidemann; then he grabbed me, and cursing—beautiful, rounded Russian curses—pushed me toward the door, and loudly threatened that I'd better never think again of trying to recruit him for my business!"

Radek grinned. He pictured the small Lenin pushing around the gigantic Parvus, and both ladies clasping their hands together over their heads and wondered whether Parvus, out of anger over the rebuff he had received, and in order to impress Radek, had not painted the scene a bit more colorfully than it had actually played out.

Parvus had calmed down. "I hope," he said, "with all the respect that you, Radek, and I have for a theoretical mind like Lenin's, and for all the friendship he's shown you, that you'll make up your own mind and come to your own conclusions."

The three blondes appeared at the end of the glass-enclosed terrace. Parvus was apparently expecting them and immediately hauled himself up from the curve of his wicker chair. "I don't want to hassle you, now," he said, once more turning to Radek. "You can reach me in this hotel until the end of the week."

Then he turned around and trudged to the staircase, making the same rowing motion with his arms as before. Radek prepared to drink the rest of the champagne. When he put his glass back on the table, he noticed the brownish envelope that Groman had already offered to him: it lay there as if by coincidence, and appeared to him to have grown thicker than it had been during the first offering.

Radek put it in his pocket. After all, he couldn't just leave it there.

5

Whenever he, in later years, thought back to Zimmerwald, he saw before him first of all Comrade Grimm's face as he triumphantly told him, after they had returned together, "And do you know, Radek, how much the whole event cost us? —Here, see for yourself: the bill from the Beau Séjour hotel, nine chambers and twenty extra beds in the attic, plus discounted full board for thirty-eight people for four days, and from our carriage driver, three open coaches Bern-Zimmerwald and back, makes a total of two hundred and ninety-seven point forty francs. Should your friend Lenin succeed in his plans—which I doubt, however—he will have made the cheapest revolution in history."

"And on top of that, the money didn't come out of his own pocket," Radek mentioned.

"He should be grateful to us." Grimm laughed mockingly. "But gratitude is not among his outstanding qualities."

"Still," said Radek, "he made sure to breathe some life into the conference."

"I thought that was more to your credit."

"Yes, but we had coordinated with each other, Vladimir Ilyich and I, already before the conference and later during the breaks."

Grimm had become pensive. "Hence his reticence ... Although he usually preaches so eagerly, and so volubly."

Radek recognized his mistake: him and Lenin; that was no business of Robert Grimm's.

"And I," Grimm continued, "had believed that you placed such great value upon your intellectual independence, Comrade Radek: You said you're your own man, did you not?"

Grimm's disappointment concerning the course of the long,

impassioned sessions in Zimmerwald was noticeable. He had made all that effort to bring this damned conference about, had, across all borders, forged plots with comrades of the most diverse currents and conspired with leftists in half of Europe and attempted to breathe his breath, war against war, into the shabby remains of the Second International, and had wandered, Sunday after Sunday, around the environs of Bern in search of a reasonably safe spot for the big meeting, and had collected francs upon francs from Swiss party friends, without being allowed to say what for, and had, bypassing the cantonal authorities, hired the carriage driver and rented the hotel, and convinced Balabanoff to write the minutes—where were there, in these times, capable women with the right attitude?—and had misled the press people hanging around all the cafes, because in just ten days, the reports would appear in his *Tagwacht*, in a special section, the "Zimmerwald Manifesto," with the addenda of the eternally carping Bolsheviks—and until then, silence. And now he had to concede that it was Radek, the viper in his bosom, who, in alliance with Lenin, had spoiled his performance, if not his entire concept.

"But you wouldn't—"

Radek sensed the fears arising in Grimm's mind. "No, Comrade Grimm," he assured him, "I won't utter a word about the resolutions of the conference or the Manifesto until you have spoken. And likewise, although Lenin will be tempted to crow about them, he will maintain discretion about the conflicts and disputes we had in Zimmerwald."

But that was exactly what Radek hadn't been quite as certain about as he pretended to be. Grimm, however, seemed relieved. "After all," he had scoffed, "you and Lenin remain the minority."

✴

They had met in Bern on Eigerplatz. Comrade Lachenmaier, from Schwäbisch Gmünd—Radek knew him fleetingly from his time in Göppingen—proudly carried a butterfly net over his shoulder and a tin box in front of his belly, until Balabanoff called to his attention the fact that the troupe was traveling as an ornithological club, and that birds were not transported in botanizing drums.

What a glorious day! He beamed in the late summer morning sun, the horses snorted in front of the three touring cars, each equipped with four hard-padded benches; the ladies sat demurely separate from the gentlemen, and comrade Grimm had sat down on the coach box of the foremost vehicle, next to Mr. Kammermann, the owner of the carriage company.

Radek sat on the left next to Trotsky who, wrapped in a cape, cleaned his pince-nez. "Don't you seek, Radek," he asked, "the comedy in the fact that the entire revolutionary social democracy of Europe can fit on three horse-drawn carriages?"

Radek gave a short laugh. "But world history is galloping at our side, Comrade Trotsky. Don't you feel the stormy atmosphere, don't you notice your coat billowing?"

Trotsky set the pince-nez back on the lightly reddened bridge of his nose. "In *Nashe Slovo*," he said, "we're printing a column with accomplished aperçus. I'm taking the liberty of publishing yours in it. With an indication of the source, of course."

Radek knew the paper, although Trotsky had never asked him to write for it. "Help yourself," he replied, nodding. "Maybe I'll think of a few more things in the next few days. That's the least I can do to honor you for the courage and acumen with which you fought on my behalf in the Paris committee investigating my youthful sins."

"The comrades in Germany appeared to have been very irritated by the fact that we declared you innocent of stealing books and pissing in beds." An expression of schadenfreude played across Trotsky's lips. "But, how is it that you're a passenger in this carriage? After your scandal at the party congress with Ebert and company, no German Social Democrat, not even the most left-wing, would have dared to name you as a delegate, and Grimm's demand was that only representatives of actually existing organizations would be allowed to participate in his conference."

The city was long behind them. The road wound through a sanguine landscape of spotted cows; occasionally, on the right or the left, a few shingled cottages appeared; it was no place for tourists, Radek thought, and certainly not now in wartime. "But it has its charms, the country here," he said, "doesn't it?"

Trotsky agreed with him. But the thought of Radek's legitimacy still seemed to trouble him. "*Nashe Slovo*," he said, in the name of which he intended to speak at the conference, was not a political organization in the proper sense either, but the group in Paris that supported the paper could at least be called a kind of association, and they made enough antiwar noise, in Russian as well as French.

Radek found the whole question ludicrous, and the fact that Trotsky, whom he had admired since 1905, persisted at it astonished him. Or did Trotsky fear that the passenger who wasn't really authorized by anyone might, at a decisive moment, take a line different than he, the great Lev Davidovich? "I am," he said, "whether anyone likes it or not, a regular delegate of the Warsaw group of the Polish party. And I have this," he put his hand on his breast pocket, "with Comrade Hanecki's seal and signature."

Trotsky raised his eyebrows. "And Luxemburg? And Jogiches?"

Radek shrugged. Was he Luxemburg's keeper? It could be that she, or her Jogiches, had underestimated the political importance of Grimm's invitation, or that the Prussian police had prevented her departure; in any case, two benches behind him, representing the Central Committee of the Socialist Party of the Kingdom of Poland and Lithuania, which was in exile in Berlin, sat Comrade Warski, who was anything but a zealot, and with whom he had a loose friendship from earlier years.

In the meantime, Trotsky had probably come to the conclusion that Radek had as much justification for this trip as he himself did. He had also discovered a new subject of interest:

repeatedly he turned to the next carriage where Lenin was sitting, together with Comrade Zinoviev, who had taken a baguette sandwich from his basket and was sharing it with the leader of the Bolshevik group.

"When you see them like this," said Trotsky, "chewing on cheese sandwiches and gulping mineral water, hardly anyone would suspect that at this minute they're planning to plunge Russia, or maybe Germany, into a civil war."

"And you, Comrade Trotsky, are not thinking of supporting such things?"

Trotsky remained silent. Finally, he said, "I didn't bring a cheese sandwich."

The horses hustled. They were going uphill now, past wooded hills that stretched up to the rock of the peak.

Radek understood Trotsky's cynical attitude, which often enough corresponded to his own, absolutely. Despite—or because—of this, he kept pushing, "what are your plans, then? If I add the hecatombs of blood that have already been spilled since last August to those that this war will cost, and count it against the blood that would be exacted by a civil war that would put a rapid end to all this misery—what would weigh more?"

"A rapid end," said Trotsky. "From your lips to God's ears."

"What faction," asked Radek, "do you think God belongs to?"

"That, we Jews," Trotsky replied in a bad mood, "should always seek to reassure ourselves!"

He had slept poorly.

He had already been rattled and overtired upon arriving in the quiet, village-like Zimmerwald, where, as Grimm still proclaimed from the seat of his coach, the conference would now take place: but instead of the bed in a halfway decent room that he had hoped for, possibly with a view of the mountains at night, he was given a mattress along with a chair and a nightstand in the attic of an ordinary hostel, together with others. Not that it affected him so much: there were older people than he, more deserving, who had a greater right to the modest luxury that the Beau Séjour hotel had to offer; but the sleeping habits of the comrade delegates in the attic, especially those from the southern countries, were quite disturbing, their snoring and moaning and farting, and even more disturbing were the thoughts in his head: What methods of political struggle did one recommend, in what words, to these people who, so diverse in character, would have to prove themselves in such different situations in countries with such differing levels of development, methods that nonetheless had to be applicable and acceptable to all?

The breakfast compensated for the lost sleep. The bread was aromatic, the coffee revived one's spirit, and the jam—ah, thought Radek, such jam for the whole proletariat, if socialism ever came. Then the plates were cleared away, the tables set, the delegations found each other, and for two or three minutes, until Grimm had taken his seat next to Balabanoff at the table of the chairman and arranged his notes, there was that tense expectation that, although they knew for what purpose they were meeting, everything still seemed to be open and any surprise possible.

After extensive throat-clearing, Grimm began; mostly platitudes, Radek thought, and only half-listened after awhile. The war, Grimm announced, had abruptly destroyed the international relationships of the proletariat and its parties—even worse, in the majority of European states, the workers' organizations had forgotten every thought of class struggle and solidarity from the day the war broke out, and had placed themselves and their press at the service of their bourgeois governments. In vain were the efforts of comrades like Karl Liebknecht, who sought to uphold the banner of socialism and remind their people of the words of Bebel and Jaurès, and of the resolutions of the great congresses of the International, which said that the workers of all countries were obligated to prevent the war by mass protests and mass strikes; abandoned intellectually and morally by their respective parties and gripped by a wave of the worst chauvinism, they had gone without resistance into the trenches, some falsely believing that they had to defend their democracy against the armies of the Kaiser, others to protect their culture and order against the tsar's hordes, whereas in truth the bourgeoisie was converting their blood into golden profit. But now, after so many futile attempts— they had gone as far as America—the selfless efforts of the Swiss and Italian comrades had succeeded in calling this conference, at which, for the first time from an international platform, socialists were again to raise their voices against the war and decide upon measures for a just peace.

Radek looked up. Suddenly he became aware that Grimm had ended and that he, despite his good intentions, had failed to note even a single one of Grimm's pearls of wisdom. And now Balabanoff, who looked particularly inspired today, was already reading off the list of participants.

At the head of the list were the Germans, who were probably also the most important in these circles, even if they still met him, Radek, who in their eyes was still the rogue of the movement, with considerable distance; delegate Ledebour, apparently something like the head of their delegation, had even announced that no German Social Democrat would sign any declaration under which the name Radek could be found.

Nonetheless, they had come, ten of them even, from the *Kaiserreich,* and against the will of their party leadership, which deserved recognition, especially when one considered that only two French delegates had appeared, both of them, Merrheim as well as Bourderon, were not even party people, but rather representatives of oppositional groups in the trade unions. However, in France it was more difficult than elsewhere to stand up against the army and government; the enemy stood deep in the country, and now, to declare oneself against the *nation* and the *party* in front of the whole world was to brand oneself a traitor in front of both bourgeois and proletarian.

It was easier for the Russian Social Democrats, who had been operating illegally for years, their only spokesmen in the country being the members of their parliamentary faction in the Duma; these had also dutifully voted against the tsar's war credits, and in this way expedited themselves to Siberia. But for all that, the party was deeply divided: between Lenin's Bolsheviks, who operated in Switzerland as the Central Committee, and the Menshevik Organizing Committee, headed by comrades Axelrod and Martov. In addition, as a representative of the Social Revolutionaries, there was Radek's bedfellow Marc Natanson, alias Bobrov, an amiable elderly gentleman who did not look like a potential bomb-planter, and who had tried to help him through the sleepless hours of the night with Yiddish jokes.

And, just as divided as their unfortunate country, through which the warring armies marched back and forth, were the delegates of the Polish party, of whose three groupings he himself represented one. The Italians, Swiss, Dutch, Romanians, and Bulgarians had it so damn easier; each one of them, sitting at the whitewashed wooden tables of the Beau Séjour, pen and inkwell before them, were allowed to have their own opinions, based on their own histories; but presumably it was they, the loners, who would cause the most trouble as soon as it came to anything concrete.

Radek was startled from his thoughts. Suddenly Grimm spoke again. In his hand, a crumpled sheet of paper, apparently a letter.

He declaimed: "Dear comrades!

"Forgive me for writing only these few hurried lines. Imprisoned and shackled as I am by militarism, I cannot come to be with you. Still my heart, my mind, my entire spirit is with you.

"You have two solemn tasks, one arising from stern duty and the other from sacred enthusiasm and hope . . ."

Radek knew this priestly language! Comrade Lachenmaier from Schwäbisch Gmünd, across the table from him, whispered reverently: "Karl Liebknecht!" Of course, Liebknecht; and Grimm, with his sense for the dramatic, had saved this letter for this ceremonial moment.

Radek let himself be carried along by Grimm's sonorous

language—broken up only occasionally by throaty sounds of dialect—which fit so brilliantly to the sublime content. Reckoning, merciless reckoning with the flag-wavers of the International, Liebknecht proclaimed, but understanding, encouragement, spurring on the loyalists who were determined not to give way a single foot in the face of imperialism, even if they were to fall to it as victims!

"The principles of our attitude to the world war can be briefly explained as a special case of our view of the capitalist social order. Briefly, I hope, since all of us, all of you are and must be united in this. The task is above all to lay down the practical conclusions flowing from these principles, and to do so unwaveringly in every country!"

And then the grand slogan: "Not civil peace but civil war!"

Despite the pathos of the language, Radek thought—which caused itchiness at the back of his hand—some things in the letter were very useful. Such as when Liebknecht demanded that it be determined how to fight, and when he fulminated not only against national unity within the various states, but also against party unity: "Every protest against pro-government politics, every sign that you reject it, every bold avowal of the class struggle and of solidarity with us, with the proletarian will for peace, reinforces our fighting spirit and increases our strength ten times over. In the same way, we in Germany strive on behalf of the world proletariat and for its economic and political liberation from the shackles of capitalism— and from those of Tsarism, Kaiserism, Junkerism and militarism, and—what is more—from *international* militarism!"

Leaving aside the man's phraseology, the case was made here for an open split of precisely those parties that had failed so miserably last August. Make an unforgiving judgment, Liebknecht demanded, on the false socialists; a new International would arise from the ruins of the old one, and they, the participants of this conference, had to lay the foundation here and now for constructing the future.

"Proletarians of all countries," read Grimm, and that was the conclusion of the message, "unite once again!," and turned his eyes to the carved wooden chandelier on the room's ceiling, and placed the refolded paper in his pocket.

Even Radek was moved for a moment. Then he thought, while the applause came, how useful feelings could be, and how much more of an effect they could produce than sober logic, and whether he would ever be capable of touching people's hearts to the same extent as their minds.

★

This, then, was his hour.

He had waited long enough for it, patiently enduring the long reports that the comrade delegates presented on the conditions in their home countries and on the changes—by no means always encouraging—brought about there by the war. And had noticed each time how they shamefully evaded the question, whenever it came up, for the sake of which the whole conference took place: What is to be done?

He felt the glances directed at him, most of them skeptical; only Balabanoff's gentle, dark eyes seemed full of admiration; and Trotsky, although he had participated in a preliminary discussion with him along with Lenin and his helpmate Zinoviev, displayed both curiosity and irony.

He decided, without much ado or back and forth, to approach the matter head on.

"Clarity!"

Too loud, he thought, too much like the call of a trumpet. But maybe his audience needed exactly that.

"A clear standpoint on the collapse of the International and on this war, and on the preconditions and aims of the peace action! Clarity not only for the participants in our conference but, even more necessary, for the masses of workers outside, who can only enter the struggle for peace when they have broken free of the spell of the policy of holding out."

So far, so good. But now, he foresaw, they would gulp.

"This struggle must be, in terms of its content as well as its means, a revolutionary one. The struggle requires: rejection of war credits, the resignation of Social Democratic ministers from cabinets, denunciation of the war-mongers from the parliamentary podiums and the columns of the press, both legal and illegal, and in the trenches. Only when the masses of workers oppose the behemoth of war with street demonstrations against hunger and poverty, and with strikes, initially economic ones and then political ones, and yes, with uprisings as well, will they be able to stop the bloodshed. I concede, this would be tantamount to revolution, and revolutions cannot be generated artificially; they emerge, especially in war, from an intensification of conditions. But one can prepare them. That is the task of social democracy today, in that it, whether legally or illegally, makes it clear to the workers that only revolution can bring them peace. And that this revolution, once underway, will lead to socialism."

The skepticism of his audience, he noted, had, with a few exceptions, given way to a kind of horror.

"We have to say all this unmistakably," he concluded, "even if prosecutors are listening in. People have to know where they're headed, and by what route. Civil war instead of civil peace!"

He admitted to himself that he had stolen this last bit of thunder from Comrade Karl Liebknecht. But weren't slogans there to be stolen?

It was about the manifesto. From the very beginning. The manifesto that was to summarize the thoughts of those gathered here concerning war and peace and announce them, concise and comprehensible to everyone, across the entire riven, blood-soaked world, calling people to action.

He, Radek, had spoken of nothing other than this manifesto. But the fellows here weren't even clear on what kind of manifesto it should be, and to whom it should be addressed: only to party members? Or to the broad masses of workers in the plants? Or at the same time to the peasants of the fields and the soldiers under enemy fire, and to the intellectuals behind their lecterns?

This, said the Swiss as well as the Italians, had to be decided first of all, since the character as well as the language of the manifesto depended on it, with the meaning remaining the same, of course. It depended above all on how much was said and how clearly.

It would be, that was beyond dispute, a manifesto of the left, Radek thought, since they were all leftists meeting here, the left opposition in the socialist parties and in the International, which had castrated itself to death at the beginning of the war. But how far left? Lenin and his people insisted, in agreement with him, on the dialectical unity of war and revolution and everything connected with that; they were the left of the left, and although not even a baker's dozen in terms of numbers, they had already threatened to refuse their signatures to the manifesto if their views, their radical views, were not duly expressed in it. And he knew that Grimm knew, as well as the others, that Lenin, to whose doctrinaire stubbornness the split of Russian social democracy into Bolsheviks and Mensheviks was due, wouldn't hesitate to split this conference, from which they hoped for at least the beginning of a development toward peace, assuming they succeeded in touching the hearts of all except for the most bellicose. And thus he, Radek, expected that they, Grimm and Ledebour and Axelrod and Merrheim, for the sake of a manifesto that was painless and acceptable on all sides, would concentrate their rhetorical fire on him, from whom—in contrast to Lenin—they hoped for at least a modicum of conciliation.

Nevertheless, he was surprised by the sharpness, no, by the insidiousness of the attack. Comrade Ledebour, who led it, was a man of mild demeanor and almost childlike features which, especially when he expressed malice, seemed especially amiable.

"In what spirit," asked Ledebour, "must our resolution be

drafted? How do we best create what we need most, an international peace movement?"

And in answer to his own question: "Here, in the propagandistic act of Zimmerwald, lies the true meaning of our conference. Comrade Radek's proposals, in contrast, which he intends to incorporate into the resolution, or manifesto if one wished to call it that, of the participants in this conference, were unacceptable."

"Unacceptable!" repeated Ledebour. "Surely, we all wish to see revolutionary actions in the war-torn countries, but the call for such actions, including detailed descriptions and instructions on how to organize them, is better left not being broadcast to the world. It's possible that such actions will really occur somewhere, but if so, then certainly not because we've called for them in a manifesto! By the way," he turned, smiling in his best Reichstag delegate manner, first to Radek and then to Lenin, "whoever signs such a manifesto must himself set a good example. Persons who, however, from the safety of Switzerland call upon others to agitate in the trenches or to march against the police in Berlin, Paris, and Petersburg, will find little hearing outside."

"*Nota bene*," he added. There had already been demonstrations in Berlin, only isolated ones, however, and this and that was being prepared in order to reach the proletarians in the trenches, but precisely for that reason one should not already trumpet what one was planning to undertake.

And then the punch: "But go ahead and publish a manifesto *à la* Radek—in the countries waging war, I assure you, its signatories and disseminators would be taken care of in no time. However, whoever wishes for something more effective to happen will, like our French brothers demand, plead for a peace without annexations, and for a renewal of class struggle as we know it and the only way it can be carried out at this time, and for a new solidarity, is in the old International."

★

He had lost his appetite, even though the beef was tender and the sauce and noodles exquisite. He had a feeling for moods, and the slightest indications, a slight change in tone, a gesture, indeed the distance between the chair of his neighbor at the table, the Italian comrade Morgari and his own during the soup were enough to let him know that Ledebour, if he hadn't already had them for the most part before, now had the majority of delegates behind him.

On the streets, black silhouettes against the darkening sky, stood groups of villagers talking, as far as he was able to understand them, about the events behind the closed shutters of the first-floor windows of the Beau Séjour; it had been quite noisy there, the gentlemen had argued loudly with each other, and that, the mamselle reported, without having drunk excessively—peculiar people, these foreigners. Beyond the street, still in soft pink, the peaks. Radek, although anything but an avid walker, would much rather have hiked up the hill to the lonely estate that promised a memorable view of the uplands of Bern in the glow of the sinking sun, than to the night session which Comrade Grimm had scheduled due to the constantly increasing workload of the conference.

"Comrade Radek?"

Balabanoff. Now this.

She hooked into him. "What will you do, Comrade Radek? You can't just let Comrade Ledebour's accusations stand!"

"Breathe, Comrade Balabanoff," he said, "breathe deeply! What wonderful air, and we're sitting there in the smoky hall. Admittedly, I contribute my share to the stench with my pipe; but still. Do you see that grove on the hill, the whitewashed one?"

"Do you envy the peasants up there?"

"A Jew," he said, "belongs in the coffeehouse."

"Or on the barricades," she said. "If he's one like you. And what will you say in response to Ledebour?"

"Nothing."

Balabanoff was unsatisfied. She needed heroes, even if only in a battle of words.

"My entire life," said Radek, "I've known what one needs to do in order to drive world history forward. And always, the majority was against it."

"But this time you have Lenin on your side."

"Then let Lenin respond." He cast a final glance at the mountains. "I'm tired."

★

"It was inevitable that things would come to a confrontation between us and Ledebour."

Lenin stood there, his thumb—a habit of his—hooked into the sleeve of his vest, and sought his adversary's eye. Despite the late hour and the delegates exhaustion—they had done nothing but talk and argue since early in the morning—the tension in the room crackled. Only Ledebour seemed but moderately interested.

"However, I must protest against the manner in which Ledebour attacked Radek. It's outrageous to claim that a manifesto with the content of that presented by Radek would only bear the signature of comrades sitting somewhere personally safe. We'll see who will be willing to sign. We already know of a few, including Germans." He raised his voice. "Also, it's an old, shabby argument that one should not call the masses to revolutionary action if one is not able to participate in the action oneself, immediately and on the spot!"

"Hear! Hear!" someone shouted, and Ledebour grinned demonstratively. This, Radek thought, was precisely what Lenin was so vocally outraged about, his and Lenin's sore spot: their exile.

But Lenin remained undeterred. "Furthermore," he continued, "I dispute that one shouldn't mention the means of struggle one intends to use. In revolutionary periods, one has never made a secret of it. On the contrary, one must present and expound these means to the masses so that they may become acquainted with them and discuss them among themselves."

He interrupted himself as if waiting for objections. Ledebour was about to speak but thought better of it and remained silent. "We in Russia," said Lenin, "have always acted on this principle; and if you think back to the year 1847, when the objective historical situation in Germany once required dealing with the question of revolution there; at the time, Marx and Engels dispatched their famous appeal from London, in which they clearly and unequivocally appealed to force—the Communist Manifesto."

"That was a different time!" Ledebour interjected.

Lenin paid no attention to the interruption. "The German socialists must decide: if today we really are standing before an epoch in which the masses are moving toward revolutionary struggle, then we must also speak of the means necessary for this struggle. According to the view of the Berlin party executive, of course, this would be pointless; people like Ebert and Scheidemann don't even believe in the possibility of a revolution. But we, who believe in it very much, should behave accordingly. One cannot attempt to make a revolution without explaining revolutionary tactics. One of the worst characteristics of the Second International was that it always avoided these explanations. That, among other things, is what broke it, and . . ."

Lenin took his thumb out of his vest and rubbed his bald head. Oh God, thought Radek, if he starts now with one of his historical lectures, everything will fall apart. But Lenin resisted the temptation. "It's like this," he said, "either real revolutionary struggle or just empty talk. To state that one is for peace means little; everyone is for peace. Our manifesto, however, has to be about how we, on the basis of our old revolutionary experiences in Germany as well as Russia, create new methods according to the new situation, and new means for the struggle for a new future."

And he sat down.

★

In the end, there were two manifestos. Two manifestos and a

commission, elected by the conference, to turn the two into one, the final one, which, they all hoped with their hearts, would go down in the history of the workers' movement—no, not only that; the history of Europe and the entire world—with its powerful message of peace.

Balabanoff, sleepless, dark circles under her eyes, had both texts in front of her, the German-French one by Ledebour and Merrheim, and the other one, the evil one, unacceptable to the majority, which betrayed the hand of her friend Radek.

Grimm nodded at her.

"This war," she read aloud, "is not our war!"

This could be affirmed by all. The wording of the German-French draft in general was such that actually no one could have any objections. That, Radek thought, was precisely the weakness of the whole thing, and that's why Lenin, as soon as Balabanoff finished, would allow the whole thing to blow up, appalling Grimm and the others.

Balabanoff again: "We take upon ourselves the express obligation to work ceaselessly in this sense, each in his own country, so that the peace movement may become strong enough to force an end to the slaughter upon our governments."

Balabanoff became increasingly restless the longer she read aloud. Radek heard it in her voice, which was here and there becoming shrill. "By renouncing civil peace, by remaining true to the class struggle, which constitutes the basis for the establishment of the Second International, we stand firm in the struggle against this terrible calamity and for an end to the genocide that dishonors humanity."

Here it came now: Lenin leaned forward. Radek would've liked to pat Balabanoff on the butt, comfortingly, but that probably would have been too much of a good thing.

"I don't wish to speak," said Lenin, "about the hollow pathos of the text. That's forgivable. What isn't forgivable, however, is that it's missing any mention of political opportunism, which is mainly to blame for the collapse of the International; also missing is any indication of the most important weapons against the war. No, comrades, neither I nor my friends will sign this."

Grimm started up. "But Comrade Lenin—!"

The others talked over each other, imploringly, or angrily, or even scornfully, depending on their temperament and general attitude. Trotsky's voice emerged from the confusion: "What does it cost you, Vladimir Ilyich—the stroke of a pen! Very well, the text is lame, but it's better than nothing, and it won't seem so bad, and one day the Zimmerwald Manifesto will be regarded with the same emotion as that of Marx and Engels."

Radek was pleased. This was the Trotsky he knew and esteemed. But Lenin was visibly annoyed. "We're not playing a game here! This is deadly serious! And we won't deign to approve this la-de-da that Ledebour et al. have presented us with!"

"Better to bust everything up!" Grimm, an angry Jupiter, arose. "Better to split than for once, just once, show discretion—isn't that right, Comrade Lenin?"

"Discretion!" Lenin hit the armrest of his chair with his fist. "About what? This isn't about any tactical tricks! It's about revolution and socialism and"—this more quietly, already an afterthought—"and peace." And to Radek: "So say something, man! It's your manifesto I'm beating myself up for!"

Radek had seen it coming, and knew what Lenin was expecting from him. Balabanoff turned to him, like the virgin, the holy one, the crucified one.

"I think," he said into the silence, "we could agree to the version of Comrades Merrheim and Ledebour—if in return they would agree to let us share our views on it in an additional statement."

Ledebour grumbled in protest, but the Frenchman smiled. "How do you say it in German? One hand washes . . . please, you're welcome to."

"Comrade Lenin?" Grimm asked.

Lenin shrugged sullenly.

"Only, Comrade Radek"—Ledebour's extended forefinger speared him—"only, you understand, Comrade Radek, that you'll never sign this beautiful, pristine manifesto together with us. There would be a tempest in the German party if you, in light of your past . . . I don't think I need to elaborate."

Radek looked around. But he didn't see help anywhere. Trotsky appeared to be amused, and Lenin's face remained absolutely rigid; no wonder, thought Radek, after the stab in the back he'd just given him. Balabanoff, he saw, pressed her handkerchief to her eye with a trembling hand. Hopefully she wouldn't get the idea, he silently pleaded, of making herself his advocate before he had paid back Ledebour and the Germans what he owed them. "May I, Comrade Grimm?" he asked humbly.

"Please."

"I come, Comrade Ledebour," he then said, "from a nation of prophets. Therefore, before I came to Zimmerwald with you, I contacted my Polish friends, and they authorized me to put, instead of my name, that of Comrade Jakub Hanecki, also called Fürstenberg, a member of the party leadership in Warsaw and known personally to several of you, including Comrade Lenin, under any document of this congress."

Outside in front of the Beau Séjour the day was dawning.

Radek breathed deeply and happily. Then he heard a light step behind him and felt the hand on his elbow.

"Ah, you prophet!" said Balabanoff. "You really discussed all that beforehand with your Comrade Fürstenberg?"

"You did record it in the minutes that way, Comrade, didn't you?"

"Of course."

Radek took her hand and kissed the ink-stained fingertips.

"Then everything is in order," he said.

6

They perched—Radek, Rosa, and Paul Levi—in a corner of the large veranda, speaking quietly to each other. Farther to the left, streched out on their reclining chairs, the patients turned their consumptive faces to the winter sun, which beamed through the glass roof from the mountain peaks; every now and then, one of the taller ones coughed and spat into a bag; below, in the valley, lay the village and square of Davos, with the train station and telegraph office, which had called upon Rosa and told her that a dispatch had arrived for her husband and that it would be sent up to the sanatorium as soon as a messenger was available.

Radek had become restless. Who, besides Robert Grimm, even knew he was here? Should he have instead remained in Bern? During his last meeting with Grimm, in the editorial office of the *Tagwacht* while discussing his next article, Grimm had made a few intimations about events in Petrograd that strangely coincided with a recent remark of Lenin's; seldom since Zimmerwald had the rumors about a Russian crisis become so intense, and Parvus, according to Levi's latest news from Berlin, had quite unabashedly allowed himself to be seen there in conversation with high-ranking German personages.

But for the first time since arriving in Switzerland, Rosa had succeeded in finding employment, even if only in this admittedly second-class sanatorium, and she was so happy to be near her husband again that he did not want to go back on his promise to finally visit her in her new surroundings. Furthermore, right at that time Paul Levi had also arrived in Davos illegally, with the most splendid reports on the situation in the Kaiser's empire, and was staying in a farmer's cottage near his and Rosa's quarters. Levi, who already before the war was part of the far left within the SPD, and in 1914 was Luxemburg's lawyer in her criminal trials for incitement to civil disobedience and for insulting the officer and non-commissioned officer corps of the Prussian army, had been one of his liaisons in Germany;

then, drafted into the militia, he had weakened himself so much through a long, repeatedly renewed hunger strike that he was dismissed from service, at least temporarily; now, with hollow cheeks and feverish eyes, he sought to gather strength for fresh resistance.

"Ah, Rosa," Levi said, referring not to the one in the doctor's coat sitting next to him, but rather the other one, Luxemburg. "Prison is taking its toll on her. Her secretary, Jakob, who's the only one allowed to visit her, told me how she's aged, her chin and nose having become so pointed . . ."

He fell silent. Radek noticed the wistful expression around the lips and the moist eyes, and thought to himself, poor Jogiches, the cuckold, it was true after all, the whispers from that time, that there had been more between Levi and Comrade Luxemburg than the simple relationship between a lawyer and his client.

"She'll have most of her prison time behind her now"—he stroked the back of his wife's hand—"by now."

"Not according to the official sentence," said Levi.

Radek disagreed. "Sentences are also subject to practical constraints."

"Which?," asked Rosa.

"How do I know?…" Radek, like an old rabbi, shrugged his shoulders skeptically. "The Kaiser loses a battle. An arms factory goes on strike in Tula. Lenin receives a message from Parvus . . . Levi knows the laws of the dialectic as well as I do, and the unexpected is added to that."

"Lenin receives—?" Levi said. "From Parvus? He told Parvus to go to hell back then! You're telling jokes, Radek!"

"Of course I'm telling jokes. I'm always telling jokes."

"And," Levi continued, "going back to old times, you still have no particularly warm feelings for Comrade Luxemburg."

An electric bell rang somewhere. There was universal wheezing and coughing, after which the patients folded their blankets and shuffled off in the direction of the dining hall. "I suppose I may invite you too, Comrade Levi?" said Rosa.

Radek found it both annoying and amusing at the same time that he and Levi, because of the announced telegram, now stayed through noon and in this way, to his Rosa's clear discomfort, had to force the management of the sanatorium to unusual hospitality. Then they sat, recognizably outsiders, three to a side table, before a plate of gnocchi each.

With the dessert, a pallid pudding with two or three apricot slices, the telegraph messenger came and, followed by numerous pairs of eyes, moved across the dining hall toward Radek. Radek put his spoon aside. The messenger got a receipt for the sealed envelope, pocketed the tip, and, once more the center of attention, walked back the same way.

Radek tore open the envelope. Just don't show any excitement, he thought; whatever the news, what was it to these people, the majority of whom might already be contemplating the grass from below when what was announced on the dispatch arrived. But precisely what that was could not be covered with feigned equanimity. It said that unrest had broken out in Petrograd. The tsar had abdicated.

"And you," quoted Levi, whose forensic talents were matched by a penchant for ceremonious declarations, "can boast you were present at its birth."

Radek waited until his heart had calmed. He knew as well as Levi that today, analogous to Goethe's observation after the Battle of Valmy, a new era was beginning; but he was reluctant to indulge in epochal thoughts, and even more so to proclaim them, in this hall that smelled like stale sauce and disinfectants and in which the ill were struggling to get their poor digestion going. And anyway, it was clear to him that as soon as the vanilla pudding was finished, the pleasant days in Davos would be over, and that he, Karl Radek, would from now on and forever be only a piece of driftwood in the whirlpool of time, which was just now about to begin in Russia surprisingly exactly according to the pattern of his expectations and those of Comrade Lenin.

The next day they—he and Levi—were in Zurich, trudging through the snow that had fallen in the morning hours and still lay fairly well preserved on the cobblestones of Spiegelgasse. Footsteps converged in front of the narrow house where Lenin lived; they weren't the first, Levi noted with relief.

Which did not please Radek at all. He did not like, when there was analysis or planning to be done, mass gatherings; the unavoidable Zinoviev, swarming around Lenin from dawn till dusk, okay; but the others were bothersome.

And indeed, a crowd of people filled the room, in the middle of which Lenin was sitting before a book, in which he was trying to decipher something that someone had apparently written between the lines. The book, someone whispered, had come during the night, with the latest news. "But even that," objected another triumphantly, "is already out of date!"

The people squatted close together on beds, suitcases, boxes, or stood pressed together against the walls or between the book-shelves; they smoked, mostly cheap cigarettes, and sipped tea and spoke in more or less muffled tones, through which here and there rang the sounds of jubilation or anger.

Lenin pushed the book aside. His gaze turned to Bronski, one of the members of his inner circle, whose article in the *Zuricher Volksrecht* on the St. Petersburg events Radek had read just before breakfast, right after arriving at the station, and shown to Levi immediately. Bronski's joyful smile died. "Just a bourgeois comedy," Lenin said. "Isn't that what you wrote, Comrade Bronski? The whole Russian Revolution just a bourgeois comedy?"

Bronski began to stutter.

"And we," said Lenin, "are sitting here, consumed by the impatience to play a role, even in just the smallest scene, in the performance!"

Radek felt pity for Bronski, who, still in Poland at the time, had taken his side against Luxemburg. "I don't think," he said, "that Bronski meant that in a contemptuous way."

"I meant"—Bronski now also sought to defend himself—"the proletariat—where then—in the whole thing—does the conscious will of the proletariat reveal itself?"

"The proletariat," Lenin announced, "*is* the whole thing!"

He jumped up and paced back and forth, without regard for the guests, with whom he collided if they didn't hurry to the side quickly enough.

"And we sit here! Sit in this Switzerland and we must struggle to catch at least a glimpse of what's going on in the distance!"

"One has to just go there," said Radek, "oneself."

"What an original idea!" sneered Lenin, remaining standing. "They'll carry us by hand to Petrograd, Comrade Radek, the English, the French. And they'll receive us with kisses in front of the Winter Palace, the gentlemen of the provisional government, and we, who are the only ones who want to drive the revolution forward, and who represent the greatest danger to the bourgeois government with our demand for immediate peace without conditions!"

Radek did not find it very appropriate to speak in the presence of so many whose attitudes might be wavering and whose reliability might be doubtful, of the alternative to the not very hopeful version just outlined by Lenin, that alternative that Parvus had already indicated to Radek months ago and whose advantages and disadvantages, Radek was sure, Lenin must have also thought through long ago, after Zimmerwald at the latest. But then, why Lenin's irritability? Nerves? If anybody remained cool at critical moments, it was Lenin. Or did Lenin really want to be convinced once again, now that the big decision could no longer be postponed, of the historical necessity of the German variant, despite the personal as well as political risks it contained for him and his party?

"The more direct way," Radek said in a rather casual tone, "appears to me in this case to also be the more feasible one."

"Perhaps you could . . ."

Lenin stopped. Now he's thinking, thought Radek, about what and how much I might know about the matter, from Grimm, for instance, or even from Parvus himself; for so far, he's kept silent, our Vladimir Ilyich, and told me nothing of the suggestions and ideas which must have reached him, through Comrade Fürstenberg alias Hanecki, his man in Stockholm—suggestions and ideas that came from Parvus in Copenhagen with the agreement of the German envoy there, Count Brockdorff-Rantzau. Lenin had kept silent probably not only because of his fundamental distrust, but even more because it must have been clear to him how extremely dangerous the project was: the phrase "traitor to the fatherland," stamped upon his forehead as soon as he traveled through German territory to the Russian Revolution for which he had worked so long, would stick to him, along with other epithets such as agent of the Kaiser, and spy, and German servant, and would destroy any political effectiveness he or his party had, not just in Russia, unless circumstances could be created for the journey through the fronts that would blot out everything questionable about the process.

"Perhaps," Lenin repeated, "you could elaborate on your earlier remark for us?"

"I'd rather not," Radek answered.

Lenin narrowed his eyes. "But I'd prefer to hear it from you, Comrade Radek. From your mouth it would sound"—he hesitated for a moment—"well, more private."

Radek saw how Zinoviev observed him jealously and how Armand placed herself protectively at Lenin's side; the tension in the room appeared three-dimensional.

"Let's say," he began, "the constellation at the moment won't return so easily. Two otherwise strictly opposed interests run parallel through the opportunity of the moment. We, this group with Comrade Lenin at its head, have to get to Petrograd in order to seize the chance that the upheaval there is offering us, the chance to take power in Russia and end the war and take the first step in the direction of world revolution, the dream of all of us; but the German military command, which, already half-beaten at the Somme, is anxiously awaiting the arrival of the Americans, also needs peace in the East so that it can withdraw its army corps and throw them into France; and General Ludendorff knows that peace in the East cannot be had with the people on the Neva that have taken the reins, Miliukov and Guchev and Kerensky and whatever their names are, all of whom dangle from English and French strings and want to keep the country at war. Rather, peace can only be had with us, since we've promised the people peace, in Russia and everywhere, and an end to hunger and bloodshed; and he'd desperately like to have us in place and will, although not very fond of us, do everything to deliver us in one piece at the Russian border. So we should, I think, use the offer. Certainly, some will cry, betrayal! Betrayal of the little mother of us all, Russia! And will slander us and insult us and attempt to clog up the minds of the peoples! But we will not let it go unchallenged. We look further ahead—a world-historical opportunity; the Kaiser, who will make possible our, I repeat, our, revolution. In Russia only at first, admittedly, but then, across trenches and mines, carried by the German soldiers and workers, turning against the Kaiser himself. Long live the dialectic! Long live the German *Eisenbahn*!'"

In Zimmerwald, Radek recalled, Fritz Platten had been, despite his office as secretary of the Swiss party, rather quiet for the most part, in contrast to his comrade, Grimm, who was constantly posing and making eloquent speeches at the table of the organizing committee, acting as if the whole conference were his personal event. Whereas Grimm, to Lenin's chagrin, sought to take a middle, not to say conciliatory, line on controversial points, Platten, when it came to votes, almost always sided with the left, to the chagrin of his Swiss, the majority of whom were Grimm's

followers and, in the conflict of the various international groupings, in favor of political prudence.

Now he sat with Platten on the upper floor of the Zurich
Volkshaus, in a room where one was relatively safe from distur-
bances, and, via a little discussion of the general situation and the
political changes that had recently taken place, approached his
real subject, the tasks that he and Lenin had assigned to Comrade
Platten.

But he very soon guessed Radek's intention, leaned back in his
worn armchair and demanded to know, "Why don't you discuss
it with Grimm?"

Because Grimm himself aspired to big-time politics, but Radek
couldn't tell it to Comrade Platten that way: the matter was sufficiently delicate even without complications with Grimm. So
Radek remained silent. Platten was tall and muscular, the features
in his tanned face striking, a mountaineer, a passionate one, it was
said, the peaks in the case of appropriate weather usually more
important to him than his party assignments.

Finally, Radek smiled. "Can't you think of why we'd prefer
you?"

Platten could. Grimm—that had also reached Lenin's ears—
had since Zimmerwald developed his own ambitions with regard
to the émigrés in the country, especially the Russians. With their
help, he sought to reach beyond the borders of Switzerland into
big-time politics, and wove threads to the socialist parties in more
than one European capital.

"Lenin," said Radek, longing for a cigar, "is reluctant to allow
somebody he doesn't fully trust to have a look at his cards."

"But he trusts me?" asked Platten.

"What counts more," Radek answered, "is that Armand trusts
you. Didn't you recently visit her in Clarens?"

"I did," said Platten, "but more by coincidence than
intentionally."

Radek shrugged. "However that may be, Comrade Armand
was impressed."

"Was she?"

Platten recalled the hour on Lake Geneva with the beautiful Inessa. Armand, this much was known in Swiss party circles, had long lived in a ménage à trois with Lenin and the very unerotic Krupskaya; the relationship had cooled, as even the most passionate ones sometimes do, and Comrade Armand seemed to prefer to cultivate her friendship with the leader-in-waiting of the Russian proletariat from a somewhat greater distance. But she was, Platten conjectured on the basis of his tête-à-tête with her, apparently still familiar with enough of Lenin's concerns to have turned the conversation there on the shore of the lake to the question: How did the Swiss comrades think, via what route and with whose assistance, could she, Inessa Armand, and the other Russian émigrés in Zurich and Bern and wherever they were, get home?

Platten had not hesitated very long with his answer. Of course, the first precondition for any kind of return, via England or Germany, via train, ski, or hot air balloon, was the overthrow of the tsar—but now he had been overthrown, and what had been nothing more than a premonition giving rise at most to speculation that afternoon at the lake, was now a fact.

"Comrade Platten," Radek's lightly crowing voice woke him from his reveries, "as soon as you're back in Bern, you'll receive a call from his excellency, Freiherr von Romberg."

"Oh—yes?"

"The name is known to you?"

"Romberg is the German emissary in Bern."

"Romberg will request that you come to him for a discussion."

"Really?"

"Yes."

"How do you know that, Comrade Radek?"

"Because I arranged it, Comrade Platten."

"Ah."

"I have a connection to Romberg, through Dr. Deinhardt, the correspondent for the *Frankfurter Zeitung*."

Platten took his case out of his coat pocket and drew a cigar from it. Then he noticed Radek's look and also offered him one. "I see you've forgotten to supply yourself?"

"Grimm turned down my last article, and my wife doesn't receive her wages until Saturday."

Radek smelled the cigar and moistened the tip. "But you'll go to Romberg?"

Platten lit it for him. "Your project is starting to interest me."

Radek blew the first blueish smoke. Suddenly, he knew how to begin. "Would you like, Comrade Platten, to escort a few dozen of us to Russia?"

This was surprising after all, even for Platten. "Don't you think, despite both of our attitudes toward him," he said uncertainly, "that Grimm would be the more appropriate one?"

"Grimm's first priority would be expediting himself to Russia, with a lot of noise, while forgetting us."

Platten grinned. "I admit, that sounds like him . . . and me?"

"You're—just different. A mountain climber. And a revolutionary one, at that." Radek, almost a head shorter than Platten, looked at him obliquely from below. "As soon as you're convinced of something, you don't deviate from your course. You'll go to Romberg and present him with certain conditions for our transport through Germany, which he and his government will fulfill for us. Then you will be our spokesman to officials and officers, both hostile and friendly, and take us in your hands and bring us completely and unscathed from Zurich to the Russian borders like your rope party to the summit of a mountain. And you'll take the same risks that we have to, arrest, imprisonment possibly, because don't believe for a minute that we, even though the new authorities have granted an amnesty to all émigrés, are traveling to Russia in order to be greeted with a friendly welcome and be comfortable . . ."

"But rather?"

"In order to take power," Radek almost said. But he wasn't sure. Power. Lenin wanted power. But power for whom? To whose benefit? As a great adventure, as Lenin once called it, or as the lever of world history, as it appeared to Radek? How did Comrade Platten see this power?

"Those who now rule in Petrograd," Radek finally said, "fear we could ruin their concept, which consists in continuing the war down to the last muzhik."

"And are the gentlemen so wrong?'"

"We've already sworn in Zimmerwald to end this war. You have as well."

"You don't have to agitate me," said Platten.

Radek, who was just then trying to reorder his arguments in order to make another go at Platten, waited.

"Comrade Armand," Platten continued, "agitates much more convincingly. And she thinks that Comrade Lenin belongs in Petersburg, at the head of the revolution."

And at her side, Radek thought the mental image of beautiful Inessa to its conclusion. And thought, if all of this, the ideas of Parvus, the desperate situation of the German military, the fantasies of a still youthful woman and the chivalrous nature of a Swiss party secretary, fit so well into the historical mosaic that Comrade Platten soon turned up in the chamber of Baron vom Romberg, holding in his hand the work of that night he and Lenin had spent in the Spiegelgasse, the list of transport conditions—and if one even imagined what would result from this in ten, twenty, or fifty years . . .

Maybe the world had lost a novelist with him. Or he saw novels where other, more sober observers only saw stupid coincidences.

★

"And do you know what he said to me after the whole performance?"

Platten stood before him as he came from Romberg's, in his dark blue Sunday suit with the white shirt and the striped tie; his expression around the eyes and mouth showed how relieved he was, and proud at the same time; as if he had just passed a test, and indeed he had; how often was it the case that somebody from his circles negotiated as an equal with a Herr von Romberg, the representative of a great power, even if one whose armies were being beset from too many sides.

"He asked who I thought I was, who intended to travel through whose territory, as if a Mr. Lenin could dictate terms to him, his Imperial Majesty's Envoy Extraordinary and Plenipotentiary to the Swiss Federal Republic."

Radek reacted sourly. "But surely Herr von Romberg will have been able to realize who is more dependent upon whom—we on him, or rather he on us?"

There it was again, Platten thought, the gigantic arrogance of these political adventurers, how many were there—fifty, a hundred?—who were barely getting by here in Switzerland until, with God's help, they would one day be allowed to return to their homeland which had been bled dry. "Ludendorff," he doubted, "do you really believe, Comrade Radek, that he needs Lenin so badly?"

Radek pondered. "Yesterday, no," he said, then, "and tomorrow, possibly once again no." But today, yes. Today, he no longer has the forces for a war on two fronts. Today he must use all means at his disposal, even the most crooked ones, to get Russia to pull out of the war. And Lenin, as soon as he arrives in Petrograd, will demand peace, immediate peace, and land for the peasants; and the Russian soldiers, who are nothing but peasants in disguise, will personally make peace with the German soldiers in the opposite position and climb out of their trenches and run home to their villages to claim their piece of land in the great redistribution, and General Ludendorff will be able to shift his troops from east to west for his last great battle."

"And aren't you afraid, Radek, that the peculiar commonality of interests between Lenin and Ludendorff, in combination with the route and mode of travel of those returning, will suggest to the whole world that someone is playing a wicked game here, and that your friend Lenin is nothing but a German agent?"

Radek tapped Platten's chest with a pointed finger. "Maybe he is? Objectively?"

He has frightened himself. His cursed mouth made him say things that one did not even dare to think among comrades. Lenin acted under objective compulsion: they all did. If it was the case that only one road to the world revolution was open to them, and that it went through German territory, then, if they did not want to lose all face in Russia, Switzerland, the West, even in Germany, they had to take this road publicly, and under conditions that could only be justified publicly, and could only hope that the great race for the historical victory, which they started by beginning the journey, would not end in favor of the Germans.

But exactly that had been the point of Platten's mission to Romberg. "The list," said Radek. "Romberg was in agreement? With all points?"

Platten now saw before him the piqued aristocratic face of the envoy. "He wasn't happy about it. But he appeared to recognize that our list didn't merely arise from idle whim."

"So: the Germans will exercise no influence upon the choice of passengers?"

"*D'accord.*"

"And there will be no inspection of passengers when crossing the German borders, in the case of both entry and exit?"

"*D'accord.*"

"The car is considered extraterritorial?"

"*D'accord.*"

"And will remain sealed during its entire passage through Germany?"

"Except for the door to the escort officers' compartment."

"Who, in turn, are only allowed to have contact with you, as the person in charge of the transport."

"Correct."

"And only you, Comrade Platten, are authorized to negotiate with any German authorities, should that be necessary?"

"Indeed."

"And nobody is allowed to enter the car without your express permission?"

"Nobody."

"And we'll pay for our own tickets for the trip, at the applicable rate per kilometer?"

"Why, yes."

"Even if some can only afford third class?"

"Romberg told me he'd rather pay the difference for second class out of his own pocket than have to enter into negotiations again with the Grand Duchy of Baden State Railway over such a trifle. But in the end, he gave in; they will provide a carriage with four second-class compartments, upholstered seats, and eight third class, wooden seats, and with two lavatories, one for Mr. Lenin and the traveling party, the other for the escort."

"Herr von Romberg, it appears, loves details," Radek observed.

"And you and Lenin don't?" Platten answered. And then, "but one more detail, dear friend: what if Ludendorff, with Lenin's help, achieves victory first? If Germany, thanks to Lenin's intervention, actually wins the war?"

"That," said Radek, "God cannot allow."

7

Until the day before departure, it remained unclear whether he would go with them. Platten too, looking at Radek's worn-out K.u.K. passport issued under the name of Sobelsohn, opined that Radek, having been born in the western part of Poland and therefore a subject of the Emperor of Austria-Hungary, would, as an enemy alien, have even greater difficulties than the others in crossing the Russian border. But since he argued that the other passengers on Platten's list of participants were also unable to produce entry permits from the Provisional Government or, of almost equal weight, from the Petrograd Soviet, Platten finally gave up his objections; and so that noon, Radek sat in the Cafe

Zahringer Hof, a full member of the traveling party, with a bundle containing toothbrush, underwear, and a few woolens beside him, and a huge package of books and magazines.

Saying goodbye to Rosa—for the umpteenth time in the course of the last few years, he thought—had been more painful than usual. She stood, her gray shawl over her white coat, in front of the train station in Davos, and suddenly embraced him and pressed him against her, and he said, "My God, Rosa, I'm not going off to war," and knew as he said it, that he very well was going off to war, or to something even bloodier, and promised her in the same breath, "You'll join me as soon as you can." But he didn't even take her to Zurich. "What would be the use," he said, "of postponing the necessary, and besides, you'd only have inconveniences in your sanatorium."

Platten rose and tapped his glass, which still had a sip of the red wine he loved. Above the voices, which only reluctantly fell silent, he announced in a sort of official tone, tinged with Swiss dialect, that he was now laying out a sheet of paper containing a declaration, which all those who intended to join the group should confirm with their signature; that neither he, Fritz Platten as the person in charge of the trip, nor any other authority could guarantee the personal safety of the individual outside of the carriage sealed by the German authorities, and that they were aware of the announcement made by the minister of the Russian Provisional Government, Miliukov, that he would have every member of Lenin's group who crossed the Russian border arrested, and that each of the signatories bore the exclusive political responsibility for his or her participation in the journey.

Lenin was the first to approach Platten and sign; after him, Krupskaya appended a ceremonial *"Frau Lenin"* under the text. Then everyone rushed in; a confusion arose, since friends, eager for a final conversation with those departing, were also in the dining room, and waiters were running back and forth with trays full of plates and glasses; luggage fell under stumbling feet, everyone grumbled and sweated, and in the confusion, Radek recognized, by the bulging forehead with the bulging nose underneath it and the restless look, an old acquaintance from the émigré cafes in Bern, Dr. Oskar Blum; Blum, of whom no one quite knew where he came from geographically, and where he belonged politically, spoke an accent-free, almost classical Russian, in which he asked all sorts of questions of all sorts of people; he was working—this was how he introduced himself to him at the time—on a book entitled "Personalities of the Russian Revolution."

Radek tapped him on the shoulder. "Are you in on this, too?"

"I very much hope so." Blum started, but immediately composed himself. "It would be the climax of my book: the personalities I write of now on the road to revolution. Or would you have any objections, Comrade Radek? Are there any laws, Swiss, German, or Russian, that exclude me from such a journey? A ticket, Zurich-St. Petersburg"—he pulled a booklet from the pocket of his jacket and held it in front of Radek's glasses—"I already bought it at the station counter."

"We didn't plan on you," Radek said.

"And who are we?"

"The faction of the Bolsheviks of the Russian Social Democratic Labor Party."

"And only members of this faction are permitted to return to the homeland?" Blum sounded a bit too shrill. "Didn't the provisional government in Petrograd grant an amnesty to all political émigrés, regardless of faction or group? And you, Comrade Radek, are to my knowledge not even Russian, and you're coming too, aren't you?"

The exchange of words attracted attention. Zinoviev inquired what was going on. Platten looked around with unease; Lenin broke off his conversation with Armand. Radek pondered. It had never occurred to anybody before that someone could have the impudence to simply force his way into the traveling party, so no one was prepared for such a case: Either this Dr. Blum was a gifted journalist who sensed an exclusive report and was prepared to take a beating for it, or an agent of the Okhrana— or both. In any case, he was—here and now—an additional risk, which had to be eliminated, if possible without causing a fuss.

Radek climbed onto a chair and called out, "Comrades! Friends! I ask for your kind attention to the gentleman here!"

Blum became uncertain; he would have preferred to have avoided being pushed into the spotlight like this.

"This gentleman, Blum is his name," Radek continued, "Dr. Oskar Blum, maybe some of you know him from the cafes of Bern, this gentleman here says he's working on a book. But what a book! What a glorious idea! A book with the title 'Personalities of the Russian Revolution'!"

He enjoyed the acute discomfort of Dr. Blum. "Who among you, comrades," Radek pushed up his glasses, "wouldn't be proud and pleased to see himself pop up one day in such a book, clearly recognizable to anyone who will be interested some day in us and our personalities!" He bent down. "If I understand you correctly, Dr. Blum, you wish to accompany us on our not so safe journey, yes?"

Blum, what else should he have done, had decided to participate in this game. He thanked Radek for his wise and sympathetic words and assured him that he was interested in nothing more than the friendly consent of his comrades to his participation in this journey, the description of which, with its already so dramatic circumstances, would form the core and climax of his work, and he asked them to accept him most graciously into their ranks and to grant him a place in the sealed carriage.

"Very good!" Radek praised him. "Very well said!" And with a calming glance at Lenin, who was gesticulating his absolute refusal, "As socialists we practice, I think, democracy. Now, how many are traveling with us? Thirty-two, among that two children? Then we'll just vote. Whoever is for Dr. Blum joining us, for literary or whatever other reasons, raise your hand."

He waited. Irony, he knew that much, was not one of the

strongest traits among the Russian Bolsheviks, and a vote, by means of which he hoped to get rid of Blum without a scandal, might therefore go wrong.

"One," Blum counted. "Two! Three!" Then a pause. Then, "Four!" That was the comrade Helene Kon from the Polish-Jewish Bund, who had been allowed to come along, because Herr vom Romberg had intimated to Comrade Platten that the traveling party would look better if it didn't consist solely of Lenin's partisans.

Then, silence.

"Cross check!" said Radek. And then, "The no-votes prevail."

Platten approached Blum and showed him the door. "Please!"

"You'll be sorry for this," said Blum. "I would have devoted a special section to you."

"Another time, perhaps," Platten grinned.

Blum bowed lightly. "I hope."

And left. No sooner had the door closed behind him than Lenin pulled a bundle of papers from his pocket and smoothed them lovingly. If he wants to read all that aloud, thought Radek, who possessed an eye for the scope of manuscripts, then we, considering the punctuality of Swiss trains, will have to hurry very quickly on the way to the main station if we're to make it at all.

"A letter to the Swiss workers," Lenin announced, "as a way of saying farewell."

Radek thought that wasn't such a bad idea; after all, the Swiss workers had many merits for the Russian émigrés, and if Lenin managed to make it clear beyond all doubt at least to them why the Bolsheviks were availing themselves of the good offices of the German Kaiser, then this would be a considerable achievement.

But it was precisely this question that Lenin skirted around. Instead, he seemed more concerned with reducing the exaggerated expectations of his listeners, or his future Swiss readers, to a realistic level. The Russian proletariat, he read from his sheet, is in no way to be considered the chosen member of the proletarian-international family; the Russian proletariat has merely, although it's more weakly organized and intellectually less prepared than the working class of other countries, been charged with the great task of opening up a series of revolutions.

And he added, in order to make sure that nobody misunderstood him, it was not any special qualities, but rather special historical conditions that had made the Russian proletariat the spearhead of the proletariat of the entire world, and that probably for only a short period of time. In any case, if only because Russia was a peasant country with large feudal landholdings, the proletariat there would not be in a position to win a social revolution with its own forces alone; at most, the Russian proletariat could give momentum for coming upheavals to the revolution that took place in February and could become the most faithful ally of the European proletariat, and of the American proletariat as well, for the decisive final conflict.

Radek, who was still a little pleased by the elegance with which he, and the traveling party, got rid of Dr. Blum, could concentrate only with difficulty on Lenin's lecture. What Lenin was offering, he thought, was not entirely new or even sensational, but it was more than simple words of farewell from club to club. For him, Radek, the question arose as to why, at this very hour, when strategy and tactics had been decided and the practicalities were ahead, the hardships and pitfalls of the journey through hostile territory and the problems of arriving at their destination, Lenin had scaled back his political hopes and himself to such an extent. Shouldn't he have instead painted a rosier picture or, even better, a deep red one, with victorious class battles forom Finland to the Caucasus and across the rest of the world, instead of assigning to the proletariat, which had after all overthrown the tsar, a role at best as a loyal auxiliary to the actual revolutionaries envisaged by the leading minds of Marxism, who unfortunately up to now had shown little inclination to overthrow their respective bourgeoisies? Or did he now, after his numerous starts—philosophical, theoretical, rhetorical, organizational—shy away from the leap, and was this letter to the Swiss workers, who in any case only understood bits of the whole, the beginning of a greater apologia before history?

And he decided to return to this question at a more opportune time.

He would find enough time for that during the trip.

✴

The rear end of the platform, from which the scheduled train departed in the direction of the German border, had been reserved for the homeward-bound Bolsheviks and their friends and family. And soon, it actually did look like a railroad station in the Russian taiga; among baskets, suitcases, and bundles—each of the passengers might take three large baskets fully packed—there were many Swiss socialists who, despite all of Platten's precautions, had heard of the great project and now wanted to wish their comrades good luck for their revolution, as well as exiled Russians, friends, but also political opponents of those departing, and the latter themselves, partly still dressed in Western European clothing, partly already equipped for the climate at home with shawls, fur hats, and felt boots; joining them were a bunch of curious people who, however, understood only fragments of the dispute loudly carried out between Lenin's supporters and several dozen patriots of various colors, who intended to return home only via the states of the Western allies and with the permission of the provisional government, and who considered the unauthorized journey through the German Empire a despicable betrayal of Mother Russia.

The scene gave Radek a taste of what awaited him and the group as soon as they set foot on Russian soil, and he was grateful to the stubborn Swiss comrades, even if he laughed at them at first: they drowned out the noisy Slav clamor of farewells and curses, first by hailing Fritz Platten, and then by singing the "Internationale," the anthem of all factions of all workers' parties, forcing even the fiercest opponents of the Bolsheviks to join in the general chorus.

However, the beautiful unison lasted only until the partici-pants of the trip began to board the carriage and, additionally hindered by their luggage, became one by one the target of renewed insults.

"Spy, German!"

"Lumpen Bolshevik scum!"

"Provocateurs"

"Agents of the Kaiser!"

"Jewish agitators!"

A long, scrawny man whose frontal vein was swollen with wrath beneath scraggly hair pushed his way to the steel side of the carriage and screeched, "Off to Palestine, you Jew sows!" and drummed with both fists against the compartment windows. Platten, next to the steps of the carriage, warned everyone enter-ing, "Remain calm! Do not be provoked!" Zinoviev, however, himself a Jew, could not be contained and shouted back insults, "Wretched Judas! We know who you are! You've taken two hun-dred francs of blood money every month from the Russian consul in Geneva . . ."

So he had feelings of the personal kind after all, Comrade Apfelbaum, thought Radek at the sight of Zinoviev's ruffled hair. Then Liliana Zinovieva pulled her husband into the carriage; and over the continued cries of protest of the long one with the swollen frontal vein Radek heard how somebody called his name multiple times one after the other, and turned around and recog-nized Paul Levi, waving a bouquet of flowers.

Levi came rushing toward him. He wanted, he said out of breath, to say goodbye to Radek one more time, as well as the others, and further had promised Rosa, Radek's Rosa, an exact account of her husband's mood and how everything played out before the departure, and so he had made a quick decision to take the early train from Davos to Zurich, and here he was; and pressed the flowers into Radek's hand with a small package of pipe tobacco, "From Rosa, and she says . . ."

He stopped. Radek felt a lump in his throat. But he controlled himself and said, "It's all right, it's all right," and then, "I think it's time."

And it was time; Lenin had also already boarded and was waving from the carriage, Armand close beside him. Radek grabbed his bundle and packages; Levi helped him; a few more steps, in the middle of a troupe of gossiping émigrés, and he was standing on the rear platform of the carriage. Levi, below, raised his fist, laughed, and shouted at him: "*Immer feste druff!*" Lenin, who assumed that Levi was addressing him, answered in imitated Berlin dialect: "*Immer feste druff!*"

But then Zinoviev came along and whispered something to him. Radek understood "Blum..." and "in the next carriage..." and Lenin said, "Then throw him out!"

Zinoviev sought to hastily explain to Lenin that he was not yet in the sealed carriage in which he enjoyed extraterritorial rights—they would only board that one in Gottmadingen, on the other side of the German border—but in a train of the Swiss Bundesbahn that was open to anyone who was able to pay. Lenin, however, already as the man in the red cap on the platform was raising his baton and the locomotive was blowing its steam whistle, hurried away through the corridor next to the front compartments and, not half a minute later, Radek saw the door of the next carriage open and Dr. Oskar Blum, pushed by an angry hand, stumble out of the already moving train; his suitcases and papers flew after him.

Radek pulled out his watch, the only heirloom from old Sobelsohn from Lemberg: the ornate hands pointed to 10 minutes past 3 in the afternoon, on Monday, April 9th, 1917.

The Swiss customs officers apparently knew nothing of the agreement with the Germans, which stipulated that no customs inspection was to be made in the case of the traveling party led by Herr Fritz Platten. They carried out the inspection in Schaffhausen, and once more directly before the border, in Thayngen; they rummaged through bundles and books and papers, and cast glances at each other, until Platten presented his passport to them and demanded at once to send a telegram to Bern. Then they contented themselves with confiscating chocolate and *Bündnerfleisch* and Emmentaler cheese. "Export is prohibited in wartime!" they said, and placed three fingers on their caps, which probably meant that they were allowed to pack their belongings again.

Then, in the evening twilight, the border posts glided past the carriage window, the Swiss one followed by that of Baden, and immediately Radek saw the weathered sign *GOTTMADINGEN* and the gray station building with the low village inn behind it, plaster crumbling from its wall. Two lonely men in field gray stood on the platform.

Platten got out and spoke a few words with the older of the two, then returned to the carriage and announced that they now had to get out with all their luggage and go to the station's guard room, where everything else would take place.

"*Allons!*" Radek said to Robert, the son of Comrade Kon, and carefully took him from his knee and placed him on the bench; Robert only spoke French, and since Radek's French, although halting, was sufficient for the four-year-old, he had won his trust; now his mother came, anxiously grasped the child's hand and wanted to know whether Radek was really sure that the journey didn't end here, at this stupid border, and that the German imperialists didn't intend to lock them all up.

He was absolutely sure of that, laughed Radek, struggling with one of Helene Kon's baskets, but he wasn't quite as sure as he pretended to be. The room they were led into also looked more like a large holding cell than a waiting room, and when Cavalry Captain von Planitz—that was how the higher ranking officer, through Comrade Platten as an intermediary, of course, had introduced himself—when Planitz even gave the order to form groups according to gender, women on the right, please, men on the left, suspicion grew among the travelers, almost all of whom had their prison experiences. The men formed a phalanx around Lenin, who, his hat pushed deep onto his forehead, pressed himself against the wall. But Planitz merely intended—since he wanted to have identification for his flock, but wasn't allowed to inspect passports—to distribute a handful of neatly cut white slips numbered from 1 to 32 and to take the opportunity to collect the fare from each of them individually, second or third class from Gottmadingen to Saßnitz on Rügen.

Radek was more interested in the younger officer who, with black-gloved fingers on the pommel of his rapier, seemed fascinated by something invisible on the wall. Radek walked up to him, stood close in front of him, and, lifting his cap, said, "Allow me, Herr Lieutenant: Radek, Karl."

"Von Bühring," with audible reluctance.

"Herr Lieutenant," inquired Radek with recognizably Yiddish intonation, "Herr Lieutenant would perhaps like to hear a nice story?" And without giving Bühring a chance to say yes or no, he began to tell of two Jews, friends, one of whom was planning to marry, but there was the issue of age difference; the bridegroom was fifty, the bride not yet twenty. "So now," Radek continued, gliding from his Yiddish-tinged German into Russian, first a few words, then completely—"So now, says the friend, when you're sixty, she'll be thirty, and when you're seventy, she'll be forty, and when you're eighty she'll be fifty, and in your ninetieth year, may the years, with God's help, be easy for you, she'll be sixty—so, why are you marrying such an old woman?"

Lieutenant Bühring, made uncomfortable by Radek's familiarity, nevertheless had to laugh.

Radek gave him time to collect himself. "Herr Lieutenant, I notice," he then said, "understands Russian? Herr Lieutenant, I assume, was picked especially for this trip?"

Bühring's face turned an angry red. "The Lieutenant has orders not to get involved with any of you, and certainly not with bad Jewish jokes. Back to your people, chap! March!"

Just then, the special German train rolled into Gottmadingen; the locomotive along with the tender, the baggage car, a cannon stove visible within it, probably intended as a cooking stove for teas or soups, and last but not least the actual passenger car, second and third class as promised, the doors of which, except for one, would be sealed by Captain von Planitz as soon as the passengers were on board.

The last compartment in the carriage was reserved for the captain and his lieutenant. Radek, holding little Robert's hand, strolled up. "And where," he asked, "does our extraterritoriality begin?"

Lieutenant von Bühring found a piece of chalk in his map pocket and drew a white line across the aisle next to the door to his and Planitz's compartment, which little Robert, suspecting a game that the adults had set up for him to play, immediately jumped over. Bühring, with his carefully ironed handkerchief, wiped the chalk dust from his black glove and said, "If you so much as place the tip of your boot over this line, I'll personally arrest you."

Radek felt a sort of pride. This ridiculous line, which little Robert was still jumping back and forth over, was a border, the first border of the territory over which he too would have some power.

"And the same applies the other way around, Lieutenant," he said.

Every time he thought back to this trip, he felt as if he had missed something, something essential, the actual historical moment, so to speak; and this despite having made a conscious effort not to miss anything that would later prove to be an image, an event, a piece of dialogue of lasting significance; such a trip, he had realized long before the incident with the meddlesome Dr. Blum, would be unique in the history of modern transportation, and he,

Karl Bernhardovich Radek, with his knowledge of the contradictions of political development, was the man, far more than the prospective author of "Personalities of the Russian Revolution," to write something valid about it.

What was remarkable, especially from the point of view of transportation, was the logistical achievement of the German railroad getting the sealed car through with its human dynamite, as Radek, in one of his conversations in Lenin's special compartment, referred to himself and his traveling companions. Considering, moreover, that it was the third year of the war and that during these years, hardly anything in the way of railroad facilities and rolling stock had been able to be maintained and upgraded in the Reich, and that at the same time, carriages and their associated baggage cars—which, with ever-changing locomotives, sometimes moved as separate units, and sometimes were joined to the scheduled trains of the various royal and grand-ducal railroads—moved from south to north, tens of thousands of freight trains—labeled with forty men or eight horses, including cannons and other war equipment to ward off the impending major offensive of the allies—had to be hastily moved from east to west, the transportation of Lenin's group on this route appeared to be a major feat. In that case, it was forgivable to have to wait for several hours on side tracks or be rerouted in a roundabout way; in Berlin alone they spent an entire night, the sleep, already restless, disturbed again and again by screeching brakes and clanking buffers, while the carriage was rerouted on God knows which route—even he, Radek, who after all knew the schedules and stations of the Berlin Stadtbahn, was not able to get a coherent picture—from Potsdam to Stettin.

The curious thing was that neither Captain von Planitz and his lieutenant nor Comrade Fritz Platten, who had a girlfriend in Berlin, were in the car that night. Comrade Olga Rawitsch, known as a blabbermouth, with whom he had been sitting in the same compartment for a long time, and who had constantly disturbed Comrade Lenin in the next coupé with her shrill laughter, claimed, however, that apart from the typical shunting noises, she had also clearly heard one of the sealed doors open, and someone, or more than one, quietly move through the corridor, entering Comrade Lenin's compartment, and then a while later taking the opposite route.

"Then, dear friend," Radek suggested to her, "I would keep my charming mouth shut about these perceptions of yours. In Stuttgart, didn't Comrade Lenin tell Comrade Jansson of the German trade unions—who intended to visit him with flowers and greetings—to go to hell? So who was he supposed to receive there on a Berlin side track at the crack of dawn? The German crown prince?"

★

Because of this Jansson, who didn't give up so easily and actually rode from Karlsruhe to Frankfurt in one of the attached normal through-carriages, Lenin had banished Radek to the baggage car. "Wasn't this Jansson," Lenin asked him, "once a delegate at the party congress of the German Social Democrats where you were expelled as a book thief and bed sullier, Comrade Radek? Some people have a memory for faces, especially for one such as yours. And you're an Austrian deserter, strictly speaking, and therefore not protected by our extraterritoriality. But, lest you go stark raving mad under all that luggage, take along your stinking pipe and a thick bundle of the newspapers Platten just bought at the station newsstand."

It was one of the rare moments where he saw Lenin exhibit humor on this trip. In general, Lenin was all too evidently under stress, and although he and Krupskaya were assigned by unanimous agreement a separate compartment, upholstered, he had remained nervous and irritable, repeatedly protesting against noise in the adjoining compartments, especially against Rawitsch's shrill laughter, and had forbidden Radek from acting, as he put it, as comic relief. And since he abhorred smoking, he

exiled the smokers to the one and only extraterritorial toilet—
which led to eternal arguments about whose turn it was, and for
what purpose, until Lenin, probably recalling Captain Planitz's
numbered slips of paper, issued identical ones, only less accu-
rately cut.

Comrade Armand, Radek had noticed from the beginning of
the trip, did not sit in Lenin's compartment, but in the neighboring coupe with Radek, the married couple the Safarovs, and
Rawitch; she also made it know that after her arrival in Russia,
she did not intend to settle in Petrograd, but in Moscow; so
the ménage à trois had been definitely dissolved; and Lenin's
irritability might be explained not only by the political risk he
had taken upon himself, but also by this circumstance. Indeed,
he even seemed to welcome it that—after the frequent choral
singing that, in Russian and French, resounded from inside the
carriage—in Mannheim Captain von Planitz finally instructed
Comrade Platten to stop the "Marseillaise," since he feared, in
his words, that this, after all the national anthem of an enemy
country, would arouse the anger of the people on train station
platforms.

That was the least of Radek's fears. According to his observations, the people here must've been almost as tired of the war as
they were in Russia when they had overthrown the tsar; there
were unmistakable signs: the state of the fields, the villages, the
cities; the conspicuous lack of men, especially young ones, in
the squares in front of the train stations and in the stations; the
tiredness of the women, their haggard faces; the look of one of
them in particular through the compartment window looking at
the white bread roll that he had carried with him, from Zurich,
and thoughtlessly placed in view of those outside; and above
all the beer, the beer in Frankfurt. They had arrived there late
in the afternoon, it was dark, and in the pale light that filtered
through the glass roof of the station concourse, they spotted a
military train waiting on the nearby track, in front of it a confusion of troops, obviously convalescents on their way back to the

front. It was unclear how they found out that there were Russian revolutionaries in the one carriage standing apart—presumably from Platten, who was stretching his legs on the platform—but in any case they broke through the thin cordon around the sealed carriage, holding mugs full of beer that they handed into the compartments, to the extent that the windows were open, and asked without any apparent shyness, "When will you finally call it quits? When will there be peace?"

The window of Lenin's coupe, Radek noticed, remained closed; apparently, Lenin intended to keep to his strict stipulation of making no contact with the Germans. Radek, however, found that these poor guys, who might soon be in some trench in the Somme, had deserved the personal treatment, and so he leaned, beer glass in his hand, far out of the window of his compartment, regardless of whether Janssen from the trade unions was still standing on the platform or not. So what now? ... A gesture of significance, a word that remained in memory ... maybe the "Internationale," arise, you wretched of the earth ... but with his hoarse, unmusical voice?

The soldiers glanced at him, questioning, demanding.

He raised his glass: "Cheers, comrades!"

★

Shortly before Saßnitz, Lenin asked him to join him.

"As you know, Radek," he said, "we did not always agree with each other."

"That can't be denied," Radek admitted.

"You're also not a party member, let alone a Bolshevik."

Radek smiled. "Already the German Social Democrats bemoaned my lax payment practice."

"Despite all that," said Lenin, "I don't know of anyone more appropriate."

Krupskaya turned her bulging eyes, reddened by sleeplessness, to the dim light on the ceiling of the compartment and acted unconcerned. What on earth was about to happen, Radek thought, and decided to keep his options open, if possible.

"You know Comrade Fürstenberg, who's in Stockholm now?" asked Lenin.

"Jakob? Hanecki?"

Lenin nodded.

"But he's Parvus's man!"

"Let that," said Lenin, "be my concern."

Radek became alert. Jakob Hanecki, alias Fürstenberg, who was never seen with anything other than a correctly folded foulard in his breast pocket, had already strewn sand in the gears of Comrades Jogiches' and Luxemburg's ultra-left sect in Warsaw. Was Fürstenberg, by nature wealthy and well versed in business, now also the discreetly placed link between Vladimir Ilyich and Parvus?

However, Lenin dropped the topic of Fürstenberg again, apparently completely unmotivated. "I have, Comrade Radek," he continued instead, "thought a great deal during this trip, and have come to the conclusion that as soon as we arrive in Petrograd, despite all obstacles and resistance of a psychological, social, economic, and other nature, we should transform the existing revolution in Russia into a socialist one, and do so immediately and directly."

"Do I understand you correctly?" Radek couldn't believe what he was hearing. "Directly? After what you said in Zurich a few days ago as a farewell to the Swiss workers?"

Krupskaya disengaged her eyes from the ceiling lamp and looked disapprovingly at Radek, who had pulled his pipe from his pocket and was stuffing it, as if absent-mindedly, with the last of his tobacco crumbs. "Yes, directly, Karl Bernhardovich."

What, Radek wondered, had caused Lenin to change his position so radically on the most cardinal of all points, socialism in Russia immediately or not? A question, incidentally, going back to old Marx. And when had Vladimir Saulovich become Paulovich? During that night in Berlin, when Rawitsch supposedly had heard the footsteps in the corridor of the carriage and the grinding sound of the door to his coupe? Or before that, in Frankfurt, at the sight of the beer glasses in the hands of the gaunt, exhausted German soldiers?

"Now as for you, Comrade Radek"— and for a second time, Lenin baffled him by rapidly changing the subject—"after careful consideration, since you are of Austrian nationality, I see no possibility at all of taking you across the Russian border with us."

Lenin paused, long enough to let him catch his breath, but too short to develop any counterarguments.

"So I propose to you, Comrade Radek," he continued, "that you separate from our traveling party in Stockholm, and then work for us there, together with Comrade Fürstenberg, as a journalist, propagandist, and however and wherever necessary."

Radek said he'd have to think about it.

"Do that," said Lenin. "You have enough time for that during the passage to Trelleborg."

Captain von Planitz and Lieutenant von Bühring stood on the quay of Saßnitz and saluted—whether to the captain of the ferry, Comrade Platten, or little Robert, who waved to them from the railing with a blue and yellow flag, the Swedish colors.

One of the ship's officers, when the German coast was still in sight, distributed questionnaires, in Swedish and English; the latter in particular seemed to have aroused Lenin's suspicions, for Armand went from one passenger to another with his instruction that it was imperative to use a pseudonym when entering one's name. Radek was the last she came to; he was standing at the bow, enjoying the ups and downs of the ship; "You're a hell of a beautiful woman, Inessa," he said, "with the wind in your hair."

She put her hand on the inside of his elbow. "And you, with or without the wind in your hair, are a rather ugly fellow; but you've got something, my dear, that works on the ladies; wit, intelligence, and a sort of charm."

"I will," he said, "have to bid you farewell in Stockholm."

"Vladimir Ilyich," she said, "always knows what he's doing."

"Really?" he asked. "Always?"

She glanced at him from the side, and was surprised by the sensitivity of his features and the almost childlike expression around his mouth. "None of what we've set out to do has ever been tried before," she said. "I'm afraid."

"You have children?"

"Five."

Radek hid his astonishment.

"And none of them are from my husband."

"I've sometimes regretted," Radek said, "not being a novelist. Especially in connection with you. But then I console myself: the most exciting novels are still those written by life itself."

The ship's officer approached them. "You wouldn't happen to know whether there might be a Mr. Ulyanov on board, would you? We have an urgent dispatch for him from a Mr. Fürstenberg in Trelleborg. But there's no Ulyanov on the passenger list."

Armand withdrew her hand from Radek and turned to the officer. "Follow me, please. I'll take you to Mr. Ulyanov."

★

Fürstenberg, grand seigneur in both essence and appearance, received the travelers at the ferry port and had them, along with their luggage, driven to the hotel, where a dinner with the obligatory Swedish smorgasbord was already waiting for them. Radek, who in Switzerland often enough had to make do with a piece of herring for dinner, found his mouth watering at this selection of fish, prepared in a dozen different ways, along with all sorts of other delicacies.

The company, all of whose members had been vegetating at the edge of poverty for years, pounced on the glittering silver table, and to the astonishment of the waiters, the bowls and plates were emptied in no time. Only Lenin, hungrier for news of the revolution than for delicacies, spurned the buffet and sat down apart from the others with Fürstenberg; but the latter had little news, especially none regarding internal discussions from the Petrograd faction of the Bolsheviks, whose ideological fluctuations, as Radek learned from the man himself, worried Lenin immensely.

Then, the next morning in Stockholm, they were received at the train station by the press and Swedish comrades, the latter headed by a gentleman in a top hat, who warmly welcomed the arrivals and invited them to a breakfast arranged in their honor by the mayor of the city at the Regina Inn. "Well," said Fürstenberg, as they sat at the table afterward, "breakfast, dear Radek, the favorite mealtime of the Swedes, and they organize one—opulent, for the most part—at every available opportunity. If one day the revolution arrives here, which I regard as unlikely, it will be greeted with a large breakfast, and then a second breakfast will be served to the departing bourgeoisie. By the way, there's an old acquaintance in the hotel here who's eager to speak to you."

"Now?"

"Go ahead and drink your aquavit first."

Radek followed Fürstenberg, who excused himself to Lenin, up the broad, carpeted stairs. In a suite on the second floor, the door of which opened without a sound, Comrade Parvus sat on a bench upholstered with red velvet.

"Surprised?"

Radek said no.

"I thought so," said Parvus. "And now that we seem to understand each other, I'd like you to persuade Lenin to see me. Tell him it's about the fate of his revolution."

"Your cigars," said Radek, "the brand that you smoked back then in Zurich; do you still have any?"

Wordlessly, Parvus held out his case to him.

Radek helped himself. "Let me tell you what will happen. Lenin will have a raging fit."

"But it's important. Besides, I have a confidential message for him from the German party leadership."

"You're taboo to him, Dr. Helphand, especially now that he's on his way to Petrograd. Why won't you understand that?"

Parvus glanced over at Fürstenberg. The latter shrugged. Radek turned to leave. "Come on, Hanecki. We have to get back."

Parvus stood up with difficulty and grabbed Radek by the sleeve. "At least try," he said hoarsely. "I beg you."

He was still looking for the actual historical moment of this trip.

In the end, he thought he had found it, on the platform in Stockholm, right before the departure of Lenin's group for Haparanda on the Finnish border. The entire troupe had already boarded; only he and Fürstenberg stood next to the carriage, in order to bid them *adieu*, along with the eingineer Worowski, with whom they would both have to work from now on, as well as, farther in the distance, a small crowd of Swedish comrades and about two-dozen members of the Russian community in Stockholm. One of them suddenly waved his huge black slouch hat and began, with real pathos—"Dear leader!"—a speech to Lenin.

On Lenin's face, clearly, embarrassment as well as anger.

"Dear leader!" the speaker repeated. "You know how much we admire you. So pay attention not to cause any nasty mischief in Petrograd . . ."

Radek nodded with satisfaction, while the train slowly started to move.

BOOK TWO

We struck them down.
It wasn't murder, it was civil war.
—GEORG BÜCHNER, *Danton's Death*

He had it good here, Comrade Fürstenberg; he lived in a suburban villa in Saltsjösbaden with a columned entrance and high, light windows, with a view of the glittering sea under the blue spring sky, and on the terrace in front of the entrance, her slender figure wrapped in a mink-trimmed housecoat, the lady of the house, looking out at the visitor, who still had not had a chance to brush the dirt of travel off his body.

"Gisa, my dear," Fürstenberg said, "I bring you Comrade Radek."

Frau Gisa nodded her head and smiled. Radek put down his bundles, took Frau Gisa's hand, and planted a kiss on it. A maid came scuttling. Frau Gisa moved two fingers toward the bundles, "To the guest room."

"If you'd like to freshen up, Comrade Radek," said Fürstenberg, "we'll see you for five o'clock tea. But please, no later."

Radek sighed. He had been looking forward to a hot bath, with plenty of reading material; and once again duty called, of the revolutionary sort. But Parvus, that was well known, did not like to wait, and definitely not for people whose room and board he was paying.

The drawing room, Radek found, after descending the winding staircase from the upper floor with a tardiness that was within the bounds of decency, was also in style: Chippendale, or something even earlier, and fine fabrics; and on a gold-ornamented little table, a porcelain vase, on which was the image of a rococo castle with colorfully dressed shepherds and shepherdesses.

"There you are!" Fürstenberg approached him. "Everything to your liking?" And led him to Parvus, who stood next to the white marble fireplace, absorbed, it appeared, in a conversation with Frau Gisa, who had to finally remind him, "Comrade Radek!"

Parvus looked up. "Comrade Radek—oh yes!" and pushed his way across the room to a highly decoratively placed seating area, into the centerpiece of which, a mauve wing chair, he sank. "What an uncouth fellow that Lenin is!" he immediately complained. "Taboo! I'm taboo for him, you said, eh? Yet he, Comrade Lenin, knows only all too well that without me and my activities, he—and you, Radek—and all that rabble would still be sitting in Zurich now, waiting on the arrival of world history! And from where, please, will he, Comrade Lenin, get the rubles for himself and his functionaries and for his newspapers, which he wants printed as soon as he arrives in Petrograd? Answer the question for him, brother Jacob!"

Parvus broke out into a sort of sing-song. "*Frère Jacques, frère Jacques! Payez vous? Payez vous?...*"

Frau Gisa laughed.

"Tell him the answer!" Parvus slapped his thigh, but he didn't even give Frère Jacques the chance to reveal the secret connections, but kept on speaking, with sweeping gesticulations, encompassing the Fürstenbergs and the entire house. "Indeed, here you see, dear Comrade Radek, my original invention—the money-laundering machine of Dr. Alexander Helphand, the first and only original apparatus of this kind, made especially for the purposes of our revolution: in the front, you push in the bloody imperialist money looted by the German foreign ministry, and in the back, Hocus Parvus!, you take out of it the clean revolutionary little rubles for the great dialectician Vladimir Ilyich Ulyanov."

He nodded to Frau Gisa, as if it were more important to him

to be validated by her than by the two men in the room. Then
he repeated, "Taboo, eh, Comrade Radek? We'll see in the end
who's taboo for whom!"

"Comrade Parvus is in a mood today," said Frau Gisa. "The
company Handels-ok Eksportkompagniet has brought a large
consignment of goods on its way to Petrograd, silk and cotton
stockings, and aspirin, and a hundred thousand pencils and several assortments of technical equipment, and a selection of used
automobiles together with their spare parts, and, not to forget,
condoms for the brave soldiers of General Kornilov's army…"

She placed a large glass of vodka in front of Radek. He drank,
but remained silent, certain that Frau Gisa, now that she was talking and in at least as buoyant a mood as Parvus, would continue
to entertain him so instructively. Fürstenberg, however, seemed
to have had enough of the whimsical chatter and took her tenderly by the shoulders, "I beg you, dearest," and pushed her out
of the salon.

That fate, the great gambler, had brought him close to both Lenin
and Parvus meant that he was granted insights into the inner
workings of politics that other people were denied their entire
lives; this undoubtedly had its charms for a man of his analytical
talents, and he enjoyed the opportunities it opened up for him;
but it also destroyed just about all the illusions people commonly
entertained; and without illusions, one became spiritually impov-
erished, even a cynic like him.

Comrade Lenin—and his travel conversations with Lenin had
only confirmed this—was absolutely indifferent to the source of
the money he needed to superimpose his own Bolshevik revolution on the first one, the one that had come about in February of
that year without the direct intervention of him and his party, and
which could therefore only be piecemeal. Radek did not consider

Lenin's indifference—not to money, but to its sources—to be a lack of moral principles; Lenin lived according to rigorous moral law; only moral values were of a different kind with him than with normal citizens; everything that brought the world revolution, the proletarian revolution, closer, was considered moral to Lenin; anything that strove for lesser goals was mere child's play, unworthy of the consideration and efforts of adults.

He, Radek, was not so monomaniacal; he also longed for the great revolution and therefore understood Lenin's attitude in financial matters, he even shared it; but somewhere, he felt, there was a given measure, up to which it was permissible to wade in dirt and excrement—up the knees, up to the belly, as far as he was concerned, but not up to the heart, or to the mouth and lips. A sealed train car, especially in light of the obvious geographical obstacles—please, of course; but thousands, or was it millions, of marks from the German Empire?...

What was a proletarian revolution worth that wasn't able to pay its own bills—from the workers' penny, *aus den Arbeitergroschen*, as they said in Germany—and instead allowing them to be paid by the bourgeoisie, admittedly, not one's own, but a foreign one, but bourgeois in any case, and offering it in exchange for pecuniary support, political dealings, strikes, mutinies: how many workers, run down by Cossacks, for how many marks, how many soldiers, executed by courts-martial, for how many rubles?

Had he thought that far, the second voice, ah, in his chest spoke up. You should have become a pastor, you damned petit-bourgeois, you, with your sensitive little soul. Wouldn't you strike and mutiny regardless of whether somebody paid your expenses or not? But they'll strike and mutiny better for you, your workers and soldiers, if you have money for the most necessary expenses. And after the victory, would anyone still ask who paid the printers' bills and where the postage money came from and the liquor for the guard of the shed where the guns were stored?

"For many years," said Parvus, "I've known but one thing: Russia must fall, the tsar, the nobility, the financiers. The greatest tyranny on earth: as long as the old Russia exists, the entire old world will exist. Russia must be smashed, broken into the pieces it has robbed over the course of its history, its structures destroyed, its army, its officialdom, tabula rasa. Tabula rasa!"

"But it would have been worthwhile for you regardless," Radek observed.

"And what objection is there to that?" Fürstenberg interjected. "Which state secretary would you receive, Comrade Radek, which great businessman would deal with a wretch like you as an equal?"

"They'll deal with us!" Suddenly Radek felt true proletarian pride. "Even if we attend with patched pants!"

"But until then?" Parvus asked. "Until you're able to afford the luxury of patched pants? I've tried this in my time; when Lenin printed the first *Iskra* in my miserable tenement in Munich, I did not in fact own a pair of unmended trousers, and life was more than arduous. Then, however, I decided to try it the other way around, that is, from the top down, and to combine politics with business, first in Turkey and Bulgaria, then later in Germany, Denmark, Sweden, and wherever else. Surely I shouldn't have to lock the doors I want to open myself, key in hand? Believe me, Radek, everything is better with money, even the revolution."

"But not with money alone."

Radek knew, already from Robert Grimm, that Parvus maintained a network of people in Russia who distributed his goods there, wholesale and retail, and who at the same time were urged to work politically for him; but the things succeeded only in business terms—commercial agents aren't martyrs—and that's why Parvus sought support from Lenin, who had at his disposal the only party that promised *tabula rasa*.

The fat man thought that was enough theorizing for now. "So, Comrade Radek," he said, "you're operating from here?"

"By agreement with Lenin."

"Journalistically?"

"I'm not a merchant."

Parvus became annoyed. On the premises of his own company, at least, he wished to be treated with due respect. "I also only make money as a sideline." He felt the pressure on his chest, took a poison-yellow pill from a dainty box and swallowed it. "You're aware, Comrade Radek, that I publish a journal in Berlin and also run a scholarly institute in Copenhagen."

"After all, you've asked me to collaborate on both," he said in a conciliatory tone.

Parvus ignored that. "But what you might not be aware of," he continued, "is that, after the most recent developments in Russia, I also have the highest confidence of, and considerable influence with, the leadership of the German Social Democrats, with Ebert and Scheidemann."

He paused, still breathing too rapidly, and observed. Of course he knew about Radek's relationship to the party bigwigs of the SPD and expected a potshot in return, a new spray of venom, a double entendre at least. But Radek only pursed his lips and declared with a smile, "Your new relationship can only prove useful."

That was even accurate, even with regard to him and Lenin. If influence could be exerted upon the leadership of the SPD through Parvus, or one could at least find out about internal party matters from him, all the better. Incidentally, Lenin had instructed him to work closely with Fürstenberg, and Fürstenberg in turn was dependent upon Parvus. And even if Parvus's institute and his journal, the stinking reformist *Glocke*, served more to enhance the reputation of their director than to disseminate Marxist thought, there was nothing outwardly dishonorable or even illegal about them, unlike his export and import business or his new connections with the German social-patriotic clique; and in general it would be difficult to prove criminal acts of any kind against him; otherwise, his numerous enviers and enemies would have done so long ago.

So Radek added, "What you were saying earlier about money laundering, Comrade Parvus, fascinates me. I only wish I understood a little more about business. But I also know how dangerous it can be to know too much."

"You already know too much." Parvus placed his folded hands in front of his belly, as if it contained political secrets that needed protecting. "But you'll hardly be able to avoid this danger as long as you live in proximity of Fürstenberg, through whom all the trade and commerce passes." He laughed to himself. "And basically, it's not so thrillingly new; what you find here in practice is the well-known cycle, money-commodity-—money, which had already inspired Comrade Marx's most profound thoughts; only, in our case, the money is in a different currency at the end than at the beginning, and probably also has a different quality. And—to a modest extent, of course—you and your dear wife will participate in the results of this cycle"—he interrupted himself to consider Radek's expression: surprise, then resistance, then, gradually, acceptance—"not because I appreciated your amusing personality so much, Comrade Radek, but because I wish to see contented people around me, and a man is most contented when he is well taken care of by a loving wife."

Radek thought of the corpulent blondes who had danced around Parvus back in Zurich at the Hotel Baur-a-Lac, and he wondered, since Frau Gisa reappeared at that very moment as if on cue, followed by the maid pushing a cart with champagne and cognac on it into the salon, whether he would really be able to bring his Rosa to Stockholm and teach her to also keep a maid.

Parvus helped himself. Then, the aftertaste of the champagne still on his tongue, he said "You will, Frau Gisa, please see to it that Comrade Radek, as soon as she arrives here, is able to prepare a regular and comfortable life for her husband; he is, I have learned, to edit a news service, and writing requires thought, and in order to think, men require calm."

"Calm?" said Radek. "Me? There has always only been turbulence around me."

"Here, you won't have any choice other than to be calm," said Frau Gisa. "In Sweden, it takes an effort to stay awake."

✳

When had he ever had this, this pleasant, bourgeois life, which stood in such horrendous contrast to everything he spoke and wrote for as the leading man of the only authorized foreign representation of the Central Committees of the Russian Social Democratic Labor Party (Bolsheviks)? When he imagined the hunger in Petrograd, which the party leaders would of course share with the people, the grueling work there, and Lenin's single pair of pants that he, Radek, forced him to acquire during his brief stay in Stockholm; Lenin had wanted to continue wearing his old battered pair, after all, he said, he was not going to Petrograd in order to open a fashion salon; but now at least he was living in the palace of the ballerina Kresinka, which a tsar had built as a small token of gratitude for services rendered, and in which the leadership of the Bolsheviks had now taken up residence.

Radek felt like a soldier on leave, especially at dinner with Rosa, who had fallen into his arms with a suppressed cry of joy upon her arrival in Stockholm, and who now, for the first time in both of their—so often interrupted—lives together, had at her disposal what she needed to show off her cooking skills: even Fürstenberg, Radek said, wiping the béarnaise sauce from his mouth, prepared himself for an illegal trip to visit the comrades; the danger point on the route, he explained to Rosa, was not so much Haparanda in the north, on the border between Sweden and Finland—there were at most a few Englishmen sitting there who could be effortlessly tricked—but rather Bjeloostrov in the south, from where it was barely a few versts to Vyborg and Petrograd, and where Colonel Nikitin, the new head of Kerensky's counterintelligence, maintained a number of agents who kept a special eye on the travelers of the company Handels-ok Eksportkommpagniet. Most recently they had stripped a few of them naked and searched them, including the anus, and the vagina in the case of Comrade Yevgeniya Sumenson, for secret messages and other objects of interest to them. Unfortunately, they had also found something on Comrade Sumenson: bank statements for the Siberian Bank in Petrograd, which, however, were legally in her name and which she openly carried in her handbag; so the statements were of little help to Nikitin, especially since they had been receipts for payments for goods sold within Russia, including large quantities of condoms for units of troops well known to Nikitin. Nevertheless, the colonel had Sumenson arrested and beaten by his soldiers, and one newspaper even reported that Frau Sumenson had made a confession and implicated the respected Petrograd lawyer Koslowski, a native of Poland like Fürstenberg alias Hanecki; but Nikitin was unable to provide proof for the original source of the money used to buy the condoms, or the route this money had taken to Sumenson, a simple authorized representative of the trading company Fabian Klingsland in Petrograd. The prosecutor's claim that it was German money that had been passed on to Sumenson by the notorious agent Parvus therefore lacked any solid evidence, which is why the new justice minister, Pereversev was his name, had not yet initiated a trial; the outcome of such a trial, according to the newspaper report, appeared to him to be too uncertain in light of this evidence and the majority in the soviet, and furthermore, he believed he had bigger fish to fry, Lenin himself, for treason and preparing an insurrection.

"And Fürstenberg still wants to go?" Rosa asked.

"I advised him not to," said Radek. "But he thinks it's urgent; something is brewing in Petrograd, and what he intends to smuggle across the border, he only carries in his head anyway."

"Frau Gisa is already scared to death," Rosa said quietly.

"They've pampered themselves long enough, the two of them," Radek answered, and knowing how brutal it sounded, added, "As have we."

"The few weeks," Rosa objected. "And you write everyday. Who is there who could do your work? And at this outpost at that?"

He stood up and stuffed his pipe, which reeked all the way across the kitchen table of the smoke of bad times past. "One day, even the smartest of us will be thrown out like useless refuse."

"I'll buy you a new one," she said.

"A new pipe?"

She nodded.

"That would be too much of a good thing," he objected. "And as you know, I'm superstitious."

As it turned out, Fürstenberg didn't take the trip. He'd received news at the last minute that Lenin had disappeared from Petrograd; within the party leadership, it was said, there had been a debate as to whether he should surrender to the prosecutor's warrant; some thought that he would get his day in court and be able to defend himself and his politics before the people, thus handing the bourgeoisie a decisive defeat. Lenin thought this was childish naïveté; after all, in this provisional government, which had been reconstituted for the third time, it was not just Kerensky who was the prime minister; behind him was General Kornilov, who was about to establish himself as the Bonaparte of the Russian Revolution, and Kornilov wasn't such a vain dilettante like Kerensky; he would shoot without hesitation.

It was bad, thought Radek, that his information here in Stockholm was so fragmentary. But he knew this much: the decisive word was peace. Anyone who credibly promised peace to the people—even if it were a separate peace with the Germans—would be supported by the common soldiers who, tired of bloodshed and exhausted from fighting with little more than their bare hands, were just then being driven into the last great offensive. And Lenin promised peace, while Kerensky, who was dependent on the Entente powers for every bullet, every piece of bread, on London, Paris, and Washington, had to prevent his troops from suddenly disbanding and, under revolutionary slogans, streaming home and taking the land on which the landlords were sitting, the latter now still supporting Kerensky, perhaps in order to support Kornilov's rise tomorrow.

The offensive, as expected, turned into a new defeat, and after that, logically, came the riots in Petrograd. The majority of the party cheered and joined in the shooting. Lenin, however, according to a report that had reached Fürstenberg, opposed the attempted insurrection; too early, he had protested, much too early. Unfortunately, the thing was unstoppable, and Kornilov had the Third Cavalry Corps, which he had kept intact until then, march on Petrograd, while Kerensky withdrew the revolutionary-minded regiments from the city. "A coup," wrote Radek, "organized by Kerensky in league with Kornilov against the workers of Petrograd; only a romantic could believe that the general will not exact his price for it."

Against these events, the reports about the successes of Colonel Nikitin in the matter of Yevgeniya Sumenson paled, especially since the actual wanted man, Jakob Hanecki alias Fürstenberg, mischievously avoided falling into Bjeloostrov's trap.

In the meantime, Lenin—although Radek didn't know this—was sitting in a lumberjack's hut in the Finnish woods; he had shaved off his reddish chin beard, and wore on his head a dark toupee topped with the sweaty, oil-smeared cap of a locomotive engineer of the Russian state railroad.

2

He had to do everything himself, and decide everything on his own. Hardly anything came from Petrograd, from the party; there seemed to be a confusion in their minds and a lack of decisiveness that did not bode well; the only thing that came with pleasant regularity were demands to Fürstenberg to deliver hurriedly, these or those goods to this or that company, by telegraph for the most part, which pointed to coming events of a most serious nature.

Despite the isolation from the comrades in Russia or, quite possibly, precisely because of it, Radek felt like he was in his element. Stockholm was a capital city; he received the reports from the press offices and mountains of newspapers, which contained the wildest news, all more or less in contradiction to each other, and morning after morning he sat, the coffee at his side that Rosa constantly brewed fresh, and sought to distill from the jumble the facts and real connections, and, more important, peel out the kernel under the surface, the revolutionary truth, which already foreshadowed things to come; and all this at a time when every day brought new surprises, when entire army corps, ready for battle yesterday, disbanded today, and when ministers in tails who had only just taken office today, were toppled tomorrow, and when large-scale military offensives, having just been announced with fanfare, soon collapsed, and even the Germans, otherwise so logical and systematic, seemed to be plagued by inner doubts . . . their victories, were they actually victories?

In short, a time that deeply suited Radek, and that demanded of him that he give more than analyses in the little paper he had christened *Bote der Russischen Revolution* (Messenger of the Russian Revolution). He was expected to provide perspectives, valid, intelligent, and comprehensible ones, which meant that he was to chart a course on maps that nobody had unfolded before him, over seas that nobody before him had sailed, to shores that nobody before him had seen, a new Columbus.

There was the leaflet with General Kornilov's appeal; in fact, the tsar's old troopers, having become corrupt adventurers, had recently even started using the forms of revolutionary agitation. Radek, fearing danger, read: but what he read there amazed and delighted him at the same time. "Rosa!" he called, "listen to this! . . ."

Rosa came.

Radek declaimed, "People of Russia, know this! Our great fatherland is dying. The hour of its end is approaching!"

He closed his eyes as if listening to the echo of his own voice.

"What writer," he then said, "could have thought this up: this language, clumsy and full of false heroism, trudging along on feet of clay! Tolstoy? Tolstoy's Kutuzov, in 1812, at least talks like a rational being. And Dostoyevsky's lunatics at least exhibited civilized behavior!"

"Keep reading," said Rosa.

Radek contorted his face into a tragic mask. "'Deep awareness of the inevitable collapse compels me, in this terrible hour, to call upon all Russian people to save the dying fatherland.' Notice, please, Rosa, the accumulation of gloomy vocabulary; here is someone playing Boris Godunov. But it gets better: 'All who have a Russian heart, all who believe in God, may pray before his altar for the great miracle, for the miracle of the fatherland's salvation.'"

"Do you think such ranting works?"

"When they invoke God, it's a travesty. And people have a feel for hypocrisy." He pondered. "Gogol, Gogol maybe could have thought up something like this; but with Gogol, irony would have come through, and this is completely one-dimensional, and whoever put together this mess, whether Kornilov himself or one of his officers, the text allows one to infer the real situation of the gentlemen; I think I'll print it. Yes, the ranting will work—but not in the way the general intended."

"Publish the enemy? In the only press we have outside of Russia?"

"Indeed!" he responded. "What do we want? To create trust! And if we constantly just publish our own chatter, we appear insecure and unreliable. But everyone recognizes Kornilov's bombast, and the thing itself weighs as testimony ten times heavier than any analysis of the situation that I could put in the paper. Just listen to this; you see him right in front of you, the hero in his braids and piping trim, how he boasts at the top of his lungs!"

Radek held the paper in front of his glasses and took a breath. "'I, General Kornilov, son of a Cossack peasant, declare to all and sundry that I personally need nothing but the preservation of our great fatherland, and I swear that by defeating the enemy

I shall bring Russia to the constituent assembly, in which the people themselves will decide its destiny and determine the new state order.' "

He interrupted himself. "Isn't that gloriously dishonest? And it gets better! 'I am not willing to hand over Russia to its hereditary enemy, the German tribe, to make the Russian people the slaves of the Germans, and I prefer to fall on the field of honor and battle, so as to not have to witness the disgrace and dishonor of Russian soil.' "

Radek reached for his cup, drank the rest of the coffee that was still in it, and promptly choked. Rosa thumped his back. "The great words," he said, when he was able to speak again, "no matter whose, always seem to end up in the wrong throat . . . and here, as a finale!" He stood up, already a monument, in his raised fist the rapier, " 'Russian people! The life of your fatherland is in your hands! . . .' "—and he clicked his heels together—" 'General Kornilov.' "

Kornilov's coup failed. The troops did not play along with their general, and the provisional government had gotten away with it once again. Prime Minister Kerensky rewarded the common soldiers and sailors by forbidding them to arrest their counter-revolutionary officers, but he himself opened negotiations with Kornilov. That, however, proved to be unproductive.

In Vyborg, they tore the epaulettes from the shoulders of the colonels, and there were shootings, as well as on the cruiser *Petropavlovsk*. At the front, entire higher staffs were arrested by the rebellious soldiers.

The readership of Radek's *Bote* consisted mostly of intellectuals—journalists, professors, civil servants—a target audience, in other words, that was able in turn to influence others. Now he sought to direct the gaze of these readers of his to a future that he, and presumably they as well, had always had in mind, but which overnight seemed to have moved from a fairy-tale distance to being within reach.

He wrote: "Capitalist Europe will not emerge from the war as it entered it. But if things come to decisive struggles for a social reorganization of Europe, questions of state reform in the capitalist countries will also assume a much sharper character."

Fürstenberg, for whom it was easy enough, had provided him with decent English tobacco. Radek lit his pipe and felt how the fragrance pleasantly stimulated him. He must, he thought, get from the form to the content, although this content was still unclear to him, a shadow in the mist, hardly more.

He dipped his pen in Fürstenberg's green-gold ink. "In Russia, the direct struggle for socialism is impossible at this time in view of the medieval condition of the agricultural economy and the low labor productivity in industry."

Here, he knew, he was contradicting Lenin, who, after that nightly stop in Berlin, had suddenly considered Russian socialism feasible; but the *Bote der russischen Revolution* was Radek's paper, only he was responsible, and he had never let others, not even Lenin, tell him what to say. Only: which forms, economic as well as administrative, should be recommended, with what content; what could be implemented at all in the foreseeable future?

Wishful thinking wasn't helpful, he thought; only facts counted. And what were the facts? "After all, the most important industries, such as metallurgy, coal and ore mining, transportation, and banking are as concentrated in Russia as in Germany and America. And if today they worked in the hands of the cartels for a small clique of Russian and foreign capitalists, they would also be able to do so for the state. Russia will have to put its hands on them if it is to overcome the social consequences of the war."

Russia, he thought. What kind of Russia? Under whose rule, whose control?

This was the central point; from here the fate not only of the country but of the whole world revolution, would be determined. "The only question is," he wrote with a hurried pen, "what kind of entity will be created: will the rule of a state monopoly be established, which will treat the masses of the proletariat and consumers no differently than the private cartels did, or will the economy be under the direction of a state in which the working class and petit-bourgeois masses of the people will have the decisive say?"

It was, consequently, about democracy, and democracy on the field where the real decisions were made: the economy. And what would it have to look like, such a democracy? Had it already existed somewhere in history, developed or in a still-embryonic state, that it could be used as a model, or would something new have to be created from scratch? And how and in what way?

"Not only will Western and Central Europe emerge from the war socially transformed," he wrote, this time rather hesitantly, "but Russia, too, will present a picture of transitional social forms far removed from what we know from previous history."

He closed his eyes. Then, all at once, the image he had been looking for came together from yes and no, downfall and utopia. And now he wrote hastily, so that nothing of his picture would escape him: "the parliamentary republic with the rule of the bureaucracy and its clique of clients cannot be the form of asserting the influences of the masses of the people. For this, local and central organs of the worker and peasant masses are necessary, which should have in their hands the administration of the state and permanent control over industry. Such a function could be assumed by the soviets…"

In his excitement, he had spoken fragments of his text aloud, and laughed, a bit embarrassed, at his inner commitment. Then, however, an idea occurred to him that was so much in accord with his hopes that he deliberately read his last sentences aloud as he wrote them down. "There might be clever people now reaching for handbooks of constitutional law to prove that the demand for a republic of soviets is utopian, because there is no example known to history of a hitherto non-ruling class having been able to exercise such extensive control. These people seem to think that history is not permitted to bring forth anything which they haven't already learned about behind a school desk."

Rosa entered the room. "Who are you talking to?"

He folded his papers and pressed them into her hand. "Read. You know how little I think of prophecies; but this one may have a chance of becoming reality."

Then, without advance notice, Balabanoff arrived. He recognize the dark voice immediately, although it was distorted by the vibrations in the diaphragm of the telephone receiver. "Yes, it's me, Angelica Balabanoff, yes, here in Stockholm; you can't imagine, Comrade Radek, how much I'm looking forward to meeting you again, I've been following your every step and your activity, which is so much in the spirit of Zimmerwald; yes, Zimmerwald is alive, didn't you receive my letter, which I sent to you while still in Switzerland; and didn't Grimm tell you that the ISC, our International Socialist Commission, is planning a new Zimmerwald conference, only larger than the first one, and this time in Stockholm; we want to be closer to what's happening in Russia than before. I'll tell you everything as soon as we see each other, and also about my impressions during my visit to Petrograd, when will we see each other, Karl Bernhardovich?"

That was her, dear Angelica, her Italian nature, her enthusiasm, and of course she would try to take up his time, although he had more urgent things to do, and again he wouldn't be able to defend himself against her attempts to ensnare him, because, at least pro forma, he, too, had been a founding member there since the days of Zimmerwald, and she was the secretary; Lenin had hung this albatross around his neck, Lenin being by no means always a selfless friend; but Switzerland had receded far into the distance since the departure from Zurich in the sealed train, the new proximity to Petrograd shifted perspectives as well as priorities.

And Grimm. Grimm had indeed informed him of the possibility of a new conference of the Zimmerwald movement, the aim of which was to increase the pressure of the Social Democratic and labor parties on the provisional Russian government and the governments of the great powers to finally make peace, a peace without annexations and tributes. Surprisingly, Grimm had turned up in Stockholm, already at the end of April; he, Radek, had just settled at the Fürstenberg house. He was, Grimm had told him, in transit to Petrograd, where he intended to negotiate with the soviet and the provisional government concerning the return home of the remaining émigrés from Switzerland; after all, Radek and the group around Lenin were only a fraction of the many hundreds who longed to return to Russia; no, Grimm assured him, he was not acting on behalf of anyone, neither the Swiss party nor the Swiss government, nor the Zimmerwald movement and its International Socialist Commission, although they all knew about his enterprise, he had informed them himself, but his mission was exclusively on his own initiative; and yet he struck a note that made people sit up and take notice. Radek didn't know if the man wanted to make himself seem interesting or if he wanted to suggest that the émigré question was only the official reason for his journey and that there was something more important behind it, secret negotiations about war and peace, for example, with him, Robert Grimm of the *Berner Tagwacht*, in the role of the *éminence grise* of world history.

Radek remembered how he had smiled at Comrade Grimm, full of sympathy and understanding—why should he spoil things with him? But in the course of the following weeks, his smile had turned to a grin of schadenfreude, for Grimm, the great diplomat, was stuck in Stockholm until well into May, when the Mensheviks in Petrograd, Chkheidze and Tsereteli, who were in charge of the soviet at the time, finally agreed to grant him an entry visa through the Russian Embassy in Sweden.

Peace, thought Radek. Considered dialectically, one had to ask, Whose peace? In the unlikely event that Grimm's efforts yielded results, and that Kerensky loosened his ties to the Entente powers, and that the provisional government, through the mediation of some sort of Swiss agency, actually opened negotiations with Ludendorff, who, given the almost pathological craving of the Russian peasants and workers for peace, would benefit? Kerensky. Kerensky, suddenly an angel of peace, together with his bourgeois backers and a few Mensheviks as decoration, would then be able to sit in the saddle of power for years to come, unchallenged, and all the effort that Lenin and Radek had undertaken to make the Russian situation the starting point of the world revolution would be in vain.

And suddenly, it flashed through his brain, a ray of light that illuminated at least a bit of the dark path: what was true of Grimm was also true of Balabanoff and her Zimmerwaldians. As cynical as it sounded, the war had to continue until the total collapse of bourgeois Russia, until from the chaos the Bolsheviks, clanking iron like Fortinbras, could emerge and sweep away all the intermediate groupings, all the compromisers, all the tearful virgins: the peace had to be a revolutionary one, or none at all.

Later, after wracking his brain for a long time about what course of action to advise to the comrades—assuming he reached them at all—on the Grimm matter, it turned out he didn't have to worry at all; the overeager dolt had somehow tripped over his own feet in Petrograd; suddenly, one read in the Russian press that a Herr Robert Grimm from Bern was an agent who maintained connections with the German authorities through the Swiss embassy and advocated to certain highly placed officials a separate peace with Germany and breaking off the alliance with the Entente powers, which after all was close to the hearts of the Russian people; and shortly thereafter Grimm reappeared in Stockholm, expelled by ministers Skobelev and Tsereteli personally, and now in trouble with the Swiss authorities and the leadership of his own party as well as Balabanoff who, as she gleefully reported to Radek, had witnessed the entire scandal in Petrograd and now, leading the recently assembled participants of the reopened Zimmerwald Conference, demanded accountability from Grimm as one of the prominent figures of the movement.

★

There she sat, in his study in Saltsjösbaden, the only room in Fürstenberg's villa in which a vibrant disorder prevailed, newspapers and brochures scattered over the carpets, a mess of books and manuscripts on tables and chairs, letting his Rosa serve her, tea and crumpets with marmalades of various colors, served on the finest china, and he involuntarily compared the two women, his and the other one in her dark silks that emphasized rather than concealed the sensuous curves of breasts and thighs, and the comparison, at least outwardly, came out to the disadvantage of his somewhat sober-looking Rosa.

"Oh, it was terrible," said Balabanoff, her voice tinged with tragedy, "Grimm, placed at the leadership of Zimmerwald by us, suddenly in touch with the Germans—we simply couldn't believe it until, in his Petrograd hotel room, he admitted it to us himself. He had, he said, for the sake of the negotiations—which he had already initiated with certain authorities—to find out what the German generals were planning; a new offensive on the part of the Germans would have ruined his whole plan; hence, and at his instigation, the telegrams between the Swiss embassy in Petersburg and his friend in Bern, federal councilor Hoffmann, which the Russians intercepted, and the campaign of the right-wing Russian press against him and Zimmerwald; he knows he'll have to account for it all, and take responsibility for everything, standing by his cause like a man."

"Oh God…" Radek broke off; he would be careful not to let on how well Grimm's foolish game fit into his political concept. Then he said, "The guy has never been able to keep it together. But somehow, his lack of foresight is also touching: the daily war dead, I'm sure, weighed on his Swiss cowherd heart and drove him to his partisan escapade."

That didn't stop Radek from attacking Comrade Grimm behind his back at this, the last of the Zimmerwald conferences, in front of the representatives of the left-wing groupings within the socialist parties of Russia, Germany, Austria, and the neutral countries; he had served often enough as a scapegoat in his own life and experienced firsthand how many political advantages could be derived from the sacrifice of such an animal.

But despite all the efforts—mainly by representatives of the Mensheviks and their German sympathizers—to cling to such a productive topic, the central focus of the conference remained the revolution on the other side of the Swedish-Finnish border, whose ever-deepening crisis threatened to draw the fifty or sixty delegates into its maelstrom; after all, Stockholm in general that autumn was a veritable nest of spies and political intriguers and journalists from the most diverse countries—often enough, all three things in one person.

Balabanoff, and Radek thought this admirable despite his private reservations about her, dominated the conference; less so by means of the logic of her thoughts, which was often lacking, than by her expressive gestures and looks. "The revolution," she said, shaking her head so that her dark hair fell back and her beautifully arched forehead showed, "what, I ask you, can the international proletariat do in this difficult hour so that the revolution of our Russian brothers and sisters is not crushed by internal and external opponents, and the comrades who struggle desperately there won't feel as if they stand alone?"

Radek knew what she was striving for: nothing impossible, really; but he also knew that this time, she wouldn't prevail with her line.

"You know, friends," she said almost pleadingly, "what the Russian Revolution means for the socialist peace movement, and you all know the saying with which, back in Kienthal, our second conference concluded, and which is all the more true today: either the revolution kills the war, or the war kills the revolution."

"You want, Comrade Balabanoff, for us to call a strike," said the Reichstag deputy Haase of the Independent Socialists, which had in the meantime split from the patriotic majority of the German Social Democratic Party and formed its own faction, "for a mass strike, indeed a general strike. But I tell you, I won't vote for that." He rubbed his broad chin, on which there was gray stubble after negotiating here all day and half the night. "I can't vote for measures where it's a foregone conclusion that they won't work—at least, not here in Germany. War means a state of emergency, and every strike, a mass strike even more so, leads to bloody sacrifices."

"And in Russia," said Radek, "we're not making any bloody sacrifices?"

"Of what use is the most beautiful call to strike," countered Haase, "if the workers don't follow it?"

Nonetheless, he remained in the minority, even among his own countrymen. The majority of delegates, wherever they came from, loudly declared, yes, mass strike; however, Radek suspected that they were leaving themselves a loophole; for it was also said, with Balabanoff's blessing, that the call for an international mass strike must be part of a new manifesto, called the Stockholm Call for Peace, and that this call for peace could be presented to the workers only after agreement had been reached with authorized comrades from the French and English parties, as well as with the Belgians and Americans; and since this could not be done easily by letter or even by telephone or cable, a messenger had to be found, a reliable one who, moreover, possessed a passport that would enable him to enter the Western countries; and this messenger had to memorize the text of the call for peace very carefully, for in times like these, there was only one container impenetrable to government eyes: the human brain.

And in fact, such a delegate was found who met the specifications, a Dane, and now seventeen of them, Germans, Austrians, Russians, Poles, Romanians, Finns, and comrades from the other countries that had remained neutral, assisted by tried and tested lawyers who helped them to avoid the worst legal faux pas, sat and worked on a draft, which, on the one hand, was to express their indignation at the reactionary measures of the governments and the demagogy of their stooges, the devout Social Democrats, and on the other hand, was to speak in stirring words of the war and its consequences, the sacrifices and suffering of the people, and all of this so briefly and easily comprehensible that the Dane could learn it by heart and then repeat it on the spot.

Not an easy task for the seventeen, each of whom was accustomed to their party jargon, and Balabanoff struggled to translate the hackneyed phrases and verbiage into language that could be understood by a general audience. "Only the masses loyal to socialism are capable," she translated the jumble of thoughts of Comrade Stadthagen, a hollow-cheeked German who coughed his tubercles across the table along with his impassioned speech, "are capable of putting an end to the war. The situation in Russia admonishes the international proletariat to take immediate action. Peace cannot be forced by isolated strikes in individual countries. The hour has struck for the march of the world proletariat! Workers, fight for mass action in every pulsing workshop, in every hut where people are starving!"

"Wonderful!" said Radek, "And so moving!"—although the pathos of the text, which resounded everywhere and was emphasized by Balabanoff's gestures, embarrassed him.

The others also applauded.

"So I will make sure," he continued, "that the appeal reaches the public as soon as possible."

"For God's sake!" Balabanoff started up, her usually tantalizing lips contorted in annoyance. "We have to give the parties not represented here a chance to speak! Only then can we—!"

"And how long do you want to wait?" asked Radek, turning to the Plenum, especially the Germans, who, agitated at the predicament he had put them in, put their heads together: Hugo Haase, Ledebour, Kautsky, Bernstein—all the leftist notables seemed to have come from Berlin this time to identify themselves, in light of new developments, with Zimmerwald. "How long do you want to wait," he repeated, "while the revolution in Petrograd is in extreme danger and our best comrades have to hide from Kerensky's bloodhounds?"

"Speak for your Bolsheviks!" shouted Axelrod, who represented the other side of the scale of Russian socialism, the Mensheviks. "With all due respect to people like Lenin, you're confusing their self-inflicted situation with the fate of the revolution!"

Radek got rough. Axelrod was nothing more—to his displeasure, he couldn't think of a more original word at that moment—nothing other than a lackey of the bourgeoisie; in reaction to this, Axelrod together with his party comrade Panin left the room in protest, and a general clamor and arguing started up. At last Balabanoff succeeded, with waving arm movements and shouts of "Silence! Silence!" in creating calm and a kind of agreement that it was better to postpone the publication of the manifesto after all, until at least an initial report on the reaction of the Western parties arrived.

So nothing remained for Radek other than to vent his bitterness in the next issue of his *Bote*. "Before the appearance of the official report, we cannot publish anything concerning the practical resolutions of the Stockholm conference," he wrote, "but we can concerning the congress of the Mensheviks, which occurred at roughly the same time in Petrograd and at which a resolution that demanded immediate peace and the recognition of the principles of Zimmerwald was rejected. Thus did the fraud of the Mensheviks' partisanship on behalf of these principles, with which they deceived the world for two years, come to its formal end."

★

That morning, the sky vaulting steel blue over the roofs of Stockholm, Radek left the villa in Saltsjösbaden with a buoyant step. The resilience of his nerves, which had suffered so long under the protracted arguments of the conference delegates as well as under Balabanoff's comforting permanent smile, was restored: even his coat, which on other days hung negligently from his shoulders, with dozens of newspapers and printed matter in his pockets, seemed today like a proper piece of clothing; the only paper he carried was an already crumpled one on which were noted the key words of the statement he intended to deliver before Balabanoff read out the statement.

But the rumor mills had been turning faster than he had suspected; no sooner had he entered the room with the paneled front wall, where the conference had been meeting for what now seemed like ages, he found himself surrounded by the delegates and pressed in the most varied accents: was it really true? Was there fighting in Petrograd? And what was the situation, who stood against whom, and who had the upper hand?

He was silent and warded them off; then, drawing the others after him, he strode forward, where, on a sort of platform, Balabanoff was enthroned behind the head table. When he had reached her, she rose solemnly, stepped around the table, spread her arms, and pressed him to her breast; her scent, partly her body's own, and partly *eau de toilette*, surrounded him, and he felt her cheek press softly against his whiskers.

"Oh, what luck!" she breathed.

He escaped from her. She was always the same, even now, dear Angelica: touching and believing, and therefore also a little ridiculous, and although she possessed an instinct for organizational power, always ready to concede on all sides. She'd be needed, he thought; the only question was: how long?

"Let me speak," he said.

She requested silence with a dramatic gesture.

Radek took his piece of paper in hand and read, suddenly more hoarse, "Declaration of the foreign representative of the Bolsheviks to the International."

He paused and whispered an impulsive prayer—dear old Jewish God, don't let my voice fail me in this hour. And he felt the mucous membranes in his throat smooth out, and his bronchials become permeable.

"Workers!"

He heard Balabanoff breathe.

"In Petrograd," he read aloud, "on the seventh of November, the workers and soldiers triumphed over the government of the capitalists and Junkers. Power is in the hands of the workers and soldiers council. The government has been overthrown which, installed by the people on the ruins of tsarism, trampled underfoot the people's interests; which deprived the people of bread in order to give charitable gifts to the Junkers; which did not touch the war loan-sharks, but instead of freedom gave the masses courts-martial and, as a scourge on behalf of Entente capital, drove the soldiers again and again into war without even attempting to negotiate peace. The workers and soldiers of Petrograd have chased out this government, as they chased out the tsar. And their first word is: peace. Immediate peace, without annexations and tributes. Immediate ceasefire! And an immediate start to negotiations!"

He smoothed out his piece of paper, folded it carefully, and put it away.

"Workers of the world," he said, now completely calm, almost as if he were speaking to some old acquaintances in a tavern, "The call of Red Petrograd is addressed to you. And now you have the floor."

Balabanoff leaped up. "Friends!" she cried into the general cheering. "After what we've just heard, I think we ought to break through the barrier we've imposed upon ourselves and ask Comrade Radek to hand our Stockholm call for peace, the result of our long joint deliberations, over to the press along with his statement."

Even Comrade Haase of the USPD,[2] quite apart from Kautsky, Bernstein, and the other German luminaries, voted for the motion, although he still thought that the proletarians of his

---

2. Independent Social Democratic Party of Germany (*Unabhängige Sozialdemokratische Partei Deutschlands*, USPD). Formed earlier in 1917 by a minority among German Social Democratic leaders who opposed the war.

country, solidarity or no solidarity, would not risk a strike for the Russians even now.

3

If one went by the way he presented himself and his attitude, Parvus was the best, not to say the only, consistent ally of the Bolsheviks in the West.

Radek even tended to accept this; but knowing that Parvus's thoughts and actions were rarely, if ever, entirely without self-interest, Radek was naturally interested in the aims the man was pursuing with his displays of friendship. Only an hour ago, Parvus had arrived at the villa in Saltjösbaden, with a noisy hurrah, and now it would become reality after all, the great social-ist revolution, joy and good luck to us all, comrades; and had called for champagne to celebrate the victory, and toasted one after the other with Fürstenberg and Frau Gisa and Radek and his Rosa, and now he sat there in his usual armchair, broad and weighty, radiating success and power, he the central star and they the lesser planets, and over in Russia, on the Neva River, still rec-ognizable in reflected splendor, his creation, the victorious party with Lenin at its head, grotesquely headquartered in an institute for the education of daughters of the nobility, Smolny.

Satisfied, he pushed one of his cigars between his lips; Fürstenberg jumped up and offered to light it. "No, no apology necessary, Hanecki," Parvus assured him, "your cable did not disturb my circles at all; by the time it reached me I had done just about everything I set out to do, and was already on my way to Stockholm. One has to take every opportunity, that's my prin-ciple, to look after things, but especially when the world is about to become unhinged. Am I right?"

Fürstenberg did not contradict him. Radek only added that the cable, which, by the way, had been drafted by both of them, Radek and Hanecki, had not come about on his own initiative; certain wishes had been brought to the attention of the foreign mission from Petrograd, all of them extremely urgent, wishes concerning the Germans, the German foreign ministry, the German army, the German Social Democratic Party.

Whereupon Parvus acted as if Santa Claus in person, opening his sack in front of the good children who had finished their revolutionary homework on time, and who now, peeking out from under his bushy beard, acknowledged the little ones' joyful amazement with "Ho-ho!" and "Ha-ha!"

And indeed, it was as if Parvus had already fulfilled the wishes from Petrograd while he was in faraway Vienna, where he witnessed the Austrian workers rejoicing over the victory of the socialist revolution, and considered the chances for an early peace with Count Czernin, Emperor Karl's foreign minister, and the next day in Berlin, when he negotiated with Undersecretary of State von Busche, and just as importantly, with Ebert and Scheidemann. In order to place his achievements in dealing with the Western rulers in the proper light, he didn't fail to mention that according to his information, which would certainly coincide with that of Radek and Hanecki, the situation of the Bolsheviks in Russia was not very rosy; Lenin and his people's commissars by no means had a majority among the people; rather, they had triumphed over a minority with a minority, and were now threatened by Kerensky's armies, who was making his return to Petrograd from the provinces, where he had taken refuge in a car belonging to the American embassy. The food supply where the Bolsheviks ruled was in chaos, and the land question had completely slipped out of their hands; moreover, in the last few days, a mass of highly dubious characters had attached themselves to the party's coattails, endangering the new order in the most grave way.

Radek sighed. "We need peace."

"And money," Fürstenberg added, and now that Colonel Nikitin's men had finally disappeared from the border near Haparanda, he was on his way to Petrograd to discuss details with the party leadership, and, almost pleadingly, to Parvus: "But I hope I can also report something positive to Lenin."

"That you can." Parvus leaned forward, his arms propped on his knees, a contented man. "I have been instructed to convey to the Bolshevik foreign office in Stockholm the congratulations of the party leadership of the Social Democratic Party of Germany on the successful socialist revolution in Russia, with the request that these be passed on to the leadership of the Russian Social Democratic Labor Party [Bolsheviks] by the fastest means possible"—at this he fixed on Hanecki, who was ready to leave. "Furthermore, Comrades Scheidemann and Ebert have urged me to inform you of the German party leadership's plan to adopt a declaration of sympathy for the Bolshevik Revolution at two mass meetings already scheduled for November 18th in Dresden and Barmen."

"If your girth didn't make it so difficult, Comrade Parvus," Radek said, "I'd hug you."

Grinning, Parvus pulled his wallet out of his jacket and took from it a piece of paper with closely spaced writing: "The wording of the declaration intended by the German Comrades for their meetings in Barmen and Dresden is by the well-known journalist and financier Dr. Alexander Helphand. *The assembly welcomes the achievements of the workers in the Russian Revolution and wishes them further success in their difficult task. It assures the Russian class comrades of its solidarity and agrees with the demand for an immediate ceasefire in preparation for a democratic peace which will secure free economic development for Germany as well as all other countries.*"

He paused, expectantly.

"Free economic development," said Radek. "The author is unmistakable." And at exactly the same moment, he sensed how off the tone and content his remark was. Parvus had wanted to make a show of himself before him and Fürstenberg; the great Dr. Helphand, who not only made the puppets dance, but even moved the stage—and Radek had found nothing better to do than crack one of his little jokes, and a most mediocre one at that.

Frau Gisa tugged her husband's sleeve and told him that everything was ready now, luggage, tickets, provisions. And it was especially intended for Parvus's ear. "The carriage is ready, Jaköble. Your train leaves in less than an hour."

Fürstenberg stood up. "You must believe me, Comrade Parvus, I would have preferred to spend the evening celebrating with you. But as you know, I serve two masters."

"I know, I know. And your trip has been planned for a long time; and Colonel Nikitin has now been forced to clear the way; and so on and so forth." An angry red spread over Parvus's face—first, Radek had spoiled his dramaturgy, and now again Frau Gisa, the preening bitch; and yet he could have said so much about his journeys throughout the war and his conversations with people who decided the fate of hundreds of thousands.

"Very well, Hanecki," he said dryly, "then inform Lenin that I've arranged in Berlin for two million Reichsmarks to be ready for collection from Herr von Stoedten, the German ambassador in Stockholm. Now we no longer need the detour via pencils and condoms, and Vladimir Ilyich can help himself directly."

Then, Radek and Parvus spent the evening in a tête-à-tête, and there was no more role-playing between them and no attempt at self-portrayal; their subject was, they both felt, too serious for such jokes. Rosa had brought a snack, various kinds of fish, and good Swedish bread, and wine, and they sat there; next to the plates that had been eaten from, there was a writing pad, on which Radek had sketched the telegram to be sent to the German Social Democrats on behalf of the Bolsheviks' foreign mission: Parvus, through the German embassy, would see to the speedy transmission of the text to Berlin.

"I'm only afraid," Parvus said, "that Herr von Stoedten will resist. It's not among his diplomatic duties to act as a letter carrier between Russian and German Social Democrats." But since he, Parvus, had himself suggested the telegram—for the sake of peace and revolution, he had cunningly explained, one must now travel on two tracks, one leading from government to government, the other from party to party—he could not avoid going to Stoedten. Radek was impressed by the fat man's new way of thinking: as if, within the few days since the coup in Petrograd, Parvus, the weaver of secret intrigues and questionable deals, had rediscovered in his breast Dr. Helphand, the man of great ideals—"And you, Radek, and Lenin with you, will have to learn to wear at the same time the frock coat of government and the shabby jacket of the revolutionary."

Radek let the clothing question drop. "From party to party isn't enough," he said. "Stoedten has to send the telegram twice: to Ebert and Scheidemann of the SPD, and to Huge Haase of the USPD."

Parvus had his reservations: the assignment given to the ambassador was already an imposition, and aristocrats like Stoedten should not be overburdened; nor did he think much of the German left-wing splinter parties; and Radek, mindful of his dispute with Haase only a short time ago at the socialist conference in Stockholm, inwardly agreed with him; but it was no longer a question of the points that had been dealt with at Zimmerwald and the old ideological disputes; it was a question of conveying to the masses of German workers the core statement of his telegram, pure Radekian text, which read—he glanced at the scrawled lines—There is still a long struggle ahead, which can only be ended victoriously by common international action by the proletariat, and it was a question of rousing these masses to action, and here, every workers' organization, whether left, center, or right, and every one of its functionaries, was dear to him.

Parvus, however, returned to the topic of the two costumes that the Bolsheviks would have to slip into from now on. He himself, he added thoughtfully, had been living for years as his own doppelgänger, and it had brought him little understanding and much mistrust. But what they were planning now was no longer an individual attempt to realize his utopia with the aid of connections, whether to the bourgeoisie or to the working class; this was now the great qualitative leap, power for the first time, the entire power of a state in the hands of a socialist party—in Lenin's hands, to call the problem by its name—and he, Parvus, as Radek well knew and could attest, had made his contribution to the fact that world history had gone in this direction and not another.

Parvus broke off. However, since Radek remained silent, he resumed. "But what now? How to maintain this power? And how to prevent an octopus from crawling out of the womb of this power, as power tends to give birth to, strangling newly won freedom? And, practically and without further delay, how and in what forms do we create a functioning economy, a commercial life in which all participate, and democracy, a new kind of democracy however, a workers' democracy?"

Radek felt a chill run down his spine. Here, before him, sat in solid flesh the elephant with a human skull he knew, yet suddenly a quite different creature, with Radek's own thoughts and fears in his heart; or was this again the fantasist who in 1905, more than twelve years ago, had presided over the first Petersburg soviet with Trotsky and who now, amid the thunder of this, the Bolshevik revolution, had come to life again?

"What I'm about to tell you," Parvus seemed to cling to his cigar, the ashes of which had fallen on his pants without his noticing, "what I'm about to tell you now, Comrade Radek, is private, and I must ask you to keep it private as well."

Radek nodded.

Parvus's widened eyes resembled two dark stones. "I want to return to Russia."

Radek was expecting all kinds of things, but not this: Parvus must have been aware of the reputation he had in the world and in Russia, especially among the Bolsheviks. A renegade, one who had become rich, at home in all alleys and quarters, whom nobody trusted. And Parvus wasn't so sentimental that from yesterday to today he would be seized by such irresistible homesickness, or such a tremendous need to heave his awkward person into struggles, other people's struggles, nota bene, the outcome of which no one could predict.

"I would like," Parvus continued, "for you to notify Lenin of my intention, personally, and him alone, you understand, so that he can arrange what is necessary."

"The reason?"

"Do I have to elaborate? After all, Comrade Radek, you are, along with Vladimir Ilyich, the one who knows best my services on behalf of this revolution. And if, as you indicated earlier, there is resistance in Russian party circles because of my policy during the war and my connections with the Germans—well, I'll give you these proofs in a pamphlet I wrote the other day, which will soon be published by my publishing house, and which you'll please read on your way to Petrograd in preparation for your talk with Lenin; and tell him I would be willing and ready to face a tribunal of Russian workers and give an account of my actions since 1905 and my aims today."

Radek accepted the envelope and thought, he does have stature, the fat man; not only physically, not only politically and in business; also as a human being. Parvus would hardly deceive himself with the dramatic gesture, tribunal, dear God; he was too intelligent for that. And he was too self-confident to dismiss his quite successful past as an aberration and to speak a pater peccavi before some party bigwigs in order to lead a new life, well-behaved and uncritical, in the new Soviet state. No, Dr. Alexander Helphand intended to play his own game, according to his own rules, which did not even appear to be that bad and undemocratic, and therefore, at the decisive moment of history, he wanted to be there, where history was made, in Russia, and to use the influence of his ideas and his power of words on the spot, in order to be able to codetermine the direction of development.

Should Radek lend him a hand? And was the question then really, Lenin or Parvus? Wasn't that exaggerated? The doctrine of the dictatorship of the working class, shouldn't it be essentially more than the plaything of ambitious visionaries?

"I will," he said slowly, "set out on the first train tomorrow. I can imagine, Doctor"—he interrupted himself, the academic title the young Helphand had acquired in Odessa had slipped from his subconscious onto his tongue and now, despite the ironic flavor, he tried to give the word a kind of intellectual connection, an inner consonance between himself and Parvus—"I could imagine you, with your experience, could be quite useful to us in Petrograd now, with our shortage of specialists—as commissar of finance, I imagine, or of export and import."

And it couldn't hurt either—a rather playful thought—to have a counterweight for later against the solitary decisions to which Comrade Lenin was prone.

"Cigar?" asked Parvus, offering his case.

Radek accepted.

In the dark waiting room of the Haparanda train station, Radek found Fürstenberg, unshaven, with a sweaty shirt collar, his red and white striped bow tie creased on both sides.

"I thought you were almost in Petrograd?" Radek put down his travel bag, sat down, reached for the bottle Fürstenberg had left on the scratched table, and poured himself a double aquavit. "It'll probably be the last until we return to Sweden."

"I've been chafing my behind on this bench for almost twenty-four hours," Fürstenberg grumbled, "and you haven't been here even five minutes and you're already complaining. Why did you follow me? Did you not trust me to be alone with Lenin? I've been working with Lenin longer than you've even known him."

Radek drank. "What's with the continuation of the journey?"

"Colonel Nikitin's agents have indeed left. They haven't been paid for a long time, according to the Izvostchiki, the coachmen, on the other side of the border. Between here and Tornio in Finland there are only hungry wolves to fear. But trains from Helsingfors or even Petrograd no longer arrive there. The revolution has shattered all travel plans."

"The K.u.K. military doctors already noticed during my medical examination that I have bad feet," Radek remarked.

Fürstenberg stretched his legs out from under the table; he wore elegant light brown boots, English goods.

"And I see you're also not equipped for the winter marches, brother Hanecki."

"I've bombarded Lenin with telegrams. In vain, so far." Fürstenberg capped his bottle and stowed it in his briefcase. "But you, Karl Bernhardovich, you don't have to come to this godforsaken place."

"I thought I'd bring you greetings from your beloved. Frau Gisa misses you to death, even after such a short time."

"Seriously, what made you abandon the agency?"

Radek had dreaded this question. He liked Fürstenberg—a clever, skillful, reliable man and loyal friend—and he knew that Fürstenberg would be deeply offended if he learned that Parvus had entrusted his message to Lenin to Radek, and not to his longtime liaison with Lenin, Comrade Hanecki, alias Fürstenberg.

"Well?"

Just at that moment a person in a shaggy fur came trotting up, waving a folded piece of paper with a large red seal, croaking from a toothless mouth, "Fürstenberg, Jakob?" Thus sparing Radek from having to answer.

Fürstenberg held out his hand.

"Furstenberg, Jakob?" repeated the person. "Eh?"

Fürstenberg dug a coin out of his vest pocket; the old man eyed and palmed the metal; the exchange of silver for paper was consummated. Fürstenberg broke the seal right between the two eagle heads, still Kerensky, or was it the tsar; the little fathers left long shadows.

"Well?" asked Radek.

"They're sending us a locomotive," said Fürstenberg. Then he began to curse, in Polish, in Russian, and finally in German. "I can toil away for twenty-four hours and nothing happens. But as soon as you appear, Radek, everything begins to move in the most beautiful way, and knowing you, they'll even hitch a carriage to the wretched locomotive, with upholstery and mirrors and porcelain chamber pots. But just you wait; the gods do not love one who has so much luck; it'll end badly with you!"

The old man in the shaggy fur was still standing in front of them. "Luggage?"

They loaded their bags on his hunched back. The host running, clamoring in some kind of Swedish—or was it Finnish? "You pay," said Radek.

"Why me?" Fürstenberg asked indignantly.

"Haven't you ever noticed, brother Hanecki?" Radek tucked his newspapers under his arm. "I'm always the second man."

The guards in front of Smolny, the majority of them Red Guards, wearing leather jackets with greasy worker's caps on their mops of hair, carried their rifles in an extremely non-military manner, one over the left shoulder, the other on the right, the third held his, the muzzle facing downward, in his elbow; the soldiers in the guard team, still in old tsarist military coats, looked feral; and all of them, even when merrily making noise or otherwise pretending to be relaxed, seemed terrifying.

Good, thought Radek, they should be afraid, the bourgeoisie, the more they were, the better; but the bosses of the guards, there were two of them, keeping a constant eye not only on their people but each other, demanded in unison, "Bumaschka!"—"Papers!"

"Not even ten days in power," Radek sneered, "and look at the bureaucracy!"

"The comrades must be allowed to protect life and limb!" Fürstenberg said, defending the new order, and wrote his and

Radek's names on a pad that the younger of the two bosses held out to him, while masses of people streamed past them, all acting as if they had just made the revolution and were now coming to get orders for the next one. Radek was fascinated by the hustle and bustle between the columns of the vestibule and in the adjoining passageways; bureaucracy had by no means won yet.

"And what brings you here, Radek?"

The head with the curly mane over the brow that was fearsome early on, and the flashing glasses in front of the somewhat too closely set eyes—this is how he remembered Trotsky, standing there in the frame of the low window of the village inn in Zimmerwald and delivering his speech, whose thoughts often enough diverged from his own, but sometimes also met with his approval, especially when passion gripped the speaker in predicting the great coming revolution, or when he spoke with cutting contempt of the Germans, who unfortunately always became pious about government at the wrong moment.

Trotsky pushed aside the two bosses of the guard. "Let the comrades through." And to Radek, "Are you looking for something to do? Because I have something for you. But no, I know, you are working in Stockholm with Comrade—"

"Fürstenberg," said Fürstenberg. "Hanecki-Fürstenberg."

"Ah, yes, Hanecki. From Comrade Lenin's stable. Then go up to him, he'll be pleased; I have to go to my new ministry. Foreign Affairs. I'm alone there at the moment; all my ministerial councilors have left, together with their department staff—only the doormen have remained; but I have the key to the safe, and the safe contains the secret contracts of the tsar with the Entente powers, interesting, isn't it?"

He waved cheerfully and walked away.

On the upper floor, the traces of soiled boots on the long lightblue carpet pointed the way to Lenin's room. The white double door stood open and gave a view of a bunch of mostly armed men talking fiercely to someone sitting at his desk in their midst.

It wasn't clear what the argument was about; Radek only

understood that the people were getting more and more agitated, until the one in the center suddenly jumped up and exclaimed in a voice hoarse with fatigue, "No, Comrade Krylenko, we will not permit the English and French and Americans to interfere in the affairs of the Russian people, and if the Allied military attachés at the staff in Mogilev should actually succeed in inducing General Duchonin to order the continuation of the tsarist war against our orders to the army, then go to Mogilev—and you, Comrade Krylenko, at the head!—and drive out the rabble and tear the epaulettes from the shoulders of Mr. Commander-in-Chief!" And then, as a friendly afterthought, "But leave him alive, please."

The delegation, or whatever it was, departed, with a hesitant step and visibly not completely satisfied, but in any case provided with marching orders it was possible to obey. Radek glanced at Fürstenberg, who must have caught sight, as he had, of the shabby green-striped sofa in the corner of the room, and the washstand with the enamel key and the towel that seemed not to have been washed since the eve of the revolution; the room, not too large, the still-life with yellow flowers and red apples still on the wall, and on the shelf, books, some of which were apparently romance novels, which had probably belonged to one of the educators of the noble young ladies.

"Why both of you?" Lenin demanded to know, "wouldn't one have been enough?"—and offered tea, brought by a young woman with a gray face and deep shadows under her eyes.

Of course one would have been enough; nonetheless, Radek would have preferred a little more rejoicing at their reunion; after all, he and Lenin—and the same applied to Fürstenberg—had not seen each other since their parting at the train station in Stockholm last spring, and many things, an entire revolution among others, had happened in the meantime, and he thought that they, too, had not done badly in their outpost, and had done their part for the success of the good cause.

Fürstenberg waited in silence; he hoped to finally learn why Radek had followed him. But Radek, too, was unusually reticent—he had been at a loss for words in the face of the meta-morphoses whose wondrous quantity and quality they would now have the opportunity to discuss with the victor of the revo-lution; or was it the aura of a head of state that had recently sur-rounded Lenin and reduced Radek's otherwise lively patter to a few meager morsels?

But Lenin did not speak of anything more consequential than the air in the room, which was thick enough to cut and smelled of unwashed bodies. "Excuse me, Comrades; too many people crowding in here, and there's only the small ventilation hatch. Life is more hygienic in Sweden."

Fürstenberg plucked at his bow tie. "Frau Gisa sends you her good wishes, Vladimir Ilyich; she made me promise to deliver them to you personally; her heart almost burst when we learned the great news in Saltjösbaden and heard of your announcement at the meeting of the soviet: 'And now we begin with the con-struction of socialism!'"

This last bit had sounded ceremonial; perhaps too ceremo-nial. But it appeared that Lenin did not wish to raise any objec-tions against the quote, or against the report of Frau Gisa's joyful excitement, so Fürstenberg continued. "And we in Stockholm are a little bit proud, Vladimir Ilyich, that we've done our part to contribute to victory, with our shipments—"

Lenin raised his hand. "No details!" Then, in the face of Comrade Fürstenberg's expectant look, he reconsidered. "Okayok, if it makes you feel good: Without your activity in Stockholm, many things would have been denied to us, many things would have become much more difficult, many things would have even failed."

He stepped around the table and embraced Fürstenberg. Fürstenberg, a good deal taller than Lenin, felt the pressure of the latter's forehead against his chest. "Not at all, not at all," he resisted the surprising demonstration of emotion. "After all, it wasn't even our money."

Lenin drew back abruptly. "Comrade Stalin," he said coolly,

"will have a conversation with you about the conditions of your future collaboration with us, Comrade Hanecki."

Radek saw that Fürstenberg had difficulty in grasping: what in God's name had gotten into Comrade Lenin? What had so changed Lenin's mood and behavior from one second to the next that he, Jakob Hanecki, collaborator and confidant for years, had no choice but to sneak away, after a brief farewell, like a chastised schoolboy?

The money, Radek suspected, the origin and further transmission of which every sensible person was silent about, and which Fürstenberg nevertheless spoke of in the exuberance of his happiness, had provoked Lenin's sudden displeasure. And although such emotion was usually foreign to him, Radek felt a moment of genuine pity for Fürstenberg; but he also wasn't sufficiently confident in his own cause to make a last-minute attempt at mediation, so he restricted himself to calling out a half-loud "See you later!" to Fürstenberg, who was already heading out the door.

Then, alone with Lenin, and interpreting his impatient hand gesture as an invitation, he settled down on the hard seat of the peasant chair that someone had placed for visitors like him in front of the baroque desk that was original to Smolny. At the same time, he was troubled by the question of how one who, in the hour of his victory, when a certain magnanimity would have suited him, could react so rudely and dismissively, even haughtily, to a completely harmless allusion—how would such a person behave if one now spoke frankly and demanded from him the full recognition and acceptance of the man who had procured the questionable money, and not only one time?

Lenin looked at him, his eyes, as so often, narrowed by two-thirds. "I was," he began, "not always in agreement with your Stockholm articles."

"That was to be expected," said Radek. "I, too, thought some of your remarks, before and after your Finnish sojourn, were unfortunate. But you won the battle in the end, and the winner is right."

"On which points did you have your doubts?"

"That would be a long and interesting list."

Lenin rubbed his stubble. "Give me the main ones. I like to learn."

"Socialism," said Radek. "Democracy."

Lenin nodded.

"And peace. They won't grant us peace."

"We'll force them to."

Radek managed a thin smile. "From your lips to God's ears."

"But surely, you didn't attach yourself to Comrade Fürstenberg's coattails to talk to me about the receptivity of the Supreme Being's ears?"

"No, but rather, about Parvus."

Radek observed Lenin, but nothing shifted on his face, except one corner of his mouth, which twitched at the remark, "He takes himself too seriously, Dr. Helphand."

"Most people take themselves too seriously."

"Granted. But Parvus had nothing more urgent on his mind than to send me his latest concoction, a rather poor pamphlet, by courier, which must have cost him a fortune. It's clear from the thing that he doesn't agree with me—and neither do you, Comrade Radek, neither do you. Yet there's a big difference between the two of you: Parvus sets up a whole program, with a different socialism than ours, and a different party, or rather, no party at all. Does he want us to abolish ourselves? Now, when world history for the first time confirms our indispensability?"

It was, thought Radek, the least opportune time to prevent Parvus's request, but there would be no more opportune one: precisely because Parvus had supported Lenin so often and so effectively, the latter would become more and more deeply entangled in his resentment of the man.

"Well," Radek took a deep breath, "Parvus has asked me to inform you that he wishes to return to Russia."

"Oh, would he?"

"And he requests that you take the necessary steps."

"Return. To Russia." Lenin tried to suppress the anger that was clearly beginning to well up inside him. "And on what grounds, Comrade Radek?"

Grounds, thought Radek. Dr. Alexander Helphand, who had a nose for great events, simply wanted to participate in them, and not just be a silent observer, but an active person, and active in a prominent position—and Lenin knew Parvus long enough to suspect exactly that. Only he, Radek, would not confirm it to him; it would be the kiss of death for the fat man.

"Grounds?" said Radek. "His services on behalf of the revolution, he asked me to tell you, Comrade Lenin, speak in his favor."

"His services, eh?" Lenin banged his fist on the table so hard that the inkwell jumped. "His German money, he must mean, from which he always took his percentage! Did he think he could buy us, and now he's coming to present the bill? To present it with his dirty hands, with all the Balkan dirt sticking to them— and blood, Turkish, Bulgarian, Austrian, German, and Russian, yes, our Russian blood too?"

Radek thought it wiser not to mention that Lenin had participated in these finances and benefited from ventures that had been suggested and arranged and paid for by Parvus. Mentioning this was also unnecessary; Lenin himself raised the point. Lenin announced, in precisely worded terms, "Please note, Comrade Radek, from the basic law and logic of the revolution: the revolution, ours of course, knows no wrong except for a wrong done to it; whatever it does, and however it acts, is benevolent; and it is therefore above all dirt, clear?"

"Clear," said Radek.

★

Next to the entrance of the villa in Saltjösbaden, instead of the modest white sign with the inscription FOREIGN REPRESENTATION OF THE RSDLP(B), there now hung a brass plate polished to a high gloss, on which a national emblem was still missing, but the state itself, whose representatives lived there, was designated with obvious pride as COUNCIL REPUBLIC.

Parvus, stocky legs splayed and head tilted sideways as far as possible, regarded the new splendor with pleasure: this, too, he thought, was a reflection of his work.

The door was opened for him, and he strode, with a touch of pride of ownership, across the soft red carpet to the wardrobe, where Frau Gisa awaited him.

"Both are back since yesterday," she said.

"I've been told," he said. "And I suppose both of them are now sitting and drinking and exulting on cloud nine." And smiling thoughtfully, "I, at least, would feel as if I'd stepped out of the fountain of youth after a visit to the revolution."

Frau Gisa led him to the reception salon.

"And your Jaköble?" he asked. "He'll have reported to you until deep into the night, won't he? For that, Frau Gisa—my compliments—you look splendid, as always."

Her Jaköble, she informed him, had had to leave the house very early. "There were so many things to arrange, he told me, for the comrades in Petrograd."

"Oh?" said Parvus, puzzled. "I didn't run into him." And after a pause, "But Radek—Radek is there, isn't he?"

"But of course! Radek hardly goes out this early."

"Why doesn't he come to greet me, then?"

Frau Gisa remained silent. There were dozens of reasons, Parvus thought, why he wouldn't come jumping from the upper floor as soon as he heard voices on the first floor, even if one of those voices was the easily recognizable one of his old friend and financier. Only today, damn it, Parvus wished that Comrade Radek would move his ass a lot faster.

But then, the light crowing, "Come up, Comrade Parvus!"

Parvus's face reddened. He paid the most for this house, in which all of them, Radek and Fürstenberg and their wives with their staffs, made themselves comfortable, not to mention half the revolution, which had also run at his expense, and there, he, for whom every step was too much, as Radek well knew, should have to shimmy upstairs there, his groaning an object of mockery for—yes, for whom?

Finally, steps. First, Radek's Rosa appeared on the upper landing and began her descent; behind her, slowly, almost as if being dragged by her, came Radek himself. As soon as he knew himself to be in Parvus's field of vision, however, he raised both arms, waved, and called out, "God greet you, most honored one, God greet you! Yes, I have news for you!"

And hurried to Parvus, took him by the elbow, and led him, carefully, as if he were a huge, iridescent but highly fragile glass ball, to the mauve armchair in Frau Gisa's seating area, his regular place.

Parvus dropped into the armchair. What'll I do, Radek thought, if he pulls out his case and dangles his cigars under my noise? As good as they are, my breakfast would come up if I had to smoke one now . . . Parvus, however, just folded his hands in front of his stomach, as usual, and asked, "Well?"

Radek looked at the two women.

"If the ladies"—Parvus coughed—"could leave us alone for a few minutes . . ."

Then there was nothing left to postpone the moment of truth. Radek sighed and positioned himself, half high priest, half commissar.

"Lenin said no."

Actually, Parvus had known the answer in advance, even before Radek's all too unhesitating, willing departure for Petrograd. Nevertheless, his forehead was suddenly wet with sweat, and he hastily wiped it with the decorative cloth from his breast pocket.

But Radek was merciless. "The Bolshevik party, according to Lenin, cannot allow the cause of the revolution to be touched by dirty hands."

"Dirty hands," repeated Parvus. His hands came off his stomach and were now flat on his knees. "He said that, yes?"

Radek didn't answer. His head was a jumble of the thoughts Parvus might be having at this moment. Dirty hands! Whose hands, Radek thought, weren't dirty? And who hadn't played his part and benefited from the work of these dirty hands? And who could presume to decide what was dirty and what wasn't? Who cast the first stone, and the many, many other stones that lay between the origin of an idea and its realization? And was anyone allowed to think himself so great and so morally elevated that he could classify and judge his neighbor, no matter who he was, as a dirty henchman, as a crook with dirty hands?

"And you, Karl Bernhardovich," said Parvus, "accepted that? Didn't contradict it? With not a single pitiful word, not a syllable, nothing?" Radek looked at his shoes, which were once again unpolished. Parvus had, with some difficulty, lifted himself from his chair.

"Damn you," he said, "all of you. Comrade Lenin, and you, Radek, and whoever today still feels victorious at the expense of those who had to dirty their hands. Those you consider your friends will turn against you, and your hopes will be dashed, and your new power will become a chain on your foot, and you will perish in your arrogance, bloody."

Then he took his case out of his pocket, took a cigar from it, and lit it. Radek saw Parvus's head, dark in the midst of the first light cloud.

He almost envied Parvus.

BOOK THREE

To punish the oppressors of mankind is mercy;
to pardon them is barbarism.
—GEORG BÜCHNER, *Danton's Death*

1

They were already waiting for him in Petrograd.

Not that Trotsky particularly loved him; they were too similar in character, both too strongly fixated on their own egos, both too convinced of the irrefutable sharpness of their own judgment and the correctness of their own ways of looking at things; but both were also experienced in dealing with people and capable of assessing the other, his talents, his weaknesses, and of behaving toward him accordingly and using him wherever necessary and possible. Even Lenin, to whom Trotsky had casually submitted the proposal, raised no objections; Radek's mission in Stockholm had been successfully completed, the transmission of the bad news to Parvus was his final assignment, and a talent like his could not be left idle for long. So why not put him at Trotsky's side?

The hindrances—not insurmountable ones—came, however, from the bureaucracy. A function as important as that intended for him, with so many independent decisions to be made, required an absolutely reliable man, and some secretary in some party office, offices of the kind being the first thing set up after the victory and staffed with the appropriate comrades, had found that Karl Bernhardovich Radek, formerly deputy head of the Stockholm office of the Russian Social Democratic Labor Party (Bolsheviks), and executive editor of its publications there, was not even a party member.

Thus, on this gloomy late afternoon, he found himself in the corner of the Smolny canteen, where someone had pinned a piece of red cloth to the wall, and was giving information about his party past to a pale, white-blond person who was dipping his steel nib far too often into a smudged ink pot and writing down with a nervous hand Radek's answers, as far as he understood them. Even more than the disputes with the wing of the Social Democratic Party of the Kingdom of Poland and Lithuania led by Leo Jogiches and Comrade Luxemburg, the expulsion proceedings initiated by the German party leadership against him for non-payment of dues and other offenses aroused the mistrust of the white-blond, causing him to ask even more probing questions.

Until Radek finally lost his patience and he shouted at the man that he should finish up this ridiculous procedure and sign the document, or refuse to do so if he wished, but enough of the questions now; then a touch of bluish red appeared on the man's gaunt cheeks and, muttering incomprehensibly, he put his signature to the precious booklet.

Trotsky liked intelligent conversations, and one could tell that he missed the Viennese coffeehouses where he, then known as Herr Dr. Bronstein, had spent hours upon hours discussing and reading newspapers. Again and again, the concise, objective nature of the discussion, demanded by pressing circumstances, threatened to lose itself in more or less amusing digressions, again and again one moved from the practical to the theoretical, or even the aesthetic, and Radek was not the man to keep Trotsky on the prosaic, sober paths. He himself enjoyed too much the winking consideration of the most diverse possibilities, the search for surprising solutions, the footnotes of thought, so to speak, so often completely overlooked by the majority of people, even within the intelligentsia, or just considered to be insignificant accessories.

"So," said Trotsky, lovingly stroking the warm, glistening brown of the edge of the desk in front of him, "you're taking over the press and news department of this commissariat. Agreed?"

"Agreed," nodded Radek, "but—"

"Your special area, and I hope to have your agreement here as well"—Trotsky raised his head and thrust his goateed chin toward Radek—"will be Germany. That is to say: the world revolution, in which the Germans will have to shape the next stage. Of course, you won't work there alone, but hand in hand with the Bureau for International Revolutionary Propaganda, which the party is organizing and which will be headed by Comrade Boris Reinstein with the collaboration of a certain John Reed, an American correspondent on location—do you know him? You'll get to know him—a believer."

"Aren't we all believers?" said Radek.

"How could it be otherwise?"—Trotsky glared at him—"after the convincing proof given here in Petrograd of the correctness of our faith. But does your faith go so far that you think it will continue to run according to plan and theory, from revolution to revolution?"

"It must," Radek replied. Then, after a moment's hesitation, "Or can you imagine, Lev Davidovich, that we'd be left alone, a reckless vanguard that has isolated itself from the majority of the troupe?"

"That's exactly why I need you." Trotsky laughed; not a good laugh, Radek thought; oppressive. "You're going to make us a newspaper, in German, you'll receive everything you need for that: paper, printing presses, and distributors at the front and in the prisoner-of-war camps—wherever Germans can be found—"

"Print run?"

"Half a million, more if you wish, your fiery appeals in its pages, Karl Bernhardovich. The readers are there and have before their eyes the example that our soldiers have offered them. And these readers will remain with us for as long as General Ludendorff doesn't withdraw them, and when he does withdraw them, they'll take our thoughts with them to the West, to Germany, to Austria, and to the Somme in France."

Trotsky had worked himself up into an enthusiasm that was contagious even to someone like Radek. Radek already saw his newspaper, the format suitable for the pockets of the field-gray winter coats, the headlines striking, the language his own: direct, convincing. One couldn't skimp on this assignment, neither with money nor with words. Socialism..., hadn't Marx already written that it would have to come first in the industrially developed countries where the proletariat was used to seeing itself as a class? Germany was such a country, and its proletarians, in the fourth year of the war, must be at least as receptive to the spark of revolution as their Russian brothers.

Must ...

He thought of Ebert, how he, stolid and complacent, had stood at the podium of the German party congress and had him, Radek, expelled by a majority of equally stolid and complacent delegates. Certainly, there were also Liebknecht and Luxemburg with their *Spartakus Letters*, and the leftists around Haase and Ledebour, who had established themselves as the USPD; but they were, like the Mensheviks or Social Revolutionaries here at home, neither fish nor fowl.

"Hardly any help will come to us from Liebknecht and Luxemburg," remarked Trotsky, whose thought processes seemed to have run parallel to Radek's. "They're both imprisoned, and apart from reservations on the part of Comrade Luxemburg against the dictatorship—of the proletariat, please note, not of the Prussian general staff—with which she'll get on our nerves, even from prison, there's little to be expected from them at present. Not that Luxemburg's reservations, to the extent as I'm informed, don't have any merit; in part, they even correspond to mine As to what ideas are haunting your head, Karl Bernhardovich, who the hell knows. The fact remains, however, that the main burden of agitation among the Germans will be borne by us, you and me and whoever else comes into question—our great advantage being that we speak for peace, indeed, that our revolution was, in the best sense of the word, an act of peace." Trotsky sighed. "Wasn't it?"

"This and that is already stirring up the Germans," Radek confirmed. "Strikes in Berlin, a revolt, but only a flash in the pan, on ships of the imperial fleet…" Radek had pulled a tattered notebook from his pocket and had begun to write. "Brothers! German soldiers!" he read to Trotsky, congruent with the hasty strokes of his pencil. "The great example of your Karl Liebknecht, your assembly and your united presence and action in your units, and finally the uprising in your fleet are guarantees to us that for the working masses among you, the time has ripened for the struggle for peace…" He paused, took his glasses from his nose and cleaned the lenses. "First page, first number," he said, and after a moment's thought, "*Der Fackel*, 'The Torch,' that's what we'll call the paper. Agreed?"

"Agreed," said Trotsky, and then, a bit mockingly, "By the way, Karl Bernhardovich, have you noticed how, despite the brevity of our conversation, your manner of speaking has already approximated mine?"

That was even true, thought Radek uncomfortably—he had always prided himself so much on his intellectual independence.

Trotsky had stood up. "Do you have reasonable accommodations?"

Radek, still preoccupied with Trotsky's remark about the weaknesses of his psyche, came to himself. "Neither my wife nor I," he said, "are very demanding."

When, later, he thought back to these first days and weeks in the new office, under Trotsky, many things got mixed up. But most of his thinking—and his feelings—revolved around the armistice negotiations that Comrade Adolf Joffe, at the head of a strangely mixed delegation, was conducting with the Germans at the fortress of Brest-Litovsk. According to Joffe, the matter resembled a chess game in which the opponents, depending on their moods and needs, took additional pieces from under the table and placed them on the board; this made the game seem highly irregular; but diplomatic negotiations between a victorious imperialist power and a proletarian revolutionary government—which had to prove itself anew every day against its domestic enemies as well as against hunger in the country and economic collapse—were also a novelty.

Joffe was also a man after Radek's own heart; one could talk and joke with him; he was cultured and well-read, interested in everything, and loved to dine and drink well—in short, a bon vivant. "Ah," said Joffe, before he departed for Brest-Litovsk, "I'm anxious to see how the gentlemen will behave when they run aground with us; perhaps they will rage in their Teutonic way, or swallow their anger; but even then they'll have nothing to oppose the general desire for peace which we embody."

This departure for Brest! Radek accompanied Joffe on the trip to the station, Joffe and Kamenev, the second man of the Soviet delegation, who before November 7 had still led the party opposition against Lenin and almost prevented the revolution with his public clamor against it—but Lenin, although hardly ever forgiving, was not vindictive in the petty sense. And now, sitting in the automobile, as they checked the list of delegates one last time, ticking off one by one the names of the specialists and the representatives of the party and the masses, they discovered with horror that in the whole flock there was not a single peasant. How could they face General Hoffmann or even the Eastern Commander-in-Chief of the German Army, his Royal Highness Prince Leopold of Bavaria, without a spokesman for the Russian rural proletariat? And where to get a reliable little peasant, now that they were already halfway to the Warsaw station?

Radek had the car stop and got out, catching a little old man who, clothed in his sheepskin and wearing a disheveled fur hat on his head, was hurriedly trotting along with a bundle over his shoulder.

"Hey, you, what's your name?"

The old man stood still and squinted mistrustfully.

"Well?"

"Stashkov, *Gospodin*, Roman Ivanich."

"And where are you headed?"

"To the Nikolaevsk train station, *Gospodin*."

"Not *Gospodin*," Radek corrected him, "not Sir—it's Comrade. It's all over with the Sirs. And where are you headed from the Nikolaevsk station?"

"Home, Comrade."

"Home where?"

The old man named a village, the name of which Radek immediately forgot again.

"And politically, where do you stand?"

"Where I'm from," the old man said carefully, "the people are Social Revolutionaries."

So a Social Revolutionary, thought Radek: wonderful—that would lend the delegation an agreeably broad spectrum in the eyes of the public. And said, "Listen, Roman Ivanich, you can still go home. But right now, you're coming with the comrades you see sitting in the auto over there, to the Warsaw station and from there, to the city Brest-Litovsk, where you're going to make a peace agreement with the Germans."

"But I have to get home, Comrade. I managed to get five long nails and needles and thread and other rarities, and they're waiting for me."

"Don't you want peace?"

The old man squinted again. "Yes!"

"Well, somebody has to make peace! Why not you, Roman Ivanich? Besides, you'll have pork to eat from the Germans, and gingerbread, and copious amounts of vodka to drink to aid your digestion. We'll send your nails and needles to your village for you. So come on, we don't have any more time to lose." And he grabbed the old man by the arm and pushed him toward the car, and the driver got out and together they heaved him into the back seat between Joffe and Kamenev, and Radek said, "This is Comrade Stashkov, Roman Ivanich," and then they were at the Warsaw station, and Joffe and Kamenev, together with their new guest, got into the Pullman car at the end of the train, and the train started and Radek waved after them until he could no longer see Comrade Stashkov, Roman Ivanich, who dutifully waved back for a long time out of the open window.

At the beginning, it really seemed as if both sides wanted the same thing—peace—and that everything would proceed in the most beautiful harmony. Joffe reported seeing long freight trains full of German troops and artillery, rolling westward from his window in the old citadel of Brest; presumably this whole force was to be used in a last great offensive in France and Belgium. Consequently, Joffe thought, General Hoffmann, the de facto supreme commander of the Germans in the East and head of the Central Powers Armistice Commission—the allied Austrians, Bulgarians, and Turks didn't have much weight—must have the greatest interest in keeping his front quiet.

Which is what Lenin and Trotsky in Petrograd also wanted. Peace had been promised to the people, peace it should be, a peace such as had been demanded the day after the revolution, without annexations and tributes, and not just for Russia, but for the whole world—and, Radek added ironically, with a perspective that differed considerably from that of General Hoffmann.

Joffe, hoping for revolutionary changes in the German army, was playing for time in Brest. That was clear from his reports, which Radek also got to read. Joffe initially proposed an armistice of six months to General Hoffmann; in that six months, much could change, and in favor of the Bolsheviks. Hoffmann, however, who intensely disliked the practice of troops fraternizing in the trenches,

encouraged by the Russians, brusquely refused, and at dinner—
they dined together in the officers' mess, the Germans with their
inferior brothers-in-arms and the Russian delegation—the main
person at the table was old Stashkov, who swallowed vodka by
the hundred grams and shoveled vast quantities of sausage, cabbage, and potatoes into the wide hole that opened up in his beard.
"Roman Ivanich," the general asked across the table in passable
Russian, "do you really want to stay here with us for another six
months, or would you rather go home to your village soon?"

Joffe, a storyteller of high caliber, described the discomfort
with which he and Kamenev and the other members of the delegation observed the fraternization between the general and the
peasant. Radek, at his desk in the room next to Trotsky's, saw
the actors of the scene as if on stage, the grinning Hoffmann and
his, Radek's, creature opposite him; Stashkov, Roman Ivanich,
weighing with a furrowed brow the limitless supply of vodka, the
paradisiacal food, and against it his fat warm wife, and the family
at the foot of the stove or on top of it; Roman Ivanich had been
away from home too long.

"I propose," Hoffmann told Joffe, "that we leave it at four
weeks, with an option to renew the armistice eight days before it
expires. And stop with the propaganda, Herr Joffe, immediately;
I won't have my army contaminated any further by you, do you
hear?"

Radek smiled with satisfaction.

Then Joffe described how he had looked at the general: like
a kindly rabbi explaining to a big strong goy, a uniformed one
at that, why God had given him more brains. And how he then
replied, "I'm not responsible, General, for the behavior of bored
soldiers, nor for the personal baggage of my couriers."

Hoffmann, whose mouth was far too small in relation to his large,
rosy round face, gasped, and, after finding words again, threatened,
"Remember, Joffe, you're the one seeking a ceasefire, not us."

★

In the meantime, the balance of forces shifted.

General Hoffmann, knowing the German situation in the West, wanted to put an end to the whole parley as quickly as possible, was not independent. According to Joffe, Field Marshal Hindenburg's advisor and mastermind, Ludendorff, was crouching behind him, deciding German policy from the great headquarters at Bad Kreuznach, as he had once done in the matter of the sealed train; and Ludendorff had tasted blood. Ludendorff wanted both peace and spoils, and that despite the fact that the Germans had conceded right at the beginning of negotiations: yes, no predatory peace. So no annexations and tributes, please, Ludendorff had General Hoffmann expressly assure once again—but then add: but what if a few of the many peoples of the Russian Empire wished to make themselves independent under German protection, the Poles, the Baltic peoples, the Ukrainians, for example? Hadn't Lenin himself promised freedom and independence to those long oppressed by the tsczar?...

For all his cunning, Joffe wrote, Hoffmann was so taken with his own successes that he occasionally vented his feelings about Ludendorff, especially when drunk; this is how Joffe learned that Ludendorff dreamed of fresh troops for his armies, recruited in the Kingdom of Poland, which would be ruled by a Hohenzollern, and of duchies for lesser German princes in Courland and Livonia, where the far-sighted quartermaster general would also then find his area of deployment against Russia in the next war, and millions of tons of grain from the Ukraine for the cities of Germany that were subject to rations, and of oil and other treasures south of the Caucasus for the German chemical industry.

"It might be necessary," Trotsky said, "to play more than one violin."

"Bruce Lockhart came to see me," Radek mentioned, "to get his copy of our *Fackel*. He's interested."

"Ah," said Trotsky. He knew Lockhart, by reputation at least. The British vice consul, Lockhart had remained in Petrograd in the company of Colonel Robins, the American military attaché, while their ambassadors had retreated to the safety of the provinces, squatting most uncomfortably in a railroad train parked on some side track. "Why don't you send the young man to me?"

Radek thought about it.

"They're putting Joffe under pressure," Trotsky insisted, "General Hoffmann and his people. What kind of peace, the fellow demands to know, do we want, and for whom are we speaking? Only for us? A separate peace, then? Or are there still threads running between us and our former allies, and a peace with us would find its continuation in a general peace? And would we, at a later date, perhaps also drag in the English and French, and a negotiator for President Wilson, to Brest? The quarters in his fortress, Hoffmann explains, are already overcrowded, his own staff already sleeping in stables and garages, and we must understand that he wishes to prepare himself in time for the expected mass influx."

"That arrogance," said Radek, "should be driven out of the fellow."

Trotsky did not comment on this point. Instead, he quoted Joffe, "*Hic Rhodus, hic salta.*" And continued, "Joffe, as you can see, is classically educated. But he's right, a jump must be made, and we can't ask him to jump in Brest on his own account."

"You revealed where we stand with our former allies, Lev Davidovich," Radek remarked, "when you handed over their secret treaties with the tsar to the public with such loud fanfare."

Trotsky shrugged. "That only shocked the Austrians, who found out that their imperial and royal patchwork was supposed to be carved up permanently. But seriously, Karl Bernhardovich, talk to Lockhart and to Colonel Robins, if you can reach them unobtrusively; the Germans are watching everything. And get ready for a trip to Brest-Litovsk."

2

No, he wasn't in a Christmas mood, even though one of the Red Guards on duty outside the commissariat had dressed up as Father Frost, with a red pointed cap and white beard, and money to collect from him and Trotsky and Adolf Joffe, who had arrived from Brest with fresh bad news as a festive gift. "It's cold, Comrades," said Father Frost, "and the crew would appreciate something warming."

Radek, knowing full well that money wasn't worth very much anymore, gave him a few bottles from the stock that one of Kerensky's ministerial councilors—who even remembered his name?—had left behind in the hurry to escape. He opened another one for his own use, placed three glasses on Trotsky's desk, and poured.

"*Nasdrovia*," said Trotsky, and Joffe, his sad eyes turned to heaven, prayed, "God, give the Germans scabies and whatever other plagues you have in your Egyptian handbook."

Joffe, Radek saw, seemed to have really suffered under the insolence of General Hoffmann, and probably also that of Baron Kühlmann, the new head of the German delegation in Brest who, after the conclusion of the armistice agreement, was now to conduct the actual peace talks.

"Kühlmann," said Joffe. "I wouldn't wish for anyone to have to negotiate with Kühlmann. With Hoffmann, you at least knew at some point what he was willing to concede and where he drew the line; with Kühlmann, everything remains hazy until facts suddenly emerge from the fog."

"So, now what is he, this Kühlmann?" Trotsky demanded to know. "Only a civilian version of General Hoffmann? Or is he pursuing a policy of his own, which at the same time would have to be directed against Ludendorff, and if it were so, could one derive some benefit from the contrary positions of these gentlemen?"

"I imagine," Radek said, refilling the glasses, "if I were sitting opposite Kühlmann, or Hoffmann, or someone else from their team—wouldn't it give me a good feeling to know that, unbeknownst to them, I still have a trump up my sleeve? All right, they have an army at their disposal, while ours is well on its way to dissolving; all right, they can, in the name of the freedom of peoples and the right of self-determination and whatever other high-sounding phrases, deprive us of all the territories they already occupy anyway—how much of a percent of old Russia, have you calculated, Comrade Joffe? But for us, do borders run along arbitrarily defined markers? Do we recognize them at all, these borders? Rather, isn't there only one border for us—that between those above and those below? And those at the bottom are always the majority, even and especially where the Germans are now planning to settle—so no great gain for them."

Joffe nodded gloomily.

"And I'm not saying that as a lecture to anyone," Radek assured him, "but to help Comrade Joffe pull himself out of his depression."

"Very noble." Trotsky scratched his temple. "But you'll admit, Karl Bernhardovich, that it would be better for us, and for the inhabitants of the disputed territories, if, instead of living under the boot of the German military or that of their puppets, they could live and work under the presumably somewhat more benevolent regime of their own soviets. As for the rest, it's our old problem: When will the German workers finally work up the nerve to make a revolution? And how long can we afford to wait to give them the chance?"

"I," said Radek, "have just had a completely crazy thought."

"Isn't it madness—" Joffe broke off and posed the second part of the quote as a question, "Or is there a method to it?"

"There is, I think," Radek replied. "Why even bother us with negotiations? Why go back to Brest-Litovsk at all? Or, if you make the effort of a trip, then to tell the Herren Hoffmann and Kühlmann and whatever else they're called, Enough! We'll no longer play along! From now on, do what you want, we're saying goodbye. We'll send our last soldiers home, too, and we won't budge. War! . . . Peace! . . . What do we care about the vocabulary of all your diplomats, the rules of your cabinets? A new time has come, and your own people will teach you . . ."

He fell silent, seized by the grandeur of his idea. And since Trotsky, like Joffe, was silent at first, he added, already somewhat more meekly, "Revolutionary, eh?"

"What," Trotsky finally asked, "is so revolutionary about the pug who lies down on his back and stretches out all fours in the hope that the big bad wolfhound with the big bad teeth will pass him by in contempt?"

Although time, place, and circumstances had fundamentally changed, some of the old differences between him and Lenin had remained. Of course, he recognized Lenin's strategic superiority without envy, his far-reaching vision, his ability to replace old dogmas with new insights and to initiate a new policy; nevertheless, if only to cultivate his own self-confidence, it tempted him to disagree at least here and there before accepting whatever particular dictum of Lenin's; and Lenin, even though he appreciated his man's talents for press, propaganda and occasional dirty work, was annoyed by the implied irreverence every time they had to deal with each other.

This was the ultimatum that the Germans, already under Kühlmann, had set Joffe: either the Western allies were to come into play by then and then, probably the sixth of January, shortly after Orthodox Christmas, or the separate ceasefire was to be followed by a separate peace—with a corresponding position of German strength, that didn't have to be explicitly added—this ultimatum had now expired, and the ambassadors of the Western allies, on their railway siding far away from Petrograd, had not even dignified Trotsky—who as Commissar for Foreign Affairs reminded them several times, with increasing urgency—with a response.

Joffe, as it had become clear in the meantime to those involved at Smolny, would not return to Brest; Hoffmann had strained the poor man's nerves too much for him to be able to offer even sporadic resistance to the Teutonic victors. But who would succeed him would depend on the tactics that the Russian delegation would have to follow, and these tactics in turn depended on the envisaged perspective: world revolution, yes or no? And if so, when?

Trotsky, as he liked to do, to the consternation of his conversation partners, posed the question directly, probably in the expectation that Lenin would help him shoo away the nightmares that would soon rouse him from sleep. Lenin, however—Radek noticed it well—did nothing of the sort. He did not confirm in any way what had become almost a cliché since October: yes, world revolution, what else, and the Germans first. Rather, Lenin returned the question to Trotsky: "You have as much insight as I do, Lev Davidovich, or even more. But I think that a bird in hand is, as they say, worth two in the bush. So stall Kühlmann, even if he shows impatience. Every day is a gain for us. Stall, always stall!"

The order was still ringing in Radek's ear on the way to Brest. It was self-evident that one wished for the world revolution with every morning sun that rose above the horizon of the vast Russian land—but also, and the thought came to him suddenly, that one began to have doubts about whether this great revolution was in the cards at all, and therefore, out of disappointment, or because after so much sound and fury one could not bid adieu to the history of mankind so easily, one now settled down to hold on to this one single, but at least real, revolution, equipped with a soviet and a few Red Guards. Was this the realization Lenin had come to, and was that the reason he had avoided answering the question Trotsky put to him before they parted at Smolny?

"You've got to be kidding me, Lev Davidovich," Radek said.

Trotsky's curly hair stood out darkly against the white-upholstered head cushion. "Comrade Lenin," he said, glancing over his glasses, "has always felt more comfortable in an area he can control."

★

Radek had known these Polish garrison towns since childhood, and hadn't expected much from Brest; but the dreariness he encountered there, combined with Prussian regimentation, was too miserable, and he secretly envied Joffe, who was in more pleasant environs in Petrograd.

Yet, as he observed, he spread life and cheerfulness, from the moment of his arrival. He had hardly climbed out of the train carriage—General Hoffmann, who had come to greet him, stood on the platform as stiff as a drill stick—when he hurried past him, a thick bundle of the *Der Fackel* under his arm, positioned himself in front of the guards, and began distributing papers left and right. Hoffmann angrily thrust his rapier on the planked floor, expecting that Trotsky would obligingly put a stop to these shenanigans; but the latter seemed to see nothing irregular in Radek's leafleting action, and accepted Hoffmann's words of greeting, uttered in a strained voice, as if he were standing at the presidium table of a lecture event and it were the most common thing in the world for a commanding Prussian general, his face discolored by apoplexy, to wish a Bolshevik intellectual the best success for their common project; and indeed, even during Trotsky's reply, which was rather monosyllabic, almost rude, a curious murmur arose in the ranks of the helmeted German soldiers, and their first questions to Radek were raised.

Hoffmann, used to Joffe's conciliatory attitude, which had made it easy for him to dominate negotiations, regarded this opening performance as a bad omen, and his report to Kühlmann was in keeping with this; the state secretary, however, knew enough about the behavior of the new rulers in Russia, who had not yet learned to properly distinguish between diplomacy and what they called agitation, and appeased Hoffmann's irritation by pointing to the coming confrontations, which would offer him ample opportunity for satisfaction.

In their quarters—Radek lived in a room adjoining Trotsky's chamber, but with the same view of the railroad tracks Joffe had enjoyed—Trotsky reprimanded him: impudence alone, he explained, was of little avail; it was only useful when paired with one's own strength, and unfortunately, this was lacking at the moment.

Radek opined that psychologically, he differed there. "Lev Davidovich," he said, "allow yourself an explanation from one whose impudence is almost legendary: impudence works most strikingly when there is nothing behind it but impudence; because most people lack imagination, and are incapable of imagining that one whose only weapon is a little bit of wit could defy them."

Trotsky laughed. "That's the amazing thing about you, Karl Bernhardovich." Trotsky laughed: " Your confidence that a bon mot will occur to you at the right time. But I don't want to make war and peace dependent on that, nor do I intend to provoke unnecessary conflicts with the German negotiators; I'm already glad that my reports say I have in Kühlmann an adversary who no longer blindly believes in a total victory for the imperial armies, and who therefore will try to practice moderation."

"So you want to be nice to him?" Radek mocked.

"On the contrary," said Trotsky, "I'm going to knock him in the head whenever I see it."

★

But that wasn't easy for Trotsky. At their first meeting, in the antechamber to the dining room, when they took off their overcoats and Trotsky noticed for the first time the evenly cut, intelligent face of the man with the carefully trimmed gray mustache and the obliging smile, he knew that the Baron was somebody capable of acting and observing at the same time, and who thoroughly enjoyed both acting and observation; and he knew what pleasure it would give him, Trotsky, to discuss with someone like Herr von Kühlmann about the state of the world and both of their positions in it.

About which he also spoke with Radek, after the latter had

witnessed Kühlmann approaching him with the words, "Ah, Herr Trotsky, if I'm not mistaken—I've heard a great deal about you and I'm glad, really glad, because it's always better to deal with the master than with his emissaries."

Radek saw how Trotsky, instead of gratefully accepting the compliment, rose to his full height and took a half-step back. "We did not come to Brest, Herr Baron," he said, and his gaze seemed to freeze, "to make friends."

Kühlmann concealed his annoyance by shoving his gloves awkwardly into his coat pocket. "As you wish, Comrade Commissar," he then said. "No one is forcing us to be civil. Nor do we have to dine together, as was the custom with Herr Joffe, and you may, if it pleases your revolutionary conscience, forgo our automobiles and chauffeurs and move about the fortress on foot." And with a "I wish you pleasant dining," he turned his back on Trotsky.

"Perhaps," said Radek, "it's not necessary to exaggerate so much."

Everyone in Brest-Litovsk, it almost went without saying, had their personal bête noire; but Radek didn't even have to try to gain the antipathy of General Hoffmann; their mutual antipathy seemed natural.

The Polish question turned out to be an excellent point of contention: not only because he, Radek, as he impudently informed the General on the first day of the Polish debate, was born in Lemberg and had grown up in Galicia, and had even been a member of the Socialist Party of the Kingdom of Poland and Lithuania, and therefore understood considerably more about the psyche of the inhabitants, Poles and Jews alike, and about their history, than anyone else at the long negotiating table here—but also because Hoffmann, as Ludendorff's governor in the East, supported Poland's right to self-determination and detachment from Russia with special verve, obedient to the Quartermaster

General, who regarded the entire Polish populated area as a German buffer zone, and dreamed of huge auxiliary armies filled with Polish recruits for his front on the Somme and Marne.

Hoffmann also counterattacked on the spot. With his claim that he possessed special Polish expertise, Herr Radek, thankfully, had already confirmed at the beginning of their conversation that he, a native of Lemberg, which belonged to Austria, and officially answerable there, was nothing but a lousy Austrian military deserter, and therefore deserved neither place nor voice at this or any table at which men of honor interacted, unless Count Czernin, as head of the imperial and royal delegation here in Brest, considered it important to include an individual of this sort among its members.

Trotsky leaped to his feet. Revolutionary Russia was absolutely indifferent to the birthplace of its comrades-in-arms, as well as to their religious faith and ancestry; moreover, a man who evaded service in an imperialist army had at least as much honor in his body as one of Wilhelm II's generals, who had only stood at attention and obeyed orders. And Count Czernin dabbed his lips with his batiste handkerchief and said in a somewhat creaky Viennese accent that his delegation, as now composed, was in a thoroughly balanced condition and did not need any additional personnel.

So everyone waited for Kühlmann. Kühlmann closed his eyes, as if the sight of the poorly lighted hall with the mostly poorly dressed people in it was hard for him to bear. Then he said in a low, precise voice, "The composition of each delegation is a matter for the government concerned, Herr General."

Radek, triumphant, moved his chair closer so that he came to sit exactly across from Hoffmann, leaned his elbows on the edge of the table, propped his chin on his interlocked fingers, and regarded Hoffmann as if he were a skewered insect. "Herr General," he said, "even if you annex Russian Poland, you'll have little joy in it. The Poles all believe they're God's gift to mankind, and behave accordingly to other peoples, Russians as well as Germans and Austrians."

Kühlmann, aware of Ludendorff's political plans, followed the duel with interest. Radek, after cunningly questioning Hoffmann's Polish hopes and thus unsettling him, now devised a new act of viciousness: he took a blackish cigar from a paper bag, awkwardly lit it, and fogged the General's head with a gray cloud. Hoffmann, a passionate non-smoker, as Kühlmann knew, would react allergically, especially since Radek's cigar also spread a beastly odor. Hoffmann also began coughing immediately, and though this did him no good, turned his face away. Finally, however, he started up: "Do you have to smoke that stuff here of all places, man?"

Radek blew a second cloud across the table. "It was the best cigar available in your army store here in the fortress, General, and my comrades have not yet tapped the reserves of the bourgeoisie."

"Herr Radek!" Kühlmann passed his own cigar case along the table through Stashkov, Roman Ivanich, and Admiral Altvater, who was attached to the Russian delegation as a military specialist. "If you wish to help yourself, Herr Radek! —from the reserves of the bourgeoisie!"

The main antagonists, however, Kühlmann and Trotsky, treated each other properly and with the greatest restraint. Trotsky even tolerated the presence of a group introduced by the Germans as a delegation from the Ukraine; in Kiev, the capital of this former granary of Russia's, under the protection of the occupying troops, a government of landowners and young academics had been formed, which called itself the Rada, and often spoke of freedom and democracy, while pledging the provisions of the local peasants, supposedly millions of tons, to the Germans and Austrians; the four or five law students who made up the delegation were courted above all by Count Czernin, who, in contrast to Kühlmann, believed in the supply possibilities of the Rada in

Kiev, had to believe in them, because the bread presently being baked in the cities of Austria-Hungary, during the fourth winter of the war, consisted of everything but grain.

"With all due respect to the slogans of the impetuous young gentlemen, Count," Trotsky warned, "you'll have to get every bit of grain yourself from the Ukrainian peasants, and a soviet of workers and sailors has already been established in Kharkov."

Czernin turned pale. The imperial and royal army, which would have to beat up these peasants one by one, was a defeated rabble that would only hold together if a ring of German troops surrounded it; and if bread, real bread, did not soon appear in the stores of Vienna and Budapest, the monarchy, of which he was the prominent and authorized minister, would be finished. Hoffmann had noticed Czernin's sudden panic and was pleased; his Germans were a different people after all, not infected by all types of inferior blood, and if agitators like this Radek were kept away from them, it would be possible to take the last sausage, the last grain of corn from Ukrainian cottages and send them to Berlin.

Thus Hoffmann accepted Radek's impudence; he was the Baron's man for rough stuff; where his regiments stood, he let the Russians know in the clear language of a soldier, they would not leave voluntarily, and they stood in the North up to the islands of the Riga Sound, a stone's throw from Petrograd, and south up to right before Crimea; how far was it from there to the oil wells of the Caucasus? Against such power, what were the leaflets of the Galician Jew whom the Russians brought with them, even if his scribblings fluttered anew every day along the front? *Peace! Down with the officers!* Hoffmann had given orders for the stuff to be collected, and whole batches of it were piled up in his headquarters; but newer, even more evil ones kept coming, and in some places, his commanders reported to him, people were starting to grumble.

And this kind of petty warfare, between him and Radek, between Trotsky and Kühlmann, had been going on for weeks

now, Ludendorff sending cable after cable: why aren't you getting anywhere? Why the hell, Hoffmann asked himself, didn't the
Quartermaster General send cables to Kühlmann? But Kühlmann
did not at all conceal that he found Ludendorff, together with his
old field marshal, stupid and tasteless, and didn't let the staff in
Kreuznach tell him what to do. And while the Rada in Kiev continued to lose power and a Cossack hetman named Skoropadsky
had to be installed as Ukrainian dictator, and in Poland even the
Jews were beginning to stab the Germans in the back, he debated
endlessly with Trotsky at the negotiating table—real stalling battles, oratorical ones that bored Hoffmann to death.

There they were arguing, he noted with a frown, around the
question of who/whom. As if that hadn't been decided long
ago, militarily above all, and as if he weren't always taking new
swathes of land under his control, without much ado and despite
the ceasefire still nominally in effect. And when Admiral Altvater
and the other Russian military officers at the table mentioned
such things, and Trotsky, flashing his fist in anger, struck the
wall map on which red and blue flags marked the barely existing front lines, Kühlmann, on the other hand, asked whether
he, Lev Davidovich Trotsky, the Commissar for Foreign Affairs
of Soviet Russia, was not aware of how much he was contradicting himself: how could he deplore the alleged imperialist
rapacity of the Central Powers and argue eloquently about every
little governorate that the tsars had annexed to their empire by
bloody force not so many years ago, and whose inhabitants now
wished to determine their order of government without Russian
dictates? Did he not trust his own theories, according to which
people everywhere, including in these lands, would rise up and
link their fate with that of the revolution which he himself had
helped to instigate?

"Ah," cried Trotsky, "what beautiful dialectics from your mouth,
Baron! Surely, it's worth discussing! But of course you see the total-
ity in a manner that's too one-dimensional." And recommended to
Kühlmann that, though he was already occupied with the questions

of nation and class, he should still read up on how his countryman Marx expressed himself on the subject, and apply it to the present; and prophesied that quite a few other peoples, as Kühlmann had so beautifully put it, would link their fates with that of the revolution, among them also the Baron's own; for the development of capitalism, together with that of its contradictions, had, as this war clearly demonstrated, become so far advanced and so palpable in Germany that the Baron might yet find an opportunity to witness a revolution personally, and in close proximity.

The dialogue, although its subject was deadly serious, had, Radek clearly felt, and to Hoffmann's disapproval, something playful about it, on Trotsky's side as well as on Kühlmann's. The Baron spoke of the chains that, according to the well-known Marxist rule, would have to be the only thing the proletariat had left to lose before it could be expected to engage in the experiment of social revolution. In Russia, he readily acknowledged, the poor were truly destitute; in Germany, however, the proletariat, ever since the days of Bismarck, who introduced the first social legislation at Ferdinand Lassalle's urging, had much more to lose than its chains. "Consult, Herr Trotsky," he said, "your friend Radek about his adventures in our Social Democratic Party, and you'll realize that your longing for a German revolution that might give you breathing room internationally and succor in your struggle against the government of His Imperial Majesty in Berlin, is the purest utopia. I would even think that you and your comrade, Lenin, in light of the situation, should be worried about the existence of your so far quite limited upheaval in Petrograd, which, it should be noted, did not come about entirely without our cooperation."

"But with whom," Trotsky trumpeted, "do you want to make peace? And you need peace! Your General Hoffmann will confirm to you that the main force even of the already reduced forces under his command is urgently needed by his boss in Bad Kreuznach."

The cigar with which Radek tormented his counterpart had

long since been smoked up, its ashes atomized on his lap, and he lit a new one. "Well, Mr. Hoffmann?" he asked.

Kühlmann, however, didn't let the General get a word in edgewise. "Peace, certainly," he said, turning to Trotsky. "But the question is, what kind of peace?"

"A just and democratic one"—Trotsky took his pince-nez off his nose and rubbed his tired eyes—"such as you yourselves have already conceded by signing the ceasefire agreement—without annexations and without tributes."

"That's how it's written," Kühlmann said.

"That's how it's written." The echo from Radek coming through the smoke.

The General sought to dispel the irritating haze with a rapid movement of his arm. Then he said, his absurdly small mouth twisted, "We've been through this two-dozen times."

"And we'll go through it again," said Trotsky, "and again and again. Because we're waiting, General, for your revolution, and Herr Kühlmann is waiting for our collapse."

"Perhaps," said Radek, not because he was thinking about it right this moment, but simply because he had an itch, "neither will happen."

3

The crisis was provoked by Radek.

He turned to General Hoffmann on this sleepy morning—they were still digesting breakfast, and none of those present expected anything dramatic—and asked ironically, "My side, as you know, is prepared, in a peace treaty with you, to grant the peoples in the peripheral regions of Russia independence and the right to determine their own domestic order. Will, in return, your government and the government of Austria-Hungary undertake not to lay any claim whatsoever to the territories of the former Russian Empire, whether or not you're currently occupying them?"

Kühlmann's smile died. For a long time, he had tolerated the fact that the gentlemen of the Soviet delegation talked as if they, and not Germany, had won the war in the East; but this time Radek's question really disturbed his already disturbed relationship with the military, and besides, it was utter insolence; and so he decided to unleash Hoffmann, who was already baring his teeth.

"You have the floor, Herr General."

Hoffmann, who had long sought the opportunity to prove to the staff at Bad Kreuznach that he could be at least as sharp as Ludendorff, was well prepared. And knowing the subject matter and the form and direction of his attack, he afforded himself deliberately calm language, without saber-rattling and the clatter of spurs. "National self-determination, Mr. Radek," he lectured, "is constantly proclaimed by your government, but wherever an independent movement even reveals itself in its sphere of power, it is suppressed." Bullets and bayonets, and if necessary truncheons, he continued, were the main arguments of the commissars, in Ukraine as in Belarus; everywhere. In addition, the ceasefire agreement, which forbids any interference by the Bolsheviks in the internal affairs of the Central Powers, was being consistently violated by them; at the locations of the German and Austrian troops, their agents spread the most malicious propaganda; thus, only recently and much to the indignation of His Majesty, they had distributed a leaflet calling for the assassinations of the highest-ranking warlord himself, as well as of several high-ranking military leaders, including General Hoffmann personally.

He broke off to allow his audience to show disgust. Radek, who had listened so intently that he even forgot to light his cigar, took the opportunity to do so. Hoffmann, in light of the air pollution, decided to come to the end without further ado. a horrible end.

"The German high command," he announced in his best commanding tone, "therefore considers it necessary to prevent by the strongest possible means any attempt to interfere with conditions in the territories occupied by us. Furthermore, I declare categorically, as Herr Radek wished, that the German high command, for reasons of an administrative nature, refuses to evacuate its troops from Courland, Lithuania, Riga, the islands in the Golf of Riga, and the other formerly Russian territories occupied by it."

He slumped back in his chair, very satisfied; not even Radek's smoke could bother him anymore.

But Trotsky also seemed to be satisfied: at last, Radek thought, the Comrade Peoples' Commissar had what Kühlmann had always denied him: the admission of the true German goals for this peace. Not freedom, nor justice, nor self-determination, nor independence—they were only concerned with loot and enrichment; but that's how the masters were . . . and how he, Radek, would write it! And what effect it would have on the masses, Russian, German, of all countries.

Trotsky's eyes gleamed behind his pince-nez.

"On the question of violence, General," he began, as if speaking from a podium, "in a class society, such as we still have throughout the world, all state power is based on violence, as Herr von Kühlmann will confirm. The difference, General, between you and us is that your friends use this violence to protect the landlords and monopolists, while we Bolsheviks use it to defend the workers and peasants. What bothers you, and so many other governments, about us is that we do not arrest the striking workers, but the capitalists who lock out these workers, and that we don't shoot the peasants who've come to take a piece of land, but the landed aristocrats and the officers who beat the peasants to death. And now, General," he asked, "could we have a map on which the annexations you intend can be clearly seen?"

Hoffmann, who had expected his words to have a completely different effect, pointed gruffly to the large map behind Trotsky's back—there, indeed, the thick black lines indicating the claimed territories had already been drawn in; some subordinate of Hoffmann's must have, at the crack of dawn, taken the trouble.

"Admiral Altvater," Trotsky said, "please arrange for the production of an exact copy of this map." And to Kühlmann: "You will understand, Herr Staatssekretär, that in view of this information on the part of the Herr General, which casts our negotiations in an entirely new light, the Russian delegation must consult with its government. I therefore ask for an adjournment."

Kühlmann looked at Czernin. "Count?"

The Count nodded. His face looked ashen; perhaps his breakfast had disagreed with him.

The snow, despite the gloomy sky, gave the bleakly flat landscape a radiant light against which a few bare tree stumps and a thatched cottage stood out as if in a black-and-white drawing, pen, not charcoal.

The short special train that had come from Petrograd to pick them up stopped; a couple of German soldiers came trudging from the cottage; the officer who had escorted them from Brest to this point stepped to their compartment door, opened it, saluted, and said goodbye.

"*Auf Wiedersehen*," said Radek. Trotsky, who was taking notes, remained silent.

The locomotive puffed out a few clouds of steam toward the sky, and the hut remained behind. It was cold in the carriage, and Radek wrapped himself more tightly in his fur. "That," he said, "was the foremost German post. We're with our own now."

Trotsky stood up and looked out the window. "But where are our own? Can you detect anything of them—a hole in the ground, a gun barrel, a trace in the snow, even?"

"Maybe they've moved their position back a bit?" suggested Radek, without much hope.

"How far back?" asked Trotsky. "Or are we still only living by the grace of General Hoffmann?"

"Some grace," said Radek.

Trotsky massaged his forehead. "Over there in Smolny, do they actually know what things look like out here?"

"Perhaps . . ." Radek looked at the Comrade Commissar for Foreign Affairs—a thoughtful type, a man of words rather than deeds. "Perhaps," he repeated, "we should let them know."

★

To his regret, Radek had missed the dissolution of the Constituent Assembly by a handful of sailors. But, he consoled himself, one could not be present everywhere the contradictory forces of history clashed; and during the night session at the Tauride Palace, when the Bolshevik deputies first left the assembly and then, at about four in the morning, Comrade Lenin hurried there to personally hand over the decree of dissolution, written in his own hand, to the guard commander, Radek had been on the train, on the way back to Petrograd.

Lenin rummaged in a drawer, found the paper with his draft, and pushed it toward Trotsky. Trotsky read it and passed it on to Radek. Elected before the November Revolution, Lenin had written, the Constituent Assembly represented the old order, not the new revolutionary one, and since the majority of its members had openly opposed the soviet and tried to prevent the distribution of land to the peasants and the takeover of the factories by the workers, and were in principle only useful to the bourgeoisie and the opponents of the revolution, it should consider itself dissolved.

"And then?" Trotsky wanted to know.

The president of the session, representative Chernov, to whom the decree was addressed, had, Lenin recounted, just enough time to announce that Russia was henceforth a democratic federal republic, when the commander of the guard, followed by several sailors, approached him, handed him the paper, and, as the lights in the hall gradually went out, told him, "Go home, Comrade."

Radek recalled: he had seen a photo, framed in mourning, of the scene in one of the bourgeois papers.

"But what effect," Lenin's brow furrowed, "will this move have on Brest?"

Radek saw that Trotsky seemed to want to leave the answer to him. "General Hoffmann will feel vindicated," he said, "and will cite the expulsion from the Tauride Palace as fresh proof of our tyranny. Kühlmann, on the other hand…"

"Kühlmann," added Trotsky impatiently, "will dismiss it with a wave of his hand." He took from his thin leather folder a carefully folded sheet and spread it out on the green felt of the table. White with colorful lines on it, circles, squares, it was Admiral Altvater's true-to-scale tracing of Hoffmann's Brest map. "Kühlmann is a pragmatist. And Kühlmann knows where the real decisions are made."

Lenin studied the map.

"*Summa summarum*," said Trotsky. "They're demanding close to 150,000 square versts."

"Sign," said Lenin.

The corners of Trotsky's mouth twitched. "If I remember correctly, Vladimir Ilyich, when we were setting out for Brest, you said 'Stall! Stall!' "

"This map," Lenin's fingertip traced Hoffmann's black line, "doesn't look like they can be stalled for much longer, the Germans."

Trotsky was silent.

"Or have you noticed that the workers are beginning to stir in Germany? Any sign of even the slightest revolutionary action?"

Trotsky shrugged.

"And where, Lev Davidovich, did you see our first outposts after you left the German lines behind?"

Again, Trotsky gave no answer.

"Then sign."

"But it would," said Trotsky, "be as good as signing our own death sentence."

"It would be, for the time being, a respite."

Radek thought of the *Levée en masse* with which the French

Revolution saved itself, and of the Russian peasants under Kutuzov, who defeated an enemy already standing in Moscow; a people's war, he thought, why not call for a people's war in this situation, a holy crusade, red flags and icons in front; the people, as soon as they learned of the German plans, would take any sacrifice upon themselves. However, then he thought, isn't this pure romanticism? Since when did he let himself be impressed by a few stirring scenes from the history books?

"Well?" Lenin said.

Trotsky suddenly straightened up and sat in an almost martial position; the bones of his skull appeared to protrude more than usual, his beard to bristle. He took the pince-nez from his nose and held it between thumb and forefinger, like a scalpel. "No, Vladimir Ilyich, we must not and cannot sign such a peace."

"And what do you propose?"

"We absent ourselves. We take leave of the war. We declare the war over and announce the total demobilization of our army and fleet by decree. And we announce that we will not participate in a predatory peace, neither with the Central Powers nor with any other states. And in light of their desire for self-determination, we confidently place the fate of Poland, Lithuania, and Courland in the hands of the German workers."

"No war, no peace." Radek giggled. "Neither-nor, nothing. Null. Zero point zero."

Once again he itched. What Trotsky was proposing here was his own idea, certainly quite witty at the time, which he, before his trip to Brest, had developed for Trotsky and Comrade Joffe and, after Trotsky's short excursion into the psychology of pugs and wolfhounds, had promptly forgotten again—until now, when Trotsky, consciously or not, appropriated it without telling him a single word beforehand.

Trotsky, however, visibly carried away by this idea and strengthened in it by Lenin's obvious surprise, was already developing it further. "The Germans," he said, "will not be able to attack us after we've announced to the whole world that we have withdrawn from the war. In any case, given the conditions in their country, an offensive against us would be extraordinarily difficult for them; haven't even Herr Scheidemann's Social Democrats made it known that they'd break with the government if it made annexationist demands on the Russian Revolution?"

Lenin appeared to weigh things; the entries on the map, plus Trotsky's own statements concerning the positions and strength of the Russian outposts, against the spark of hope that offered itself with the risky project of Dr. Bronstein, who was otherwise quite prudent in his deliberations.

"We can drag out the Brest negotiations for another three or four days," said Trotsky. "Then it's all over."

"Your proposal," said Lenin, "and I have nothing better to offer—sounds quite attractive; if only we could be sure that Hoffmann will indeed be unable to march his troops against us. But what if we can? Already, there's nobody in our trenches, didn't you say that, Lev Davidovich?"

"The troops," Trotsky said, "have demobilized themselves."

"We'll submit your proposal to the Central Committee," said Lenin.

On his way out, Radek wondered whether he should remind the People's Commissar for Foreign Affairs of the origin of the great idea. But then he thought: precisely because I came up with it, it'll probably go wrong; Trotsky, please, should take the blame for its failure.

Somehow word had gotten around that the stakes were high that morning, and so in Smolny's dining room everyone who would come was there from the comrades in the headquarters and out-side: Trotsky first of all, as one of the main actors, and next to him Bukharin; and among the others Zinoviev and Kamenev, who played a subordinate role in Brest; furthermore, Lenin's faithful supporter Kollontai, and the Hungarian Bela Kun, and Pyatakov, and last but not least, Radek himself, who was meeting many here for the first time, Comrade Stalin, for instance. Stalin caught his eye because of his low forehead under the hedgehog haircut and because of the uncertain smile with which he greeted those sitting around him; only his eyes didn't smile.

Already within the first half hour, Radek sensed, factions were forming, one, strong in numbers, around Comrade Bukharin, whose fiery eloquence also gripped Radek, although the holes in his logic were clear enough; another around Trotsky, and the third around Lenin; the latter the weakest numerically, as was often the case in the debates of the last few weeks. Lenin, when it seemed necessary to him, represented even the unpopular views, and possessed sufficient stamina to wait until his way of thinking prevailed, even against considerable opposition. Which didn't make him more popular, certainly not with Radek, who loved someone whose opinion consistently proved to be correct and then, mischievously, didn't even find his high success rate worth mentioning.

How much more pleasant Comrade Bukharin was, with his noble head and noble speeches. Certainly, even he had to admit that the natural allies of the Bolsheviks were at present on standby; still, he said, the proletarians of the West remained in that calm that precedes the storm; but if they didn't fight, but rather, as recommended by Vladimir Ilyich, went down on their knees before the imperialist robbers, it would be said throughout Europe that Lenin and his party had always been the Kaiser's secret agents, at least since that train journey across Germany. No, they couldn't just write off what they had achieved so far, the first tentative steps of the revolution, the sacrifices made, the cherished hopes, and simply hide behind the stove, provided that the stove was still standing. No, they had to take up arms! War, indeed! Not the old war, begun by the tsar, with the old army that had already disbanded—a new war, a revolutionary one, with new, revolutionary people! In any case, as had been clearly shown, the boundaries between war and revolution were fluid, and one revolutionary bullet from a revolutionary gun barrel outweighed ten from imperial weapons. To wait, to stall, as had been done up to now, or even to sign this rotten peace agreement, did not bring the world revolution one day closer; but a struggle now, standing up to the German generals too, after having beaten one's own, would rouse the German proletarians from their lethargy, their deadly lethargy, and the French, English, and American ones, too. He who did nothing, who played dead, would achieve nothing, destroying himself.

War, Lenin said, against the Germans. And, as so often, he leaned on the podium with one hand and stuck the thumb of the other into the armhole of his vest. War, with what army? And left the floor to Trotsky. And while Trotsky, with much shrewdness, offered the no-war-no-peace project as a way out of the dilemma, Radek thought, with a feeling in his stomach as if his bowels were turning over, and what if all this, all the theatrical thunder, Lenin's, Bukharin's, Trotsky's, and whoever else's too, was only to prevent the world from ever finding out how and for what purposes Dr. Helphand's dirty money had been smuggled into Russia? War, he thought, yes, war! General Hoffmann should have crushed the whole revolution, including his, Karl Bernhardovich Radek's, precious person—if only they were honest about it!

"Trotsky's idea," he heard Lenin say, "is appealing but too risky. Stay sober, Comrades. We must hold onto what we have, our revolution; we must not jeopardize it with any plan, no matter how beautiful and adventurous. We are realists, revolutionary realists. And precisely for this reason we must sign this peace agreement, the peace of General Hoffmann, and fulfill its conditions until world history gives us a better one."

"I protest!"

Radek was terrified; that had come from him.

He stood up. "I believe," he said, "that Comrade Bukharin's attitude is the only one possible for a Bolshevik revolutionary, and if there were even a dozen men here in Smolny with honor in their bodies, they would take heart and arrest Vladimir Ilyich."

Everyone froze. "Comrade Radek!" Lenin spoke softly but sharply. "It may be that arrests will be made here. But I think it'll be your turn rather than mine."

Many others, Radek thought, would have punished him with contempt or worse after this clash, and would have held a grudge for years to come; not so Lenin; Lenin was, even his opponents acknowledged, not a vindictive man; or he simply had too much on his mind to also keep lists in his brain with names on them whose bearers had to be paid back.

From all that Lenin said in the two days during which the question of war and peace or neither-one-nor-the-other was discussed in the highest circle of the party, and from the theses that Lenin presented, it became clear to Radek: the man had come to the conclusion that a world revolution would not come about for the rest of their lives and that, in order to save at least the Russian Revolution, a separate peace had to be concluded with the Germans as quickly as possible and under whatever conditions.

Logical?

Logical, certainly, Radek admitted: but the devil was a logician, and Bukharin, who never tired of proclaiming with a raised fist that no true revolutionary could make such a shameful peace with the imperialist robbers, sounded much more seductive.

In the case of the first vote—no, Lenin was in no position whatsoever to impose his opinion on the members of the committee—Radek, together with Kollontai and Bela Kun and Pyatakov, voted for Bukharin. Lenin, supported by Stalin, received a total of 15 votes; Trotsky's proposal, which Lenin described as an international political demonstration that unfortunately could not be afforded, 16. Bukharin: 32.

"Lenin is someone who practices realpolitik," Trotsky said, looking through the compartment window at the blurred outlines of Brest. "And since, as you'll have noticed, I am too, we agreed,

Lenin and I, and with your vote, Karl Bernhardovich, and those of a few more people who finally saw the light of reason, we beat Bukharin's suicide club."

Radek stood up, took his small suitcase from the luggage net, and put on his fur. Trotsky's victorious smile, recognizable despite the half-light in the compartment, amused him.

How he looked, would by the providence of fate, from a joke that Radek had allowed himself, became a piece of history.

There they all were again, Kühlmann, General Hoffmann, Count Czernin, the Turks, Bulgarians, Ukrainians, and also, on the Russian side, the familiar faces, including the contented, shining one of Roman Ivanovich Stashkov, the representative of the working peasantry, who had received the German hospitality rather splendidly. But there was nothing left of the old bonhomie, which at times had been at least noticeable; there was a new tension in the atmosphere, whether emanating from Trotsky or from Hoffmann; everyone knew that the old stalemate that had prevailed for so long no longer applied: the hand of history was descending to sweep the pieces from the board.

Kühlmann opened by complaining once again about the constant Soviet attempts to incite the German army to mutiny, but then Trotsky took the floor. "The hour of decision," he said, "has struck."

Hoffmann, Radek saw, hooked his right arm over the back of his chair and crossed his legs; hour of decision meant, for him, confirmation, with signature and seal, of his total victory.

Radek enjoyed the picture; it would be the last of its kind in his life, from such close proximity. He even abstained from his cigar so that Hoffmann's complacency would remain intact, and dutifully awaited the things to come. Trotsky rose, leafed through his papers, only to push them aside immediately, and said, "Gentlemen! The conditions under which your side is prepared to grant us and the war-weary world peace are cruel and predatory, and in no way correspond to the agreements we made at the conclusion of the armistice: no annexations, no confiscations. But what else could be expected from the rulers of an imperialist state!"

Hoffmann grinned. Radek could imagine the kind of thoughts the guy's limited brain was now producing: so this, Hoffmann would triumphantly think, was probably Comrade Trotsky's farewell aria; let him rant, the People's Commissar, about imperialism; he would have to sign in the end.

Trotsky's eyes behind his glasses sought the imperturbable face of Baron Kühlmann. "But we," he said, "are withdrawing from the war, our armies, everything. The peasants, now still in uniform, must return home to the land which the Revolution has taken from the great landowners and given to them to feed the people, and the workers, who served in the army, must return to the factories, so that they may produce there, not for more destruction, but for the good of the people—and both peasants and workers may build a new state, a socialist one."

Kühlmann raised his head, his nostrils flaring as he smelled mischief; Hoffmann's arm came loose from the back of his chair, and he leaned forward, suddenly suspicious; Count Czernin alternately kneaded his chin and earlobes.

"We will no longer participate in this war," Trotsky continued, "and will inform the governments and the public of all countries of our step. We are demobilizing all of our forces which at present still face the troops of Germany, Austria-Hungary, Turkey, and Bulgaria, and are waiting, with a hand held out in friendship, for the response of the other peoples, firmly believing that they too will follow our example."

Then he took the topmost of the papers he still had before him in hand, and read aloud, with emphasis on every word: "In the name of the Council of People's Commissars, the Government of the Russian Federal Republic informs the governments united in war against it and their peoples, and at the same time the states allied with us as well as the neutral states, that Russia, refusing to sign a treaty of robbery and annexation, declares the state of war with Germany, Austria-Hungary, Turkey and Bulgaria to be over. The corresponding orders will be issued simultaneously to our troops."

He then sat down.

Radek listened: nothing, not a sound, not a movement. A silence like in a wax museum. Just a shake of the head, an "Ah!" of surprise, a collective murmur—and he would have breathed a sigh of relief; but as it was, the atmosphere slowly became eerie. Yet, God knows, he had experienced enough assemblies in his years and heard enough speeches to endure even these without heart palpitations; but here he sat, still spellbound, like the others in the room, by Trotsky's voice and Trotsky's words: his own words, in the clear light of day.

Then: "Outrageous!" Hoffmann, his broad face glistening with sweat. "Outrageous!"

The band constricting Radek's chest burst. "Outrageous!" he crowed, leaping from one leg to the other, a veritable dance of triumph. "Outrageous, outrageous! You'll have—hurrah, Gloria Victoria!—many outrageous things under your nose soon, General!"

Hoffmann turned away. "This person has gone insane," he said to Admiral Altvater. "Please show him out."

Altvater didn't stir.

It was all indeed insanity, thought Radek. From the very first day of this war, up to the moment of this peace.

4

And again Lenin's fears came to pass. General Hoffmann gave marching orders.

Radek read the reports coming to Petrograd from all along the completely broken front and felt fear—for the first time since he had plunged into revolutionary action: real, piercing fear.

The enemy advance seemed unstoppable, its pace depending only on logistical conditions, the condition of the railroad lines and roads, which, however, were miserable; the number of available carriages and locomotives, draft animals and vehicles, the amount of supplies or ammunition and fodder that the Germans had to transport, and their ability to replenish them. The piled hair crowned by Anna Karenina hats, suddenly promenaded on the boulevards of the capital, like in the old days, ladies dressed with distinction on the arms of gentlemen in well-kept furs; through the wide windows of the luxury restaurants along the Nevsky could be seen the shadows of hurried waiters swinging napkins, bowing to the idlers on the *fauteuils*; and behind the patrols of the Red Guards, who, in their worn jackets, occasionally still appeared on the streets, the stream of light-hearted bourgeois, already celebrating the arrival of the approaching Germans.

Radek imagined the grinning triumph of his intimate enemy, General Hoffmann—where was the resistance, why did nobody do anything! He wanted to shout out loud, protest, anything, if he hadn't known how nonsensically weak his voice was against the facts that Hoffmann was creating on the ground with every new hour that the clock in Smolny struck, and how horribly futile the appeals that he, little Radek, wrote with a feverish hand were, already outdated before they even came off the printing press.

Stop playing games, Lenin demanded. Sign the treaty, now, immediately, regardless of what Hoffmann demands! And Hoffmann demanded: the entire Baltic region, plus Finland; Ukraine a German protectorate; and jurisdiction over everything that had fallen into his troops' hands. In Berlin, the German princes were already well groomed and spurred, in order to ride eastwards and take over the duchies and kingdoms Ludendorff had awarded them.

Bukharin, supported by Radek, proclaimed in the assemblies that the people would rise up as soon as the enemy had penetrated deep enough into Holy Russia; but the people did not know what was happening to them; confused, despondent, they still longed, now more than ever, only for peace; the seeds sown by the Bolsheviks in the days of Kerensky and Kornilov had sprouted and now bore bitter fruit for them.

Trotsky, who considered himself partly responsible for the Brest debacle, was correspondingly contrite. He resigned from his post of People's Commissar for Foreign Affairs; and in this way, he thought, one could at least document that the Soviet government was serious about the hand it was offering the Germans for an unconditional separate peace; another, less fixed and determined than he was, such as Comrade Sokolnikov, was to lead the new delegation to Brest with the sole task of putting the Russian signature to the treaty; he, Trotsky, was ready to do penance for past arrogance by taking over the most difficult, the most thankless portfolio that the Bolshevik government had to offer, the Commissariat of War, with the obligation of creating, from the total defeat of the old one, a totally renewed army, a Red one.

At the beginning of March, Hoffmann finally allowed Comrade Sokolnikov to sign the treaty in Brest, and both men's signatures were now emblazoned under the document, the contents of which Lenin compared, in front of the Central Committee, to the Treaty of Tilsit dictated to the Prussians by Napoleon in 1807, which had elicited such hot tears from the eyes of the noble Queen Louise; and see, wrote Radek in *Izvestia*, how short the period of time was that passed before Tilsit ended on the trash heap of history. Only, Hoffmann also feared exactly this, and therefore marched on and on; he seemed determined to grant no respite to the enemy, and therefore no opportunity to draw breath; the treaty was signed, he let Sokolnikov know, but it still lacked ratification by the All-Russian Soviet, the only body which, according to the law of the new rulers in Petrograd, was entitled to do so.

★

One could calculate when Hoffmann's advance guard would enter Petrograd, and the cheers of anticipation of the remaining aristocrats and bourgeois grew measurably louder. Trotsky had his Red Guardsmen drill in the city's front gardens and practice street fighting on boulevards and canal bridges; Lenin, however, relied more on Russian distances, and opted to move the necessary government and party cadres to Moscow. Exactly eight days after the signing of the peace treaty, Radek again boarded a train car in which Lenin was also sitting, an unsealed one this time; and this time his Rosa was allowed to accompany him, in his compartment even, so that he had his own audience, a not necessarily grateful one, by the way, for his opinions and explanations, and for the old bitter jokes.

"I let Vladimir Ilyich know several times," he said, "that I consider the move to Moscow psychologically wrong. Smolny, I explained to him, has been filled with our spirit over the last few months; in people's minds, Smolny and the revolution are one and the same concept; to abandon Smolny is, in practice, to abandon the revolution. But he responded: without us, Smolny is what? A half-withered finishing school; and now, as soon as we're sitting in it, the Kremlin, instead of Smolny, will become the global symbol of revolution."

Rosa laughed, not mockingly, so as not to hurt her Karl, but rather tenderly. "You should," she said, "before you argue with Lenin, percuss your arguments more thoroughly."

The verb *abklopfen*, Radek realized, came from the doctor's vocabulary. He remembered her hard fingertips on his hairy ribs the last time he had the flu, and grumbled, "Lenin would run the country from a circus tent, too, as long as he gets to play director."

"That was ugly," she said.

"But true."

Radek stood up and stretched his cramped limbs.

"Must I," he said, "also love the people who constantly prove their superiority to me?"

Besides, despite its inner logic, the thought was still alien to him that the troupe that not so long ago had boarded the special train car in Gottmadingen on the German side of the Swiss border and was now once again—increased by a number of heads, that of Comrade Stalin, for example—traveling together, could ever reside in the Kremlin as masters of the house.

★

Then, after a journey with constant interruptions—at least this way, Rosa had the opportunity to see something of the country that was to be her home from now on, of the forests that seemed so much higher and darker than those of Germany, the endless fields upon whose gradually melting snow the scarce huts crouched, and the strangely heavy, immobile clouds on the horizon—Moscow.

If, in Petrograd, there had been an almost unbearable tension, the days full of angry curses and boisterous laughter, the nights full of fear of gunshots where no one knew who fired, in Moscow there was a leaden calm, and, when darkness came, a hopelessness interspersed with drunken outbursts. The convoy, hardly noticed by the people, which brought the arrivals from the train station across the city, exhausted by war and hunger, to the Kremlin, resembled to Radek's eye a funeral procession rather than a column of revolutionaries who were to give a new turn to developments in the country starting tomorrow; and in the shadow of the Red Gate, through which they now entered the still magnificently luminous residence of the old tsars, he felt: what gloom!

He put his arm around Rosa's shoulder. "Never forget this, this princely entry into the Middle Ages."

His laugh, then, sounded uneasy.

★

Outside of Petrograd, Trotsky, who had stayed behind in the old capital, nevertheless managed to hold off the advancing Germans with a few handfuls of Red Guards, the embryo of his new army. Hoffmann, who was more interested in grain and coal, oil and rolling stock than in the thousands of hungry mouths he would somehow have to feed if he took Petrograd, left it at that; and Radek, lodged in one of the white-and-gold suites of rooms in the Cavalier Wing of the Kremlin, in a chamber close to Lenin's rooms, celebrated the victory in his leaflets and pamphlets, the first of the Russian Revolution against German military power. He prophesied that the backbone of Hoffmann's hordes had been broken; now the fortunes of war would turn, but they did not.: Elsewhere the German troops were already approaching the coal mines in the Donbass; their further goal, visible to all, was the Caucasus.

Trotsky obtained Lenin's permission to renew his connections with Bruce Lockhart, the English consul general, and Colonel Robins, the American military attaché. If ever, then now, at the last minute before the ratification of the Brest treaty, Trotsky let the two of them know, was the chance for the allies to draw the Bolsheviks, who had been so hard-pressed by Hoffmann, to their side, and once again to put a pincer movement on the Kaiser from the east and west at the same time, and reverse the entire situation, the calculations of the Germans and the predicament of the Soviet government; only they needed to provide help, the English and American gentlemen, with men and material, directly and immediately, via Arkhangelsk or Vladivostok, it didn't matter; and Lockhart and Robins, who had long since advocated this strategy at home, promised, urgently and over the heads of their ambassadors, to intervene in London and Washington.

Lenin, however, to whom Trotsky had hurriedly communicated this promise by the two, remained skeptical. We'll see, he said; but there was a deadline by which the tragic business had to be done, otherwise the Germans could, with the appearance of justification even, penetrate even deeper into the country.

Four days after the government's arrival at the Kremlin, the All-Russian Soviet met there for its decisive session, and this time, for all the passion, even Bukharin's tone and that of the Social Revolutionaries were less shrill, muffled by the damask curtains, the heavy carpets, the wainscoting of the hall where once the nobility of the empire met and where the delegates of all the councils now sat in their shabby smocks and tattered blouses.

Basically, it was clear to everyone, and Radek in any case, from the beginning what one of the delegates, a red-bearded Cossack, was saying in a rough voice. "Comrades! We've fought for four years. We're exhausted. We have no army left, no supplies. But the Germans have one, and it's only a few versts from Petrograd and Moscow, on the go. We're defenseless. Do you want war, or peace?"

Silence. Radek was aware that if there was no promise of help from the West, ratification was the only option. Nevertheless, there was only one motion for and five against. The debate dragged on; and from the weary applause for one speaker or the other, it was impossible to tell which side of the issue the Plenum would vote for in the end.

Then came Lenin.

Radek observed how he, in passing, leaned down to Colonel Robins, who was crouched most informally, with his back to the comrades in the presidium, on the front edge of the stage.

"Has Lockhart heard from London?"

Robins shrugged.

"Or you from Washington?"

"No, sir."

Lenin straightened up. "I'm going to speak now. *For* this peace. And it will be ratified."

★

And yet—no respite.

Hoffmann did not adhere to any treaty or signature anymore. As soon as the weather improved, he took supposed violations of the Brest Treaty by the Bolsheviks as an excuse—and of course, the comrades violated the fine print wherever they could—to advance again; but the movements of his troops became more erratic as the summer wore on; his army, thinned out by the Western front, where Ludendorff was burning it up in hopeless battles, was barely able to hold its elongated rear lines against sabotage and gunfire from partisan rifles and peasant revolts that flared up here and there.

Radek followed the new developments, lying in bed in his room in the Kremlin, covered with a ragged duvet and two to three-dozen capitalist newspapers, which he shifted back and forth, tearing out reports and filing them in an order that got mixed up every time he moved his legs. What did Hoffmann want? Did he still believe in victory in an enterprise that looked more and more like his private war, with the noble goal of overthrowing Trotsky and him, Radek, personally? Or was the usually cool calculator—especially after the assassination of his commander in Ukraine, General von Eichhorn, by an excited crowd—no longer capable of logical thought?

Signs of decay everywhere. Radek rubbed his unshaved chin and reached for pen and writing pad; perhaps the new German ambassador, Count Mirbach, who had come to Moscow after the ratification of the Brest Treaty, could be greeted with a leaflet; short, sharp sentences, understandable to everyone, Germans and Russians alike, beginning something like this: Welcome, Mr. Count! You, too, will soon understand what is happening before everyone's eyes in seemingly defeated Russia!

But there were also signs of decay on the party's own side: that party, already not always united in the great days of October, split into constantly shifting factions, not only over the question of whether to kneel before the Germans or pursue a revolutionary people's war, despite everything; also over what the state, the new one, should look like, and the role of the state in general, which one wanted to abolish completely; and socialism: was socialism feasible in a single country; it had always been said, no, that probably wouldn't be possible; but weren't the banks, wasn't industry, to the extent it still existed, concentrated in a few hands, so that they were quite ripe for being taken over by the proletariat, or should they rather wait to take action until the revolution had come in the West too, and, in alliance with the workers and peas-ants there, dare to take the step toward real socialism even here, even in the still semi-feudal Russia of the muzhiks? And all this mental confusion showed itself everywhere, in the commissions and delegations and councils, factory councils, peasants' councils, soldiers' councils, and was expressed aloud in the voices of the Mensheviks and Social Revolutionaries, both left and right, and even in their own party, which broke up into revolutionary-heroic, technocratic, pragmatic, and whatever other soon larger, soon smaller groupings.

What a delight it would be, thought Radek, to live in this unrest—if not for the fact that at the same time the enemy was in the country, the Germans—and the domestic enemy, the class enemy, who, under the table, as Comrade Dzerzhinsky's new secret police, the Cheka, reported, were opening negotiations with the Germans and arming themselves and only waiting to put an end to the revolution and its most revolutionary element, the Bolsheviks.

On this day—the black clouds, in which the lightning already flickered, promised a heavy thunderstorm—the fifth All-Russian Soviet Congress convened. Not that Radek expected this congress to bring any clarifications; but what was a revolution, he thought, without long, impassioned speeches, and each of the factions hoping to strengthen its forces through the debate.

The contrast of the red and gold tones of the interior of the Bolshoi Theater, where the delegates were meeting, with their own faded clothes, excited Radek in a strange way; and the scent of the costly perfumes that the society ladies had once spread here during *The Queen of Spades* and *Boris Godunov,* or during the dance of the Pavlova, was displaced by the pungent odor of peasant and soldier sweat, which was more familiar to him. These peasants and soldiers and workers sat beside him in the pit; on the stage before them, in the solemn glow of candles, the Presidium of the Congress, behind them the members of the government.

In the boxes and on the balconies, Radek recognized the privileged foreigners: the observers of the Allied missions, Lockhart, Robins, the Frenchman Sadoul; and above them, not only in rank, the representatives of the Central Powers, with whom Russia was now formally at peace, Ambassador Mirbach with his Austrian, Turkish, and Bulgarian counterparts. Radek had put the press, since he had been responsible for their placement, in the tsar's box, not, although the idea suggested itself, in order to humiliate the former ruler yet again, , although the idea suggested itself, but because he hoped that the newspaper writers would feel flattered and thus give better grades to the Soviet Republic.

A Bolshevik spoke, Vardin-Mgeladse; Radek knew his slogans, one of the heroic faction. "A war," Vardin cried out, "a revolutionary one, aye! And if they beat us, what does it matter if we die! In any case, it's better to sacrifice one's life in open battle than to surrender one position of the revolution after another to the enemy without a fight!"

Radek knew that this would set the tone not only for the Bukharin wing of the party, but also for the petite bourgeosie gone feral of the Social Revolutionaries. These now appeared, one after the other, led by their martyr, the aged Spiridonova, who had once been raped by a whole troupe of Cossacks, and attacked the government—for the death sentences it was passing, for its disregard of peasant interests in the still outstanding settlement of the land question, but above all for its policy toward the Germans. The forefront of the attacks was directed at Lenin, who was now sitting on the government bench with his head resting on his hand, and, as an object of demonstration, against Mirbach.

Lenin stood up and responded; but his words, otherwise so convincing, had an effect only for a few minutes. Then Radek saw Kamkov, *the* rhetorical great of the Social Revolutionaries, step forward: the drama was approaching its climax. Kamkov spoke with apparent calm, restrained the anger in his voice, sparing nothing and no one; the delegates of his party, and not only that one, jumped up and turned nosily and with curses against Mirbach up on the balcony, "Down with Mirbach! Away with the German murderers! Tear up the hangman's noose of Brest-Litovsk!"

Once again, Radek was torn between emotion and reason—his heart beat for all those, even among the Social Revolutionaries, who demanded a liberating strike against the predatory imperialists; his mind, however, slightly ironic, thought, let them shout, the heroes; an army has never been defeated by great feelings alone, and certainly not a German army. Nor could he fail to admire Mirbach, who sat in his box, very erect, frowning at the threatening din; only his lips quivered slightly, whether in contempt for the mob or in nervous tension, it was difficult to say.

In vain, Comrade Sverdlov, who presided over the meeting—one of Lenin's men—swung his bell; he was unable to restore order even halfway, and after a whispered exchange with Lenin he summarily broke off the meeting and adjourned it until the afternoon.

Later, Radek found out about the circumstances of the assassination from the testimonies of Embassy Councilor Riezler and Lieutenant Mitter, Mirbach's interpreter, and from the statements of the perpetrators themselves. Blumkin, a short fat man with blond curls and a round child's face, whose words mostly came in such a hurry that saliva sprayed from his lips, and the gloomy, long-haired Andreyev, both well-known Social Revolutionaries, had gotten past the guards during the enforced break of the congress, during which Mirbach had retreated to his embassy on Deneshny-Pereulok; they must, they said, warn the count urgently of an assassination plot against him. No sooner, however, were they in his study on the ground floor, where Mirbach intended to hear them out, than they drew their pistols and began to fire; neither of the two was a skilled marksman; out of seven bullets, only one hit the ambassador, but it was fatal.

In the meantime Lenin, accompanied by Radek, had gone to the Kremlin and had Trotsky and Sverdlov come to him to discuss the further tactics of the government. Sverdlov was too enervated to come up with any useful ideas. Trotsky proposed to stop negotiations with the opposition and to crush it, by force if necessary. Lenin was still deliberating when the telephone buzzed.

Radek, who knew Lenin's imperturbability, was startled by the man's sudden pallor. "A car, Radek," Lenin said, "quickly." And, already on their way to the German embassy, "now Hoffmann has the pretext he's been waiting for. We have to get in touch with Berlin at once to prevent the worst."

In Mirbach's study, the first thing Radek saw was the dark, damp stains on the carpet; in the shards of glass on the threshold of the door to the terrace, over which the assassins had probably fled, the light of the afternoon sun sparkled. Lenin spoke German to Riezler, who was still visibly shocked. "Please, Herr Botschaftsrat, let me immediately convey to your government the deepest sympathy . . . *Mitleid, Mitleid*, is that right, Radek?"

"*Beileid*," Radek said.

"Convey to your government the deepest condolences," Lenin concluded.

And on the ride back to the Bolshoi, after a long silence, to Radek, "I've decided, Karl Bernhardovich, from now on the Bolsheviks will bear the burden of the revolution alone."

5

And the burden was heavy.

Sleep eluded him that night in August. It was as if the party, to which his life was chained, had nothing but enemies: at home, on the constantly shrinking territory on which they clung with difficulty to power, and in the world outside in any case. They were encircled, that's what one read in the foreign press; a word, Radek thought, that seemed invented especially for the Bolsheviks: encircled by the Germans on one side and the Western allies and their auxiliary corps on the other, the Cossacks of Ataman Kaledin and the hordes of the resurrected General Kornilov and General Denikin, and the Czech Legion, marauding through the country on armored trains and spreading terror in the name of democracy, and by the Japanese, who were preparing to land far to the east. The main enemy, however, was hunger, and the chaos in trade, transportation, and administration that accompanied it, and the fatigue of the revolution—all of which was increased to hypertrophic degrees by the agitation of the Social Revolutionaries and the Mensheviks, and the taunts of the bourgeoisie who were crawling out of their corners everywhere.

Radek tossed his dressing gown over his shoulder, closed the door of the room behind him, cautiously, Rosa sleeping fitfully, and descended the poorly lighted staircase and entered the wide courtyard of the Kremlin, laid out for the prancing horses of the Imperial Guard and for the splendid carriages of the nobility.

He winced.

What was that? An echo? Or something more tangible? Were there, in the glow of the moon, the old ghosts dancing?

And indeed, over there: a man, alone, moved like a shadow, hurriedly and yet apparently aimlessly, first to the left, then to the right, and finally, after a sudden turn, toward the Moskva River, which flowed beyond the broad wall, gray and sluggish as ever. The man wore neither cap nor scarf, and his jacket was open: the night wasn't so warm after all, Radek thought: but that wasn't the only piece of recklessness Lenin practiced: where was his personal guard: a stab from the dark, a shot in ambush . . . Radek was outraged. The purest temptation of fate.

So he decided to talk to him, although Lenin might have wished to remain alone with his thoughts.

He coughed audibly.

"Oh, you!" the companion who suddenly became matter out of the pale light of the summer night did not appear to be unwelcome to Lenin, who anticipated his question: "Headache," he said. "A headache. And you?"

"I've been suffering from bouts of insomnia for some time now," Radek said. "It seems everyone has their problems."

"I'd like"—Lenin waited until Radek had matched his stride—"to have your problems." And after a short laugh, "Have you ever been booed from the stands during an assembly?"

"You?"

"Recently. Almost. People were raving. But not with enthusiasm."

"Where should they get enthusiasm? When they can't even get bread anymore!"

Lenin lowered his head, as if Radek had blamed him for the calamity.

But Radek suddenly felt very close to Lenin and would have put his hand on his shoulder and embraced him, had it not been for the inner distance that the other wore around him like armor.

"The worst thing," Lenin continued, "is the silence." He tilted his head as if listening to a distant voice. "We talk and talk," he said gloomily, "about the dictatorship of the proletariat. But our Russian worker has gone limp. Or has turned away. He only sees the difficulties, and not the miracle that we've held our ground so far, and even have allies, the vast mass of poor peasants, and the proletarians of the Western countries, even if they're also forced to wage war against us…"

Did Lenin himself believe that? Radek thought of the peasant uprisings in the Penza governorate, where they fought back bloodily when the Bolsheviks came to requisition grain; and as for the working class, the international, the less said about it, the better. But Lenin, even if his audience only consisted of one person, Radek, seemed to have overcome his depression and lapsed into his public speaking mode. "We must see, Karl Bernhardovich: the spark of revolution had spread to all countries and will ignite the fire. Our situation may be difficult at the moment, but we shall hold the banner we have unfurled firmly in our hands, whatever the cost—and alone, if we must. Don't you think?"

Radek took the resisting man by the elbow. "Let's go back to bed. We both need to sleep."

✴

It couldn't, it couldn't be, thought Radek, that a movement of this magnitude rested on the shoulders of one man, however powerfully built he was and however quick and sure his perception. And yet it looked as if that were exactly the case. What an error of world history!

At the same time, however, he also asked himself: to what extent did his feelings influence his judgment? What would the loss of that man, who was lying on his bed here in the Cavalier Wing with the bullet in his neck, cared for by Dr. Rosanov and a few other doctors who had been brought in rather by chance— what would the loss of this man mean to him, Radek, personally? What did he feel for him? Reverence, even love: did his heart warm at the thought of him, his sayings, his moods, his temperament? Or did he only see him as an excellent thinker, whose brain worked precisely and flawlessly?

Who the hell knew.

And if they had to do without him tomorrow, whose side would Radek take? Trotsky's? Zinoviev's? No, not him, the schemer, the vain one. Or perhaps Stalin, the sinister crony?

In any case, the world, and indeed the entire world, was focused on one Vladimir Ilyich in those hours; diplomats, editors, correspondents, accredited and freelance, came from everywhere. Mr. Radek, the details, please. When, how, where, who, the details! Has the perpetrator, or have the perpetrators, been arrested yet? And what is Lenin's condition at this hour? Is there a chance he'll survive the wound? What do the doctors say? A bulletin, when can we expect a bulletin?

Radek shared as much as he knew, or as much as he thought it was good to communicate. That evening, he reported, Comrade Lenin had already spoken at two large rallies. But then, in the industrial area on the far bank of the Moskva, before the workers of the Michelson works, he appeared a third time using what was left of his energies, and spoke, with the greatest passion, of the events in Ukraine, on the Volga, in Siberia, in the Caucasus, where the Whites, after the withdrawal of the Soviets, had immediately abolished the eight-hour day, reinstated the old tsarist police, and returned the land and businesses to their former owners.

"The assassination attempt, Comrade Radek!" someone admonished him. "Not the whole story of creation again, please!"

But Radek was not disturbed and continued to quote Lenin. "If among you, Comrades, said Ilyich, there should still be uncertainties about the question of who is doing what to whom, I recommend you look at these territories: the bitter answer will become clear to you, quite without explanations on my part."

Radek sensed the displeasure among his listeners. As much as he liked to lecture the guys from the embassies and the press, too much of it might be counterproductive.

So he gathered his words. "Even now," he said, "Lenin's final sentence rings in my ears, spoken shortly after midnight, eight minutes exactly, according to the clock on the wall of the great hall of the Michelson works: *We have only one choice—victory or death!* And while Ilyich, passing through the crowd, was looking for the way to the exit from the hall, one of the assassins, a certain Novikov, pushed aside the bystanders, thus creating the space for the gunwoman to aim at Lenin—and to fire."

"Gunwoman." The tone was sarcastic. "That's not how the little one looked."

Radek remained conciliatory. "Rather delicate and girlish, I know. Miss Fanny Kaplan, of the right-wing Social Revolutionaries. And where, pray tell, is it written that a terrorist must look like a butcher's wife?"

"Terror—that's your speciality, in fact!"

Radek straightened up. "Is that any wonder?"

"And where is Miss Kaplan now?"

Radek looked at the new questioner, a not particularly pleasant type, and certainly not a sympathizer. "In the Lubyanka. Under heavy guard, I suppose."

"You're going to put her on trial?" That was the first one again.

"Justice will be done to her. But why are you more interested, esteemed sir, in the perpetrator than in her victim?"

"Because a bullet to the body is an occupational hazard of the professional revolutionary."

"Strange." Radek felt how dangerous the ground was that he was treading on, but an inner voice dictated his answer. "Strange," he repeated, "Lenin said the same thing after he came to under the hand of Dr. Rosanov."

Her visit was to be expected, Radek said to himself: Vladimir Ilyich probably would have wished it so, if someone, Krupskaya, for instance, had asked him about it; such a close encounter with death would have touched the emotional life of even the toughest revolutionary, and basically it didn't matter whether he had sent for Armand or if she had come on her own: Kaplan's bullet had hit more inside him than just a piece of tissue between his spine and esophagus.

The day before, Balabanoff had already turned up, directly from Stockholm, and hadn't allowed herself to be brushed off, despite the medical objections: the physicians, who, with the exception of Rosanov, had been called in more by chance than by professional considerations, were unsure of how to behave: both could have unfortunate consequences for them at such a time and with such a patient, and Balabanoff knew how to place herself in the limelight in such a way that the intimidated doctors soon considered every one of her demands, even the most exalted, to be law; only Rosanov, in conjunction with Krupskaya, succeeded in wresting Lenin from the effusive embraces of the gentle Angelica.

And now, Armand. Couldn't he, Radek, take care of Inessa,

Krupskaya had requested, at least until it had been established whether Vladimir Ilyich was up to the stress, both physical and emotional, of such an encounter.

So they both sat together, Radek and Inessa. Inessa had become gaunt, he found: pale and gaunt; the Swiss bloom, product of alpine air and alpine milk, had wilted and given way to a haggard expression around the eyes and mouth. Or was it that, living with her family, with whom she had moved in after her return to Russia, she found herself deprived of the drama she enjoyed in Lenin's environment?

"I haven't," she said, "heard from Vladimir Ilyich for so long. And now, you understand, I'm half-mad with worry. What's his condition? What are his prospects? Can we speak to him? Or at least see him? And would they allow me?"

Would, in this case, meant: would Krupskaya allow her to, thought Radek. But Nadezhda Konstantinova didn't have that much influence over events and the sick man at all. Only, if not her, then who? Trotsky, the successor, if there was to be one, hurrying from the military front that was just forming? The Cheka, which had failed so visibly at the Michelson plantworks?

Radek sighed. He felt sorry for her, the once so beautiful Inessa, really and truly. Not that Krupskaya had emerged from the contest with her as the radiant victor; there was nothing radiant about the gray bags under her eyes and the features marked by constant disappointment; he had always brought women only misfortune, the sick man who had never had a heart for those who loved him, and who was now fighting for his life not far from this room, with the bullet in his left shoulder and a second one in his right sternoclavicular joint, which Dr. Rosanov did not dare to remove.

Dr. Rosanov came in, rumpled coat, unshaven. "Fifteen minutes," he said. "And no long conversations, please, especially ones that might excite the patient."

Lenin and no conversations, thought Radek; Ilyich, as long as he had even a remnant of breath in his punctured lungs, would develop theses. And since Radek didn't know whether Dr.

Rosanov included him among the admitted visitors, he simply joined Inessa and Kruspkaya without asking the doctor first.

Having barely crossed the threshold, he was terrified down to his heart: the drawing pen of death, the merciless one, had been at work: the white, sunken face, tiny above the thick bandage around shoulders and neck; the eyes, deep in the dark sockets; if he survived this, Lenin would never again be who he had been.

Something similar must have been going through Armand's mind: the man she loved, struck down at the moment when his fight was at its peak.

"You," she said with an intensity that reminded Radek of fortune tellers he had heard in his youth, "will live. And I'll cheer for you in Red Square on the day of the Revolution's victory."

"Someone like me," said Lenin, but it was more like a croak, not the familiar tone from him, with the usual sharpness, "someone like me doesn't step down so lightly." And, after a pause, a little stronger. "Besides, there's still Kaplan."

"Kaplan?" Inessa didn't immediately understand. "What about Kaplan?"

Radek suspected: the old superstition, a life for a life. They were all superstitious, the Russians, and hadn't Lenin's brother also met his end on the rope, under the tsar at that time, in retribution?

Krupskaya was suddenly agitated. "No, you won't tolerate that, Volodya," she said in a trembling voice. "A revolutionary doesn't have another revolutionary executed."

Armand's features became hard. Oh, the effusiveness of this woman! "Terror against terror," she said. "Isn't he your husband, Nadezhda Konstantinova!"

Lenin, with a barely noticeable movement of the hand, refused. "Others... will... decide that," he said with effort.

Others? thought Radek. Who? And over Lenin's head?

But how beautiful were the rumors that circulated, and how useful! A special train, with Kaplan on board, had left Moscow for the Urals; Lenin, in the face of death, had granted mercy before justice; the great act of reconciliation had begun, with the Social Revolutionaries, the Mensheviks, with all. A new Jesus, Vladimir Ilyich, lay pale in Krupskaya's arms, the blood dripping from his wound.

Inessa stood up and bent over the sick man. He closed his eyes and smiled. She kissed his lips, a breath, hardly more.

★

"Comrade Malkov," said Radek, "the truth, please. The truth, and how to present it, is one of my functions."

The large, heavy red hands on the edge of the table. The striped shirt under the coarse cloth of the dark jacket. The narrow eyes, used to identifying even the most distant ships.

"I was ordered to remain silent on the matter."

"Then I'll tell you how it went down; correct me if I'm wrong. They came to you and said, go to the Lubyanka and pick her up there and take her to the Kremlin in a barred car, and lock her up there under strict guard, in a secure cell. And then they showed you an ukase from the Cheka: Kaplan is to be executed; the sentence will be carried out by Kremlin commandant Malkov."

His hands moved, but soon rested again.

"Isn't that right?" Radek asked.

"Shooting a person," Malkov said, "especially a woman, isn't an easy thing. It's a heavy duty, a very heavy duty." He pondered. "But the verdict was just. And I, Pavel Dmitrievich Malkov, Communist, sailor of the Baltic Fleet and commandant of the Moscow Kremlin, carried it out with these hands."

Later, Radek would attempt to describe to his Rosa what he felt at these words of Malkov's; he didn't succeed. What a business, the revolution!

He reached for a piece of paper. "Death to the White Terror!" he spoke half aloud, while he was already writing, "that should be enough, as a headline in *Izvestia*."

Malkov nodded.

Then, later in the text, Malkov had trouble following: "On so-and-so September of 1918, according to the decision of the All-Russian Cheka, the member of the right-wing Social Revolutionaries, Fanny Kaplan, who shot Lenin, was executed."

"And that's it?"

"That's it," said Radek.

When the news came over the telegraph, news not to be misjudged in its importance—they were on strike in Vienna and Berlin, the troops were refusing service, there was mutiny in the fleets—he thought his heart would burst: too often, the hopes he had cherished had been dashed, the expectations he had clung to had been disappointed, too often he had been stranded with his promises, proclaimed in public, that the workers, the German, Austrian, Italian, French, English, and so on, would come to the aid of their comrades in Russia at their lost post—and now, suddenly, it was supposed to be reality, the great prophecy, and from the balcony of the Berlin Palace—according to the ticker tape—from which the Kaiser usually exhibited himself to his people, Comrade Liebknecht had proclaimed the socialist republic!

Voices became loud in the corridor. Rosa came rushing into the room. "Lenin wants to go out! To the street! To speak! To everyone! Everyone! Everyone!"

Radek jumped up. He had expected someone to come, Dr. Rosanov perhaps, or Krupskaya, to call him to Lenin.

"My coat," Radek said, "quickly," and put it on, already hurrying down the corridor after a couple of larger-than-life figures, in the midst of which, he more sensed than recognized, was Lenin.

Then, in front of the entrance to the house, they pushed Lenin into a car; Radek attempted to squeeze through to him, but they shut the door right in front of his nose, and shortly thereafter, there was only the big crowd in front of the crenellated wall, and then outside, in front of the gate, on the wide square, tens of thousands, close together, the shouts, the flags, the banners, hastily written, the cheers.

They marched late into the night, from the factories and workshops, tenements, the shacks of the suburbs, men and women, many with their children, and armed squads already in the coats of the new Red Army. The world revolution had come, Radek thought, the people heard its iron step. Our loneliness is over.

He put his hand in his pocket, feeling the pipe. But he had neither tobacco, nor matches.

BOOK FOUR

We can play-act all the way through, even though we're
stabbed in good earnest at the end.
—GEORG BÜCHNER, *Danton's Death*

H e wasn't the only one who believed the fate of the revolution would be decided in Germany. As early as 1917, during Red October, and in the following months, there had been voices, even at party headquarters, in Lenin's immediate environment, that advised calling off the whole undertaking: a hopeless cause until the impetus for it came from outside.

But now it was here, the long-desired collapse of the Imperial Army, which promised liberation from General Hoffmann's stranglehold—world history in action, and we can say we were there. One even heard of councils, formed by the German troops according to the Russian model, and before Radek was the telegram from Comrade Joffe, who had been sitting as Russian ambassador in Berlin and there, assisted by Bukharin, was engaged in grand politics. He had just learned—Joffe cabled—without even making the effort of enciphering his message—that the German government had offered an armistice and peace negotiations to the Western allies. And he had been expelled twelve hours later, one of the last official acts of that government.

When Radek later thought back to those days, they seemed to him like a singular triumph of his efforts. What he had thought and written in Bremen, Leipzig, Bern, wherever, was confirmed, and gloriously fulfilled, what he had worked for from his youth, not always with the cleanest means.

After that night, when the news arrived of the upheaval in

Vienna and Berlin, the Moscow newspapers were all already printed and delivered, but special editions at least, Radek knew, would be expected of him before daybreak, and where to find a printing house capable of gathering its workers at this hour and in that hullabaloo of rumors, hopes, and vodka, until finally Comrade Bela Kun arrived with typesetters and printers he had recruited from among Hungarian prisoners of war: on the morning after that night, then, the masses really entered the stage, now already at least partially, under the direction of the party, streaming toward the House of the Soviets, and he, Radek, at one of the huge windows on the upper floor—what spirit, what movement on the broad street!—and crawling through the middle of the crowd, a shiny black insect, the car, with Lenin in it.

Radek grabbed Kun by the hand and they actually managed to get out of the building and to Lenin. He also recognized them, despite his exhaustion, and told the driver to stop.

Radek jerked the door open. "I beg you!" he said. "You don't just look sick, you *are*!"

"I've never felt better, Karl Bernhardovich, than here and now."

Radek had been much too close to him in the last few weeks and months to believe him. And Lenin himself knew perfectly well that it was the cheers and affection that reached out to him from the masses, even stronger the later it was at night, and probably also his own feeling of immense relief at the eventual turn of events, which had always buoyed him up when the wounds began to ache and his heart threatened to tighten.

Radek spoke with great intensity: "Give the order, Ilyich," Radek sproke with great intensity, "to take you back to the Kremlin, to Dr. Rosanov! You have to go to bed."

"This here"—Lenin's hand movement seemed to encompass the whole people—"brings me the best cure."

"Then at least come with me and Kun, out of this commotion, and into the House of Soviets there so you can lie down for a few minutes!"

This time Lenin agreed. As he got out, he felt that he could barely hold himself up, and inside he leaned on Radek and Kun and groaned heavily several times, allowing two of his personal guards to grab him on either side and almost carry him up the stairs. As soon as he reached the top and caught his breath, however, the drug that had kept him up all night—the drug of victory—took effect again, and he demanded to be led to the window and allowed to enter the narrow balcony, the wrought-iron grating of which a young painter had recently painted in a golden color, as if in anticipation of future triumphs of the world revolution.

It was indescribable, the eruption among those down in the street when they became aware of the deathly pale, obviously fever-ish man behind the gilded bars. Radek had never before experi-enced such feelings becoming manifest, not in Warsaw in 1905, and certainly not with the good old SPD, and never again, he suspected, would he experience anything like it. The Bolsheviks, who had held out in Moscow over the last year under terrible pressure, clamoring and debating, and often enough despairing, had become the source and focus of a new kind of energy.

Radek had his way of gripping people. When he spoke, there were currents, similar to electric ones, which seemed to emanate from him to those assembled; he only had to take care that the first contact was made, had to find with a quick glance among the faces in the circle the most indifferent, the most tired, whether it was that of a man or a woman, and speak to that face, and only to that one: if you had that one, you had the hearts of all.

In the hall of the Prokhorovo factory, a weaver, gaunt with narrow shoulders, her age unclear; she had probably not had a particularly happy life. No, he did not idealize poor people, as Luxemburg so often did; that led to human and political mis-judgments; but this woman, as he observed her, her facial expres-sions, her gestures, turned out to be a real medium, one might say. The revolution in Berlin, he instructed the woman, and through her all of his listeners, was a decisive victory not only for the workers there and the German village poor, but also for them here, the Russian proletariat; but at the same time, it placed an enormous responsibility on them. They, the workers of Moscow, had felt more than once what it meant to starve; their German class comrades, however, had lived for a long, long time on an eighth of a kilo loaf of bread and a few turnips a day.

The question of why the German proletarians had only just now chased off their government, and not earlier, he didn't even allow to come up, not even in his own head; it would only have brought the woman to wayward thoughts. Now, however, as he stood at a telephone in the Commissariat for Foreign Affairs, which was constantly breaking down, picking sentence after sentence out of the fragmentary words of his interlocutor with nerve-racking patience, he had the woman before his eyes again, her hand stretched out to him as if she held in it a piece of that dark, bran-like bread that was available in Moscow, if any was available, in the second year of the victorious October Revolution.

Comrade Chicherin next to him, who had replaced Trotsky in his function as Commissar for Foreign Affairs, was a man of little patience. "Demand to speak to the minister! Who do you have on the line there—the German Foreign Ministry, isn't it?"

"I don't know if they even have a minister again. There's a people's representative speaking on the other end, Delegate Haase, I know him, a leftist."

"And what's he saying, your friend, the people's representative? Don't keep me waiting so long!"

"I'm trying to understand what he's saying!"

"Tell him, we want to have Joffe in Berlin again. And we call upon him to make sure that Joffe gets his *agrément* back!"

"I'm talking about something else with him right now!"

"About what?"

"About bread!"

"Are you crazy, Radek?"

"Bread is a revolutionary topic!"

Chicherin uttered a more than annoyed "Oh! . . . Tell your—
what's his name?—Haase, it wasn't him and his government, but
the old imperial one, which expelled Comrade Joffe from the
country barely four days before it went to hell itself!"

"I beg of you," Radek slammed his fist on the table, "please be
quiet already!"

Chicherin swallowed, but remained silent. Radek listened
again; the connection with Berlin had improved, Haase's lecturing tone was clearly audible. Then, suddenly, the conversation
fell apart; but the most important thing had been said. Radek put
the receiver down. Then he looked at Chicherin's irritated red
face with a smile.

"Do you know, Comrade Chicherin, what People's Deputy
Haase said about our offer of active solidarity? He told me they
knew there was even more hunger in Russia than in their own
country, and he asked us to give the bread we were planning to
sacrifice to the German revolution to the starving in our country . . . You wouldn't happen to have anything to smoke, would
you?"

Chicherin held out his cigarette case.

"Now listen, dear friend, to what this Haase in his stupidity has
revealed to us." Radek sucked hungrily at the commissar's self-
rolled cigarette. "The president of the United States, he bragged,
guaranteed Germany the import of so much wheat and so many
fats that they'd be able to get their entire population through the
winter with it."

Chicherin didn't seem very interested. Did the man need to
have everything explained to him? Radek wondered. Haase's
haughty words revealed the great plan they were concocting in
the West: they'd keep the defeated Reich, barely but nevertheless,
in line, and at the same time rein in the German Revolution—
not much was needed anyway—and try to let the Kaiser's old
army, still present and still clustered deep in the Russian interior,
march eastward again like it was 1914—but now in alliance with

the West and in order to crush a still embryonic socialism under their hobnailed boots.

"What's with Joffe!" urged Chicherin, who had understood absolutely nothing. "This—what's his name? Haase?—can't presume to totally cut off the Commissariat for Foreign Affairs of the Russian Soviet Republic from what's going on in Berlin!"

For a moment, Radek thought he heard again the woman from the Prokhorovo factory, voiceless echo of his own appeal for bread: "We will starve, Comrade Radek, but we'll help our German brothers!"

"Maybe," he said, "a few of us should go to Berlin without the express permission of the Comrade People's Commissar."

2

The invitation to Berlin was kept rather cool, cool and correct, as one was wont to do from party to party, when there had already been several quarrels between them; there was little to be felt of brotherhood in tone or of revolutionary solidarity or the like; the signatory's name was Molkenbuhr, and he bore the heroic first name Brutus. Radek still knew this Brutus from SPD times, a dry fellow, always afraid of committing himself; that such a person should have risen to leadership of the Berlin Workers' and Soldiers' Council and even become its secretary seemed strange.

"And you'll accept the invitation, of course," said Rosa, "and set out immediately for Berlin."

Radek faltered; the tone—her tone had been a little too pensive, too reserved. He smiled. "You know me, I'm like the stone in the biblical slingshot." And continued: accept the invitation, yes, what else, and get through the still existing front line of General Hoffmann as quickly as possible, as difficult as that might be—or had he already been replaced by another commissar? ... At this first German Congress of Councils, the revolution would be constituted; perhaps this or that could be steered in this or that direction.

"I'm pregnant," she said.

He swallowed. "Are you sure?" he said; of course she was sure, after all, she was a doctor. He stood up. "I'm going to take you in my arms now and kiss you and dance with you across this room. That's what one does, in the case of such news."

"Stay seated," she said, "I noticed your fear, and I understand. But I want to have this child. Because it's yours, and it will be a new little person."

"I didn't say that I don't want it," he objected.

"I know what you think," she replied "You've said it often enough: in these times, these are no times to bring children into the world. But then: who are you making a revolution for?…"

"Yes," he admitted and felt ashamed, "when I think of the word revolution, I always think of humanity as a whole, but you're thinking of a single human being that you're going to give birth to. And maybe you're even right…"

"Don't worry," she said, "I'll take it all on myself, the entire burden: and you'll be as free as the stone that flies through the air, hurled here and there by history."

He took her hands. "If it's a girl, name her Sophia, after my mother."

She pulled free and stroked his head. "Oh, my little Lolek …"

★

They sat together with Lenin in his room around the green-covered table—him, Joffe, Bukharin, and two other comrades, the entire delegation that had been selected for the German Council Congress, plus Sverdlov. Ilyich lectured them on the line that they should attempt to push through in Germany. Radek only half-listened; he thought of Rosa, not his Rosa, but rather the great passionate one, Luxemburg, whom he too had once admired, and who had pushed him away, and who would now be back in Berlin, just released from prison in Breslau, and then again of his Rosa, who was now pregnant by him, and still it touched him strangely that the two women had been destined to bear the same name; and he sought to imagine Karl Radek as a father, the mewling welp in his arms: Karl Radek, of whom they said he couldn't even pull up his pants because he was constantly carrying the *Times* and the entire French and German press tucked under his arms; but hadn't she, his Rosa, said, that she would take on the whole burden herself . . .

Sverdlov, sitting to Lenin's left, explained that the delegation would receive a special car and provisions from the All-Russian Executive Committee's rations room. Oh God, Radek thought, how many conferences had he been to now, how many congresses had he attended, delegated by how many groups, how many groupuscules, all of which have since passed and faded away? This time, however, he came with more gravitas than ever, as the messenger of a really existing revolution and as representative of a really existing power.

Afterward, Ilyich took him aside. He looked worried. "Grave times are upon us."

And what, Radek thought, had the times been up to now? Fun?

Lenin's voice sounded hoarse, the after-effect of Fanny Kaplan's bullet and the renewed strain. Germany, Lenin said, had been crushed, but this also opened the way for the Entente into Russia, with or without German auxiliaries, via Hungary and Romania into the Ukraine, or via the Dardanelles.

Radek assured him that he saw things the same way. At the same time, however, he felt the need, as so often recently, to prop up the afflicted man before him, and assured him: "If the Entente powers manage to get their expeditionary corps to Russia before the revolution has infected them as well, then we will smash their troops in our country, just like we did to their German predecessors."

"Hopefully," Lenin answered.

And he began to give him instructions for the case that he would have to stay behind alone in Germany, as he had stayed behind once before, in Stockholm that time, after all the others who had traveled with him in the sealed train went on to Petrograd. "You'd be standing all alone, Comrade Radek, behind enemy lines, dependent only on yourself. Intervention against us is inevitable, and its outcome may well depend on the situation in Germany, and you'd then have to influence this situation, by any means necessary, you, on your own."

Lenin's confidence flattered him, but he did not share his assessment of the situation. "The German Revolution," he replied to Ilyich, "is too great an event for us to regard it merely as a means of diverting another, greater enemy."

"I'm not suggesting that you force events, Karl Bernhardovich." Lenin looked at him strangely. "They'll develop according to their own laws."

The delegate of the Dünaburg soldiers' council was a stutterer, and what was more, he stuttered in one of the many German dialects; but this one seemed familiar to Radek's ear, from his time in Göppingen; it was with this inflection that the typesetters and layout designers of the *Freie Volkszeitung* had spoken, where he had acted as editor-in-chief for a few months; what hadn't he done and written and spoken in those years to get the German comrades moving?

"You can't t-t-trust them, the Herr Of-f-ficers," said the delegate of the Dünaburg soldiers' council. "They say one thing but th-think another, and have only g-g-gone over to the revolution for sh-sh-show; but," he promised, "Dünaburg is the b-best route into Germany, and we'll bring b-b-bring you through, Comrades."

It was possible that he even believed what he said, the delegate of the Dünaburg soldiers' council. But for now, they were stuck in Dünaburg. The provisions from home, it turned out, consisted of a barrel of porridge and one of honey, the diet of the children of Israel on the march through the desert, Radek remembered, and hoped that the journey to the German revolution would not take forty years. The stutterer didn't return. In his place, a captain pretending to be a Social Democrat appeared and invited them to a meeting of the soldiers' council; he was the chair of the council, he explained, democratically elected by the men, and asked whether one or more of the Russian comrades would like to make a presentation in their circles; no, unfortunately, he could make no commitments with regard to their further journey; here in Dünaburg, they didn't make any decisions; decisions came from Berlin.

Joffe spoke first; his German was a bit too professorial for those present at the meeting. Radek spoke himself after Joffe, and was forced to realize to his annoyance that he also missed the effect he was aiming for, despite his proven recipe; whoever he fixed with his gaze in the round, whichever face he chose, none of the guys reacted.

Then in the night he was suddenly awakened; a beam of light fell on his face, behind the flashlight a monocle, diagonally below it, a blond brush could be recognized. Major Baron von So-and-So, the name incomprehensible. On behalf of General von Falkenhayn he had the honor, indeed, Major Baron von So-and-So had said "honor," to inform the Russian gentlemen that unfortunately they could not be allowed to proceed through German-occupied territory, and from there to Berlin; rather, they would be expedited via Minsk back to the territory held by their comrades.

That, Bukharin replied, remained to be seen. In any case, he pointed out to the major that he was dealing with a high-ranking delegation traveling on behalf of a government at least as legitimate as that of the present government of General von Falkenhayn. And now enough palaver; let our locomotive dock.

"It would be more agreeable to me," said the Baron, "if you wouldn't force me to arrest you."

"Arrest?" Radek reached into his coat pocket, pulled out the pistol he carried next to his tobacco pipe, a dainty thing with silver fittings from Tula, on loan from the Kremlin armory. He had never fired at a human being in his life, not even in 1905, in Warsaw, during the attack of the mounted police, and he felt in advance the satisfaction with which he would point the little pistol at the fellow. And to Bukharin, in Russian, "We're not going to let ourselves be arrested by some arrogant Kraut Junker!"

Bukharin, who didn't want to leave the hero's role to Radek, also drew a gun.

"Gentlemen, please!" the major objected, also in Russian, smiling amiably. Then he opened the compartment door. Outside, in the circle of light from the platform lamp, stood half a dozen German field gendarmes.

But even without them, any violence would have been absurd in a region where the roads and railroads were still completely in the hands of the Germans.

The trip turned out to be a nightmare. It was cold in the coupe, they kept stopping at the strangest stations, no one knew why, apparently not even Lieutenant Stieglitz, the commander of the escort that Major Baron von So-and-So had given them, whether for their own protection or to prevent them from taking an unauthorized change in route. The escort consisted of a handful of grumpy older people who occasionally became threatening, but who were obviously also afraid not so much of them, the handful of Russian civilians, as of what they represented; never again, one of them suddenly shouted, would they get out of this Russia; they'd perish here in the cold like Emperor Napoleon.

The Napoleon legend seemed to be rampant in the German eastern army in general; in Wilejka, also one of the pockets where the train suddenly stopped, heavily armed men loitered about waving their fixed bayonets after learning who the gentlemen were who were there in person; Bolshevik swine, they called them, they probably wanted to go to Berlin to drag Germany into a new war, and Liebknecht and Luxemburg, obviously known to the men, were cursed along with them, the red whore; then, Radek heard these soldiers speak with concern about Napoleon. Lieutenant Stieglitz remained missing; he probably didn't want to be held responsible in case something happened to those under his protection; after they had finally moved on, he reappeared; grinning sheepishly, and allowed himself to be lured by Bukharin into a discussion about imperialism, in which a few people from his crew also took part.

Later, in Molodechna, the locomotive was decoupled; that was it, it was over. Night came, and Stieglitz announced that if they should suddenly hear machine-gun fire, they shouldn't be alarmed; there was a train coming towards them from Minsk, of which it was not known under which flag and under whose command it was not known, nor who had sent it. When the train arrived, a bunch of Germans, officers and men alike, were hanging from the carriages, and the carriages that were crammed with hastily gathered goods; in Minsk, the exhausted men reported, a ragged mob appeared without warning, most of them barefoot, and pounced on them, and their fellow soldiers who had not run away fast enough were massacred and robbed of their boots and coats. The Red Army, it seemed, had entered Minsk.

Radek's eyes sparkled behind the thick lenses of his glasses. "Herr Lieutenant," he said, "surely you'll permit us to contact Minsk via the stationmaster's teletype at the location."

Stieglitz looked over at the train of fugitives; he probably was already seeing himself in a similar situation. "Please," he said somberly.

The new stationmaster in Minsk took a while to understand the message that Radek had ticked through. Delegation? Who? What? To where? Radek remained patient. Then, at last, the redemptive message: SENDING LOCOMOTIVE MOLODECHNAMOLODYETSCHNA.

Joffe, his neck wrapped thickly with a woolen scarf, was waiting for him at the door of their compartment. They embraced each other as they had done that earlier night before, when Joffe, expelled from his Berlin embassy, exhausted by the fugitive-like journey and full of the most contradictory news, arrived in Moscow; and, as on that night, Joffe again smelled, although unwashed and with a feral beard, of the finest *eau de cologne*.

3

Radek saw that, basically, both Joffe and Bukharin felt relieved to be back with their own people. Of course, their appearance at the German Congress of Councils would have been a sensation, Bukharin's especially, the dialectician, whose words could make even the most firmly established theses of an opponent crumble, would have achieved many things, and Joffe could have reestablished the connections that he had had as an ambassador to the Kaiser's last government and that had been broken by his expulsion by that government. But, they consoled themselves, they had done what was possible under the circumstances to get to Berlin; after all, they, men of office and dignity—Bolshevik office, Bolshevik dignity—could not try to sneak between post lines and trenches against the will of a still-functioning Prussian military apparatus; it would have been pure adventurism, as well as life-threatening.

Couldn't they? Couldn't he, Radek, at least, who had always operated on the fringes of norms and laws, a marauding knight in the realm of party, press, and government bureaucracies?

He discussed the question with Adolf Joffe, in whom he preferred to confide rather than the cool Bukharin. Joffe wheezed that he had a problem with his heart; and how, he asked, was he to be helped out again if he got into a bad situation?

Then—what a wonderful invention, the telegraph, and what a miracle that such devices were still ticking away despite the turmoil of two revolutions occurring at the same time—he managed to contact Moscow, not Lenin directly, but Sverdlov at least, and Sverdlov spoke to Ilyich and telegraphed back, saying, please, Comrade Radek, you have Lenin's blessing, but the risk is strictly your own.

In the meantime, he had looked around Minsk and had come across German comrades who, like him, were urgently trying to get to Berlin as quickly as possible. He already knew one of them, a certain Friesland, but his real name was Ernst Reuter and he belonged to the USPD, the Independent Social Democratic Party, thus a leftist; the man had been taken prisoner of war, and he, Radek, had picked him up in the camp, hastily indoctrinated him and used him for propaganda among the other prisoners. The second, Felix Wolf, although not having gone through his school, had been similarly active: even before the war as a clerk in Russia, he had ended up in Siberia, where he joined the Bolsheviks in 1916; in 1917 he fought as a partisan until he was sent to the Western front to agitate among the Kaiser's soldiers behind the German lines, just as he was now doing in Minsk. Wolf obtained false papers, identity cards of German prisoners of war; Radek's had belonged to a Sergeant Hähnlein; how many names was this now? Radek thought, but he could no longer remember all his pseudonyms.

Joffe and Bukharin traveled from Minsk back to Moscow in an upholstered compartment. Radek brought them to the railway station, then, amply provided with money from the formerly joint treasury, he, together with his new companions, boarded a much less luxurious train leaving for Lithuania; they were seated in a rickety freight car, with people of all kinds, most of them dressed in scraps of ragged uniforms and all of them hungry and lousy; no one knew how long the journey would take and where and into whose hands they might end up; nevertheless, everyone hoped to reach the desired destination. There were no checkpoints anywhere, military or civilian, no one paid any attention to him and his companions, the shabby clothes of unclear origin, which they had procured in Minsk, offered protection against curiosity; he sat on the plank floor of the car, leaning against Friesland-Reuter's lean chest, and tried to sort out the fragments of conversation that reached his ears from right and left and front and back.

The people complained that they were still waiting on peace, for the sake of which the revolution had been made; now, one—peasant that he was—wanted to at least return to the piece of land that the Bolsheviks had promised, or back to the family that had been scattered in the war, or even just an oven to crawl on top of, some hole where a spoonful of grits could still be had. And yet, thought Radek, even in this most miserable guy, there was a potential, somewhere in these hearts there was also a longing, for justice, beauty, joy, or did he only hear it from the rough sounds above the pounding of the wheels, he who secretly still carried the same longing in his heart?

In the middle of nowhere, they had to get out of the train, out of the thick haze that had offered at least the appearance of warmth, out into the wind that swept over the icy stubble. The power, what a grand word, *power*, of the Red Army reached up to this point; beyond the station, it was said, near the thatched roofs visible over there, stood the Germans. Radek turned up his collar, pulled his cap down over his ears and gripped the bundle tighter, in it the canned food and the crust of bread; he trudged on across the field, Wolf in front of him, behind him, as rear guard, Reuter, alias Friesland; at any moment Radek expected the German "*Halt, wer da!*," but nothing of the sort came. In one of the dwellings, earth piled up around charred beams, crouched a peasant and his wife; they looked ancient, but that was probably the suffering and hardship, for, from one of the beams, there hung a cradle with an infant in it, the little face wrinkled, the eyes festered. Radek put a can on the table and half a loaf of bread; the man grabbed it hastily, even stuffing the child's mouth with dark crumbs. Then they became more trusting. On this spot, the woman said, had once stood their house; now it had burned down, by whom, who should know, and now they lived here this way; in the spring, they'd see; the main thing was the land. A horse? A sleigh? Not with us! But a little faurther on, there was someone who was better off than they were, maybe he could help.

It did in fact smell like a stable, after they found the other man's cottage. For minutes they knocked and shouted to lure the farmer out from behind his door, and he bargained long and hard, eyeing each bill before saying, okay, he would drive them.

And then they crouched behind the broad back of the man in his fur, watching the clouds pass by in the occasional moonlight; at dawn they recognized their first Germans; columns in retreat, dispersed into clusters of the fatally exhausted, staggering through the snow, bent over as if under infinite weight, and not even looking up as the sled slid by. Toward the Germans came other columns, even more miserably dressed, their feet wrapped in rags or bare in wooden slippers: Russian prisoners of war who had fled from the German camps. They were freezing terribly, but the cold, like their hunger and fatigue, seemed to affect them less than the Germans; their march was home. In the marketplace of a still somewhat intact little town stood an abandoned column; around campfires, here one, there one, huddled field- gray soldiers, holding their hands to the flames. "Why don't you go into the houses," Radek inquired, "and warm yourselves?"

"Too dangerous."

"Why's that?"

The man stared at him. "They'd kill us."

"Ah, so."

"What haven't we taken from them in this war, the coats from their bodies, the scarves from their necks, butter from the dish, goats from the stable. We were also hungry and cold, weren't we? And we had to send food to the women at home to go with the turnips. Now we'll pay for it; we'll die here like those under Napoleon."

Napoleon again, thought Radek. They must have had their experiences with the partisans, Wolf suspected, and strode toward the tavern across the street. The taproom was empty, there was nothing to get here; behind the bare counter an old freezing Jewish woman sat next to her son.

Reuter, who also called himself Friesland, flopped onto the hard bench in front of the cracked wall. Didn't she at least have hot water, he asked, for tea?

The old woman observed Radek. "Are you a Jew?"

"How do you know?"

"The eyes. And how you stand there, with your tired feet. Are you a Bolshevik?"

"I'm a Bolshevik."

"They're coming, the Bolsheviks, and things will be better for the Jews."

"And for humankind," said Radek. "I promise you."

The old woman nodded to her son. He left and came back after a while, a bottle of yellowish vodka in his hand. They drank and warmed themselves. Then they paid the peasant the rest of his wage and hired a Jewish carter who owned a sleigh and who swore to them by God Almighty that he would take them as far as the city of Vilna.

In the suburbs of Vilna they found an inn, half in ruins, but two or three windows showed light. Felix Wolf, who had developed into a sort of travel marshal, summoned the servant of the house, or was it the owner? He examined them with squinted eyes; but since the carter, having just been paid, praised his passengers as great gentlemen and able to pay, the fellow grumbled, well, maybe there's a room, with two beds only; however, they would have to arrange it.

Wolf and Friesland-Reuter went into the city in order to investigate the situation; Radek suddenly felt how exhausted he was, went to the room, which still smelled of a perfume, a cheap one, lay down on the soiled sheet without undressing, and tried to sleep; but sleep wouldn't come; he began to think about the revolution, the Soviet revolution, which was in part his creation, and Comrade Parvus's, and about the terror that his Polish mentor Dzherzhinsky had instituted in Russia after Fanny Kaplan's assassination attempt on Ilyich, and about the German revolution, which he was on his way to and which, if it were to prevail, would probably also need a pinch of terror, despite Rosa's well-known democratic airs. He thought in German. He thought in three languages—Polish, Russian, German—depending on his subject. When he thought about the revolution and socialism, he fell into German as if of his own accord; the most important part of his political education had occurred in Germany, and from the very beginning, with conflict and contradiction.

He woke up in fright; the door had opened a crack. "Is sir unable to sleep?"

The servant of the house, or was he the owner?, entered on quiet soles. "Would sir like," he whispered with a salivating tongue, "something for the heart? I have something very beautiful, very sophisticated too, daughter of a general, a Russian one, a real one even, if it's agreeable, such are the times nowadays, the gentleman understands, and pleasantly plump, as it should be."

Radek felt the blood rush to his groin. Lolek, his mother had taught him, hold back, such things are for the Goyim; but life had brought him enough temptations; and after all, he was neither a rabbi nor a monk.

"Get out of here!" he shouted.

Then he turned to the wall. It would have been embarrassing if Wolf or Friesland Reuter, or both, had caught him in the act with one of the general's daughters.

The noise on the street woke him up, shouting, gunshots. Would he have to go out again as soon as he had warmed up in bed? He pulled the blanket over his head.

Wolf came. "What are you doing lying there and playing hide-and- seek with yourself?" He laughed. "But it's nothing serious, the Germans are having a drink before they leave. I made friends with a few of them. They showed me where their delousing facility is, and told me their field gendarmerie won't let anyone into their German empire who can't prove, with an official stamp, that he's been washed and deloused."

"Now that's what I call *savoir vivre!*" Radek put his feet on the rag which, with much goodwill, might be called a bedside rug. "But what kind of revolution is that, without dirt and without lice!"

"Let it go," Wolf said. "A delousing certificate is better than no paper at all."

"How's that?" Radek wanted to know. "Suddenly our papers are no good anymore? They were expensive enough!"

"A change of costume," said Friesland-Reuter. "Better safe than sorry."

"All right," Radek said, and went off with the two of them to be deloused by the Germans. Naked among the naked, he stood in the steam and suddenly thought: Who am I here? Speaker of the revolution, writer of the revolution, Lenin's trusted advisor for press and agitation—and how was he supposed to prove this? If someone switched with him, flesh for flesh, some higher-up with braids on his sleeve, or a corporal in the dressing room who had the idea of playing with fate—what use would his protests be to him, and who would ever know what had become of the real Radek? But the wrong one would arrive in Berlin and be welcomed by the comrades there as the delegate of the Soviet party and government, and would preach deceit and betrayal at the German Congress of Councils, and everything would go wrong with their German revolution, as so much had already gone wrong in this Germany, while he, Sobelsohn, Karl Bernhardovich, the only real and true Radek, wandered through the city, a new

Kasper Hauser, earning laughter all around when he called out to the people, yes this and no that, but not at all like the fake one preaches it to you!

"Here, put this on!" Wolf tossed him a bundle. "A masterpiece."

The masterpiece was a uniform of the Imperial and Royal Austro-Hungarian army, which he should have been wearing for the entire war, had he not left for Switzerland at the last minute in 1914. Wolf said he had established relations with a cavalry captain of the Honvéd whom the fortunes of battle had brought to Vilna and who, on the basis of their delousing certificates and for a sum of money, would confirm with signature and seal that they were Austrian prisoners of war on their way home and had the right of transit through Germany, and that the German authorities were obligated to assist them in their journey and to provide for them according to the applicable regulations.

Comrade Friesland or Reuter, whatever the case may be, had his bony wrists sticking wide out of his sleeves, but Radek's k. und k. uniform fit perfectly.

4

To Germany? From here? From Vilna?

The stationmaster, knowledgeable about politics, as it turned out, began to grumble: first the gentlemen made revolution and abolished all order; but without order no railroad; as soon as a few carriages arrived and a locomotive, someone came and confiscated them; tomorrow perhaps a train would leave for Königsberg via Eydtkuhnen, or maybe not. At what time? Was he a prophet? And what, pray tell, do you mean by time? The gentlemen had taken four years for their war, so what was the hurry now, their Kaiser was up and gone anyway, along with Empress Zita and his Imperial councils, but there were now councils of a different sort in Vienna, workers' councils; only there was no order, and without order, no railroad.

Even here in Vilna, God help us, there was a workers' council, they learned. Felix Wolf went and made inquiries. When he returned, he reported that there was a certain Cichocki in this council, who claimed to know Radek. Cichocki, Radek thought, feeling something like an emotion: Comrade Cichocki had already been a mature man when he, Lolek Sobelsohn, listened with him in the educational circles of Polish workers to the fiery speeches of the young Dzherzhinsky, and wrote with a childish hand notes on the subjects of Hegelian dialectics and Marxian economics in a dark blue school notebook.

Then the three of them, Wolf, Reuter-Friesland, and Radek, sat in Cichocki's whitewashed sitting room drinking turnip tea and eating bread spread with a sweetish mass, and Cichocki reported that the German general Falkenhayn was arming the local bourgeoisie, and that Colonel Pilsudski—who had once been a socialist, a Polish one—and his people were planning the conquest of Vilna. At this, he looked at Radek, an expression of naive confidence in his still clear, bright eyes, as if to say that this was all nothing but alarm, a trumpet blaring in the background and of little importance, for weren't there the Red Army and Soviet comrades, always ready with fraternal aid?

Radek had pushed the tea aside and approached the bookshelf: printed matter, especially when piled up alongside each other, attracted him like the legendary magnetic mountain attracted ships. They were all there, mostly in Polish, the illegal pamphlets and books from which the boy from the ghetto of Lemberg, no sooner had he become Bar Mitzvah in the temple, realized that only socialism could provide a remedy for the myriad ills under which oppressed humanity suffered, and that this socialism, for good reasons easily recognizable to anyone with half an understanding, would not come through pious prayer and patient waiting, but only, and exclusively, through revolution.

The others seemed to sense what this room and the weathered shelf with the treasure of carefully guarded printed matter on it meant to him; Friesland, actually Reuter, thought that he and Wolf had better return to their quarters now; Radek could go ahead and stay for the night, if he so desired, and tomorrow morning they would pick him up; and Cichocki added that for someone like Radek, it was safer in his dwelling.

Radek nodded and reached out for the fresh tea that Cichocki pushed toward him. To his right and left, literature piled up on the old sofa. Then he leaned back on the sagging cushion and closed the tattered notebook on his lap. "I'm not a patriot, you know, old man, in the usual sense. As a high school student I burned for Poland; now, what is Poland to me?" He spoke very softly. "And yet, when I flip through these pages, I hear the voices of our martyrs in the tsar's courtrooms, and I feel as if the entire path of Polish socialism is appearing before my eyes. How young they were then, the comrades, when they were sentenced to prison and forced labor. In 1889, on the hundredth anniversary of the French Revolution, they believed someone would come to liberate them. But no one comes to bring freedom to anyone. One has to take it, and when one is finally close enough to it, to reach for it…" He looked up. "Remember, old man, 1905 . . . ?"

In 1905, like Rosa—not his; rather, Luxemburg—he had returned to Warsaw, hoping that what had happened so magnificently in Petersburg would now also happen in Poland. He adored Rosa: she was the master of the revolution and its genius; in her writings, her speeches, the tangle of ideas of revolt and human happiness came together in a perfect system; it was an almost aesthetic pleasure to follow her thoughts; but she paid no attention to him because he was too young, and not a guy like Tyszka, who she then served, and who ruled the party that he had split off from the Pilsudski crowd, he the pope of the new sect and Rosa its apostle.

But that, Radek recalled, had only really become clear to him the following year, when he was in prison in Warsaw and had time to think and learn Russian and to write—he had always been able to write, unlike Jogiches, whose hand shook when he had to put more than ten words on paper—and to write not only for random pamphlets of ephemeral groups, but, among other things, for the great Kautsky's dignified *Die Neue Zeit*, in which the prominent figures of social democracy of all shades held their journalistic rendezvous.

And now the Russian Revolution had come a second time, and this time, unbidden, permanently—and he, Mama's little Lolek, was its messenger to the German revolution, indeed the European revolution, without which, Rosa had also always emphasized, the Russian one was doomed to perish or, throughout its life, lead a crippled existence.

★

They marched to the station like a troop of real k. und k. infantry, in unison to the "Radetzky" march, ta-ta-tam, ta-ta-tam ta-ta tam-ta-tah, which Felix Wolf belted out in front of them. Then they hopped across the tracks to the railway siding where the train was still standing without its engine, and found an open compartment and spread out in it like princes.

But their happiness only lasted a short while. Then, at the platform, the carriage was stormed: it was hardly possible to breathe. A German military doctor, who was constantly staggering into him, concluded from Radek's restrained reaction that he must be some kind of intellectual, and, between curses and apologies, engaged him in a discussion. Radek remained cautious; he didn't praise the Bolsheviks, only saying that they were taking from the rich in order to give to the poor, and Friesland-Reuter mentioned that they had established a stable order and were in the process of crafting a disciplined army out of a bunch of wandering peasants and deserters. This last bit in particular met with the approval of the military doctor and the other Germans in this and the neighboring compartments; they were all in favor of order, and the military doctor even spoke confidentially: Hindenburg, he whispered in Radek's ear, had ordered, when there was talk of councils among the troops, to go ahead and allow them to be elected, but to take care that the councils were replaced by competent non-commissioned officers and officers loyal to the military leadership.

Radek took note of this with interest; if this information was true, he would have difficulties at the congress he was on his way to. Then the train stopped; the military doctor fell against his chest; outside someone shouted, "Eydtkuhnen! Civilians to customs!"

But nobody stirred, civilian or military; nobody could have stirred, and nobody came in order to carry out checks on those in the train.

After Königsberg he fell asleep, despite the crowded confinement. It was a rare, deep sleep that befell him; when he came to, he had no idea how long this sleep might have lasted; someone slapped him on the cheek with the back of his bony hand, Friesland-Reuter, as it turned out, and in the blackness behind the dirty window, a sign swayed by, poorly lit, BERLIN; it remained illegible which of the many Berlin stations it was.

They split up. This had been discussed in Vilna; none of them knew who had the upper hand in Berlin at the moment, the right, the left, the independents, the generals, nor whose troops were patrolling where, and so they decided to split up for the time being; one man could be replaced; three couldn't. "Sobelsohn," Radek repeated at their departure, so that they would remember it. He still had his old passport in the name of Sobelsohn, his only real documentation: "Karl Sobelsohn, Hotel Central."

Then they submerged into the current of the gray crowd, the cheerful, inventive Wolf and the rather morose but reliable Ernst Reuter alias Friesland; Radek found the station's restroom, disappeared into one of the smelly stalls, tore off his Austrian uniform and, carefully balancing so as to not get it dirty, stepped into the black trousers that he had been carrying in his bundle since Vilna, along with the jacket that was already quite worn at the sleeves and collar. Then, as he looked at himself in front of the spotted mirror outside, the reddened eyes behind the round, nickel-rimmed glasses, the messy hair, the three-day beard, he suddenly felt very alone, and almost helpless; yet he was used to moving about in foreign cities like a native, in Paris or Bern or Stockholm; but those had been cities in a state of static calm, bourgeois and sedate; this Berlin, however, was in a state of revolution, in a whirl, the currents of which he had only guessed at until now, although the revolution here was also his in more than one sense, desired and instigated by him; and yet, who was there for him now, who should he approach, where was someone waiting for him with open arms? He knew the Hotel Central, somewhere adjacent to Friedrichstraße, at least from the last time he was in Berlin, when the wretched vote of his Social Democratic brethren in favor of the Kaiser's war credits had made it seem inadvisable for him to remain at the heart of the German military machine. The Central—he hoped that it had not gone out of business in the meantime—had had atmosphere; behind the wall to the neighboring room there was groaning and squeaking every half hour at night, two girls shared the use of the bed there; one was named Rieke; he never learned the name of the other, considerably prettier one.

While still in the taxi on the way to the hotel, he opened up *Die Rote Fahne*, which he had managed to get hold of with some luck at the station kiosk, and devoured the headlines in the flickering light of the sparse gas streetlamps.

"It's all just words," the driver grumbled, "paper, empty promises." The man had a deep, purple scar on his skull, a shell fragment apparently. "It's already over, the revolution, and once again we're the fools."

The front page of *Die Rote Fahne* said the opposite. According to it, the workers would march tomorrow, or if not tomorrow, then the next day, in endless columns, and sweep away the government, the Eberts and Scheidemanns; but Spartakus, carried by the will of the masses, would triumph in Berlin and throughout the empire. Radek felt anxious; he knew the need of comrades, especially the leftists among them, to take their own wishful thinking for the real situation; he had indulged in the inclination himself often enough; the practice was also quite legitimate, as long as there was no danger that someone might take the battle cry seriously and follow it, plunging with bared chest into the enemy's bayonets.

The Central still existed, and a sum of money in excess of the usual fee procured him a room key; but he only stayed long enough to wash off the grossest dirt. Then he was on his way to *Die Rote Fahne*; the editorial address was—that touching affection for the law on the part of Germans—actually printed on page 4 at the bottom of the paper, and he was pleasantly surprised when discovering, upon his arrival at the house indicated, Zimmerstraße 41, that the comrades had taken up quarters here of all places, on the premises of the *Berliner Lokalanzeiger*, the pet newspaper of the Kaiser's loyalists; at least this one act of usurpation testified to a bit of revolutionary spirit.

But otherwise, he encountered little that looked like the dictatorship of the proletariat, no bulletproof bunk for the guard, no posts, no controls, only a great confusion prevailed in the corridors, out of which an excited female voice suddenly called his name.

He knew the elderly girl, she was called Fanny, and she had been a secretary in one of the organizations that he once had something to do with; Fanny seized him and pushed open a door on which a note was stuck, the writing of which couldn't be deciphered quickly; and there Liebknecht sat, staring at him. "Radek!"

Radek laughed, but he felt more like crying. Then they embraced and held each other, silently, to control the ardor of their feelings; so many years lived through, first as a gravedigger at the front and then in prison, while the other engaged in dangerous activity, spinning intrigues and plots; and he really felt Liebknecht's breath, smelling of cold cigar; and the prickly mustache pressed against his cheek. "We'd only been told," Liebknecht said at last, "that those fellows had turned you away at the border."

"I came anyway," said Radek. "To the Council Congress. In order to speak there."

"Too late, unfortunately. The congress is over." Liebknecht took the pince-nez from his nose and wiped the moisture from the corners of his eyes. Then he led Radek to a polished door behind a dark green curtain, and said, noticeably too loud, as if to drown out something tormenting him, an inner doubt perhaps, "Rosa will be extraordinarily delighted!"

So Rosa's attitude toward him was still the same, and Liebknecht knew it. And probably not just Liebknecht, thought Radek; who in the party—the German, the Polish, the Russian parties—had not been interested in Luxemburg's sentiments and her hostility toward him; only he had hoped that time, the time of war, the time of revolution, every month like a year, would have allowed the resentments of earlier times to subside.

She sat at her table and wrote, completely absorbed in her thoughts, it seemed. Radek hardly recognized her; the hair, though still full and, as before, coiffed upward from the nape in a beautiful wave, had turned white, the complexion prison pale; the facial bones stood out more than ever, and the wrinkles at the mouth and around the tired eyes had dug in deep.

But she had definitely noticed him, for all at once she laid her hand flat on the sheet of paper, as if to conceal her text from his eyes, and greeted him frostily. "So there you are. I guess it couldn't be done without you. Did Ilyich send you?"

"At least, he had nothing against me coming."

Liebknecht thought he had to compensate for the lack of warmth in her words; he put his arm around Radek's shoulder and said with an enthusiasm that wasn't even feigned, "And how useful he would have been to us at the Council Congress!"

Luxemburg left that unanswered.

"Oh, Rosa …"

She raised her head. What a sound from the fellow, suddenly!…

"I know, Rosa," he said, but didn't elaborate on his knowledge, "I know what moves us, both of us."

It wasn't hard, he thought, to guess Rosa's feelings; he, who had been formally rejected by the parties of two great countries, who had spoiled her carefully cultivated relations with the German comrades to the best of his ability with a poisoned pen, and had deepened the split from her and her Jogiches in the Polish party, and who had internationally spread the news that her clique was finished, and then, seeking protection from her and Tyszka's retaliation, had nimbly clung to Lenin's coattails—here he was now, the representative of the victorious Russian Revolution, and endowed with Ilyich's authority!

"I hope," she said pointedly, "you don't find anything wrong with our actions."

"How could I," he said. "All my knowledge comes from today's edition of your newspaper."

"And that"—Liebknecht scratched his mustache— "isn't enough, you think?"

"I wonder"—Radek felt uncomfortable, since once again he found himself, as before, on a collision course with Rosa—"I wonder how much bite there is to your bark?"

Luxemburg's brow reddened. She pushed her chair back and straightened up as best she could. "We stand here," she said, "you too, Karl Radek, at the cradle of a new party. And when a healthy child is born, it cries out, the louder, the better."

5

At first she didn't want to go at all to the meeting with him; Jogiches had to convince her first. Jogiches, Radek found, had changed; he had mellowed with the hard years that lay behind him; he had led the illegal work of the Spartakus League from its beginnings until he had been arrested after the great strike in January 1917—the first in Germany, which showed that the proles were no longer willing to endure the Kaiser's war unquestioningly and without complaint; and the Kaiser's juridical apparatus had known whom it had in its clutches, and had treated him accordingly.

Since when, Radek thought, had he and Tyszka not spoken to each other? Ah, yes, since the Polish split back then, the split of the Social Democratic Party of the Kingdom of Poland and Lithuania, in which he, Radek, had diligently participated from Germany and from wherever an effective word could be interspersed. Of course, Jogiches had not forgotten; Jogiches never forgot, a memory like an elephant; but now he mentioned nothing more of the old quarrel, at least not here, in the dignified premises of the *Berliner Lokalanzeiger*. Rather, Jogiches, organization man that he was, immediately wanted to know what he was planning now: to just sit in with them as a representative of the Bolsheviks, or, as before, to work politically alongside them?

For a man of his stature, Tyszka had much more delicate hands. Radek imagined how those hands touched the naked body of Rosa Luxemburg with desire; but there had been more between the two of them than just the physical, and anyway that was a long time ago.

"Oh, this congress!" exclaimed Jogiches. "Congress of workers' and soldiers' councils!—a singular scandal!" And the whole thing had ended as scandalously as it began—with the decision of the delegates, for God's sake, not to carry on the revolution that had fallen into their laps! They'd rather dutifully participate in a national assembly, in which every high school teacher and every stinking lawyer would walk all over the people, and the bourgeoisie would cook up quite a constitution.

"And yet," said Radek, "I'd have really liked to listen to the congress, after receiving the kind invitation of Comrade Brutus Molkenbuhr."

"Brutus!" sneered Jogiches. "Oh, they didn't stab Caesar;

they rose from their chairs and sang the "Internationale" and dispersed. You arrived too late in Berlin, Radek. We didn't have a faction in the Plenum either, not a single one of ours got in there in an orderly fashion, maybe a few who sympathized with Spartakus were present in the hall; the Comrade Social Democrats had done all the work."

"And you weren't able to assert yourselves? I know you and your people, Tyszka, you're not shy otherwise!"

"That's easy for you to say!" Jogiches scolded. "Who was there who could have prevailed?" And thought to himself, more restraint, old boy, we still need the messenger from Moscow. Then he continued, hoarsely, "When Comrade Liebknecht proclaimed the socialist republic from the balcony of the palace, do you know how many members we had? Not one hundred and fifty, in all of Berlin!" He nodded vigorously, confirming the unbelievable. "And when Liebknecht demanded entrance to their congress, they told him at the door that it was a meeting of workers' and soldiers' councils, and you're no longer a soldier, Karl, just like Rosa's not a worker."

"Rather flimsy!" Radek suppressed a grin; the right-wing Social Democrats had also used such methods against him—only at the time, at the party congress in Chemnitz, at the instigation of Comrade Luxemburg; and then the verdict had been: expulsion.

But Jogiches had already changed the subject; he spoke of the precautions that everyone had to observe now: Radek, too, should beware: the Kaiser's secret services were still operative, and the Freikorps were looking for victims; how often had he preached to Karl and Rosa that they should live illegally, as he did, and keep their connections conspiratorial; but the two of them were like lambs, without guile; at the next best opportunity they'd be arrested, and then . . .

And now they were assembled in the back room of the Fröhliche Freiheit—a worker's pub; Bebel, a brownish-tinted reproduction of an old photograph, hung on the wall; directly under the picture, Paul Levi sat like Christ at the feet of the

Father; and indeed Levi, upon further consideration, resembled Leonardo's Jesus: the suffering expression of the narrow face, the tolerance with which he accepted the actions of the apostles at the table. Occasionally, when their eyes met, a smile, a secret one, drew itself around Levi's lips: perhaps he was thinking of the dining room in the sanatorium in Davos, where they both, he and Radek, had received the news of the tsar's abdication while eating; or of the train platform in Zurich, their breathless farewell in front of the compartment door of the special carriage of the Swiss Bundesbahn, in which the history of the new era began.

The waitress came with a large tray, on it plates of potato salad, proportioned fairly; but Radek saw that the woman had hidden a morsel of gray meat under Liebknecht's portion; he was obviously her favorite.

Rosa took the floor after they had heard his report from Moscow. He had kept it short and not glossed over anything when speaking of Lenin and the assassination attempt on him, and of Trotsky, Zinoviev, Dzherzhinsky, and of the unpleasant, not to say precarious, situation in which they found themselves, and how the German upheaval had come to their aid just in time—a historic example of militant solidarity in the service of the world revolution: you have our eternal gratitude, comrades. But Lenin was determined, he added after a moment's reflection, to hold out even without help from Germany, with all, even the toughest means; and then, knowing with what satisfaction Rosa would receive this, he quickly prophesied that the Bolsheviks, whom fate had chosen as the vanguard of the international proletariat, would be spared many terrible constraints if they continued to receive the urgently needed political support from the workers, peasants, and soldiers of the new German Republic.

Even if, he thought, he wore the shoe on the other foot than good Rosa—who in her innermost being probably believed that Lenin had started his revolution much too early and in too dictatorial a fashion: the indirect confirmation by him—Radek, of all people—of her theories about the world revolution, would at least partially reconcile her with the evening forced upon her by Jogiches. So she explained without her usual acerbity that she could understand that Lenin would not shy away even from the harshest means; Lenin had in his character much of the great St. Just. But her Felix! Felix Dzerzhinsky, the otherwise so sensitive, musical man, as the chief and main executor of the Cheka! No, no, no... "And on principle," again with indignation, "terror is not a suitable means." She poked at her potato salad. "Have they been able to destroy us by terror? And for every Kaplan that you shoot, ten others will come."

Radek hesitated. He hoped that Levi, who had followed the discussion with excitement, would intervene, or if not Levi, then Liebknecht, even if the latter often argued in a sloppy way. But they were both silent, Levi and Liebknecht; people didn't like to mess with Rosa Luxemburg, in this circle and in general.

So he finally replied, "Terror, Rosa, always has two sides, and in Russia especially, as you very well know: ours, and that of the others. That Ilyich is still alive was a matter of a millimeter and a half. And how many of us have already been killed by shots from an ambush? What do you demand, in the name of your humanity, that of all parties to the conflict, we're the only ones who shouldn't defend ourselves?"

"Blood," she said, "leaves behind ugly stains."

"Your blood too, Rosa, if the shots hit you."

"Do we," said Levi, "have to discuss this topic of all things?"

"Perhaps we do," said Jogiches.

Radek, who had just eaten his last forkful of potato salad, lit the cigar he had procured from the Central's porter at great expense. Then he said, "In our country, they're counting on the world revolution, just like Rosa is—but what if we have to wait a long time for it? If, here, in spite of the best preconditions, you don't even succeed in accomplishing the small German part of the revolution? How then do we survive the years we'd have to hold out alone in Moscow until the next chance?"

"But all this cruelty and injustice!" Luxemburg's lips twisted in disgust. "I just can't imagine how Felix …"

"And I'm telling you, Rosa"—Jogiches laughed suddenly, a coarse laugh—"if you have to, you too could be cruel and unjust."

Radek choked, the cigar was no good: this, from Jogiches! And how concerned he had been about her just a moment ago!

Luxemburg also needed time to get over this blow from her Tyszka. Then, however, she seemed to realize that Comrade Radek's arrival in Berlin had set more into motion than a few lapsed personal conflicts.

"Oh, Leo," the voice an echo of past tenderness, "how often have I told you: if power has to be based on such preconditions, then it's better to renounce it!" And to Radek, "That's what separates me from your Lenin: the power he wants and the party he's formed for it accordingly. No, I renounce this kind of power. I would accept power only from the hands of the masses, and only if they demand of us: seize it and exercise it, for us and with us."

A poet, thought Radek, a utopian one. But the reality, as could be said after the Russian experiences, was different: the great ideals, if they had ever been valid, vanished into ever more distant horizons, and we were left with the stony path, which dragged on endlessly. And all at once he felt fear—not for himself, but for Rosa; even if she detested him and he paid back the stings she gave him in the wicked political game, she remained the fire spirit, descended from the spheres to him and the gray creatures around him.

Listening to her again, he realized that she, too, was extremely worried, but her worries were not so much about developments in Germany or even about herself, but about freedom, for the sake of which the revolution was made, and about his party, the Russian party, and its policies, and about Lenin. "Without a critical press, however, without the right to free speech and assembly, a role for the masses in political events is inconceivable. Freedom only for supporters of the government? Only for the members of a single party? Freedom, Comrade Radek," she postulated, "is always the freedom of those who think differently."

"Correct." Radek blew a smoke ring toward the lamp. "Absolutely correct. But what if your coddled dissidents then take the liberty of bashing our skulls in?"

"But violence convinces no one!" she countered. "Lenin's means will prove ineffective. Moreover, he didn't invent them; dictatorship already existed sufficiently in the executive of the old Social Democratic Party. But you in Moscow extend the system to the state as well, spreading fear and terror with the punishments you impose on all who dare to try to resist the bit. Which in turn leads to the suppression of all political initiative; in the villages and towns, in the offices and factories, even in the soviets, life dies out; what remains is a sham life in which only the bureaucracy's activity unfolds. A relatively small number of leading comrades with inexhaustible energy behave as if they were in control of things; but the real leadership is in the hands of a baker's dozen of mostly self-appointed functionaries who, when the occasion arises, call together a few hundred or a thousand carefully selected representatives of the working class and have them applaud and confirm their decisions, unanimously, of course—the rule of a clique, then, a dictatorship, but not of the proletariat, but of the apparatus; and the result of it all will be a total brutalization of the individual as well as of society."

Radek noted the warning glance that Levi tossed her way; presumably Levi sensed the danger that lay in her thoughts; or they even originated, at least partially, with him—Comrade Levi, as true to the cause and reliable as he was, liked to think outside of the usual templates.

Then the waitress came and cleared off the table.

★

The three of them went walking along the evening Friedrichstraße and through the passage where the whores did their rounds, to the magnificent boulevard with the poetic name Unter den Linden, Liebknecht, Paul Levi, and him. Liebknecht played the cicerone: the public here, he explained, had become very different these days; it lacked the dignified gentlemen and ladies, the dapper officers, the strolling *jeunesse dorée,* the whole bourgeois ambiance that one could enjoy just a short time ago in front of the café on this corner; the soldiers who know, singly or in squads, pushed their way along the edge of the sidewalk showing the marks of war on their gray faces, and seemed, together with the poorly dressed, mostly already elderly workers, who were visibly uncomfortable here, to be waiting for something, a bundle of recent rumors, or a demonstration that might form; Levi thought that this was the peculiarity of this revolution, the informality, the volatility, the constant back-and-forth of alliances and factions.

There actually was a demonstration in the Tiergarten; the speaker was ranting about some criminals, and people were shouting *"Nieder!"* Down with whom?, Radek thought, then he understood that it was against Ebert and Scheidemann, against the government, and Liebknecht explained that it was a demonstration of the USPD. But weren't the USPD themselves in the new government, Radek wanted to know.? But these, Leibknecht smiled, were Berlin USPD members, who were still to the left of the party and who were making common cause with the revolutionary shop stewards, who had played a leading role in the uprising and, without a unified program or recognizable goals were pushing more and more into the foreground. Radek then inquired whether it would not be better to leave Spartakus as a loose alliance until the situation had been clarified; otherwise they might suddenly find themselves alone and isolated. Jogiches, it seemed to him, also had his doubts as to whether in this situation the transformation of Spartakus into an organized party would be correct and useful. But Liebknecht, quoting Rosa, replied that the vanguard of the working class longs to no longer march cowering in the ranks of any other party, but to march into battle with its head held high and under its own flag. Then, feigning an appointment, he departed, leaving Radek in the hands of Comrade Levi; in truth, he had probably been annoyed because he had not succeeded in convincing Radek of the necessity of founding an independent communist party in Germany.

Levi dragged him to a meeting of metalworkers in the north of the city, at the end of Chausseestraße, and although Radek resisted, Levi let the bystanders know: a comrade from Moscow, from the land of the soviets. And so he had to speak whether he wanted to or not.

Radek knew what Levi expected of him and what these workers wanted to hear: the voice of the revolution, firm and sure of itself and pointing the way amid the Berlin confusion; but the devil possessed him, or was it that he was still troubled by his meeting with Luxemburg—he began to speak, instead of the victories of the Bolsheviks and their heroism, but of the suffering of the Russian proletariat and of the difficulties the comrades had to contend with, of hunger and cold and tears and blood, and the White Terror, and the pincer maneuver of the armies of the Western imperialists, which, like the imperial Germans a while ago, threatened to suffocate Red Russia, until an obviously drunk person shouted at him, "Shut up, whiner!"

Then he was startled, and brought his speech to an end as quickly as possible.

★

The very fact that the founding party conference took place in the Plenary Hall of the Prussian parliament gave the whole thing a very special touch: the vanguard of the working class, who were allowed for the first time to loll about in the armchairs upholstered to the dimensions of Junker asses, felt as if they had conquered the stately building themselves; yet nowhere in the darkly paneled room was there even a rifle or a trace of blood or gunpowder in the pleasantly tempered air; rather, it smelled of badly washed bodies and sweaty underwear; and the rent for the hall had been paid, as it should have been, down to the last penny by the future executors of the victorious revolution, thus burdening the treasury of the Spartakus League to the extreme.

Radek sat crouched in one of the back rows; he preferred to keep a low profile for the time being. A few of the comrades from earlier—Duncker, Pieck, Meyer—nevertheless noticed him; they were, it seemed to him, quite aged since he had left them behind in Germany at the outbreak of the war, and stood in striking contrast to the youthful appearance of most of the delegates; have the years, Radek thought, also marked my features so clearly?

The noise that the three of them made when greeting him from far away was all the more inappropriate; he had to fend off the spirited Duncker with both hands, otherwise he would have fallen around his neck. As soon as he had taken his seat next to him, Meyer began to rail at the fat Ebert, who, Radek remembered, had already had him thrown out of the editorial office of the party newspaper in Göppingen because of the handful of marks that were missing for the subscriptions to continuation of the paper; Fritz Ebert, bookkeeper that he was, and forever clinging to the apron-strings of the bourgeoisie—Meyer was very proud of this description of his character—remained true to himself throughout the war; always hurrah and new credit for the Kaiser and the Reich; now, as a reward, he would probably become president of the republic. If, yes, if the communist party that they would launch today, did not throw a monkey wrench in the works.

The scene was getting uncomfortable for Radek; his speech, his presence in general, was meant as a political surprise; and here the guys were talking all in one go and audibly from afar about their memories of him, while in the corridors the press people were roaming: SENSATION! RADEK WITH SPARTAKUS! SOVIET STRING-PULLER IN THE PRUSSIAN PARLIAMENT!—and that was that.

Only, the German press proved not to be so alert; the six or eight earnest gentlemen who lingered nearby, clutching their pencils, apparently did not even suspect what the dispute was about that was being carried out among the Spartakus celebrities at that very moment, and was the reason why Luxemburg, on the platform in front, was so visibly nervous, shuttling back and forth between Liebknecht and Jogiches. Radek, on the other hand, who was watching the proceedings through half-closed eyelids, knew only too well what was being negotiated there, albeit indirectly—the course of the still nascent party; whether to go it alone for the time being, or allying with the USPD and the shop stewards; participating in Ebert's national assembly, or boycotting it; accepting the bourgeois republic, or smashing its structures before they took shape, with all the risks that such a policy entailed for all concerned.

Jogiches, this much Radek knew, did not see power as fruit for which one only had to stretch out one's hand; remnants of the Imperial Army that were still strong existed, reorganizing themselves as Freikorps and publicly claiming that a stab in the back by the left robbed them of their victory in the field; and the huge apparatus of German Social Democracy still existed, cumbersome but firmly established, with its interlocking links in every factory, every village; but Luxemburg was infected by the enthusiasm of the youth in the hall and by her own impatience: how long had she had to wait in her fortress cell in Wronke, and later in the penitentiary at Breslau, for this experience; she still carried the echo of the freedom bell in her ear, or had it been the tinny sound of the little bell in the narrow tower of the prison chapel?

Liebknecht, however, had told Radek himself that he went to bed at night with the firm resolution that he would never, ever enter the national assembly, never allow himself to be degraded to a puppet in the puppet show that was to be staged there to mislead the working class; but then he woke up in the morning, day after day with the same concern: whether it wouldn't be politically wiser to play along with the artificial thunder and take advantage of the tribune that was offered even in a bourgeois parliament.

★

He was startled. Behind him, short of breath, stood Comrade Pieck, "They're waiting for you!"

Radek followed him down the wide, carpeted center aisle toward the podium. He felt their gazes at the back of his neck and heard the murmur; even if the delegates in their majority did not know him either by appearance or voice, the journalists had their wanted poster: the restless spirit of German Social Democracy, who in earlier days had so often and with such relish shaken it out of its complacency, partner to the business of the notorious Parvus, who smuggled Lenin together with his male and female entourage to Petrograd in 1917, Trotsky's sharp-tongued assistant at Brest-Litovsk, who drove General Hoffmann nearly to madness with his quipping arrogance, and now the Bolsheviks' sharpest pen.

Then he stood at the podium, leaning heavily on the top, with the unsteady rows of delegates in front of him. No, he thought, they did not look like a party; there was a lack of toughness in expression, resulting from a long focus on the common goal; the inner firmness that also shows itself outwardly, the result of the sum of dangers that one has gone through, and the often cynical serenity that comes with the knowledge of the dangers that one sees still ahead; the young people down there, even if this or that one had held his own bravely in strikes and demonstrations or even on the barricades, had not yet been confronted with that political logic that results from the knowledge of human dependencies, and that which swiftly causes all unclear sentiment, all mere phrase to wither away.

"When news of the German Revolution reached us," he began, his voice measured yet audible to the farthest corners of the hall, "the workers of Russia were seized by rapturous joy."

He wasn't even exaggerating there: in that hour, illusions had shot up like a flash in the pan.

"And we didn't just rejoice," he continued, "because your victory had broken the ring that the imperialist powers had formed around us, but because you made us feel that the German proletariat, our older brother, as it were, from whom we had learned so much, would now work with us hand in hand in order to build socialism."

Luxemburg's mouth puckered; mocking woman, thought Radek; I'll be careful not to get involved in your quarrels; you know your weaknesses even better than I do: despite all your heroic sayings, the old German inability to assess oneself correctly.

But then Rosa's face changed; her gaze seemed to seek help from him as it had once done when he had cornered her in a dispute about some internal affairs of the Polish party, and he felt pity; poor Rosa, how she clung to her illusions of the approaching Red millennium, despite pain and doubt.

"Nevertheless, you too," he cried, "can learn from us! One year of the Russian Revolution, one year of the rule of the working class in our country, has provided the decisive test of the example and the answer to the great fundamental question of whether the proletariat is capable of taking power and holding on to and exercising it!"

Luxemburg, he saw, had understood, despite her reservations. But did the others understand what he was driving at? This one or that one, perhaps, who had come across a pamphlet by Ilyich or one of Trotsky's writings, possibly even an article from his own pen, hastily put to paper in Stockholm, or later, on his greasy table in the fortress of Brest.

"You'll be accused," he warned, "of being agents of the Bolsheviks, and nothing but imitators of our revolution. But what's so bad about imitating what has proved to be good and useful? The system of councils that prevailed among us resulted simply from our everyday experience; but our thoughts were nourished and fertilized by the disputes which had long since been conducted among you in Germany, and elsewhere, about the tactics and strategy of the future struggles of the working class; and if there are those who call you agents of Bolshevism, please, are we not all agents? Agents in a common cause, you and us? And among my Russian comrades, many are very proud of the fact that not so long ago, they worked hand in hand with your Rosa."

At first, his listeners had felt uncertain, and marveled at him as if he had descended to them from another world. But now, as he held out his arms to their Rosa as the culmination of his message of salvation, they burst into thunderous applause, and their enthusiasm increased until he—and how he played the scene!—stepped down from the podium and walked toward Luxemburg.

Then it became silent. Only from a distance one could hear the doors suddenly falling shut and being locked by the hall security, so that the representatives of the press didn't all rush out at once and, *Radek, Radek, Radek,* notify their editors before he could leave discreetly.

"We have been allies," he said into the silence, "since the day Karl Liebknecht was the first to raise his voice against the war from the tribune of the German Reichstag. And I promise you— as soon as you really take power in your hands here in Germany, our Russian workers will make this alliance reality and stand shoulder to shoulder with you wherever necessary, in the Urals, on the Don, on the Rhine."

He swallowed. He had really allowed himself to get carried away by his own pathos: how could he, who should have known better, conjure up such a grandiose vista before the eyes of this bunch of dilettantes! But now they had all jumped up and hung on his every word; Liebknecht pushed himself into the picture, waiting for the words that would now have to come from him, Radek, in order to bring the assembly back to earth.

"The world revolution will continue to advance!" he said, soberly, as if he were talking about a sack of cotton. And to Liebknecht, with an ambiguous smile, "Only, no one can calculate its tempo in advance. We've had to wait more than a year for the uprising of the German workers that led to the overthrow of the Kaiser; in the meantime, we've been forced to defend ourselves alone, with our teeth and claws, until today, rifle in hand, we can say, yes, we've seen fulfilled what your Karl Liebknecht cabled to our Congress of Councils at the time: COMRADES, WE'RE COMING!…"

Luxemburg, obeying her impulse, stepped toward Liebknecht and grasped his hand. Radek, who in spite of all his inner distance from her was nevertheless moved by the gesture, exclaimed, "The Russian Revolution may be taking place however many miles away from you, but its spirit lives in your breast!" And with an arm raised imploringly, "I see the day dawning when not only the workers of Germany and Russia will have liberated themselves, but at the same time socialism will have become, in fact and in practice, a global task."

The central door flew open with a crash; the gentlemen from the press, their notebooks bulging with notes, rushed into the vestibule. But before the police could come to their senses and enter the meeting hall from the corridors and arrest the illegal speaker, he had disappeared.

7

The cheerfulness was forced.

The Germans were like that, though Radek. Everything ran along preordained lines: at Christmas they were contemplative, on New Year's Eve they were bursting at the seams with noisy cheerfulness. Even in the Liebknecht home, the pattern could be discerned: but where else should he have fled to on this night, which heralded the year of Our Lord 1919, the next in a series of fateful years, which now washed him along since the beginning of the war, a year that held new dangers for him and—this as an afterthought—for the master of the house as well.

Liebknecht leaned toward him now, sweating slightly, his gaze a little uncertain from the wine. "I float," he said, searching for a simile, "like the spirit above the waters."

"I wish," said Radek, "that I could also feel like a spirit for once, above or below or on the waters. But I lack the imagination for it, the poetic one. The lofty feelings that inspire one like you, brother Liebknecht, become with me sober premises with predictable consequences that, emerging one from the other, move between categories of a thoroughly familiar kind."

"And there are no miracles at all?"

"The whole thing is a miracle—that we dared to do it back in October, and that we've survived to this day against all reason, including my own. But you can't count on something like that."

"Maybe you're right," said Liebknecht, "to make fun of me."

"I didn't make fun of you. I'm too afraid to do that; afraid for you, for me, for all of us. And there's no escape. Where to?"

He broke off. How could he talk like that, in front of Liebknecht, who was so sensitive to every nuance in tone! Was it the night, this particular one? The uncertainties of the year that was coming up?

Liebknecht threw his lips open like a defiant child. "We're not as weak as you might think. The Social Democrats may be stronger in numbers than we are, but their brains are ossified, and they still haven't grasped that the world turns; the youth, however, marches with us, and already the USPD find themselves forced out of government and into opposition. From now on, things will develop faster, faster than you think."

Radek, who had hoped for a conversation with deeper substance, felt bored. "Develop—in which direction?"

The question seemed to upset Liebknecht. His breath came in short bursts and smelled of the sour wine that was being served. "*Mit uns zieht*," he sang, swaying his glass rhythm, "*die neue Zeit* . . ." Then he blinked fiercely behind his glasses, ". . . and time, my dear Radek, as we know, moves only in one direction."

★

Four days later, the struggle began.

Radek guessed Ebert's plan: Radek could easily put himself in his opponent's head: he possessed that gift. As head not only

of the Social Democrats but also of the new provisional government, Radek reasoned, Ebert couldn't leave the relatively
well-equipped Berlin police under the command of Comrade
Eichhorn, a left-wing USPD member, and relieved him of his post
overnight; but the police chief, this too was foreseen in Ebert's
calculations, would hardly accept this and, risk-taker that he was,
would arm the more radical among the Berlin workers and, ahead
of them, together with Ledebour and perhaps even Liebknecht,
would attempt a coup. Then, however, he, Ebert, could have
the Freikorps, and whatever other troops he had at his disposal,
intervene militarily and drive out the Bolshevik mob's desire for
civil war once and for all.

Radek found his suspicions confirmed by Philips Price, who,
against all rules of conspiracy, turned up unannounced at the
door of the small apartment in Steglitz assigned to him by the
editors of *Die Rote Fahne* and crowed loudly in English, "Never
expected to see you here, old boy!"

Radek hastily pulled Price into the room. The man still looked
exactly like he had in Moscow: the yellow tweed jacket with the
leather patches on the sleeve, the crumpled trousers, the thick
tobacco-smoked mustache; Price, correspondent of the London
Daily Herald, had come regularly for his briefings, and they had
both gone afterwards to Price's quarters in the Arbat to drink
whiskey; over the whiskey, Price had him outline the glorious
future of communism. Now his paper, he told, had sent him to
Berlin, and in the editorial office of *Die Rote Fahne*, they had
sent him—Radek winced: my God, what dilettantes!—directly
to Radek in Steglitz. But at least Price knew the answer to what
Radek was most interested in at the moment: Eichhorn's successor, a certain Ernst, had declared at his press conference that
morning that if the Eichhorn people did not hand over their
weapons, they would be dealt with by force.

In exchange for such valuable news, Price now demanded
to hear what he, Radek, thought of the situation, and what the
new conflict signified; Price must have sensed the tension that

lay over the city. "Don't ask me," Radek replied, "Don't ask me what's brewing; in Germany you never know; but whatever, good things rarely are."

Then he grabbed his coat, cap, and pipe and told Frau Bondy, his landlady, that he had to leave urgently; and if she would please give his guest, before he also left the house, a cup of tea from the good Russian tea in his personal tin in the kitchen cupboard.

He went to the Central Committee in a roundabout way; he changed streetcars twice and took a cab as well; only then did he believe that no one had followed him. So he missed the beginning of the meeting; they were already talking about a general strike when he arrived. "*Alle Räder stehen still,*" declaimed one, "*Wenn dein starker Arm es will!*" "All wheels stand still, if your strong arm so wills!" Others, excited by their own exuberance, demanded, "Mass protests! Factory workers to the streets!" Resistance on the part of police loyal to the government and Social Democratic officials had to be broken, by force if necessary; in the end, the decisive word would always come from the barrels of guns.

Luxemburg had a pile of books in front of her, one of them open; but she wasn't reading; rather, absorbed in her thoughts, she stared at the flag draped obliquely in the corner of the room. At last she seemed to notice him; the sharp wrinkle on her brow deepened.

"And what, please, Rosa," Radek coughed, "do we want to achieve with our strike?"

She remained silent, feeling awkward. She probably hadn't expected that so directly, he thought; or had she not even asked herself the question yet?

"A general strike," he said, "is no child's play; ring around the rosies, a pocket full of posies, ashes, ashes—"

"We all fall down," she said. "Or not? But it's deadly serious for us: a protest strike, on a large scale. We want to know now, how far does Ebert intend to go, and how the working class will react; after that, we'll see."

"So it is a game," he said.

Later, in an adjoining room, he ran into Liebknecht. Liebknecht took him aside. "You musn't," he said, "unsettle Rosa anymore; she has it hard enough without that. Of course we can't form a government of our own now; we're still too weak for that. But a government supported by the USPD and the revolutionary shop stewards with a base in the factories, under Ledebour, say, is conceivable."

"Everything is conceivable," said Radek.

The demonstrations were enormous.

There must have been, Radek estimated, well over a hundred thousand people marching at the same time through the streets in the government district and behind Alexanderplatz, not always through the same streets, and not always the same people. And what a feeling to march among them!—seeking the deeper, political meaning in their coarse laughter, their raucous shouts, their snatches of occasional song—what a feeling! What did they hope, what did they expect; did they have plans, a conception, and if so, what. Were the seeds sprouting here that he and Ilyich and Parvus had sown in Zimmerwald and Stockholm and Petrograd? Shouldn't they, Radek wondered, with this crowd, this mood, have seized power on the spot? Ebert, squatting in Wilhelmstraße with two or three of his ministers, had only a few squads of aged reservists standing in front of the Reich Chancellery, and they, it seemed, were less than enthusiastic about the prospect of having to protect the head of their provisional government.

A general drove up in his open car, without cover; Radek recognized him, Groener was his name, the visage had been seen in several newspapers yesterday—a bourgeois; the nobility kept itself in the background these days. They'd probably now conspire with each other behind the cloudy flounce of the mezzanine floor of the Reich Chancellery, his, Radek's, old intimate enemy from the party apparatus and the military man of a new type, technician and psychologist rather than swashbuckler, and therefore all the more dangerous, agreeing on what to do and when: should Ebert flee the capital, to Döberitz, for example, where Groener, as Radek had learned from Price, had assembled an almost war-ready division, and place himself under the protection of the army, which was now called the Reichswehr, or should he hold out in his official residence and wait until the general arrived with his troops—what else could they have parleyed about?

And how much time did this still leave the revolution? The demonstrators in the streets gathered and occupied the building of *Vorwärts* and chased away the editors, although the editorial office and printing house of the Social Democratic Party paper were of no strategic importance; but nothing serious came from the headquarters of the USPD, nor from the revolutionary shop stewards, nor even from the newly minted Communists; nobody showed the people better targets. In front of the Hotel Eden, where, trimmed to a wasp waist and spurred and booted, officers were coming and going—from the Freikorps, the porter readily told Radek—he met Comrade Duncker, who was passing anxiously, held him, and invited him for a drink in the hotel, but Duncker cringed: the lion's den, was that necessary? But Radek, who was attracted by such situations, convinced him that no one would look for him there, and pushed the reluctant man into the hall and invited him to sit down at one of the small round tables, and ordered aperitifs for both of them; expensive fun for the illegal Party treasury, but it improved the mood. "Now then," he asked, almost cheerfully, "what will happen today, what do the comrades think?"

Duncker swallowed. Rosa wanted to wait, he finally reported, until the workers outside Berlin had also risen up; and Liebknecht told him that he, Radek, should stay in his apartment and not move from there, because if he were caught by the enemy, it would be just as embarrassing for them in Berlin as for the comrades in

Moscow. The Russians, it would then be said, were staging the entire German revolution.

"Do you know," Radek asked, "Comrade Friesland, who also calls himself Reuter?"

Duncker didn't understand.

"Through this Reuter, alias Friesland"—Radek smiled,—"I'm in contact with a group of former Russian prisoners of war who are leading a sort of partisan life here. And again from them, I know that a German military staff has been meeting in Dahlem since last night, joined this morning by Ebert's bosom buddy Noske, Herr Armeeminister, in anticipation of his reinforcements moving in from all sides."

Poor Duncker, who up to that point had kept his nerves reasonably under control, started to run away without even sipping his aperitif.

"And," Radek continued, "please inform Comrade Liebknecht: unless he plans to take state power immediately, he should not get involved in armed altercations; they could end very badly. And he should stop the protest strikes and call for new elections; only in this way can the Party save its chances for tomorrow and the day after."

He didn't know if Duncker had understood him or even listened properly, Duncker was getting ready to go; now he rushed to the wardrobe and pushed his way through the revolving door to the street, leaving Radek to settle the bill.

Nothing remained but to sit in the room and read and make excerpts. Frau Bondy, who as a doctor's widow had an eye for uneasiness, inquired sympathetically: was it his nerves?

No, his stomach.

Then perhaps a little spoonful of valerian?

A spoonful, please.

A schnaps, he thought, would do better, but he swallowed the valerian; Frau Bondy had been told that by profession he was an independent scholar, and so it was written on his police registration; hence the work at night, the irregular departures, the late visits, the long morning sleep and his sensitivities.

Then Paul Levi arrived, a package wrapped in brown paper under his arm. Ever the gentleman, he kissed the hand of the widow, who had opened the door for him; after the landlady, blushing, had retreated, he hastily told Radek that he had come on Rosa's behalf; Liebknecht had gone into hiding and his connection to the Central Committee had been severed, and the last anyone had heard from him was from the Bötzow Brewery, where he had been negotiating with representatives of the USPD on further steps. Rosa, however, had taken note of Radek's recommendations. "Rosa is of the opinion," Levi continued, "that we shouldn't be the ones to sound the retreat; the USPD will already do that."

"That's not politics," Radek said, and, indicating the package, "What have you got there?"

"For you," said Levi, "just in case. Government troops have already moved in to storm the *Vorwärts* building."

Radek untied the package. A uniform: common soldier, infantry, dirty and worn.

"Put that on," Levi said. "I'm going to Friedrichshain now, to a workers' meeting; I hope we can get a few men there to support our people at *Vorwärts*."

Radek put the jacket on and looked at himself in the mirror. "This," he said, "I cannot do to the widow Bondy."

"Maybe you'll have to," Levi said, and left.

Radek kept reading, but remained restless. After a while, an hour, he estimated, Levi returned—Levi had achieved nothing, the meeting in Friedrichshain had dispersed before he could address it. Radek suggested trying to see if they could reach Rosa. Levi thought it was risky, three or even more leading comrades in one bunch; but every move was risky now, every word.

They found Luxemburg precisely where she wasn't supposed

to be: in the editorial offices of *Die Rote Fahne*. She sat there in the canteen, Liebknecht, who had just returned, sitting opposite her, spooning pea soup with apparent peace of mind.

"We still have some in the kitchen," she said, and called out "Lina!"

Lina Becker was one of the editorial secretaries.

"Would you also like a bowl, Comrade Radek?"

Radek was suddenly hungry. Lina Becker, gray blouse, gray hair, gray face, entered with a tray, on it a large bowl, chipped at the edge.

"Comrade Radek," Luxemburg introduced him, "from Moscow."

Becker snapped her eyes open.

"This isn't the new style in Moscow," Radek said, scratching at his pants, "this is my personal touch."

Liebknecht laughed. Radek reached for the spoon; he was grateful to the women, both the gray one and the pale one with the dark, fervid eyes.

Levi became impatient. "What is it? Don't you know the situation? The Freikorps will march here next, if anywhere. You have to leave, all of you—no more jokes, no more palaver, no more discussions, leave, and leave immediately. Radek has his costume and his illegal quarters. But you, Rosa, and Karl, where are you hiding? Do you have conspiratorial apartments? You'll need them."

Lina Becker walked out. From the corridor there were excited voices, hasty running, evidently people were starting to organize there. "We will," Liebknecht said almost cheerfully, "find protection," and then more thoughtfully—"in the great heart of the working class."

The back-and-forth outside started to subside; just a few more shuffling steps; a man, countless wrinkles under his stubble, heavy, low forehead, entered the canteen, said, "Here, I'm supposed to bring you this," and laid a newspaper, still damp with ink, on the table: the latest issue of *Vorwärts*.

Liebknecht tugged at his tie. Rosa Luxemburg began to read aloud, first page, banner headline: "PROVOKATION!" Below, a facsimile apparently: "*Ebert and Noske overthrown! Liebknecht and Ledebour take over the government!*" And then, also in italics, commentary, the how and why: the will of the class, the masses in motion, now or never, long live the revolution! And then, the signatures, likewise in facsimile: *Liebknecht. Ledebour.*

Radek whistled lightly through his teeth. Luxemburg remained silent, embarrassed. Then she looked up and said tonelessly, "Does Ledebour know, at least?"

"No," said Liebknecht.

Again the silence. Then Levi, as a sort of attempt at consolation, to Liebknecht, "Tell us."

Liebknecht began, became muddled, finally he got his stuttering under control. As a last attempt at a rescue operation, he had picked up a squad of armed men, mostly young boys, in order to occupy the War Ministry at their head, and when the officer on guard there confronted them and wanted to know whose orders they had, Ebert's or Noske's, the minister's, he had simply replied that they no longer existed, and in response to the order "in writing, please!," dictated the text that was printed here, on a piece of writing paper, and put his and Ledebour's name under it, a stratagem of war.

"A stratagem of war," said Levi. "Ah, so."

A stratagem of war would have been in order, even more so in a civil war! Unfortunately, Liebknecht's men, while he was still negotiating with the guard commander, had all run away.

There was gunfire in the city. One heard it clearly now.

"Let's go," said Luxemburg.

8

Gunfire echoed everywhere in the city. The echoes, sometimes distant, sometimes alarmingly close, drove him again and again into the street; but the directions from which the noise of battle came also changed; and although his ear was trained by old experience, it was impossible for him to determine exactly where the fire was concentrated and how the fighting was developing.

But evil was in store for him. He forced himself to stay in his room and work; he wrote and tore up the paper, wrote and tore up the paper; he had to wait for the messenger from Jogiches. Jogiches, foreseeing future mischief, had created his own network of liaisons, eight or ten comrades, no more, but unfortunately without practice in the field of illegal communication.

The messenger, it turned out, was Lina Becker, the editorial secretary. The old girl was terribly excited; her nose protruded redly from her pale face, her bony hands trembled; nevertheless, she still managed a winning smile as she stood in the doorway of the widow Bondy's apartment; she hoped that the professor was at home—yes, he was? and already at his desk? Always busy, always busy, the professor! But as soon as she was alone with Radek, her knees gave out; she sank onto the nearest chair and began to sob.

Radek stroked her straggly hair.

"Rosa and Karl"— Becker blew her nose—". . . arrested."

"Both?"

"Both."

A peculiar emptiness spread under Radek's skull, and his hands and feet suddenly froze.

"When?" he asked.

No, she didn't know, Becker said, when Karl and Rosa had been arrested and under what circumstances, nor where they were now; but they had been seen, it was said, by passersby, once near the Tiergarten, another time in front of the Hotel Eden, and both times surrounded by soldiers; and Comrade Jogiches was very worried.

Radek closed his eyes. He saw himself surrounded by steelhelmeted figures, pushed back and forth between them, bleeding under the butts of their rifles, his lip torn by their punches, the gaping wound on his forehead, oozing darkly.

Then his blood pressure dropped again; his pulse slowed down; thoughts began to form anew. At the moment, there was no possibility of mass actions to liberate Karl and Rosa; General Groener's troops were probably in the process of crushing the last workers' militias, and in the factories, people kept their heads down if they still wanted to work there. Perhaps a coup d'état? But for that, you needed much more information, and people who were attuned to one another, and technology and hiding places and money.

"Could you, Lina," he asked, "get hold of Comrade Levi?"

She flinched. "I'll try."

"You have to find him," he implored her, "and tell him to summon whatever Central Committee members he can reach. We have to clarify what's happened here, and where Comrade Luxemburg is being held, and Comrade Liebknecht, and their condition. That's the most important thing, after that we can think further. I'll get to the meeting somehow."

Becker went, silent and hunched.

He should have offered her tea, thought Radek. At least that.

The meeting, he found out, would be held on the premises of a Dr. Bornstein; not a comrade, the doctor; but he had sympathized with Spartakus, and who would suspect anything if several people went to a dentist's office in quick succession.

Radek, who had had a hasty cup of coffee for breakfast, nothing more—his stomach would have refused anything more solid—bought, as he did every day, the morning newspapers on the corner and put them, bundled, in his coat pocket; he opened the one that happened to be on top, however, and began, while already walking, to read the first page; at the bottom, the message of the Wolff telegraph bureau: the well-known Bolshevik leaders Liebknecht and Luxemburg had tried to evade arrest, ordered by martial law, by fleeing; the soldiers carrying out the arrest had been forced to use their firearms; in the process, the two were killed.

He kept walking, mechanically, the newspaper still between his fingers. He'd known it; he'd already known it when he discovered the two of them, harmless as children at play, in the editorial office; it was bound to happen. A conversation came to mind that he'd had with Liebknecht, how long ago was it?— certainly before the war—about the various translations of *Peer Gynt*; Liebknecht had only known Passage's and found it incomparable, but Radek gave him Morgenstern's to read, and Liebknecht sat down with him on the sofa and read, in succession, until he then jumped up and, deeply moved, began to recite the passage where Peer Gynt seems to hear in the whispering of the leaves the lament of the songs he never sang, the tears he never wept, the battles he never fought. "Oh, Radek, Radek," he had cried, "the cursed half-time that one is granted to live all of one's life in!"

"Oh, Absalom!" thought Radek. He'd lived a whole life in the time of barely half of one, the wild boy; but perhaps it was better that way, for his memory; one couldn't imagine Liebknecht as he would one day become after all; dignified gait in the halls of power and the usual phrases on his lips; how they all became as soon as they succeeded in the ranks of the party, the German socialists.

The comrades sat around the tattered magazines on the low table in Dr. Bornstein's waiting room; Paul Levi, in silent dejection, Eberlein, straining his hobbyhorse, the connections to the countryside that absolutely had to be restored, and the grumpy Thalheimer, who was subjecting Comrade Pieck to a kind of interrogation; how had it been possible for him to escape from the Hotel Eden, while Rosa and Karl, as he himself had just confirmed, were each surrounded by heavily armed guards. But Pieck only expressed himself very ambiguously in response to

Thalheimer's probing questions; had Pieck, Radek thought, paid a price to the military men for his life, and if so, what price? Only once did Pieck become concise: suddenly, he reported in his ponderous way that he had found himself alone in the corridor of the floor, had run to the elevator, which had fortunately just arrived, and had then lost himself in the confusion of the entrance hall.

They were still waiting on Jogiches. Radek was worried about him; Tyszka was caution personified, but that was precisely why he might have gotten caught; fate shuffled the cards it dealt according to its own system. Then he went next door; there stood Dr. Bornstein's dentist's chair, uninviting; Radek sat down in the corner, picked up a sheet of paper, thought for a moment, and began to write: You've sprinkled his dead body, whose wounds cry to heaven, with tears, covered it with the red flag of the world revolution, and laid it up in your hearts so that it may rest there forever. He loved life; uninhibited and unconcerned, he seized it where it lured him. There was so little of philistinism in him, so little of hypocrisy, so much of childlike joy...

He laid the pen aside. Nothing about Luxemburg? Not a word about Rosa . . . to whom the party—and he himself—owed so much, the brilliant mastermind, who had now made the highest sacrifice herself? Why only Liebknecht? Why the sudden lapse of memory? Because her body, it was said, had not yet been found, while Liebknecht's martyred face was already glaring at the proles from the pages of the capital city's newspapers—in order to frighten them? But yes, Radek promised the old Jewish God, he would write about Rosa too, just not today, just not now; what did he actually feel for her, in general and at this hour in particular, what a tangle of feelings; besides, no one could expect that of him, more than one obituary a day, and on such a day; and if he idealized the dead, who could blame him for that, at the sight of that maltreated face?

Levi came to take him back to the meeting; the situation wouldn't tolerate any further delay; the decision had been made not to wait any longer for Jogiches. Radek folded up his half-finished script and followed Levi; the meeting began; he even participated in it, but what he said was not very coherent; he couldn't concentrate, he kept seeing the colorful prints that Dr. Bornstein had hanging on the wall—all kinds of dentures, palates, throats, muscles, nerve cords.

Nor did anything concrete come of it; only hollow resolutions, eloquently concealing the absence of any conception and the lack of organized forces; from all angles, defeat stared and paralyzed thought, and even he, washed in so many waters, felt incapable of developing a practical idea.

And then, after they had already given up on him, he showed up after all: Jogiches, on whose gaunt shoulders the coat of party leadership now fell. The police had already had him in their hands, he reported; but they had not been sure who was among the numerous arrested, and he escaped before anyone could identify him.

Radek embraced him. It was obvious what Tyszka had gone through in these two or three days; his eyes, red-rimmed, sat deep in their sockets, and around his mouth the pain showed, the bitter pain that he must have felt at the news of his Rosa's death; *his*, whose else, and if ever, if not now again, *his*.

"My head is bursting," Tyszka whispered to him, "thinking about how those guys must have tortured her before death came, and how she must have looked at the end..." And then, "Writing, Karl, is difficult for me, you know that. So you write it, the farewell to her . . . She was a great, a wonderful person. And so lovable, so lovable . . ."

Of course, it was wrong from a conspiratorial point of view, but nonetheless they, he and Jogiches, left Dr. Bornstein's office together; Jogiches knew of a little Dutch tea room near Nollendorfplatz, so quiet and bourgeois that neither of them, and certainly not both of them together, would be looked for there. But no sooner were they on their way there that they again got into the old quarrel—Radek didn't know how, later he thought maybe it was his fault—about the course of the prewar Polish party; Rosa, Jogiches claimed, had been completely in the right at the time to have him, Radek, expelled from German Social Democracy; and only when they sat down at the little table with the red-and-white checkered tablecloth did first Jogiches, then Radek, start laughing: how grotesque it all was at the time, when people were at loggerheads over such things.

The server brought the tea. For a while they sat in silence, then they talked about Rosa, half aloud; Radek admired Tyszka, who suddenly spoke of her and of her role in those years with a very peculiar detachment.

"She would have been," he said, "a part of world history."

Radek glanced at him. "Instead, her murderers are."

"But a senseless part."

"That indeed," Radek confirmed.

"World history will have to do without Rosa," Jogiches said with resignation. "It'll be harder for the two of us. So many questions, so many doubts . . . I'll miss her answers."

Radek was silent for a moment. "We'll have to wait," he then said, "until history itself provides the answers to our questions."

"But then," said Jogiches, "it might be too late for humanity." Then, abruptly, "you have to leave Berlin, Radek, absolutely, preferably today. The government wants to destroy us, politically and psychologically. Go to Leipzig, or better yet, to Bremen, you know your way around there, you have friends there from before."

"And why don't you disappear, Tyszka?"

Jogiches smiled. "Someone has to stay behind after Rosa's departure, to hold the banner high."

Radek patted his newly regained friend on the knee. "I see things less dramatically. Someone has to stay behind to put together a new editorial staff for the party paper. And that someone, as things stand, would be me."

They paid and left. At the corner, in front of the column were notices were pasted and the billboards, Jogiches stopped. "There—you see?"

Radek saw. In letters several inches high, imitating Russian letters, the question WHERE IS RADEK? And below it, smaller, INVESTIGATIONS ON THE STAY OF THE BOLSHEVIK LEADER RADEK HAVE NOT YET YIELDED RESULTS. Radek grinned, although he felt uneasy, and read on that for the capture of Radek, Karl, or for more information that led to his capture, a—and now again in big, thick, black letters—REWARD OF 10,000 MARKS was offered.

Ten thousand marks, he thought. That wasn't bad by German standards.

9

After a few days, the nervousness subsided; only at night did he wake up in terror, oppressed by the images of his imagination: he and Luxemburg as one, the shattered face hers and his at the same time, a common cry from both of their tortured bodies.

He forced himself to write. The widow Bondy, who brought tea to his table and a plate with something he ate without tasting, saw him bending over manuscripts and praised his erudition, and when he took off his round glasses and massaged the bridge of his nose, her heart filled with pity and she begged him to take a rest.

He analyzed, mainly for his own encouragement, the reasons for the defeat that had been suffered, which he saw mainly in the difference between the character of the Russian and German revolutions, and, analogously, between the German Communists and the Bolsheviks. His own people in Moscow, he wrote, had come to power in the struggle for peace, bread, and land; they therefore had the soldiers on their side, and the rulers in Petersburg weren't able to defend themselves in the way the German bourgeoisie had been able to, the latter still having parts of its army at its disposal. But the more bloody the repression of the German working class now, the more terrible would be the revenge whose seeds were being sown.

He then gave this to Comrade Lina Becker to copy, who came to him for dictation, alternating with a girl named Dorle. Lina and Dorle, both colorless and inconspicuous in their worn coats, were at the same time a link to the party, the only one he had left; the arrangement apparently proved itself, so that he began to believe it could be endured in this way until—well, until something occurred that called him back to direct action.

Then, when he was hardly expecting it, rumbling sounded in the stairwell, wild ringing, and the shout, "Open up! Police!" followed by a tearful "Yes, yes! Yes, yes! At once!" from the widow Bondy. Radek's throat, dry as sand, contracted; something tightened in his abdomen; just not that, he thought, please, God, it's so embarrassing; and then the door flew open and three men rushed into the room at once. The foremost proclaimed, "Hands up!" and waved a hand grenade; Radek suddenly felt the ridiculousness of the whole scene and said, "You don't want to blow yourselves up with that gentlemen, better put that thing away!" And noticed with satisfaction that his bowels were about to calm down and his throat was functioning again.

"Herr Radek is right," noted the fattest of the three, who seemed to be in charge of the undertaking, and to his assistant, "Will it be soon?"

The hand grenade disappeared into a briefcase. The two less corpulent ones, Radek saw, had begun to rummage through his papers, those on the table as well as those in the drawers, and produced from a corner a few medicine bottles, which they showed to their boss with expressions indicating significance.

"Poison, eh?" he said.

"Stomach drops," said Radek.

The fat one wiped sweat from his nose. "So you're the wanted Radek, I presume."

Radek pointed to his manuscripts. "My writings, both Russian and German, are mostly inscribed with my own name. And please don't get the pages mixed up."

Insolence, he thought, is everything. And since his visitors wore civilian clothes, ill-fitting overcoats of different colors, only the hats uniform, matching, so-called bowlers, stiff and black and obviously governmental, he concluded that the gentlemen did not belong to any semi-legal paramilitaries, but were normal Prussian criminal investigators, and that there was no immediate danger to life and limb.

The fat man's eyes disappeared between bulging lids. "Papers," he said, "are always an indication of guilt. We therefore appreciate them."

"Correct," Radek confirmed, "no papers, no sin. And no revolution." He waited for the fat man to grasp the full magnitude of this thought; then he asked, "And what happens now?"

"Now," said the fat man, "we ask you to please come with us."

Only in front of the house, down in the street—the frightened expression of the widow Bondy in the corridor remained in his memory—did it occur to Radek to inquire where they were going, and the fat man said, to police headquarters, and Radek said, "But not on foot?" And the fat man said they were keeping a cab on standby as a precaution, and waved it over, and Radek was bundled into the back seat with a horse blanket around his knees; and then he listened to the clop-clop of the hooves on the cobblestones and asked the fat man how the police knew his whereabouts, to which he answered with a grin that there was no such thing as somebody disappearing without a trace; in the youth group, the communist one, the comrades blabbed that a Lina Becker worked for him, Radek, and then they only had to find said Lina Becker and trail her, and a Frau Dorle as well—child's play, the ladies didn't follow the rules of conspiracy even in the slightest.

And now, Radek said, he assumed that Oberkommissar Diedrich and his two men were entitled to the 10,000 marks reward offered for the arrest of Radek the Bolshevik agitator, and recommended that they collect it as soon as possible; because of the inflationary course of the German currency, money was constantly losing value.

The cab stopped in front of the Presidium, and the driver stuck out his demanding hand, and the fat man said, "If you would please pay the man, Herr Radek …"

The events at police headquarters remained hazy.

He had assumed that he would be taken to somebody of higher rank, if not to the police chief himself, where he could have then complained about the unlawful invasion of his privacy, but the fat man shoved him into a rickety elevator and, after one, two, three flights of stairs floated past, dragged him out of the booth again and down a long corridor into a quite un-Prussian, filthy office where a uniformed man sat behind a typewriter.

Your passport, please. The whole thing started in a highly trivial way; Radek soon lost interest and confirmed the requested data in a bored voice. Radek, Karl, born 1885 in Lemberg, birth name, nationality. They had never seen a Soviet passport before and showed the most moderate curiosity; number, date of issue, valid until, the blurred photo. He was also carrying Austrian papers, but they were stuck in the lining of his jacket, not even his pockets had been searched so far; the uniformed man continued to type with two fingers, monotonous clattering; Radek was getting sleepy. The fat man nudged him: reasons for his stay in Germany?—Business? Other?—Other, Radek said and smiled, Other, the fat man dictated to the one typing, and added for Radek's benefit that he was taking the wording of the questions from the form for the arrest report; they were therefore regulation and not part of the actual interrogation. As soon as that had begun, he, Radek, would answer in more detail; of that he, Oberkommissar Diederich, was sure.

Radek signed the report, his pen nib firmly on the low-quality paper. Oberkommissar Diederich seemed to know more than what he was saying, and Radek wondered whether he should keep teasing the man; perhaps he'd find out how long he'd have to wait in this dull room and where he would then be sent; but suddenly he felt sluggish and lazy; a kind of fatalism took hold of him, and he wondered whether Luxemburg had experienced such a moment on the way to Golgotha.

★

For Radek, this moment ended with the appearance of an army officer, who, pistol belt around his accentuated waistline, displayed a smug expression.

"That's the prisoner?"

The fat man confirmed. "*Ja wohl*, Herr Oberleutnant."

He approached Radek. "Von Trettwitz," he said, "may I?"

"Radek," said Radek. "And I call your attention to the fact…"

But by then he already felt Trettwitz's hands, like skin-colored butterflies, flitting over his body. He saw that the only thing they uncovered was the booklet bound in green Saffiano leather, which he had quickly pocketed before he was taken away from the home of the widow Bondy; he didn't know why he had actually done that; how much opportunity to read would he have, wherever they were taking him.

Von Trettwitz raised his fibrous brows. "Faust," he said, "and in German! Who are you trying to impress?"

"When I'm not openly carrying a Bolshevik dagger between my teeth," said Radek, "I sometimes occupy myself with Goethe."

"We know you," said Trettwitz, "your reputation as a comedian precedes you."

"And what, do you think," Radek asked, "is behind the comedian?"

"We'll find out."

Although spoken softly enough, that was a threat.

★

This time, they drove in a gray-painted automobile, apparently from army stock; Von Trettwitz next to him, on the auxiliary seats opposite, Oberkommissar Diederich and his two men; the fat man's bowler had slipped.

Radek didn't know the streets through which the car rattled.

In a moment, he feared, the familiar silhouette of the Hotel Eden would appear, and the fear he thought he had subdued sat in his guts again. But instead of the Eden, there was suddenly a broad, sprawling brick building, dirty yellow, with long rows of barred windows and an equally barred gate.

"Moabit," said von Trettwitz.

The gate opened,

"Moabit," repeated the fat man, and adjusted his hat. Radek didn't know if he was supposed show gratitude for the double information; Moabit was the great city prison of Berlin, notorious for the severity of its enforcement; now it also served, he had read somewhere, the purposes of the Freikorps and similar organizations.

"Go on," said Trettwitz. "Hurry."

Booted men stood everywhere, most of them very young, rifles in their arms as if going off to battle. "Come on," they shouted, "hurry up!" and together with the Oberkommissar they chased him up the stairs; Radek heard the fat man's gasp and saw the looks of the men in boots, and drew his skull between his shoulders, although it was clear to him that if they hit him with their rifle butts, there would be no escape for him any more than there had been for Luxemburg or Liebknecht.

"Halt!" said Trettwitz.

A cardboard sign hung in front of the paneled door at the end of the hallway, *STADTKOMMANDANT*. A sentry stood at attention. Trettwitz said, "Colonel Reinhard is expecting us," and with all his own fear, Radek wondered what fears must be plaguing Colonel Reinhard to cause him to barricade himself like this in the high-security wing of a high-security prison.

Then he faced the man: the colonel was sitting in a huge room behind an iron desk, on which there was nothing but a telephone and a yellow, sharpened pencil; the pencil was the exact center of the whole tableau of officers of the most diverse ranks, who had posted themselves there to the right and left of their boss and were waiting for events.

"Would you kindly put your hands behind your back?" The soft, polite voice from the background: Trettwitz; but the meaning of the request became clear to Radek only when the handcuffs pressed his joints together. The colonel's blood pressure seemed to have only waited for the double-click sound; the broad, scarred face turned bluish, and he shouted, "You should turn that guy over to the troops."

Radek felt his heart stop. Then it pumped again, hastily and irregularly at first, as if it wanted to make up for what it had missed, and he thought, so that was how it has gone down: they had been handed over to the troops, first Liebknecht, then Rosa, or vice versa, or both at the same time, and now it was his turn. In a side door, to which he had paid no attention before, a cluster of steel-helmeted heads appeared; in the next moment the associated bodies would detach themselves from the frame, wildly swinging arms would grab him and tear him to the ground, nailed boots would crush his brain and ribs and Adam's apple and eyes.

And then, from wherever, the memory of Brest-Litovsk came to him, of General Hoffmann, whom he had driven to red hot anger with his pipe, and he shouted, "You idiot!" And as Reinhard looked up, dumbfounded, "Yes, you, who else! I know what you plan to do with me; but you know nothing, not even who I really am, and that your people will hand you over to us without the slightest scruple when the time comes!"

That was a bluff, of course. But it had an effect on the man, and on his subordinates. These, instead of rushing at Radek, still stood as if nailed to the floor. Radek straightened up. "I am the official representative of the Russian government, Colonel, if you will please take note, with the rank of ambassador, and stand before you not as a prisoner, but under the protection of the Berlin police, and there is an official report about this, and if you

wish to parley with me concerning my rights and your respon-
sibilities, then take me over, as is proper, against receipt from
Oberkommissar Diederich here, and from then on you alone will
be responsible for my welfare and for the integrity of every square
inch of my body. Clear?"

Reinhard puffed himself up, but could manage nothing but an
indignant croak. From the adjutants and staff officers to the right
and left of him, came neither word nor movement; only their lips
twitched. And the squad in the doorway, all giants compared to
him, also seemed impressed by the insult to their commander;
they pushed forward rather hesitantly until their step faltered
altogether.

Radek doubted, however, that this deep Prussian sleep would
last long; one sharp order, whether from Reinhard or one of his
officers, and everything would awaken abruptly.

But it was the civilian who came to first. Oberkommissar
Diederich shuffled over to Reinhard's desk, and Radek actually
heard him say, "The receipt, please."

Reinhard jumped up, has massive skull lowered like a bull's,
so that the fat man hastily removed his bowler from his head;
he stood there and said in a dangerously hoarse voice, "Am I a
prison guard?"

The question could hardly be answered, even by Radek. Finally,
von Trettwitz stepped forward, said "May I?" and reached for
the colonel's telephone, picked up the receiver and spoke a few
words into the mouthpiece. Shortly thereafter, a scrawny little
man with a toothbrush-like mustache under his nose introduced
himself, identifying himself as the director of this prison; and
since the colonel was still too agitated to give proper instructions,
Trettwitz took over and explained to the little man what a dangerous Bolshevik agitator was standing before him in the person of
this prisoner, and with what care he was to be kept in custody.

The director rocked from one foot to the other. His prison,
he explained, was hopelessly overcrowded, the time requirements, the difficult, ah, the colonel certainly understood, and one

couldn't simply let such a prisoner lodge in the cell corridor; but the Lehrter Straße jail not far from his, he knew reliably, still had capacities.

Reinhard sat down again, visibly disappointed; a nightly interrogation here in the building, Radek suspected, with all the pleasures it offered, might have been on the lad's mind. Then he saw the clumsy fingers reach for the yellow pencil and move it over a sheet of paper that an adjutant had hastily placed in front of him; the sheet, folded crookedly, was handed to Trettwitz.

Then the running of the gauntlet through the corridor, which was filled with grinning uniformed men, was bad, perhaps the worst thing of the day. And to not even be able to raise one's arm in defense! A kick, a well-aimed punch, and he'd be lying on the floor, at the mercy of this scum...

Suddenly, he flinched: the animal whine, the pathetic *life! Life! Let me live!* came from him himself, from his own chest! And he thought, horrified, whether *she* too, during her last bloody moment of fearing death, whimpered like that, and then he thought, no, not *her*, she had that pride, pride to the core, which I, poor Lolek Sobelsohn—where would I get it?—never had . . .

The fat man commanded "Square!," and the three police officers and von Trettwitz formed a protective square, in the middle of which he, Radek, staggered along, and so they maneuvered him through the uniformed mob in the sandy courtyard and out to the gate, and hoisted him onto the truck there, on which a dozen or more callow youthful Freikorps men swung, shouting noisily against him, but refraining from fisticuffs in the presence of Trettwitz and the three bowler hats, and after three or four minutes, half an eternity to him, the fat man delivered him to the entrance gate at Lehrter Straße to the prison staff there, against receipt, of course, but von Trettwitz continued to cling to him, with Colonel Reinhard's note in his hand, so in a trot then, with a new, even more threatening escort, through the convoluted corridors of the ancient building, and down endless staircases, deep to the lowest cellar, where, in the haze of a dim electric lamp, a three-part lattice cage opened up, in the middle of which was a bucket and a narrow bed, on it a worn mattress and a thin, dirty brown blanket.

They pushed him in there. One of the guards took off his handcuffs.

"Strip!" Trettwitz ordered.

"Naked?"

Trettwitz nodded.

Radek shivered from the cold. He was no beauty, he knew that, and certainly not when naked; with his scrawny ribs, and the straggly tufts of hair in his armpits and around his long, circumcised penis, he resembled a plucked chicken rather than a defiant hero. The only consolation was that he knew the procedure; it was the same in every country he had been to, and he held his spread anus in front of the youngest of the guards, who was already squatting behind him.

"That will do," said Trettwitz, "thank you," and after Radek had dressed again, handed him the Saffiano-bound book, "your reading for the night."

Just then, Radek felt himself grabbed and held in a stranglehold. Four men, he saw, dragged an iron plate, in the middle of which was a ring, and let it crash on the stone floor next to the bed.

"Chain the man!" Trettwitz ordered.

Steel manacles closed around his wrists and ankles.

"A bit medieval, don't you think, Herr von Trettwitz?"

"You forget," he replied, "that we saved your life." And, turning to one of the guards, "move the prisoner's bucket closer to his bed, if you please."

10

He was totally exhausted and, despite his chains, would have fallen asleep; but the noisy bickering outside about the best way to dispose of him kept him awake: a bullet through the peephole?

Smash the lock in the door, into the cell, and slit his throat? Or bash his skull in?

And the like. Then one of them, probably the sentry, shouted, go to hell, all of you; the lieutenant said he was sticking his neck out, being liable for the red son of a bitch. And then someone actually put a bullet through the peephole, and dust trickled from the wall opposite where it had hit.

After that, everything gradually calmed down.

★

"Come on, get up!"

Radek blinked; a visibly ill-tempered guard, his chin sown with stubble. The man took off his chains, grabbed him by the elbow, dragged him up, and then limped beside him to a hutch, where, in the light of the gray morning that fell obliquely through a narrow window, a sink and water pipe were visible. Radek washed himself while shivering, and while he dried himself with the thin towel thrown to him by the guard, he listened to his complaints about the times and his superiors, who gave him nothing but trouble; he had been in the judicial service since 1890, and here on Lehrter Straße since 1903, and he had never seen them keep a prisoner in custody chained up, and this in a cell where they usually only locked up addicts.

Radek wasn't quite comfortable with this information; but one day they'd have to talk to him, and for that, they'd have to take him to better quarters—or they'd simply take him away to treat him like they had Liebknecht, and even for that purpose, they would by necessity take off his chains.

But no one came until the midday soup, which was pushed through to him and which he spooned out himself despite the iron cuff, and after that only the limping guard came to fetch the bowl of food again; he did not engage in any conversation, not even a short one.

Radek made himself comfortable, as well as he could: he

squatted on his cot, his free leg bent, and tried to scratch his back with his free hand; at last the door opened. A table with a stool and an office chair were carried in, and soon after someone dragged in a typewriter. The corresponding clerk, black pads at the elbows of his shabby jacket, placed the stool in front of the table and sat down awkwardly. Radek coughed.

The clerk raised his head. "Sit up straight. Herr von Ziethen attaches great importance to correct posture."

"And who," Radek asked, "is Herr von Ziethen?"

"In your place, I wouldn't mess with Herr von Ziethen."

"Yeah?"

"Herr von Ziethen is"—the clerk on his stool assumed a sort of guarded posture—"the investigating magistrate."

"Then he'd better make sure," Radek suddenly sounded angry, "that someone comes and takes these irons off of me!"

But Herr von Ziethen was already standing in his cell, and Radek interrupted him before the man could utter a word. "In whose hands," he demanded to know, "am I, please? The military authorities? The judiciary?"

"For the time being, in mine." Ziethen took a seat in the chair and pulled a document from his briefcase, which he placed on Radek's knee. On the neatly circled label of the file was written—Radek read it, bureaucracy promised security, with satisfaction—INVESTIGATION IN THE KINGDOM OF PRUSSIA VS . . . and then in handwriting, *Radek, Karl, alias Sobelsohn.* "The *Kingdom*," Ziethen explained, "you should please consider stricken. *State* of Prussia. In view of the general state of shortage, our courts are required to use up in official traffic all of the office materials still available from previously."

Radek grinned with schadenfreude. "Revolutions, even German ones, have consequences. But before you start your investigation, Herr von Ziethen—that's who you are, isn't it? Tell me, on the basis of which paragraph of which law do you put prisoners in chains?"

"From my side, Herr Radek," Ziethen leaned forward with a

slight groan and retrived the file KINGDOM OF PRUSSIA VS RADEK, KARL, ALIAS SOBELSOHN, "there are no grounds for keeping you in chains."

Just then, the door creaked again; a dignified gentleman with blond whiskers and a gray-silk tie under his studded collar entered the cell and, looking over the glittering pince-nez, caught sight of the chained prisoner.

"Radek, my God!"

Whereupon he took off the pince-nez, carefully put it behind the white cloth in the outer breast pocket of his frock coat, and threw his hands over his head.

"Herr von Ziethen," Radek turned to the investigating magistrate, clinking his hands, "I'm pleased to introduce Dr. Weinberg, one of my attorneys."

Weinberg was wealthy and sufficiently prominent to afford leftists, whether USPD, soldiers' council members, or even Spartakists, as clients; in the days before New Year's Day, Radek had already had Paul Levi put him in touch with him, and asked him to take care of him in case he needed legal help; and now, like the deus ex machina on the theater stage, there Weinberg stood, his hands still raised.

"The guard commander!" ordered Ziethen.

The clerk hurried. But instead of some senior guard, von Trettwitz appeared, who, before Dr. Weinberg could start to protest, explained with a brutal smile that Herr Radek was in chains by personal order of Colonel Reinhard and would remain so until further notice; furthermore, that apart from the investigating magistrate and the guards, no one should have access to the prisoner, and certainly not a lawyer, and a Jewish one at that.

This, Weinberg decided, was even worse than under the Kaiser; and he clamped his pince-nez back on his nose to hide the hatred behind the lenses—the hatred that his forefather, the old cattle Jew—had shown to Trettwitz's ancestor, the lord over cattle, and over man and soil; and he called out to Radek, "That remains to be seen!," and left the cell with fluttering coattails.

Radek enjoyed the scene, the first joyous one in a long time, rattled his chains, and said, "Herr von Ziethen, if it's not you who's in charge here, but the Herr Oberleutnant and, indirectly, Colonel Reinhard, then I see no point in a conversation between the two of us."

Ziethen slid KINGDOM OF PRUSSIA VS. RADEK, KARL ALIAS SOBELSOHN back into his briefcase and said, "I'll sort it out," and while on his way out, "Is there anything else I can help you with?"

"You can," said Radek. "Take a few marks of my money which was confiscated, and buy me a volume of Shakespeare."

The investigating magistrate approached him; he seemed moved and squeezed his hand, the chained one. Radek cast a sidelong glance at Trettwitz; he was probably now thinking of the copy of *Faust* in the green Saffiano, and no longer found the stunt original.

With next morning's malt brew came the Shakespeare, in English, a thin-printed edition in two volumes. He leafed through the second, paused:

> *Macbeth shall never vanquish'd be, until*
> *Great Birnam Wood to high Dunsinane hill*
> *Shall come against him*

and thought, how long had he been waiting, were Ilyich and Bukharin and the others in Moscow already waiting, for the Birnam Forest to start moving on Dunsinane and Macbeth to fall at last; but these had been Scottish revolutionaries who had camouflaged themselves there with green branches and attacked, and not the Germans, by whom the trees in the forest stood meticulously lined up, and showed no intention whatsoever of marching against Dunsinane or any other bastion of the oppressors.

"Radek?"

The door screeched on its hinges; footsteps, firm, self-assuredness personified.

"Ah, Herr Oberst."

"Hi, Radek!"

"Hi, Reinhard!"

Reinhard clenched his right hand. "If it was up to me, Radek, I'd have you hanged with the greatest of pleasure. But the goddamned Jews, this Ebert, this Scheidemann, are afraid of the Bolsheviks, and I have, God hear my lament, orders to treat you like a porcelain teacup, and even to take off your chains."

"I know Ebert," said Radek, "I was a member of his party until he personally tossed me out. You can accuse him of many things, but not of being a Jew. Likewise, to my knowledge, no Israelite blood flows through Scheidemann's calcified veins."

He thrust the steel handcuff in front of Reinhard's stomach. "Will it be soon?"

Reinhard controlled his outrage and told the guard to get going.

After some fiddling with the key and lock, the chain rattled to the floor. Radek massaged his aching wrist. "Why, Colonel, are you so eager to see me hang?"

"Spys are hanged."

"And what," Radek pushed his still-chained foot toward the guard, "is left in Germany to spy on? You don't even have an army anymore!"

"We don't have an army," grumbled Reinhard, his brow swelling with anger, "because the Jews, damn them, have plunged a dagger in its back; and now the Entente is enslaving the defenseless German people."

Radek, finally freed from his chains, stretched out his limbs. He could have hopped like a flea, that's how light he felt, and his brain, freshly infused with blood all at once, began to produce new ideas with renewed vigor. "Spy or no spy," he sneered, "suppose I were here on behalf of my party and my government."

Reinhard was triumphant: the guy had said it himself—he was a spy!

"And if that were so," Radek inquired mildly, "do you think it advisable for your beaten and disarmed Germany, by the brutal treatment of my person which you, Reinhard, ordered, to also affront its only potential ally, Bolshevik Russia?"

Reinhard hesitated. From that point of view, he had considered neither the matter itself nor the disgusting man who, chained or not, with his sloping shoulders and erratic movements and unsteady gaze, eluded his, Colonel Reinhard's, grasp, again and again.

"Allies, potential, eh?" he finally said. "What are there, then, for commonalities?"

Radek left the question unanswered. If, he reflected, it dawned on even this dumb clod that there might be some common ground between the two losers of the war isolated from the rest of the world, then it might be worth pursuing the idea of a German-Soviet rapprochement, however remote it might seem now.

But he still felt very weak on his legs, and the guard had to support him up the gloomy stairs and across the courtyard, where the cold air flowed down from the icy blue of the sky. He greedily inhaled the air that cleansed his lungs, oblivious to the mobs of Freikorps thugs lying around, and felt the ray of light that fell into his new cell like a gift from God, and was delighted by the little dust motes dancing around in it; then he walked around the cell, its length and width: what humane dimensions! And the bucket freshly painted, even pink! And at the table there, on which a green-shaded lamp stood and a package seemed to already be waiting for him, he could read and work; he would be able to buy paper and have books sent to him and subscribe to newspapers, not just the German ones, which reeked so penetratingly of the provincial, but also the French and above all English ones, since *Pravda* didn't come into the country. And he had to make sure it was possible to receive visitors, if not exactly the members of the Central Committee, if it still existed, then others who could stimulate and inform him about the political situation and how things stood in the party—and, of course, his lawyers, Dr. Weinberg and the grave Dr. Kurt Rosenfeld with the hedgehog haircut and the prickly little beard on his chin.

But for the time being, only investigating magistrate von Ziethen came, hanging his coat on the hook next to the door and—"Satisfied, Herr Radek?"—indicating with a sweeping gesture the advantages of his changed domicile.

Radek, who was about to open the package, enjoyed the aroma of smoked ham inside, and asked Ziethen, who was also sniffing, whether he knew from whom the delicacy came; and when Ziethen told him, "from a Herr Levi," he was touched, for he remembered how Comrade Levi had once spoken to him of his parents' little farm somewhere in Württemberg; noble Levi, who, even while going underground, slipped him such a rarity; there was still hope for humanity after all; and he considered whether he should offer a slice to the investigating magistrate, but decided against it, because his own stomach was more important to him, and second, because Ziethen might interpret such generosity as an attempt at rapprochement.

The typewriter was brought in again; the clerk with the elbow-patches placed it exactly where the ham had been a moment ago, and Herr von Ziethen rubbed his hands together, "Well, let's have it!"

Apparently in the belief that the best way to approach intellectuals was through their intellect and by demonstrating to them how much one was interested in their ideas after all, Ziethen began by engaging Radek in a chat on the topic of the famous historical necessity of socialism and revolution, taking into account possible democratic aspects.

Radek, for his part, regarded the investigating magistrate's affability, even if it was only mere show, as a possible lever for further improving his circumstances and, mindful of the tactics Trotsky had used in Brest-Litovsk vis-à-vis Secretary von Kühlmann, decided to respond to Ziethen's questions, which were initially rather verbose.

In agreement with most of the leading spirits of socialism, he therefore declared that he regarded man as a social being who, collectively and individually, strives at the same time for salvation from his misery and for personal self-determination. Assuming favorable natural conditions, the foundations for the attainment of said goals are created as soon as a society, through the organization of labor, has achieved a volume of production that guarantees the physical existence of the population as well as its higher development. Only at this point—Radek's index finger jabbed in the direction of the investigating magistrate's heart—did the actual history of humanity begin.

"And from that point on," Ziethen said, smiling, "everything then runs like clockwork according to historical necessity?"

"If only it did that!" Now Radek smiled too. "How comfortably I could arrange my life, then!"

He continued: "Capitalism had advanced the forces of production to such an extent that poverty and hunger on earth could be eliminated, but that did not yet mean they would be eliminated. The prerequisite for that was for the masses, at least in the industrialized countries, to recognize their damned historical duty to undertake this task. If they didn't do so, or if they failed at a solution, capitalism, with its craving for profit and gigantic contempt for mankind, would continue to proliferate. But it was precisely in the wake of this war that the chance for the self-liberation of the masses and a real change of the whole disastrous system presented itself . . ." "only," and now a tone sharper, "humanity also has to seize the chance!"

"And that," said Ziethen suddenly, having followed Radek's thoughts with mute fascination, "is exactly the point."

Radek froze; there, in his enthusiasm for the logic of his own lecture, he had provided reason and proof for the government's accusation that he and Luxemburg and Liebknecht had plotted a coup to take power in Germany.

But then, after a very long moment of shock, the redemptive argument: "Nowhere, Herr von Ziethen, at any conference, meeting, or demonstration, have I asserted that this opportunity presented itself on the streets of Berlin on January 9, 1919, of all days, nor had I called upon the masses to seize it just then."

The investigating magistrate guessed that his prospective defendant was about to elude him, and countered, "Doesn't a revolutionary occasionally take a risk, Mr. Radek? Think of the sealed train car in which you once traveled; to my knowledge, you and your friends have never been entirely averse to a little *vabanque*."

"You flatter me," Radek hesitated. "In reality, Herr von Ziethen, we followers of Marx conduct our activities on a scientific basis."

"Indeed?"

"Indeed."

But wasn't science itself, thought Radek, the greatest risk? And wasn't it necessary to act anyway? Only in this case, as he'd already realized after his first nights in Berlin, success was as good as impossible: in the only German workers' organizations that could be considered for such an undertaking, the councils, the Communists were a tiny group; the leadership of the struggle would have fallen to the old Social Democratic cadres and, possibly, to the USPD; there was therefore no question of the party seizing power; and if—after a successful putsch in Berlin, for example—power had nevertheless been seized, how long would it have been possible to hold it, given the balance of power?... Accordingly, he had warned the Central Committee to not even attempt it. But the comrades, it turned out, understood little of science. The majority of them were laymen, and even Luxemburg and Jogiches, who had written in their *Spartakus Letters* that one could only take power when supported by the majority of the working class—which, by the way, was also questionable—also hadn't been able to stop what had already started rolling.

★

"There is, Mr. Radek"—Ziethen gave the clerk a wave—"a well-founded suspicion that you assisted Herren Ledebour, Liebknecht, et al during the unrest in January of this year in committing a number of crimes, such as breach of the peace, violations of the law on explosives, and the like; in short, in preparing a violent coup d'état. Would you like to comment on this?"

"Yes."

"Please."

"I'd like to know," said Radek authoritatively, "whether the Prussian prosecutor's office has nothing better to bring against me than that? Does it not have any effective evidence of a plot inspired by me, for instance, to cut off Comrade Ebert's stupid head or set fire to the Reichstag? Or does the prosecutor's office only have the belief, peculiar to this authority, that a Bolshevik, a Russian one at that, cannot help but be implicated in every violent crime in the book? Did your police, who searched my rooms and rummaged through my pockets, not find anything? No bombs, no calls for violent overthrow in my handwriting?"

Ziethen remained silent.

"Or was there something of interest to you after all: a copy of a letter, namely, in which I advised against any act of political violence, although the government provided sufficient provocation?"

"That," Ziethen told the clerk, "we'll leave out."

"Or do you want to indict me," Radek continued to press, "for hiding under a false name in order to avoid the fate of Liebknecht and my friend Luxemburg?"

"I beg you," Ziethen became angry, "Germany is a civilized country!"

Pause.

Finally Radek, quietly. "That, too, has yet to be proved."

11

The longer the interrogations dragged on, the more clearly Ziethen suffered. The material that the investigating magistrate confronted him with either came from idiots or from provocateurs; sometimes both in the same person. One witness had allegedly recognized him at the head of a horde of agitated workers who were trying to storm the Alexander Barracks; only, the description of Radek in this testimony, as even Ziethen must have realized, in no way corresponded to that of the Radek now sitting before him; three trade union officials swore that they had seen him going in and out of the headquarters of the Hamburg Communists during the week in which Liebknecht and Rosa Luxemburg were murdered, that is, at a time when he had long since sought refuge with the widow Bondy; other informants of the public prosecutor's office had given even more untenable evidence.

After the investigating magistrate had exhausted his reserves of such reports and circumstantial evidence, he returned to the warning letter to the Central Committee of which Radek, just freed from his chains, had perhaps spoken of a little too hastily. "At the time," Ziethen remarked, "I thought such a piece of correspondence was a product of your imagination. In the meantime, I know you better, and I quite trust you to have written such a letter; besides, it's been reported to me that it existed. It's not part of my duties as investigating magistrate to advise you, but confidentially, the original, or even a copy, of this document might well absolve you."

Radek remembered the wrinkled hands of Dürer's mother laid flat against each other in the picture on the wall of his room at the widow Bondy's, behind the frame of which the copy of the letter to the Central Committee that Ziethen desired was hidden; and he answered, "And it's not part of my duties as a detainee to prove my innocence; the prosecution has to prove that I acted culpably, and where and when. Besides, and vice versa, such a letter could be used by you as a piece of evidence that I was the inspirer and secret leader of the whole January events. No, you'll have to use your own informers, Herr von Ziethen."

The investigating magistrate was annoyed. That this person refused to understand the seriousness of his situation, or even to consider that he, Ziethen, could wish to show fairness even to him, Radek! "So, where can I find this letter, or at least its text?"

Radek closed his eyes and remained silent.

The investigating magistrate frowned. The Prussian government could neither put the Soviet citizen Karl Radek on trial with any chance of success, nor could it let him go. He saw a months-long debate coming, gradually degenerating into a routine, between him and this agonizing man whose brain was an heirloom of generations of rabbis washed in every Talmudic water. Oh God, thought Ziethen, perhaps a *Landsknecht* like that Reinhard had been right, and another corpse in the Landwehrkanal would have been the more practical solution.

Then he wiped the thought from his mind. No, not that.

★

In March, there was unrest again, the echoes of which reached the prison; Radek, who was about to make his rounds in the inner courtyard, huddled in a protected corner, close to the guards, while from the barracks opposite, the shots whipped over and against the walls. In the barracks lay the Kessel Brigade, a troupe of select killers who mercilessly abused their freshly delivered prisoners; the screams of pain rang in Radek's ears every time; nevertheless, he ordered an Easter cake from one of the lads, who had boasted of his wife's baking skills, for a small fee; but he took the precaution of letting the man taste it first, and only when he showed no signs of poisoning did Radek eat it himself.

After a while, a quiet agreement was reached with Herr von Ziethen: they both knew that further questions regarding the prosecutor's charges would yield as few results as the ones they'd already gone through repeatedly, and so they spent the hours set aside for the interrogation in contemplative conversation, especially about the problem of dictatorship in revolutions, both past and present, and about the present political situation, about which Radek was well informed, since he spent a large portion of his nights with notations and excerpts from the most diverse newspapers. Accordingly, his files piled up into towers, and his card index which, solid researcher that he was, soon filled several cardboard boxes. In view of the increasingly threatening confinement in the cell, Ziethen said with a touch of irony that he, Radek, might have to be assigned a second room for the library and archive.

Radek felt the sudden pounding of his heart. "Do you expect such long delays?"

Then he got a hold of himself, rummaged hastily through his papers, and held out to the investigating magistrate the newspaper clipping he had been looking for. "There—I'll translate: 'Moscow—The well-known journalist Karl Radek, currently being held in a Berlin prison, has been appointed the full and authorized ambassador of the Ukrainian Soviet Republic to the German Republic.'"

Ziethen gulped: they obviously didn't know that at the ministry, otherwise they would have told him.

"No congratulations, Herr von Ziethen?"

"That's a hell of a joke."

"The London *Times* is a serious paper."

"Nonetheless, it's a joke, Herr Radek," insisted Ziethen, "because the territory of the state that you claim to represent is almost entirely in the hands of a certain Skoropadsky, a Cossack general."

Radek saw his triumph melt away and reacted viciously. "How much longer, Herr von Ziethen, of this pretend investigation? How much longer my isolation, my only pleasure being our dialogues, the content of which is also becoming exhausted? No, correction; once, by coincidence, on the way to my round in the courtyard, I ran into old Ledebour of the left wing of the USPD, in whose lap the January upheaval fell, and who now sits four cells to my right; your guards tried to tear him away from me, but he roared like an ox, and so they had to let us speak a few hasty words." Radek took a breath. "Well, I have the greatest understanding for your dilemma, Herr von Ziethen. Yes, if you could have succeeded in presenting to your superiors something that would have enabled them to drag me before your courts with some chance of success . . . But as it is, your bureau dreads losing face in Berlin and the surrounding capitals were it to so easily release his excellency the ambassador of Soviet Ukraine. So what do you suggest, in my interest and yours, Herr Investigating Magistrate?"

"Write a note, Herr Ambassador, to his excellency the foreign minister."

Radek laughed. "Cute idea; for his excellency Hermann Müller, the foreign minister, is also an old acquaintance of mine from my Social Democratic days."

Then he pulled a leather case from his pocket, in which, in a row like brown soldiers, were half a dozen good cigars.

"Care to?"

But Ziethen declined.

Since he could think of nothing more suitable at the moment to improve his mood, he actually wrote a long note to Hermann Müller, on prison paper, seven pages long in his spidery handwriting, and beginning with the emphatically disrespectful salutation, Herr Reichsminister!

In it, he complained that not only did the German government recognize the Junker-capitalist White Russian clique under the tsarist Hetman Skoropadsky as the legitimate rulers of Ukraine, but also supported them by sending German weapons, instead of allying with the Ukrainian Soviet government, the only authentic representative of the Ukrainian masses, which had appointed him, Karl Radek, as its diplomatic representative in Berlin; and why, pray tell, did he learn of this appointment from the press and not from Comrade Müller's ministry, as would have been right and proper?

Whereupon he lectured Müller on the political consequences not only of this conduct, but of the whole process of harassment to which he, Karl Radek—who at the time was not yet an ambassador, but who had been a delegate of the Russian workers' and soldiers' councils—had been subjected after his absolutely unlawful arrest.

It was a literary exercise rather than a diplomatic document, and Radek by no means believed that it would have any beneficial effect on Müller, if it managed to reach the foreign ministry at all—they knew each other too well for that. But over the course of a week, a trusty showed up, a well-known robber and murderer, as he immediately revealed, who removed the pink tin bucket that cut into Radek's flesh every time he sat on it. This having been taken care of, a retinue of prison guards entered, nodded to each other and looked around the cell; one groped for dust flakes and the edge of table and bed with index finger erect, another complained about the dirty window. Finally, the prison warden appeared in person, the trusty at his heels, the latter carrying a large object wrapped in brown paper. The warden approached Radek, clicked his heels together, according to the old custom, said "Ballkopf" and waved to the robber-murderer. The latter revealed the small present: a porcelain chamber pot crowned with a wooden ring of dimensions that promised Radek a comfort he had not known for a long time.

"And what, Herr Ballkopf, have I done to deserve such attention?" asked Radek.

"My staff and I," the prison warden raised his brow, "will always try to do our best for you, Mr. Radek. By the way, this afternoon we're moving you to a double cell, which you can set up as you wish."

★

This was now already a sort of apartment, only with barred windows: the one cell a salon including library, the other the bedroom and study; the robber-murderer, who considered himself his personal servant, since he was allowed to empty the luxury chamber pot that morning, suggested hanging curtains, and also procured some.

The first visitor from the outside world was Karl Moor. There they stood under the hands of Dürer's mother—Radek had arranged for the picture including the letter concealed behind it to be brought to him from his room at the widow Bondy's— and looked at each other; Moor's eyes became moist, and Radek, although seldom plagued by waves of emotion, felt a twitch in his throat. How long had they known each other, he thought—since 1904, probably—the rebellious scion of wealthy Austrian nobility, who had adopted the name of the noble chief robber from Schiller's play, and the Jewish Polish lad with the socialist ideals. They met again in Bern, where Moor, as a young revolutionary, had already frightened the respectable bourgeoisie with his affairs with women, but the local foreign police were tolerant of him, knowing that Moor had just inherited his parents' fortune and, as the Swiss authorities preferred, had also invested it in Switzerland; however, he now spent larger sums less on escapades in Gstaad or Vevey than on cultivating his extensive political connections and supporting the most diverse émigré groups; this in turn annoyed Lenin, who would have preferred to have had all that nice money exclusively for his Bolsheviks; and indeed, it was rumored that Moor, along with Comrade Parvus, had also had a share in the provision of that scandal-ridden, sealed special train car.

As if wishing to confirm this, Moor said musingly, "Do you remember the platform in Zurich when you left, the dim lights?"

"I confess, I missed you then."

"There were too many agents of too many secret services there."

Radek nodded understandingly. "And today it was just the Prussians?'"

"And they were courtesy personified!" Moor enthused. "But first I had a lot to go through! You've been my only hobby since the day of your arrest, believe me. I've been besieging the gentlemen in their offices; after all, for a while, it was a matter of life and death; your life, my boy, your death. And you try convincing half the Prussian bureaucracy that their plans are flawed and their actions futile, and that, furthermore, seven Germans who are being held hostage in retaliation for the hard-pressed treatment in Berlin of the Soviet Ukrainian ambassador would only be released when you were safely back home in Moscow."

Radek's brow furrowed. "In the Kremlin, ah, yes . . ." The idea that he and Rosa, his Rosa, indeed now resided at the Kremlin still didn't quite register with him.

"You've earned room and board at the Kremlin," Moor said, "more than most of the heroes who are quartering there now."

"Ach, old friend . . ." Radek's joyful excitement at the visit had given way to a kind of foreboding of disaster that might await him in Moscow. "Even my mama, God rest her soul, used to say that the higher you rise, the lower you fall."

Soon, word got around that the authorities had granted Radek certain privileges, and that he was ready to receive friends and acquaintances, though of course not every Tom, Dick, and Harry.

Enver and Talaat Pasha did him the honor, one a brigadier, the other a colonel, two Young Turks with God knew how many Armenians on their conscience, and who now, after the British victory over the Ottoman Empire, were seeking safe exile in Moscow and thought that he, Radek, could further their travel plans. Radek found them amusingly repellent; his penchant for intelligent power mongers was in conflict with his sense of solidarity for the humiliated and persecuted; a pogrom was a pogrom, whoever the victims being slaughtered. The two of them—who with their dark, red fezzes perched on hair parted with military precision, brought a dash of exoticism into the gray of his prison—were important to him mainly for their symbolic value; coming to a nebbich—which he had been until recently—for help.

His new status was confirmed a few days later. The man who entered the cell, after much bowing and scraping by the guard, well groomed in appearance from the high forehead passing into baldness to the dull polished English boots, politely stated his name and title, although he could assume that his well-proportioned features must be as well known to the prisoner as his reputation as a mastermind of the democratic wing of the German bourgeoisie: Walter Rathenau, chairman of the supervisory board of AEG, the Allgemeine-Elektrizitäts-Gesellschaft, and, during the war, organizer of the supply of raw materials for the Kaiserreich.

Radek surmised that Rathenau had come to learn directly about Russia, to supplement his own information: personal impressions by a participant in the events, characteristics of the rulers of the new polity, economic and military forecasts; but to Radek's astonishment, Rathenau, as soon as he uttered his first sentence, hardly allowed himself to be interrupted, and talked for more than an hour, in a well-modulated, sonorous voice, to which he seemed to be listening at the same time.

May he, he opened the conversation, explain to Radek his thoughts on the world situation?

Radek expressed regret that he couldn't present his guest with a decent cognac.

An elegant hand movement—unnecessary. Rathenau acted casual; his posture indicated: trust for trust. Contrary, he explained, to most of what the German press wrote on the subject, Soviet Russia would not be defeated: tsarism had been totally rotten from the inside, the muzhik had not the slightest cause to once again place himself under the yoke of the large landlord, and as for the Russian bankers and industrialists, they had always been too feeble and fearful. "But," he raised his finger in warning, "do not overestimate the historical significance of your Bolshevik victories. Even the Huns," the comparison obviously pleased Rathenau, "the Huns fought one victory after another until their little horses had run themselves to death and their empire broke up."

Radek liked the man: Rathenau acted as if for him there were no doubts, no ambiguities, no possibility of wrong decisions. He sat, one leg crossed over the other, demonstrating superiority. And maybe that wasn't even an act; maybe it was second nature to him. And suddenly, it hit him: vis-à-vis him he saw in this educated Western European Jew, although outwardly so very different, his mirror image, his double. Wasn't he, Radek, also aware of the excellent quality of the gray matter in his skull, which was able to subdue even the most complicated things, at least in thought? And the clearly recognizable self-love, which all too often turned into contempt for his neighbor, wasn't it also, like Rathenau's, one of his most outstanding qualities?

"The question is," Rathenau continued to pontificate, "whether your people are capable of creating a new order in place of the old capitalist one, to which there is no return. All social relations are breaking down. The world is at a crossroads."

He waited, as if Radek would now have to raise his objections. Radek, however, somewhat surprised by the other's analysis, which he hadn't expected to be so radical, could only agree with Rathenau, with the reservation, however, that he believed the future of mankind would still be best in the hands of the working class.

"The working class?" Radek felt his self-confidence crumble under Rathenau's pitying gaze. "Your working class can only destroy; true creativity is a matter of the brain; only under the guidance of the aristocracy of the mind can your working class build a new society. And this will not be a society of equals; human equality is impossible. But hereditary right won't exist anymore either, the new order will destroy it"—brief laughter interrupted the flow of speech—"and you can believe me, the heir of the AEG dynasty, Mr. Radek. The leaders will be the most intellectually capable, in turn giving room to the most talented from the ranks of the rest of the people—"

"And how"—this time Radek felt superior, being on Marxist ground—"do you intend to organize the new production?"

"Reading about that in my books!" Rathenau went over to Radek's book table and reached for one of the volumes as if by chance. "Marx, if you please—but Marx only created a theory of destruction. With me, however, you'll find a theory of constructive socialism. I took the first scientific step in this direction!"

Radek bowed. "My compliments."

"You can take my findings seriously, since they're based on Marx's," Rathenau replied, piqued. "And on this basis, develop them further. In Germany, a revolution like the Russian one is impossible for decades to come. The German worker is a philistine. But how will you secure victory for your Russian revolution without German help?"

"We'll have to try," said Radek.

12

His situation began to amuse him.

If at the beginning he had been considered a kind of bandit, with murder in his eyes and hatred for all that was sacred, but now, to an ever-increasing degree, the reputation of a guru became attached to him, a witty one at that, from faraway lands where wondrous, albeit dangerous changes were taking place. At the same time, cut off from the comrades conducting politics in Moscow, he was totally left to his own devices: his own adversary on questions where more than one point of view was possible, and the supreme authority, because the only one available, concerning judgments that had to be made about people and situations.

Of course he was clear about the fact that he was also serving as a lure for the Prussian police, and he took care that none of the top officials of the German Communists, most of whom were living underground, would think of seeking an audience with him under whatever guise; the news he received from them indirectly was enough to confirm his worst fears: the leadership of the party was a confused bunch; Paul Levi, its most intelligent mind and, after Jogiches was murdered, its leader, found little appeal among the masses; he isolated the party from the trade unions, which, after all, were the working class's only effective organizations in times of retreat.

"Does Levi not see that?" Radek moaned, and glanced, demanding approval, at Ruth Fischer who, plump and young and bright-eyed, hung on his every word.

Comrade Fischer had come from Austria and was now touring Germany to agitate the proles with her genuine, or at least seemingly genuine, revolutionary enthusiasm. The German party, she confirmed to Radek, was a club of rebellious fellows, courageous in the majority and ready to fight, but incapable of inspiring the masses. And gradually, she added, their members were losing faith that a tiny but determined minority of professional revolutionaries could manage to seize power; on the other hand, they had no idea how their handful could become a mass revolutionary movement. Defeated in the streets, they therefore planned to shift their activity to the factories; the power in the factories they hoped to conquer would then become power in the state . . .

Radek liked how Ruth Fischer presented things and how her speech found expression in the movement of her body at the same time. When was the last time he'd had a woman?

She waited for an answer.

"But the unions," he said hastily, "are embedded in the factories. The first revolutionary wave in Germany has ebbed away. And until the next one . . ." He felt her being carried along by his words, prosaic as they were, and sought to give a personal touch to the text he was reeling off. "That means, first of all, taking over the trade unions and the works councils, and dominating the city and district councils." He pulled several sheets of paper from under a pile of books. "I sketched all this out in the expectation that someone would come along to whom I could"—he rolled up his manuscript—"entrust it." Then he stepped close before her, took her hand, and closed her fingers, one by one, around the little paper roll. "If I ask you nicely?... Surely they won't search your tempting body ... ?"

She shook her head, her dark curls dancing. Then she opened her blouse.

Radek noticed his tongue going dry. "The party will be grateful to you," he said hoarsely.

If there was anyone with a higher opinion of himself than Radek, it was Maximilian Harden. But while Radek often relativized his strongly developed self-confidence to others by means of critical-ironic or even disparaging remarks about his own person, Harden—also a pseudonym, Witkowski was his original name—displayed his greatness demonstratively: he, editor of the *Zukunft*, and by virtue of his pen Germany's supreme judge in matters of good taste, political finesse, and literary perfection.

For this reason alone, like and like usually didn't go well together, Radek had his reservations about Harden; and he felt all the more flattered when the man who had not shied away from openly attacking the second Wilhelm from the moment of his accession to the throne, and who had made his paper the leading intellectual journal of the empire, asked if he might have an audience in the Lehrter Straße.

"There have to be heroes in history," Harden said, "but I love to pick them myself."

By then they had been talking for a while, a conversation that had been started with caution by both sides; knowing the mental dodges each of them was capable of, neither Radek nor Harden wanted to embarrass himself in front of the other.

"Object all you want," Harden continued, "I've been a socialist long enough to know your reasoning. Aren't you yourself, Radek, and your party constantly on the lookout for figures of light to beguile the masses—whether or not the one you've chosen is suitable for the role? Think of Lassalle, how he let himself be built up by his workers, and he had by nature the heroic gesture that today's workers lack! What is your Lenin, with his accountant's persona and accountant's language, against somebody like that! But be that as it may—your boring anonymous forces, to which you attach so much importance in history: well, I confess, humus is needed everywhere: but why does the great, the historical, grow elsewhere, with so much barren fruit in the case of you materialists?"

No wonder, thought Radek, that old Mehring, his teacher at that time within the German Social Democracy, couldn't stand Harden, Harden's stilted diction, his bloated thoughts. The Wilhelmine era, which had produced such figures, was dead, had gone under in the blood and muck of the world war; Harden, however, had survived, a last witness to vanished splendor. And he had shown courage as the advocate of the aged Bismarck against the loudmouthed young Kaiser; and later, in his paper, he had picked apart the imperial legends that had served industry and the military as justification during the war; and, only recently, his was the only one of the country's bourgeois journals to name the murderers of Liebknecht and Luxemburg.

Now, however, it seemed to Radek, tones of weariness, even resignation, had crept into the cultivated pathos. "Ah, Germany," sighed Harden, "what's left that could give us cause for hope. German Social Democracy, which crawls on its belly before the industrialists and bankers and doesn't dare to clear away the old bureaucracy? Everything is perverted, democracy is nothing, the national idea is a brutal farce; defeat, for other peoples an occasion for settling accounts with one's own past, leads here only to the search for scapegoats and vindictiveness of the lowest sort. Yes, Versailles! I grant them Versailles, I welcome it! Perhaps the imposed treaty will be a lesson to this people who have never learned anything from history, except new mistakes. And would they have behaved as victors, the Germans?" He interrupted himself: "Ah, I forgot, Brest-Litovsk was, after all, your personal battlefield."

"An instructive episode," Radek nodded. "On the other hand, neither Trotsky nor I had any illusions about these victors."

"Parochial as ever," sneered Harden, "the German gentlemen! Even a Commissar like General Hoffmann should have realized that the future of Germany, if there's to be one, can only be based on cooperation with Russia. And even now they don't want to hear anything about the possibility that a new historical force could be in the making over there…"

Rathenau had already expressed similar thoughts, and Radek found it only logical that Harden's thoughts, which ran parallel to his own, also found expression. And concluded if this was the case, wasn't it his damned duty, whether as a prisoner on remand or as a fictitious ambassador, to carry out this new policy, though for the time being little more than a scheme, in real life? And said, "Ideology, the German one in particular, aside—let's talk about what your bourgeoisie really understand, honored friend: coal, grain, timber, hemp, linen, cotton, and the possible profit to be gained from them."

Harden sat up and took notice: despite all differences, a kindred spirit! It had taken him years and the reading of thick books, including several by the convoluted, finicky Marx, before he had been willing to grant the products that Radek enumerated, certainly not without disgust, a certain, albeit limited, place among the factors shaping history.

"But," he asked, "under the new conditions in your country, and those are the decisive ones, will your muzhiks be willing and able to produce the necessary quantities of the goods you mentioned, plus others that would have to be available if a modern state is to be established?"

Radek remained silent. Harden became unsettling to him. As unsurprising as the question he had asked was, coming from a bourgeois writer, here and now it touched upon the very point that had so often given him, Radek, food for thought, thought he wasn't sure why and since when, exactly. Of course, with the enemy in the country, and with the country itself being cut off from parts of the Ukraine, the Caucasus, and Siberia, this question was more hypothetical, but that was only true as long as there was a civil war and violence was the supreme law. But after that? Along what trajectories would it function, this socialism?

Finally he answered, and it was embarrassing to him to hear how much he was bragging—nor more, however, than Harden had been before—"I mean, we can rely on the hundreds of thousands of proletarians who, in two long bitter years of revolution, must have realized that the difference between a capitalist and a socialist state does not consist in the fact that in the latter one lolls about on the stove and allows people to work whenever they feel like it."

Harden played with his heavy gold cuff link. "So where do you see the difference, then?"

"In the power of disposal over labor and its results. In a socialist state, workers no longer leave this to a few dozen financiers and corporate masters; rather, they take it over themselves."

"And you replace the despotism of the gentlemen large capitalists with what—the despotism of the comrade people's commissars?"

That sounded almost like Luxemburg's warning that evening in the pub in Berlin, what was its name, Zur Fröhlichen Freiheit—the appropriate name for a barroom dispute about the Red Terror and its necessity. And what did Harden really know about this despotism, which until then had been little more than a shadow on the wall, a threatening one; presumably Harden drew his insights from the world of the Prussian bureaucracy: apparatus was apparatus; and then Radek thought, please God Almighty let the despotism of our People's Commissars at least be an enlightened one. But aloud, he said, "Once it's in its hands, the working class will not allow itself to be dispossessed of the power of disposal over its own labor."

Harden looked up. "Could you write something about that for me?"

"Do you think your readers will swallow that? Won't their horror of the author put them off?"

"The German bourgeoisie had come to terms very well," Harden again played with his cuff link. "Very well, I said, with Russian feudalism; why shouldn't they, then, as soon as the initial shock is over, be able to come to terms with Bolshevism?"

"Especially since even our People's Commissars should have learned by now that if you want to keep wolves peaceful, you have to feed them."

Harden agreed: wise commissars, well-behaved wolves.

"And should your bourgeoisie be embarrassed about supplying us directly"—Radek smiled—"I imagine that the Jews of Warsaw, for a modest fee, would perform the transfer."

"But you should probably leave that out of your article."

"I know how far I can go in depicting the realities."

Harden rose. "With you, Herr Radek, I could increase my circulation numbers considerably."

Karl Moor, always eager to make new connections, introduced him to his latest acquisition, Baron Eugen von Reibnitz.

"You may, Herr Radek"—Reibnitz's vowels had a nasal overtone—"describe me with confidence as a National Bolshevik."

"National Bolshevik . . ." Radek fixed upon the little mustache Reibnitz wore under his nose. "The most interesting hybrids are created in Germany."

"What appears to me to be just as important," Moor mentioned, "is that the Baron is, from his days in the Cadet corps, friends with General Ludendorff."

Externally, Radek found, Reibnitz exhibited little that was aristocratic; however, the narrow nose, the bow legs that betrayed the cavalry man, and the vowels fit the cliché.

In his circles, Reibnitz quickly assured him, there were quite a few gentlemen, active officers among them, who, like him, advocated for a continuation of the revolution in Germany, because the central task facing the German people, the renewal of its greatness, required the restoration of the productive forces of the country through their nationalization, which in turn could only take place with the assistance of the workers' councils and, consequently, in cooperation with Soviet Russia.

Radek felt the touch of fate almost physically. If this Reibnitz, who, no sooner had he met him, assailed him with such a program, wasn't a psychiatric patient into whose brain good old Moor had dripped that stuff, and if there were indeed German officers, perhaps even high-ranking ones, who thought similarly and were prepared to act, then the great dream that began in October of 1917, the fulfillment of which presupposed a German revolution, might yet become reality, although via a completely different path than the expected one: not through the proletariat, but from above, from this strata that, half intelligentsia, half state parasites, suddenly seemed to develop thoughtfulness, even a sort of conscience.

"Phase one," Reibnitz dictated, as if he were standing, a commander's baton in hand, in front of a map, "the factory councils must, even before nationalization, train the workers for the new mode of production. After that, and partly simultaneously, phase two, the radical moral transformation, in the course of which, through pressure on the part of the intelligentsia and the proletarians, now with a completely new motivation, the owning class will be forced to divest itself of its property, with adequate compensation, of course, a settlement, so to speak, to nobody's disadvantage; our revolution will be as radical as it will be bloodless."

"Hopefully," said Radek, thinking, a lunatic after all; and his sense of having witnessed the origin of a great turning point crumbled.

The Baron, too, apparently became uncertain. "Didn't your Comrade Lenin also speak in those terms when he outlined the tasks of the Soviet power?"

"I remember," said Radek, "a spring evening." And, as if to comfort him, he put his hand on Reibnitz's shoulder. "One of the rare ones, where all of Moscow has the scent of blossoms. But Lenin made his speech, you'll note, after," emphasizing the *after*, "we had seized power."

Reibnitz acted as if he had understood what Radek had meant, and maybe he even had. Then he looked questioningly at Moor, but did not wait for his reaction, saying instead, "I'd like to invite you, Herr Radek; you could stay with me, my house is spacious, and for me it would be most delightful if, in the case of the future of Germany and Russia, we could . . ." He couldn't think of a fitting verb.

" '. . . . . .' arrange it?," Radek proposed.

★

His salon—that's what he called the gray room, and the German press adopted the name—became an institution. Philips Price, correspondent for the London *Times*, came, and was even more interested in a discussion about the perspectives of the world revolution than in his, Radek's, experiences. Radek, however, tried to make it clear that the world revolution was more inhibited than supported by the ultra-left tendencies of the English Communists.

"If you wish," said Price, "I could inform Comrades Gallagher and Murphy of your criticism."

"Do that," said Radek, "but emphasize that these are my personal views; I'm not Lenin's representative on earth."

"No?" said Price. "One sometimes gets that impression." And offered him, as if it were a tribute, his leather pouch, in it the fragrant English tobacco.

And there appeared a certain Thomas, his ears protruding, light blue eyes bulging from under his carrot-colored brows, who introduced himself as a contributor to a Jewish newspaper in Vienna that Radek had never heard of, and who began to ask him what the situation of the Jews in Russia was like now, and whether they were really better off than under the tsar, or, as one often heard, worse, and what the Soviet government was doing to solve the Jewish question.

Something, Radek thought, wasn't quite kosher with the man. He glanced at the prison guard who had brought the visitor and—which rarely happened—had stayed in the cell, and now stood there with mouth agape; mere coincidence? Or as an official overseer?

And Radek said, "The Jews, Mr. Thomas? The Jews are condemned to suffer, whether in revolution or counterrevolution or whatever, until the Messiah will come riding at the head of the Red Army like our Budyonny, only the Messiah will drink and curse less and will be a more beautiful man than our Budyonny, with eyes that will shine like the candles that my mother, God rest her soul, lit on the Holy Sabbath."

"You're like a real poet, Comrade Radek."

"Life," said Radek, "is a poem."

"Only without rhyme."

"But with a rhythm."

At that, the overseer seemed to have had enough, turned on his heel, and retired. The man who called himself Thomas leaned over the table and said *sotto voce*, "I'm in Berlin illegally, but the publishing house I'm organizing here for the Comintern will be strictly legal, and I hope you've used the time in your salon, Comrade Radek, to get some writing done?"

So was this Thomas real after all?… Besides, there was something about the guy that tempted Radek to produce something in front of him. "In the last few months I've written," he enumerated on his fingers, "apart from a bunch of smaller things: an article on the tasks of the German Communist Party; a pamphlet, a vicious one, against Kautsky's 'Dictatorship and Terror'; a critique of the Communist left on the role of the party in the proletarian revolution; and a study on the development of world revolution and the tactics of the Comintern." He enjoyed Comrade Thomas's astonishment—if, as he hoped, he really was a comrade—and added, "A whole work, you might say, no?"

Then, accompanied by four solidly built justice officers, Herr von Ziethen presented himself.

"Ah, we meet again!" said Radek.

"You haven't missed me, have you?" Von Ziethen smiled, and told him in an emphatically binding manner that he'd now stayed long enough in the Lehrter Straße, and that he, the prisoner on remand Radek, should please get ready to vacate the cells that had so long been his home.

"Is it time"—Radek's breath came in bursts—"to go home?"

"Not yet, unfortunately."

"Where, then?"

Again the smile. "Allow yourself to be surprised."

"I"—by now Radek had gotten a hold of himself—"protest!"

"Really?" Ziethen, who had been honestly pleased to be able to break the news to his prisoner, sounded offended. "Why?"

"Because, Herr von Ziethen, I'm not able to pack an entire archive, complete with leaflets and and notebooks, on such short notice. For that, I need a certain amount of time, which you will please allow me."

The bonhomie that the investigating magistrate had displayed up to that point again gave way to Prussian sternness: the man was obviously under pressure himself. "I'm sorry."

"You wouldn't use force, would you?"

"Force!" mocked Ziethen. "We brought you here by force, we can take you away by force."

Radek grinned at him as if to challenge him. Ziethen beckoned to his assistants. Two of them clasped their enormous hands at the level of Radek's behind; the other two grabbed him and placed him on the improvised carrying seat, and so they transported him out of his refuge, into the hostile world.

13

"Welcome!" called out Baron Reibnitz.

Radek saw him standing there under the portico, raising his hands in greeting. One of the judicial officers folded down the steps of the barred green coach in which he had arrived; he got out, and now they, all four of them, moved in single file behind him through the hall, under Reibnitz's stag antlers up to the dark walnut guest room, three windows overlooking the Tiergarten, and planted themselves, fat and bow-legged, on the leather corner sofa.

Reibnitz had an anger attack. "Out!"

"It has," replied the one who wore a little mustache like the Baron's, "been so ordered."

Reibnitz disappeared. After a while, Radek heard him on the telephone, but only understood a single thing from the angry tirade: "Insolence!" Back again, Reibnitz announced, "I let Noske have a piece of my mind! What does that lout think he's doing, the *sozi*, just because we allow him to play army minister! And now, Herr Radek, if I may invite you to a quick bite."

Radek ate with an appetite, smoked salmon, fried eggs, white bread rolls, and talked to the Baron about the work that, he assumed, was waiting for him in Russia: a press agency he planned to organize for Lenin, with branches in Berlin, Paris, London. In the afternoon, his four guards suddenly toddled off and were replaced by a modest little man, almost a dwarf, who introduced himself as Commissar Schmidt, Gustav Schmidt, who, on his little chair in the vestibule, melted into the shadows. The next morning, over breakfast champagne—since he had been by Reibnitz, Radek had been served more alcohol than was good for him—his host asked if they could be joined by Colonel

Bauer, commander of the German artillery toward the end of the war and a close confidant of General Ludendorff.

At once, the Colonel entered, a man with feline movements and a velvety, entirely non-military voice, dressed in soft English tweed, and, no sooner had he taken his seat, he spread the word about the lively interest with which he and his great friend, General Ludendorff, had always followed Herr Radek's views, insofar as they were public and knowable.

Radek returned the compliment by expressing his appreciation for the power of a speech in which the general, under attack just recently in one of the Reichstag committees because of how he conducted the war, not only countered the accusations of the democratic representatives extremely effectively, but had totally destroyed them; which Bauer in turn acknowledged by pointing out that the said representatives had also argued too much like dilettantes and that in Germany, no state could be made with democracy, literally or figuratively.

Radek then wanted to know if the rumors were at all based in reality according to which a section of generals, inspired by Colonel Bauer's great friend, were heading for a *coup d'état?*

"Why, no, what's the point?" The Colonel squirmed like a cat whose back was being scratched. General Ludendorff thought it would be child's play to get rid of Herren Ebert, Scheidemann, and Noske; but then there might be resistance on the part of the workers, and at present it wasn't possible to govern against the workers; the workers would first have to be disappointed by this republic, then they would realize that Germany could only be saved by a dictatorship—a dictatorship based on a social agreement between the workers and soldiers.

Radek, who, theoretically as well as practically, hadn't thought much of bourgeois democracies and their social democratic appendages for some time—after all, who was running the interventions against the Soviets?—raised his glass in the direction of the Colonel and told him that he found Ludendorff's perspective at least worth considering.

"*Prost!*" said Colonel Bauer, and "*Prost!*" said Reibnitz, and the Colonel added that on this basis, *à la longue*, cooperation by the German officer corps with Russia and even with the German Communists was conceivable; after all, they were natural allies against the victorious Western powers.

Radek enjoyed the champagne on his tongue, which was dry with excitement: what Bauer was presenting to him was clearly some kind of offer of alliance, and the man seemed to truly believe that he, Radek, possessed some kind of authorization. A mistake, unfortunately, probably also favored by the ambiance in Villa Reibnitz, which gave his insinuations and allusions a completely different weight than they had in reality; if he didn't save himself as quickly as possible, he might get into hot water.

So he said, "Then, Colonel, let the General make his proposals openly to the German workers! And he'd have to negotiate with the Soviet government in Moscow…"

A clumsy maneuver, actually unworthy of him.

A cat's hump seemed to form beneath the Colonel's tweed; the ruffled hair and the sudden yellow in his eyes completed the picture. The guy hated him, everything else had been a masquerade; and he felt relieved when Bauer set his glass on the tabletop, stood up with a jerk, turned around, and left.

The Baron continued to be courtesy personified, but from that point on the conversations they had lacked the nice candor they had at the beginning, and Radek's sarcasm, when he did use it, sounded rather forced. Also, his inner tension, increased by the continued delays in his departure for Moscow, could hardly be controlled; he became irritable increasingly often.

Ziethen had let it be known that the stumbling block was the Poles; they refused Radek transit. Pilsudski had been one of his most personal enemies already during the time when he, Radek, had been close to the PPS, the old Polish Social Democracy;

such enmities are preserved over the years and spread in one's consciousness; and now that the man was tussling with the Red Army, victoriously even, and had appointed himself Marshal of Poland and was the de facto head of the new, albeit bankrupt, state, he had let the comrades in the Kremlin know that, according to the Treaty of Trianon, Karl Bernhardovich Sobelsohn, the applicant in this case, was no longer a citizen of Austria and certainly not an ambassador of any Soviet Ukraine, but, since he was born in Lemberg, now Lvov, was a true Pole, and therefore required Pilsudski's highest permission to cross the Polish-Russian front line. And now the gentlemen in the Foreign Office were trying to organize a flight in which he and a similarly endangered fellow passenger, the Turk Enver Pasha, would not touch Polish territory at all, but only the airspace above it; reasons enough to shake the composure of a man who had a lot behind him and who was drawn to his wife and, as he'd learned in the meantime, newborn daughter.

Furthermore, the constant comings and goings of his increasingly numerous visitors and their demands gradually became a burden on the Baron; Radek tried to limit their number, but often enough they came unannounced; the Reichstag representative Ernst Heilmann of the SPD, with whom he had already quarreled before the war, and who proclaimed in a stentorian voice that in Germany a socialist revolution was completely out of the question; Friedrich Stampfer, editor of the official party newspaper *Vorwärts*, who assured him that even in the event of an attempted coup by the right, the Social Democrats would refuse to enter into an alliance with the Communists, even a merely temporary one; and, brought to him by Rathenau, the aged Felix Deutsch, chairman of the supervisory board of AEG and one of the country's cleverest industrialists, who spoke rather skeptically of the possibilities for any economic order other than the capitalist one.

"But you do acknowledge," he said, disputing Deutsch's thesis, "the evolution of the savage in the primeval German forest into the director of AEG? How then, can you deny that a biped who has scaled such peaks could not reach still higher ones?"

Deutsch, who saw his ancestors in the hills of Judea instead, raised a prophetic hand. "At all times there has been a stratum of leaders and organizers; it's indispensable!" Reibnitz, mindful of his own standing, nasalized approvingly, while Rathenau, who was anxious to talk with Radek about future trade deals in case the Soviet power remained for a long time, tapped his foot impatiently.

When the two gentlemen from AEG had left and he and the Baron were sitting in the library with coffee and cognac, Radek surprised the Baron by telling him that he had found quarters which, although less comfortable than his rooms in this house, still relieved him of the feeling of being indebted to someone else, no matter how friendly.

Reibnitz protested; what an undeserved lack of trust; couldn't they have settled disagreements, which are always possible, together, rather than pulling up stakes? And who, then, was the happy new landlord?

Radek smiled. The Baron was taking the whole thing a little too tragically. It had all happened quite suddenly, a chance conversation in the shadows of the antechamber with his dwarfish guard, who, by the way, held the rank of police commissioner and was named Schmidt, Gustav Schmidt, and, being typical of the lower middle class, also had many things to report of high sociological value.

Reibnitz smoothed his little beard. And when, please, should the move take place?

"First thing tomorrow, would be best."

"Oh well then"—the Baron seemed really depressed—"have a pleasant final night in the Reibnitz house."

Radek escaped from the cushions of his armchair. He wouldn't find a piece of furniture like this, in which one disappeared in such a luxurious way, too soon.

★

In his own home, Schmidt was able to indulge his passion for potato pancakes even while on duty. He fried the grayish-yellow pancakes himself and cut them into strips, which, sometimes smeared in puree, sometimes *nature*, shoving them between his little teeth, a chain eater, so to speak, while the smell of the repeatedly used frying fat permeated the small apartment and rose unpleasantly to Radek's nose.

Sometimes Schmidt also brought Radek a plate of potato pancakes, along with a napkin of bright white damask, a last heirloom, he explained, from his mother's household, and Radek demanded to hear more about the old woman, and starting from her, who had sewn buttonholes for a shirt manufacturer until she went blind, the conversation continued, from which Radek, who had learned to listen, was able to extract a maximum of information about the situation of the working classes in Germany before and during the war, and about the police service of the young republic and the loyalties of its officials; and his dwarf's confidence in him grew so much that Schmidt was induced to procure for Radek a leather jacket and a Mauser pistol of considerable caliber from police stocks, at very acceptable prices.

Schmidt's attitude was also helped by the sort of people who, after Radek had moved out of the Reibnitz house, now came to his modest home to have long discussions with the subtenant, as he now regarded his private prisoner. He was instructed to take down the personal information of these people, and was surprised to find that they appeared, in dress and bearing, and presumably character, rather bourgeois, and in any case far less threatening than the Radek entrusted to his care, from whom surprises might still come: an escape attempt, perhaps, or a sudden appearance as the head of a Bolshevik putsch troop; but he preferred the better kind of visitor, distinguished from the other by attitude and manner of expression, and something more difficult to define: Rear Admiral Hintze, for instance, who, though almost as diminutive in stature as himself, especially impressed him.

But Radek, too, seemed impressed by Hintze, saying after the latter's departure, "Don't you notice it too, Schmidt, despite his petite figure, the power that emanated from that man, and his charisma, despite the immobile, almost Chinese face!"

The commissar compared himself to Hintze in the stained mirror he had hanging in the hallway: petite? He was used to mockery from Radek, but not such tones. And all of a sudden he remembered the word for the quality he had not been able to define until that moment: "Style! The Herr Admiral has style!"

Radek was amazed that the dwarf even knew the word at all in that sense, and attributed this to his own beneficial influence on him. "Style, yes, you could say that. After all, Hintze was an attaché to the tsar's court before the war, and therefore influenced by the old Russian ways. But I was even more interested in what he thinks today. He's worried about Germany; but so are you, Schmidt, only you don't own estates in Silesia like he does, with hundreds of Catholic day laborers, who, he told me, lectured him about the injustices of the capitalist order; they no longer wanted, they told him, to slave away as before, but rather to organize a new life, and that would then be the real revolution; and he asked me what I thought of such farm workers, and whether I believed that there could ever be such a revolution in Germany."

"And how did you respond?"

"What would you have told him, Schmidt, in my place?"

"*Herrgott!*" The dwarf jumped up. "My potato pancakes!"

When he returned from the kitchen, with a tray, on it two large portions, each with a blob of beet jam, he said, "Revolution? Here?" And offering Radek one of the plates, "A real, true revolution?... Tell the Admiral to give his day laborers better payment, and the church a nice donation; and that we, here, pardon me, Herr Radek, are not Russians, but orderly people."

Finally, it was said that an airplane would soon be ready to fly him and Enver Pasha to Moscow. But "soon" was an elastic term, and dragged on, and his patience was exhausted, and when even, conspiratorially, as they called it, Clara Zetkin and Paul Levi suddenly appeared at his door, he lost his temper and shouted at them and at his dwarf at the same time, who certainly wanted to see their papers, and the scene would have turned very ugly if Schmidt had not suddenly winked, "But we know each other, Frau Zetkin, and Herr Levi has also long been in our wanted books, in profile and *en face*; so come in already."

After this entrée, a touch of comedy—which Radek in particular felt—spread over the grave formulaic language of the "Theses of the West European Bureau of the Comintern on the World Situation and the Tactics of the Communists," to which the three of them now drafted their own theses; every tactic, they admonished their comrades, had to proceed from the assumption that a revolution on a European scale would be a process of long duration. And when Zetkin, the finished document in her pocket, emotionally clasped him around the neck, although he himself was equally moved, he was also overcome with laughter at the thought of the expression on Comrade Zinoviev's face in Moscow when he got to read this passage, and the hysterical tones with which Zinoviev would denounce him at the next meeting of the bureau after his—with luck!—return.

Yes, this return. Finally, provided the weather was good, the when and where of the departure was perfect, and the pilot had introduced himself: a young man with an open, clear gaze: in the last year of the war he had flown a Fokker, but the luck of taking an enemy out of the sky had never been granted to him. No harm would come to Radek from him—or would it? The boy also spoke too lyrically about the beauties of flying: the earth deep below, the curve of the horizon, the landing gear gliding over the towering white of the clouds, man's age-old longing finally fulfilled. And on the same day, the telegram, for the attention of Karl Radek, Berlin, sender a Captain Berner, Warsaw: urgent request, for safety reasons, notification of exact departure time and route of the aeroplane D-233F, signed, Berner, Ignatz—who was Berner,

Ignatz, where had he heard of him? Ah, one of Pilsudski's people, his head of defense, even. With that, the plan unfolded: to get him from the sky, alive, with the help of the youngster with the warm-hearted look; or dead, and at the competent foreign ministry, the gentlemen responsible would deeply regret the unfortunate accident.

"Schmidt!" he called.

Schmidt hurried over.

"Schmidt," said Radek, "see to it that this letter reaches Herr von Ziethen immediately."

The letter stated that he, Radek, believed that the investigating magistrate von Ziethen, as well as his office, would prefer that their former prisoner be returned to the Kremlin safely and in one piece, and would therefore allow him to travel by train instead of by airplane, despite the risk involved, and he politely asked Herr von Ziethen and his office to make the necessary arrangements.

Which they did.

In the meantime, he packed, four large suitcases full of everything he had been able to procure in the field of economic literature, and the socialist press, and, most dear to him, the writings of Albert Einstein, completely unknown in Russia at that point. His own belongings, plus a little jacket and dress for the baby, fit into a travel bag.

Schmidt and two other officials escorted, which was useful since they could heave his luggage into the compartment; then, as a representative of the Foreign Ministry, embassy counselor Hey introduced himself; Hey did not seem to particularly appreciate either his assignment or his charge, and showed it in unguarded moments. But first, since Radek's final release and the date of his departure had been made known to the press, Hey had to fend off the journalists who, along with Paul Levi and Clara Zetkin and the widow Bondy and Comrade Lina Becker, the innocent party responsible for his arrest, crowded Radek. Radek would not have been averse to an impromptu press conference; the embassy counselor, however, feared the public attention and dispatched the two broad-chested assistants of Commissar Schmidt against the noisy crowd in front of the compartment window.

The red-capped conductor raised the signaling disc.

Radek let himself fall into the upholstery and watched the steel posts slide by outside, slowly, then faster and faster.

★

The border station was called Prostken. There, the stationmaster handed a sealed telegram to embassy counselor Hey.

"From your ministry?" Radek inquired.

Hey made an effort to appear composed. "We're getting off here."

"The train isn't continuing on?"

"The Poles are taking you from here."

Radek moistened his lips. "That wasn't the plan."

The embassy counselor was already giving instructions to unload the luggage. Then Hey turned to his charge. "I had also hoped to have the pleasure of further providing you with my company. But," this while—indicating the telegram that he still held in his hand—"as I've been informed, my task has been fulfilled," and, thinking he knew what fears Radek was nurturing, "If you'd like, you may return to Berlin with the commissar and myself."

Radek grinned at him. "And disgrace myself for all time?"

"Let's go eat," Hey proposed.

The train station hotel in Prostken had been a dilapidated shed even before the war, and the war hadn't made it any prettier; but having seen the special carriage awaiting an engine on the Polish side of the tracks, the innkeeper had tied a white apron around his belly and stood in front of his door, and with numerous bows, he talked about how he had been expecting the gentlemen from the Inter-Allied Border Commission for a long time, and had prepared a meal for them which they wouldn't be ashamed of in Paris or London: "Non, Messieurs, Prostken won't disappoint you, and I graciously ask you to come in, your Lordships."

Radek decided to get drunk; what he had wanted to avoid, namely being left unprotected at the mercy of the Poles, was now awaiting him, and there was nothing left but to trust in the old Jewish God, whose existence had already been doubted by Marx and Engels and all the Enlightenment thinkers before them. The innkeeper brought vodka, contraband, and all kinds of wine; but the food was so fatty it soaked up the alcohol, and in Radek's brain only a pleasant whirl remained rather than the total stupor he had hoped for. He hugged Hey, who was sitting next to him on the right; he assured him that he would only remember him fondly when sitting in the lice-ridden Polish cell; and then to his left, he patted little Schmidt on the head and prophesied that he wouldn't have as interesting and entertaining a prisoner to guard again anytime soon; then he saw the train coming into the station from the Polish side in the last twilight of the afternoon, locomotive, tender, a carriage. Shortly thereafter, a tall officer stepped into the dining room, marched up to him, raised his outstretched fingers to the brim of his square, gold-trimmed cap, and announced, "Allow me, gentlemen, Captain Berner."

Radek's dizziness remained, the head of Pilsudski's military defense, in person, in order to take him off embassy counselor Hey's hands.

The trap shut.

Now they had been riding for hours over the flat, gray countryside; his flat, gray fatherland, Radek thought, his Polish one, for which he had been so enthusiastic as a boy, reading Mickiewicz and the other poets who sang of the homeland; and what did he

feel now, as he sat opposite Captain Berner on the dusty upholstery of the former luxury train car and listened to the music of
the cultivated Polish this man spoke?

But after a while even Berner fell into silence. Radek closed
his eyes. Everything had turned out quite differently than he
had feared: not a note of triumph, not even in the moments of
lowered vigilance, in Berner's voice: the captain showed himself
interested in his German adventures and his observations on the
mood of the German military and the conditions of the German
judicial institutions; but every time he, Radek, brought the conversation to the intentions Berner's superiors might have for him,
the latter's finely curved lips twisted in annoyance, until at last he
declared, "For your reassurance, Herr Radek, the Marshal has
decided that it is not worthwhile to expose himself to political
liabilities on your account."

By then they were in Bialystok, and the train stopped, and an
attendant in white linen livery brought bread and hot tea, and
Berner served the tea and said, "Now we part ways." Shortly
thereafter, he grabbed his little suitcase and left the compartment.

Radek thought about Pilsudski's remark. But Pilsudski had
always been an arrogant man, even more arrogant than Radek.
But if, thanks to Pilsudski's megalomania, he escaped imprisonment and possibly worse, so much the better.

Then someone yanked open the compartment door. Outside,
about ten men took up their positions with bayonets fixed. Then
orders: they spread out in the carriage. A younger officer climbed
into the compartment, threw his cap, belt, and saber on the seat,
gruffly declared that he was in command here; but no sooner had
the train started moving, he leaned toward him: "Don't you recognize me, Comrade Radek?"

In what fire, thought Radek, had he once again gotten into
from the frying pan? But the lad did not appear to wish to provoke him. "Once upon a time," he said, as if beginning a fairy tale,
"I was a guard in Smolny."

From the jumble of faces in his memory, this one emerged,

with the vivid dark eyes and the stringy hair and the brownish forehead; furthermore, the gate at Smolny and the man inside saluting, Dzien dobry, Towarzysz.

"And your name is Jasinski!"

"Jasinski, that's right," he confirmed, "and now a lieutenant of the Polish army."

"And how, Comrade Jasinski, did you end up in this army—from Smolny?"

The question wounded Jasinski's pride. He straightened up, his voice sounded harsh: as a Pole—and wasn't Radek one too?—there was only one duty for him, to fight for the freedom of Poland, even if it was shoulder to shoulder with the Bolsheviks. But now that a free Poland had risen from the ashes of war, he had joined the ranks where he could directly serve the fatherland: in the Polish army.

The old Polish romanticism, to which he had also once adhered . . . and its heroes in novels, to whom young Sobelsohn owed the name Radek. And said, "You're serving against the workers, Comrade Jasinski, both the Russian and Polish ones."

As long as counterrevolution threatened from Germany, Jasinski argued, no socialist revolution could be made in Poland; its newly won independence had to first be secured; but neither the Marshal nor the young Polish officers wanted war with the Red Army; they were particularly afraid that the Bolsheviks, as soon as they had won in Russia, would make common cause with the Germans, and then what, please, would be left of Poland?

Jasinski's concerns were uncomfortably close to reality, Radek thought, since he himself had spun the first German-Soviet threads in his Berlin cell, and in the Reibnitz house, and in the tiny apartment of the tiny Commissar Schmidt.

But he said, "Nonsense, Jasinski!"

However, the thought of his deceit sat agonizingly at the back of his mind during the entire rest of the agonizingly slow journey; soon the locomotive failed, soon the tracks were blocked; one lived on stale bread and here and there a goose stolen from a farmer, and wherever the train stopped there were military, the officers, a few English and French among them, most hostile, but also curious and always ready for debates about the Soviets and Polish independence, recent and already once again threatened, and how could he, himself a Pole, side with the Bolsheviks—well, he was a Jew, after all. Once, at a godforsaken station, Polish soldiers drove a squad of captured Red Army soldiers—ragged, starving, blood-crusted—across the track, and an old peasant woman pleaded to St. Michael the Archangel, "Children of a tsar, and strike each other dead!"

What fatherland, Radek thought. The workers have no fatherland. He had already preached this when the Cossacks rode through the streets of Warsaw and before he met Luxemburg for the first time, in the glorious year of 1905. And he said this now to General Sikorski, the commander of the staff of the front, who invited him from the train to tea at the station in Luninec.

Sikorski marched with a spring in his step across the carpet in his parlor car, lengthwise and back and lengthwise again; obviously he saw in him, Radek, someone with whom he could communicate, despite their antagonisms. "You Bolsheviks won," he lectured, "because in Russia the peasant allied himself with the worker. But in Poland"—he pounded his fist on the table so that Radek's tea glass jumped—"in Poland we won't allow that; we'll implement an agrarian reform ourselves!"

Radek held his glass firmly. "And your large landowners? What a clamor, what an uproar, when you start your reform! And your generals, in-laws and cousins as they are to your nobility, will rise up against you."

Sikorski tightened. "The interests of the state," he proclaimed, "stand above class interests."

Radek pondered: should he take the trouble to argue against the General's social theories; but Sikorski evidently thought he had now put forward his panacea for warding off a Polish revolution, that was enough of that discussion, and he allowed Radek to turn to more personal concerns, especially the question of when they intended to at last turn him over to his comrades on the other side of the front.

"Ah, again and again these delays!" complained Sikorski, and indicated to his underling to prepare him fresh tea and bring white bread and caviar from some secret stock; then, sliding the can generously across the table to Radek, along with the vodka, he said, "Not our fault, Towarzysz Radek; something is brewing on your side, and since, as long as you're with us, we have responsibility for your dear skin, we would like to avoid you entering the thick of battle unawares." He heaped the caviar on his plate and poured himself the Russian hundred grams, which he drank in one go. "But I offer to submit to Trotsky a telegram in which you suggest that he postpone his attack on this sector until we have shuttled you over to him."

"I don't know, General"—Radek blinked skeptically— "whether my person seems sufficiently important enough to Comrade Trotsky to cause him to change his strategic plans. But perhaps we can radio him that I am with your staff, and request notification of the place and hour of my transfer."

Sikorski was tired of the conversation. "As you wish!"

The snow upon which the pale moon drew the silhouettes of the shot-up trees, crunched underfoot, and somewhere behind him, where the patched track ran, the distant locomotive spewed its sparks to the sky.

Radek stumbled, panting, across the field where one offered a target to every lurking rifleman; he couldn't fall behind his companions. In response to his telegram, a Red Army commander had appeared the day before yesterday with the authority of the front commander to clarify the details for Radek's transfer; but where was the patrol that was to receive him? Very well, they'd been delayed; the rendezvous was supposed to take place sometime yesterday, but the artillery on both sides had been active until dark. Now, at last, there was silence. Lieutenant Jasinski, who had taken it upon himself to escort him to the very end, gestured to his men, "Hurry up!" Radek smiled to himself: a whole war had been stopped for the sake of little Lolek Sobelsohn.

Then, as if growing from the white ground, they suddenly stood there in their long coats, their faces masked against the cold under their red-starred, pointed caps: our own, Radek thought, our own again, after such a long time, and he felt a lump in his throat and a tear running down his icy cheek from under his glasses.

One broke away from the troops and came toward him. "Comrade Radek?"

"Yes," said Radek, "here I am again."

The man started to greet him, but before he had uttered two words, Radek suddenly started to laugh, completely senselessly; it was as if he were in a dream, the parts of which couldn't be fit together and everything therefore seemed to be distorted in the most peculiar way, and in addition Jasinski suddenly embraced him, and Radek thought, oh brother, what will become of you, and then he saw the Red Army commander's frozen face, but he didn't find an opportunity to explain the situation to him, because fraternization had come about, from both sides, and they were smoking machorka together and arguing. "Yes, we're proud of the eagle!"—"The little bird on your cap won't fly far, but our red star will shine over the whole world!"

Then the Red Army commander took him by the arm and pulled him along, and it was like an exodus.

★

The dream lasted a while.

There he was, riding in an armored train belonging to Comrade Aralov, the political commissar of the southwestern front. On the table, next to Aralov's pistol, were a piece of smoked fish and a crust of bread that smelled of bran, and under the table were bulging sacks. "This," said Aralov, "is our money, our new money," and showed him a fistful of bills on which the most striking thing were the zeros.

"You carry such high sums of money around with you?" said Radek.

"We're distributing the little ruble among the people," said Aralow seriously.

At the train station in Gomel, Radek paid a hundred rubles for a pack of matches, which shocked him. A detachment of student officers arrived in parade formation. They were, he learned, men steeled in many battles, who had come to honor him. Then Aralov disappeared with his armored train, and Radek got into a rust-stained carriage with slashed upholstery, but in it, oh wonder, oh joy, was his luggage, all four suitcases and the travel bag.

Beyond Gomel, the locomotive got stuck in the snow, and the railwaymen took him to the soviet of the next village, where a meeting was immediately called, at which he was, of course, obliged to speak. The chairman introduced him to the peasants as Béla Kun, the famous Hungarian internationalist whom the comrades in Moscow were eagerly awaiting. So Radek spoke as Béla Kun and received great applause. An old man gave him a pot of beetroot puree as a thank you and a snack. Then, on the train, which in the meantime had been dug out and was slowly rolling along, he fell asleep, the sweetish taste of the stuff still on his tongue, and woke up only when the compartment door was noisily opened and a voice he recognized as Bukharin's called out, "Such a day, and he's asleep, this guy!"

And then he was back at the Kremlin. There was the Redeemer Gate, through which they entered, and the Cavalier Wing, in which, as Bukharin immediately informed him, he had been allotted larger quarters as a recent family man, and on the broad sweeping staircase, going up, he nudged Bukharin in the side and said, "Do you think we belong here, really and truly?" and just at that moment he caught sight of Rosa, his Rosa, running toward him, the child on her arm. He took his cap from his head and moved his face close to the little creature, who looked at him from astonished eyes. "So small," he said admiringly, "and so thoroughly complete!"

"I wanted to name her Sophia," said Rosa, "as you wanted it, but at the registry, I don't know why, they registered her as Sonja, and now everyone calls her that. I hope you'll love her anyway."

"Sophia—Sonja," he said to the child, "which do you like better?" and felt the little girl's little fingers close around his finger. And to Rosa, "I can try to get an official correction for her."

Rosa smiled, a motherly smile. "Maybe we'll try for the revolution first—for her."

BOOK FIVE

We are puppets
and unknown powers
pull the strings.
In ourselves, nothing.

—GEORG BÜCHNER, *Danton's Death*

Lenin was ill, very ill.

And Lenin was the last among the heroes of the revolution in whom one could believe, the last who even now, in year VI after Red October, cared more about the cause than about his own influence and advantage. If you spoke with Lenin, you didn't have to fear that a second, secret meaning might be concealed in his words, or that he might interpret such a meaning into your speech. With the others—and he, Radek, was by no means an exception—one wasn't so sure on this point; a more or less subtle change had come over all of them at the same time as the power they were now allowed to exercise, which clung to them like mildew on the leaves.

At the same time, the harmful infection was probably at its lowest level in his own case; what personal power did he already have that was worth struggling for; after Balabanoff's resentful withdrawal, it was not he who was installed as secretary of the Executive Committee of the Communist International, but rather his traveling companion from the sealed carriage, Comrade Zinoviev, Grigory Yevseyevich, who sat and rearranged the leading functionaries in the Western European parties from top to bottom and bottom to top as he saw fit. His contribution to the preparation of the coming world revolution. To him, Radek, such games meant little. He had come to the conclusion, after intensive observation of economic developments in London,

Paris, and Berlin, that the capitalists had managed once again to overcome their crisis after all; even in Germany, a tentative stabilization was in the works, quite perceptible to the expert, precisely because there, the mark had fallen to a trillionth of its original value, and the printers of the central bank, simply by refusing to supply the daily tonnage of zeros, thus depriving him of his means of payment, had overthrown Reich Chancellor Cuno. When the common worker started to even demand that even his wage be calculated on the basis of gold according to the stock exchange index, inflation completely lost its appeal to the bankers and industrialists.

For the men leading Russia, whether they sat in the Politburo or in the Executive Committee of the Comintern, the famous ECCI, this restless activity in the West had something exotic about it; they registered it—if they were concerned with it at all these days, since quite different questions were at stake in Moscow and Petrograd—and analyzed it, but according to rules shaped by the classics of Marxism, and that had been expanded and substantiated in protracted disputes with Revisionists and other Deviationists; and they generally gave comfort and strength to the comrades in the developed industrial countries amid their turmoil, and funds, and directed them according to the experiences they themselves had when they were still a conspiratorial troop of rebels in an exhausted peasant country.

He was all the more astonished when a letter from Krupskaya reached him, not in the Kremlin, but in the editorial office of *Izvestia*; a still young comrade, according to the description of the post office resembling a peasant girl, had left it for him personally—"personally" was underlined twice. Speaking, wrote, Nadezhda Konstantinova, was difficult for Comrade Lenin, and Stalin, in his new function as General Secretary of the Party, had expressly forbidden visits to the village of Gorky, with the best of intentions, of course, so a little caution seemed appropriate. But Vladimir Ilyich had expressed an urgent desire to see Comrade Radek once again, and therefore, despite possible misgivings, she asked him to come to her husband's sickbed quite soon.

Everyone knew that Lenin, in order to take care of himself after his strokes, had been moved from the Kremlin to Gorky, near Moscow, where, with the window open, he could enjoy the oxygen-rich forest air in the park of the country house of a former factory owner. In the Kremlin, Radek reflected, the visit would have been an easy one, a few steps across the corridor in the Cavalier Wing, past the usually strictly locked door to Stalin's apartment; in Gorky, however, the undertaking required a great deal of forethought and organization.

The guards at Gorky were uniformed, but without any badges. The strongest among them blocked his way. Radek tried to push him aside; the man dodged and did not waver.

Krupskaya had stepped out of the house and stood there, helplessness in the look of her bright Basedow eyes.

"I've dealt," Radek said to the uniformed man, "with completely different guards, twice as wide as you, by God, fed every day on German sausage."

"Comrade Stalin has ordered—"

Radek interrupted him. "Can you read?"

Of course he couldn't; Stalin collected illiterates; they were more reliable.

Radek pulled a piece of paper out of his pocket, with scribbles on it. "It's written there, in his own hand: Stalin, Josif Vissarionovich."

"Vis-sarion-ovich," repeated the man, as if he was actually spelling it out. "Go ahead, Comrade."

"There, you see!" Radek boxed him appreciatively in the belly. "Competent, competent!" And to Krupskaya, "As the master, so his people. Still, one shouldn't underestimate the Comrade General Secretary."

By then, they were in the hall of the house, where several Impressionist paintings were hanging; the factory owner had had taste. Krupskaya stopped. "Perhaps first I should—"

"Better not. Is the doctor present?"

"No, but Fotiyeva is."

Fotiyeva, he knew, was one of the four secretaries who had the right to take dictation from Vladimir Ilyich. Radek knew her from the Kremlin: one of the overzealous ones. "Ilyich is upstairs?"

Krupskaya nodded and preceded him up the stairs to the upper floor. Her husband's illness, and probably her recent quarrels with Stalin, which were whispered about in the inner circle, had made her eyes even gloomier and her movements even more sluggish than they had been before.

The door to Lenin's sickroom was blindingly white, the baroque embellishments on it freshly gilded. Krupskaya knocked softly.

In the crack of the door, in a bluish pallor, Fotiyeva's pointed nose showed. "He's sleeping!"

A sound from the depths of the room, half a guttural moan, half a gurgling protest.

Radek pushed the door open, letting Krupskaya go ahead.

Fotiyeva screeched, "How could you...!"

"I can!" said Radek, and, following Krupskaya's footsteps, stepped up to Lenin's bedside, and realized that he had come to the wrong side of the bed: Vladimir Ilyich's right hand was lying there on the gray wool blanket, a crab-like animal with five legs that looked as if someone had wantonly trampled it; the left, however, was moving as if to signify to him: Come here! Come! Closer! Closer still!

Fotiyeva attempted to drag him away. "It's forbidden for Comrade Lenin to—"

Radek shoved against her lean chest; Fotiyeva staggered and backed away; he shoved again, suddenly furious, and again, until, squealing and croaking unintelligibly, she escaped through the still-open door.

The living half of Lenin's face showed unmistakable interest in the grotesque scene; his eyes sparkled as in his best days when he pulled the rug out from under his opponent with a well-placed point.

"What is it that is forbidden for Comrade Lenin?" asked Radek, and went to close the door behind Fotiyeva.

"It's forbidden for him to have conversations with strangers," said Krupskaya, "especially political ones."

"Even Stalin knows"—Radek carefully took his place at the edge of the bed—"that I'm no stranger to Vladimir Ilyich."

Lenin moistened his lips with an awkward tongue. "And what, if not politics," the syllables slipped into each other, he struggled for each word, "if—not—politics, should one talk about with old comrades?"

"To me, Vladimir Ilyich," said Radek, "you speak understandably enough."

Lenin placed his living hand on Radek's knee. "Germany? Tell me!"

"Don't you receive any reports?"

Lenin moved his head, tortuously slow, from side to side.

"But that's criminal!" protested Radek.

Krupskaya stroked the paralyzed hand. "The doctors warned: no excitement, absolutely none, after this third stroke!"

"Am I a vegetable?" Lenin clenched his living hand into a fist. "The doctors forbid me from thinking, and then they're surprised when I get excited! . . . So, Germany. What's going on?"

"All sorts of things have been set into motion there; and in our favor, many think."

"And what does Stalin think?"

"Stalin remains silent."

"Ach . . . And what do you think, Karl Bernhardovich?"

The patronymic crumbled in Lenin's pale mouth, which now stood half open in the bloated face. Radek would have liked to scream, but he didn't; he said, "You and I know, Vladimir Ilyich, in Germany the old norms taught to us by history no longer apply."

Lenin once again managed to form understandable words. "But when," he asked, "if not now?"

The same question, Radek thought, that he had so often asked himself in his political work, in Moscow, in Warsaw, in Baku, and in Germany. And what had he not done to advance things in Germany, even trying to establish a link with the radical right, calling in a public speech a provocateur named Schlageter—who had blown up a railroad train in the French-occupied Ruhr and had been executed for it—a brave soldier, albeit of the counter-revolution, and had referred to the riffraff of the Freikorps as wanderers in oblivion, tragic figures who could find a home among the Communists. But General Seeckt, now head of the Reichswehr and secret protector of the fascists, had found fat Ebert more acceptable than him, Radek, and put an end to the game.

"It distresses Ilyich," said Krupskaya, "that he can't intervene."

"We miss him; his advice, his guiding hand …" Radek interrupted himself; what was he talking about, as if he was already sitting at Lenin's grave! "How much, Nadezhda Konstantinova, does he know what's going on?"

"He knows that they're divided in the Politburo on all questions important to the future, and that Zinoviev, Trotsky, and Stalin are at odds over his succession. And he, he's not allowed to dictate more than twenty minutes daily."

"To whom?" That had come out too hastily. "Fotiyeva?"

"Her too."

Lenin cleared his throat. "Everything confidential—stay with—Nadezhda Konstantinova."

And the copies, thought Radek, who receives the copies?

Behind the forehead with the pulsing, brittle veins, his mind was at work. "The letter, Nadya, the letter, you know which—"

"You want him to read it?"

"Yes. Hurry up."

Krupskaya shuffled away. Then she returned, a red leather briefcase under her arm, which she carefully unlocked.

Radek held the folded sheet of government paper, usual quality, between the tips of his thumb and index finger. Explosives, he thought, this is what it felt like to handle explosives these days. "Should I really read it, Vladimir Ilyich?"

Lenin closed his eyes. "Please."

The letter contained, Radek soon saw, a number of characterizations, apparently written down for the use of a larger body, let's say, the Central Committee: characterizations, if one compared the names contained therein, of the candidates for the succession to party leadership after the foreseeable demise of the present holder of this position. He was tempted to put the letter back on the bed with the stipulation thank you, I'd rather not. There was special knowledge that, rather than being helpful to the person in the know, might plunge him instead into an abyss full of snakes. But curiosity prevailed, and a kind of serene self-esteem that the terminally ill Lenin had chosen him of all people from the inner circle to receive knowledge of his political testament, since that's what the letter was.

Nonetheless, he was startled as he read: Comrade Stalin, having become Secretary-General, has unlimited authority concentrated in his hands, and I am not sure whether he will always be capable of using that authority with sufficient caution. And a bit later: Stalin is too rude and this defect, although quite tolerable in our midst and in dealing among us Communists, becomes intolerable in a Secretary-General. That is why I suggest that the comrades think about a way of removing Stalin from that post ...

★

"And Germany?" Lenin couldn't be dissuaded from the subject. "The truth—about the—German situation!"

But what if, Radek considered, a copy of the secret letter had long been on Stalin's desk, thanks to Fotiyeva, who, having just read Comrade Lenin's observations on figures of the party and government, could calculate who among the half-dozen candidates had the best chance of becoming the new leader?

"Ger—many!" The paralysis began to act again, clearly audible, on the sick man's tongue. "Please!"

And what if, Radek thought, Comrade Stalin, through the same Fotiyeva, learned about his visit to Vladimir Ilyich? And about the red folder? And silently added two and two together? They'd never liked each other very much, the overly bright Polish Jewish boy and the Georgian cobbler's son from the Orthodox monastery school.

"Ilyich is concerned about the legacy." Krupskaya poured drops on a little spoon and fed them to Lenin. "What will become of the revolution? Into whose hands will it fall? How will it change, if, for years to come, it remains confined to a single country?"

Radek, who had never heard such thoughts, and formulated in such a way, from Krupskaya's mouth, listened up.

"But a German uprising, a victorious one," Krupskaya continued, "that would be like an elixir for Ilyich, and would make Comrade Stalin and his apparatus a subordinate figure."

Lenin, after swallowing the medicine, seemed to feel more comfortable and nodded approvingly. What insults, Radek wondered, must Krupskaya have suffered after the removal of her husband from power, so that she, the most benign of women, turned with such sharpness against anyone, even Stalin.

"Germany!" admonished Lenin, whose thoughts seemed to run only on this track, for the fourth or fifth time already.

Radek decided: the elixir. And even if the brew failed him, things couldn't get any worse than they already were now for Vladimir Ilyich. "I quote you, Comrade Lenin," he said. "When, if not now!—And I reply: yes, now. Not only because—and this is the news which made the comrades of the Politburo break off their vacation in the sunny Caucasus and hurry back to Moscow—not only because the new government in Berlin, under Herr Stresemann, has turned to the French and the English for help and is ready to sacrifice us for this help, and sacrifice the treaty of cooperation which it concluded with us in Rapallo, but because it can be expected that after all the strikes and the unrest in Germany, and the inflation and the unemployment, a revolutionary situation has at last arisen there."

He cast an appraising glance at the sick man: had he really followed his heated tirade? And did he believe him? Or did he distrust his, Radek's, sudden conversion from doubting Saul, always urging alliances, always thinking up new maneuvers, to fiery subversive Paul, who sneeringly disregarded all misgivings?

But Lenin had apparently understood him and had gained hope; instead of the deathly sad expression around the eyes that he, Radek, had already noticed at their greeting, the cunning wink of former times showed up again; perhaps Ilyich already saw the discomfort of Comrade Stalin, who had relied upon the mono-revolution, probably because he thought it was easier to control by a man endowed with sufficient energy; now Stalin would have to adjust to people and processes of which he was in no way certain.

"And you," asked Lenin, "will also—put that forward—in the Politburo?"

Radek hesitated. If here, in front of the sick man, he committed himself to the course of armed insurrection in Germany, but then, in front of the Politburo, in light of the overwhelming risk, he advised against the undertaking—how would he stand before Vladimir Ilyich or—if he should no longer be able to receive the last report of Karl Bernhardovich Radek, soldier of the revolution—before himself, when he brushed his whiskers in front of the mirror in the morning?

"As you know, Comrade Lenin," he said, "I'm not a member of the Politburo."

A despicable remark, Krupskaya thought, especially to her husband, who had always seen to it that Radek was called in to the meetings whenever the comrades dealt with the German question. "But surely," she said with surprising irony, "even if the comrades there don't love your cheeky remarks, they won't want to dispense with your experienced advice?"

He suddenly felt miserable. Unless the old Jewish God changed his mind, this was probably the last time they would see each other, he and Lenin, before they parted ways forever, and he was unable to summon up the human magnanimity that the hour demanded after all the quarrels they had had together and the crises they had faced together.

"I'm full of doubt," he said.

"Doubt?" Lenin turned his head, with effort, until he could look Radek in the eye. "Doubt, you? What should I say, so briefly before my exit?"

"Forgive me," said Radek. "I was always a fool."

Now, one was already used to the meetings without Lenin. The first few times, the empty chair had been a shock; but then, when the hope faded that Vladimir Ilyich would soon sit there again, slightly bent over as usual, and no one, not even Stalin, dared to occupy the vacant seat, some administrator gave orders to remove the chair.

Radek regarded the gap at the long table as an impiety; on the other hand, he said to himself, in the long run this chair without a person would have been an all-too-painful memento. And even worse, he noticed that at critical points of the discussion, he involuntarily looked around for the piece of furniture that was no longer there, as if a hint could still come to him from there, a late echo of words long since lost.

Trotsky spoke. There was, Radek noted, the same gesture, the same rhetoric as in Brest-Litovsk at the time; even the theme was similar, the future of Germany, and the inevitable German revolution with which Trotsky had already in such a fiery manner threatened Secretary of State von Kühlmann. And with equal fieriness he demanded, but now from the Politburo of the Russian Communist Party, that the leading German comrades, whose arrival in the Kremlin could be expected any minute, be given the unmistakable signal to go on the offensive at home.

"The German comrades," Trotsky's voice cut through the smoky air, "the German comrades will confirm that in Saxony alone there are fifty to sixty thousand class-conscious German workers, organized in units of hundreds and ready to march on Berlin as soon as our comrade ministers in the government of Saxony hand them rifles and machine guns from the armories of the local police; and we too, I tell you as Commissar of War, will not be lazy when the time comes to rush to the aid of the fighting German proletariat."

Trotsky took the pince-nez from his nose; his face had reddened. "Or should we wait," he asked, "until Ebert has consolidated himself in Berlin and first smashes our German party and then, Rapallo or no Rapallo, allows his Seeckt to attack us as the spearhead of the Western allies?"

Radek looked around the circle. Bukharin, his features still youthful, held back. Zinoviev, who as the top man of the Comintern, should have welcomed the long-awaited opportunity to prove his policy, did likewise. Was it because the call to struggle had come from Trotsky, and they feared being identified with his actionism? Or did they simply think it was too early in the morning to commit themselves yet?

"Well, Comrade Radek?"

He felt the piercing gaze; the brow was raised mockingly.

"What does our specialist for German questions think?"

"Since when, Comrade Stalin, are you interested in the thoughts of specialists?"

"Since we're being tormented with highly amateurish remarks. Or don't you remember, Comrade Radek, Trotsky's warning only recently in the Central Committee, of which you are a member"—this was already vicious, and Stalin paused; then he leafed through a notebook—"The leadership of the German party is good for nothing, it is steeped in fatalism and sleepiness, and further, Trotsky's own words, the German revolution is therefore doomed to failure . . ."

Trotsky jumped up, "That was in a completely different context!"

"But you were right, Lev Davidovich!" Stalin pressed his broad fingertips against each other. "I, too, believe that the German party is not ripe for seizing power, and any attempt to do so would lead to catastrophe."

Radek thought of the promise he had made to the ill Lenin. The terrible thing was, he also shared Stalin's opinion, at least in this respect. And not even Lenin's chair was still there, the empty one, to which he could have turned. And Stalin did not release him from his claws, Stalin was merciless.

"Well, Radek?"

But he was spared from having to decide, for the moment at least. A secretary appeared and announced that the delegation of the German Central Committee had arrived, and Kamenev, who was charing the meeting, interrupted the debate.

They left it to him to take care of the German comrades. He saw to it that they got something to eat and drink and informed them, as far as this was possible in such a short time, about the state of the discussions.

Ruth Fischer's bosom, he found, had increased in girth at least as much as her temperament had grown in passion since they met in his Berlin prison cell, and the pale, spongy Arkady Maslov, Russian by birth but already at home in Berlin for years, was visibly more than just politically dependent on her; Comrade Brandler, Paul Levi's successor as chairman of the German party and on its right wing, was obviously less susceptible to her charms.

Radek smiled at them all, quite the gracious host. Fischer immediately grasped the constellation in the Politburo from Radek's few hints and, washing down a piece of smoked sturgeon with a Russian portion of vodka, said that she and Maslov, and probably also Comrade Brandler, knowing what was going on in Germany, would support Comrade Trotsky one hundred percent; never before had the situation been so critical for the German bourgeoisie, never before had the working class been so eager to strike out as just now. Brandler could testify to that.

Brandler testified, somewhat too rashly, Radek felt. Yet Heinrich Brandler, the first true proletarian at the head of the German party, was rather someone who hesitated, averse to all risks. But he was now destined to become a minister in Saxony, and if the uprising succeeded, he would probably rise considerably higher still.

Accordingly, after the meeting had resumed and he had satisfied himself that Zinoviev and Bukharin, with due caution, of course, were also tending in Trotsky's direction, Brandler provided the information desired by the Russian comrades: Fischer even spoke of a bright future.

There was silence. Stalin tapped out his pipe. "You accept that, Radek?"

He had known that something like this was coming. And the familiar inner voice warned, you know the conditions, little Lolek, and neither Mama nor anyone else will be able to help you if you bear false witness now. But there was the spark of hope that kept Comrade Lenin alive; should he stamp out the spark? And should he really agree with Stalin, he of all people, and here of all places?

And maybe he'd be lucky, and the German uprising would succeed?

"We would," he said with mouth askew, "reproach ourselves forever if we failed to seize the revolutionary opportunity presented to us."

"Very true," said Trotsky.

"Good," said Stalin. "Then we request, Comrade Radek, that you direct the undertaking on site."

2

The name was a household word: Larissa Reissner. Trotsky had called her an Olympian goddess; Boris Pasternak, meeting her for the first time on the deck of a warship, the only woman— and what a woman!—in the midst of a crowd of red sailors, had been fascinated by her voice, which suggested a personality of a special kind. And Vadim Andreyev, the son of Leonid, the poet, had described how on the streets of prewar St. Petersburg, every third man stopped as if rooted to the spot when she, then still a young girl, passed on the sidewalk.

Strange, thought Radek: he alone, although he knew and appreciated much of what she had published, had never met her face to face; it might have been because she had been hanging around for so long on the fronts of the civil war, whether in Svyazhk, where Trotsky organized resistance against the Whites from his tank platoon, or on the ships of the Volga flotilla commanded by the massive Feodor Raskolnikov, her lover even then, and later her spouse; the story was still told of how she stood on the bridge of the minelayer *Pryktis*, side by side with the sailors, while the shells of the shore batteries howled around her head.

But he had always maintained indirect contact with her. A woman like her, beautiful, spirited, clever, and a Communist in a very demonstrative way, was too valuable to his work within Russia and outside of it for him not to have paid her the attention she more than deserved; and it was he who had launched the legend of Larissa the political commissar of the Baltic fleet, if not invented it, at least on the feuilleton pages of the European Sunday papers. And she had also directed the fleet, not in any kind of political function, but through her Raskolnikov, Fyodor Fyodorovich, who, appointed commander-in-chief of the Gulf of Finland, was still as passionately devoted to her as he was on the banks of the Volga and Kama.

Akhmatova, with whom Larissa had a poet's friendship, a rapturous one, had told him about the apartment in the Admiralty that the couple occupied; Fyodor, still the simple red sailor at heart, and she, with the refinement of the ladies of the finest Petersburg families. So there they were drinking tea from English cups, as Akhmatova described it, she and Larissa, in Larissa's salon, which was also her workroom: three large windows with a view of the Bronze Horseman, and below the windows, on the opposite side, far away, the Neva, which glittered in the evenings.

★

And now she sat there in front of him, in his paper-littered editorial room, one leg crossed over the other, the little hat slanted on her reddish shimmering hair, and acted as if her face were not the most extraordinary thing in the world, flat and sober as a postage stamp. You're not going to have your heart touched, he thought, by Madame Reissner; she's been through rencontres like this dozens of times, and expects from you the usual measure of compliments, no more and no less; so pace yourself. But he knew he couldn't quite control the lust that had suddenly taken hold of him; and even the thick glasses that had often served to camouflage his eyes wouldn't be able to hide the expression in them from her.

"Strange," he said, "that we've never met, you and I; yet, if I remember correctly, life offered us enough opportunities."

"Strange," she repeated, "on the way to see you today, the same thought occurred to me almost verbatim."

"Anyone who, himself a writer," he interjected, "makes the acquaintance of a colleague in the field through their verse or prose is likely to come closer to them than over dinner, or at a meeting, or even on the deck of an armored ship. And what you, in particular, have written, Larissa Michaelovna, makes a more lasting impression than even my best ever did."

"Very nicely said." She seemed genuinely pleased. "I, in turn, could enumerate some things of yours, Karl Bernhardovich, from which I've learned: precision of thought, sharpness of formulation, wit—wit not in the ordinary sense; wit as a weapon, and as an aesthetic pleasure. On my scale of values you are, and this is one of the reasons for my trust in you, one of the greats."

As much as her words flattered him, they sounded too controlled. "Reading most of what's printed in this country today, Larissa Michaelovna," he said, "I get as impatient as you do. Whatever the genre—the eternal empty phrases of revolution!"

"Intelligentsia!…" She shrugged.

"I know you have your reservations about your own people." He smiled. "Since you made yourself available to us, before Smolny, probably the most elegant volunteer of the Revolution, your literary hero has been the man with the calloused fist, the soldier, the worker, and the woman with the haggard features. All well and good. But I see more essential things in your texts, much more essential: moments from inner life, motifs, feelings, the description of which gets to the kidneys of even such a hardened guy as myself…"

Her face, he noticed, had taken on a different expression; her features had become softer and more open at the same time.

"I admit," he said, "I've tried to prepare for our meeting."

From under a pile of magazines and pamphlets on his work table, he pulled out a stapled booklet, recognizable as a product of War Communism.

"Astrakhan," he said. "I had no idea I would ever read from it, and certainly not to the author. Still, listen to this: 'When children die, perhaps their whole unlived life appears to them in the mirror of their dreams. In an agonizing hour, in a night of confusion and fever, they relive a whole life and give it up without regret, like a glorious garment worn only on a festive day and now discarded forever and with all its flowers and fragrances …' "

He stood up, approached her, took her head between his hands, and kissed her on the forehead.

They both remained silent. Then she said, "It's not true."

"What's not true?"

"I was warned about how ugly you are. And you even cultivate this ugliness, because you find it interesting."

"An ugly Jew, no? That's what they said?"

"Yes."

"So at least on that point I haven't disappointed you."

"But you don't seem ugly. At least not to me. If I saw you some-where, at a landing place on the river, for instance, among the porters, or in front of a tavern, your kvass in your hand, I would say, he has a story, and go up to him and let him tell me what he's done and experienced, and what he thinks and feels and wishes, and of the women he's had, and his views on the good Lord."

"And he would tell you, the sacks that I have to carry are heavy, and fate is heavy, and it presses upon my back, and what on earth do you want from me? You come to me like an angel, with your white feet on my dirty earth, just so that once, once in the course of my days, I may see something as glorious as you? Are you so generous by nature, or is it your curiosity? What in the case of one person are the hands coarsened by labor that impress you, in the case of another are perhaps the inner doubts, or the capac-ity for suffering that you find noteworthy. And either way, I can't do much for you: I can only try to help you in your expeditions into the human heart—and into its contradictions—so that you may find what in the end confirms you and me: that which is revolutionary."

She waited.

But he seemed to have said what he had set out to say, and in doing so had come close enough to her purposes and aims: so close, in fact, that she wondered, to what extent does this man read thoughts, or, if not that, then to what extent have I myself betrayed my thoughts to him?

"When are you leaving—and would you allow me to accom-pany you?"

So it's like that after all, he thought, and thought about how it would look, the scene at the Belorussian train station, he and Rosa and the little girl, and I'll be back soon and take good care of yourself, and next to him Larissa's suitcase in the care of Raskolnikov, who wouldn't miss the chance to take her to the train, this woman, radiant in splendor and beauty; no, they would have to meet somewhere else, perhaps in the train car after departure; but that wouldn't work either, they were, all of them, celebrities, and stood in the public eye, and the public would figure out everything worth figuring out; but then it occurred to him that Raskolnikov, Fyodor Fyodorovich, would fill the whole platform with the force of his personality, and leave no room under the dusty, smoke-filled station roof for the unworthy talk of functionaries and journalists.

"So when are you leaving?"

"What, in God's name, are you hoping to gain from this trip?" he asked.

"And what are you hoping to gain? You're not being sent as a tourist! Recently Tukhachevsky told me about the preparations he's making…"

"For this trip?"

"For this trip," confirmed Larissa. "And he quoted Stalin to me. He said that if we succeed in winning Germany this time, the center of the revolution will shift."

"Really?" asked Radek. "From Moscow to Berlin?"

"From Moscow to Berlin. And I want to be present for the event." She added, thoughtfully, "Maybe one should renew one's faith in the revolution from time to time."

"In Germany?"

"Don't you believe in the German possibility, Karl Bernhardovich?" And after a breath, "So will you take me with you?"

Life, he thought, had spoiled him with women, beginning with his beautiful mama, up to his Rosa and little daughter, and in between the others who had loved him, one night or a hundred nights; which of them had been the one that had told him: you possess the wisdom of love, and although you can't be trusted, not for a minute, one puts oneself into your hands without hesitation and feels safe with you, in warmth and security. That was her instinct, he reflected; women are guided by their instinct, and I don't know why it is that I have such an effect on their instinct, perhaps something feminine, familiar to them.

"This trip," he said, "is not without risk."

"At Kazan, behind the White lines," she said, "captured by the Cossacks, that was no stay at a spa, either."

"Think of Luxemburg," he said, "washed up on the banks of the Landwehr Canal. And you, Larissa Michaelovna, are infinitely precious to me."

"I," she said, "accept the risk."

He bent down and grabbed her hands, slender hands with beautifully shaped fingers. And thought: what are we talking about? It's all so simple: it's just that the lightning struck me. Why complicate it then? Why not just explain it: Larissa, Larissa, Larissa.

"But if it came to that," she said, "to the revolution in Germany—that would be, after all—correct me if I'm miscalculating—that would be, definitively, the new stage of world history." Her face lit up. "A new world, wouldn't it? And by your side."

Dear God, he prayed, please let me be wrong with my accursed doubts. Please don't let anyone destroy this woman's hope, no German general, no incompetent functionary, no stupid coincidence.

"We'll travel together," he said, "into this new world."

The act of creation of the new world, Heinrich Brandler—now the top man of the German party—had let him know, was to take place at the all-German conference of workers' councils in Chemnitz, but without him, Radek; his presence, Brandler had feared, would frighten the participants of the conference very much, and that was not wanted; too great an effort had been made for that, to finally push beyond the narrow ranks of the party into more representative layers of the working class: the trade unions would be represented at this conference, and parts of the Social Democracy, some of its right wing even, and delegations from factories and mines, and whatever other allies could be gathered. This was, he thought, in real terms Radek's united front policy, which he had practically imposed upon the Comintern and its head, Comrade Zinoviev, and Brandler planned to call for a general strike from the tribune of the Chemnitz conference: a general strike, however, under the conditions of the state of emergency that Reich President Ebert had proclaimed, and with more than one division of Reichswehr advancing on Saxony and Thuringia meant open insurrection and the beginning of revolutionary events. And tomorrow evening he and Larissa, disguised as a married couple, Nathan Fischbein and wife from Lodz, would meet Comrade Brandler in Dresden, at the Europäischer Hof.

Radek had chosen the route via Prague; a detour, but at the Czech border the German border police, alerted by the state of emergency, would hardly expect him. So they drove over Karlsbad, and he and Larissa decided to interrupt their journey here for the half day and night that remained until their rendezvous with Brandler; he knew the path along the Eger, which Beethoven and Goethe had already walked, there was a plaque in the rock with the poet's words; the little river babbled; and through the trees, the October sun cast spots of light on Larissa's face and shoulders, and her little boots brushed through the falling leaves …

He had fallen for this woman, her body, her soul, with his body and his soul. When she pressed him against her and they became one, he and she, one being, one thought, one blissful ache, he thought: life. Everything up to now had been a mere prelude, but this was fulfillment; if death came now, he, Radek, would say: d'accord, regretting the premature end of joy, but satisfied that he had received everything he had a right to demand from fate.

They set at the bank, the babbling water at their feet. He turned to her. "Happy?"

"And you?"

"I wonder," he said, "how is it, by what merit of mine, that this has been given to me, this night, these miracles."

"Just accept it."

"You are what I need," he said. "And will be what I need, not just this night: always."

"Really: Always?"

"As long as I breathe," he said.

"I've been thinking," she said. "about Raskolnikov and me, about you and me. Those are different planes. It's like the earth and the stars."

"And no collision?"

"No contact."

A leaf fell from the tree and fluttered to the ground. There was the farewell of the two couples at the Belorussian station: Raskolnikov and her, kiss and embrace, come back to me safe and sound. And his Rosa and he, kiss and embrace, come back to me safe and sound.

"Why don't you ask why I don't ask: what about your wife?"

A second leaf fell, and another, farther away. "Those are different planes," he said. "It's like the earth and stars."

"And no collision?"

"No contact."

3

Shortly after their arrival in Dresden, a second train came in on the other side of the platform carrying Lieutenant General Alfred Müller, commander of military district IV (Saxony); Müller had been the highest state authority here since Reich President Ebert had issued a declaration deposing the state government of Saxony, including its three Communist ministers, a few days earlier.

Soon, the platform, on which Radek had been looking in vain for a porter, was filled with military men of all kinds, whose metal ribbons and braids and cords lent a festive atmosphere to the whole confusion and turmoil. From the overly loud remarks of the gentlemen—which referred, among other things, to the woman at his side—he was able to infer that the General intended to stay at the Europäischer Hof on Prager Straße; the General preferred a decent hotel to the more Spartan conditions of a Reichswehr barracks, and Radek thought with discomfort of Brandler's feelings if he, coming from his factory council conference, then entered a hotel with such occupants to meet with his Soviet advisor.

But the appointment couldn't be changed; and besides, the whole thing had its good sides: the service there would be reasonably pleasant, and neither the political police nor Müller's own staff would suspect a Red Bolshevik like him, Radek, in a hotel where their highest boss was staying, and in the company of the wife of the famous Raskolnikov. And as for Comrade Brandler, Radek thought it would only be useful for him if he practiced moving inconspicuously near the armed forces of the class enemy, especially if the indications about the outcome of the conference in the little newspaper he had bought at the border station turned out to be true.

When he finally found a porter among the uniformed men on the platform and got hold of a cab for himself and Larissa at the station entrance, he also gave the Europäischer Hof as his address, thus rising visibly in the esteem of the coachman. Larissa found the room they had reserved from Karlsbad a bit too pompous, but that's how the bourgeoisie was, she said.

And soon Brandler also arrived; a bellboy announced him, which Brandler did not seem pleased about; he looked around shyly, but no one else was in the corridor, and the sight of Larissa in her negligee completely confused him. Brandler looked quite rattled and tattered; he had driven the bumpy road from Chemnitz, without stopping, in a defective rental car, and that after the nervous tension of the conference, and he now felt, he said, glancing at Larissa, as if Radek had suddenly transported him to another world.

Then he reflected and asked, "Where can we talk?"

"Here," said Radek.

Brandler hesitated.

"I don't think," said Radek, "that the military people in the hotel are watching us; they've only recently arrived themselves; and you can trust Comrade Reissner completely."

Brandler became embarrassed.

"Comrade Reissner was already involved in secret missions when you were just beginning your party work."

"How should he know that about me?" said Larissa. And to Brandler, "Wouldn't you like to freshen up a bit after your trip?"

Brandler nodded with gratitude and disappeared. Radek rang for the room attendant, who was momentarily breathless, even though ladies in this or that state of déshabillé were nothing new to him. Radek cleared his throat. "Coffee, for three. And the most recent newspapers, please!"

Brandler stepped out of the bathroom shortly after the waiter had brought what had been requested. Radek, no longer paying attention to his coffee, sat with the newspaper in front of him and cursed. Then he held the paper up in front of Brandler's noise. "There—uprising in Hamburg! Did you know about this or not?"

"Me? . . ." Brandler scanned the report. "No. Or maybe yes. But . . ." Brandler's face had lost all color. "Uprising in Hamburg . . . but that's impossible!"

"Sit down!" said Radek. "And report!"

Brandler slumped over. Then he giggled, and his giggles intensified, shaking him. "Misunderstanding . . . everything a misunderstanding. From the beginning, the whole idea . . . uprising, hah!"

Radek saw that the man was completely distraught. "What," he asked in a brittle voice, "did they actually decide in Chemnitz, at the conference of factory councils?"

Everything went wrong, said Brandler, a miserable scene. No decision had been made; they had simply dispersed. But at least he managed to keep party comrades together.

"Everything went wrong?" asked Radek. "Despite the thorough planning?"

"Everything!" said Brandler, panic now clearly in his voice. Everything. The united front, prepared for so long, had been shattered, his call for a general strike rejected by the majority of the delegates; his ministerial colleague in the government of Saxony, the Social Democrat Group, had even threatened to destroy the whole conference if he, Brandler, insisted on his motion after the advanced guard of the Reichswehr had already arrived in Dresden. But all the activity of the party in the districts, all measures and marching orders, and the arming of groups of hundred, would have depended upon the realization of the general strike …

"Why the hell didn't you call for it, then!" said Radek. "Even without the Social Democrats! Why did you get involved in this conference in the first place? Out of fear of your own courage? Whoever wants to make a revolution has to be able to strike out, even without uncertain allies! You had the weapons, you had the organization …"

He interrupted himself.

"You had weapons, right?"

Silence.

"Why were you even a minister in the state government of Saxony in the first place?"

"I tried my best. The others sabotaged it."

"And what did you decide that night, after your united front broke down and the conference of factory councils dispersed— you and the party delegates that you had held together, after all?"

"To maintain the party. And to call off the uprising! Completely! And to notify the districts accordingly, immediately and by courier."

"Hamburg too?"

"We sent three men to Hamburg with instructions: stop everything! But Thälmann, with his goddamned sectarianism and his me, me, me, seems to have struck out anyway and put his whole district at risk, as well as the whole party…"

"And you can't do anything, anywhere, to help Hamburg when they've already started out there?" asked Larissa. "No solidarity action? No partisan act? Not even a little leaflet?"

Brandler glanced at Larissa, helpless.

But he, Radek, Moscow's emissary and responsible in his comrade's eyes for the new stage of world history, sat pale and discredited under the wonderful eyes of this woman, failed by the tepidness of a short term-minister in Saxony and the adventurism of a would-be Napoleon from the docks of Hamburg.

★

Brandler declined Larissa's invitation to dine with her and Radek; he had, he said, already tempted the gods enough by entering this hotel at all; besides, he had a place to sleep in a Dresden suburb where he felt safer; and in Berlin he and Radek would know how to find each other again.

Then he fell into silence and stared at Larissa as if he were only now discovering her strange charms, but found her presence in the hour of his humiliation all the more incriminating for that very reason. Finally, since Radek made no effort to comfort him, he left.

Radek sighed and threw himself onto the bed. This was the catastrophe. As things stood now, defeat was already a fact, and defeat without a struggle, shameful. And they'd blame him for it, the comrades in Moscow, and perhaps they were right; he rushed forward, he, little super-smart Lolek, instead of letting the others make world history when they felt like it. And when he thought about it, he even felt himself partly to blame for the failure of the whole enterprise, although for other, historically justifiable reasons: hadn't he supported this united front policy that Brandler had failed at?

But he couldn't tell anyone all this, not even Larissa. Larissa sat down with him. "Too bad for you, Larissa," he said.

"I thought too bad for you!"

"Who knows how many more futile attempts the revolution will require…" And thought, oh poor you, there will be no revolution in this country that could remove your doubts, nor march columns, no proletarian Germans, as a subject for you. And then he thought of the gray, lifeless hand of Comrade Lenin, which had lain on the edge of the bed in the sickroom in the dacha in the village of Gorky, and sought to remember who it had actually been that morning in the Politburo who had driven him, Radek, into the situation in which he now found himself. Trotsky or Zinoviev, or even Stalin.

She kissed him, and he thought, to hell with everything that was bothering him, ministers and generals, functionaries, secretaries, the whole power-hungry horde.

Then her lips left him. "I'm afraid, dearest, we'll have to part."

"Why"—his heart faltered—"for God's sake?"

"Because I'm going to Hamburg."

He had feared this from the moment he had read the reports on the front page of the newspaper the waiter had brought him. The uprising had struck fear into the hearts of the Hamburg bourgeoisie, but had been de facto confined to less than half a dozen working-class districts; the rebels, initially equipped only with a mixed collection of revolvers and hand grenades, had unexpectedly appeared before daybreak in front of a number of police stations, had taken them by surprise, and had carried off the infantry weapons stored there. But that was all; the mayor and the police chief announced that the insurgents were being crushed by strong forces and that their action would therefore hardly spread to other districts of the city or to the shipyards and port facilities, let alone to other German provinces; moreover, police reserves and volunteer units as well as larger Reichswehr units were arriving to reinforce the forces of order, so that it could be expected that the Communist specter would be done with in the shortest possible time.

"And that's where you want to go," he said hoarsely.

"Yes."

"In order to write about it."

"Yes."

"What Comrade Thälmann has set into motion there is nothing but a heroic blunder!"

Larissa smiled. "A heroic blunder is still heroic—and more appropriate for writing about, than Comrade Brandler's retreat…"

The old Italians, thought Radek, painted such a smile, with such finely contoured lips; only, this smile wouldn't fit the gruesome subjects, nor the garish hues she would see in the shot-up streets of Hamburg's suburbs.

"And who was wrong?" she asked. "I came to Germany with you to write about an uprising; I did demand of you that it be a victorious one."

"But they won't print anything about a non-victorious one in our publications, Larissa. If you see what's happening now on the bloody pavement between the barricades in Hamburg, and then write it as you saw it, and someone prints it anyway—no, that would have consequences, consequences of a political sort, for those who set the game in motion, for Comrade Zinoviev, for example, or for Trotsky or—"

"—or Comrade Radek?"

"Him too."

Her smile faded. "Fine, I won't."

He took her in his arms. He had maneuvered himself, and Larissa, into a trap. How to get out again?

"Of course you'll go there," he protested with forced cheerfulness. "Only, I'd rather stick my own neck out for my foolishness." And thought, how noble of me; and feared that in the end he himself would have to censor away what she would write about Hamburg . . . And therefore added, "But please see, dearest, that your own head at least remains intact."

"Shall we go eat?" she asked.

Either the news from northern Germany had become known to Müller's staff, or it was simply that the gentlemen had found time to establish themselves in their rooms and were now resuming their routine: in any case, the previously so pleasantly casual atmosphere of the Europäischer Hof had become more military; not that the soft oriental carpets in the entrance suddenly smelled of boot polish; but the cute bellhops and noiselessly hurrying waiters who had previously dominated the scene in the hall and salons had been supplemented by the heel-clicking of officer cadets.

His Excellency Lieutenant General Alfred Müller and entourage entered the dining room. Radek watched as the man let his eyes roam until his gaze fell on Larissa; Müller's figure and physiognomy reminded him of the perpetually irritated General Hoffmann from Brest-Litovsk days; both men obviously came from the same stratum, upwardly mobile middle class, and therefore sought to appear all the more aristocratic. Müller now moved his head in Radek and Larissa's direction in a hint of a greeting; so Radek nodded too, just as politely condescending, noticing how Müller, before taking a seat at the long table reserved for him and his staff, sent an adjutant to the reception, and Radek surmised that at the moment Larissa was probably the main object of the inquiries that were being made, and noted regretfully how few opportunities remained for him to spoil the General's victorious mood, thanks to Brandler's pusillanimity and lack of risk-taking.

"Do you notice how they're staring at us?" Larissa asked.

"At you," he corrected. "You have to imagine what a rare phenomenon you are in the lives of these types. It's all right with me; I can disappear behind your splendor."

Larissa remained serious. "Aren't you concerned at all? . . . It would hardly be pleasant if someone suddenly found out who we really are and what brought us here."

Radek swallowed the rest of his aperitif, waited until Larissa had also drunk her sherry, and then turned his attention to his broth. "If I otherwise have little confidence in Zinoviev, his forgery workshop is first class. And Herr and Frau Nathan Fischbein of Lodz, traveling on business in varous European countries, not only possess impeccable Polish passports; an equally impeccable financial reputation precedes them with all the responsible German authorities."

She laughed. "Fischbein!—your invention? But you haven't

even trimmed your beard, let alone wear a cute blonde wig. All it takes is for someone to come along who knows you from the old days . . ."

"Larissa, star of my soul—you know I've always only led double lives. But whether Sobelsohn, Radek, Carlson, Childe, Porebski, Arvid, Struthahn, Parabellum, Bremer, and whatever else—I've learned all the names by heart—I've always remained little Lolek from Lemberg with his great longing for beauty and light…"

"Beauty," she said, "light . . . I believe I'll love you very much."

They had both had a bit to drink, just enough to at least partially blot out what was bothering them: political failure, with the sacrifices it would cost; Hamburg, and the separation that lay ahead of them; and the scene in the dining hall after the meal, running the gauntlet along the General's table, the officers following the passage of Herr and Frau Fischbein with lewd grins.

"Guys, disgusting ones, in whose presence you already feel sullied …" She pulled him to her. "What are you thinking about?"

"Not about this scum …"

She played with his unruly hair.

". . . nor about Brandler's conference or the Politburo." He took her hand and held it tightly, kissing her neck, shoulders, breast, stomach. "Forget everything except our feelings," he said, breathing harder. "Away with all that. And just the one thought: you, and what you are, and how you are."

Then, a pounding at the door.

"Open up!"

Rattling. Clank of the handle. Kicks against the wood.

A voice, outraged, "They're actually sleeping!"

Larissa whispered, "Police?"

"Unlikely."

She detached herself from him, took her handbag from the nightstand, and suddenly had a pistol in her hand, silver work from Tula, a delicate piece, with traces of use.

"Give that to me!" he demanded, and threw on his robe. "In a shootout you'll get the short end of the stick."

"You won't?"

But she let him have the gun. Outside, another screech. "Fucking around in there, huh? While Germany burns, huh, and the *Kameraden* sacrifice themselves! Open up, or there'll be trouble!"

Suddenly the latch gave way, the door flew open, in its frame a whole squad of officers in various stages of drunkenness.

Radek unlocked the pistol.

"Aäch, Fischbein!" bleated the one standing front and center. "And with his *schikse*. How about it, Fischbein—let us have a go, huh? A Jew might want to have a monopoly on socks and underpants for the army, but not on a woman, such a splendid one!"

A second chortled. "Up and at it! And don't be afraid of syphilis! As the Herr Chief Medical Officer said: do you want to live forever, dogs?"

And another, this one a few percent less drunk, clicked his heels together and saluted. "Pardon, *der Herr, die Dame*. We were looking for *Kamerad* Kinkel, Major Kinkel, and walked into the wrong room by mistake, idiocy in any case, military next to civilians, a man has to know where he belongs . . . !" The voice tipped over: "A Jew to the Jews, the *schikse* to a brothel!"

Radek had turned chalk white. He pointed the barrel of the pistol at the man and commanded, in sharp Prussian, "Dismissed!—About face! March!"

The officer's jaw dropped. But then he pulled his own revolver from the holster: the hammer clicked. Then there was shouting and yelling, general pandemonium. Radek saw the distorted maws, thought, how stupid, and, thank God for Larissa, and that you were granted that; and then: why don't you defend her, why do you stand there like a pillar of salt, shoot already, shoot already! But his damned hand was paralyzed.

Someone gently pushed him aside, tenderly, almost like a caress: Larissa.

Then she pranced two or three steps toward the gentlemen, stood there for a moment, sneering—and slammed the door in their faces.

For a while, they continued to rampage outside; then it became strangely quiet.

"That would mean it's over," she said.

He turned to her. "I bow, my brave one, to you. I, in contrast to you, was quite nervous." His laughter sounded hysterical.

She went to her dressing table and took a small bottle from it. "Cognac?"

They took a seat on the causeuse, a rare piece of furniture that Larissa knew from her apartment in the Admiralty, said "*Na zdorovie!*" and drank, Radek glancing at the door, her, at the window. "Nevertheless," he said, "we should have played it more like Herr and Frau Fischbein from Lodz: both squatting in bed, frightened, covers pulled up to our chins, and complacently laughing along with the guys at each dirty joke. But that's how they got suspicious. And even this toy." He weighed the little pistol on his flat right hand. "Was it at least loaded?"

In a single swift movement, she took the weapon out of his hand, aimed, and shot. The middle part of the folding mirror above the dressing table shattered; the shards flew, glittering dangerously, through the room.

After that, he had no argument left against her trip to Hamburg.

She didn't need him. She could protect herself on her own, and she was smart and experienced enough to do the right thing even under the most adverse circumstances. And he, whose photo—in profile and *en face*—could be found in every properly kept German police card index, would probably endanger her even more than she endangered him by her striking beauty or the way she moved.

What else could he do—the morning was already dawning between the window curtains—but tell her how much he cared for her: not that she'd be convinced; but did one always have to be able to provide reasons for each of his feelings that convinced the other? Perhaps he should simply tell her that he didn't want to part with her again, after waiting so long for her to come back into his life; but she would naturally ask back: why don't you come with me, even without a party mandate, if you want us to stay together now?

But she didn't ask the question, leaving him alone with his doubts of conscience.

And so, he defended himself without having been accused. "I fear that this Hamburg affair, the result of the ambition of a local functionary, will turn out to be more than just a lost battle in the great class struggle; it will prove to be decisive, the categorical turning point, the change from quantity to catastrophe, call it what you will. And I don't want to have to see it, I don't want to witness, without having the power to intervene and the corresponding authority, the beginning of the destruction of all our hopes."

Then he pulled the curtains aside. The incoming light drove away the shadows from Larissa's forehead.

4

No, he had nothing to reproach himself for: he had supported her plan, as far as that could be done from under conditions of illegality in Berlin, and had tried to put her in touch with the right people in Hamburg in time; but basically he was glad that she only got there when the uprising had already been put down. What could be more nonsensical than injury or even death in the last hour of retreat from a final, lost suburban battle?

She described this battle to him, according to the accounts she had received herself: when the signal came to end the fighting, it was not because the insurgents had been defeated, but because there was no sign anywhere of a general revolution in Germany or even in Hamburg; and when the comrades then retreated from their positions behind the hastily made barricades, or the blocks made out of human bodies in front of the entrances to the bridges, or the defiles behind the narrow windows in the winding walls, and over the peaked roofs, the way in other, rougher countries, partisans disappeared over the mountains, while the superiority of the police and Reichswehr—two to five hundred, heavily armed, against tiny squads of ten or twenty with rifles or pistols—while this superior force waited cautiously until, at last, an initial patrol had crept upon a quarter long abandoned by fighters, and the mass of uniformed men began noisily, hand in hand with informants, of which there were many among the population, to comb through the tiny houses of the little people and the gray, narrow tenements.

She had her notebook on her lap, but she rarely leafed through it, mostly to check some detail, a few remarks about the tactical situation in one of the three suburbs, Barmbek, for example, which she intended to write about in her reportage, or the face of a woman, aged far beyond her years, saying goodbye to her husband, who before dawn followed the order to the party soldiers' post, or the description of a wounded man whom the comrades dragged into the shelter of a house entrance. She carried most of it in her head, or, judging from the tone of her words, in her heart, and drew from it so that she must have quickly recognized her problem: the dichotomy, on the one hand, between the incompetence and confusion in the ranks of the German party, exacerbated by the faulty instructions of the members of the Soviet Politburo and the Comintern, the members of which were willing to sacrifice the German comrades for their own ambition—and, on the other hand, the necessity and inner compulsion to present what had happened in a way that would keep her readers' faith in the party and revolution, which had been propagated with such effort.

★

"Oh, Larissa," he said, thinking that the painful feeling in the area of his heart must be communicating itself to her as well. "But I warned you—remember?—already in Dresden. It was already clear that nothing would come of it. And you could have spared yourself so much suffering and annoyance, apart from the fact that every hour of separation is a loss for both of us, an irretrievable one."

"Surely you're right, dearest," she said, leaning toward him, and he thought, what's the use of all this talk, come into my arms, which makes considerably more sense.

"But I experienced so many important things there," she continued, "among the people, and learned so much in the way of new things that will help us later."

"Later, later!" He sounded irritated. "Does anyone know if we'll live to see this later, you and I?" And faltered: how did he arrive at this question, and at this moment? Wasn't Larissa in the prime of her years, and in the bloom of her beauty? He must, he thought, have endured more anguish for her after all than he had admitted to himself.

"For example, the barricade," she said. "I thought I knew pretty much everything about the meaning and structure of the barricade—from the history of the structure: the woman with the glowing face under the Phrygian cap waving the bullet-riddled banner, the student pressing his lace scarf on his mortal wound, the worker who had just fired his last cartridge…"

Ah, Delacroix, he thought; but she portrayed the scene with such uplifting temperament; continue speaking, Larissa, he thought; as soon as we're back home, they'll drive your romanticism out of you.

"Or ours, in 1917," she said. "But these, in Hamburg, were

different again. Maybe, I can imagine, the tactics of civil war depend not only on the historical period in which it develops, but just as much on the cities in which the people turn out to fight."

She speaks in almost finished texts, he thought. Only her pathos would have to be reduced by a certain amount, her high-minded prose would have to be given sober tones, which, through the contrast of content and form, would create the real effect; but that was already editorial work and would be easy enough to do.

She spoke to him of the city, which, like a freshly caught fish, still twitched in the net, and the smoke of revolution still hanging over it; or, another image, standing piled up like an ancient colossus, its huge legs splayed across the banks of the Elbe, that old, filthy inn for the hoodlums of the ocean. For kilometers along the water, nature was as good as extinct, and where a tree trunk had survived, it was more like a mast left over from a shipwreck. Two of these trees were particularly memorable to her, one at the pier, cramped and bent over like a woman fighting the wind; the other in front of the office of Blohm & Voss, the largest of the Hamburg shipyards. The shipyards, it should be noted, where hardly anything was stirring, while bloody fighting was going on in the suburbs.

Just as, by the way, business continued as usual in St. Pauli, and people continued to offer living flesh for sale in these alleys with unaffected simplicity; visitors came to look at the goods on display from one little shop window to the next; then they entered, in a more or less drunken state, to have the most divine of lies, love, acted out for them, and flying out after a while onto the pavement, accompanied by the noise of heavy curses.

★

So, the barricade . . .

Larissa was back on her subject; she had, probably remembering her time during the civil war, this interest in tactical questions.

The barricade had taken on a different function; it was no longer like a fortress wall between the guns of the revolutionaries and those of the government; in general, it no longer served as protection for anyone, but rather as an obstacle for everyone; now it was nothing but a largely permeable wall made of trees, beams, stones, overturned carts, concealing a deep trench from the armored cars of the government, the most dangerous enemies of the uprising. It was precisely this trench that was the purpose of the modern barricade, she instructed him; thrown across the street, it deprived the army and the police of a view of the real events behind the disheveled backdrop, drawing the troops' attention to itself, and serving as the only recognizable target; with its empty chest, it received all of the fierce fire directed by the government's forces against its invisible revolutionary opponents.

How wonderful, he thought, how passionate, and how tactically clever!—Only, to have to hear and recognize all this now, from the loser's perspective, made it seem doubly senseless; but she didn't seem to notice that; she was so immersed and absorbed in her insights and realizations that she wanted only one thing: to pass them on to someone whose mental world would be able to absorb and process it all; she forgot that her listener might never be able to benefit from it for the future; in order to learn from the course of history, be it an episode or an entire epoch, one had to be in a position to learn from it and then apply its lessons. But would he be left in such a position, or would he instead be removed from it as soon as possible, precisely because he had shared responsibility for the emergence of these lessons?

"Oh God," he sighed, "how stupid . . ."

She raised her head. "I know, dearest, I know . . . and all the victims, in vain . . . and how unjust it all is . . ."

"Continue."

He seemed to genuinely want to know, and not spare himself; he was someone who could abstract from his own person when it came to larger questions. "And another interesting thing emerged," she said, "a very novel change in civil war strategy and tactics."

She felt the gaze of his eyes; these minutes belonged, and would only belong, to him and her for all time, and it was up to her to bring them to life—whether or not one was aware of the irony that lay in a conversation between lovers about the technology of modern street fighting.

The workers, he lectured, had become invisible, elusive. They almost no longer fought in the streets, which they left to the police and troops. Their new barricade, with hundreds of secret passages and thousands of reliable hiding places, consisted of the network of working-class neighborhoods with their cellars, floors, and apartments. Every window in the upper floors was a firing post, every attic an observation post, every bed in every worker's household a sickbed, on which an insurgent could count in case he was wounded. This was the only explanation for the numerous casualties on the side of the government forces, while the workers, in the Barmbek district for example, had only about a dozen wounded and a handful of dead. The troops, however, had been forced to attack in the open street; the workers fought in their own homes. For an entire day, the Reichswehr's attempts to take Barmbek failed because of the widely scattered positions of the workers who, hidden behind shutters of some kind, chose their targets while below, the military's guns pelted the empty barricades with fire . . .

✳

The condition of the illegal apartment in Berlin, where Brandler had finally placed him and Larissa, contributed considerably to Radek's depression. He didn't believe that the worn-out bed and the broken chairs were Brandler's retaliation for the splendor of the Europäischer Hof in Dresden, which he had had to endure for an entire afternoon, and in the immediate vicinity of General Müller—the completely humorless man had no sense for such malice, and besides, he was clearly far too concerned with his own—and the party's—future to worry about personal acts of revenge; rumors were already circulating that Thälmann, the Hamburg party leader, was boasting of the dedication and strategic talent with which he had led the uprising, in spite of the most adverse circumstances, for which he was not responsible; now, in spite of the resounding defeat in his district, or precisely because of it, Thälmann was seeking to replace Comrade Brandler in the top position of the German party and was seeking the help of the comrades in Moscow for this purpose.

Brandler, Radek indeed recognized, had come to him out of his own insecurity, seeking consolation; only, he didn't know that the one from whom he was seeking consolation was as much in need of it as he was; so Radek said, "Let it rest for a while, Brandler; if we listen carefully now, both of us, we'll learn more, and more valid things, from Comrade Reissner's report than if we were to waste our time with our combined assumptions and hopes. Comrade Reissner has experienced more significant things in Hamburg than you and your entire apparatus, and she knows how to piece together sketches from small details that, taken as a whole, allow us to see reality. Please, Larissa."

"This," said Larissa, "has become known to me from reports by eyewitnesses. This happened in the large corridor in the Hamburg Rathaus, where the prisoners from the Schiffbek police station had been brought, in the last days of October, to be shown to selected guests, press, members of government: brought on heavy trucks, three, four, five layers of people, piled on top of each other like slaughtered meat, from which the blood drips down on those suffocating in the lower layers."

Radek saw Larissa leafing through her notes, apparently searching for a detail, a phrase; her mouth was contorted in pain. "They fought bravely and chivalrously," she read aloud, "a few against a superior force, and yet they spared their prisoners and released the wounded. But they were treated like cattle: the police and the Reichswehr trampled on their bodies with their heels, beating their skulls with their rifle butts."

"Larissa," he said, "enough."

She looked up from her notebook. "A filthy, bloody epilogue," she said, "and yet no soldier's boot will be able to trample the traces of the events of those three days in October in the history of the German workers' movement."

Brandler choked up, moved. These were his comrades, after all, and this young lady, whom he had initially assumed to be nothing more than a pretty traveling companion of Comrade Radek's, seemed to have considerably more substance after all, and her assessment of things would also lend a little historical weight to him, who was actually a simple person, upon whom they were all now heaping censure.

"There was this girl from Schiffbek," she reported quietly, "Elisabeth had been her name, they said, laying there in the long white corridor where the drunken soldiers ran gauntlets over the living piece of revolution they had captured, and people ran against the walls in pain and despair. Every quarter of an hour a new squad of military came into the room and pulled at her until she regained consciousness, to come at her again with curses and their rough hands. Communist whore! Red sow! And that went on until a sort of miracle actually happened . . ."

Radek looked at Larissa's disturbed face. What did it matter how much of her tale was fact, and how much of it was nightmare?

"The miracle," she said, "the voice suddenly, thin, at the same time non-human and prophetic, exclaiming: Rosa Luxemburg."

Radek felt a chill run down his spine.

"Yes," repeated Larissa, "Rosa Luxemburg. Thus spoken and proclaimed by the girl Elisabeth from Schiffbek, who squatted there tortured and humiliated in the whitewashed corridor in the Hamburg Rathaus. Of course, no one could tell anymore which of Luxemburg's words the girl spoke: only just Luxemburg; and that the people there began to listen to her, even the soldiers, even those very ones . . ."

"Comrade Brandler . . ." said Radek.

Brandler winced.

"I'm very glad," said Radek, "that we came to Germany, Larissa and I, even if it didn't do us or your party much good. For me, at least, there's been an arc from the time with Luxemburg to here and now."

He stood up, went to Larissa, took the notebook from her hands and kissed her fingertips.

5

The news of the failed German uprising had long since preceded them on the way to Moscow, and there, mixed with all sorts of rumors, it had been whispered through to the last corners of the last ministries and bureaus—how couldn't it, since everyone knew that the weighing of the various contenders for the succession to the dying Lenin was influenced by the outcome of the enterprise that had begun with so much hope.

Radek therefore took time—for himself and Larissa—to return; he could still prepare for the daggers already drawn for the ambush; and every day together with Larissa was a gift from the gods. But then the matter couldn't be postponed any longer; he also learned that Comrade Ernst Thälmann was already on his way from Hamburg to prepare the ground in Moscow for his own purposes. Perhaps, Radek thought, as he watched the snowy expanses of Russia glide past the window of the carriage, Larissa sitting opposite him, perhaps it had been a mistake that he had hesitated so long with the journey home; whoever wanted to keep his position in politics—and what else was left, once one had gotten involved in this business—had to be the first to arrive at the place where decisions were made, and the last to leave.

There she was now, his Rosa, the child in her arms, looking at him over the little head, saying, "No, nothing's come from Stalin, no call, no notice, written or verbal; were you expecting something like that?"

"No," he had to admit, "actually not."

He had the feeling that Larissa's scent still clung to him, even though after his arrival at the Kremlin, he had thoroughly soaped and showered himself off; and he thought, how is this going to work out à la longue? I can't and don't want to do without either my beloved or my family; well, the constellation was familiar, and not just from literature, and the favorable thing in this case was that none of the participants, including Raskolnikov, ever conducted their marriage according to the ancestral pious way of thinking; the revolution had developed its own moral code; but nevertheless, even the loosest form of cohabitation—and how long had he been living with his Rosa?—creates bonds that can't be dealt with capriciously without causing hurt; and forbearance and toleration are not synonymous with indifference, and reproaches, however silent, remain reproaches.

"Only Zinoviev came by," Rosa said, "the day before yesterday, and asked if I knew exactly when you were coming, and played with the little girl, knelt down with her on the carpet and pushed the cart with the little doll in it back and forth, and said, 'Call me Uncle, Sonja, little heart, Uncle Grischka,' and pulled a bag of candy out of his pocket for the child, real honey candy; the comrade who manages his dacha keeps bees, he explained."

Zinoviev, thought Radek—there already was the first of the pests waiting to pounce on him: how, please, did it come to the debacle, you can tell me, you can trust me, you'll need someone to stand by you when they begin to question you: everything was so favorable, the government in Berlin helpless, the party and the workers organized and ready for battle; why, then, when it was time for action, this strange restraint; and was there no one, except in Hamburg, who could have kindled the fire that was glowing there into a conflagration?... It would sound like that, or similar, and that was still the mildest version among the imaginable possibilities.

"And Béla Kun was here," said Rosa.

"Kun?"

"Yes."

Why Kun?, he thought. Kun, representative of the Hungarian party to the Comintern, had been living in Moscow since his expulsion from Hungary after the fall of the Soviet Republic and, proletarian victor in the making, had been spreading his professional optimism at every international conference, every meeting, every congress. But where did his interest just now come from?—Kun had hardly ever maintained close ties with him. Did Kun, who had the reputation of being a permanent failure, want to strengthen his self-confidence by trying to prove to him, Radek, whose political reputation also seemed to be endangered now, how much they both resembled each other, as well as their respective situations?

"Béla Kun," said Rosa, "told me to tell you that he's going to organize an evening in his apartment for Comrade Thälmann, and whether you'd like to be there—together with me, by the way."

"How kind." Radek's old cynicism rose in him like stomach acid, and he thought that people could not be thought low enough. But seeing Thälmann should be worthwhile: what role had he, one of the few genuine proles in the leadership of a Communist party, played in the Hamburg days, and how far had the uprising and the tactics, of which Larissa spoke with such respect, been his work, and how would he behave now that the comrades in Moscow were discussing the defeat from all sides and looking for culprits?

"Maybe I should go," he said.

"Without me," said Rosa. "I have a night shift. Take Larissa."

Radek looked at her: she had spoken without any emotion. "Whatever you say," he said.

★

Both Kun and Thälmann seemed to feel unsettled by Larissa's presence: yet the two were otherwise quite different from each other: Kun dainty and nervous, unable to keep his limbs still for more than a minute or two, and constantly trying, with some exclamation, a laugh, a cough, to interfere in other people's conversation, or even in their silences; Thälmann a mountain of flesh, a muscular one, with a head that looked as if the Creator, in shaping it, had been content with the crudest; and as head and body were, so were speech and thought: slow and awkward, with frequent pauses, of which it could not be said whether they were the result of thoughtfulness or of black holes in his brain; one generally had the feeling with regard to all his utterances that one had already heard them at some time; which didn't matter, since he didn't take the reaction of his listeners into consideration, if he noticed it at all.

"You were in Hamburg?," said Thälmann to Larissa, twisting his wide mouth into a kind of friendly grin. "Why didn't you come to see me?"

"Unfortunately, the comrades I dealt with there," she apologized, "forgot to mention your existence."

Thälmann coughed gruffly: that had hit him after all. Kun gesticulated animatedly. "I find it rather praiseworthy that the comrades in Hamburg don't reveal the names and functions of their leading comrades to everyone who comes along, not even to such a beautiful woman."

"Nicely said, Comrade Kun," sneered Radek. "The great unknown who pulls the secret strings from the shadows of illegality—only, he appears too often in the columns of the party press."

"That's in fact the difficulty for us," Kun countered, "that people like Ernst Thälmann are popular, and at the same time have to work in the background."

Larissa grew impatient. "If I couldn't meet you then, Comrade Thälmann, why don't you explain to me now the reasons for the defeat in Hamburg?"

Thälmann thought it over: the question couldn't be dismissed. Of course, Kun had told him on whose shoulders Zinoviev and most of the relevant people in Moscow wanted to put the responsibility for the disaster, and he had the perfect answers ready; but Reissner, who had gained civil war experience years ago, and with her journalist's eye had now looked around Hamburg herself, would hardly be satisfied with that. So he replied sullenly, "The reasons? The reasons for the defeat? Your friend Radek should be able to tell you better than I can. After all, he and Comrade Brandler, from whom our instructions came, were huddled together while we were at the front, in battle." And after a pause, "Alone."

"At the front," repeated Radek, "in battle. You. Personally?"

Thälmann remained silent. His blood pressure, suddenly rising, discolored his face. What had this unpleasant broad really learned in Hamburg about his participation in the fighting, and what part he had played in the leadership, and the part played by the other comrades?

Kun realized that the conversation wasn't going the way he thought it would. He jumped up and crowed in his Hungarian inflection, "That's not the point! The important thing is that Thälmann at least started the uprising, if only in Hamburg, while—"

He suddenly stopped.

"Whereas I concurred with Comrade Brandler, who stopped the whole damn thing."

"And that"—Kun hopped up and down with excitement—"even though your mission was to finally get the German revolution, long overripe, started."

"Under the conditions I encountered upon arriving, that would have meant the destruction of the German party."

"What's the saying in Germany," Kun crowed, "Better a horrible ending than a horror without end."

Just then, Kun's wife entered with a tray, on it, vodka and small glasses and a platter with Hungarian specialties. Thälmann turned to the refreshments. "I don't know," he said with his mouth full, "what the devil got into Radek that he allowed Brandler to call off the action. I, on the other hand, thought our revolution was worth attempting. He who doesn't dare, as we say, doesn't win."

Kun raised his glass. "Bravo! Lenin too, never hesitated when action was needed. And aren't we all, Radek included, disciples of Lenin?" And with one of his nervous laughs, "Only some have learned better from the master than others. Prost, Thälmann!"

That was rather cheeky, thought Radek. Kun obviously knew that there were people in the party apparatus who would try to conceal their own failed policy by unanimously sounding the horn against him, Radek; otherwise Kun, who had never been a model of courage, would have refrained from such jibes.

But Larissa thought it was time to protest. "Comrade Kun?" She smiled.

Kun smiled back. "Comrade Reissner?"

"Explain to me, Comrade Kun, what your services to the revolution consist of? You were defeated in Hungary, along with your party, and fascist terror now reigns in your fatherland."

"I'm not sure you can blame that on Comrade Kun." Radek now thought it would be a good idea to demonstrate generosity. "How far, and when, can the individual influence history at all? As far as the German revolution is concerned, however, I think I can say that it'll only have a chance again when Comrade Thälmann and his people have learned to deal with their Social Democrats without constant head-on clashes."

Thälmann, to whom dealing with Social Democrats appeared in any case to be nothing worth thinking about, crammed his mouth with stuffed paprika, and looked questioningly at Kun; who, in turn, knew that he would have to help the helpless giant out of the ideological jam if he didn't want Radek to prevail in the dispute. Kun therefore inquired mockingly, "And until Thälmann has learned to be gentle with the German Social Democrats, do we keep our comrades there on a leash and make them wait until Radek graciously allows them to make a revolution? Until forever and a day? What did Danton say, Comrade Reissner?

"*De l'audace, de l'audace, de l'audace!*" she answered hoarsely.

"Precisely the audace that Comrade Radek has demonstrated more of in his life than half the executive committee of the Comintern."

"We don't want to exaggerate," Radek said. "But you can take note, Kun, that by supporting Brandler, I've at least ensured that a piece of the German party will still be there for a next attempt at revolution."

"How nice!" said Kun. "How useful!"

Thalmann had stood up from his chair and looked first at Kun, then at Radek: then he reached for the bottle, poured himself a glass, and began to laugh noisily. Ho, ho, ho, ha, ha, ha!, and didn't stop, until Larissa took two steps until she stood right in front of him, and began to hammer on his chest, which sounded like a hollow barrel, and shouted at him, almost hysterically, "What are you laughing at, lummox, you clod?"

Thälmann grabbed Larissa's slender fists with his dockworker's paws. "It's a joke, girl!—a Polish Jew and a Hungarian one, getting into each other's hair, in Moscow, over the German revolution! Ho, ho, ho! Ha, ha, ha!"

BOOK SIX

We do all our work these days in human flesh.
It's the curse of our times.

—GEORG BÜCHNER, *Danton's Death*

1

It was no opera, although the performance took place in the red
and gold splendor of the Moscow Bolshoi, and the intrigues
contained in the plot would have been enough for more than
a musical drama, and the events not only on stage, but also on the
parquet and in the terraces, were followed by the audience with
the greatest excitement.

Among the stars, all of whom performed their arias and recita-
tives without tonal accompaniment, but often all the more shrilly
for that, Radek was indisputably the most respected. Certainly
others, the German Ernst Thälmann, for example, seemed more
heroic, and Grigory Zinoviev, whose somewhat soft face in the
limelight resembled a wax image, was more prominent than
Radek, and the speeches and interjections by which the great
man conducted himself therefore had more weight, but since
at the same time the smell of a Comintern official clung to his
words, the boredom they produced in the rotunda of the huge
house was predetermined.

One should have expected that boredom would be the last
thing that would come up today among the delegates to the
long overdue congress of the Communist International, who
had come from all over the world to learn profound insights for
their party work in their respective countries from the debates.
And indeed, there were a number of solo acts that had entertain-
ment value even for the more-hardened comrades: Thälmann's

performance, for example, who, in the glorious halo of the futile Hamburg uprising, made an ardent commitment to world revolution in his powerful dockworker's bass voice, or the prophecies of old Clara Zetkin, who, with her admonition to sober reason, even succeeded for a short while to curb Comrade Zinoviev's zeal to seem more revolutionary than he was, or the splendid demonstration of theoretical wisdom by Comrade Bukharin, who in a truly masterful manner demonstrated speech from both sides of his mouth and showed how, with the appearance of the most beautiful objectivity, the legs could be knocked out from under the intended sacrificial victim; nor were the many-voiced choruses, marked by loud dissonances, without charm, especially those of the Germans, who bore witness to the doomed split between the party left, under the passionate Ruth Fischer, and the more moderate ones around Comrade Brandler; a split whose consummation would only just barely be avoided in the days just before the congress, and then only by using political brute force against poor Heinrich Brandler.

And as always, thought Radek, there were those striking parallels between the factual contradictions of events on the one hand, and the animosities of the leading comrades on the other, and the various cabalistic philosophies, which were expounded by their opponents with a doggedness that indicated their secret pleasure in such pastimes—such as when Bukharin supported Zinoviev, lecturing at length about the united front from below as well as from above, and about united fronts of an honest and dishonest sort, the latter being only a political maneuver. He himself, Radek, as well as Brandler and Zetkin, on the other hand, endeavored to speak intelligently to all present, though without earning much applause; but it wasn't easy for many of them to accept in simple words the simple fact that the enemy had won the battle—planned as the great decisive one in the European class struggle—in October of the previous year, and that the party had failed to take part in this battle at all. And this against such a despicable opponent as the fat Social Democrat Ebert, who imposed a state of emergency on the Free State of Saxony, and then on the Reich, and for this purpose mobilized the entire soldateska of General von Seeckt and, as Brandler had shown from the stage of the Bolshoi, supplemented it with the fascists of the Black Reichswehr, plus the racketeers and swindlers who had shamelessly enriched themselves during the inflation that had just ended; plus that part of the German proletariat whose members were, opportunistically, simply glad that they had been able to keep at least one job amid all the turmoil, and now had neither the slightest interest in the theses of these Communists, nor in upheaval and civil war or even the dictatorship of their own class, but at most in the few bills of new money that they were paid at the end of the week.

Radek straightened up and looked from the red velvet-covered podium out over the crowd in the glittering rotunda; his eyes lingered on the second row in the middle of the parquet, where Larissa had taken the place he had given her and was now waiting for the things that would necessarily concern her too. Earlier in the intermission, as he stood in the gallery of the theater, surrounded by journalists and other curious people, she had forced her way through the crowd to him and had said, audible only to him, "Right after this they're going to slaughter you," and he replied, equally quietly, "The sharpening of the knives has been clearly heard." The solemn glow cast by the lighting upon the audience, and the inner tensions discernible on Larissa's features, caused her face to acquire a very peculiar expression which touched him deeply at just that moment.

Now he also noticed the pointed expression with which Ruth Fischer—as one of the more prominent participants in the congress, almost directly next to him on the stage—followed his gaze. She breathed heavily, and her plump bosom quivered, and he almost wondered whether there was perhaps a remnant of the flush he thought he had recognized in her when she had visited him in Moabit prison, and her little girl's admiration for him and his courage had flooded her heart; and was there, besides her instinctive jealousy of Larissa, a second motive for her new hatred of him? A kind of disappointment at the cowardice which, she claimed, had been the reason that he, together with Brandler, had kept the German party—with the exception of Thälmann's Hamburg, of course—from plunging blindly into the civil war the previous year?

"Earlier today," he began, "Zinoviev explained that after all, nobody blames Comrade Brandler and me for the fact that the party suffered this grave defeat last October. That, Zinoviev said, could happen to anyone."

"No," Fischer immediately butted in, "we don't criticize you because you were beaten, but because you didn't fight in the first place. Yet the situation was revolutionary to a boiling point, and the party stood ready, and still does today, to lead the masses into struggle!"

"Ready! Ready!" Brandler, on the parquet, had leaped up. "Without a military organization? Without weapons? I ought to know! After all, you sent me into the government of Saxony to procure the weapons for the uprising, and in my brief time as minister, I did nothing but search for these arsenals—unsuccessfully."

"The workers would have already obtained weapons!" Fischer called out. "They did in Hamburg, too!"

"Comrade Reissner!" said Radek "Larissa Michaelovna, you were in Hamburg…!"

Larissa was startled, but got hold of herself and stood up. Camarade Treint, the Frenchman who was presiding, already raised his hand defensively, but then, facing Larissa, lowered it again. "I bow," she said, "out of feelings of solidarity and admiration, before the few hundred who fought in Hamburg. But there were fourteen thousand party members in Hamburg at the time, and only these few took part in the uprising. The rest preferred to walk past them every morning on the way to work, fists clenched, of course, but in their pockets."

"Because they had no weapons!" roared Thälmann.

"Exactly my point," said Radek, "and whoever's thinking of Petrograd in 1917, forgets that at the time, there was still a war going on and an army was shattered and weapons were lying around everywhere in abundance…"

He cleared his throat; and now, the conclusions. "Comrades, whoever says we'll get the weapons 'then' underestimates the technical preparations for an insurrection, and whoever claims out of the blue that the task of the Communist International is to organize the revolution tomorrow morning, or the day after tomorrow at the latest, and that we'd be ready at any time to lead the masses into the struggle for full state power, is simply spouting phrases."

A pause; rhetorical.

"What are you waiting for then, Comrade Fischer, if, as you say, you're ready every day to take up the struggle for power?"

Fischer started up.

"No," he declared, "it's also true for Communists that one isn't prepared to do what one doesn't have the strength nor the means to do." And to everyone, "and as for the boiling point in Germany, the revolutionary one, not just Comrade Fischer and other comrades on the ground, but also we here in Moscow—including myself—have misjudged the entire German situation, and have accordingly planned wrongly and set wrong dates—and I myself went to Berlin as a result, on behalf of the Comintern."

He contemplated. Yes, he had been uncertain at the time and had vacillated: to strike out or not? But there had been poor Lenin's final wish and the pressure of the Troika, the emerging new leadership of the Russian party—Zinoviev, whose political actions and speeches were still influenced by the sense of guilt that had clung to him since 1917, when he betrayed the date of Lenin's revolution to the bourgeois press; and the much more popular Kamenev; and Stalin, the coolly calculating one, whose name, despite his ever-increasing power over the apparatus of functionaries, both in Russia and in the International, had not even been mentioned at this meeting today.

★

"My friend Zinoviev"—he turned to Larissa, with a smile that the audience might also interpret as addressed to all of them— "whenever Zinoviev and I argue, we explicitly assure each other of our friendship. Zinoviev, then, has said here that I'm of the opinion that the world revolution has paused, and that we'll see in fifty years. Zinoviev exaggerates. But unlike those of you who declare that nothing has changed after the great defeat, and that the proletariat still has full confidence in its own strength and in the wisdom of the party, I submit that at present, we may be in a trough between two revolutionary waves, and should use this time to prepare ourselves for the next historic occasion, and not to convince ourselves that we're riding the crest of the wave, when in reality a torrent of dirty water is being poured over our heads."

Zinoviev was annoyed. "Very funny!"

"Radek's jokes," Fischer supported Zinoviev loudly, "are known to be the best. Maybe we should make him editor of a humor magazine, under strict political control, of course, instead of allowing him to spread, as in *Pravda* recently, the notion that the German revolution is already done for."

"Enough!" Radek struck the podium with the flat of his hand. "I demand of communists, even you, Comrade Fischer, that they recognize political reality, and behave accordingly."

Larissa applauded, but only a few joined her; it had become too clear in the course of the congress on which side of the argument the weight of power in the Party and the Comintern would fall.

★

But, he promised himself, he would still tell them the truth. Zinoviev and the other grandees, even Trotsky, who had just appeared in one of the boxes, apparently, after urgently questioning him yesterday about the reasons for the German defeat, in order to have his revolutionary illusions reinforced today by the day's speakers. After all, it wasn't just about Radek's personal fate; it was also about quite decisive struggles over political direction. And besides, since Trotsky had placed his bets on an early world revolution, the German party's shameful retreat before the armed power of the bourgeoisie was highly detrimental to his chances in the intrigues over succeeding Vladimir Ilyich—while Zinoviev, as well as Fischer and Thälmann, and probably Stalin too, hoped that the new constellation would be advantageous to their position in the grand tussle between functionaries.

"We've suffered serious setbacks," he began again, in a lapidary manner, "in Germany and elsewhere. But whoever would blame Zinoviev for this is a fool. Brandler, and to some extent, I, made the decisions on the ground."

Larissa pulled her head between her shoulders. He gave her a comforting nod: self-criticism, like the sacrifice of a pawn in chess, could sometimes be useful.

And continued: "I don't underestimate my possible theoretical mistakes; I'd just prefer it be proven to me that my decisions were erroneous before being slaughtered."

Zinoviev remained obliging. "Your merits will save you from beheading, Comrade Radek. And your talents, for oration, mainly."

"Thank you," Radek replied. "But now to fundamental matters, to the German question, which you claim, Comrade Zinoviev, is solved by the establishment of the new party leadership in Berlin. The German question is defined by the degree to which this new party leadership, promoted by you, Comrade Zinoviev, and the majority of the Executive Committee of the International, represents the entire German party."

He stroked his beard, in which more and more gray threads had recently begun to appear, and said: "The fact is, comrades, after the inflation, which completely drained him, the German worker is now receiving real money again. It's filth, but it no longer melts between his fingers. He can buy something with it. And what could we observe in the last German elections? That where unemployment decreases, so does the Communist vote."

Now that, he thought, fit little to Ruth Fischer's idea of the future of the German and Russian parties and her own role in it. But he'd offer her, and the delegates suddenly listening in the house, something even better.

He pulled out a newspaper page, small format, from his pocket. "*Der Funke*," he said without particular emphasis. "Party newspaper in the Berlin suburb of Neukölln. The article from which I'd like to read to you, if I may, is by a young comrade, Thomas his first name, who, I am told, serves as secretary to Comrade Fischer, in her Berlin office…"

"I'd like, Camarade Treint," Ruth Fischer announced to the chairman, "as soon as Comrade Radek has finished, to be allowed to speak as long as he has."

"Do that, comrade," said Radek, "do that. The Comintern practices, wherever possible, democracy. But to the matter at hand … Why, just now, writes young Thomas, this passivity in the party? And answers: not only because the comrades are breeding rabbits in their garden allotments, not only because they want to go for a walk in their new shoes, not only because spring fever is stirring, not only because of their long unemployment and because the situation is rotten, but because a whole lot of our comrades no longer understand the tactics by which we seek to wage the struggle against capital …"

Radek raised his head. "So it's not just philistine stories, but political differences, but they don't express themselves in discussions or functionaries' meetings. Our Comrade Ruth Fischer's secretary describes it like this: the comrades no longer openly confess what they think, but simply declare passive resistance, stay comfortably at home or in their garden allotment and, without the slightest remorse, put the party's circulars in the oven, because—because everything is nonsense after all—because, as they say, Det ja doch allet keen'n Zweck hat."[3]

His Berlin dialect was almost perfect. They grumbled in the German delegation, and from the grumbling, noisy protest emerged.

But Radek was undeterred. "And how," he read in a sharp voice, "are the meetings? How do the comrades behave there? The majority declare with honest conviction: oh, quatsch, we run there and listen to lectures we've heard a hundred times before, about the united front policy as a synonym for the dictatorship of the proletariat, or whatever, and then we run home again."

He turned with an ironic shrug of the shoulders to Zinoviev, who had spoken a long time on precisely these views of the dictatorship of the working class and how to bring it about the day before, and then quoted Thomas further: "We'll never achieve anything that way. Nor will we achieve anything if, in the factories or on the streets, we present the workers with long-winded resolutions on this or that issue, or call on them to hold demonstrations or counter-demonstrations. Why, they ask, don't our leaders put themselves at the head of the demonstrations? And suggest that it would be better to do 'something real'... One can't shake the suspicion that these comrades are always thinking only of the others, who are supposed to do 'something real'..."

He broke off. He saw there was concern in Larissa's eyes; she knew, and he knew, how little this reading of young Thomas's observations fit into the concept of the congress organizers. But that was precisely why he had to end now with a bang—a weak exit would have been the absolute political end.

And said: "Comrades! This article in the small Communist paper from the district of Neukölln confirms what I myself experienced when I was in Germany the last few times, and which you can read in my report from that time: that a part of the membership of the German party, the anonymous ones, namely,

---

3. Translator's note: Berlin dialect; "There's no point to any of it."

without rank or influence, who are supposed to take care of the striking and demonstrating and in the end also the shooting, that they stand almost in a kind of class opposition to their new party leadership. And here lies—indeed, Comrade Fischer!— the German question for the international workers' movement, and here Zinoviev and the executive of the Comintern should begin probing."

2

The closing session of the congress had been memorable for various reasons.

First, because he had been allowed to participate, even though he no longer held an official position in the Comintern, he, one of the co-founders of the Third International. There were whispers. One didn't know on that last morning at the Bolshoi: Was his presence in the building, despite his new status—which was less than that of a messenger boy in Zinoviev's office—a sign of a budding tolerance, or was this something like a collective bad conscience on the part of the grandees that was being expressed, or was he being flaunted: Look, this is what happens to whoever kicks against the pricks.

Second, because as he sat there for the last time in the illustrious circle on the stage of the former court opera of the tsar, he suddenly became aware that he had reached a turning point and that from now on his fate would take a downhill turn, steeply or less steeply, to God knows what depths—unless he decided to switch out a good portion of the principles by which he had lived and thought up to now, and with them, probably also many a friend and comrade-in-arms with whom he had stood side by side over the years.

And third, because at this congress, despite all the radical talk by Comrades Zinoviev and Fischer and others, a turning point quite similar to his own had occurred in the development of the revolution in Germany, in Russia, and elsewhere: so that he was overcome with astonishment at the linking of the personal failures of little Lolek Sobelsohn from Lemberg with the great events of the world.

But his entrance had already been dramatic enough. Whether he had been looking for Trotsky in the vestibule, or Trotsky had been looking for him, they met there in any case, and after a few words of greeting, Trotsky indicated with one of his imperious gestures for Radek to join him. Which he did; and no sooner had he entered the interior of the theater, following at Trotsky's heels, than he saw, half concealed behind the red silk curtain of one of the magnificent boxes, Comrade Stalin, who seemed to have decided to finally consecrate the congress with his presence; and in Stalin's shadow, uniformed to seam, button, and piping like Lev Davidovich, only clumsier, Voroshilov, Stalin's confidant in the Red Army and presumptive successor to Trotsky in his office.

Voroshilov crowed, "Ah, here comes the lion—Lev—including his tail!"

So it had come to this; a nitwit like Voroshilov was allowed to crack jokes about him in front of people who knew him as a clever and discerning comrade—and, moreover, in front of Larissa—and rage seized him, and he stepped out into the light behind Trotsky, shouting, "Better at the lion's tail than in Stalin's asshole!"

It was as if the bystanders had had their breath taken away. Radek felt the devious look that Stalin usually hid so carefully, and he understood the fear that even a Lenin had of the man in the final days of his life.

The phenomenon wasn't new, he had observed it often enough: the sudden fall from the heights, caused by one's own fault or by circumstances that seemed to have conspired against the unfortunate, or both: and then the nothingness—the daily routine, to which one was, physically as well as psychologically, accustomed, before it could take place; the intellectual world in which one had previously moved, and, involuntarily, still moved, had become a hollow shell, and the only real business left was the attempt to convince oneself of the reality of the state into which one had fallen, the devil knows how.

As mentioned, the phenomenon wasn't new to him; however, up to now it had always affected others, whom he then also, if it was possible, inconspicuously gave aid to: a few rubles here, a little package there, with a book or a bottle in it, to let the poor wretch know he wasn't completely forgotten. But he, Karl Radek, he had assumed, was too experienced and cautious, and too clever, for such mishaps to happen to him; and if he was forced, as the profession sometimes entailed, to risk his position and reputation, he had at least understood how to keep his risk to an acceptable ratio to the possibility of success.

This time, however, he realized in retrospect, he had had no chance at all; everything and everyone had united against him; they just needed someone on whom they could place the burden of their own misjudgments and bad decisions in order to be able to hold their own on the slippery ladder, or even to climb it one or two steps.

He found himself alone. When, ever, had he been alone recently, alone with himself and his thoughts or, what was even more precious to him, with Larissa? Every such precious hour had cost him cunning and planning in advance, and how often had it eluded him just before its fulfillment—a hurried article, an urgent correction, or some busybody's request for information that would supposedly not brook any delay.

And now the silence. No more calls to someone who still had a telephone with a direct connection to the government on his desk. The silence of the two typewriters, which tugged at his nerves more than the hectic double clatter. No impromptu conferences with members of soviets and commissars, with embassy counselors and delegates of the most exotic foreign bodies and with representatives of organizations and parties. One could enjoy the silence, certainly. But then, by leaps and bounds, the memories began to torment him, the images without context, the questions without context and consequence.

He paced back and forth on the trampled carpet, or also in circles. He had not acquired any treasures, no paintings, gold coins, or antiques, and the furnishings of his apartment were less than luxurious. His pants, hardly ever touched by an iron, flapped around his ankles, the pockets of his jacket, battered by the bundles and newspapers he carried in them on other days, imparted a sort of clownishness to him; in the end, they had all laughed at him at the Bolshoi; an evil, almost threatening laugh.

He shooed all that away: he would, he decided, use the time, God's most precious gift. A book. He would write a book, the story of a revolution that was also his own; who, if not he, knew about its turmoil and contradictions, who, if not he, would be believed, here in Russia and beyond its borders?

He sat down, opened the notebook, bad, gray paper: it was a gray story, illuminated only here and there by glaring, flickering flames. And where should he begin? Through whose eyes should he look at it, through whose brain explain it?

... The voice! The accent!

"Am I disturbing you?"

Radek turned around. "I don't have any appointments."

And thought, if only the guy smoked better tobacco; Stalin's sense of smell had probably been corrupted by the multitude of holy scents he had to inhale day after day in the monastery churches of his childhood, and he therefore didn't know what he was inflicting on his surroundings; or he knew it only too well, and thus demonstrated his power over people.

Stalin sat down next to Radek's desk. "Since we live in the same building, I thought an informal visit might be possible, and perhaps even useful." He pulled the leather pouch from the breast pocket of his litevka, opened it thoughtfully, pointed to Radek's pipe stand with his broad fingertip, and asked, "Would you like any?"

"Thank you." For his part, Radek slid a tin can with English writing on it across the table and offered its golden contents to the uninvited guest. "I prefer mine."

Stalin turned up his fleshy nose at it. "I don't know the foreign varieties. Ours are enough for me." And said abruptly, "I've made sure, of course, that nobody will bother us."

Radek confirmed, "One can't be too careful," and thought, while he stuffed his own pipe with feigned equanimity, the old bandit, how many of his guys has he placed around my door; and silently compared the encounter with encounters he had had with Lenin, especially the one when, with the dying man's shaky signature, he learned of the latter's fears about the abuse of power that the new General Secretary would exercise, and then, in the next paragraph, his suggestion to the Politburo that the comrades should think about a way to remove Stalin from such a position of responsibility. And had Stalin now come to hear from him, the heavily beaten one, how much he knew about such internal matters, and what exactly, and to offer him a deal?

But Stalin blew a thin stream of smoke through his nose and remained silent, content. The man, Radek thought, clearly enjoyed unsettling his respective counterpart; a primitive psychology, yet probably successful among the people in the apparatus, whether party or government, from whom he drew his ever increasing power. Finally, Stalin nodded meaningfully. "You know, Karl Bernhardovich, my private hobby—the study of people and their relationships to each other, and their ambitions, strengths, weaknesses, and considerations of how best to use them for the benefit of socialism."

What wonderful frankness, thought Radek; but this just showed him how sure Stalin thought he was of Comrade Radek after his fall, which Comrade Zinoviev could not have brought so smoothly across the stage of the Bolshoi without the express approval of Comrade General Secretary. And he thought, now it's coming: confidence for confidence, Comrade Radek—what did Vladimir Ilyich tell you then, eh?... and then his offer.

But it turned out differently, and quite surprisingly. "On the basis of this favorite pastime of mine," Stalin continued between two clouds of smoke, "I'm aware that the Party and the government simply cannot afford to let somehow like you, with so much knowledge and talent, enjoy the pleasures and comforts of rural life in some dacha, in the company of one of Russia's most beautiful women, even, while the international proletariat is shedding its blood and sweat for the world revolution."

"I thought, after the German defeat, you're betting on socialism in a single country?"

"And what are you betting on? And on whom?"

"You'll forgive me, Josif Vissarionovich, if I don't make a commitment right here and now."

Stalin laughed. "Knowing you—and I've been watching you—you can't resist playing with fire."

"But I can tell you one thing, Comrade Stalin," Radek reached for his notebook, noting on its front page, in neat script, Fundamental Principles, "that I'd rather go into an Arctic mine than do or say things that I can't reconcile with my political conscience."

"My way of thinking entirely!" Stalin's thick brows touched each other; so Arctic mines frightened Comrade Radek. And said, "I conclude from your words, Karl Bernhardovich, that we can make use of you again?"

"I'm a Communist, Josif Vissarionovich, and a member of the party." Radek curled his lips. "Still."

Stalin tapped out the pipe on the heel of his boot. The "still" wasn't lost on him, any more than the reference to the mining industry in the polar zone had been; but he preferred not to respond directly. Then he slid the pipe into his breast pocket beside the tobacco pouch. "I hope you'll understand that we can no longer use you in German affairs, in the near future at least; but how does China sound?"

China, thought Radek. If they let him take Larissa ... And China had its charms. As one of the Comintern secretaries, he'd heard a lot about China, and occasional visitors, such as Comrade Dalin, Sergei Dalin, had told him: in China there was more excitement than anywhere else in the world; in China the revolutionary element was interwoven with the colors and forms of a truly ancient culture; in China, even if the Politburo didn't want to admit it, the basic rules of Marxism had only the most limited applicability.

"How does China sound?" he repeated. "A Communist, Josif Vissarionovich, goes where the party sends him."

Stalin's facial expressions, Radek had noticed over the years, were rather monotonous; but now the skepticism was unmistakable. "Don't panic, Karl Bernhardovich," he said. "We don't plan to ship you off to Peking or Canton. You'll stay in Moscow, and serve your way back into Comrade Zinoviev's good graces as a well-behaved school principal; and there'll probably be a place in your school for the lady of your heart."

And with that, he stood up, and in an almost military trot, plodded toward the door. Then he waved again at his new ward. As if he were an ape in a zoo, thought Radek, receiving his piece of sugar.

She warned him: he should restrain himself, for God's sake, and not trust any of them and their words, even if he thought they were, for once, up to no evil.

For he was already at the top again after his conversation with Stalin; they can't get along without me, he said to her, without my oversight, with my experience, my knowledge, Larissa dearest, they grope around as if in a maze.

"What maze—whoever has power just declares the greatest insanity to be the norm and, that's the craziest thing about it, people even accept it, or at least they pretend to."

He laughed. He felt flattered that this clever, creative woman, who certainly had her own style, was increasingly succumbing to his diction, adopting his view of people and things, and his form of irony. Here, however, she insisted on her position: "With Stalin, always look for the most evil motive possible; he is selfishness personified. And if he picks you up after letting you fall, and puts you back on your feet, ask yourself: what does he hope to gain?"

"He's a small man, you know," said Radek, "who struggles tremendously to walk in a great man's boots. So he wants to use me as a crutch. Lenin, he thinks, already used me in that way. He did, but like a Lenin, with critical distance. And now that I've fallen deeply, he wants to pick me up, Comrade Stalin; I can be had cheaply, he believes, and would obey orders, if only to enjoy his patronage . . . daring combination, eh?"

"Did he actually say something like that?"

"He's crude, a crude peasant. But he's not that crude. But I saw how he appraised me: like a Gaul at the horse market."

"Nonetheless," she said, "or precisely for that reason: protect yourself, dearest."

Since nothing happened in the next few months to indicate that his combination would soon be realized, he did what Stalin had indicated: left his wife and little daughter in the Cavalier Wing of the Kremlin and went to the dacha of Comrade Joffe—who had been devoted to him in friendship since Brest-Litowsk and remained loyal to him even now—in order to enjoy there, in the company of one of Russia's most beautiful women, as Stalin had disapprovingly remarked, the pleasures and comforts of country life. But he still trusted Stalin's words to the extent that he carried a suitcase full of literature on China: geography and history, economics, social affairs, characteristics of warlords and revolutionaries, both often the same person, and reports from the Comintern archives: the latter, even read in context, were so scanty and contradictory that he wondered how comrades working in the field could ever distill a coherent policy from them.

And it was only natural that for all the really existing differences, he drew comparisons between Germany and China, and the dependencies of their respective Communist parties on the Russian one; Larissa sat there by the crackling fireplace, her pretty feet in elegant slippers on the hand-embroidered footstool; and he imagined the lumps of crippled bones that a woman of her standing would have displayed there in China, and shuddered.

"They'll need a long time," he said, "to extricate themselves from their past."

"And us," she asked, "how long will we need?"

He added a piece of wood, a few sparks flew up. "What do you know about Sun Yat-sen?"

"He's the Chinese Lenin."

"You could put it like that, to simplify. And like Lenin, he died recently. And his successor in the party he created, the Kuomintang, is General Chiang Kai-shek."

"At least they already have a successor there," she commented suggestively.

"But he has serious competitors. And every one of them possesses his own territory, and his own army. And additionally, there are the Communists of different varieties."

"And that's where you're supposed to get involved," she said doubtfully. "When do you expect they want to send you there? First school, then praxis, or what? In any case, please, arrange for me to come with you; I want to write about it."

But her tone didn't sound as confident. He glanced at her. "Nothing is definite yet, I told you. And there's no school at all yet. Just a high-sounding name that someone came up with, Sun Yat-sen University."

"And who came up with it?"

"The people's worthy inventor of names, Stalin."

The more he read about the history of Soviet-Chinese relations, the less clear everything seemed to him. On his walks with Larissa on his arm—not that he was much of a walker—he tried to figure out the basic facts that made up the whole puzzle.

China, fact number one, was a semi-colonial country. Which meant twofold oppression of the people, twofold exploitation: first, by its own bourgeoisie, its own lords, who had their wealth in their own enterprises, their own land, but at the same time also acted as agents and representatives of foreign investors; and second, by the foreign imperialists directly themselves, who had a foothold on the coasts of China and also owned their concessions and special territories in the interior of the country, and outside those borders their banks, railroads, shipyards, trading houses, as well as corresponding shares in Chinese enterprises. Yes, there was even a separate trade union of Chinese workers in foreign companies, one of the largest and most radical, by the way.

From all this emerged fact number two: the dual face of the Chinese revolution, brutal and fearful at the same time, and the ambivalent attitude of the Chinese propertied classes and their officialdom and military. For they, who sought as best and as vigorously as they could to break up the feudal structures, of which there were still enough in the vast country, and who strove to get away from under the domination of foreign capital, at the same time already felt threatened by the lower strata of the people, who had paid the main blood toll for the rather incomplete freedoms that the revolution had brought, politically, economically, and in general.

"China," said Radek, "is stirring up the entire Politburo, Larissa. It is, you'll admit, a special kind of pleasure to sit here in the countryside and watch them quarrel: Stalin, who no longer has any use for revolutions elsewhere because he wants peace and quiet for socialism in a single country, is suddenly in favor of the united front with the Kuomintang in China, the same united front whose German variant, there with the left Social Democrats, the same Stalin strictly rejected; Trotsky, who sees his permanent revolution, beautiful as the dawn, already rising off the waters of Canton, attacks Stalin—in front of the whole assembly, imagine—for his kowtowing to Chiang Kai-shek, and insults the Comrade General Secretary as the gravedigger of the revolution; Stalin, in turn, threatens Trotsky with expulsion, storms out of the meeting, cursing, and orders the Chinese Communists to submit to the discipline of the Kuomintang in accordance with his new united front, and forces Zinoviev, who is very uncomfortable with this intervention by the supreme leader, to admit Chiang to the Executive Committee of the Comintern as a member with a seat and vote. You see, Larissa, it's time for us to return to Moscow."

And in fact, the next morning one of the Central Committee's long, heavy limousines arrived, its chauffeur delivering two envelopes to Radek, one containing his certificate of appointment as rector of the university named after Sun Yat-sen, the other a letter from the editor-in-chief of *Izvestia*, containing a request to him to write a series of longer articles on foreign policy topics; these would be specified in both cases.

The chauffeur stowed both of their suitcases and Radek's hastily assembled papers in the luggage compartment; Radek made himself comfortable in the back of the car next to Larissa, and a feeling of happiness flooded through him when he saw the finely carved profile in the light of the sun's rays slanting in between the birch trees. He smiled at her: "Is this victory?"

She stroked his hair. "Whatever it is, you'll have to pay for it."

3

University!... either one didn't take the whole thing seriously—one had to hibernate somehow until better times came along—or one saw in the matter, as remote as it seemed, a real task, to which one devoted all of one's energy and thoughts.

Radek wavered at first on how to behave, and his first weeks and month as rector were more like occupational therapy than the exercise of a real profession; he as an administrator and

pedagogue—for Chinese people, even! a crude Stalinist joke—
and more than once he was tempted to borrow a costume and
pigtail wig from one of the Moscow theaters and appear as a
learned mandarin before his students, and before the guests,
who, eager for sensation, always turned up.

Soon, however, things in China went from isolated tremors to a
continuous quake, the shock waves of which radiated in all directions, and especially to Moscow, shaking people and opinions
all the way into the sacred spaces of the Central Committee and
the Comintern; and without having wanted to, he found himself
again at the center of events.

Trotsky, who, because of his frequent ailments, which doctors
seemed unable to cure, spent more and more time in convales-
cent homes, had allowed himself without resistance to be relieved
of his post as War Commissar, and had thus renounced any real
influence he might have possessed in the bodies of power; only
his brilliance as a political thinker and his reputation as a victor
during the revolutionary war remained with him—Stalin's lack-
eys could have printed so many feature articles and produced so
many films about the Battle of Tsaritsyn, in which their client,
like Trotsky before him in the legendary defense of Svyazhsk,
directed the action at the front in a beautiful commander's pose
from the footboard of the staff car of an armored train and, as
soon as the thunder of the battle had died down, wanted to report
to Comrade Lenin on his victories.

Trotsky came to visit him at his university.

Trotsky looked around the sparsely furnished office, nodding
approvingly; and then grabbed the ebony horseman from the
middle of the bookshelf, a gift from the father of one of Radek's
students, carried it to the window, and let his fingers glide
thoughtfully over the masterfully crafted figure: the armor and
the horse were inlaid with silver; behind the precious saddle, an

armored monkey balanced on the horse's bare back, carrying the horseman's standard with one hand while clinging to him with the other—just as he, Radek, had often clung to Trotsky in the past.

Trotsky's dark silhouette against the bright square of the window reminded Radek of a very similar impression from the similar meagerly furnished quarters that the Germans had provided for them both in Brest-Litovsk—what hadn't happened since those days: what a steep ascent! What a deep fall!

"Why, Lev Davidovich," he asked, "did you resign from the War Commissariat so abruptly? And why, back then, during Ilyich's funeral, did you stay somewhere in Crimea and leave the field to those here, Stalin and Zinoviev and Kamenev and consorts?"

Trotsky placed the horseman back on the shelf. "Why do you think?"

"At the time remember, Lev Davidovich, when all the papers were full from the first to the last line with eulogies about Vladimir Ilyich's service on behalf of Soviet power, I was the only one who recalled your merits, so that many already began to suspect that I was preparing the people for you as the Bonaparte of the post-Lenin phase of our revolution. And who the hell knows, that may even have been my intention …"

"I confess to you, Karl Bernhardovich, there are moments when I myself am disappointed with myself. No, I won't become a Bonaparte, although I have sometimes thought about holding a little Thermidor in the face of the shameless appetites and vanities of the so-called vanguard of the proletariat that's forced its way to the top in this country."

"To overthrow Stalin?"

"Stalin is a pest."

"And I was just about to suggest to you, Lev Davidovich, that you reconcile with him, indeed ally with him—against Zinoviev, who is an even bigger pest, and a fool to boot."

Trotsky swallowed. His beard seemed to bristle.

"Think about it, Lev Davidovich: maybe we'll have to live for a while with the grandiose socialism in a single country of Comrade Stalin."

"You say that, the man with a direct view of China? You, the educator, the prospective one, of the Chinese revolution?... Don't be ridiculous. There is no socialism in a single country, no matter how highly Stalin praises it to us. Do you know Saltykov-Shchedrin's comedy *Pompadours*? There, Saltykov has a guy whose most burning desire is to introduce liberalism in the Russia of the tsars, and because this proves impossible, he then settles for a Russian governorate, then an oblast, then a town, and finally an alley in a town ... Onward, Karl Bernhardovich, onward together with your friend Stalin toward socialism in a single alley!"

Radek knew the play, and Lenin already had, on appropriate occasions, as well as inappropriate ones, quoted from it; and had nevertheless declared, in October 1917, with the revolution victorious only in some sections of the country: "We are now proceeding to the construction of socialism!"

But he wasn't eager to continue the eternal debate just now, since he didn't yet know enough about the balance of forces in China and the chances for victory of the individual groups there; in Europe, at any rate, people were better prepared for a longer period of the continuation of the existing order with all the consequences that this would have for their behavior.

"Wouldn't you like, Lev Davidovich," he announced with a friendly smile, "to give a lecture or two at my university, on this very question?"

Trotsky scrutinized him. The sparrow was sticking his head out of the dirt again and chirping, and quite cheekily at that!

On two days of the week, usually Tuesday and Thursday, he held a jour fixe; whoever among his students felt like it, came to him in the large anteroom and sat down at small tables, or remained standing, and drank tea and talked. Larissa, serving little cakes with it, unobtrusively guided the conversation; she was no less interested than he was in the information received about China in this way; he himself was more reserved, fearing that his guests, who were often still young, might prefer to remain silent out of shyness in front of the respected person he represented from their point of view; in any case, the Chinese, their sense of rank and superiority still sharpened from feudal times, tended to be extremely reserved. Additionally, there was the language problem: some of them, mostly from wealthy circles and sent by the Kuomintang to study, had a tolerable knowledge of English or Russian, and the others, industrious as the Chinese were, learned quickly; but often enough interpreters had to step in, and then there were the dialects: Southerners didn't understand Northerners, and Northerners didn't understand Southerners; they wrote, improbably swiftly, with the pointed finger of one hand their ideographs on the outstretched surface of the other, and the interlocutor deciphered it without difficulty; but what if one couldn't read, like so many who had been delegated by the trade unions to study in Moscow, or by the Chinese Communist Party or the workers' militias?

Gradually, however, despite all the difficulties, he succeeded in forming his own picture of the real conditions in their country from the contradictory descriptions and reports of his students; this, however, didn't agree at all with that of the Comintern, on which, it turned out, the rigid policy of the Russian Politburo toward China and the various factions of the Chinese party and the Kuomintang was based.

But there were also a few female students, one of them of extraordinary grace, her face as if made of porcelain, the fragility of her slender-shouldered figure emphasized by the tight-fitting pastel green garment with the high collar at the neck. Shen Hsi-kao was drawn to Larissa, and Larissa to her, and several times after the jour fixe, Radek sat with them and enjoyed the tête-à-tête with the two so dissimilar beauties, even if what they talked about was completely different from love and poetry.

Shen, who had already studied in Shanghai—her father was a silk merchant—and had been influenced by Communist ideas through her studies at the Beida, Beijing University, expressed her fears: in her parental home, where connections were maintained not only to higher Kuomintang officials, but also with Western businessmen and colonial officers, there was unabashed talk that the merchant class would no longer allow itself to be restricted in its freedom of action by the workers and the trade unions: rather, as soon as they felt strong enough, that is, as soon as General Chiang Kai-shek approached from the south with his armies, they would renounce any compromise with the lower classes and make a clean sweep with the oppressors—but the Communist functionaries, partly out of their own conviction of the immaturity of the Chinese proletariat, partly on instructions from Moscow, blindly submitted and obediently did what her father's friends demanded of them—"Like coolies!" she exclaimed angrily—even if this kind of policy weakened the workers' cause and endangered the party; and she, Shen Hsi-kao, feared a bloody end: one couldn't imagine in Moscow what cruel villainy the Chinese bourgeoisie and its military rulers were capable of.

Shen's insistent chirping had quite an affect on Radek, even more than on Larissa, who kept asking and learning more and more details from Shen until she finally turned to Radek, agitated to the extreme. "And what do you say? Aren't you going to do something about it? Or do I, or Shen, still have to explain to you what this is all about?"

He sighed. "I know, I know, and not just since yesterday. And the ones at the top know it too, as well as you or I do. But before the Comintern authorities set their lazy brains into motion and their entrenched theses start to vary, and the bureaucracy around Stalin begins to stir from their armchairs, the catastrophe has to break out first."

"And you also want to wait that long?" Larissa grabbed him by the elbow. "You know, I like the Chinese, at least as much as the Germans, and I don't want to have to experience again—"

She broke off. She had suddenly turned ashen, and her face, otherwise so youthful, seemed to decay for his and Shen's eyes.

"What's the matter, dearest?" He jumped up. "Are you ill?" He felt for her pulse; it was beating disturbingly irregularly. "Speak, Larissa, tell me!"

Little Shen hurried away and returned with a water-soaked cloth, which she placed on Larissa's forehead. Then she massaged both of her temples, following a certain pattern, it seemed, and then began to apply rhythmic pressure on certain points in the neck and sternum and back of the hand, also according to a system.

Larissa gradually began to show color again. She straightened up, her breath came more forcefully, and her gaze fixed on Radek, as if she hadn't seen him in a long, long time, and then on Shen Hsi-Kao, and she whispered, "He must . . . go to Stalin. He must . . . do something. Don't you think so, Shen?"

"But of course," said Radek hastily, "certainly..." Stroking Larissa's hands: "anything you want." And consoled, "Besides, at the moment, in fact, only Stalin can make a difference there, and why not turn to him—then at least he knows that we know, and may feel compelled to act . . ."

He became aware that little Shen was still with them, listening to his deliberations; but that didn't matter now; what was important was to give warning, and demand changes to the Comintern's disastrous China policy, and that something change; and even more important, to finally take Larissa to good doctors, military doctors if necessary, even if Raskolnikov had to be called upon.

He decided to write to Stalin and to deliver the letter himself to Stalin's apartment so that it would reach the addressee safely; all he had to do was climb one floor higher in the Cavalier Wing of the Kremlin.

He wrote very carefully. Stalin, as rough and ruthless as he was to others, was highly sensitive when it came to respect for his own person; any half-tone that even hinted that one might harbor doubts about the wisdom of his judgments had to be suppressed, any appearance of rebellion avoided. "Josif Vissarionovich," he wrote, "in the position which you have entrusted to me, affairs necessarily come to my attention which, without evaluating them myself, I nevertheless wish to bring to your attention."

And so on, in this submissive manner. Radek grimaced. Such self-relinquishment wasn't easy for him, especially in the face of Stalin, whose abilities—except when it came to manipulating people—he didn't rate too highly. And he feared that the Khosyain, the boss, as he had been calling himself more and more frequently lately, would read the letter from his freshly minted China specialist, but, since it implied criticism of his own political decisions, would put it aside angrily and do nothing decisive—except perhaps against him, Radek.

He was all the more surprised when Stalin announced that he would pay him a visit at his university. Since neither the date nor the hour were mentioned, Radek assumed that he would be informed; but nothing of the sort; the door suddenly opened, and Stalin appeared, by coincidence or not, right at a jour fixe, and with a small entourage, the most prominent of whom was Comrade Molotov. Stalin stood there and looked around, serious, but with a touch of feigned benevolence; then his eye remained fixed on the middle circle in the room, where Radek and Larissa were; he encountered loud laughter from there.

Radek raised his head. Protocol, he considered, protocol probably required that he break away from the circle and hurry with Larissa toward the Khosyain in order to greet him, but before he could make up his mind, Stalin was already coming toward them both. He stopped in front of Larissa, bowed a little, and said, "Comrade Reissner, I presume? I've heard about you."

"Only good things, I hope, Josif Vissarionovich."

"Only the best." And to Radek: "I hope I'm not disturbing. I just heard you all laughing heartily. What about, please?"

"I told the young comrades how it came about that I became rector of the university named after Sun Yat-sen."

"And the young comrades found that so amusing?"

Radek grinned. "When someone previously sitting on a high horse suddenly falls off—that does have a certain element of comedy about it, Comrade Stalin, doesn't it?"

Stalin's face darkened. "Some, Karl Bernhardovich," he replied harshly, "sit more firmly in the saddle than others."

Hell, Radek thought, does he have to make every instance of sarcasm about himself? In any case, he had now jumped out of the frying pan into the fire, as the saying went. And he said, "Nevertheless, if one has to fall, it's better to let him fall softly. We imagined, when we were laughing like that, that perhaps we could found a Jewish university, named after King David, and appoint you, Josif Vissarionovich, as its rector ..."

Larissa was alarmed. Stalin fixed Radek with his piercing gaze.

"But why Jewish?" asked Molotov naively. "Comrade Stalin isn't a Jew!"

Radek tapped himself on the chest. "Am I Chinese?" And he realized that in this moment, he had blown any possibility of effecting a change in Soviet policy toward China.

This time they met on a weekend, at Joffe's dacha: he was on one of his diplomatic trips; so the secret observers, whom Radek had noticed nearby, at least couldn't associate good old Joffe with him and Trotsky when they reported to Stalin.

Larissa, wrapped in a woolen blanket, rested on the terrace; despite the uncomfortable heat on her forehead and cheeks, she was freezing; Radek had brought her a thermometer, but she refused to use it; she was afraid of illness.

She looked at the two of them as they walked away. Trotsky, straight like a soldier, walked along the path between the birch trees, beside him her little frizzy-haired man, trying to keep up; he seemed a little ridiculous, the poor man, with his stumbling gait.

Larissa could imagine what they were talking about; during those days there had been enough hints at the table and in the evenings at the edge of the bed: the structure at the top of the party and the Comintern was in flux, and Trotsky would demand that her beloved get involved again.

Then the two of them disappeared from her field of vision.

★

"It seemed unreal," said Trotsky, "but it was reality: grown men, old comrades, beaten through so many party feuds and always climbing back to power—there they sat before me, Zinoviev on the left, Kamenev on the right, two of the triumvirs of the great Soviet Union, totally distraught, and they told me excitedly—in retrospect, still shuddering, they said—about the rude insults with which Stalin had mistreated them, and the dangerous threats which he had issued and which he would put into practice if they did not obey orders."

Radek imagined the scene: Kamenev, with the gray hedgehog hair on his high skull, a quiet man, actually, but he also had his past, his conflict with Lenin, but that was long past and didn't affect him, Radek, in the slightest. But Zinoviev! Zinoviev, recently enthroned in the middle of the stage of the Bolshoi, grinning in triumph! Zinoviev was enemy number one, and the troika, which had been in the driver's seat since Lenin's death, was about to gallop apart, and one would fall, Stalin or Zinoviev, but more likely Zinoviev, since Stalin's elaborate bureaucracy weighed much more heavily on the scales of power than the Comintern clique on which Zinoviev leaned, or the Leningrad Soviet, of which he had been chairman since the days of the Revolution.

"And you want my advice?"

"More than that, Karl Bernhardovich—your support."

Radek hesitated. Then he took his glasses from his nose and polished the lenses. "How great, tell me please, Lev Davidovich, is the influence of a school director?"

"You can't be serious."

"Oh, but I am. I think that a little restraint suits me better than big appearances at the moment. But I'll tell you: both Stalin and Zinoviev are looking around for allies; use the opportunity, make Stalin an offer—he'll be willing to make concessions."

To the right of the path there was a small wooden bench, crudely assembled, offering space for two. Trotsky sat down on it. "And from you," he asked, "did Stalin receive an offer?"

Radek sat down next to him. "Not a general one. I decide on a case-by-case basis."

"I've always known," Trotsky wrinkled his nose, "that you have an opportunistic streak, Radek; but aren't you indulging it a little too strongly now?"

"Maybe my drive for self-preservation is just better developed than yours."

"You could say that," Trotsky said, irritated.

"You'd rather be completely booted out, honored one, and end up somewhere far away in Turkey?"

"Why Turkey?"

"Or China. Or wherever."

Now Trotsky was really annoyed. "We will struggle," he declared programmatically.

"There were better opportunities to do that earlier, Lev Davidovich; you missed them. And anyway, one has to set priorities. It's Zinoviev's turn to fall."

When they returned to the dacha and opened the door, they found Larissa slumped on the floor.

The second of panic. The swirl of apprehension. The helplessness.

Radek's hands shook, his knees threatened to buckle; he wanted to pick up his beloved, take her in his arms and cradle her like a child—but what was the use. What should they administer now, what drops, and where could they be found? Or cardiac massage? Respiration? Vodka? Vodka was in the cupboard, but how would they get her to drink it?

Trotsky, however, had already gone into action. He knelt down next to the fainted woman, opened her dress, and listened for her heartbeat; one sensed that he knew his way around, a military man. Radek was deeply grateful that Trotsky was present and obviously able to take care of Larissa; suddenly, however, a blazing shot through his mind: what if she died now?

And then: dear, dear God, not that, I beg you! You've created her! Her, Larissa—youth, beauty, strength, sensuality, life! Death; not her! You can't let this happen. I beg you, God . . . !

Trotsky stood up. "So, you can bring your vodka now."

Later, on the way to Moscow, with Larissa stretched out in the back seat of Trotsky's car, Radek noticed for the first time the wrinkles around her eyes and mouth—wrinkles of suffering, wrinkles of age?—and heard her say in a pained voice, "It was a dream, dearest, wasn't it?"

Radek already wanted to say yes. But Trotsky, less sensitive than he was, beat him to it again. "It must have been your circulation, Larissa Mikhaelovna," he announced, "you'll need a more thorough examination."

4

The great battle took place at the Fourteenth Party Congress, and Radek had the pleasure of watching it without having to participate himself. He watched the deployment of the armies and listened to the clang of the weapons and the battle cries of the men—World revolution! Socialism in a single country!—both lofty slogans, which concealed, however, the offices and posts of power in the party and soviets and army, and in industry, that, agonizingly slowly, arose from the sweat of the people.

He was involved in a different way: with his nerves and heart. Not that he would have preferred one of the protagonists, Stalin

or Zinoviev; but the longer the arguments dragged on, all conducted in the pseudo-Marxist terminology with which he was
all too familiar, the clearer it became to him that decisions were
being made here about historical processes that would shape his
century, and the consequences of still incalculable dimensions
would emerge from the tiny coincidences of the most private lives
that had formed the less attractive characters of the two men who
determined the confrontation—shouldn't one suspect a *Weltgeist*
behind the whole thing? A dialectical materialist one, of course.

In those days, visitors piled into his workroom at the university;
they brought him reports from the scene of the action, the great
Congress Hall, where the struggle was still going on. Gradually,
it became clear, at first from seemingly incidental observations—
who dared to make fun of whom, for example, or who assured
whom of his deepest respect, or from the tone at certain points
in the long speeches that *Pravda* published daily—in whose
favor the fortunes of battle were tilting. The decisive factor was
a more psychological one, expressed less in pithy words than in
occasional asides: back then, in 1925, the delegates to the Party
Congress, most of whom were embedded in secure civil service
positions, preferred a quiet existence in the firmly established
socialist order of a country protected by a strong police force to
the risks of revolutions that might, after all, go wrong, endangering their own position; and so, in the end, it was Zinoviev who
lost the final, most important vote, and who, bowing his head,
left the stand, and Stalin who, in the name of the entire party,
announced the new political line: Stalin's.

★

Comrade Sergei Dalin, Soviet Vice Consul in Shanghai, was an
inconspicuous man; one met him and minutes later had already
forgotten whether his sparse hair was blond rather than dark, or
even already gray, and what color and shape his eyes were; as for
the rest, he possessed a shrewd judgment of his surroundings,

and his powers of observation as well as his memory were phenomenal—the ideal messenger on a confidential mission for someone like him, Radek.

On the way to the government hospital, where Larissa, feverish, had finally been given a bed for proper diagnosis, Radek visited Dalin in his Moscow quarters, a small room in a dilapidated communal apartment where the damp wallpaper peeled from the walls and the alcohol stove polluted the air. He placed the bouquet of flowers—which he had obtained by trading two bottles of black market American cognac—on the rickety table, dropped onto the woven straw chair seat, and stretched his legs.

"Those aren't for me," said Dalin, "the flowers?! I can hardly believe that this room has ever seen such splendor." He took the tea from the stove and poured it with great caution into two old Russian teacups.

"No, not for you," said Radek, "as much as I'd have liked to give you a small pleasure. But take comfort—these flowers are for the most beautiful woman in Russia, who, unfortunately, is seriously ill at the moment." And then asked, "How long have we known each other now, Sergei Pavlovich?"

"Four years," Dalin sipped his tea, "for four years now, we've been running into each other repeatedly."

"And each time, we've dealt with important things together."

"And every time, Karl Bernhardovich, I've had inconveniences afterward."

"You've survived them."

"I'm a survivor. You too, by the way."

Radek patted him on the knee, smiling. "This time," he said, "I'll hardly endanger you. All I want from you is a report, and a reliable one at that. And I want it soon."

"About China? I'm on my way there."

"I have other sources, of course. But my informants are in the majority dilettantes, unfortunately, or base their information on the observations of dilettantes, and what I get from them is piecemeal, and usually delayed."

"I haven't been in China for six months; take that into consideration."

"For precisely that reason, Sergei Pavlovich. One sees more clearly with fresh eyes. And I need to know if I have to act, and when."

"Act. In what regard?"

"Stalin is sworn to Chiang Kai-shek. But I don't trust Chiang. What is the guy planning? And for when is he planning it? Find out for me, and find a sure way to let me know. Understood?"

"Understood."

"And now, if you'll excuse me, friend—I have to go to the hospital."

Dalin understood. "You love her a lot, don't you?"

Radek shook his hand.

There he stood with his flowers in his white smock, dressed in white, his feet in government slippers; the hospital management attached the greatest importance to both gown and slippers, fearing infections transmitted from the outside world to the patients by the visitors, and in front of him sat the ward doctor in her not entirely clean office, a gaunt, bad-tempered person, who was visibly unwilling to answer his increasingly urgent questions about Larissa's condition, and about the results of the examinations so far, and what the prognosis would be, if there was one: the professor would be there soon, she said, and he should ask him about it; she, a simple ward doctor, was not authorized to give information of that kind without his express permission.

And he became more restless with every minute.

What was that? Just the usual bureaucracy? Or was Larissa in such a bad state that only someone with the consecration of higher authority could inform him? And he hesitated to go to her bedside without knowing at least approximately what her condition was, and what the causes of her illness were: of course, once at her side, he would radiate cheerfulness and good courage; no, it's nothing serious, believe me, Larissa dearest, just a little infection, an insignificant one, the professor told me himself just a few minutes ago, they'll give you baths and powders, chemical ones, the newer kind of mixture, and a few injections, should they prove necessary, and in one, at the most two, weeks, you'll be as good as new, he promises.

But to tell her this, or something similar, without the slightest clue, no, that wouldn't do, it would be unconscionable, and she'd never trust him again if she found out that he had told her falsehoods, even if it was with the best of intentions; but what should he do now, he was already glad that the scrawny witch there, who visibly enjoyed her ridiculous power over him and Larissa, had allowed him access to the patient Reissner as soon as the support staff had finished cleaning the patient's room.

She had her own room; that, at least, he had been able to obtain after intervening with Comrade Stalin's private secretary—it was more like a compartment, better suited for brooms than for the ill, with just enough room in it for the bedside table next to the bed and a chair, the narrow window leading onto a light shaft, so that Larissa, who loved nature so much, did not even have a leaf before her eyes, a green one with a bit of sky behind it, but rather just gray, dirty brick work.

Her face was blazing. He had found out the day before that her fever had risen dangerously, but this was frightening. Apparently she needed time before she found her way back to reality from whatever fantasies, opened her eyelids, moved her lips, "Ah, my little one ... you've come ... and what beautiful flowers ..."

One hand felt over the bedspread for his, the other stroked the flowers. "What colors! You know, I see colors here only in my dreams, and my dreams torment me."

He sat down beside her on the bed, felt her hot forehead, and held her hand, the joints of which seemed to have become even slimmer.

Her mouth twisted.

He, concerned, "Are you in pain?"

She seemed absent. Her glance wandered.

"Does something hurt?" He leaned over her and kissed her tenderly. "Tell me, dearest. Surely there's something I can do for you?" The pain that she wouldn't admit suddenly pierced his heart. Perhaps this hospital, too—the best in Moscow; they all admitted themselves here, the great and powerful, and let themselves be cured—but where did they die?—perhaps this hospital wasn't quite the right one for her.

A gust of wind in the air shaft shook the window pane.

"Sometimes it does," she said, "sometimes it does. Hurt."

"Badly!"

"Sometimes."

"And where?"

"In the abdomen. And in the chest often. And in my head and joints …"

"And since when?"

"Since when?…" She thought about it, but apparently came to no precise result. "You must have noticed how bad I was feeling. Or you didn't want to know…"

He didn't want to know. He didn't want to know of his responsibility for her, and even now it was unbearable to him, helpless as he felt, to have to hear and see and sympathize with how she suffered.

The door opened, squeaking, and the professor came prancing into the room, he really had that jaunty step that indicates the inner joy of someone who rejoices in his successes and the recognition paid to him by humanity. Radek moved aside, because behind the prancing man was the entourage that every great scientist drags behind him, crowding the narrow room: the senior physician, the scrawny ward doctor, assistants and nurses.

The professor reached for the chart at the foot of the bed and cast a frowning glance at the curves. Then he felt Larissa's pulse, then knocked the covers off her, folded her shirt up and palpated her slightly bulging belly, on which reddish pustules appeared. At the end, he chuckled, "Well, we're doing much better, Comrade Reissner!" and then growled in the direction of his entourage. "We'll continue with the therapy as before, which is of course only a provisional one. If there are any changes in the patient's condition, I request immediate notification."

During this examination, which seemed to him far too perfunctory, Radek, standing on tiptoe, sought to catch Larissa's attention over the heads of those present, and saw that, in spite of the fever that clouded her vision, she recognized him and his facial expressions, and guessed his message. And I put you in this hole, my poor angel, he conveyed to her, any village healer would have done you better, or I should have raised hell to have a specialist come from Berlin to treat you, or from London, or Paris, but it was all too late already, I realized too late how bad it was, the old malaria again, someone told me, or whatever, and I already no longer had the influence that even the most necessary things require here in order to be fulfilled, let alone special wishes, forgive me, my heart, my everything; and she, in the language of her eyes that shone feverishly, I will live, I want to live, for you, beloved, the happiness we had was too short, they can't do that to us, not even this professor, this prancing busybody, but you stay with me, a while longer, don't leave me, I'm modest, I don't ask for much, please…

But he went out with the others, and in a few steps was at the side of the prancing man, and seizing him by the sleeve, hissed, "Now, honored one, now I want to speak to you," and the professor was startled, and his feet remained rooted for a moment, and he said, "Yes, Comrade Radek?"

"Your diagnosis, and briefly."

"Typhoid fever."

★

This was also one of the lessons of his life: a worry seldom came alone.

As if his head wasn't already full enough with thoughts about Larissa—what would become of her? What were the chances that she would overcome the illness, the terrible illness? And to what extent was it his fault that it had come to this with her, what were his failures?. . . In addition, Bukharin had moved up to the head of the Comintern, to Zinoviev's spot, and was now pursuing Stalin's China policy, absolute adherence to the Kuomintang, with the most obedient zeal, and was immediately opposed to every attempt that he, Radek, made to thwart this policy. And it was foreseeable that, given the nature of Chiang Kai-shek and the character of the contradictions in the East and South of China, both military and economic, this policy must be heading toward a total disaster for China's Communists—which Dalin also confirmed in his first letter to him, sent from Shanghai. And not just that; Sergei Pavlovich further reported to him that Chiang Kai-Shek had demanded from the Chinese party a list of all of its members working in the ranks of the Kuomintang and shoulder-to-shoulder with it—why the list?—and that Bukharin and Stalin had both strictly instructed the leadership of the Chinese party to comply with Chiang's demand.

Also, the external appearance of the letter was a cause of further concern to him: by signs that were unmistakable, it could be seen that it had been intercepted; but why then had the trouble been taken to restore the letter so that it resembled its original state, and deliver it faithfully to the addressee? To lull him and Sergei Pavlovich into a false sense of security? To continue to monitor their correspondence? And to strike in due course? But against whom? Against Dalin? Against him, Radek? Against both of them?

"I'd like to help you so much …" said Rosa, his Rosa.

He was moved; her tone was genuine, there was nothing artificial in it, nothing that was supposed to indicate to him, here, look, what a noble woman I am! No, this tone came from the heart, there was, and he wasn't just imagining it, the old connection, though she had, in the course of time, turned to other men in her discreet way, one of them, to his annoyance—for the man, handsome and courageous, commanded even his respect—Comrade Unschlicht from Trotsky's international military staff. "You can help me," he seized on her question, "if Larissa…"

He broke off.

"If Larissa … ?" she repeated.

"Should anything happen to her, please prevent me from shooting myself."

She looked at him. It was clear that he was suffering. "You're not the type to shoot yourself," she said.

Fyodor Raskolnikov came, filling the whole floor of the hospital with his broad shoulders, his chest, his commanding voice.

Radek wondered how Raskolnikow knew about Larissa's illness, or even that it was approaching crisis, and came to the conclusion that he could have only learned of it from her: there must have therefore been continued contact between her and her husband—for how long? And despite the great love she always showed for him, Radek? Not that he should have been angry with her for that—after all, he himself led a double existence: one with his wife and little daughter in the Cavalier Wing of the Kremlin, the other in a two-room apartment with bathroom and toilet on the upper floor of his university, to which he was entitled as its rector and which Larissa had furnished according to the upper-middle-class taste of the Reissners.

He and Raskolnikov encountered each other right in front of the hospital room, a different one, by the way, from her first one, in a different section of the building. Raskolnikov, whose mind was still under the impression of the misery in which he had found Larissa and the words she had wrested from him, stopped and stammered, "Ah, Radek! Also on the way to see her … good, good … she longs for you, she said …"

Radek pulled him aside. In his mind he could already hear the reproaches: if you took her away from me, couldn't you at least take better care of her? But Raskolnikov only looked at him sadly and asked, "What can we do, you and I, to make her well again?"

As if I wouldn't have undertaken it long ago, thought Radek, if I only knew how; and then, the man's *we*, *us* promised a kind of fellowship; and he felt something like relief, since Raskolnikov seemed ready to assume part of the responsibility for Larissa's recovery.

"If we got her out of here," Raskolnikov suggested, "and I took her to the Crimea! Sea air! What a wonderfully healthy woman she was when I had her with me at the Black Sea. Admit it, Radek, the first signs of her suffering already appeared on the journey with you through Germany—one only had to read what she wrote about Hamburg, the pathos bordering on hysteria! Pathological! And now? Sensitive as she is, she recognizes, as do you, Karl Bernhardovich, and I, into what abysses the Revolution threatens to plunge! And let's admit it, it's in the brain of man that the diseases of his body originate. But I see, you trust the doctors more than one to whom Larissa once meant everything"—he swallowed—". . . and perhaps still does today."

Radek asked back, "Have you discussed your offer, Fyodor Fyodorovich, with Larissa as well?"

Raskolnikov laid his heavy hand on Radek's shoulder. For an entire moment, Radek feared for his shoulder bone; then Raskolnikov let go of him and said, "Go in, she's been expecting you for a long time."

He hadn't suspected that this would be the last time that he saw her; soon after, her heart failed—in the middle of the night, she had been alone at that hour, he would never forgive himself for that, no hand to hold hers, no one to press a final kiss on her forehead—and afterwards, when he stood before her again, she was already no longer herself: was rather an image, white, cold marble, with certain similarities to a woman he had known and, with all of his soul and body, had loved.

And in fact, it had looked as if there had been an improvement in her condition during that recent visit. Her temperature had dropped, her pain had lessened; she had even eaten a little broth with a piece of white bread and kept it with her, and she seemed to be at inner peace, so that he thought he could dare to tell her about his meeting with her husband, in the corridor outside, and that he and Fyodor Fyodorovich had talked to each other, and that Fyodor Fyodorovich had told him about his idea of going to the Crimea with her, Larissa, so that the sea breeze would rub the poison out of her lunges and intestines; but he thought that as soon as she felt well enough, she should travel with him, Radek, instead, to the Caucasus, where, on the terrace of the sanatorium, they could enjoy the sunshine and the great silence until she had completely recovered. And so beautifully and touchingly had he described the scene, and such hope had he awakened in her, that the fears with which she spent her days receded from her and a glow of anticipated happiness lit up her haggard face.

The professor also came hopping in for the evening visit, almost without an entourage today, and, after a brief auscultation, still spread optimism, without, however, committing himself to a definitive prognosis regarding the duration of the disease or its course and outcome, whereupon he patted Larissa's wrist and, turning to Radek, asked if he was now more satisfied with Comrade Reissner's accommodations—more space and much better equipment, yes, and the view from the window above all; the trees in the garden, with the snow glistening on the branches; and the ward doctor a more affable person than the previous one, open-minded and warmhearted; oh, he already knew what was appropriate and what Comrade Reissner was lacking, and, as Comrade Radek would probably have noticed, he had arranged the necessary things on his own; what he concealed, however, was that this new, considerably more pleasant room was part of the intensive care unit of his hospital. Then he pranced out.

Radek sensed that it was time for him to leave as well: Larissa seemed exhausted, her gaze fixed on distant places where he couldn't follow her. But when he rose, she took his hand and clung to him, and he said, "But dearest, it's better that you rest a little now, so that you may regain your strength; if you wish, I'll sit with you a little while longer, until you're asleep; and by the way, we'll see each other tomorrow."

He kissed her. Her lips, formerly so plump and rosy, felt like bark, and her breath came shallow and hasty. After a few minutes her eyelids closed; she seemed to have fallen asleep; carefully, he withdrew his hand from her, got up and crept to the door. One more look from there: she was lying so peacefully, and he thought he saw a smile on her face, and was full of good hope when he closed the door quietly behind him.

It was unreal, unbelievable; everything in him resisted that a person so bursting with life should suddenly no longer be, her voice, although already distorted in the past few weeks, now completely silenced, her gaze frozen, her thoughts evaporated, to where, no one knew.

He walked around, in his university, in the gates and court-yards of the Kremlin, in the alley of the city, its parks and boule-vards, aimlessly; what god had struck him like this, and why him? And how was he to live, without warmth and beauty, and without the thoughts, the suggestions with which she enriched him?

Rosa tried to give him support, which he took note of, without the feeling of emptiness changing. He took care of the external stuff—the documents, the notification of friends, the final resting place, the final journey—that kept him occupied, but didn't help him to bear the loss or the questions about his failures: would it be possible for her to still be alive if he had acted sooner, recognized the seriousness of the illness sooner, consulted other, better doctors, even the miracle healer from the village?

Then the day came when they followed the cart pulled by two heavy black horses to the Vagankov Cemetery, and loaded the coffin on their shoulders at the gate, he and Boris Pilnyak and Comrade

Yenukidze and the other three, six bearers in all, as custom dictated, and carried Larissa to the Communist section, the front row, where the tomb gaped at him, to the left and right of it a pile of yellowish earth, on top of it wooden beams, so that the cemetery workers would stand securely when they lowered the coffin into the pit, and the mourners would have support for their feet when, one by one, they poured their shovelfuls of sand onto the deceased.

"Immortal sacrifice, you are descending…" The melody, carried in Russian minor key, did not leave Radek's mind during the slow march to the grave with the burden on his shoulder, and even afterward, while they stood there, black against the gray February fog, so that he could not follow the words, beautiful and worthy no doubt, spoken by the poet Pilnyak, and only felt the burning in his eyes.

And now she was immersed in the darkness from which there was no return, his wonderful beloved. He might have cried out, but nothing escaped his throat but a croak, of which he was strangely ashamed; and then he caught sight of, half hidden in the bare bushes: Raskolnikov. Had he come to demand her back from him, Radek, or to punish him, since he had not been able, in his recklessness and egoism, to hold on to her?

But Raskolnikov approached him and hugged him and kissed him on the cheek, and Radek felt that Raskolnikov's cold face was wet with tears and said, "Please forgive me, Fyodor Fyodorovich, at least you; I can't."

"It's still too early to write the biography of this high-minded woman," he began, sitting at his work table in the university named after Sun Yat-sen, seeking to conjure up this high-minded woman from his memory and knowledge of her, so that she would at least remain in his words until someone could be found who could appreciate her in a worthy manner, and whom his notes would then serve.

And wrote, "Among the tiny number of intellectuals who joined the struggling proletariat in 1917, aware of the world-historical significance of the events of October, with deep faith in victory, even with a cheer, was Larissa Reissner. Although she was only twenty-two years old when the hour of death struck for bourgeois Russia, she did not live to see the tenth anniversary of the Revolution, in whose ranks she fought, so death-defying, weapon in hand, whose battles she described as only one can who is at the same time a great human being, an artist, and a great fighter... a few slim volumes remain as Larissa Reissner's legacy. The October Revolution is her only subject. And as long as fighting, thinking, feeling people feel the urge to know how it really was, they will reach for those lines and not let them out of their hands until they've read them to the end ..."

And continued, after a short pause: "She did not fall in struggle against the bourgeoisie, when death often looked her in the eye; she fell in struggle against nature, which she loved. In her final hours, she still rejoiced in the sun, which took leave of her with warm rays through her window. She spoke of how beautiful it would be in the south when she went there to recover, and how good it would be then to fill her head, which had been harried by illness, with new thoughts. She promised to fight for her life, and only gave up the fight when she lost consciousness ...

5

Despite his mourning Larissa, he noticed the new unrest among his students. Groups formed, they argued loudly with each other, the chirping of their language was mixed with shrill sounds, and there was even violence in the dormitories and classrooms, and Comrade Pavel Mif, who Stalin had assigned to him as an assistant—overseer would have been the more correct word—demanded that he create order at his university.

There was no *jour fixe* anymore, not since Larissa's illness; he couldn't imagine anyone other than her in the role of hostess, and had therefore dropped the whole arrangement until his beloved would return to her work in good health—he still believed that at the time. So he called in the students who had particularly caught his eye and questioned them one by one, but most of them seemed to have some knowledge of the conflicts between the Soviet authorities, and remained taciturn; they had hardly heard from family and friends for some time and could therefore tell him little; but that little was enough to confirm his worst fears.

That day, the dainty Shen Hsi-kao appeared. She had avoided him recently, probably feeling that her presence would remind him of the hours spent together with her and Larissa, and would weigh down his heart uselessly. So they sat there at first, without either of them saying anything of importance, until Radek said that he knew that the loss he had suffered had also hit her hard, and that he understood her reticence, as she probably understood his; one didn't like to touch open wounds, and how could she have consoled him, when there was no consolation?

She nodded sadly. Yes, she would remember for the rest of her life this wise and beautiful woman who had shown her so much kindness; and just now, when bad things were happening at home, she felt all the more painfully the void that Larissa had left behind.

"Bad things?" asked Radek. "In what regard?"

Shen reached into her shoulder bag, Chinese embroidery, and brought out a little letter, ideographs, finely painted, "from my father," and began to translate to him passages from it that she had marked in advance: how pleased my father was that his greatest wish had been granted and that his silk spinning mills were finally safe again and in his own hands, after he had already had to fear that the workers' militias with their soviets, which they were already threatening to establish, would deprive him of them; now, however, these same workers' militias had, thank the ancestors, opened the city of Shanghai, which had been completely under their control except for the foreign concessions, to the troops of the Kuomintang Party and welcomed General Chiang Kai-shek as their ally; but a few days later, in agreement with the merchant class, both nationalist and allied with the imperialist powers, he turned around and ordered the workers' militias to hand over their weapons to him, and then had thousands of them arrested and locked up in jails, together with all the Communists who could be found, and her father and his business friends, joyfully excited by their confidence in Chiang, now awaited the next step.

This was the coup: Chiang Kai-shek, Stalin's confidant and an honorary member of the Comintern presidium, had plotted against the Chinese Communist Party. Radek felt the blood leaving his head; he had seen the betrayal coming, and again he had failed to find ways to publicly disavow Stalin's China policy and thus thwart it; but he had been incapable of action; his mind completely preoccupied by Larissa's illness; or was that also just an excuse to himself; and the real reason for his failure was his fear of an open confrontation with Stalin?

He decided to assemble his students in the large lecture hall—without informing Comrade Mif of his intention, by the way—and to tell them what he had gathered from the letter from Shen Hsi-kao's father, and to ask them if there were not some among them who, on the basis of their own information, could confirm or supplement his conclusions.

Which, to his surprise and much to the horror of Pavel Mif and other lecturers, caused a veritable storm: hands shot up, people shouted across the hall, people argued for the floor and confessed that they had learned in the meantime that in their circle of friends and family, and not only in Shanghai, but also in the provinces, many had become victims of the events; and one girl reported in a kind of singsong that the Kuomintang soldiers had burned the captured comrades alive in locomotives, and others spoke of other atrocities; and everyone had questions and held views, opposing ones for the most part, as to why the murders had come about, and what was still to be expected, and how to act, in China or here in Moscow; and the result of the excited confusion was the urgent request to him, Radek, to speak out about the whole thing.

A few months ago, he would have probably hesitated; but now that Larissa was gone, he saw no reason whatsoever to make any allowances and avoid inevitable confrontations.

"I myself," he said from the lectern, "feel partly guilty. I distrusted the Kuomintang from the start, especially General Chiang Kai-shek, and as you can see, I was right; had I not repeatedly demanded that the Comintern and Comrade Stalin, who had always been aligned with Chiang, review their tactics."

He straightened up and threw his head back. "And I will continue to do so, in the hope that all is not yet lost in China and that the world revolution may regain a foothold there. I will stand up and criticize Comrade Stalin, and will demand that this policy be changed immediately."

He saw how Comrade Milf diligently took notes, and was tempted to show him his bare bottom; but he couldn't really do that in front of his students.

Comrade Sergei Dalin had been ordered back from Shanghai to report to the Commissariat for Foreign Affairs, it was said, but both he and Radek suspected it was more to keep him under wraps and prevent him from divulging the embarrassing Chinese truth: Dalin had arrived in Vladivostok on a Soviet steamer, which had hundreds of fugitives from Chiang's terror on board, and from there had taken the Trans-Siberian Railway to Moscow, his memory a veritable treasure trove of facts which he, having satisfied himself that no one was listening at the door, now spread out before Radek.

Yes, it was true, the comrades had literally been burned alive; he himself had been in the Chapei district, near the railroad station there, and had seen the transports and the faces of the prisoners, and had heard the whistle of the locomotives, and had talked to railroad workers until Chiang's army police drove him away, and had told the Soviet advisors about it, who were still serving on Chiang's staff at Stalin's behest; but he had only received a shrug of the shoulders; we're just among half-savages, what do you want, Sergei Pavlovich?

"Among half-savages," added Radek, "who attempted a revolution on their own initiative."

"Which we prevented," said Dalin.

He hadn't expected that—the message from Comrade Mif, which he presented with a crooked smile: Comrade Stalin wished to speak to the students of the university named after Sun Yat-sen, and he, Radek, together with the responsible comrades of the Party Secretariat, was to make the necessary arrangements, on such and such a date.

So thanks to Mif, his threat to criticize the official China policy had reached Stalin's ear, Radek thought, and he had decided to take the bull by the horns before the beast could become dangerous to him.

In the following nights, to his own astonishment, Radek slept deeply and soundly; it was as if the tension with which he awaited the duel with Stalin had strengthened his nerves; controversies calmed him down, he realized not for the first time.

Stalin came inconspicuously: no motorcade, no large entourage; the greeting at the gate, a committee of students with a single banner, *WELCOME!*, in Cyrillic and Chinese script, and then into the building and with him, Radek, in the lead, up the stairs together with Molotov and Ordzhonikidze and bodyguards, but then all alone in his workroom for a brief *tête-à-tête*.

They looked at each other. Radek saw the hard face; the man had not yet been in power long enough for fat to be deposited under the angular chin and around the mouth, which tolerated no contradiction.

"And how should we proceed?" asked Radek.

Stalin obviously found the question out of place. "You'll introduce me. Then I expect applause. Then I'll speak."

"And then?"

"What, then?"

"No response? No questions?"

"Who should respond? Who should ask? You? The students?"

"For example."

Stalin moistened his lips under the thick mustache. "The suggestion has already been made to me, Comrade Radek, to change your position: from rector to lecturer."

Radek knew that Stalin was expecting a shocked expression, a plea for forgiveness, something along those lines. But he begrudged him the pleasure, and instead declared, "That doesn't scare me, Josif Vissarionovich; the Chinese don't know the difference between R and L anyway."

Stalin stared at him; it was a little while before he understood. Then his brow reddened. He stood up and said, "Let's go."

★

Stalin spoke in his usual manner, his vocabulary simple, with a monotonous raising and lowering of the voice, the thoughts, where it was possible, repeated a second or third time for the purpose of strengthening their persuasiveness, and the only oratorical effect the dialogue with himself, where the answers, to no one's surprise, followed with an undertone of triumph to the self-posed questions: What a source of wisdom I am! … This liturgy, Radek assumed, Stalin considered the highest form of dialectics.

The gist of Stalin's speech, although he must have had at least a passing knowledge of the recent gruesome developments in Shanghai and elsewhere, was that, contrary to certain assertions of Comrade Radek and his ilk, the China policy of the Soviet government and Comintern had from the beginning been based on a correct analysis of Chinese history and of the still semi-feudalistic conditions in the country, which precluded the creation of workers' and peasants' soviets, and required alliances with sections of the national bourgeoisie; this policy therefore remained necessary, even if it sometimes appeared that there were setbacks and unforeseen conflicts; and if one or another of the Chinese generals with whom we cooperate should turn out to be a disappointment, there are enough other leaders on the left wing of the Kuomintang, such as general Wang Tsing-wei, Chiang Kai-shek's old rival, who will continue to make common cause with us and lead the great Chinese people in the only historically correct direction, as is desired by their vanguard, the Communist Party.

This even allowed, Radek noted, continued cooperation with Chiang; but what kind of policy was this anyway, which left the fate of a people and its vanguard to the arbitrariness of some eternally corrupt military, instead of supporting the revolutionaries among the workers and peasants and stimulating them wherever possible to independent action!

Stalin ended with a rather lame attempt to celebrate the future of the Chinese revolution, which was marching forward arm-in-arm with that of the Soviet peoples; the applause, triggered by Comrade Mif, remained substantially below the length and volume due a party General Secretary, and all eyes, including Stalin's, were now on Radek.

He dithered. What now? A reply, as he had announced to himself and his students, in this same hall? Or the end of the event, with expressions of thanks? Not quite an hour ago, Stalin had threatened him with demotion . . . Oh God—he had already fallen deeper in his life, and there were values other than rank. But was there any point in talking back now, and what could be achieved by it in view of the balance of power; a small school principal and occasional writer of articles, alone and without allies, against the recognized head of the entire party apparatus?

Nevertheless, he felt something like shame, before himself and before his Chinese students, when he now stood up, strode to the lectern and, with a slight sideways bow to Stalin, thanked him for his clear and wise words, which so thoroughly illuminated a most complicated situation and which, by this alone, would provide counsel and aid in abundance to the comrade students and to all who might otherwise learn of the contents of this speech.

After that, everyone dispersed. At the head of the entourage, he escorted Stalin down the stairs to the entrance gate. There, the great man turned to him once again: "You were quite reasonable, Comrade Radek."

Never again alone, he swore to himself; he would never again have to stand alone before the powerful; from now on, he would see to it that there were people—no matter how personally unsympathetic to him—who, out of their own interests or whatever motives, it didn't matter, would stand by him and cover and protect and support him. A faction, please—even if, Radek thought, factions were still so frowned upon in the party and Stalin, for good personal reasons, railed against them—and was even proud of the fact that he had already made the decision to organize resistance before, in the early morning of the next day, after the trip from the Kremlin to the university named after Sun Yat-sen, he found his books and papers, neatly arranged and piled, in front of the door to his workroom, and Pavel Mif sitting behind his desk, telling him that he could have his personal belongings brought to the room where the late Comrade Reissner, who was also greatly mourned by him, Mif, had worked.

Radek stuffed his pipe, lit it, and blew the smoke in Comrade Mif's face, as he had done in his time to the German General

Hoffmann. So this, he thought, was Stalin's shot, and it had been fired even though he had accepted without objection the ramblings by the party's General Secretary concerning his China policy. "Let Josif Vissarionovich know that I consider educating young Chinese people with the theories he prescribed to us yesterday to be a counterrevolutionary activity."

Mif grew pale. He knew that from time immemorial, tyrants ordered the bringer of a message, and not its sender, to be beheaded.

What was he still worth? What was he still good for? Dismissed from his post as rector of his university, he was cut off from his own news about China, which, as he knew, could be used to conduct splendid politics in Moscow. And at the same time, he learned from the editors of *Izvestia* that his services as a commentator on international affairs were no longer needed.

What would he live on? He didn't receive a pension like many other Old Bolsheviks who had adapted to the apparatus and now consumed a modest pension, and when money had flowed to him from this or that source, he had always spent it with a great gesture. Now, he depended on his Rosa, who, when the occasion arose, performed substitute services at night in hospitals or polyclinics and was paid little enough for it, while he squatted at home in the Kremlin and guarded the child's sleep.

And somewhere, in the same Kremlin and at the same time, Stalin was sitting, but now in larger palatial quarters, working, it was said—but more likely getting drunk in the company of his cronies—waiting for him, Radek, to come crawling to him and repeat the act of humiliation he had already performed once at the end of their joint event in the university named after Sun Yatsen; this time, however, the kowtowing was not for the enlightenment of a few hundred young Chinese people, but for his, Josif Vissarionovich's, and his drinking buddies', own pleasure.

So he pulled himself together and went to Zinoviev on the floor above in the Cavalier Wing and, after knocking briefly, entered and dropped into the leather armchair in which he had already sat when it was still part of the furnishings of Zinoviev's office on the premises of the Comintern, and said, without greeting or introduction, "Grigory Yevseyevich, now I'm ready for you."

Zinoviev jumped up, leaned over the table, and stretched out his hand to him. "It's about time. We can use you."

There was the sudden familiar form of "you," Radek thought, after all that had gone before. Zinoviev's still soft features showed an expression of suffering, the exact opposite of the triumphant grin when, at the end of the famous Comintern congress, he forced Comrade Radek to leave the stage in disgrace. Now they met again, both Hirsch Apfelbaum and Karl Bernhardovich Sobelsohn, equally humiliated by Josif Vissarionovich Dzhugashvili, and equally forced to fight for their bit of human dignity and for the future of the revolution. "We can use you, you said. Who is 'we'?"

"Me," Zinoviev listed, "Kamenev. Trotsky. Joffe. And others, spread throughout the whole party. We haven't lived and worked for nothing."

Did he really believe that? Radek asked himself. If they were so strong, why had he and Radek allowed themselves to be hurled from their safe place in the ruling troika into powerlessness, leaving them only Trotsky to cling to, Trotsky, who had already gambled away his own power as well?

No, it wouldn't be a pleasure to work in this new association, whose only unifying bond was opposition against the usurper of control of the party apparatus; and every word that he, Radek, said from now on, every step he took, had to be carefully considered, if he didn't want to fall even lower that he had already fallen—but the attempt had to be made, there was no going back to Stalin: he was implacable.

They went, individually or in pairs, threes, or even all four at a time, to the factories, clubs, army units, and party cells, and spoke, on anything: they were clever people and skilled speakers and knew how to entertain their audience, and they avoided frontal attacks against Stalin; only the barbs in their words stung painfully, and the Khosyain, the master of the house, the boss, did not order them, the authors, punished, at least not for the time being, but rather the comrades who gave them a platform for their dissenting speeches; these then lost their posts and functions, and their lamentable fate became widely known, and the opportunities for critical utterances in any public forum soon dwindled.

So it was decided to break out of the cramped meeting rooms and go where revolutions have always been made, to the streets, to the masses; the date and occasion were also given, the coming tenth anniversary of the great October Revolution, on which the people were to celebrate themselves and the brilliant Comrade Lenin, and implicitly, his at least equally brilliant successor, Josif Vissarionovich Stalin.

Maybe, thought Radek, he too should celebrate the day in his own way, with his pen, and write an appropriate encomium; he knew only too well that Comrade Stalin was receptive to such stuff, and with that, he might conciliate him; but no, no, no, not he, who had been one of the passengers on the trip through Germany in that sealed carriage and had made history at night in league with Vladimir Ilyich.

Trotsky and Kamenev were to march in Moscow at the front of the demonstration, whereas he, Radek, and Zinoviev would appear and address the people in Leningrad, where the latter had been chairman of the Soviet for years. Later, he learned what was happening in Moscow: some people, from Stalin's secret apparatus, of course, shot at the car in which Trotsky and Kamenev were riding to the demonstration, and Trotsky, in sudden panic, ordered the driver to turn back before they were even in sight of the gathering crowd, let alone in Red Square.

Things were similar, and yet different, for him and Zinoviev in Leningrad. Already on the night train there, in front of the sleeping compartment, he recognized the men following them lurking nearby; they were under surveillance: and no sooner had they both reached the Winter Palace in the morning, coming from the railroad station, where exactly ten years ago workers and sailors had set out to storm over the high ornamental lattice, than his nocturnal observers were around him again, and soon a militia captain, with a whole platoon of uniformed men behind him, approached him and Zinoviev and said, "If you'll please follow me, Comrades."

The Leningraders in the vicinity recognized Zinoviev—after all, he had been the boss here long enough—and awaited things to come with growing interest.

Radek was also anxious. Here, on the home playing field, so to speak, Zinoviev had to prove what he really stood for, and show what strength and courage he had in him. Zinoviev stared the militiaman in the eye; the latter, knowing what loss of face he would suffer if he failed in this test, stared back and said between his teeth: "I have handcuffs with me, Grigory Yevseyevich; do I have to put them on you?"

"You won't do that!" Radek thought it was time to intervene. "No one, including you, Captain, knows how things will turn out today, here and in Moscow, and whether tomorrow Comrade Stalin will still be—"

He broke off. That was the ultimate challenge, the consequences incalculable. But the militiaman didn't think in Radek's categories: he knew only that he had his orders and he had the necessary men: but the two troublemakers from Moscow, prominent as they were, had nothing and no one behind them, and he had to get them out of the way before any of the crowd thought of taking their side; so he turned to Radek and said in an official voice, "I am taking you and Comrade Zinoviev into custody," and added, "for your own protection," and gave his men a wave, and Radek heard Zinoviev's hoarse cry, "Citizens, to the rescue!" and saw that there really were demonstrators rushing toward them, and that scuffles were beginning, and felt himself being grabbed by the arm and shoulders and dragged away, and found himself, after a short ride in a locked car, in the cell of a militia station, together with Zinoviev, who was crouching on a stool and gloomily looking at his knees.

"Don't be depressed, Grigory Yevseyevich," he said, "the Comrade General Secretary was ahead of us by just a single step. We'll do better next time."

"I doubt, Karl Bernhardovich," said Zinoviev, "that there will be a next time."

He wrote. Now and then he raised his head and looked out of the window at the wide courtyards of the Kremlin, thinking that such a historical setting might be stimulating for what he was planning: a history of the revolution presented by one of the original participants. Only, how much longer would he be allowed to enjoy the view? There were rumors, spread from the doorman to the floor woman: what were people who no longer exercised any government function doing in the quarters of those in power? Freeloaders, all of them!

That evening, Rosa came home from her clinic with a note in her hand, on it a smeared stamp and the notification from the Kremlin administration that Comrade Radek, K.B., together with his family had to evacuate apartment number 43 in the Cavalier Wing of the Kremlin by November 17, 1927, at the latest.

"I'm sorry," he said, after reading the scrap of paper; what, other than these relatively decent quarters, had she had of her life with him in the course of these years; she had to share even his love with another; and yet had stood by him and provided for the child, as well as the necessary money; and then he thought, where to put the three of us, and the closets full of papers, all irreplaceable, condensed work and foundation for new things, and felt a pang of shame in his heart and the back of his knee: where, without a relationship and protection, could one find an apartment or even a room in this city?

They met at his place, the small group which in party circles was called "The Opposition": Trotsky, Zinoviev, Kamenev, whose hair had turned white over a few weeks; and Adolf Joffe, once chief negotiator at Brest, then leading the Commissariat for Foreign Affairs, and now stripped of his position because of his declared sympathies for Trotsky and for him, Radek.

None of them knew what to do. Joffe declared, "They'll have to carry me out of my apartment."

Radek was startled. "What do you mean, Adolf Abramovich?"

But he remained silent. Did Joffe, Radek thought, mean that he would only give way to violence, or did the always amiable, cheerful man have in mind the gruesome connotation that the term "carrying out" also had?

But the others also didn't address Joffe's announcement, nor did they discuss political matters: each was too preoccupied with himself and his own future and how to cope with the sudden change in circumstances of his life.

Until Radek, gripped by sudden anger, exclaimed, "And me? What should I do with my papers? I tell you, I'll sell them all— maybe someone will pay me something for them! What idiots we've been! None of us has even a kopek; and we could have set aside a nice war chest. Now the lack of money is killing us. With our famous revolutionary ethics, we're nothing but stupid intellectuals!"

Soon after that, they went their separate ways, without any firm decisions, and without any feeling of togetherness.

★

Sleep avoided him that dark night; not only did the fears of the future weigh down on him and the thought of the final act of packing that still had to be done; Joffe's ill-boding words, the ambiguous ones, wouldn't leave his mind, "They'll have to carry me out"; and the longer he lay silent, listening to Rosa's breathing as she slept next to him, the more the second, terrible meaning gained in probability, until he crawled out of bed, slipped into his pants, and, with felt slippers on his feet, left the apartment and hurried up the stairs to Joffe's quarters.

And still on the stairs he heard the noise, hurried footsteps, calls for the floor woman, who also came running. "Open up! Unlock it!" Oh yes, they had duplicate keys, all those guards; he took the last steps, in spite of his slippers, two, three at a time, and ran down the corridor and got to Joffe's door just as the fat woman in the nightgown opened it, and heard someone say, "A gunshot! It could be heard all over the floor! He'll have killed himself, such a good man, always a heart for the working people."

Radek pushed them all aside and with two steps was in the room. Joffe lay on the bed, his eyes like mother-of-pearl, a trickle, dark red, from the hole in his temple down over his ear to the pillow.

Then he saw the letter on the table, addressed to Trotsky, and pocketed it. In a few minutes, the GPU would arrive and search everything, and the orderlies from the government hospital would load Adolf Abramovich onto a stretcher and carry him out of his apartment, just as he had predicted. It was better then that he, Radek, took the letter.

Later, after handing the envelope to Trotsky, the latter read to him: "Don't give up, Lev Davidovich, and tell the others, too, not to follow me, but to keep fighting …"

When moving out of the Kremlin, still sheltered from the rain by the great archway, he met Zinoviev carrying an object wrapped in brown paper under his arm. They stopped and greeted each other, joking aloud about the escort of overseers that Stalin had assigned to them and who were standing just within earshot. Then, more cautiously, he spoke to Zinoviev about Joffe, and how he was lying there, at peace with himself.

The little one tugged on his sleeve. Her feet were freezing, she complained.

"Soon, soon," he said, "we're going soon, and outside the gate there's a car waiting for you and Mama and me." And to Zinoviev, "What are you dragging along, Grigory Yevseyevich?"

Zinoviev unwrapped the paper. Radek recognized the features; what the man was taking from the Kremlin was a plaster copy of Comrade Lenin's death mask. Zinoviev had always had a penchant for the symbolic.

BOOK SEVEN

Will the clock not be still?
With every tick it slides
the walls closer round me,
till they're as narrow
as a coffin.

—GEORG BÜCHNER, *Danton's Death*

M oscow's housing problem was supposed to solve itself. He had feared something like this: Stalin's mills ground slowly, but they ground terribly fine; and in this case they didn't even do it that slowly, as he pointed out to Rosa: after Joffe's funeral in the cemetery of the Novodevichy monastery—the GPU swarmed among the graves, but over a thousand comrades, all oppositionists except for a handful of officials of the Commissariat for Foreign Affairs, had come to listen to Trotsky's funeral oration, the last speech the friend and confederate in Moscow was ever to deliver—after that funeral, it was all in one fell swoop; what a winter!

Trotsky, standing at the grave, read from Joffe's letter, which he, Radek, had saved from the secret police: "One doesn't lie right before death," Joffe had written. "My death is an act of protest against those who have brought our party to its present disgraceful state. Moreover, a politician has the right to depart from life if he believes he can no longer be of use to the cause he has served. But don't follow me! Follow Lenin! Carry on the struggle, the common struggle, which I no longer had the strength for: remain unyielding! In revolutionary loyalty—A. A. Joffe."

After that, Stalin, taking for granted the approval of the next Party Congress, the fifteenth, decreed the expulsion of Trotsky and Zinoviev from the Party. And Radek, reading the *ukase* in *Pravda*, said, "This is only the beginning, Rosa," and stroked his hand over the rough-planed table in Comrade Dalin's room, in the alley behind Kuznetzky Most, where the family had taken shelter while Dalin was away on business. There was paper and a pen in front of him, a few words already sketched out, but he had changed his plans: no more history of the revolution, the subject was too big; but it would become a biography of Lenin, a testimony to the almost blasphemous difference between Vladimir Ilyich and the successor, the legacy hunter.

Little Sonja came and sat on his lap.

He stroked her dark hair. To Rosa, he said, "Stalin can't help it; he must eliminate the opposition, especially its heads. He can't tolerate anyone beside himself in the party. Especially not now, when he is facing the greatest turning point of his life, his accursed life. The economy is breaking down under his hand, the market collapsing, while the speculators in the economy are allying themselves with the bureaucracy; he can give the craftsmen nothing with which they can produce goods, because the kulaks supply him with nothing, and the kulaks supply him with nothing because he can't supply them with anything for their grain and their cattle, not pants, not shows, not plows. And the industrial workers at their rotten machines are tired of the whole system, from which they have nothing. Thus, the only support left for him is the *apparatchiki*, who can still cling to the remaining corners and gorge themselves. And the village poor and the proletarians grumble. One even hears of strikes. That's why he'll have to resort to terror, in the countryside, in the city, no longer the revolutionary terror of the past, which had its justification then, but rather a quite ordinary state terror, although he'll call this a revolutionary act and steal the idea of the permanent revolution from under Comrade Trotsky's shirt, a permanent revolution, however, limited to poor Russia; headline: the new, perfected socialism in a single country; and he'll bring hunger and misery upon the people, even more than the people already suffered in war and civil war—and we can't do anything about it, because he dominates the party and we still, in spite of everything, believe that the party is the great upholder of the revolution. This party? This one party? Why not a second party; a third?"

"You're talking shit," Rosa said.

"I'm talking shit," he agreed, and thought, what audacity! Not even Trotsky, although he was already outside of the magic circle of the party, would allow himself such rebellious thoughts; conquering the party from within, that was still allowed according to the Leninist codex, but one did not found a second empire; one didn't go that far, under any circumstances.

Nonetheless, in those December days, he waited on a call, however hesitant and timid, from Rakovsky, from Smilga, Serebryakov, Smirnov, and all of them, the old ones, who had been there from the beginning and who bore the scars on their bodies from the past battles: let's raise the torch against the darkness that's falling around us, let's do something, now, before it's too late—but no cry was heard, nothing; the only sound audible was the dutiful applause for Stalin at the Party Congress.

But from there came the news about the expulsions. Trotsky's and Zinoviev's expulsions were confirmed by the delegates, as was proper, and the congress decreed a long list of other expulsions. He read the list, all of them good names, many of them he knew personally. He forced himself to calm down and counted, seventy-five in all; number fifty-two: Radek, K.B. And he almost felt relieved that he, too, was one of the sinners—how would it have looked if his name, of all names, had been missing! What a coward, sycophant, lickspittle he would have been taken for!

And yet—what was the use of noble character? Despite all the difficulties he suspected that Stalin would have in the next few months, it was quite possible that he'd survive the winter, and not just this winter, also the following one—and then it would be demonstrated that Trotsky had been the wrong horse to bet on. He called himself to order: was one allowed to regard the fundamental conflict over the future of socialism as a horse race? Is that what they had lived for, and lived according to noble principles?

And he was seized by a great anger toward Stalin. Stalin forced

one to confront everything that was low and dishonorable in
the human soul. Stalin was like a boil that infected all the tissue
around it.

After dinner, he slipped into his coat, explained to Rosa he was
going to catch some fresh air, and walked through the darkness
around Red Square. There, under the starry sky, lay Comrade
Lenin in his new, electrically illuminated mausoleum, very dead;
even his brain, which had thought so many clever and complicated things, had been scraped out of his skull, and he, Radek,
his traveling companion, was standing here, alone, watching the
cars come crawling out of the Kremlin gate, one by one, with their
shadowy faces in the back. The congress had just ended, and the
delegates were being driven home, and he wondered how many
historical moments this now made in his career, which was so
rich in historical moments, and thought to himself, what a twist
of fate it would be if Zinoviev met him again at the gate; but neither Zinoviev nor Kamenev nor any of the opposition members
stuck their noses into the cold that night; only he, Radek, was so
foolish, and he finally turned away himself and returned to his
worn-out mattress in Comrade Dalin's room, in the alley behind
Kuznetsky Most, and to the breast of his poor Rosa.

However, at that hour, he later learned, Zinoviev and Kamenev
had already made their confession of remorse, at the last possible moment of the congress, just before the iron curtain fell,
said Bukharin ironically, who had presided over the meeting; and
they had documented their contrition with a long letter, peppered
with Marxist-Leninist phrases, to Comrade Stalin, who regarded
it like the sugar dots on a chocolate cake crowning the banquet of
the higher cadres at the conclusion of the event. In the letter, the
two of them stated how mistaken they had been when they had
recently failed to recognize the profound wisdom of Comrade
Stalin's thought; but now, under the impression of the arguments

and explanations put forward in the speeches and discussions of the congress, the scales had fallen from their eyes and they had become convinced of the complete correctness of the line of socialism in a single country, and that their own views had been erroneous and anti-Leninist, and so they were now asking for a review of their expulsion from the party, and for readmission to it.

Stalin, however, was not somebody who forgave and forgot so easily, and one could imagine him snapping his broad finger as he remarked, without particular emphasis, that it might be useful to allow for a certain period of time to elapse first—six months, say—for probation, before reintegrating the renegades into the ranks of the party, and even then only with due caution...

And if those two thought they would be spared the journey into exile in the middle of January, in a poorly heated, rickety railway carriage, they were mistaken. Just like Radek, K.B., Zinoviev G. J., and Kamenev, L.B., had to go to the Kazan railway station that morning, according to the GPU's instructions, except that Radek's travel order, which the chief of the escort handed to him, stated next to the words *Paragraph 58 (Counterrevolutionary Activities)*, that the destination was Tobolsk, and *for an indefinite period of time*, whereas Kamenev was to be transported to Penza and Zinoviev to Tambov, both of which were still in Europe . . . while Tobolsk . . . where the hell was Tobolsk? Somewhere behind the Urals, Radek remembered, quite far north, but not yet in the Arctic Circle; at home he had owned an atlas, but there was no more home anymore, and he had sold the atlas for kopeks; but in his mind's eye he saw the big book still lying there, open, the broad green area, on the left side of the map the brown hatched mountains that formed the divide between Europe and Asia, and close to it, on the right side, and already no longer part of actual civilization, the black dot next to the thinly meandering line, Tobolsk on the Tobol River.

And what would become of Rosa and his daughter Sonja, standing there on the station platform to see him off, and already separated from him by a thin cordon of GPU guards?

He sought Rosa's gaze and beckoned to her and the child, and felt the choking in his throat. He loved her, after all; who else did he have in the world but the two of them? That's what he had written to Stalin, and to Ordzhonikidze, complaining in a kind of despair: why this punishment too? Even under the tsar, wife and child were allowed to accompany the exiles, but in Soviet Russia, where the family was praised as the cell-form of socialism, their bonds were to be broken with brutal wantonness. Beyond the guards, he saw, something was gathering. A collection of dubious figures, some of whom appeared to be in costume. This was a common site on the streets now, and he had already seen it in Leningrad, during the failed demonstration that he and Zinoviev undertook there in November: the beatings were organized by GPU provocateurs—pogroms, they used to call them—and he was afraid for Rosa and the girl, and for his own bones, and ran to the chief of the escort, although he was probably in cahoots with the bandits, and demanded protection, and screamed and waved his fists, until the big-boned man grabbed him and pushed him toward the carriage and yanked open one of the compartments and pushed him violently into it and threw his suitcases after him and slammed the door shut.

Rail journeys, the longer ones at least, were like punctuation marks set by fate: departure and arrival, and the stretch in between, marked the stages of life.

He wrapped his coat around himself and hid in a corner of his compartment. It was as simple as that, Radek off to Siberia; just a moment ago, through the dirty window, he had seen Zinoviev and Kamenev standing on the platform—they would probably, he assumed, be loaded onto a later train, which would relieve him of the necessity of arguing with them for hours, perhaps even days, because of their timidity—and had caught a final glimpse of Rosa, to whom the child was clinging, and now the Russian endlessness was passing by outside; where did Asia begin in this country, and wasn't Stalin at the same time the displacement of Europe from the Russian Revolution by Asiatic despotism?

Right before departure, a dozen or so men had been brought to the carriage, whom he easily recognized as future fellow sufferers; but they had been put into other compartments, presumably to isolate him, or out of consideration for him, because of his former rank, who knew? So he sat, alone with his thoughts, and with his outrage. It had really been so easy to banish him; where would resistance come from, who would provide it? The net that Stalin had woven in the few years since Lenin abandoned his great work, long before its completion, was tightly meshed and impermeable; the fish wriggled in vain. And now the historical circle had closed, and it had come to the point that the authors and advocates of the revolution, who had already been banished to Sibieria under the tsar, were sent there again, only now the tyrant was called something else; and he, little Lolek, who had only ever wanted to break out into the boundless, found himself among the enclosed.

In the night, when outside the window the tall black trees swayed from one darkness to the next, his thoughts were even blacker, and he shivered, from cold and from horror, pressed into the pillow Rosa had given him, longing for her, and at the same time thinking of Larissa and the night with her in the hotel in Dresden, the noisy Reichswehr officers outside the door. In the morning, one of the guards, a peasant in a sweaty blouse and lambskin jacket, brought bread and a battered kettle of hot water, and Radek thanked him in a friendly way—why upset the people you were taking leave of?—and brewed tea leaves, this also being a precautionary gift from Rosa.

Warmed by the tea, he became bolder and demanded of the commander of the escort that he allow him to visit his traveling companions; his influence in Moscow, he mentioned, still reached far, even if he was now being sent to Siberia; well, said the officer after some reflection, he would let a few of his charges drop in, and indeed, after a while, three of them came, among them Comrade Smilga, formerly a member of the Central Committee in a capacity responsible for industrial administration, whom he knew casually, and they greeted each other with accentuated cheerfulness, keeping the conversation neutral as long as the GPU man, who already seemed to regret his generosity, hung around—"Where are they sending you, Comrade? And you, Comrade, Where?"—Smilga's place of exile was Narym, a sad nest, but Radek's Tobolsk didn't have a much better reputation either—until their overseer, bored, finally slipped away to attend to another one of his duties.

Whereupon they turned to more serious matters—how to keep in touch with each other, no matter where they were displaced in the vast country; those inner forces that kept people going grew out of information; it was essential to know how the individual was doing in his place of exile and what was happening to him and what could be done for him if he needed help. Moreover, Radek agreed, a real exchange of ideas had to be organized, a permanent exchange of ideas, what do you think of this and that, and what do you think will become of it; it was a time of internal turmoil, and the expulsion from the party and the deportation to distant provinces of so many independent-minded comrades testified not only to a new vigilance on the part of the bureaucracy and Stalin, its supreme representative, but also to the fears of new antagonisms, through which the opposition could again become a dangerous force to the rulers: all the more important, therefore, for the exiles to be in contact with each other.

But, Smilga said, letters, telegrams, and telephone conversations all ran over routes—and anyway, for long distances—that were easily visible to Stalin's secret apparatus.

Radek smiled. But of course, Ivar Tesinovich, and perhaps one could occasionally even use this way to send a visible message to Stalin's apparatus if one wished to know its reaction; in this way, one could try to influence what was happening in the party—and indirectly, one's own fate...

He sensed that his proposal seemed too Machiavellian to Smilga and the others. But he also knew that many in the party and outside it regarded him as a gambler; a gambler, however, who often didn't fully calculate his risks; he and his ideas therefore had to be treated with caution, it was said in Stalin's circle as well as among Zinoviev's friends; only Trotsky had the confidence to keep him, Radek, on the path of reason and virtue.

★

The second night was even worse than the first. This was already Siberian cold now, which relentlessly penetrated the carriage, and he was ill-equipped for it, his coat sufficient for Moscow or Leningrad, perhaps, but not for the Urals, on whose heights the two locomotives, one at the head, the other at the end of the train, swept along.

And then, once again one of the short days had passed, the mountains had been overcome; the last screeching curves downhill, sparks flew into the dusk, the train stopped; a shed grew out of the icy landscape where a siding branched off from the main line, and there were shouts and commands. "Dawai! Dawai!" and within minutes, he was standing, bewildered and breathless, next to his suitcases and boxes in the hidden snow; not far away, a hooded squad of new GPU people, the replacements who had seemingly appeared out of nowhere, eyeing him curiously as the train with Smilga and the others slowly rolled on, toward new horizons.

Radek approached the people, picked out the one among them who seemed the oldest and who wore a feral beard, and addressed him: "Are we traveling together from now on?"

"If you attempt to flee," said the man, "we'll shoot you."

"Flee—where?" Radek wanted to know.

"There's nothing here you can flee to," warned his new guard, "only Steppe. You'd be like a rabbit in a bare field."

"I'm cold," said Radek. "When do we go on?"

A shrug. But then the sergeant—for that was what he was—stirred, and pushed open the door of the shed, and Radek saw a red-hot stove inside and a table, on it a Morse device, and next to it a bench of the simplest kind, such as was to be found in railroad stations, on which the telegrapher was squatting, his greasy civil servant's cap pushed down his neck. The telegrapher nodded to him to sit down. Radek accepted the invitation.

"You're Karl Radek?"

So he was known, even here. "Radek," he confirmed, and began, enjoying the warmth radiating from the stove, "Karl Bernhardovich."

The telegraph operator indicated the shaggy fur thrown over the back of the bench and the thick felt boots standing there. "For you."

"For me?..." So simple. Radek swallowed. So simple—and yet a miracle. Since the application of Paragraph 58 (*counterrevolutionary activities*) to him, everything was reduced to the simplest: apparently, someone was sitting somewhere directing his fate, and this someone at the moment apparently did not wish for him to freeze to death in Siberia. And he was therefore not only allowed to partake of the fire, around which, in the meantime, the guards had grouped themselves, but also to be equipped with the necessary clothes.

"For me?" he asked, as if he wanted to be completely sure. "From whom?"

"Orders," said the telegraph operator.

From Stalin himself? Or Orzhonikidze? Or one of the GPU bosses? Or a person further down the official ladder, who remained humane?

"Comrade Stalin," said Radek, suddenly almost cheerful, "give him my thanks."

"You know him?"

"Of course." Radek stroked the thick shag of fur with relish. "We have regular discussions, Josif Vissarionovich and me. He has his views, and I have mine."

"If I," said the telegraph operator, "would have discussions with Comrade Stalin, I would never contradict him, not at any price."

"Maybe I'll behave that way as well in the future." Radek grinned. Then he had a new idea. "Would you," he asked, without much hope of anything coming of it, "send a telegram for me—to Moscow, to my wife?"

He waited, with mounting tension. But when no derisive laughter came, no "what are you thinking?" he began to look for a scrap of paper in his pocket, and a pencil.

The telegraph operator turned to his machine. "The text?"

The text! He couldn't believe it. But the man was really sitting there, stretching out his hand.

Radek shook his head and got hold of himself and wrote, *Rosa dear outright miracles today have just been given a fur and a pair of felt boots long live the Soviet power, kiss, Karl.* And took two fingers full of his small supply of tobacco from his pouch and stuffed his pipe and lit it with a splinter of wood that he briefly held to the stove and sucked the first smoke in celebration of the miracles of this day.

The telegraph operator began to work; Radek, fascinated, watched the little hammer moved by the man's finger; from that finger, if the authorities would only let it go through, the coded message would go out to his Rosa, the first to receive it: *I will survive.*

He sniffled from inner emotion; yes, he would survive; what had happened here, the fur, the boots, the telegraph operator, even the sergeant with the feral beard, was a sign. He went to the door, opened it, stepped outside and looked up at the stars, thinking, little Lolek Sobelsohn, he's become sentimental in his old age, that's what loneliness does, the terrible loneliness of exile.

A wedge of light flashed, a locomotive puffed in the distance; the train approached, two cars only, old army stock, for horses or soldiers. The sergeant, too, turned out to be a humane person; he ordered his men to heave Radek's luggage up into the car; they themselves got in behind, and they camped, guard and guarded together, in the freshly heaped, but already musty smelling straw.

The next day, the train arrived in Tobolsk. The station sign was still perforated with bullet holes from the civil war.

★

"Dear Lev Davidovich," he wrote to Trotsky. "Greetings of solidarity, from the bottom of my heart. The greatest enemy here is boredom; the newspapers first arrive after weeks, and then one hardly finds anything worth reading in them. And yet I sense even here there's unrest in the population; all the more painful that I'm completely cut off from everything that's happening. Do you have anything new, anything pleasant, to report?—the Boredom, as I said, and in addition the loneliness, and the cold, which prohibits one from spending a longer stretch of time outdoors, no matter how warmly one is dressed. I also soon caught a chill, and have kidney pain, for the first time in my life. The doctor I went to looks like a butcher and probably is one; he gave me powders, but they were of no use, and mumbled something about surgery if nothing else would help. I live in a wooden house, a hut really, but with carvings over the door, and an old woman comes and heats the stove and cooks for me, lots of cabbage, hardly any meat; people don't have it themselves. The local GPU chief is a brutal fool . . ."

He deleted that; the man could make life here impossible for him.

"Tobolsk has a Kremlin, once a noble building, quite untypical for the area, and which needs to be restored. And what is Stalin planning? Does he really want to give the peasants their private property, and create industry out of thin air? I shudder to think what that would require! Above all, imagination . . . And do you trust Stalin to have that kind of imagination? As

I see him, he only has imagination enough to manipulate the people . . ."

He also made this sentence unreadable; then he ended the letter with, *With old faithfulness—Radek.*

Nonetheless, only this GPU Chief, Luzhkin by name, remained for him as an interlocutor and source of news—the doctor and whoever else might be considered as belonging to the intelligentsia in Tobolsk—the Party Secretary, the Chairman of the Soviet, the school director and a few teachers, two or three semi-legal priests, the managers, or were they even the owners, both Jewish, of the grocery and general store, the former lawyer who did the paperwork for the old women of the town and the peasants in the surrounding countryside, the engineer in the machine and tractor station, and finally the rabbi—all hardly came into question for any serious thought; and Luzhkin possessed certain useful information, since the secret police made sure their full-time employees were oriented toward the tasks that would come their way. And anyway, he had to report to Luzhkin at regular intervals, first daily, then weekly, although he lived only about three hundred steps away from his official residence, directly under the eye of the police, so to speak. But the most enticing thing was that Luzhkin had a telephone, and you could attempt to get him to let you use it—not too often, of course—for a call to Moscow or somewhere else.

"Konstantin Samuilovich," he began, after putting his signature in Luzhkin's big log book as a sign that he had still not fled Tobolsk, "I won't say that we've become friends in the time since I've been under your supervision; your position in the world and mine are too opposite for that; we sit, one might describe it, one at this end of the table, the other at that end—but, after all, at one and the same table."

Luzhkin furrowed his low brow. At the same table with Radek: what would the people one step higher up say to that? And yet there was really no objection to this assessment of the situation, since, seen in this way, the distance from him to Radek was the same as that from Radek to him, and the answer to the famous question that Lenin had already asked, the question *Who, Whom?*, remained completely open; and no matter how clever Radek thought he was, he, Konstantin Samuilovich Luzhkin, after the special training he had received, was quite confident of his ability to deal with him, and sure, therefore, of his superiority, He announced: "You'll see for yourself, Radek, that your dreaming of all kinds of revolutions in all kinds of places hasn't paid off; it's all a question of organization; you simply have to know where to be at what time with how many men and for what purpose; everything else is idle chatter—idle chatter and a danger to what we have to deal with. But thank God, man is so built that he loves to see the result of his labors: the tailor his pants, the mason his house, the militiaman his prisoners: so everything has its order, and we see to it that it's preserved."

"Bravo!" said Radek, apparently genuinely pleased that Luzhkin had conjured up the opportunity to applaud him; Luzhkin's chest, however, swelled; in his provincial policeman's existence, he had so far seldom experienced being allowed to bask in the recognition of his peers, especially when they had been sent to him with the label *Political Opponent*; his own people were not so generous; medals, especially if they came with bonuses, hardly ever reached him; you had to fish for them yourself in the winter ice, and often enough you got your behind wet.

"Bravo!," repeated Radek, "you are a useful citizen," and decided to leave it at that; he had to avoid the suspicion of Comrade Luzhkin that he, Radek, wanted to put him in the light of glory in order to lead him by the nose once he was sufficiently dazzled.

"Ah, yes." Luzhkin sighed. "We are needed." And leaned forward, with a confidential gesture, "You mean, perhaps, what a big deal it is, a tiny nest in Siberia, what does it matter, a transient every few weeks to be registered, an exile here and there to be reported on; but don't forget, around Tobolsk the district, the villages with the kulaks, each one an embryonic bourgeois, you don't suspect, Karl Bernhardovich, what riches are being hoarded there in huts where one suspects nothing but a stinking stove on which the unwashed guy sleeps away the winter..."

Radek's ears perked up. Where were these tones coming from? This topic?

"But not for long!" continued Luzhkin, his broad face reddening. "Maybe the big life will be over soon, and the proletariat will strike!"

"You mean?"

A superior grin. "Luzhkin, Konstantin Samuilovich, is not a talker."

"I've also," Radek admitted, "heard of such things, and one of the reasons I'm sitting here, torn away from my wife and child, exiled to the Siberian wasteland, one of these reasons is that I and my political friends have long demanded steps of this kind. Vladimir Ilyich and myself, I can attest to you from my own experience, did not sweep away the big landlords in order to prepare the way for a class of fat large farmers..."

Unnoticed by Luzhkin, he had moved over to his side of the table. "The revolution," he continued, "has gone over from the young, who wanted new relations in 1917 and who waged the civil war for that purpose, to people of more moderate habitus, to the slow and quiet who, averse to all risks, always call only for security and even lose what little they have which was achieved with toil and trouble. But I have kept in my heart the youth that has become inconvenient to the types of officials in today's Moscow and in Omsk and Tomsk."

He paused and observed Luzhkin; but he didn't seem to consider himself such an official. "Incidentally," he then continued, "I believe that you too, Konstantin Samuilovich, are constituted quite similarly to how I am, otherwise you'd hardly be so hotly anticipating the developments to come . . ."

He reached for the telephone receiver. "May I?"

Immediately, Luzhkin felt uneasy again. But the man in front of him was, as it turned out, a secret sympathizer, and besides he, Luzhkin, was present and listening, and not through a special device connected somewhere, but directly, controlling every word that came from Radek's lips; and what could be so dangerous about the conversation of a husband with his wife, who, from Radek's tone and the content of his words, had something very pleasant to tell him?

Finally—Luzhkin was already gesticulating—Radek hung up, turned to him and said, beaming, "Do you know, Konstantin Samuilovich, what my wife has just told me? She thinks it will be approved for her to come to me in Tobolsk, with the child!"

Luzhkin nodded. "I already knew."

"What?" Radek's voice momentarily trailed off. "Since when? And you didn't tell me anything about it? And just let me ramble on about kulaks and revolution and youth and whatever else?"

Luzhkin, proud that he belonged to the stratum of those in the know, and was treated accordingly, rubbed his hands. "The world will find out about our plans and intentions soon enough."

"I'm not the world. I'm Radek."

"You are, pardon me, a completely ordinary prisoner, Paragraph 58, counterrevolutionary activities. And now get lost, Radek, I have work to do."

So, she'd come. The worst thing, the loneliness, would be taken from him. Or not. Since when did employees of the apparatus entrust state secrets—and this was one—to the wives of deportees or to some provincial policeman? Only when he saw them in front of him, his Rosa and little daughter Sonja, under the station sign with the inscription *Tobolsk*, would he believe in his happiness; he had learned that much in the years of the dictatorship of the proletariat, to whose power structure he himself had belonged, even if only as someone of the second rank; that there neither rules nor laws applied equally to everyone, and that even promises of an official nature could be interpreted arbitrarily, the arbitrariness of the superiors.

The longer he thought about the new turn that had been announced to him there, and always presupposing that it would become reality, the closer he came to the conclusion that someone higher up was playing a game with him; letting him fall, but just before the fatal impact, catching him; punishing him, but at the same time, within certain self-imposed limits, favoring him, quite similar to a teacher in a seminary, who tried to tame his unruly pupils by means of the stick and an occasional piece of carrot—and that this pedagogue, who was concerned with the weal and woe of little Lolek Sobelsohn, must be Comrade Stalin himself, who had his own intentions with him—and possibly even his own inner ties to him. Had he, Radek, not had a very special relationship with Lenin as well? And didn't Stalin know about it? And didn't Stalin also need a person—*one* at least—who didn't just tell him what he wanted to hear? So he made a kind of bet with himself; if his wife and child really came to him in Siberia, if the news had not been a deliberate deception, spread through Rosa and through stupid Luzhkin, in order to test how far his power of resistance reached, then it would become clear who it was that held the hand over him, and he would know the point of reference according to which he could set course and sail.

The next few weeks, even months, he spent in inner restlessness, increased by the never-ending winter. He wrote, by the dim light of the oil lamp, letters, for the censors; articles, for the desk; chapters of his book, for the future; his kidney troubled him, with each day he felt more tired, he stayed in bed longer; only the visits to Luzhkin, which he had to complete, forced him outdoors, and even Luzhkin noticed his bad condition and put him off until spring, which had to come at last, even here in Tobolsk.

And spring came. Suddenly there was a different blue, and streams trickled, and buds appeared on the birch trees, and Radek took a cloth and cleaned the windows, so that it would be brighter in his room, and the old woman swept the floor, and gave him a bundle of green branches with colorful ribbons, for Holy Easter, she said.

On that day, Varga appeared. Luzhkin brought Varga with an indifferent expression, as if it were the most natural thing in the world for a Hungarian professor of economics based in Moscow to go specifically to Tobolsk in Siberia to pay a brief visit to an indefinite exile. "Allow me to enter, Comrade Radek," said Varga, "the last time we saw each other, if you'll recall, was at my lecture at Sun Yat-sen University, you delighted me greatly then with your observation that you had seldom heard such clear and at the same time interesting words from your podium."

"Eugen Varga!" Radek cried. "Welcome!," and hurried to put on water, wishing that Luzhkin had already gone to hell, though he would have been only too glad to learn from the latter why the sudden guest, and at whose instigation, and whether he, Luzhkin, had this time also been informed of the matter in advance. "You must tell me everything, Varga, what's going on in Moscow, and where you got the idea of calling on me in the great void, and are you still …"

"Yes, I am still," responded Varga, removing his paletot and sitting down at the table; Luzhkin remained standing, but kept close by, the eternal overseer.

Radek had certainly sensed the point in his guest's insinuation: wiser and more cautious than he, Radek, Varga had avoided openly taking sides in the great debate and had therefore, although Hungarian and Jewish, been left in the function into which he had stumbled—without planning to—over the years; one of the few experts on economic matters who still had something to say to those at the top.

"And you just," Radek asked, "made a detour to Tobolsk on your way to I don't know where? Just by chance?"

Varga turned to Luzhkin with a look that the man promptly reacted to: he took a step back, said, "I'll see to your quarters for tonight, Comrade Varga," and disappeared.

"How beneficial a little power can be," Radek commented, preparing the tea, and Varga fetched a bottle of vodka from a briefcase, and now they were sitting opposite each other, almost like old friends, and Radek lost a good part of his mistrust when the other smilingly admitted that no, he had not come by chance; on the other hand, he had not come on someone's direct order, either; indeed, there had been a conversation with one of the now leading people . . .

"Who?" Radek wanted to know.

Varga raised his glass; it doesn't matter; maybe the whole thing only rests upon his interpretation of a side remark in said conversation . . .

"And because of your personal interpretation of a side remark—so many kilometers into the wasteland?"

"Yes!" said Varga indignantly. And emphasized again, hoarsely, yes, it had been his own decision, not an order of any kind from above. In view of the developments he foresaw, he believed that a clever man like Radek was needed, not in Siberia, but in the center of power, his voice, his power of words; but how could one expect a Stalin to fall to his knees before him and beat his breast, *mea culpa*, Karl Bernhardovich; no, the first step would have to come from Radek; and what was worth more to him: a small loss of face, or the return to Moscow?

"Face!" said Radek disparagingly. "How much face does anyone have these days? But there are loyalties."

"And there are facts. Would you like to hear how the economy of this country is really doing . . . ?" Varga pulled a few sheets of paper from his briefcase, on them columns of figures and curves of various kinds, and spread them on the table in front of Radek. "We are accustomed," he explained, "to glossing over reality, especially in our public pronouncements; it makes life easier and sweetens one's sleep; but I can't afford such tactics, even at the risk of offending one or the other . . . You see . . ."

His index finger glided over the entries as he lectured Radek as if he were the head of a government institute or even a ministry and not a deportee beyond the Urals. It was clear from the lecture that the Soviet Union, despite its vast resources of men and materials, was facing economic bankruptcy, which would come tomorrow rather than the day after, and that no help was in sight, either at home or abroad, either from proletarian masses in Germany or China or India filled with revolutionary spirit, nor from Western investors inspired by their business acumen, "And to strike a military blow of liberation against capitalist encirclement: we don't have the necessary industrial base for that either ... So ..."

So, thought Radek, the full justification of Trotsky's theses was being proven; the approaching collapse confirmed the speeches and actions of the opposition; and if Stalin were consistent in his crudely knit thinking for even ten kopeks, he would have to think of a comparison with Trotsky. "So," he took up the sentence begun by Varga, "socialism in a single country is nothing," and felt hot gloating rise within him, but immediately suppressed it; whose revolution was going to hell in a handbasket, if not his own?

"According to all rules of logic," Varga admitted, watching Radek stuff his pipe with trembling fingers, "according to all the rules of logic you would be right; but we're not dealing with logic here, honored one, but with the desperation of a man of power who has decided on a *tour de force*; and I, strictly a logician, have come to the conclusion that under the given circumstances this *tour de force* is the only logical thing to do, and have entered fully into the mad enterprise and have collaborated in the drafting of a first Five-Year Plan for the industrialization of the Soviet Union and other such plans to follow, and for the conversion of agriculture from the individual cultivation of private plots to a common, collective, large industrial land area—whatever you want to call it—which at the same time will give us the opportunity to control the recalcitrant producers down to the last peasant and his last acre ..."

Since Radek had forgotten to look at the clock, he didn't know how long they sat together that night over the vision of a highly adventurous future, despite the dry figures and formulas on which it was based, but he did remember the elation that filled him because someone of Varga's stature was wooing him, as if the success of the whole great project depended on his, Radek's approval—which was possibly, he thought, even the case, at least from Varga's point of view: for he was probably not as self-confident in his heart as he appeared to be on the outside.

Then he escorted his guest over the muddy paths of Tobolsk to his lodgings near the Kremlin, on whose squiggly roofs the moon cast white shadows, and they embraced each other, and then, at a short distance, he caught sight of a dark shadow, motionless, spectral, almost—the representative of the secret police, Konstantin Samuilovich Luzhkin.

But nothing followed from Varga's visit, remarkable though it was; the days passed, the weeks; the late Siberian spring set in with milder airs; he wrote, to Trotsky, and to other comrades-in-fate, seeking to uplift them and himself at the same time, and to exhort them to continue bravely to bear their adversity; the coming events, he prophesied, would prove how right they had been and were to persist in their oppositional attitude.

And when he thought of the hand that, as he imagined, someone was holding over him, and of the bet he had made with himself, a bitter laugh came over him; why then had Rosa not arrived long ago with the child? And why Rosa's evasive answer to his every time more urgent request, by letter and by telegraph? Since Varga's visit Luzhkin denied him the use of the GPU's own telephone—why the endless waiting? Only because in Russia, as was known, every official procedure took three times as long as in the rest of the world, or because Rosa's joyful news, together with its confirmation by Luzhkin, had been based on a rumor instead of reality?

But then, the pain in his back and his restless thoughts deprived him more and more often of his nightly sleep. There was a knock at the front door early in the morning, and Luzhkin stuck his head into the living room to ask if he could enter, on official business; and when Radek, in a bad mood, replied that the police usually exercise their rights without permission, he entered, positioned himself with his legs wide apart next to Radek's bed, and said, "I have the agreeable duty, Karl Bernhardovich, of informing you that your wife and daughter Sonja will be arriving here later today," and letting an already opened telegram flutter on Radek's bedspread, added, "I had expected, if I may say so, an outcry of happiness, or at least a more cheerful face!"

"What do you care about my face!" said Radek, who reached for the telegram, sat up, stretched his legs out of the bed, and read. His breath came hastily. Yes, that was her language, that was real; and at the same time he was annoyed that this policeman already knew the text, had forced his way in between him and his wife, and was delighting in both their feelings, *Finally! Forgive me for keeping silent for so long. Love, great love! See you soon.*

"We'll have to get a bed for my daughter." Radek slipped into his pants. "Go to the carpenter and see if he has one for sale, otherwise have him make one. And as soon as possible. And anyway, you don't expect, Luzhkin, that the three of us will live in this primitive hut without the slightest comfort. You're responsible for me, your superiors will have told you that—responsible as well, therefore, for my and my family's living conditions. And the fact that my wife and child are now coming to me should have set certain thought processes in motion even in your brain!"

An evil light glinted in Luzhkin's eyes. "Very well, Comrade Radek. See you in the afternoon, at the station."

"And get a carriage, please."

He already saw her from afar; she leaned out of the window and beckoned to him, and he ran with his awkward steps to the carriage and pulled open the compartment door and helped first her and then the little one to climb down and embraced both in his arms, and said, once to each, "Thank God!" and, "Now everything will be all right again!" and turned and called, "Luzhkin!," and Luzhkin came up, uniformed now, and on his breast the two medals he possessed, but before he could introduce himself to Rosa, as was proper, Radek said, "Luzhkin! Why don't you take care of the luggage?" and Luzhkin pulled himself together and clasped the suitcases under his arms and carried them over to the carriage, where the coachman he had hired was standing by, and the three of them got in, Radek with his wife and little daughter, and Radek turned to his guard once more, "Please see to it that the rest of the luggage is brought to us as soon as possible!" and to the *izvostchik*. "Drive off!" And the duped Luzhkin, who had intended to claim the fourth seat in the cab for himself, remained behind, angry.

"No, Sonja," said Radek, trying in vain to keep the dust that rose from the bumpy road away from his daughter, "no, how tall you've grown! And how pretty!"

And indeed, she had reached the years when her childlike features began to change to those of a young woman, and she sat there, wrapped in her coat, the fur-trimmed ruff turned up, and around her head a checkered shawl, looking around her with wide, wondering eyes.

"It's all very rustic," he said, "but that's how they live here." And, encouragingly, "And how have you both been in all this time? Have you missed me as much as I've missed you?"

Suddenly, a tear rolled down the face of the little one, who was no longer so little. It was the wrong question, he thought; he was no longer used to familiar interaction with the only people who were his.

And he cursed Stalin with one of those long, rolling, Siberian curses that Luzhkin had taught him. Rosa shook her head, while Sonja marveled at him, wiping the almost dried tears from her cheek with the back of her hand.

"Excuse me," he said, "I promise to improve myself."

3

Later, most of the individual details would blur in his memory, the when, the how, and the where, and the sequence of events; he'd only remember certain highlights.

Such as the move to Tomsk, which followed the arrival of his wife and child, necessarily, as it were; for, Radek reflected, if someone proceeded with him according to plan and intention, then that someone had to lead him out of Tobolsk, where, left to himself, without connection to any others, he could have done nothing but continue to crawl along in tracks formed long ago and to ruminate in patterns solidified long ago. In Tomsk, however, already a larger city, but still in Siberia. he was joined by a few people who, like him, were troubled by the apparent futility of their existence and longed for change, in their own lives and in the life of the country. And here lay the danger that they posed to the rulers: change was everything to them; the permanent revolution that Trotsky saw in the life of peoples was in their blood; and whoever wanted to eliminate the danger, or even take advantage of the energies created by their instinct for change, had to let such people have their way—or exterminate them.

However, the move didn't take place so quickly. It took time for Luzhkin to decide to inform Radek of the council of the gods; after all, Luzhkin had no one else to give him importance and even to bring visitors of the quality of Professor Varga to his domain. Thus, Luzhkin was in no hurry to shuttle his personal charge and his family to Tomsk and leave them to his colleague in the field there, and pleased himself in pretending to a Tobolsk social life, at the center of which he placed the Radek couple, surrounded by half a dozen splendid specimens of the local intelligentsia—he himself, Luzhkin, brought drinks and food, as he had provided the bed for Sonya and the new larger house on the road by the river, and his wife, who could not deny her peasant heritage, cooked and served at the festive meal.

But ultimately, Luzhkin arrived, and told Radek that the

authorities were having him and his family transferred to the city of Tomsk, which already offered certain amenities and stimuli, and, with a broad grin, "I myself will escort you to your new place of exile and hand you over to the care of Comrade Poltorenko."

"How caring!" sneered Radek, thinking that this, then, had been the secret about which the guy kept dropping hints; and the improvements in his and his family's situation, which would undoubtedly occur with their departure from Tobolsk, had been spoiled for him by the way in which he was passed on, like a leper, from one personal informer to another.

"And this unpleasantness," he said to Rosa, "will now remain with us for the rest of our years," and tried to cope with it by his usual irony; but he didn't quite succeed, and even Rosa, who thought that at times at least they'd be able to shake off the riffraff, and in the meantime the lads might let themselves be used for this or that practical purpose, was not able to tear him out of his depression.

★

But the doctors at least, the doctors at the hospital in Tomsk were able to help him. They took care of his kidney and, after a thorough examination, ruled out the need for surgery and prescribed medicines and a diet that gradually improved his condition; he regained the desire to work, encouraged as well by Trotsky, who admonished him from Alma Ata, "I advise you to live sensibly in order to preserve yourself. At any cost. We are still very, very much needed . . ." And sat with Sonja, who was now going to school in Tomsk, at her homework; and at night he and Rosa loved each other anew; after a long time, until then, relaxed and reasonably happy, they both fell asleep.

And a few weeks later, Smilga arrived from Naryn and Preobrazhensky from his place of exile, one after the other, and the three of them, mostly on walks in the woods, braved the eavesdropping attacks of Comrade Poltorenko, Fyodor

Fyodorovich, who not only looked and acted like Luzhkin's one and only twin, but also seemed to be so in all his expressions of life. Preobrazhensky had received news of Trotsky's recent serious illness, malaria, with complications, and the three of them discussed how to help their friend in faraway Kazakhstan, and Preobrazhensky, whose otherwise mild voice suddenly hardened, proposed an appeal in the matter of Trotsky, addressed to the Central Committee, but indirectly addressed to the world public—without regard to what might happen to them afterward.

Smilga, who had long been one of Trotsky's most faithful, raised his bushy, already graying brows: even if he no longer made a secret of the thoughts he had developed in the isolation of Narym, and which had begun to deviate considerably from the political line of the opposition, he nevertheless agreed with Preobrazhensky about Trotsky's person and his illness. And Radek, who did not have a guilty conscience, but an uneasy feeling in his body because of his increasingly clear distrust of Trotsky's theses, announced all the louder: "Yes, an appeal! And in clear language, such as one has not heard for a long time!" Let Stalin see how he'll cope with the text when it goes from Tomsk across the country to the groups of oppositionists, and from them to all citizens and beyond the borders; in any case, it would be a great relief to him, Radek, if he could finally give vent to his heart. And reaching for a sheet of paper, while watching Comrade Poltorenko lurking at the window of the neighboring house, he wrote the beginning of the appeal and, pen still between his fingers, read it to the other two. "Having learned of the illness of Comrade L.D. Trotsky . . . we appeal to the Central Committee of the Party with the request . . . to transfer Comrade Trotsky to a place . . . where the possibility of his treatment is given!"

Smilga's gaunt face twisted. "Perhaps a bit more personal! Let's talk about ourselves, too! Like this: The older ones among us have been expelled from the party and banished as counter-revolutionaries, although we have fought for communism for a quarter of a century, and we have to eke out a living on thirty rubles a month; but the treatment of Trotsky during his serious illness is the outrageous climax!"

Radek glanced at Preobrazhensky, who was again smiling quietly to himself. "And you, Yevgeny Antonovich?"

"Ah," he said, "I'm thinking something very simple to myself, but appealing to the emotions. Here: We've seen Comrade Trotsky on all fronts of the civil war. And although we no longer have a party book, but only an identity card with the seal of the GPU and the note Paragraph 58, we raise our voices to save Comrade Trotsky and demand the lifting of his banishment and, at the same time, that of all Bolshevik-Leninists."

The light at Poltorenko's window went out, but the shadow of his head remained. "And do it, dear Comrades," Radek added to the letter, "as soon as possible."

They signed: Smilga, I.T.; Preobrazhensky, Y. A.; Radek, K. B.; and the next day they delivered the brief to the post office, with Poltorenko as their witness.

In his speeches, Stalin forgot to mention that the treatment of the poor peasants and industrial workers, which he now promised to improve as quickly as possible, had been one of the essential points of the opposition: the opposition had shown how from the NEP, the New Economic Policy—which Lenin had launched in order to bring about some kind of production in the destroyed country—a quite potent exploitative society had developed, with which both government and party bureaucracy were interwoven and intertwined. And precisely in this lay—as not only Trotsky and he, Radek, but also the majority of the Old Bolsheviks saw it—the secret inner structure of Stalin's rule, and if they had opposed and demanded remedy, and harsh taxation of the rich large peasants and merchants, and control over the bureaucracy, and elimination of indirect taxes on peasants who had neither horse nor plow, and workers who had only their own hands, the logical answer of the apparatus—Preobrazhensky and Smilga fully agreed with him—had to be the new terror, of which the three of them, among many others, were the victims here in Tomsk.

It did good to analyze current events among like-minded people—and also, where possible, with one's own wife—and to draw conclusions about one's own behavior in the immediate future. For Stalin, according to his, Radek's, experience, was by nature incapable of moderation. The news piled up indicating that the government's new steps, wherever they pointed, went beyond reasonable limits. "We had suggested at the time," Radek mentioned, "to tax the wealthy peasants heavily; he's having them exterminated, as a class and even physically, and the consequences are already being felt, bread is getting worse and scarcer."

Smilga leaned forward. He could talk very intensely when it came to his area of expertise. "In industry—the same gigantism! He can't leave it at one factory, one plant, no, it has to be a whole collective combine, and built out of thin air! No matter what it costs, in money, in human lives."

"And while hunger is rampant in the country," Preobrazhensky mentioned, "food is exported abroad at giveaway prices to bring in gold to finance technology." And added almost tenderly, "And yet it's our old general line . . ."

"So?" Radek pursed his lips. "What are you trying to say? Doesn't the success of an enterprise depend primarily on who carries it out?" And, satisfied with the punch of his argument, stuffed his pipe.

But Smilga countered, "But the fact is that neither you could carry out the new program, nor Preobrazhensky, nor I, nor even Trotsky. We have allowed ourselves to be catapulted out of the positions from which history is made, and instead we are clucking in this Siberian chicken coop."

"I wonder," Preobrazhensky had become reflective, "what a Lenin would have done in our situation . . . You knew him, Karl Bernhardovich . . ."

Radek looked after the smoke that he blew out in thin clouds. "Lenin, I suppose, would never have allowed himself to get into our situation—at least not while he was healthy—and not by the games of a man like Stalin."

"But if need be?"

Radek thought of the Zurich main station, the special carriage, in front of which the noisy emigrants. "If need be, he would have done everything to return to the scene of action at the first opportunity."

"Everything?" asked Smilga.

"Everything."

"You see," said Preobrazhensky.

It was inevitable that Rosa sensed the approaching changes in her husband's thinking; they brought conflicts with them, psychological ones above all; one couldn't begin to have serious doubts about Trotsky's permanent revolution without, at the same time, undergoing a painful process of detaching oneself from him psychologically as well. Which did not at all mean that he, Radek, was already willing to defect with flying colors to Stalin's socialism in a single country. What kind of socialism was that, he asked Rosa, from which more and more people were turning away, so that they had to be forced by violence or, in individual cases, by bribery, to yield their labor power? —But Trotsky's thesis did not bear fruit either: wherever any fruit began to reveal itself, a leading comrade, especially chosen for the task, knocked it from the tree before it matured. And where was the new Lenin, who developed from the ineffectual doctrines a new, sensible one, which promised to bring results?

In that same spirit, he wrote to Trotsky—in the form of questions, not of fixed opinions—and hoped that his letter would reach his friend between two attacks of his malaria and that he would thus receive an answer; and indeed one came: Poltorenko brought it himself, read by the police, and remarked with a cheeky smile that he, Radek, would probably not find much that was new in it, whereupon Rosa angrily ordered the GPU man out of the house; Radek, who in the meantime had leafed through the contents of the thick envelope, said, "But the fellow is right!" and pushed the papers toward Rosa: Lev Davidovich had had the fun of compiling on his typewriter a good dozen lengthy Radek quotations, all of which declared permanent revolution to be inevitable and socialism in one country to be total nonsense.

Rosa knew how much the sick man of Alma Ata must have hurt Radek with this missive; never one to readily admit his weaknesses, her Karl had probably confided to Trotsky, and apparently the latter, God knows why, had misunderstood the display of confidence as a poorly veiled attack on his most sacred theory, and had defended himself accordingly. Nevertheless, she refrained from stroking her husband's soul and said to him, "Be big enough to accept the lesson Trotsky has taught you. You've faltered. And that makes you vulnerable to people like him, or even Stalin. You're going to have to make up your mind whose side you're going to take—and until you do, don't give yourself away."

"And which side do you advise me to take?"

"I don't know," she said, "neither will bring you happiness."

"I want to live," he said. "To live at least until it's revealed whether what I've done in life has been in vain."

"That," she said, "is the long view."

Everyone here in Tomsk had their secret aims.

Preobrazhensky wanted to organize. He wanted to make people out of numbers: the right people with the right tools in the right place, so that the right thing would come into being; now and here he wasn't even a spectator. "Karl Bernhardovich," he said, "how long are we going to wait?"

Smilga pressed his wrists together as if someone had chained them together. "I want to build," he said. "They should let me near where they're building the new factories. What do I care about the ideological differences, the damned theses and comments, and speeches and rebuttals."

And Rosa said to Radek, "You, too, could do more useful things than you're doing now, and I could support you. All right, I help Sonja with her schoolwork, and keep us together, body and soul; but is that enough? Let's discuss it."

Poltorenko, however, already saw himself, similar to his predecessor Luzhkin, raised several notches on the GPU's official ladder as a reward for his work with and on Radek; not for nothing had Radek told him, "Wait until I capitulate, then you'll experience something!" And, seeing Poltorenko open his mouth, added, "That was a joke, of course, I'm famous for my jokes, they'll have told you that much!"

Upon which, Poltorenko sat down and with his clumsy hand wrote a clumsy report, with a copy to Moscow, to the effect that the exiled Radek, K.B., was showing clear signs of a change of heart, which is why he, Poltorenko, requested new instructions.

Radek withdrew. In the past, he had mostly done this when he was preparing a coup and wanted to be clear about its contingencies; now, it wasn't a coup in the true sense of the word, but rather a thoughtful essay; one considered what if, the possibilities, the consequences, and all that was seen through one's own glasses and presented—yes, for whom? First and foremost, for himself, although he owed Rosa just as much an answer to the question he had in mind: after all, it concerned her and the child's future to the same extent as it did him. And Preobrazhensky, and Smilga, and hundreds, thousands of others.

On his solitary walks, the leaves were changing color early in these parts, he caught himself in fragments of soliloquies, and mocked: What are you dramatizing, Lolek, the ascent from the depths into which you have plunged yourself; no one has pushed you but yourself, your enemy was your own folly.

Then he had the idea. And it grew with perfect logic out of the book he was working on anyway, and the parallelism of the conflicts of those times and these times—and the question had already been put to him: How would Lenin . . .

Radek had returned to his house and pulled the door of his chamber shut behind him. Yes, how would Lenin decide, today? At that time, when the decision really lay with him, and him alone, Vladimir Ilyich, like him, Radek, had known that socialism in a single country, and one like Russia at that, was still less than a utopia—an impossibility!—and yet on that October evening he had proclaimed: We are now proceeding to build socialism!

There was a difference between arguing about an idea in a coffeehouse and being confronted with the real necessity of guiding the fate of millions along this track or that one, or into the abyss.

And wrote: Vladimir Ilyich, as I knew him, would have chosen socialism in a single country in our situation. Comrades, he would have said, this is the hard road, but it is the only one, and since when do we shy away from a few stones and potholes?

And knew how Stalin would lap it up; but was one allowed to conceal or distort the truth just because it suited Stalin? And how could one get ahead? He himself, above all. His, Radek's, interest was: to survive. Survive personally. But it was also the survival of the Soviet Union; it was also the survival of socialism. That was the new Holy Trinity, he, the country, the idea, whose Paul he would become when he imputed such a speech to Comrade Lenin. But also, who could prove him wrong? Trotsky? Or resent his quotation of Lenin? Wasn't the end a good one?

"They won't print it," said Smilga after reading Radek's text, and Preobrazhensky agreed with him. "We've been stamped as non-persons—not to be remembered, as the Bible curses such people; you can submit the most beautiful piece of prose, Radek, the purest joy for the Politburo; as long as it bears your name as author, or one of ours, it will inevitably go to the furthest corner of the filing cabinet, after being noted by the competent authorities."

"Maybe being noted is precisely what I want?" replied Radek, and sent his article to Comrade Trotsky in Alma Ata, with good wishes for his recovery, and a copy to the editorial staff of *Izvestia*, knowing full well that the manuscript would have been handled by the secret police long before it arrived there.

By then it was January, and winter, already his second in Siberia, lay like a white carapace over the land, and together with Poltorenko, the bringer of news, a gush of icy air entered the room.

"Can't you shut the door?" Rosa scolded.

"I know I'm not welcome." Poltorenko brushed off his felt boots, which soon left a puddle on the wood of the hallway. "But I am obliged to return this letter to your husband. The addressee has moved."

He put the envelope on the table with the address facing up. Radek read: *Alma Ata. Trotsky, L.D.*

"Moved?"

"Yes, to Turkey. To Prinkipo."

Turkey, thought Radek, feeling the heavy throbbing of his heart. And thought: Prinkipo. Already the Roman emperors had sent their exiles to the island.

And now it was beheaded, the Russian opposition: a Trotsky abroad was no longer their Trotsky, was a foreigner, no matter how sharp his thoughts still were, and how sensitive.

"He was taken aboard a Soviet ship," Poltorenko said, "and now he's gone, and he won't return to us. By order of the government."

"I'd appreciate it, Poltorenko," said Radek, "if you'd leave us alone now."

★

"This is the height of shamelessness!" Smilga looked around: no one contradicted him. "And it's the public admission that the Politburo can't cope with the opposition, that our thoughts are stronger than Stalin's clichés, even though he has everything on his side, the printing press, the apparatus, the privileges of power."

"We must protest!" shouted Preobrazhensky. "All of us! In all the places of exile! And wherever else there are comrades of ours! And our protest will stir up the people of the country, and they, too, will raise their voices and ..."

He fell silent. He had spoken too rashly, and too loudly: such proclamations came a dozen to ten kopeks, and everyone here was clear about their value and effect, he Smilga, Radek, and Rosa—it was better to keep silent.

"Of course there must be protest," Radek assured him. "As long as you have a pen and a piece of paper and a way to get that piece of paper into circulation—always protest!" He laughed, a bit too shrill. "There's still time to commit suicide."

Rosa was startled. But, she said to herself then, he wasn't the type.

And immediately he also explained, "I'm talking about political suicide. There are two forms of it: exile and surrender."

"And you think we have a choice, Karl Bernhardovich?" inquired Preobrazhensky.

"If you call it a choice, Yevgeni Antonovich!"

They sat around the table, and none of them spoke anymore. Radek saw before him the solitary man on the rocky shore of his Turkish island, the sparkling pince-nez, the sharp profile that had been so familiar to him since Brest-Litovsk, the graying shock of hair. Then he got paper and pen and began to write, first one sheet, then the next, with a few short pauses for thought, while the others deliberately avoided looking over his shoulder. Rosa got up and refilled the tea cups. At last he put aside his pen, read over his two drafts, and nodded.

"Do you want to hear?"

He expected no answer, and received none.

"Version one," he read: "*To the Central Control Commission of the All-Unionist Communist Party, Bolshevik. We, the undersigned, raise a vehement protest against the expatriation and*

*deportation of Comrade Trotsky, L.D. We swear that we will
not rest nor pause until Comrade Trotsky, L.D., who more than
anyone else in his person embodies our revolution, has been invited
by the Government of the Soviet Union and the Central Committee
of the Party to return to the rightful place of his political activity.*
Signatures follow."

He took a deep breath, but did not look up, as if he was not
interested in Smilga's reaction, nor Preobrazhensky's, nor that
of his wife.

And recited, "Version two: To the Central Control Commission
and so on: *We, the undersigned, hereby declare our agreement with
the general political line of the Party and our break with the theses
and assertions of the Opposition. We declare that we no longer have
anything in common with Trotsky's theory of permanent revolution and his related doctrines, and withdraw our signatures from
the documents of the Opposition, and hereby ask to be readmitted
to the Party.*" He raised his head. "And again the names."

Rosa stood up, stepped behind him, and gently stroked his
stubborn hair and neck.

★

Eventually, he knew, they would choose the second version. But
until then, time would pass, months, the better part of a year, a
time full of inner conflict, full of turmoil and agony: was one a
man of character, or a dog that crept along the edge of the road,
shy-eyed and tail between its legs?

Fate was named, how else, Poltorenko.

Poltorenko came with an official-looking document, which
turned out to be an order for five tickets of the cheaper class from
the city of Tomsk in Siberia to Moscow's Kazan Station; in addition, the stipulation, read out by Poltorenko with audible gusto,
that the voucher was valid only for the specified date; otherwise,
if one wished to travel on the route, one would have to pay the
fare out of one's own pocket.

Exactly in this way and not otherwise, Radek thought, by an administrative act of a state enterprise, a bureaucrat like Stalin would indicate to him and his people that their banishment had been lifted and that they were once again free Soviet citizens: no court order, no ukase of the party, or even a personal message, even if it was only signed by a subordinate secretary. To such people as he, who until recently had stood up for creatures like Trotsky, not even the satisfaction of writing: We, the Khosyain, the master of the house, have found it necessary to change our mind and to give appropriate orders; such traces are not left in history by a great man!

Comrade Poltorenko, however, received certain instructions, which he didn't comment on, but which kept him fully occupied until the departure of the Radek group; and when, at the various stops of the train, in Kochenevo, in Chany, Taltarsk, Maryanovka, there appeared with striking regularity clusters of exiles—oppositionists, that is—such as he and Smilga and Preobrazhensky had recently been themselves, when, despite the presence of the local police, the members of the traveling party were loudly summoned to the window of the carriage or dragged out onto the platform and justification was demanded from them for their sudden departure from the old ideals, Radek began to suspect that the organization to which Poltorenko and his predecessor Luzhkin belonged might be connected with the origin of this turbulence, whether on Stalin's or someone else's behalf. They were interested, obviously, in his behavior under the new circumstances.

In Marjanovka, one of them, standing out from the others on a wooden box, a red-haired man with a bright, youthful voice, shouted, "Here, listen to what Comrade Trotsky has written to us, and you, Radek, Preobrazhensky, Smilga, over in your train to Moscow, listen! You, once destined to endure the war and the October Revolution with honor, have erased yourselves from the book of the living. You have deprived yourselves of the most important thing that distinguishes man: the right to trust. No one will give it back to you, no Stalin and no Central Committee!"

Radek, at the compartment window, behind him his wife and daughter and the two traveling companions, felt anger rising in his chest, bitter anger. "Trotsky!" he shouted back. "Who is Trotsky anymore—a failure! A loser! And remember for your own lives—it's not the duty of a politician, when he's said A, to always say A! Sometimes he must say B, and sometimes even Y! Or he can also explain that he never said A at all!"

The hissing of the locomotive, the clanking of the couplings on the carriages, the screeching of the axles, and above it all—the train was already moving—from the platform the noise of indignation, the shouts and curses. He stepped back from the window, dropped onto the bench and covered his head in his coat. After a while he felt Sonja's thin, hot fingers comforting his hand.

If he thought his ordeal would end after his return, the Party taught him otherwise. The Party deposited him and his family in a basement apartment—apartment was a euphemism—a damp hole that reeked of rot, with a broken sink, rotten pipes, wallpaper flakes falling from the walls, and a view of the passing feet of the population: At the moment, the comrade from *Izvestia*, who had picked them up at the train station, remarked, nothing more luxurious could be offered to them; he, Radek, knew what sacrifices the Five-Year Plan demanded from the population; besides, he should prepare himself for his appearance at the *chistka*, the great purge, which was now being carried out throughout the country, and especially in Moscow.

He had gotten out of the habit of getting angry at every mean thing that was done to him; raving did no good, and people were increasingly losing their sense of the polished word, his own weapon.

"Let it be," said Rosa, "the man is right: first the *chistka*."

The *chistka* occurred in the assembly room of the print press of *Izvestia*; for such events, the competent authority preferred to choose a workers' locale and a workers' audience; thus, the questions that made up the *chistka* could be asked by some people down below who were not even aware of how highly embarassing these questions were, and, in addition, the ruling class got the feeling that they were really allowed to exercise dominion over those who were thrown before them as victims.

At first, Radek was worried when he stood there on the podium, and next to him, comfortably reclined in their imitation leather armchairs, the inquisitors, selected apparatchiki, and in front of them the printers and typesetters and machinists, skilled workers with a certain experience; and some of them still knew him from the time when he had corrected their own articles in the typesetting room and then watched them paginate, and helped with final changes; and there were indeed a few with whom he thought he felt sympathy: They accepted his answers to the probing questions with which the Party representatives put him, although he often enough avoided the point of the matter—they were content with superficialities; how much income he had had, how many hours of work per day, and how long had he known this, that, or the other person, and Comrade Lenin, he had known him, too . . .

But yes, and perhaps they would like to hear more about it, the journey in the sealed carriage from Zurich to Stockholm . . .

The faces of his inquisitors contorted angrily, but they did not dare to refuse his offer in front of all the people, and when he then began to tell about the night's journey through Germany, and about Vladimir Ilyich's plans and thoughts, and when he saw the first glow flare up in the eyes of his audience, he knew he had won.

Then he noticed the hand that rose, a worn hand discolored from so much handling of printer's ink.

The chairman, a Party man unaccustomed to spontaneous requests to speak: "Yes, Comrade?"

The hand remained, and the accompanying voice, calm, humane. "Comrade Radek, thinking back today—have your expectations from back then been fulfilled?"

It became very quiet in the room. Radek looked at the questioner once again. No, he wasn't a provocateur. He was simply someone who wanted to know. Just that.

But the chairman jumped up and hit his wooden hammer three times on the table. "The session is ended."

★

Why did he do this, the master of the house, the leader of the world revolution? Why this meeting, which, even if it took place at night, cost him time and distracted him from work, or from his pleasures; what did Stalin expect from it, what benefit? Personal satisfaction? Let's see how small he's become, this Radek, how low he's learned to stoop, how humbly he crawls?

The question did not leave Radek's mind as he sat, every nerve painfully taut, facing the other who was sucking on his pipe, his eyes fixed on the tapestry above the sofa, a Caucasus Mountains landscape.

"A free hour," said Stalin, "presented itself. And I wanted to see for myself what effect—what was it, Tobolsk? Tomsk . . . ?"

"Both, Josif Vissarionovich."

". . . what effect your Siberian sojourn had on you and your thinking."

The Caucasus landscape lost his interest. Radek noticed how the hard eyes turned on him, demanding.

"We know some things," Stalin said. That, Radek thought, was probably meant as help: the kind of help a Stalin gave.

"I, too," he said, "have endeavored to give you this and that in the way of information, Comrade Stalin."

"It could have been more."

"Caution," Radek said, helping himself from the tobacco pouch Stalin held out to him, "was in order."

"Caution," said Stalin, "is always called for. And what, do you think, should happen now?"

He could dare, Radek thought, to venture forward a little bit.

And said, "In socialism, especially that which is built in a single country, man, even one who has once stumbled, should be given the opportunity to make his contribution; also, bread tastes better when it's earned."

A declaration of principles, and beautifully phrased; and if he had correctly assessed the great man, and his inflated sense of self did indeed prove stronger than his natural distrust and insecurity toward him, Radek, then such a thing would also work favorably.

Stalin seemed to be thinking. "You are a clever fellow, Karl Bernhardovich," he said at last. "But for the time being I want to trust you—besides, it's to your own advantage if you behave sensibly. You'll write for *Izvestia* again. But one thing I ask of you: from now on you'll suppress the little jokes with which you used to amuse Moscow, at least as far as they relate to my person, understand?"

Radek bowed his head.

"After all," this added as a footnote, "I am the leader of the world revolution."

Radek knew the answer he would now give the man was a mistake that could never be taken back, but it came to him from his deepest Jewish soul, like the flame from Moses' thorn bush, and wouldn't be suppressed: "*That* joke, in any case, Josif Vissarionovich," he said, "is yours."

4

They were still living in their hole, as Radek had christened the miserable chambers in the basement that the Party had placed at his and his family's disposal; no wonder that his kidneys were making themselves felt again and that daughter Sonja, hardly having survived one flu-like infection, was already getting into the next one. Only Rosa seemed to be able to bear these kinds of life circumstances to some extent. "We will," she said while caring for her two patients, "not be broken by the harassment of these thugs." And when the proof of his first article written again for

Izvestia came to the house for final corrections, "You'll see, Karl, from now on everything will be sorted out."

Then, however, the editors returned the already corrected text, giving very flimsy reasons, and when Radek, with a sad-triumphant smile, showed her the oblong paper marred with red pencil, she took his head between her hands, kissed his forehead, and proclaimed, "The main thing is that this is still sitting on your shoulders."

So he kept working, what else should he do with his time, and waited for things to happen. Late that morning, with Sonja at school and Rosa on her way to get the most necessary groceries, he sat alone in front of the rickety kitchen table, busy with a new article conceived for *Izvestia* on the effect of increased industrial efficiency on the quality of life of Soviet man—and he suspected that this work, too, would probably be rejected again— when he heard the timid scratching at the door, as if a stray cat were seeking entrance. He rose with a groan—when he had squatted too long on the hard chair, his limbs stiffened—and went and unlatched the door. The face that grinned at him with accentuated friendliness seemed familiar: there was something childlike about it, with the thick-lipped mouth under the freckled little nose, and yet he didn't know where to place it.

"You don't recognize me"—in an ingratiating voice.

"In fact, it seems to me, Comrade, that we have met, only I don't remember where; perhaps you'll give me a hint . . ." And stepped aside to let the visitor in.

The other laughed. "I escaped through a terrace window minutes before you entered the room where I was working, and you encountered me, or my official photo, at most on the pages of a dossier, labeled *Dangerous Social Revolutionary, armed,* of the tsarist Okhrana or even of its successor, the Cheka. Allow me, Blumkin, Yakov Grigoryevich."

Blumkin! Radek thought, Blumkin, an unforgettable name, Blumkin, the assassin, who in league with another, Andreyev, had shot Count Mirbach, the first German ambassador in post-revolutionary Russia; and in his memory the images of that time came back: the wild ride, he at the side of the highly excited Lenin, from the Kremlin through the dark streets of Moscow to Djeneshnyj Pereulok, to the Imperial German Embassy; and the count's blood, which, seeping into the carpet, was still clearly visible; and the embarrassed expression of Lenin, who, standing next to the rest of the puddle, tried to put his feelings into protocol-correct words to the embassy counselor Reizler, for the purpose of transmission to Berlin— *"Beileid,"* as he, Radek, corrected, not *"Mitleid."* So this was Blumkin, and why in hell was Blumkin looking for him, today and here in this hole, after so many years?

"I assume, Yakov Grigorievich," he said, "that you, too, did not lead such a quiet life after you escaped across the embassy terrace?"

"One goes underground," replied Blumkin with a touch of irony, "and emerges again. Illegality has been my milieu, so to speak, ever since I undertook to put a bullet in the belly of his majesty Kaiser Wilhelm, in Berlin, in a very amateurish manner and therefore in vain. Later, however, I turned my back on my friends, the Social Revolutionaries; your people, the Bolsheviks, seemed to me more likely to succeed in the long run—more solid, more purposeful, if you know what I mean; and he who wants to change the world cannot constantly change the direction in which he thinks."

"A praiseworthy decision," commented Radek.

"I also found"—Blumkin pulled up the second kitchen chair, sat down, and crossed his legs comfortably—"in Comrade Trotsky a man quite after my own heart, bold and cunning—it was a pleasure to listen to him and feel how his thoughts and mine complemented each other . . ."

But this didn't seem so likely to Radek; Trotsky and this killer with the child's face in spiritual camaraderie, hatching plans together; but then it occurred to him: at some point he had heard of a young man of letters named Blumkin in Trotsky's staff and wondered whether there might be a relationship between him and the murderer of Count Mirbach, but had considered the idea so absurd that he never asked Trotsky about it.

"I was," added Blumkin hastily—his speech often coming in such a rush that he sprayed droplets of saliva between his words—"I was, you might say, Trotsky's man for everything he wished to keep confidential."

The uneasiness that had already crept over Radek at the first sight of the visitor intensified. Trotsky's man for confidential things—now of all times. Couldn't the guy imagine that he, Radek, was kept under surveillance even and especially after his Siberian stay, and that everyone who knocked on his door was from that moment on also an object of police surveillance?

As if he'd read Radek's thoughts, Blumkin emitted a muffled laugh, "Hi—hi—hi!" and raised the hand that once held the pistol out to Count Mirbach. "Just don't worry, Comrade Radek, about me or even yourself, for God's sake! I am, as they say, secured. On all sides, secured. When the staff of Comrade Trotsky was disbanded, our friends from the GPU selected the most talented of his aides, headed by Blumkin, Yakov Grigorievich, and integrated them into the ranks of the secret police."

He turned his head and quickly looked around as if to catch the eavesdropper behind him; but there was no one there to overhear them, and he nodded with satisfaction. "And so," he said, "I've been on Comrade Menzhinsky's payroll ever since, carrying out his orders and, whenever it so happened to be the case, Comrade Stalin's at the same time." He pulled a checkered handkerchief from his pocket and wiped his mouth. "And am still in that capacity now."

"It is," Radek assured him, "extremely kind of you to draw my attention at the very beginning of our conversation to your relations with the present head of the GPU, Comrade Menzhinsky. I was about to point out to you that a visit to me, in this period of Soviet history, could result in the visitor being followed by anonymous figures."

Blumkin's gaze darkened. "What if I'm already being followed?"

Radek was startled. But he composed himself, "Then you would be even more unscrupulous—and stupid—than I had suspected from the moment of your appearance."

Blumkin doubled over as if he had received a blow to the neck. "But let me explain to you . . ."

"And you think I'll believe your explanation?"

"You must, Comrade Radek, you must! You're my only hope!"

"You're pinning your hopes on me? Why me?"

"Because both of us—and Comrade Trotsky . . ." Blumkin again fell into his hurried way of speaking: "Listen, listen . . . I was sent to Turkey several months ago with the task of establishing contact with Lev Davidovich and regaining his confidence, and to establish myself in his circle and find out there what I could about his plans, and"—this even more hastily than before, almost incomprehensibly—"if the opportunity arose—" He broke off and moved the flat of his hand, like a blade, across his throat and concluded with his strangely neighing "Hi—hi—hi!"

Radek raised his chin and offered his Adam's apple to Blumkin. "And with me, now, such an opportunity arises, in all discretion; I assure you, Comrade Menzhinsky, and even more so Comrade Stalin, would highly credit you for it!"

Again Blumkin cringed. "How can one—how can one misunderstand so much! At least hear me out! As soon as I arrived in Turkey, I went to see Comrade Trotsky and embraced him and kissed him on the cheek, and that was not feigned, you can believe me, but genuine feeling, and I confessed to Comrade Trotsky there and then who had sent me to him and with what commission, but that the moment my eye fell on him, Lev Davidovich, all my old affection for him reawakened, so that I was still quite touched, and told him with tears in my voice, Lev Davidovich, I said, do what you will with me."

"Comrade Trotsky, then, it seems," said Radek, "had no difficulty at all in turning you!"

"To turn!" Blumkin's mouth twisted: the word from the jargon of agents was not to his liking. "One has one's loyalties, and especially to such a noble person as Trotsky—what personality, what genius!"

Radek paused. Loyalties . . . Was Blumkin, who had first broken, then restored, his loyalties to Trotsky, giving a broad hint to him? But Blumkin was already back in his hasty suasion. "To turn! I didn't need to be turned. I offered myself to him! Of course, said Comrade Trotsky, I must test you, Yakov Grigorievich. Lev Davidovich, I asked him, who should I get rid of for you? Stalin, Kirov, Molotov, Ordzhonikidze? But he waved me off, with his smile, which you know, Comrade Radek, he waved me off and said, not immediately and not necessarily so bloody, Yakov Grigorievich; it will be enough for you to return to Moscow, and I'll give you some stories to report to your employers, Comrade Menzhinsky, and through him, Comrade Stalin, for their satisfaction, because neither of them is overly clever, and both are therefore easily satisfied, and you, Yakov Grigorievich, will use the main part of your time in Moscow to re-spin the web of opposition that these criminals have damaged by my banishment from the country; and I asked at what point should I begin, and immediately you came to mind, Comrade Radek, and so I suggested your name to Comrade Trotsky as the first contact, but Lev Davidovich showed such abysmal contempt for you that I thought, we'd better take a few others first, we'll find quite a few—"

"And how," Radek finally interrupted him, "how is it that you're now sitting here in my basement after all, endangering me and yourself by your presence?"

"It's because of Vera Petrovna," said Blumkin, blushing.

"Vera Petrovna?"

"Vera Petrovna is one of the most beautiful women in Moscow," answered Blumkin, "if not the most beautiful," adding modestly, "and she loves me."

"And what do I, pardon me, have to do with your Vera Petrovna?"

"Immediately after my return to Moscow"—he smiled wryly—"especially you, Karl Bernhardovich, with your sense for feminine beauty, will understand this, I went to see Vera Petrovna, but it was as if I had found a completely changed person: depressed, even harried, unable to speak freely, to think freely, unable to love. I told her off the top of my head that Menzhinsky had sent one or more of his people after her. But no matter how urgently I questioned her, she admitted nothing of the sort to me, only: her changed nature, so clearly noticeable, was there and weighed on me, and I began to see, with the eye that our kind have in the back of the head, the fellows lurking in some corner or other and archways and side streets and the like, ready to jump out in ambush, and don't tell me, Karl Bernhardovich, that I'm seeing ghosts, and that in reality my Vera Petrovna had only taken another lover while I was with Trotsky in Istanbul and Prinkipo; I know what I'm talking about, I've been in the underground since the days of the German Kaiser Wilhelm."

"All the worse," Radek said gloomily, wishing Rosa were finally back from her shopping so he would have someone to strengthen him against this murderous individual.

"And I need help," cried Blumkin, "your help. You are the only one who can help me. You have the necessary connections—to the opposition, as well as to the officials, don't deny it, Karl Bernhardovich, that's a fact."

Now Radek really panicked. The man was either a provocateur, sent by the police, or he was insane. With such an order from Trotsky in his pocket—assuming that he had at least spoken the truth there—to arrive in Moscow and immediately and unhesitatingly throw himself into the bed of his old lover, the first person the GPU people, if they wanted to catch him, would have approached, and then, after he had discovered during the act of love or shortly afterward that they were on his heels, to appear at his place, Radek, who was in the process of reestablishing himself, and to whine to him, "Help, Comrade, Radek, help!"—what, in the name of the old Jewish God, should he do? Deliver Blumkin to the knife, or himself, or both?

He still hoped that his Rosa, with a full shopping bag, would come already, but she stayed away longer than planned, and anyway there was neither comfort nor advice in this situation.

"Listen carefully, Blumkin," he finally said. "I can neither hide you nor conjure you out of the country, nor do I know anyone who could. I can only advise you not to wait until the authorities strike. You have to beat them to it. You know the name Ordzhonikidze?"

Blumkin nodded. "Control Commission?"

"That's right," Radek said. "Sergo Ordzhonikidze is head of the Party Control Commission. He's a roughneck, but not necessarily an evil or dishonest man, and he, like Stalin, is Georgian, and Stalin, one hears, considers him, as far as that is at all possible with him, his friend. So go to Ordzhonikidze and confess to him. If anybody can, he can do something for you. And don't hold anything back from Sergo; he is sensitive about that. Maybe that way you'll at least save your life."

Blumkin stood up. He looked as if all the air had escaped from his round body, and none of the words that usually came so hastily and moistly from his lips would form. Then he shuffled to the door, opened it hesitantly, turned once more, looked sadly at Radek, and left.

Radek was about to close the door behind him, but suddenly Rosa stood in front of him, shoulders a little slouched because of the shopping bag, and said, "Who was that person?" And seeing Radek's face, "A new problem, again?"

"I hope not," he said.

But instead of one, or even several, new problems, they experienced what might be called a kind of lucky streak. Not only did his articles begin to appear in rapid succession in *Izvestia*, with almost no editorial nagging about the manuscript, but other publications, in the end even the central oracle itself, *Pravda*, asked for his cooperation, and all of them paid him punctually and without him having to haggle over every ruble, the usual fees for prominent journalists. Rosa was finally free of the most pressing financial worries and could dress herself and the child in new clothes—expensive fun in Moscow, if one did not, or not yet, belong to the nomenklatura that had access to the special section of the GUM, the big old department store on Red Square.

And then, oh, joyful surprise, the messenger from the Economic Department of the Central Committee, Personal Provision Section, a young man with rosy complexion, dressed in pinstripes, who, after a cursory inspection of the hole in which the Radeks had had to spend their days and nights, wrinkled his nose, brought to their attention his name and patronymic, Ivan Ivanovich, and then something unintelligible, and, handing Radek a typed paper, said, "This, Karl Bernhardovich, is the order for your new apartment. You can move in there at any time."

Perhaps Ivan Ivanovich expected thanks, but an inner voice advised Radek to express himself, if at all, only in the most general terms, which he did, his eye fixed on the official letter without any sign of emotion.

Ivan Ivanovich, however, seemed satisfied: no, the document did not require a receipt, and wishing Comrade Radek and his family happiness in their new domicile, he turned on his heel and disappeared, very upright and aware of his importance.

*

The apartment was in the Dom Pravitelstva, the House of the Government, as it was called, although no governmental activity emanated from it; it was simply a residential barracks for higher cadres, set without any special architectural effort on the bank of the Moskva opposite the Kremlin, with an entrance hall smeared by boys' hands and scratched elevators and the usual guards at the gate and on the floors; and yet, what an unimaginable difference from the basement, which, thanks to the understanding of whoever, they had finally been allowed to leave! And what a joy that he had room again for his books and notes, so long kept secretly with patients of Rosa, the basis of his work, and for a reasonable desk on which his disorder could spread!

In addition, another blessing, the apartment was located on one of the upper floors, so that the wind blowing from the east across the river could bring cool air, not to mention that from the middle of the three large rooms—yes, that's how many they had now, plus kitchen and adjoining rooms—one could enjoy the view of that part of the Kremlin in which Comrade Stalin had his working and probably also some living quarters. And on more than one night, Radek suddenly found himself watching from his window the play of shadows at the window over there with a mixture of fascination and reluctance that was quite new to him.

"I don't know," Rosa said to him one morning while ironing the white collar of Sonja's school uniform, "don't you sometimes feel that there's too much of a good thing happening to us all at once?"

"They owe us more than the few favors," he replied, but silently admired the sensitivity with which Rosa guessed the internals of his subconscious. "Where is the reparation, where is the position, the official one due to me? And as long as the black silhouette on the other shore stares at us, where should I recognize the signs that we can feel safe after all that's happened to us?"

But instead of messengers from on high with promises of eventual restitution, Comrades Smilga and Preobrazhensky came by to see how he was doing, they said, and dutifully admired the new quarters. "And there"—Radek's finger pointed—"you see that window there, the seventh from the left on the second floor from the top, through that one I communicate with the big boss directly, the Khosyain; there are, as you know, psycho-energetic streams from one man's brain to another's, even over longer distances, and mine are carried by such strong emotions that I can make the dark man there in the yellow Kremlin light across the Moskva do the strangest contortions during my nights . . ."

They looked at him. Preobrazhensky shook his head, barely noticeable. Smilga said, "You know, Karl Bernhardovich, that Blumkin was executed by the GPU? They didn't make much of a fuss about him; they arrested him on his way to Ordzhonikidze, interrogated him, put him before a compliant judge—and what judge isn't compliant?—and shot him."

Radek gulped. "How do you know that?"

"In Moscow," said Preobrazhensky, "such news doesn't remain secret. Not outside of Moscow. Perhaps you're too concentrated on yourself, Karl Bernhardovich, you don't meet enough people. Here . . ." He presented Radek a crumpled piece of paper, a hectographed leaflet. "Such stuff is in circulation at the moment."

Radek read. The diction was familiar to him, as was the hatred, the cold hatred that spoke from the text: Trotsky. And the one against whom this hatred was directed was him, Radek. Judas Radek, the informer, the traitor, who turned the noble young poet Yakov Blumkin over to the GPU.

So, thought Radek, he had also written verses, the lad; but he hadn't made anything about that known that morning. But the matter was bad enough: now they had him, Stalin and Stalin's people, they only had to follow Trotsky's line on the leaflet: look, he's ours, this Radek, heart and soul, plays the agents of the opposition into our hands; hadn't he sent Blumkin to Ordzhonikidze? What did it matter whether Blumkin was still talking to Ordzhonikidze, who handed him over to his henchmen, or whether he was arrested before he had even been to Ordzhonikidze? The bullet of the firing squad, which blew out his life, hit the messenger of Trotsky justly, as a punishment, as a warning, for others, whatever, and the role that he, Radek, played in the process, or better, that Trotsky said he played, the role of Judas Iscariot, was indelibly fixed for all, for opponents as well as for friends.

"What do you think," said Radek, "I should have done? The guy told me himself when he came to me that he was already under observation, and he was a danger to anyone he blew his saliva bubbles in the face of, he was a veritable sitting duck, and not even a beautifully feathered one . . ."

"The worst thing for you," said Smilga, "isn't the leaflet at all. The worst thing is that from now on you are between all fronts, because why, if you weren't also his potential confidant despite your official protests against Trotsky, did Blumkin come to you of all people? And there's no one left to protect you—"

"Except for the one at the window above the river," Preobrazhensky interjected. "Only I don't know if brain waves from shore to shore will be enough in your situation . . ."

5

They readmitted him to the Party: one of them. But this was no longer the Party that had been his, and sometimes he felt that they, too, considered him a foreign presence, although they also let him travel again, even on official missions, and gave him assignments for editorials and essays that came close to matching his talent and experience.

He was drawn to Germany, back to the stage on which he had so often played his part and experienced his disappointments, Germany, whose Left, as he saw it, had prevented the long over-due world revolution by its inertia and its unwillingness to think anew and, for that very reason, had conjured up developments the immense dangers that even in Moscow few could have foreseen. He let Stalin know of his wish, in a roundabout way, and stated on record that an informational trip, such as he was planning, would be extremely useful in general and for his press work in particular; and after not even an unduly long time he was informed that the project was being reconsidered and that they would let him know.

The condition attached to the official approval was then: no interference, even indirect, in the affairs of the Comintern depart-ment responsible for Germany or of the German party; restric-tion to observations and exploratory talks; and, outside these, even if this was difficult for him, strict restraint.

Of course, from the very beginning of his stay, he noticed the surveillance—both German and Soviet—of his person; but since he had expected both, it didn't affect him; and in general, the whole enterprise was more a kind of sentimental trip down memory lane for him than the large-scale research he had requested at home; he suspected that this would probably be his last visit to Germany, and that was exactly what he said, sitting on the train from Karlsbad to Dresden, to the traveling companion he was dreaming of.

Ah, Larissa, he said, what has become of our former hopes? And at the Europäischer Hof in Dresden, where the boorish staff officers of General Müller had so rudely interrupted his being with her, and where he, in memory of their two nights of love, had also stayed this time, he met in the dining room an equally boorish, noisy company of higher Nazi officials, who burst into derisive jeers at the sight of his Jewish appearance.

Walking through the streets, in the Weiße Hirsch quarter as well as in the working-class neighborhoods, and later in Berlin, and especially reading the business pages of the newspapers, which hardly any of the local Soviet representatives knew how to analyze the way he did, he realized what a dire crisis the country was in, and how completely without a clue the German government was in the face of the millions of unemployed and their psychological consequences, and how in the banks and industry, and in the army even more so, the idea of handing over power to Private Hitler was being toyed with; and in the Romanisches Café on Kurfürstendamm as well as in the workers' bars in Wedding and Prenzlauer Berg, and at occasional meetings with old acquaintances, he learned nasty details about the rift that had formed there on the left through the fear of contact on the part of the Social Democrats on the one hand, who preferred to build armored battleships instead of pushing for social change, and, on the other hand, the sectarian attitude of Stalin and his shield-bearers in the German Communist Party, who steadfastly refused to cooperate with the Social Democrats, even to fend off Hitler's National Socialists.

But to whom should he turn, to whom should he hand over his findings? Larissa, dearest, he lamented that night, as he stood leaning against the railing of the canal in which Luxemburg's body had once been found, and he saw in the album of his sub-conscious the gruesome image of the bloated body wrapped in rags, and immediately afterward Larissa's slender, beauti-ful hands caressing him: in vain, Larissa, dearest, he lamented, everything is in vain, and disaster, it seems, is unstoppable.

He returned to Moscow, deeply depressed, and wrote a report to which no one ever responded, and several articles from which even the bit of political criticism contained therein was deleted; only the clichés remained, the prescribed ones.

★

He did not rebel, although that would have been his obligation, his revolutionary obligation, to spread the findings he had made in Germany to everyone, everyone, everyone.

And since he kept quiet, he was left in the apparatus as a travel cadre, that's what it was called, and in the international informa-tion department of the Central Committee of the Party he was called in, in an advisory capacity, and he gave his advice, which nobody listened to, and he thought, your revolutionary duty, Karl Bernhardovich, is now just to survive, just to survive, until the times change in this country and it will be possible once again to be a Communist.

They sent him to Geneva as a member of the Soviet delega-tion to the disarmament commission, and his anxiety grew when he heard the Germans making their demands around the con-ference table; but he enjoyed the international ritual, the buffet receptions in particular, where ironic allusions could be made to this and that, and once or twice he even managed to escape his monitors by getting into the car of an attaché of a foreign power at his invitation—which was noted harshly by the head of his delegation.

When he himself was sent to Warsaw at the head of a cultural delegation—culture, what was that?—the Nazis were already in power in Germany, and the speeches, his as well as those of the Poles, sounded hollow in light of the fact that no one knew what game Hitler intended to play with the Poles and with his, Radek's, own government.

At home in Moscow, however, people did not seem overly concerned about the Nazis; only the newly arrived emigrants from Germany—several of whom he knew from earlier times—were full of excitement. They reported bloody atrocities in SA locales, police stations, prisons, and camps, but bravely asserted that Hitler, under pressure from the proletariat, would be able to hold on only a short time, and showed disappointment at the apparent lack of interest in them on the part of the respective Soviet authorities. Only Radek took a closer look at them, invited them to his house, interviewed them, explained that the local comrades were more interested in developments in their own country than in fascist brutality, in collectivization, for example, and the successes of the Stakhanovite movement, and tried to get them a few rubles in addition to their official support by finding them work at one or another magazine. Only to one, the writer Gustav Regler, did he point out the shadow at the illuminated Kremlin window and say between his teeth, "There—see him—there sits the man who is responsible for all this misery."

When the editors of *Pravda* asked him for a longer tribute to Comrade Stalin, which, from his pen, would be more interesting and pleasant to read than the dozen pieces whose monotonous clatter filled the gray columns of the press and the stuffy air of the meeting halls, he agreed, after a brief hesitation. "Stalin loves the smell of incense, and will hold in the highest esteem the one who wields the little cask most skillfully," he said against Rosa's misgivings.

"Most skillfully—what do you understand by 'skill'?"

"What is it, Rosa," he said, pursuing the new line of thought that had come to him, "what is it that creates stomach aches for us in the excessive praises of the very highest people and their deeds and influence? It's not the frequent repetition—habit has a dulling effect. Not the triviality of the phrase—the vocabulary of the average comrade is meager, and he is pleased every time he finds familiar things again in the public announcements. It's the lack of reality that's disturbing: everyone sees that the successes attributed to our Josif Vissarionovich are anything but that, even on cursory examination, and in the end the applause that resounds on all sides may not sound entirely authentic even to the ear of the great leader."

He pondered. "Objectivity!" he then announced. "Objectivity! Authenticity! One would have to find a way to give the whole slimey prose the appearance of objectivity and thereby authenticity. And when, I ask, can a judgment be made in history, an objective one? Not today! People in the present experience reality—what a disadvantage for statesmanlike necessities, what a nuisance! But the future is different! The judgment of those in the future can't be verified—at least not by those living in the present. One must believe the ones from the future, since their judgment is a retrospective one and therefore contains the possibility of objectivity. Logical?" And confirmed himself, "Logical."

Rosa's glance contained something of the admiration that he had always longed for from her, but which she only all-too-seldom granted him.

"And at the same time—how pleasant!" Then added, "The future tense relieves me of commenting from a present point of view on the deeds of our hero—the mendacity of which would be obvious to all." And straightening up, "To work, then."

★

The year 1967 seemed to him to be the auspicious date: exactly half a century after the great October Revolution; socialism—even if it did not yet look like it today, there was still, in terms of time, a chance for it. Socialism had triumphed all over the world, and interest in the history of this victory was correspondingly lively, in the School of Interplanetary Transport as well, whose premises and facilities he imagined to be quite similar to those of the university named after Sun Yat-sen and whose rector he had been.

The lecturer turned to the students. "In the previous lecture we dealt with the historical moment when the news of the premature passing away of our great teacher and leader Lenin shook the whole world, with the moment when the mortal shell, lifted on the shoulders of his best friends, floated over the heads of the masses of millions into the colonnaded hall, being there for days the destination of the pilgrimage of the workers and peasants of our great country and from everywhere."

A good, a worthy beginning, he thought, from which the leap to the main character of the play could be ventured without further ado. Josif Vissarionovich, to whose judgment the text was calculated, loved pathos, precisely because it always seemed an artificial contrivance in his own utterances.

"The air still resounded with the words . . ." No, the word *word* was not enough, not for Stalin . . . "From the oath, chiseled as if from granite, which Stalin . . ." The title! Don't omit the title, he pays attention to his titles . . . "Which Stalin, the Party's General Secretary, had taken in the Bolshoi Theater, words that meant that the Party would remain faithful to Lenin's legacy of struggle against capitalism, that it would lead this struggle to its victorious end, consolidating the dictatorship of the proletariat and guarding the unity of Lenin's ranks like the apple of its eye."

Radek read over the draft. The apple of the eye, which was guarded there, was a Stalin quotation, and he would notice it with pleasure; but Stalin's spirit also floated otherwise, breathed there, in the lines.

"Today," he let the speaker continue, "we want to deal with the years following Lenin's death, during which the proletariat of the Soviet Union and its Leninist party . . ." Don't forget, Karl Bernhardovich, under Stalin's leadership; so, "Its Leninist party, under Stalin's leadership, built the foundation of the socialist economy and armed itself for the great international struggles that would later consolidate the final victory of socialism."

Again he interrupted himself. And how, he compared in his mind, did things look in reality, now, in 1933, what were the true perspectives? And a horror ran through him; what if this eulogy was taken at face value not only by Josif Vissarionovich, as he had intended, but also by the others whom he had in mind, the thoughtful ones in the country, who had a sense of irony, and whom he hoped to make understand that here was someone writing who, without at the same time casting doubt on the historical achievements of the workers, intended to expose all the tacky fuss, the personality cult, and the man around whose person it was conducted? What, for God's sake, could be done to make it evident, at least to the more intelligent among his readers, what was meant here and what was to be communicated to them—should he lay it on even thicker, surpass all previous records of jubilant bluster and self-praise, flatter Stalin ad nauseam?

"Maybe you think"—this was the rhetorical question of the 1967 speaker—"that the work of those years was a matter of course, that neither the proletariat nor its leaders demanded anything qualitatively new? What an error, but one that must be eliminated if you want to recognize the full magnitude of the Stalin period"—brilliant idea to name an entire period after Stalin!—"to appreciate and understand the full magnitude of the period of building socialist society, and the gravity of the work accomplished by the proletariat in that period, and the historical greatness of Lenin's successor, Josif Vissarionovich Stalin."

If, he thought, they gave him a good cigar for every mention of the hallowed name, he would be taken care of for months to come. And continued, "Certainly, the Stalin period stood firmly on Lenin's shoulders; Stalin was the executor of Lenin's legacy. But to fulfill this legacy, Stalin and our party had to make decisions independently, not inferior to Lenin's in boldness." Boldness was an exquisite quality for someone like Stalin. "In boldness, they had to develop Lenin's doctrine independently, as Lenin developed Marx's doctrine . . ." There was also the biblical pedigree—and now quickly something poetic for the greater glory of the prophet: "The Soviet proletariat had to soar a second time on the wings of the greatest enthusiasm to the heights of the October Revolution and fan the flames of the world's fire more strongly."

Good? He asked the shadow at the window over there, and answered himself, very good, my dear boy; and put the pen aside for this evening.

When he awoke the next morning, he felt elated; the tightrope walk he had undertaken challenged at the same time all the cunning and wit that was in him, and that he had developed to a certain level of perfection in arguments with opponents of various kinds, and in years of journalistic practice.

The next point of his treatise, to which he intended to devote himself, was the question of the construction of socialism in a single country; this, above all, because here was the opportunity to present Stalin as a theoretician of the highest rank, although he was nothing less than an original thinker; he even inserted quite unashamed other people's scribblings; see the "Fundamentals of Leninism" by the fool Xenofontov, already revised by half a company of professors. And quite incidentally he, Radek, by degrading himself to the status of a small erring human being, could safely move away completely from Stalin's grand theses and theorems.

"For Radek," he thus had his interplanetary speaker report to the audience of 1967, "for Radek, who came from the Luxemburgian camp, the construction of socialism in a single country seemed as ridiculous a thought as the idea, ridiculed by the famous Russian satirist Saltykov-Shchedrin, of the introduction of liberalism into some district of tsarist Russia by a well-meaning governor. International capital"—he gave the speaker an old Radekian phrase to quote—"would inevitably destroy the socialist hearth in the Soviet Union if the international revolution did not mature. Radek, like Zinoviev and Kamenev, who considered themselves executors of Lenin's will, did not understand that the possibility of socialism in a single country is the Archimedean point in Lenin's strategic plan!"

Archimedean point, he thought delightedly, what a concept. But now to Stalin, "who," he wrote—using the wrong metaphors, as the great man himself liked to do, just swirling around—"who had unfurled Lenin's banner of building socialism as the task of the October Revolution," and had the lecturer of the School of Interplanetary Transport recommend this point to the special attention of his listeners, "since here the whole greatness of Stalin as the successor of Marx and Lenin appears, his whole greatness as the theoretician of Marxism-Leninism and as the leader of the world revolution"—Stalin's self-designation, he recalled with amusement—"and, finally, the entire greatness of the Party as a weapon in the victory of socialism."

But this vein, Radek felt, carried even more gold; one had only to dig a little. And he wrote, moving his lips like the old Jews at prayer, "Stalin elaborated and developed Lenin's doctrine of the possibility of socialism in a single country. This alone would have been sufficient to establish the historical significance"—significance, yes, and historical at that!—"significance of Stalin as Lenin's successor. But Stalin added another merit to his great merit for the elaboration of Lenin's strategic plan"—not enough merits could be attributed to Comrade Stalin. "In grandiose historical struggles he put Lenin's strategic plan into practice and realized it. He not only led the proletariat into battle for the fulfillment of the, so to speak, national tasks of the October Revolution, but also built a fortress of the proletariat, which facilitated the international victory of socialism. Thus, Stalin became the great architect of socialism."

He breathed deeply. *The great architect of socialism.* No one before him had ever given that title to the shadow at the Kremlin window; that would earn him quite a bit, and there he had two birds with one brilliant throw of the stone, the title of his article at the same time.

After the architect came the war hero.

The only difficulty was that the war hero's name was actually Trotsky, who could only be mentioned, if at all, in connection with highly negative epithets. Unfortunately, all too many people knew that Stalin had mostly been involved in logistics during the civil war, in other words, he had been what the troops called a "rear-echelon motherfucker."

But such a person could still be transformed into a heroic figure with a little imagination and the appropriate fervent words. "Just as he not only learned Leninism from the books, but absorbed it at the sources of Lenin's teaching, already building up the Leninist party in the tsarist period and leading the struggle of the revolutionary proletariat, so also in the years after October, Stalin was seen less in the staff headquarters of the revolution than in the firing line of the struggle." Now the details of the firing line: "When the noose of hunger tightened around Moscow, he brought in grain; when the opposing forces gathered in an ever tighter ring around Tsaritsyn, he organized the defenses there" — organized them, but without himself taking part in these defenses! "And when Petrograd was threatened with danger, he checked the bastions there." And now the whole thing in a nutshell: "He does not see the revolution from reports, he looks it directly in the face; and here, eye to eye with the revolution, the final development of Stalin as leader of the revolution was completed."

And, not to be forgotten, as an apparatchik, brutally pushing all his rivals out of the way and seizing power in the Party. "He directed the battles of the Party at moments," he then wrote, "when victory makes hearts beat faster and swells the sails of hope. And remained free from giddiness at successes. He led in moments of defeat and retreat. Where fear seizes even brave hearts, he remained steadfastly calm."

And let one after the other of his critics walk the plank. But how did one say that without having to walk said plank oneself afterward? Perhaps like this: "Precisely because he was the best representative of creative Marxism, to use an expression of his which he applied at the Sixteenth Party Congress, Marxism-Leninism in his hands proved to be not only a means of analyzing the main phenomena of the epoch, but also a means of leadership in the greatest revolutionary struggles. In this fearless and at the same time cautious and bold leadership"—what a splendid synonym, Radek thought, for the dirty work of factional intrigues— "Stalin understood how to organize the struggle for the historically necessary goals, to create a functioning organization of struggle, to distribute the fighters to the decisive front sections and to place the most suitable leaders at their head."

And now, careful, old boy, careful! Any wrong nuance now might lead to a crash in his tightrope walk between cult and fact, between hero and usurper—

"Only the union of sharp, clear, farsighted Marxist-Leninist thought with this most intimate attachment to the main cadres of the Party created the leader of the revolution capable of replacing Lenin . . ."

He tasted the sentence. No, that couldn't be all, that wasn't enough, not for Stalin, and certainly not for those who knew his true nature. And he added, going to the limit of double meaning, almost exceeding this limit: "The political leaders come to their place in the Party and in history not on the basis of elections, not on the basis of appointments. The true leader of the proletariat is formed in the struggle for the Party's line of struggle, for the organization of its coming battles. And Stalin, who was already among the first in the Party leadership during Lenin's lifetime, and who proved to be the theoretician and politician of the proletariat, became its recognized and beloved leader on the basis of the outcome of the years-long inner-Party struggle, which was of the greatest principal significance . . ."

That had to be enough, he thought.

★

At *Pravda*, where they were at first astonished, if not shocked, by Radek's basic futurological idea, the appeal of the novelty, combined with the versatility of the content and the dazzling effect of the language, soon began to work all the more strongly the more often the comrade employees read the learned lecture at the School of Interplanetary Transport to each other; they decided to approve its publication in the New Year's issue of the paper, provided that it was accepted by the supreme authority, and when not only no objection was heard from his side, but on the contrary a few cautiously approving words, the generally positive attitude of the editorial staff escalated to clear enthusiasm.

In the days after the beginning of 1934, "The Great Architect" became the talk of the town; the workers were prepared to hear the whole thing chewed over again at the next works meeting, and the intelligentsia admired the extent of the turn Radek had taken and the skill with which he had pandered to Stalin: someone should try to imitate that! And so it was no wonder that the publishing house of the trade unions obtained permission to publish the extraordinary piece of literature as a brochure in an initial print run of 225,000 copies, and Radek himself, as a sign of the personal favor of the hero of his work, received two invitations, one to a speech at the Seventeenth Party Congress, the other to the Writers' Congress.

He sought consolation in alcohol. Now, he was a Jew and had been brought up as such, and Jews did not drink, at most a little glass on the Sabbath, and he also found no taste for vodka with comrades, even if there had been an occasion to celebrate. But now he began drinking in earnest, and it did not escape Rosa's notice how his face changed as he poured wine and beer and schnapps down his throat without rhyme or reason, and she demanded to know, "What's the matter with you? Why are you drinking?"

"Humanity makes me want to cry." Snot dripped into his cognac. "That's why. And I tried so hard . . ." He sniffled. "My own daughter tells me, Papa, she says, how could you! Even at school they talked about me and how comprehensive—comprehensive, in fact, our little Sonja said—I appreciated Comrade Stalin, who sent us to Siberia . . ."

You don't know a damn thing about that! he had hissed at Sonja; the next moment he would have liked to slap himself and ask for her forgiveness; the child had reached the age, her small breasts were already visible under her school uniform blouse, the age when she had the right to demand that serious things be seriously discussed with her.

But it made one despair! From everywhere, this disgusting recognition! Or contempt from those who still adhered to oppositional thinking. Didn't this people understand? No, they didn't get it, they were, all of them, for years already so adapted to the language of the bootlickers, and so weaned from any lateral thinking, that they took his work from A to Z for a serious historical evaluation and simply did not understand the ambiguity of the matter, the intricate *no*, which he hid in the acclaiming *yes*, the dialectic of the whole.

Rosa, to whom he was explaining this with a heavy tongue, grew pale. Inwardly, she thanked God that people were blind and deaf to the true content of her Karl's hymn-like prose, and prayed that only a little naïf somewhere would not get the idea of declaring the splendid clothes that Karl had tailored for the Great Architect to be a web of mockery and scorn.

"Stop drinking," she said, "I beg you. Or do you want to ruin yourself, and me, and Sonja, a third time?"

He laughed, in a way that was new to her, unpleasant. "What do you want? Josif Vissarionovich, may he go to hell, is so full of himself, and at the same time so insecure, that he'll always need me to confirm his greatness. I am his *Hofjude*, his court Jew, you see, and court jester in a single person. But this piece of writing will be like a beacon in the future, and a proof that at least some-one was there, in this time, who recognized him and who stood up to him."

BOOK EIGHT

We didn't make the revolution,
the revolution made us.
—GEORG BÜCHNER, *Danton's Death*

1

The instruction came: This, the Eighteenth, was to be called the "Party Congress of the Victors." The kulaks were defeated, industry was being built up, the opposition had surrendered; for the first time in the history of the young Soviet Union, a certain relaxation was felt among the population, and life, as Stalin himself had proclaimed, had become better, more cheerful; and if it had not been for the fear spread by the omnipresent GPU, one could have almost spoken of normalization.

But appearances, as Radek knew only too well, could be deceiving, and he kept his distance from those—by no means oppositionists, all of them well-behaved apparatchiki—who thought that, in view of the hard-won consolidation in the country, the people could be given a little more breathing room, and who, since a new policy probably also required a new man, thought about whether Comrade Stalin should not be asked to withdraw, at least partially, from administrative work and, on the occasion of the Party Congress, to give the post of General Secretary to another comrade, Sergei Mironovich Kirov, for example, the secretary of the Leningrad party organization. Not that they intended to overthrow Stalin—on the contrary, they would place him on an even higher level of the Party and government apparatus, which, however, had yet to be created, a presidency, for instance, and raise him, who was gradually getting on in years, to the rank of an elder statesman, a kind of second Lenin, Radek thought with a grin, only not yet mummified, and indeed, so the rumor went, Ordzhonikidze and Mikoyan and a few others had also made their way to Kirov; but Kirov had shrugged it off in horror; he did not trust the plan.

What was then considered certain news in the editorial offices of *Izvestia* was that Stalin had sent for Comrade Kirov and asked him, "Why, Sergei Mironovich, did I not hear about such things from you?" To which Kirov replied that he thought the whole thing was idle speculation, not worth wasting a thought on, and, moreover, he was convinced that Comrade Stalin was still the best man for the post of General Secretary. And Stalin had replied to him, "I prefer that people stand by me not out of conviction but out of fear; convictions can change."

The report to the Party Congress, presented by Stalin himself, was a singular enumeration of successes, all attributed to his own beneficent work; and all who had ever brought even a breath of criticism to their lips confessed their errors and swore eternal correction.

Kirov announced that the report of the Central Committee to the Party Congress, given by Comrade Stalin, had proved to be so comprehensive and correct to the last point that there was no need at all to discuss the individual points; it would be better and more useful for the work of the Party Congress simply to elevate the report, such as it was, to a resolution; and he moved, in addition, that it be decided that all Party organizations should be guided in their future work by Comrade Stalin's proposals in this report and the tasks he set forth in it, and should regard them as Party law.

Radek didn't believe that this kowtowing would help Kirov to get back in Stalin's favor; and neither, he thought, would the impassioned speech of Kamenev, who took the floor soon after, serve that purpose. Kamenev declared from the rostrum that the era in which they lived would go down in world history as Stalin's, and he, Kamenev, considered the old Kamenev, who had been foolish enough to fight the Party line between 1925 and 1933, dead and gone, and would be damned and cursed if he carried his rotten corpse around any longer. Radek heard Kamenev's curse, and he remembered old Moses, Thou shalt not take the name of the Lord thy God in vain, which saying Kamenev, born Rosenfeld, must have known, and in his mind's eye he saw Kamenev struck down by Stalin's henchmen and dragged away by him, Kamenev, himself; and he was horrified.

Bukharin spoke a bit more soberly, although still full-bodied enough. Bukharin, who seemed to want to emphasize what about him was outwardly reminiscent of Lenin—the little beard, the look, the gestures—in celebration of the Party Congress, named Stalin "Field Marshal of the Proletariat" and awarded him the title "Best of the Best," and confirmed what an honor it meant for him, Bukharin, to be allowed to participate in this moving event, which was christened "Party Congress of the Victors," with full rights, despite the disagreements of the past.

Only, Radek thought, if everyone in the hall was the victor, then who were the defeated? But by then they were calling him to the tribune, and he climbed up and saw the eyes directed at him from the hall, the curious and the bored, the lurking and the mocking, and a few actively participating ones, signaling that there was one or the other among the delegates who sympathized with him after all—and to his right, Comrade Stalin's eyes, cold and hard as stone.

He pulled up his pants and tightened his belt; his pants were always threatening to slip down, much to the amusement of his listeners; he didn't mind amusing them, but prefered to do so with a polished, ironically dazzling word. And so he began to speak about how and by what means he had cured himself of the disease of Trotskyism, with the help of Comrade Stalin's wise thoughts, of course, and thus enabled himself to return to his real

profession, journalism. Thus he had the transition to the subject
he was given: the tasks of the Soviet press in the period of building socialism in a single country, Stalin's period that is. He spoke
off the cuff; he knew the old clichés by heart, so often had he
used them in his articles and his speeches, in front of workers and
students, and in front of newspapermen, local and foreign, especially the latter. But then he did deviate from the routine. After
all, something extraordinary was expected of him on this extraordinary day; and he was not like the others, the already broken,
docile, in their penitent shirts; he wore the fool's dress, the colorful one, with the clasps sewn on it and the ridiculously tiny bit of
freedom that this dress gave him.

He straightened his shoulders. "Everything we have experienced in the last few years has shown us that the working class"—
he felt the growing tension—"after destroying the freedom of the
press and all other bourgeois freedoms"—enjoying the general
shock—"the working class, under the leadership of the Party and
its General Secretary, Comrade Stalin, has created such others
in place of these freedoms, for the creative activity of the workers
and peasants, as the world has never seen before."

Downstairs they were still holding their breath at his most
daring antithesis. Stalin was silent; then, however, he stroked his
mustache like the cat that has had its saucer of milk. The small
gesture was enough; it produced a laugh, a liberated one, and
applause here and there, which soon spread all over the hall.

He had won once again.

With regard to the organization of the Party, the traditional
forms were followed: the delegates to the Party Congress elected
the members of the Central Committee, who then elected the
Politburo and the General Secretary.

But Radek, although not a delegate himself, noticed the small
differences that the old Politburo, Stalin that is, had introduced

for the purpose of perpetuating its rule—as if someone had seriously threatened it! There was the inconspicuous fact that on the electoral list, the number of members and candidates to be elected corresponded, so that a real election became practically impossible. Also, those nominated to higher offices did not appear on the list in alphabetical order, as was customary in the past, but according to an arbitrary key, which presumably corresponded to the value that Stalin and his coterie attached to the person in question: number one was, of course, J.V. Stalin, followed by Kaganovich, who was also responsible for checking the ballots, Kirov, with his power base in Leningrad, and Andrei Zhdanov, who was said to be capable of reading even more complicated texts. In addition to this, Stalin—later Radek would make his jokes about it—personally collected the ballot from those whom he considered particularly unreliable, and slid it into the slot of the cardboard box he carried under his arm, looking deeply into the eye of the frightened delegate.

Counting would then take some time. But this time dragged on unduly; apparently there were some difficulties, and Radek wondered what they might be. Then unrest spread through the corridors at the buffets, whispers ran from group to group, under the seal of utmost secrecy, of course. The vote had gone differently from what the highest authorities had wanted, but in what way differently, surely one would not, we should not, no, impossible, "no" votes against Stalin, and not just three or four or half a dozen, but over a hundred, no, two hundred, no, even more, yes, that is reliably confirmed, although it already borders on, yes, on what, on counterrevolution, and what will the Khosyain do now, the master of the house, the boss, Josif Vissarionovich, beloved and adored by all?

"Wait and see!" said Radek. Wait and see! And they marveled at him in the corridors and at the buffets: he, Radek, this calmness, he, who otherwise at every opportunity, suitable or unsuitable, was brimming over with malice and irony, did he have nothing else to say than, "Quiet!" and "Wait and see!"?

He trusted, he replied, in Comrade Stalin; and when he saw Comrade Ordzhonikidze, who came striding through the hall, paler than usual, a sick man, it was said, he approached him, grabbed him by the arm, supported him, asked how he was, and Ordzhonikidze said, barely audibly, that he was afraid after what had happened at this Party Congress, simply afraid; a crack had appeared, an initial one, in the edifice of power that Josif Vissarionovich had erected, and this just now, after it had been thought that strict rule could be softened a little in favor of the comrades in the Party who had labored over the years for the revolution, and for the benefit of the people of the country.

"Do sit down, Grigory," said Radek. "Take care of your heart."

But by then the bell sounded; people poured back into the hall; and then when silence fell, a silence in which tension crackled, Comrade Kaganovich began to read out in a hoarse voice, "Stalin, J. V.—three votes against out of one thousand and fifty-nine; Kirov, S. M.—four votes against."

And no one stood up and demanded a recount of the ballots.

"I won't bet," he said to Rosa after this Party Congress, "a cent on Comrade Kirov keeping his head. In fact, only three delegates voted against Kirov at the Party Congress, and two hundred and sixty-seven against Stalin."

"He won't dare," said Rosa. "Kirov is the favorite of the Party. And in Leningrad, they'll protect him with their bodies."

"In Leningrad," Radek said, "they replaced the top of the GPU, which was subordinate to the Party organization there, with new people. Kirov then protested to Stalin."

"And Stalin?"

"Stalin said it was a measure in the course of internal reforms of the Ministry of Internal Affairs he couldn't concern himself with . . . He, who concerns himself with everything."

"And what about your head," Rosa said, "if Kirov loses his?"

And in what a banal way—later he saw it that way himself—had fate taken its course!

✴

At the Writers' Congress he spoke, in a strangely wooden and unoriginal manner, as several of his listeners found, about socialist realism, its content and method, and, although he had hardly read anything by the man, and what little he had read rather bored him, he let loose about James Joyce as an example of all that was damnable. "What is the basic feature in Joyce?" he explained in detail, "his basic feature is the conviction that there is nothing big in life—no big events, no big people, no big ideas; and the writer can give a picture of life by just taking 'any given hero on any given day,' and reproducing him with exactitude. A heap of dung, crawling with worms, photographed by a cinema apparatus through a microscope, such is Joyce's work."

He himself, he laughed to himself in the middle of his speech, had shown how to write about great men, and had been thoroughly misunderstood. He really came to life at the evening party at Maxim Gorky's house, to which the most prominent participants of the congress had been invited, and where there was hardly any discussion about literature, but all the more about politics, and where the best alcohol produced in the country was served.

Of which he filled his glass repeatedly until he felt what little inhibition he had brought to the party dissolve into pleasant nothingness. He reproached the German writers who, together with Gustav Regler, had flocked around him, with how effortlessly the intelligentsia of their country, no better than the workers, had allowed themselves to be brought into line by the Nazis; traitors all, traitors to the Revolution! And Andre Malraux, who had shone at the Plenum of the Congress, he insulted as a miserable petty bourgeois; it was easy for Malraux to talk, Malraux had no one above him to control him, no one whose limited brain he had to take into account day and night. And he became weepy: everything, everything, everything was turning to misfortune, and no one understood him . . .

Mikhail Koltsov, from *Pravda*, came up to him, grabbed him by the lapels, shook him, hissed, "Shut up, man! You're talking your head off! Don't you see—there, Molotov! There, Kaganovich!"

"So what!" Radek burst out laughing, shrilly, frighteningly. "Let them hear! You printed the stuff in your lousy paper, didn't you! The Great Architect! Don't you understand anything? Isn't there anyone among you who even knows how to read properly?"

And again the laughter, which then suddenly broke off. Koltsov led him out, past the silent guests.

★

Throughout the year, expecting disaster every day, he nevertheless sought to work. But he produced nothing that would have given him any satisfaction, in terms of style or ideas; nothing flashed and sparkled, how could it, when his thoughts would not stop revolving around the Great Architect, and how he must have raved after reading the brilliant piece a second time, only now from the other, the subversive perspective.

It was like Chinese water torture: one waited for the drop to fall, but the drop didn't fall. Perhaps, Radek thought, Stalin had more, and more important, things on his mind than to take punitive action against poor little Lolek Sobelsohn, who had not received a single vote in the election to the Central Committee at the Party Congress, simply because no one had thought of nominating someone like him to the Central Committee. Rather, Stalin would wonder what to do with Kirov, or Zinoviev, or Bukharin; or—but this was less likely—Josif Vissarionovich spent his thoughtful hours planning for the prosperity of the economy, it was said that bread stamps would be abolished, and everyone should be able to buy bread in abundance and stuff themselves with it; Or he was worried about the march to the East, for which Hitler, according to secret reports, was preparing his army—there was enough besides his, Radek's, person for the great man to occupy himself with . . . But Radek had the nasty feeling that Stalin had him standing there next to the inkwell on his desk behind the window over in the Kremlin, a little figure formed out of clay or plastic or something, into which he stuck needles every night before going to bed, until there would be no more room even for the thinnest, shortest needle and he would smash the entire object with one blow of his clumsy fist . . .

A fruitless year. As far as possible, he refrained from making any statements on internal Party matters and confined himself to foreign policy; the phenomenon of National Socialism provided enough material, as did the question of how it came to power despite the numerical strength and power of the German Communists; but there, too, he had to be careful not to offend Moscow sensibilities, and as for the effect of his tirades against Hitler, at home and abroad, he might as well have left them unprinted, they had so little effect; not for nothing had Comrade Kaganovich declared, and certainly not on his own account, that if the German government wished to establish relations with the Soviet government similar to those that existed before the Fascists came to power, they would be glad to do so. And the foreign correspondents, whose visits and interviews had earlier served him as a kind of confirmation of his role in the country, began to bore him—forever the same questions about the same people and the same events.

And then the lightning struck, and a rumble of thunder followed, spreading to all areas of life.

As fate would have it, he was in the editorial office of *Izvestia* when the news ticked over the telegraph: *Kirov Murdered*.

There they stood, half a dozen comrades, in the office with the honorary diplomas on the wall and the heavy upholstered furniture, only Bukharin, who, probably to test his loyalty, had been appointed editor-in-chief of the paper after the Party Congress, sat behind his desk, getting more and more nervous as more of his people rushed in with newly arrived information: the assassin, equipped with an old GPU passport, had entered the Smolny, the headquarters of the Leningrad party organization, and, without being stopped by the guards, had climbed the stairs to the second floor, where Kirov's office was located, and had lurked in the corridor until Kirov stepped out of the door; then he had fired at him; Kirov had immediately slumped down dead. That had been in the afternoon, at 4:30 p.m. A hurried government statement said that the murderer had been sent by enemies of the workers' movement, that he would be identified. A miserable dilettante, thought Radek, the author of this statement—Stalin himself, perhaps? How could they know who the murderer was sent by when he was still being identified? And wasn't there a bodyguard or at least a guard on the second floor of the Smolny?

All eyes turned to Bukharin. He stood up, agitated, and said, stammering slightly, "The attack on Comrade Kirov was an attack on the working class."

To which someone asked, "And what do you think, Comrade Radek?"

Radek shrugged his shoulders.

"You've already," continued the questioner, "witnessed at close quarters the assassination of Comrade Lenin, and that of Count Mirbach."

What was this, Radek asked himself, a provocation? And answered, "They'll let us know what to think."

And said goodbye with a wave of his hand.

✱

At home, in Dom Pravitelstva, was Rosa. And Sonja. Sonja hugged him. "I'm scared, Papa."

"You don't have to be afraid," he reassured her, "especially not for me. Comrade Kirov had enemies."

"And you have none?"

"Me?" he said "No one takes me so seriously."

Then he went to his room. The window over the river was dark. "Murderer!" he said, but not loud enough for the two next door to hear him.

2

Stalin, accompanied by Molotov, Voroshilov, and Zhdanov, went to Leningrad the night after the attack in order to take the investigation of the crime into his own hands, and from there he issued a decree, personally and without confirmation by any government or party authority, but with legal effect, instructing the competent organs to expedite cases of carrying out or even preparing acts of terrorism, and to execute the death sentences to be pronounced in such cases immediately after pronouncement of the verdict.

With which, Radek thought, first of all the Kirov assassin was out of the way, young Comrade Nikolaev, and within the shortest possible time, and could no longer point out the strings by which he had been manipulated; nor would he be able to give clues to the band of henchmen of the planning mind behind the plot: to the man who had tracked him, Leonid Nikolaev, and brought him in and worked him until he was ripe for the deed, and name the one who lent him passport and pistol, and the one who cleared the way for him to his victim by detaching the sentries inside the Smolny, and the one who prevented Kirov's faithful bodyguard, Comrade Borisov, from being on duty at the very hour when the early darkness of winter bathed the halls and corridors of the Smolny in dim twilight—so many accomplices, so many confidants; there would be a bloodbath in and around Leningrad; and besides, Radek thought, instigators for the murder had to be found, behind whose confessions and avowals in court the real culprit could hide.

He no longer slept. Rosa prescribed him the strongest sleeping pills available; they all did no good, in his nights he woke up—weren't they already knocking at the door: Karl Bernhardovich, will you please follow us, or do we have to use force? And hadn't he said and written enough that, given the Comrades' way of thinking, could be interpreted as incitement to terrorist acts? Whoever denigrated the Great Architect, as he did, was engaged in double-dealing, and that was the first stage of betrayal of the Party and its great leader, and perhaps, it would be said, he, Radek, would not be so displeased if, after the murder of Kirov, a murderer were also found for Comrade Stalin.

But the ax didn't fall on his head yet. Rather, it struck Comrades Zinoviev, Grigory Yevseyevich, and Kamenev, Lev Borisovich, and about a dozen of their closer and more distant acquaintances, all of whom had once belonged to the opposition group around Zinoviev but had long since renounced it. Radek was relieved to find that these two were the more logical candidates for the conspiratorial role and more likely to be considered for it than he; had they not already publicly opposed Lenin in 1917 in setting the date for the uprising, which then grew into a revolution? And, in later years, had not Zinoviev spoken most blasphemously against Stalin and, as head of the Comintern as well as chairman of the Leningrad Soviet, offered him noticeable opposition; even then, claimed the comrades of the NKVD who embarrassingly questioned Zinoviev, he and his friend Kamenev had spun the threads for the network of the Leningrad and Moscow centers, both of which, directly or indirectly, had instigated the terrorist bloodshed.

Izvestia reported that during their interrogations Zinoviev and Kamenev bravely replied to the accusation that they had known about the terrorist sentiments within the Leningrad Zinoviev group, the former saying he did not feel responsible for the counterrevolutionary freaks who had launched a fascist attack, and the latter that he could not plead guilty to a crime committed by perpetrators with whom he had no relations and could not have had any.

They could protest for a long time, thought Radek; whoever provided the questions to the interrogators used that bogus logic which irrefutably followed the bogus accusations which had been invented long before the investigation; and those who sat there, confronted with the questions—if they were allowed to sit and not forced to stand during the endless interrogations—squirmed under the C and the D and the E that mercilessly followed the A and the B, and so on until the Z, when the poor man signed his confession, although he was aware that what he was signing were only half-truths and entire falsifications.

Then in the trial, which was able to take place already six weeks after the murder—so successful had Comrade Stalin's investigative activity been—Zinoviev and Kamenev and seventeen other members of the Trotskyist-Zinovievist opposition were sentenced to prison terms of between five and ten years. The reason, Radek learned from the press release: the defendants had engaged in illegal, anti-Soviet activity with the aim of replacing the existing Party leadership and Soviet government. To this end, they had declared themselves leaders of their Moscow Center and allied themselves with the Leningrad Center, where the assassination of Sergei Kirov was prepared and organized.

So it was that easy, thought Radek. But he had never thought much of the imagination of his opposite in the Kremlin.

★

And yet he was a more contradictory character than Radek had thought until then, for, although it would have been easy for him after the conviction of Zinoviev and Kamenev and the other alleged members of their alleged center, Josif Vissarionovich had still not had him removed from his modest post; on the contrary, Stalin, through Comrade Kaganovich, had offered him a most honorable position as one of the co-authors of the new Stalinist constitution, which, according to Kaganovich's description, was intended to be the most progressive, democratic, and humane in the world. And, Kaganovich added with a thin smile, another prominent member of the commission that would be responsible for the text was to be Comrade Bukharin, Nikolai Ivanovich—Bukharin, Radek thought, who, in his highly precarious seat as head of *Izvestia*, was regarded in initiated circles as an even more questionable figure than he was.

Radek lit one of Bukharin's cigarettes. "Perhaps, Nikolai Ivanovich," he speculated, "Stalin possesses a sense of humor, albeit a peculiar one, and both of our appointments are a manifestation of this quality, which, however, has hardly come to light so far. What a team, you and I—or don't you also see in the constitution already named after our universally revered Josif Vissarionovich a fun plaything for the master rather than a project to be taken seriously?"

Radek's cynicism, so openly displayed, did seem to shock Bukharin. "Couldn't it be," he defended himself, "that Stalin, precisely after the rapid destruction of the double-dealing Zinovievist center, as he christened it, wants to demonstrate something to the country and the world with this constitution? Namely, that we feel safe enough again to return to legally standardized conditions? And to prove such an intention had just the two of us, who still have a certain reputation as independent minds, brought in to work on it?"

"Independent heads," said Radek, "if I may mention it, are the first to roll."

"Nevertheless, Karl Bernhardovich"—Bukharin pulled out a sheet of paper and inked it with a half-dozen paragraph marks—"nevertheless, I think the matter would be worth trying. Sometimes laws, especially when they meet people's needs, acquire a weight of their own, a dynamic of their own, if you will. I imagine that some kind of barrier could be put up against the arbitrariness that now prevails by certain provisions in the code of a constitution—what a joke of history, if Stalin's plaything were to gain such a life of its own precisely through our work, our thoughts, and the word of the law were thus to become a material force?"

"Illusions," said Radek, "are not at all always a bad thing. But illusions about Stalin . . ."

He stopped. Couldn't he also use a spark of hope, and wouldn't it be appealing to him to let his imagination run wild and imagine a socialist state that would be ruled by law and order, even a democratic one, instead of by ever-increasing dictatorial violence?

"Let's give it a try," he said.

★

They met as often as they thought necessary—that is, not too often—while the commission met periodically to hear their proposals and add its own, mostly insubstantial ones. The work progressed, albeit slowly, the sections on the form of government of the Soviet Union, its administrative structures, property relations, rural ones in particular, and on the equality of citizens in terms of race, religion, and sex, and on their social rights and duties, had already been worked out, and Kaganovich, who mostly attended the commission's meetings in silence and then delivered the papers to Stalin, seemed satisfied. It was clear to all, however, that these first chapters offered little cause for conflict; it would become more dramatic when it came to questions of justice and policing, and to the rights and liberties of the individual citizen vis-à-vis the state, which on the one hand was a dictatorship—of the proletariat, all right, but who was the proletariat?—and which would hardly tolerate any abridgment of its dictatorial power; but on the other hand, with this constitution, claimed for itself to represent the highest, most welcome form of democracy.

They had dragged this out until even Kaganovich showed signs of impatience. Finally Bukharin said, "I am in favor of taking the bull by the horns—either the Politburo wants a constitution, a democratic one, in which case it must swallow it, or it wishes to receive a phrasebook—the good fellows can have that too, but not from me; and I don't know if you want to supply them with one, Comrade Radek."

Radek deliberated for a moment. Then he replied, "The

comrades in the Politburo want a constitution, and it really should be the most democratic that can be conceived. But they'll treat it like twaddle, and afterward you and I will be ashamed of having supplied them with the text for their mendacious theater."

Bukharin eyed him mockingly. "Are you capable of being ashamed at all, Karl Bernhardovich?"

"I still can," Radek said sharply, drawing a thick line through the sentence he had jotted down on the sheet in front of him. "But I see the day coming when shame means nothing to me, and all I want to do is survive."

Bucharin grew pale. "What did you just cross out?"

"Here you go," Radek cleared his throat and read: "All citizens are equal and free before the law, and no one may rob them of their freedom without a valid legal decision."

"But that's completely correct!" protested Bukharin.

"And who decides," said Radek, "what a valid legal decision is, and who can issue legal decisions? Stalin?"

"I'd like," Bukharin massaged his forehead, "I'd like for us to do our duty."

"One is allowed to have doubts," said Radek.

At their next meeting, it was Radek who would not tolerate any more delay. "I want to finish it," he said. "I have a bad hunch they won't be patient much longer."

"You're afraid that Stalin…?"

"I fear that Stalin may have other things in mind for us than his constitution."

"Then," Bukharin said thoughtfully, "it would be all the more important that we put a few more stones in his path so that he at least stumbles before he tramples us."

"So let's write," Radek said, drinking from the tea Bukharin had brought and reaching for his pen. " 'Citizens of the Union of Soviet Socialist Republics are guaranteed the sanctity of the person. No one can be arrested other than by court order or with the permission of the prosecutor.' Agreed?"

Bukharin smiled. "The language is unambiguous."

"The meaning, I think, too. And further: likewise, the inviolability of the citizen's home, like his secrecy of correspondence, are protected by law."

"Allow me, Karl Bernhardovich, to return once again to the judicial system…"

"But of course, Nikolai Ivanovich."

"I would insert here: 'The trial shall be public in all Soviet courts, the accused being guaranteed the right of defense.' "

Radek let his pen fly across the paper: ". . . guaranteed the right of defense." And added, "And judges are independent and subject only to the law."

"And the prosecutors, Karl Bernhardovich, also perform their functions independently of any other organs and are subordinate only to the Prosecutor General of the Soviet Union."

Radek put the pen aside, stepped around the table, and, tenderly almost, put his hand on Bukharin's shoulder. "What do you think, Nikolai Ivanovich: which of us will be the first to be forced to invoke these provisions?"

"I was . . ." Bukharin withdrew his shoulder from the touch of Radek's hand, carefully, not wanting to offend him, "I was, when we still thought in such categories, a right-deviationist, and you a left one. Who do they think is more dangerous today, in your opinion?"

Radek returned to his chair. "I could probably answer you better if I were a medical doctor and more familiar with the effects of paranoia and such ailments of Communist officials."

"You really think . . . ?" asked Bukharin.

"Sometimes"—Radek reached for his pen again—"sometimes I think so. But aren't we all a little neurotic?"

Bukharin changed the subject. "And now the freedoms!" he said hoarsely.

"All right," said Radek, "and let's make it short: the citizens of the Soviet Union are guaranteed by law freedom of speech, freedom of the press, freedom of assembly, and freedom of demonstration." He looked at Bukharin as if seeking help. Then, when Bukharin did not answer, he continued to write, half reading aloud, "For the exercise of the aforesaid rights and freedoms, the public streets, squares, and buildings are placed at the disposal of the working people and their organizations, as well as the news media, together with the printing presses and paper supplies and all other materials which may be necessary for the aforesaid purpose."

"You'll take away their power with that," Bukharin said.

Radek nodded. "That's intentional."

★

The members of the commission were silent for a long time after Radek and Bukharin had read out the last of their paragraphs and presented the text, neatly typed, to them. Perhaps they did not immediately grasp the magnitude of the moment, this revolt in paragraph form, or, fearful as they were, they preferred to wait for Comrade Kaganovich to speak.

But he simply put his copy of the transcript in his coat pocket and said, "If none of you wish to comment on the draft, then I guess I can say good night to you all."

Two days later he summoned Bukharin and Radek.

"Sit down," he said.

Radek tried to find out from the man's face what was going on inside him; in vain, Kaganovich had learned to wear a mask.

"Comrades," he finally said, "I am instructed by Josif Vissarionovich to thank you for your efforts and to tell you that he has seldom laughed so much as when reading this document." And as if to illustrate Comrade Stalin's laughter, he too began to laugh, overloud and from a hollow chest; it sounded like the shriek of a hyena.

Then he fell silent.

Bukharin was the first to overcome his reluctance. "And what will become of the constitution?"

"Why do you ask, Comrades? This constitution is the most progressive, democratic and humane ever written, and it will, of course, go down in world history as such, Stalin's. You understand, don't you?"

"I think we understand," said Radek.

3

The old principle that one could not be prosecuted twice for the same offense did not apply for Stalin, whose concepts of law and order had been formed at seminary in his native Georgia.

Radek learned from the editors of *Izvestia* that Stalin had sent a confidential letter to the members of the Central Committee informing them that in January 1935, Zinoviev and Kamenev had admitted only moral and political responsibility for the murder of Comrade Kirov. In the intervening year and a half, however, it had turned out that during that first investigation of the murder, far from all the facts of the treacherous counterrevolutionary White Guardist and terrorist activity of Zinoviev's people had been uncovered, nor had the Trotskyists' part in it been fully clarified. However, on the basis of new information from the Ministry of Internal Affairs, the NKVD, it could be considered a fact that Zinoviev and Kamenev not only inspired the terrorist activity against the leadership of the Party and government, but also gave direct instructions both for the murder of Kirov and for the preparation of assassination attempts on other leaders of our party, first and foremost Comrade Stalin.

The phalanx of adjectives, lined up like tanks in the field, the merciless battle array of incongruous assertions and accusations: this, Radek realized, was Stalin's highly idiosyncratic language, just as the direct bloc with Trotsky and the Trotskyists—an alleged new discovery of the NKVD—had sprung more from the world of ideas of the great leader than from the brain of some subordinate functionary. The latter, Yezhov, who, because of the failure of the secret police in the first prosecution of the group around Zinoviev and Kamenev, criticized in Stalin's letter, had had to take over the post of head of the NKVD in addition to his function in the Ministry of the Interior, was now to lead the already recognized and unmasked bloc of Zinoviev's people with Trotsky and the Trotskyists, the instigators and executors of the terrorist actions, and to produce the evidence with which the members of the bloc could be convicted of their outrages in court.

Radek went to Bukharin's without prior announcement. The latter seemed to have just removed the papers with which his desk was otherwise littered; only his desk set, silver, a work from Tula, stood on the green-covered desktop; Bukharin himself lay, obviously exhausted, on the sofa in the corner, his hands clasped at the back of his neck.

Radek excused himself.

"It's all right." Bukharin rose up, tired. "I see you've also read the stuff Stalin thought up."

"Only skimmed," said Radek, "and not even completely. They acted very secretively in the editorial office. But the brief insight was enough for me." He pulled his pipe out of his pocket and sought to plug it with trembling fingers. "Anti-Soviet united Trotskyist-Zinovievist center . . ." he quoted. "That's the name of the enemy now. What a word salad! And yet how rich! And what follows next?"

Bukharin looked up. His laughter was anything but cheerful. "Did you know, Karl Bernhardovich, it is already being spread that the conspirators, besides their very own, the united Trotskyist-Zinovievist, have created a reserve center—in the new terminology, a parallel anti-Soviet Trotskyist one—which, however, they're alread on the trail of."

"I suspect"—Radek lit his pipe—"the establishment of centers of this kind with subsequent trial and obligatory death sentences will become a dear habit to them." Radek choked on the smoke of his pipe and coughed for a long time. "And do you already know, Comrade Bukharin, whom they have planned as the main characters in this parallel-and-so-on center?"

Bukharin was silent.

"Me, perhaps, Nikolai Ivanovich?"

"I only know," Bukharin said unwillingly, "that Stalin's entourage is thinking about me as one of the accomplices in the misdeeds yet to be defined. They have also already summoned me to a meeting of the Central Committee, whether as a member or as a prospective defendant is still open." Bukharin pointed to his table. "You see, I've cleared the decks."

Radek thought of his own desks, the one in his little room at *Izvestia* as well as the one at home, which were cluttered with all sorts of highly compromising papers.

"I, at any rate," Bukharin straightened up and tightened his shoulders, "I, at any rate, will defend myself. They won't bring me to my knees."

"I'm on your side, Nikolai Ivanovich. I promise you that."

"I hope, Karl Bernhardovich, you'll always remember this promise."

★

There he stood in his study, the conscious window of the Kremlin in front of his eyes, and with nervous fingers he tried to put things in order in and on his desk. Where to put all the paperwork: Deshurnaja, the watchdog outside in the corridor, would dutifully register every basketful. Maybe the stoves? But even that would be too conspicuous with the smoke emission....

Rosa entered, looked at the mess and asked, "Should I help you with that?"

"Some of it has to be sorted out," he said, adding, "for posterity, if we should be granted one. The rest must be put away. Perhaps in Sonja's satchel?"

"It's probably too small for these amounts." She smiled.

"Bukharin has already cleaned up," he said, "and he swore to me they wouldn't force him to his knees. At least the man has composure."

"And you don't?" said Rosa. "Incidentally, it is unclear to me how they want to implicate you in the matter and, above all, what for? They are primitive, admittedly, and they think primitively, but they must tell themselves that you are more useful to them in *Izvestia* than in any dock."

"In the minds of these comrades, I fear, our logic does not prevail. And don't forget, Rosa, they've already once renounced my talents and sent us to Siberia," and wondered at the cool tone of his voice, while inside everything was screaming Parallel Anti-Soviet-Trotskyist center, him and him and him—and Radek, Karl Bernhardovich.

Suddenly she began to sob, and he kissed her, tasting the salt on her cheek.

"Don't cry, please don't," he attempted to console her. "We've already gone through so much together; we'll survive this too."

She had regained her composure and returned to her question from earlier. "What do they want to achieve? That you, with your clarity of thought, confirm their delusions: confirm that the country is riddled with conspirators who have nothing more urgent to do than to take the lives of the noblest comrades on the instructions of the chief conspirator, Trotsky? Is it enough for them to bear false witness against this or that person, who you might deliver to them if the pressure becomes great enough on body and soul?"

"Perhaps," he said, "they want me, who until now was considered a reasonable and witty person, to confess that I lost all reason out of hatred for the great Stalin and for the Party that, despite all my predictions, was establishing socialism in a single country, and therefore had become one of those Trotskyite-fascist-White Guard and what-else bandits? So that they can kill me with a semblance of justification?"

"What if they promise to spare your life? Promise that

somewhere out of sight of the world they'll let you spend your last days in peace and quiet, and that while they're at it, they might even give you a chance to write?"

He stared at her. "Where do you get these ideas!"

"I read your articles. And in the night I hear what you dream." Her eyes filled with tears again.

"I know you'll be brave," he said, "if anything happens to me."

At about the same time, when the new second trial of Zinoviev, Kamenev, and their associates before the Military Collegium of the Supreme Court of the Soviet Union was pending, he learned that his column in *Izvestia* was to be discontinued; he was not given any formal reasons for this, not even by Bukharin, who could hardly be seen in the editorial office.

He wrote to Stalin, two and a half pages of impassioned assurances of his unbreakable loyalty to the working class and his loyalty to the great master of Marxist-Leninist thought, the uncompromising champion of socialist construction in a single country and defender of the Soviet people against all challenges from the Trotskyist traitors at home and abroad; then, without having shown Rosa the draft or even spoken to her about it, he tore it all up; he could not foist a Great Architect on Stalin again; and so he confined himself to quiet tones and calm assurances, knowing full well that Stalin would not appreciate an appeal of this kind. Stalin would probably not accept any more letters from him at all; the man would have long since made up his mind about Comrade Radek, Karl Bernhardovich.

The guards in front of the courtroom blocked his access; one needed a special *propusk*, and he did not have one; one of the secretaries of the court, who he went to see about it, said sarcastically that if Comrade Ulrich, the chairman, or the prosecutor, Vyshinsky, wished to see him in court, they would send him a summons. And there was still no word against him in public; he almost wished that someone would already attack him with any accusations, whose baselessness he could then prove.

"I have to anticipate them," he said to Rosa. "I have to speak first. I have to create a position from which I can defend myself."

She didn't know any better advice for him. She herself felt what was building up against him and saw the desperation with which he tried to defend himself against it, and she said, "They haven't attacked you yet."

"They will," he said, "they will. They need a group for their Parallel Anti-Soviet Trotskyist Center, and I'm afraid I come in quite handy as a relatively prominent member."

He was not yet banned from the premises of *Izvestia*. Although most of the editors he sought a conversation with remained very reserved, he nevertheless learned this and that: Zinoviev and Kamenev defenseless, not even a last stand, two sick people on the verge of physical collapse, in addition to the other defendants' compliant statements. The main thing, however, was that his colleagues helped him to take a look at the trial reports and to get a picture of the intention and course of the trial from the behavior of the participants in their roles, their stiff dialogues.

Then he sat down to write.

★

He wrote for his life.

He wrote, thickly underlined, of the Trotskyist-Zinovievist fascist gang and its hetman, Trotsky—naming him a hetman, he thought, as captain of a squadron of Cossacks, of all things, was an idea quite to Stalin's taste—and wrote of the stench of decay spreading all over the world from the defendants in the hall where the Military Collegium of the Supreme Court of the Soviet Union was hearing the case. He described Zinoviev and Kamenev as depraved cowards who had conspired to make a criminal attempt on the life of the builder; he hesitated, "builder," that was very close to the Great Architect, but it was the title that the prosecution had given to Stalin in its indictment—that is, criminal attempt on the life of the builder of socialist society, Stalin, and the leader of the Red Army, the locksmith Voroshilov. He wrote that the defendants themselves had testified how they had drawn up the murder plans, selected the perpetrators, and established the connections with the Gestapo in Germany, thus making it impossible for their leader Trotsky, who was sitting there in Norway, to wash the blood of the noble Kirov off his hands. And he wrote, quoting Lenin, of the steep and difficult road the Bolsheviks had traveled, holding each other firmly by the hand, and how it therefore seemed impossible to them that there should have been scoundrels in their ranks who, using as a cover the faith of the rank-and-file fighters in the Party, crept up on the leaders of the Party with gun in hand.

And to what higher end? he wrote. Did they have had a program, a political one? No, they had long since lost touch with the working masses, had no content to offer and no faith. They had only one aim: to clear the way for themselves to conquer power by murdering the great champion of socialism. And they knew about the consequences of their actions, he wrote. They knew the international situation. They knew that the leaders of the fascist-military cliques on our borders were preparing war against the fatherland of the working people, against the land of socialism, and that the slightest deviation from the Party line, the undermining of confidence in Stalin's leadership, and certainly the assassination of any Party leader, especially that of the brilliant leader of the Soviet peoples, Stalin, was direct work for war and fascism.

He had started sweating and was drying his forehead with the fresh handkerchief Rosa had tucked into his jacket, as she did every morning. Rosa, he thought; what would Rosa say? Then he read again what he had written so far, and was shocked; his text could well serve the prosecutor as a plea; yes, his words were much better than the clumsy gibberish of Comrade Vyshinsky, whose stupid logic could be seen through immediately by anyone with some intelligence.

And now further, further. He had gotten involved in this business, now he wanted to bring it to an end. And so he wrote: "Destroy the vermin! It is not only a matter of a few with ambition, who were personally determined to commit the most abject crime, it's a matter of liquidating agents of fascism who were ready to ignite the fire of war and to bring about the victory of the fascists, in order to receive from their hands at least a mirage of power!"

This was real pathos, he thought; it would have an effect, perhaps even on Stalin; where else, if not in him, Comrade Radek, did Stalin find such an eloquent advocate of his theses?

And concluded: *The proletarian court will pass upon this gang of criminals dripping blood the sentence they have deserved a hundredfold. People who raised their armed hands against the lives of the beloved leaders of the proletariat must pay for this monstrous guilt—with their heads. However, the main organizer of the gang and its deeds, Trotsky, is already nailed to the pillory of history.*

The printer's messenger, a spiky-haired boy, knocked on the door. "Comrade Bukharin would like to let you know"—Bukharin, thought Radek, was Bukharin in the house again?—"if you want the article in the paper before the end of the trial, he needs it now." Radek skimmed over his last lines; then he handed the boy the stack of scribbled pages, complete with deletions and additions, and said, "The proofs in an hour at the latest, yes?" and thought that these then, the long strips of rough paper, on them the handmade impression of the just-submitted article, would be his last chance to jump off the already rolling train.

★

"You'll probably tell me," and with that he handed Rosa the set of proofs, "that you don't kick someone who's already down. I'm not proud of this work either, God knows; I've thought over every word back and forth, and still the whole thing is below me; but when someone reaches for a life preserver, it doesn't matter to him how it's painted; the main thing is that the thing carries him."

"Let me read already," she said. "I know you're not comfortable."

"Nobody can help those two anymore anyway," he defended himself. "They're done for, and I suppose they know that as well as I do and won't resent my ranting. Besides, would either of them, Zinoviev or Kamenev, spare me if they could save their lousy lives with a few statements against me? But then why the breaks in my text, the false tones, the uncertainties? If a villain, at least I prefer to be a perfect one . . ."

At last she came to read, and he watched her with anxious attention: her face lost color, her eyes widened, and, then, as she spoke, her lips quivered. "This—this is . . ."

"This is what?"

"The dual . . . this dual possibility of applying it! To whom do you pronounce judgment when you write 'destroy the vermin'? And when you demand that people who raised their armed hand against the beloved leaders of the proletariat must pay for their guilt—with their heads! To whom are you saying it, please? To Zinoviev and Kamenev and their miserable co-defendants, or to yourself, too, when tomorrow they drag you before the same court on the same charge? Can't you already hear Vyshinsky shouting your own words at you at the end of his plea?"

He panicked. "I must have been blind," he said hoarsely, "not to have realized it myself, and dull in the brain. But it's not too late. I can still prevent this stuff from being printed! Give me the proofs!"

And grabbed them and ran down the stairs to the Dom Pravitelstva exit and all the way to the editorial office of *Izvestia* and, completely out of breath, rushed into Bukharin's office, who was already on the move and, besides, seemed to have his own worries, and, pointing to the printing proofs, said, "We have to take this out. It's far too dangerous. For me, and in the end, for you, too."

Bukharin closed his fur coat. "Karl Bernhardovich," he said, "do you think I haven't noticed? But it is still the only way in which you can possibly save your skin. Besides, the higher-ups have long known what you've written there, and they would be most astonished if we didn't print it."

"Oh God," said Radek, "God of Abraham, Isaac and Jacob, why all this?"

"This God," said Bukharin, "is nothing but an interested spectator. Can I give you a ride in my car? Who knows how long I'll still have my privileges?"

★

The next day, by special courier from the Supreme Court, he received the long-awaited *propusk*, the invitation to attend the trial of the Anti-Soviet United Trotskyist-Zinovievist Center, with a seat in the front row of the press section, where everyone in the hall could clearly see him, his colleagues from the press, especially the international press, the judges, the defendants, and Vyshinsky.

So his article, he wondered, though not yet published, had already had an effect, and perhaps this small favor was meant to signify to him that it had had an effect in not such an unfavorable sense? Only Rosa remained uncertain, although the *propusk* was a fine specimen of Soviet printing art, two-color with national emblem and squiggled border.

"Couldn't they," she opined, "have placed you there in the middle of it all to have a special punch line in their show?"

"Punch line? What punch line? What do they know about punch lines?"

"But they hate you."

And when he left for court in the morning, she watched him with an anxious look and wished it was all already over and done and he would be back home for a late snack, which she would prepare for him with great love, while he described his impressions to her in his ironic way.

★

Some took pains not to stare at him as he squatted there, seemingly at the center of the action: but most made no secret of the fact that they regarded his presence as the only entertaining thing in an event that had become routine: Vyshinsky the prosecutor's questions, which already implied the answers expected from the defendants.

A bad play, he thought, as he followed the dialogue: the text was police-speak, the dramaturgy amateurish; he would have done all this much better and much more credibly if someone had commissioned him, and even occasionally let slip, in the manner of his great master architect, who was behind it all and what they intended by it.

At the same time as these thoughts, he grasped with a journalistic eye what was going on to the right and to the left and on and in front of the tribune; yes, secretly he even enjoyed observing how, in spite of the enormous pressure under which he stood, the mechanism in his brain was functioning: only it had to be ensured, under all circumstances, that this precious world spirit was preserved for future times. Suddenly he flinched: there in front, morbidly pale, with barely any shoulders, and shrunken, Zinoviev stood in front of the burly Vyshinsky and said in a toneless voice, "I confess, underground groups of the right as well as of the so-called left have sought contact with me and with Kamenev . . ."

"Louder, defendant," Vyshinsky said disapprovingly. "Clearer and louder."

Zinoviev coughed. When his voice carried again, he said, "Even outside the groups individuals approached us, Smilga, for example, and to a certain extent Sokolnikov . . ."

Radek froze, despite the stifling heat in the hall. Smilga, he thought, Sokolnikov. He had been with Smilga in Siberia . . .

"Defendant Kamenev!" sounded Vyshinsky. "Step forward!" Kamenev pushed his way toward the rostrum: head bowed—that head which he, Radek, had demanded in his article.

"Defendant Kamenev, what have you to add to the testimony of your accomplice?"

"Since we feared," said Kamenev, as if he had rehearsed it dozens of times, "since we feared that we might be discovered, we chose a small group to continue our terrorist activity. For this purpose we appointed Sokolnikov from our side. And on the side of the Trotskyists, it seemed to us, the most suitable people for this purpose were Serebryakov and Radek . . ."

The trap had been sprung.

4

It was a beautiful autumn, warm and sunny, and he had time, a lot of time, and more than once, when he walked through the streets and went to the parks, where the leaves began to change color, he thought that this would now likely be the last autumn he experienced, and he felt the sadness that wrapped itself around his heart like a gray veil. The only disturbing thing were the pursuers, who kept at such a distance that he could just notice them when he looked around; sometimes he managed to shake them off by quickly turning a corner or darting through a backyard to avoid them; then, not two minutes later, others appeared from another direction and of the same appearance and with the same casual attitude, and attached themselves to him.

Several weeks passed in this way. Rosa packed the little suitcase he had already carried on the trip to Siberia and put in it whatever she thought he might need in the Lubyanka in the first few days, until it became clear what he really needed; always provided that they allowed him to keep any articles of a personal nature at all, and did not immediately put him in prisoner's jacket and bast shoes; one had heard many a thing from the great remand prison; but they seemed to have treated each person a little differently, also differently at different times; they were variable.

Perhaps the respite they now allowed him was already part of the ordeal; should he worry about their intentions and sink deeper and deeper into the morass of uncertainty so much the easier it would then be for them to bring the notoriously slippery spirit of Radek, Karl Bernhardovich, into line. But what was that line, he pondered; and there was no one to ask or to talk to; whoever recognized him avoided him; all that remained for him were the newspaper boxes in the streets where *Izvestia* was posted, or *Pravda*; there he listened to the half-loud remarks of the citizens, who preferred to buy two fingers full of machorka for the few kopecks the paper cost.

Then, when they came to fetch him, it was still dark outside; while he was hastily dressing, he caught sight of Sonja in the doorway, her light blue robe thrown over her shoulder, and saw the startled back-and-forth of her eyes between him and the leather coated ones, "Papa, when are you coming back?" and heard his own hoarse voice, "Soon, child, soon," and Rosa's anxious plea, "Can I give him a cup of tea only, a single cup, you did get him out of his sleep," and the answer, "He's arrested, ar-rest-ed, you understand." Then she gave him his little suitcase and quickly kissed him again, and Sonja cried, and then he found himself on the stairs, on the right and on the left a man each, and one behind him, who kept stepping on his heels and at the same time pushing him in the back, so that he stumbled; suddenly they were in a great hurry.

★

The German cell had been cleaner: a veritable salon toward the end of his imprisonment on Lehrter Strasse; but then he had been imprisoned by the class enemy, and the ones holding him now were his own comrades, and they didn't have to be considerate to anyone or anything. But at least he was alone here; they could have put a guy in his cell to report his every word, not that there would have been much to report; probably he would have learned more from the informer about the intentions of the justice system than the latter would have learned from him about secret crimes he had committed; the charges against him would be fabricated anyway, and badly fabricated to boot; and he himself would not confess anything to the authorities that they could use for their purposes.

Three steps to the window, three steps to the door; if one stood crosswise and stretched out one's arms, one almost reached from wall to wall—window, that wasn't a window, that was a barred hole, through which only at certain hours a thin ray of daylight came in, and the naked electric bulb on the wall was screwed into its socket in such a way that its light must catch his eye and, when he lay down on the narrow, hard cot, rob him of sleep. In addition, there was a stool, and in the corner a tin bucket; next to it was a bowl with a pitcher; furthermore, there was a board on the wall, a kind of shelf, and under it a folding table, chained up at the time.

Only now, when things were so tangible, he realized what they intended to do to him; until now everything had been only visual or auditory: Kamenev, Zinoviev, Vyshinsky, the court; but this, now, was physically palpable with the tips of his fingers feeling the splinters in the wood, the cracks in the lime, and the rough tissue with which he had sought to protect his tired body in the night—night? What was day here, what night?—against the damp cold of the masonry. And that, for how long? Only now he became aware how completely helpless he was at their mercy, their whims, their arbitrariness, because there could be no question of logic and reason, unless one called logic what resulted from their madness, and reason what derived from their lies and falsifications. But this trial would happen without him, he swore to himself; they would have to do this business without his cooperation; and not because of any ties to Comrade Trotsky, against whom the whole web had been woven by Stalin, or out of any feelings of solidarity he, Radek, might have toward friends or like-minded people, but for his own sake; he was not the buffoon he sometimes appeared to be; he was, damn it all, a Communist.

There was a clank in the lock that tugged at his nerves; then the door opened.

"Come along!"

A guard, pistol on his belt; another guard with bayonet fixed, who would escort him, probably to the interrogation, his first this time. He threw on his coat, which had been left for him, and followed the two. The guard, Radek noticed, stayed behind in his section, but the one with the bayonet trudged on, close behind him, occasionally tapping him on the shoulder, right, left, now straight ahead again and up the stairs there. Then they had arrived: at the end of a lime-green painted corridor, an office, bare except for a poorly colored portrait of the great Stalin, below it a man who turned to him: "Radek, Karl Bernhardovich?"

"Luzhkin, Konstantin Samuilovich!"

"Surprised?"

Radek pulled up a chair.

"Remain standing!" Luzhkin ordered him. "This is an interrogation, not a chit-chat session like in Tobolsk, back then."

"It wasn't a chitchat session then either," Radek corrected. "Even if you believed that."

Obviously the investigating magistrates, or interrogators, which they were in reality, had orders to treat him only moderately brutally. They didn't beat him—probably he would have collapsed immediately had they begun to do so—nor did they inflict other bodily punishments; at most they grabbed him and shook him with a rough fist when they became angry at his intransigence; otherwise, however, they applied finer means, nervous exhaustion above all, which caused his thinking to dull and him to forget what feints he was already using and how he had fended off this accusation and refuted that claim and what he had conceded to them and what he had not. They themselves, Luzhkin and young Kedrov, who constantly radiated a kind of restrained friendliness like a bridegroom on his way to his betrothed, and the others who came to relieve them, called their method a conveyor belt system, and each of them scraped a little more at the sensitive spot of his consciousness before passing it on to the next.

It didn't take him too long to get an idea of the aims and purposes of his interrogations; Luzhkin had already mentioned them after he had told him about his career in the NKVD, which had only really taken off after he, Radek, had been released from small, cozy Tobolsk, first to Tomsk and finally to Moscow. The Interior Ministry headquarters seemed to have taken a liking to Luzhkin's detailed and, as he himself put it, analytical reports on the soul of the exile Radek, and had brought him to Moscow and given him a short additional training and then placed him in this position. Coincidence? Radek had asked; or had it been known in advance that old acquaintance loosened the tongue? Whereupon Luzhkin had only grinned all over his coarse face; grinned and continued his questioning.

However, the confession that Luzhkin demanded from him was also a too clumsily arranged story. Following the written and oral instructions of the arch-heretic Trotsky, the Parallel Trotskyist Center, with Yuri Pyatakov, Grigory Sokolnikov, Leonid Serebryakov, and he, Radek, at its head, intended to help bring about the defeat of socialism in the war against the Soviet Union, which was expected in the near future, in close cooperation with the Nazi-German and Japanese general staffs, and as a reward, obtain power in the country from the victorious enemy, which power they would in turn use to grant the Germans and Japanese major concessions of a territorial and economic nature and to reintroduce capitalism in Russia; until then, however, they would render an initial service to their allies by terrorist attacks on the leaders of the Party and government, especially Comrade Stalin, and by a series of well-directed acts of sabotage in industry and transportation in the Soviet Union.

"And," asked Radek, whose feet and back ached most terribly after hours of standing, "you believe that yourself, Comrade Luzhkin?"

"Not 'Comrade,'" said Luzhkin, "citizen."

"So do you believe this nonsense or not, which is the reason for the interrogation, Citizen Luzhin?"

"We ask the questions here, Citizen Radek. And I ask you about the instructions you received personally from the traitor to the fatherland Trotsky—you received them by letter?"

"I have had no correspondence with Trotsky since the time you and I spent together in Tobolsk, Citizen Luzhkin, and you yourself read it at the time."

The young man in the corner of the room, sitting at a special little table with his shorthand pad, asked, "Do you want me to write that down, too?"

Luzhkin's face flushed red. "You're making fun of me, Radek! You are a provocateur! But you'll see how far you'll get with that!" And shouted, "Kedrov!"

Kedrov appeared in the doorway, smiling cheerfully.

"I want everything from today in the minutes," said Luzhkin, "everything, as usual."

Kedrov took the stenographer into the next room, and soon the staccato of the typewriter, Kedrov's voice, and the murmur of the stenographer's reply sounded from there. Radek could hardly hold himself up, but after his quarrel with Luzhkin, he knew, he would let him stand until his knees gave out. But just then the door was torn open, and into the room stepped, accompanied by assistant and secretary, Prosecutor General Vyshinsky.

"Ah," said Vyshinsky, "here is our prospective defendant! Sit down, Radek! How far have we come with our confessions today?"

Radek dropped into the chair, stretched his legs and groaned in relief.

"Kedrov!" exclaimed Luzhkin. "Kedrov—the protocol!"

Next to it the short buzz of the roller: The sheet was pulled out of the machine. Kedrov entered, in his hand the typed paper, recognized Vyshinsky, greeted him submissively and handed him the product of his, and Luzhkin's, and their assistants' toil of the day. Vyshinsky reached for it, skimmed it, laid it, satisfied, on

Luzhkin's table, and said, "All that's missing is the signatures."
And to Radek, "Comrade Luzhkin will lend you his pen."

"Please," said Luzhkin, dipping the pen into his little barrel and offering it to Radek.

"I can't sign anything," said Radek, "because I haven't testified to anything."

"Nothing?" said Vyshinsky. "Nothing about your plans? About the structure of the Center? The connections with Bukharin? Your talks with the German military attaché? Your terrorist apparatus? About Ukraine and the Primorje region, which you were willing to cede to the German and Japanese imperialists? All the great treason against the fatherland that you and Pyatakov and Sokolnikov and Serebryakov were planning? Surely these are facts!"

"These are not facts," Radek countered. "This is a poorly conceived script for a bad crime movie. And if you're its author, Comrade Vyshinsky . . ."

"Citizen Vyshinsky!"

". . . you should be ashamed of yourself, Citizen Vyshinsky—I could deliver you a far better one. But I'll deliver you nothing, and I'll sign nothing for you. And now, if you'll allow me to retire to my cell . . ."

"You're making a mistake, Radek." Vyshinsky rose. "You're in our hands, we're not in yours."

★

His constitution was not that ironclad. When they let him sleep for a short time at night or in the early morning, which was rare enough, the faces of the interrogators haunted his dreams: a gallery of devilish grimaces, all the more devilish because none of these faces, considered alone and for themselves, had anything distinctly devilish about them; rather, they all appeared highly normal, faces of men in their prime, family fathers, half or three-quarters educated; and in precisely this normality lay their horror.

And they changed their tactics. They no longer pressed him, nor did they threaten him; they did not even seem overly interested in any confessions on his part; they just ran to fetch him from his cell, every day at a different hour, and had a file lying on the table of the respective interrogator: They read it out to him and made sure that he also listened attentively, and showed him the signatures of the persons concerned, undoubtedly genuine signatures, and the note next to it indicating how long the individual had held out until he finally gave in and pleaded guilty with all the details that they wanted to hear from him: Yuri Pyatakov, one month and three days; Serebryakov, 3 months and 16 days; Sokolnikov, one month and 10 days; and Muralov, 7 months and 17 days; but he had been an old soldier, and had been in Trotsky's army all through the civil war, and had been in the Lubyanka since April, at a time when Radek was still writing foreign policy articles for *Izvestia*. If he, Radek, so wished, they told him, they could also confront him with one after another of his co-conspirators, so that he could have their statements confirmed by them himself; not necessary, he replied, even without such demonstrations he believed the NKVD staff to be capable of extracting from any desired person any desired confession of guilt.

And suddenly he began to scream hysterically and to pound with his fists on Luzhkin's table. And while he flinched in fright, they came running from all sides, the interrogators with their assistants and guards, and clung to him and grabbed him by the wrists and held him so that he could not move. The foam came to his lips, "Yes, I confess! I confess everything, everything!—that I intended to have the entire Politburo murdered and to crown Hitler personally as tsar in the Kremlin, but that there was still someone who was part of my plot, closely at my side, inspirer, confidant, accomplice: Luzhkin! Luzhkin, Konstantin Samuilovich! Yes!"

He drew breath.

"And I tell you, Comrades, if I demand Luzhkin's head, Yezhov, in order to have a confessing Radek at his trial, will easily have a dozen heads like Luzhkin's cut off. Or don't you think so?"

Luzhkin's eyes came out of their sockets, and he trembled all over his solid body: he knew Radek's threat was serious.

"I will," said Radek, "write to Stalin, and all of you, including Luzhkin, will vouch for me that Comrade Stalin will also receive my letter. And now take me back to my cell and serve me a decent soup and a large portion of pelmeni and a hundred grams of Stolichnaya. Have I made myself clear?"

That was on the seventy-seventh day after his arrest.

The letter went through the official channels, via Yezhov, and Yezhov sought him out in his cell, a petite man with thinning blond hair and veiled eyes, and let him know: Not like that! His letter was completely useless! How could he assume that Comrade Stalin regarded these trials as theater, the direction of which was up to him, Yezhov; for Josif Vissarionovich, what was discussed in the trials was gravely serious; and had not the assassination of Comrade Kirov been a reality, just as the threat to socialism from the internal and external enemy was a reality, and had not Trotsky himself announced in his writings, published for all to read in capitalist foreign countries, what tasks his followers would face here at home after the violent overthrow of Stalin's bureaucracy? Or did Radek really believe that Comrade Stalin, who knew how to direct people so masterfully, was suffering from a split consciousness, what doctors called schizophrenia, or even from the disease of paranoia, and was having Old Bolsheviks condemned and executed on the basis of some imaginary facts? ... So his advice was to change the letter in the indicated sense; after that it could be that Comrade Stalin would like to declare himself ready for a conversation with him, Radek.

Radek thought about it, and after an hour he called for the guard and asked for a pen and paper and for his table to be folded down, and wrote to Stalin: *Esteemed Josif Vissarionovich, after an abundant two and a half months of obdurate silence on my part, endured by the government and the Party with the utmost long suffering, I have come to the conclusion that my attitude is unworthy of a Communist, which I still believe I am, and which I have learned after thirty-five years in the labor movement, that I am obliged to abandon my individualism, which has led me into the company of criminals and traitors, and to contribute to the truth, and especially that concerning the Parallel Anti-Soviet Trotskyist Center, reaching the people in our country as well as those outside its borders. How I can best make this contribution of mine, I would like, if you can lend me a little of your valuable time for this purpose, Comrade Josif Vissarionovich, to discuss with you.*

And the signature.

By the respectful manner in which they treated him when they picked him up, he realized where the journey was going, and like a student before an exam, he repeated in his mind once again the points he assumed Stalin would respond to: repentance, but without an excess of contrition; readiness to make all the confessions demanded, insofar as they were credible: confirmation of all the great man's political theses, especially his findings concerning Trotsky; willingness to make amends for all the damage done by him, Radek, by openly stating the background of his participation in the plots for which he was being indicted.

The large building in which the NKVD had set up its headquarters was terrifying by the sheer force of its architecture, and he wondered if that was the reason that had induced Stalin to receive him in this of all places: in any case, he was brought through a series of corridors, one always more luxuriously decorated than the previous one, to a magnificently carved double door, padded from the inside, behind which was Yeshov's service room, in which two armchairs were set up, one large, throne-like, shining dark leather, the other lower and narrower, evidently intended for a subordinate; in front of these two armchairs was a kind of poor man's chair.

Radek bent down to inspect the primitive furniture. Then he caught sight of the soft noble boot shafts in the doorway and, after a turn of the head of the associated man, who, Yeshow obediently following him on his heels, silently strode across the carpet and settled down on his throne, his hands with the broad short fingers wrapped around the knobs of the armrests like the paws of a sphinx.

"Sit down." Stalin nodded, though it was unclear whether the order was for Yeshov or Radek or both; in any case, Radek crouched down on the little chair and waited for the move that would open the deciding game.

But Stalin took his time. Finally he said, "So you've come to your senses, Karl Bernhardovich?"

"The truth, Comrade Stalin," Radek said, "prevails in the end."

"And why then," Stalin raised his brows, "your long hesitation?"

"What kind of truth would that be, requiring only a nod of the head? How long did it take you, Comrade Stalin, putting one of your insights on top of the other like stones of a building, to develop your great, overwhelming truth from the initial, the core idea; to comprehend all this, the six or eight weeks it took me are not too long a period at all."

The idea seemed to interest Stalin: in fact, the whole complex construction according to which he conducted his politics and led his trials had also taken years to develop; he had already begun his first deliberations during Lenin's lifetime, when the others were still making fun of him; one had even said, leave the theorizing, Koba—they called him Koba in the early days—you don't know anything about theory, Koba; ah, but he did know something about life, and about struggle, about the struggle for power.

He blew the smoke of his pipe into Radek's face and watched him suck it in as if it were a precious gift; it was, for one who sat in the Lubyanka and feared for his miserable life.

"And now I," said Radek, "will testify to this truth; I shall be believed in the country and outside in the world if I tell of the great conspiracy which Trotsky instigated and in which I took part together with Pytakov and Serebryakov and Sokolnikov, and of the plans to get rid of you, too, Josif Vissarionovich, just as Zinoviev and Kamenev had Comrade Kirov killed in the most nefarious way by a hired assassin . . ."

"Not only I," said Stalin, "was on the list; the whole Politburo collective was. And why this terror, I ask you?"

"To dispossess the Soviet proletariat," Radek said, thinking, if I ask him for some tobacco, he has plenty of the best, and would he give orders to give me back my pipe? "The Soviet proletariat, which is successfully building socialism and at the same time arming itself against the future attack of the German fascists and the Japanese military, with whom, on the directive of Trotsky, my co-conspirators and I intended to cooperate in order to receive from their hands governmental power in the country after the lost war."

And thought, don't speak as if you know it by heart, act as if you're searching for your words: he must believe that you believe what he thinks you believe.

And continued, "I know there will be many, out in the world, and many a one here in the Soviet Union, who will entertain their doubts about the indictment and our confessions..."

Radek interrupted himself, cast an appraising glance at Stalin and continued. "How is it possible, they will ask, that men who fought for the idea of socialism all their political lives became traitors and saboteurs and treacherous murderers in the span of so few years and in such large numbers?"

"Yes, how?" asked Stalin, leering. "Perhaps you, who are known for your clever answers"—smiling ironically under his mustache—"perhaps you will find us an explanation which will be as simple as it is generally acceptable."

Yezhov became agitated. "But this has all been known for a long time, and is supported by dozens of testimonies!"

"To your satisfaction, possibly," Radek knew what he risked with this objection, "but to that of Comrade Stalin as well?"

Stalin chewed the mouthpiece of his pipe; the script and direction of the trials had been, in their conception at least, his work.

"All the more important," Radek added, "and all the more necessary for the purposes of Party and government, that one should come with new arguments."

"The old ones aren't glamorous enough for you, eh?" asked Stalin. "Besides, I know the nature of your arguments; I had a whole pamphlet full of them printed in a high print run—remember?"

The Great Architect—that was all he needed. For a moment Radek panicked. Then, however, he got hold of himself: there was only one thing, he thought, to bet on a rogue and a half; and laughed, a little too long and too loud, and said, "I am not one of those who step in the same river twice."

Stalin asked, "So you think my truth needs improvement?"

"The truth," Radek replied, "can't be improved. The truth is true, or it is not. But a line of evidence can gain a great deal by new and better evidence, and by the way in which one produces it."

Stalin looked down at Yezhov. The latter raised his head and cocked his ear. "You have Radek's confession?"

"It's as good as ready."

"Then let him read it," said Stalin. "Since, as he informed us, he has recognized the necessity of our procedure, he will be able to supplement and perfect it a little here and there. After all, with him we are dealing with an experienced writer."

He rose, tapped out his pipe in the ashtray on Yezhov's table, nodded to Radek, and left, as silent as he had come. Yezhov hurried after him and yanked open the heavy door.

★

Luzhkin seemed to have been taken off the case; Kedrov, the second man, asked the questions that remained to be asked, ordered the answers and how to record them, and Radek signed.

That morning, however, Radek being prepared for a new session in the manner of the previous one, Kedrow entered the room, a heavy fascicle under his arm, ordered that a chair be brought and a table, and announced, "Here, Prisoner-on-Remand Radek, your statement together with the prosecutor's questions."

The tone of expectation was unmistakable in the brief announcement, and Radek himself was eager to see how the authorities had solved their assignment; he sat down, leaned the volume of files diagonally against the table top, adjusted the lamp, and began reading.

But oh, after a few pages already, what gray boredom! What a hollow tone! What emptiness of thought! What lifeless vocabulary, what bumpy style! Above all, what a hodgepodge of improbabilities and breaks in this text! In the previous trial, he had already noticed the wooden speech, the superintendent-like stiltedness in the dialogues between Vyshinsky, on the one hand, and Kamenev and Zinoviev, on the other, but here he was unquestionably dealing with the efforts of semi-illiterates who, driven by literary ambition, tried to clothe highly inadequate documented facts in a mixture of Marxist-political and juridical phraseology.

"Your pen, please!" he turned to Kedrov, who looked at him suspiciously.

"You can't, forgive me, leave it like that!"

Radek began to cross out and rearrange, and replace one word with another, and then parts of sentences; "A Sisyphean task," he said angrily, folding the notebook shut. "With all due respect for the efforts your friends have made, is this how we are going to convince mankind of the villainies of the Parallel Trotskyist Center, and mine in particular?"

Kedrow's expression spoke of the misfortunes Radek had plunged him into, and he looked at him helplessly.

"Well then!" said Radek. "My proposal: I will rewrite the whole thing from scratch, including Comrade Vyshinsky's questions. This will then have a hand and foot, and if necessary we will adapt the statements of the other defendants and possible witnesses to our dialogue, so that the thing looks authentic and perhaps even gets a little shine. And provide me with decent working conditions, Citizen Kedrov."

✱

He worked as if in a fever. He became especially heated during the Radek-Vyshinsky dialogues: Vyshinsky had to be portrayed as the seemingly superior one, who was always given the last word, so that in court the victory of the prosecution, of the good, and thus Stalin's victory, would appear as naturally given.

Vyshinsky: Can you qualify the transition you planned from individual to group terror?

Radek: This was a new extended tactic, which we began to think about in 1935.

Vyshinsky: You call it a new extended tactic. But in the language of the Criminal Code it's called murder.

Radek: I'm not so familiar with the Criminal Code; therefore, I express myself poorly in its language.

Vyshinsky: I believe that after the trial you'll know the Criminal Code very well.

Radek: And I think that after the trial I will hardly have an opportunity to occupy myself with the Criminal Code.

Vyshinsky: That will depend on the verdict of the court. In any case, you'll know more than you do today ...

Radek broke off. He did this from time to time, simply to make sure that the Radek in his text was not some puppet on some puppet stage, but himself, little Lolek Sobelsohn from Lemberg, who had imagined that he could help determine the fate of the world revolution, and whom this revolution, having perverted itself, had spat out into the Lubyanka.

★

Then he had finished his work and leafed through the manuscript again, inside that strange mixture of pride—if a trial, then at least not the bungling one the judiciary would have arranged—and fear that what he wrote here with such intensity might be his own death sentence.

All that remained was the letter to Rosa, which he had already begun, and which, if only he drafted it wisely enough, might even reach the addressee. From under the sketches and notes he had discarded, he pulled out the sheet: "Dearest Rosa!" and then the personal part, the feelings for her and Sonja, and continued, "In the next few days my trial will take place. So that what happens there does not hit you unexpectedly, I asked for a reunion with you, in vain. Read then what I can communicate to you…"

And what Yezhov will allow, he added in thought, and continued to write. "I have admitted that I was a member of the Parallel Center and took part in its terrorist activity, and knew about the connection of the Trotskyists with German and Japanese agencies, and will corroborate all this in court. It is not worth affirming to you that such statements could not be wrested from me by force or by promises. You know that I would rather die than buy my life with such confessions . . ."

"I will simply testify to the truth . . ." Perhaps he would rather tear up the letter? The truth . . . Yeshov's truth . . . Stalin's truth . . . Would Rosa understand? "If, dearest, this truth should be unbearable to you, remember me as you knew me; but you have no right to doubt even one word of the truth established by the court . . ."

And if he did go a little further, just a hand's breadth, a finger's breadth? "If you think carefully through what will take place in court, especially the international part of the revelations, you will understand that, again, I had no right to hide this truth from the world."

Was that clear? Too clear, perhaps? . . . And now, in conclusion:

"However the trial may end, you must live, Rosa—if I should remain alive, in order to help me, too. But if I have to die, you should help the country through socially useful work. And know that whatever comes, I have never felt so closely connected with the cause of the proletariat as I do now."

And thought, even if those for whose political benefit and piety he would lead the trial against himself in the next week or the week after, sneered upon reading this assurance, it was the pure truth, in the face of death.

5

It was the evening session, and they were still working on Pyatakov. Vyshinsky did not let on how much he enjoyed having before him someone whose power of resistance had long since been broken; except for an expression of slight reluctance, no emotion showed on the prosecutor's roundish face, and the deliberately sober tone of his speech, intended as a special touch and sign of juridical objectivity, would also have made it very difficult for him to express any human feeling.

Radek had known Yuri Pyatakov for years, even if there had been no close relationship between them; Pyatakov came from the business world, heavy engineering, where he had sat in leading positions and had even had the opportunity to travel abroad; in this respect, his choice as one of the chief defendants in this trial even made sense, if one wanted to blame the breakdowns and collapses of Stalin's five-year plans on a gang of conspirators directed by Trotsky.

Pyatakov was testifying about his connections with Bukharin, who, Radek reflected, would probably be the central figure of the next trial, which, considering Bukharin's known earlier deviations, would have a new right-wing Center as its subject—an ideological dependence on Trotsky, however, would be difficult to prove there.

Radek inconspicuously looked around the room. There they

sat, on the one hand the apparatchiki, some of whom probably feared that in the distant future they might suffer the same fate as he; and on the other hand the diplomats and the corps of foreign correspondents, some of them known to him personally, among whom, as at the trial of Zinoviev and Kamenev, the number one topic of conversation would be: why do they confess?—the most frequent answer: because they are Russians, it's the Russian penitent soul that is acting out here. And there was Lion Feuchtwanger, the famous German novelist, driven out of his homeland by Hitler and now here on a reporting tour; Feuchtwanger had recently been received by Stalin; and Radek tried to imagine what one great man might have confided to another great man on that occasion.

Pyatakov was again questioned about Trotsky and reported how much Trotsky's ignorance of the real conditions in the Soviet Union, especially the strength of the Red Army, had worried him and his co-conspirator Radek; Trotsky was still harboring his illusions and was betting on defeat, which is why it had become necessary for someone to meet with him.

Suddenly Vyshinsky directly addressed him. "Defendant Radek, did you receive two or more letters from Trotsky in 1935 or even a little earlier?"

The familiar script. Radek threw a slice of lemon into his tea glass and drank, "One letter in 1934, in April, a second in December 1935. I wish I could have given them to you for your evidence, Citizen Vyshinsky; but I burned them both as soon as I received them."

"But the content of these letters," Vyshinsky prodded, "surely the content corresponded to Pyatakov's remarks just now?"

"In principle, yes. In the first letter Trotsky mentioned that it would be desirable to bring about the war, which was approaching anyway, more quickly; the Trotskyists would come to power sooner that way; then in the second letter he described the two variants of coming to power: one without, the other with war: whereby he considered the first less likely."

Radek turned; the tension in the hall, especially among the foreigners present, was palpable: he especially noticed Feuchtwanger's questioning look. "Of course, this was about tangible concessions to the victors," he continued. "For neither Germans nor Japanese would deign to cooperate merely for the sake of Comrade Trotsky's beautiful eyes. Then, in the second letter, there was talk of social and economic policy, which Trotsky described as an integral part of such cooperation after his own had come to power."

Vyshinsky chipped away: "What was the essence of this policy? And no excuses, please."

"In the return to capitalism. This, however, remained concealed. In the second letter there was also talk of contributions, through the handing over of entire enterprises that were of value to the Germans and were to be administered capitalistically. In Trotsky's first letter there was still no mention of a social program; it consisted of a whole three pages and dealt exclusively with the bringing about of the war and the tactics of defeatism; only the second letter then contained the complete Trotskyist social program and was therefore written on eight pages of thin English paper. There was no third letter."

Vyshinsky said, "You will be able to comment on this point during your interrogation, Defendant Radek. Now I just want to know from you: In the main, do you confirm Pyatakov?"

"In the main, yes."

Pyatakov gave him a pained look.

"And in this second letter," Vyshinsky again adhered to the given text, "were there enumerated the conditions which the Parallel Center group would have to fulfill toward the foreign states after its assumption of power? More precisely, did Trotsky speak of territorial concessions?"

"Trotsky said that they would probably be necessary."

"Ah, yes?" triumphed Vyshinsky, recognizing the wording Radek had supplied him with. "And which ones, please?"

"I intend," Radek announced, "to speak more fully on the

complex in due course." And sat down. He felt exhausted; but he had again shown Vyshinsky who was directing.

★

Vyshinsky, however, in agreement with the presiding judge, Ulrich, decided despite the late hour not to let Pyatakov out of his clutches yet. With whom, he wanted to know, had he talked about his terrorist connections?

A tired movement of the head. "With Radek."

"Comrade Chairman," this from Vyshinsky, "allow me one more question to the defendant Radek?"

Ulrich fixed upon Radek through his pince-nez. "Go ahead."

"Defendant Radek," Vyshinsky bent over, "did you have a conversation with Pyatakov regarding a certain Dreizer?"

They had agreed on Dreizer, he and Vyshinsky. Dreizer had been a go-getter, a terrorist by trade, allegedly, and Dreizer was dead, executed already after the trial of Zinoviev and Kamenev; which was advantageous for all involved: anything could be said about dead people.

"In 1935," Radek said, "in July, I think, Pyatakov and I talked about Dreizer. When we met for the first time after Kirov's murder, we wondered whether it was pointless to liquidate the leading comrades one by one."

A short pause, for effect.

"One only, and then another—that would not bring about anything revolutionary, but would only result in the destruction of our organization. So it was necessary to clarify whether or not there were forces for a larger-scale action."

In the hall they held their breath. This, from Radek, and so casually!

Vyshinsky inquired, "Do I understand you correctly: assassinating Comrade Kirov was too minor for you; one would need at least half the Politburo . . . ?"

Ah, you hypocrite, thought Radek, proclaiming, "Either

renounce terror altogether or organize it in a serious way, as a mass act, which would then next raise the question of taking power."

"So you mean, defendant, either *en gros* or not at all?"

"The number is not what is really important here. Rather, it's a matter of principle: if terrorist acts serve the purpose of obtaining power; in that case, one must envisage, without much flinching, the destruction of the top echelon of the government."

Vyshinsky, with almost genuine horror, "Entirely?"

"Of course."

"And what did you decide?"

"To send for Yefim Dreizer, who had extensive connections among the terrorists. Depending on the picture he would give us, we were going to decide."

Apparently Vyshinsky was now developing ambitions of his own. "Is it true, Defendant Pyatakov?"

Pyatakov looked around him like a hounded animal. "Everything," he said hoarsely, "happened at Trotsky's direction, who demanded an act aimed against a whole group. The question was: could the existing cadres do it? If so, Radek was also in favor of it."

Vyshinsky was apparently not even able, Radek thought, to conduct the interrogation along the agreed upon lines. And said reproachingly, "Pyatakov is confusing everything for us. There are differences to what is recorded in the investigative material."

Whereupon Vyshinsky lost his composure and started tattling on himself, "The investigation material is based on your facts! Whose facts?"

Joy flashed through Radek. Could the game that was being played here be made more clear to those in the hall? But would this audience also listen properly and understand correctly?

And said, "We're contradicting the material, ours and yours. We have testified that Trotsky's directive on terror against the whole government leadership arrived in January 1936. However, Dreizer was not available at that time, and I never met him again later, and without Dreizer nothing could be decided."

"But you were aware that there were groups in Moscow engaged in preparing terrorist acts?" Vyshinsky asked.

Did Vyshinsky think that he, Radek, wanted to escape from him with the help of Dreizer, who was nowhere to be found? So he confirmed, "One of them was even under my leadership," and for the second time he felt how they opened their mouths in the hall.

"And what did this group of yours deal with?"

Couldn't Vyshinsky think of anything better? If only he, the fool, had stuck to the agreed texts! But now the prosecutor gave him, the state criminal, the opportunity to make the wonderful statement: "I don't think it would be in the interest of your prosecuting authority if I developed in public how such acts of terror are most practically carried out; that also does not correspond to my views of correct behavior before a high Soviet court."

"Your views on this"—at last Vyshinsky thought he had an answer befitting Radek's impudence—"interest me less than your activities at that time."

"You didn't want to hear me through to the end!" countered Radek.

"I'm asking you, what were you doing with your Moscow group?"

The guy, Radek thought, had finally found his way back to the agreed upon wording, and so he also answered according to the script: "They were working on the preparation of cadres; the objects were also already envisaged, but without a deadline."

"From your professional-criminal standpoint—what does that mean, *objects*?"

"Since the foundation of the Parallel Center, the circle of persons against whom our acts of terror were to be directed was known."

"And in January 1936," Vyshinsky mimed the dispassionate legal scholar, "the question of expediency arose in your mind?"

"In January 1935."

"Fine. In any case, the question came up. And how did you and Pyatakov decide this question?"

"We didn't decide it at all. After all, we had no basis for such a decision, no connection with Dreizer, our man for terror, who for half a year simply did not get in touch." And added, outside his text. "The terrorists of a country just can't be much better than the rest of the means of production."

★

And his own interrogation was still ahead.

He said to himself, sleep, you must sleep, otherwise what is still holding you together will break apart. The couch they had given him for the duration of the trial was a sanatorium bed compared to his cot in the Lubyanka, so the sleeplessness was not due to that; his restlessness came from within: after careful consideration, he had decided on a course that would justify him, at least before history—a little word here, a little word there, for those who came later—no, more than a little word, deep traces, unmistakable, inaudible, and these not only for those who came later. Anyone who could even think halfway had to understand what he, Karl Radek, had undertaken to reveal to the world by contrasting his confessions with the statements of the other defendants, extorted by torture or otherwise, and by his duet with the prosecutor: the absolute absurdity of it all. This was the most perfect sabotage, because it was pure dialectics—the overloud, overused Yes! Yes! Yes! from which a tiny, stubborn No nevertheless peeled out in the end, his No, which would then endure!

The thing was excellently conceived, he told himself, but would it work as he had planned? Had his essay on the Great Architect, which he had knitted according to roughly the same pattern, the effect he had wanted to achieve with it? Or was the power of power more powerful than all cleverness and cunning, were assertions already credible by the fact that the power of the state stood behind them? What was man's natural doubt against his need, indeed his desire, to comply? Especially since he was supplied with the official Party reasons for the police pressure?

But if that was so, if his idea—truth through absurdity, revolt through genuflection, negation through affirmation—was not understood by this people, what remained for him? To stand up tomorrow morning in the courtroom and crow out: Lies! Lies! My confessions—lies! The confessions of all here—lies! There is no conspiracy, no Parallel Trotskyist Center, and Kirov was killed by Stalin's own hired assassins, and . . . and . . . and . . .

But by then they would have long since pounced on him: a madman, they would have said, a shot, quickly, and that would have been it—with luck. And Trotsky would write something secretly malicious in his little paper as an obituary; criticism, Radek's criticism above all, Trotsky forgave no more than Stalin forgave; and in the West they would use his, little Lolek's, appearance to turn his words against socialism; and that was the last thing he wanted at that time . . . Oh, poor us!

He must have slept a little, a few minutes, hardly more; a barber came, in prison clothes, and soaped him up, spraying him with an eau de cologne after shaving. Throughout his interrogation, he would not get rid of the cheap smell.

★

Today was his day; everything was concentrated on him, listening to his answers, information, stories. In his head, however, it looked like a kaleidoscope: pictures followed one another; each of extreme sharpness of the figures and clarity of the colors, but without coherence and jumping from one to the next at the lightest touch.

"When did you, Defendant Radek," Vyshinsky asked, "learn of the existence and activity of the United Center?"

"Trotsky wrote me about it as early as February 1932," said Radek.

"What did he write to you then?"

"He said he had it on good authority that I was ready to return to the struggle. He did not yet use the word terror: he spoke of eliminating the leadership. Then, at the end of the year, I really decided to rejoin the fight."

Radek knew the letter and text of Vyshinsky's next questions, and in front of, again, a large audience, they went through the individual sections of the fable together: how he, Radek, forewarned by this letter of Trotsky that he would be approached, then gave his promise to the contacts, and how they, in the well-known conspiratorial manner, formed their group and began preparations for action, creating and gathering terrorist cadres, and appointed said Dreizer chief of staff of the operation, and, foreseeing the sacrifices it would require, placed part of their people, including just him, Radek, in the status of a temporary reserve.

Now the Kirov murder would come up. And right on time Vyshinsky asked, "Were you aware, Defendant, against whom the terrorist acts were to be directed?"

Radek spiced his answer with a pinch of mockery. "It was no secret to me who was at the head of the Party and the government: Stalin, Kirov . . ."

"So you knew even before the nefarious crime was committed that the Trotskyists were preparing the assassination of Comrade Kirov?"

"I even knew that the deed was to be carried out by Zinoviev's people. Kirov was in Leningrad, and in Leningrad Zinoviev's supporters also had their stronghold, so everything was clear."

Vyshinsky, however, wanted things more specific. "What connections did you have with Zinoviev?"

"Before Kirov's assassination, I met with him three times," Radek said readily, adding for good measure, apparently to lift the prosecutor's spirits, a list of his meetings with the still-living conspirators: with Sokolnikov, in the summer of 1934; with Pyatakov, from 1932 to 1935, an average of once a year, the last time in January 1936; and with Serebryakov in 1933, 1935, 1936.

In the field of such statistics Vyshinsky felt comfortable and therefore let Radek continue reporting: who was subordinate to whom, and who collaborated with whom, and in whose hands the majority of the threads converged: namely, in his, Radek's.

"And with whom did you discuss these activities of yours?"

"With the members of the Center."

"And from the group of the Right?"

"Of course, I was in contact with Bukharin."

"Of course even. And conducted what kind of conversations with him?"

"Well, in the manner of members of two different centers making contact with each other. I asked him, 'So you've also embarked on the terrorist path?' Bukharin replied yes. Then we saw each other right after the murder of Kirov, people crowded Bukharin's office at *Izvestia*, I had to wait for a favorable moment to exchange a few words with him. Who this Nikolaev really was, the murderer, neither of us knew at the time, but it was clear to us that the attack must have been the work of an organization, his, mine, or Zinoviev's."

Radek, though still following the given text, had fallen into that state of excitement in which man suddenly abstracts from himself, and felt the unreality, even ridiculousness of the scene he was reeling off there for Vyshinsky's show. Vyshinsky, however, seemed to be satisfied, especially after he, Radek, as intended, continued to talk about the subject. "Bukharin, by the way, was also of my opinion, either we stop the individual terror now and go over to terror against the whole government, or we give up the enterprise . . ."

"What did you mean, you and Bukharin?"

Radek took a small step forward, toward Vyshinsky, and casually slammed his arm down on the barrier of the witness stand, "You see, Citizen Prosecutor, neither Bukharin nor I have any terrorist practice; but based on a knowledge of the history of terrorism under the tsar and in Poland, I did wonder, can we achieve our goals by shooting at individuals, and only at long intervals?"

Vyshinsky said understandingly, "I may conclude, therefore, that you are not a supporter of the partisan method?""

"Individual terror is completely lacking in seriousness." So, there at least he was established as a wholesaler in terror.

★

And now, Vyshinsky followed point by point his protracted scenario: the appearance of the enemy of the people and traitor to the fatherland. "I wrote," Radek reported, "through *Pravda*'s New York correspondent to Trotsky: if our bloc intended to seize power, this could not be done in a vacuum; above all, one had to decide whether one wanted to come to power in the wake of a war or even help to bring about the war oneself; therefore, one had to learn what the imperialists were planning and what they intended to demand; Trotsky should therefore seek the appropriate contacts."

"That was in May 1934?" asked Vyshinsky.

Radek nodded. "Then in the autumn of that year, at a diplomatic reception, a representative of a Central European country known to me sat down—"

"No names, Defendant!" interjected the chairman. "I warn you!"

"So the representative of that country sat down with me. It is disgusting, he said, how our press and yours argue with each other on a daily basis; how should one negotiate with each other? In any case, he said, he knew at home that Mr. Trotsky was striving for a rapprochement, and his Führer was inquiring what this effort of Mr. Trotsky's meant. Perhaps it was only the dream of an emigrant in sleepless nights? Or who was behind the thought?"

Radek had fresh tea brought and sipped the hot drink. "But since," he then continued, "our kind could not hold long conversations with foreigners at diplomatic receptions, I briefly informed him that the political realists in the Soviet Union, that is, we, understood the need for such a rapprochement and were prepared to make concessions to his government in return. . . . For a Soviet citizen, of course, a conversation of this kind was inadmissible."

"But it was connected with the correspondence you were carrying on with Trotsky?"

"Like the whole international side of our plans," Radek conceded amiably.

"And you told your co-conspirators about that, too?"

"Exactly. About the inevitability of the war of the Germans and Japanese against the Soviet Union, and the inevitability of the Soviet defeat, which would permit our coming to power, which is why we would be most interested in an accelerated beginning of the war."

Radek hesitated. Eliminating an entire government leadership by assassination would have been a *coup de main* for which one could have taken some credit. Helping to bring about a defeat of the fatherland, on the other hand, would have generated much less sympathy. But he had now directed his conduct of the trial to such absurdities, and Vyshinsky now, it had to be acknowledged, stuck to the agreed text. "And this conduct of yours was a conscious one?" he demanded to know.

"I have," Radek assured him, "except in my dreams, never acted unconsciously in my life."

"And this, unfortunately, was not a dream?"

Radek was amused by Vyshinsky's naive joy that he had been allowed to appear funny for once, and confirmed to him, "No, this, unfortunately, was not a dream."

"This was reality?"

"Sad reality"

"Truly sad, sad for you, Radek."

The back-and-forth dragged on. There was talk of Hitler's and the Mikado's demands, to which, according to Trotsky's letter of 1935, the Reserve Bloc would have to yield. Perhaps, thought Radek, I should have made the whole thing shorter; but this doctrinaire lot wanted everything treated double and triple, that's the way they are, and I'm not the judge, only the accused, trying not to cut too ridiculous a figure.

"What," Vyshinsky finally demanded, "did Trotsky's program amount to this year?"

"As I have already said—toward a return to capitalism," Radek replied.

"And that gave you food for thought?"

"More than that, it made me think that the situation in the country had changed in the meantime."

"In what way?"

Radek began his short talk on the success of Stalin's Five-Year Plan and the rearmament of the Red Army, which Vyshinsky had specifically requested. Pyatakov, too, Radek reported, had thought that it was necessary to discuss the new development with Trotsky, and so one of them would have to go to Oslo to confer with him. He had left this trip to Pyatakov, because Trotsky's last directive had shown him that the latter had lost all sense of reality; when Pyatakov then returned to Moscow, he had brought with him even sharper instructions from Trotsky; had he, Radek, communicated these to a wider circle, they would have blown up the whole bloc.

"Restoration of capitalism under the conditions of 1935," he said, "just for the sake of nothing, just for the sake of Trotsky— when I heard that, I felt like I was in a madhouse. And if I had explained to our people that they would have to carry out all this—treason against the fatherland, sabotage, terrorist attacks— in order to end up serving as police station supervisors in the reestablishment of capitalism in the Soviet Union, that would have been the end. So the four of us, Pyatakov, Sokolnikov, Serebryakov and I, felt that we could no longer take responsibility for carrying out the Trotskyist directives, and we agreed to convene a conference of our bloc. We arranged how to organize it, determined the circle of participants, and who should notify whom."

All this had sounded realistic enough, he thought, and now he was quite exhausted. "As for me," he concluded, "this was my last meeting with the other three, the last in freedom."

★

He felt his concentration slipping. Dear God, he prayed, don't let me faint.

But then he heard Vyshinsky's agonizing voice. "So one can conclude: as long as you thought socialism was weak, you were allowed to betray it and work toward war and defeat. Then, when you realized that this same socialism had consolidated, you lost your faith in Trotsky's theses."

Was this guy starting to stray from the script again, Radek thought, and replied, "You read very deeply into the human soul, Citizen Prosecutor; yet please allow me to comment on my thoughts in my own words."

Vyshinsky's face flushed red. "I know that you have a sufficient vocabulary, Radek, to hide your true thoughts behind it. That is precisely why I ask you to speak here no longer as a journalist specializing in international issues, but as one accused of high treason . . . So it is true that in 1934 you were in favor of Trotsky's program of defeat because you thought it was possible in real terms?"

"Yes," said Radek.

"In 1935, however, you considered this program unreal and were against it?"

"Yes."

"Your conversation at the diplomatic reception in 1934 with that gentleman from a Central European embassy was therefore, if I'm not mistaken . . . ?"

"Treason."

"So you concede that? And yet you had your conversation with the said gentleman?"

Radek held himself up with an effort. "From whom, if not from me, did you learn about the encounter? Surely that means, Citizen Prosecutor, that I had the conversation with the man!"

"And thereby knew that it was tantamount to treason against the fatherland?"

"Yes."

Vyshinsky straightened himself up, the brooding conscience in person. "And that didn't dismay you?"

"Of course it dismayed me. Or do you think treason is a daily habit with me?"

This last exchange had been impromptu; and yet, thought Radek, what beautiful, dense dialogue! And where else would they have found so perfect a defendant!

Judge Ulrich rose and put on his beret. "We'll take a break."

During this break they sat in an unadorned room behind the court-room, seventeen in number, the defendants of this second great trial, eating their soup and bread. And again, since the guards ordered them to be silent, Radek could do nothing but look from one to the other and try to guess from their facial expressions what they thought of him and his testimony—though he found this most difficult with those he had never met before his interrogations in the Lubyanka: Some unfortunates who had caused an industrial accident and had thus fallen among the saboteurs, or police creatures who appeared in court in the role of active terrorists, which after all must have existed in a Parallel Anti-Soviet Trotskyist Center.

Especially Serebryakov and Sokolnikov—Pyatakov was sitting there completely apathetic—seemed to want to ask him what he actually intended by the manner and the content of his confessions, and the tone in which he made them; and he would have eagerly told them and explained his great historical game to them: only how and where? And then a court messenger appeared and led him to Vyshinsky.

He was sitting in his private workroom, enjoying himself; the remains of a beef roast were still on the table, and the vodka, and a half-smoked cigar was lying there, and Vyshinsky noticed Radek's greedy look and asked affably, "Want one?"

Radek understood this at the same time as an invitation to sit down, and said yes, he would certainly appreciate a cigar, and at the first smoke already felt the slight dizziness that came from his weakness and the long withdrawal from nicotine.

"I don't agree," Vyshinsky got down to business, "with your deviations from our text, Radek . . ."

"The first deviations," said Radek, "came from you every time, Andrei Yanuaryievich."

"No excuses," he parried. "Sometimes it seems to me that you want to signal to the public that there is something—you will be familiar with the word—not quite kosher about your so nicely formulated confessions."

Vyshinsky, at least, Radek thought, had thus noticed something.

"But I warn you, Radek. Even if, as I suppose, you hope to escape with your life, it's by no means certain how the matter will turn out for you."

Radek's hand, holding the cigar, trembled. This was the first thing he had heard in regard to life and death, his life, his death, and even this seemed more an *à propos* than trustworthy information.

"I don't have to mention particularly," Vyshinsky continued, "we want to create a certain image, which is difficult enough to create, and we don't want to have it destroyed."

"Then why don't you avoid your attempts," Radek replied, "to portray me as a petty scoundrel before our audience. I know you already have to deal with petty criminals by profession; but, in the first place, I'm not one, and, in the second place, although Comrade Stalin will not see it that way, it's better and more effective for your trial, too, if you behave as if you had political brains before you and not tramps."

"What do you expect from this," Vyshinsky asked back, "if you stand up to me? In this situation, Karl Bernhardovich, I'm your only friend!" He stood up, "Let's go. Ulrich doesn't like long lunch breaks."

✴

There they were again in their old places. Vyshinsky, high above him, said, "We were talking about treason. So that's what you committed?"

"That was not my original intention," Radek replied.

"But you do not deny having told the gentleman from the Central European embassy at the reception in 1934 that he could not expect any concessions from the present Soviet government?"

"That was the meaning of my statement."

"That his government, however, could count on concessions from political realists in the country?"

"And that Mr. Trotsky was entitled by us to negotiate for just that."

"Is that treason?"

Radek shrugged. "Of course it's treason."

"But in 1935 the situation in the country presented itself differently to you, and you considered this one betrayal enough. Did I understand you correctly?"

"Yes."

"And what did you do then?"

"I made preparations so that the others would no longer commit treason either. And to decide further."

"And what did you plan," Vyshinsky said, emphasizing each of his words, "what did you plan to propose to your co-conspirators?"

"To go to the Central Committee of the Party and confess everything there."

"And you counted on them following your advice?"

"A number of them did."

"But you alone and for yourself did not want to confess?"

"I considered that this question would have to be decided collectively."

"And at that time did you reduce your own anti-Soviet, counter-revolutionary, and criminal activity to any recognizable degree?"

Radek pretended to have to think. "In 1936 I was something like the head of the Center. In January 1936 I met Pyatakov once again, and from March on I didn't see any of the bloc people. But I also did nothing to undo anything. I simply remained, until my arrest, a member of the Center . . ."

This waiting, he thought, this terrible doing nothing, had indeed been the content of his days then. But for quite different reasons.

"So you have not," Vyshinsky drilled again, "gone to the Central Committee to take up arms?"

"No, I didn't."

"And then they arrested you."

"They arrested me." Radek saw the scene before him in Dom Pravitelstva with Rosa and the child. "And I immediately denied everything. From the beginning to the end. Everything. Won't you ask me why?"

Vyshinsky did not like the direction so clearly now. "I know," he said irritably, "you will always find answers. So you were questioned and had the opportunity to confess to your actions."

"I didn't think the timing was right. I can explain it to you . . ."

But Vyshinsky interrupted him. Vyshinsky, Radek saw, had become very nervous, which must have had something to do with their lunchtime conversation. "Comrade Chairman," Vyshinsky said, "please arrange for the defendant not to make speeches, but to answer my questions."

Ulrich was pleased that he could finally interject. "Defendant Radek, you may make a total of two speeches: one your defense speech, and before the verdict is pronounced, your closing speech."

Radek bowed.

Then Vyshinsky said very measuredly, "You told us, didn't you,

Defendant, that you had a desire to go to the Central Committee and expose yourself?"

"Yes, sir."

"And that the only reason you didn't do it was because they beat you to it and arrested you?"

"Yes, sir."

"I'm asking you now, Radek—on September twenty-second, you were first questioned by examining magistrates. Did you have a chance to confess to your crimes then?"

"But I didn't."

A dead silence fell in the hall.

"You were told the charges against you. You were asked if you pleaded guilty."

"I answered not guilty."

"You were asked if you had been associated with any other persons, and those persons were named to you, and you were confronted with them."

"I already told you, I denied everything, from beginning to end."

"And on November fourth, you were questioned about details of your activities."

"They questioned me until December fourth, day after day, and I kept denying."

"For how many months?"

"Almost three."

Vyshinsky's voice sounded punitive. "You, who had wanted to expose yourself completely and, as you claim, just couldn't make up your mind to hand your people over to the hands of justice, when you found yourself in the hands of justice yourself, categorically denied all you had done? That's how it was?"

Radek felt the gravity of the moment. "Exactly."

"And doesn't that, Defendant Radek, cast doubt on everything you have told us about your deliberations and inner fluctuations?"

Radek raised his hands. "Certainly. But only if you leave aside the fact that you learned about Trotsky's program and instructions, and in general about everything on which your evidence is based, only through me. And you will not want to deny this fact, because"—his voice became cutting—"what would become of your trial otherwise?"

Vyshinsky seemed to freeze. As if, Radek thought, the curse of God had struck him as it had Lot's wife.

6

He began to count his days, his hours. The ukase issued by Stalin after the Kirov murder, which stated that convicted terrorists were to be shot within twenty-four hours of the verdict, was still in effect and would remain in effect until the unfortunate end of the Great Architect—so how many days and nights did he have, Radek, to think about his life and about the life after, in people's memory or wherever else this most shadowy existence played out?

And in the face of all this, he had to endure in this crowded courtroom.

This plea had been written by the Chief Prosecutor himself, without Radek's help: and so it was, lengthy, rambling, full of circumlocutions. "You started with a tiny anti-Party faction!" He went back to the early years of the Revolution and tried to prove that Radek had already then, in Brest-Litovsk, been an opponent of Lenin and the Party; and then only after the death of the great teacher and after the takeover of the Soviet affairs of state by Lenin's master student, the brilliant Stalin. Even then Radek denied the socialist character of our Revolution, denied the possibility of establishing socialism in a single country at all, and sneered that it was like the satirist Saltykov-Shchedrin's introduction of liberalism in a street of a country town in a tsarist governorate; and at that time the betrayal had already been in the offing which had now come to a full outbreak and, via Trotsky, had led to Radek's and the other conspirators' alliance with the German and Japanese fascists, organized in the Parallel Center.

"This trial has shown," Vyshinsky cried, "with what serpentine cold-bloodedness, with what criminal deviousness, the Trotskyist bandits have waged and are still waging their struggle against the Soviet Union, stopping at nothing, be it murder, sabotage, diversionary attacks, espionage, terror, treason against the fatherland!"

Then the variations on the theme came and repeated themselves; Vyshinsky himself seemed to sense the boredom he was spreading, and even more the first major weak point in his argument, and bravely tackled it. "Comrade judges!"

Radek became attentive.

Vyshinsky, through his glasses, fixed his gaze on him. "When we have just heard from the mouths of the leaders of this gang the confession that they actually received directives from Trotsky for the reestablishment of capitalism in the Soviet Union and accepted these directives and directed their nefarious activity accordingly, the question arises, how can men who fought for socialism for so many years and who called themselves Bolshevik-Leninists, how can such men be accused of such monstrous crimes? Is not such an assertion perhaps proof of the worthlessness of their confessions and of the fact that the charges against them are falsely brought and that here men are accused of something which, by the very nature of their earlier revolutionary, socialist, Bolshevik activity, they could not have committed?"

Radek acknowledged Vyshinsky's question with a friendly smile. Yes, how could one really accuse people in such a way?... But Vyshinsky made the answer to his rhetorical question too simple: the accused, he claimed, were by no means such great, noble revolutionaries. Rather, they had always deeply hated the Soviet order, but had known how to camouflage their true feelings, to conceal their true views; they were, as they themselves then admitted, duplicitous.

And he, Radek, especially. Vyshinsky's description of Radek was almost poetic: "Double-tongued and grimacing, he described how Trotsky at that time wanted to tempt him to flee abroad, and how he, Radek, was horrified at the thought of appearing against the Soviet Union under the protection of bourgeois states, and therefore preferred to stay at home. At that time, in 1929, when he reported in our press about Trotsky's plans for robberies of our trade missions abroad, he was in freedom; no Cheka, no GPU, no People's Commissariat for Internal Affairs, no examining magistrate and no public prosecutor bothered him with interrogations; he was a free citizen, he was a journalist, in freedom he smoked his pipe, or cigars, everywhere, and blew the smoke into the eyes of his interlocutors."

Radek thought that he could hardly have described himself better. But Vyshinsky could not find an end. And what else had Radek written at that time? he asked further. That Trotsky had wanted to get money for his anti-Soviet work through these robberies . . . Yes, for what? Radek thought, for vacation trips? And watched the contortions on Vyshinsky's roundish face. "I mean," he said, "you can't help but believe this confession from an authoritative source, made before the Soviet public not from the dock, but in the columns of our press!"

And now, Radek foresaw, the prosecutor would again fall into his old "contradiction." Vyshinsky had to build him up as a key witness, that is, grant him reliability and truthfulness, and at the same time accuse him of duplicity and hypocrisy. "But Radek lied!" proclaimed Vyshinsky. "Radek only pretended. He condemned his own friends to divert the attention of the authorities from himself. Following the method of inveterate criminals, he shouted, Stop thief! and thus tried to escape his responsibility. Over the corpses of his friends he tried to get out of the stinking cesspool in which he himself had long been stuck. The proletarian court, he wrote in reference to Zinoviev and Kamenev, will pass judgment on this gang of criminals dripping with blood. People who raise their hand against the lives of the beloved leaders of the proletariat will have to pay for their boundless guilt with their heads . . . Do you remember, Radek? With this you also wrote your own judgment . . ."

Radek lowered his head. No, he did not look good now.

Vyshinsky had managed to escape from his own contradictions and in return had forced him, Radek, into the corner of hypocrites, opportunists, and denunciators, who committed every villainy just to save their own skin . . . Vyshinsky would sacrifice him ruthlessly.

★

There remained the question of evidence. Everything, the whole trial, was based on confessions, and only in the case of his own confession did he know how it had come about. But were confessions enough? Didn't Vyshinsky—and Stalin—need something more tangible?

Radek was curious; how would Vyshinsky tackle this, his main problem? Vyshinsky began rather awkwardly by explaining that the character of each criminal case at hand determines in advance the nature of its possible proof. He then asserted that it had been proven that the crimes listed in the indictment had been committed and their perpetrators had been conclusively convicted. "We have before us," said Vyshinsky, "a conspiracy, and we have before us a group which intended to carry out a *coup d'état*; but where are the documents? one might now ask, where is the program of which you speak? If such an organization actually exists, where are its material traces—bylaws, minutes, stamps, and so on?"

Vyshinsky straightened up and puffed out his chest. "I dare to state, in accordance with the basic requirements of juridical science, that in criminal cases for conspiracy, for *coups d'état*, you cannot demand, show us minutes, resolutions, membership books, nor demand that the criminals have their activity confirmed by a notary's office."

Then, Radek noticed, Vyshinsky had finally created a little merriment in the hall. "Of course," the prosecutor continued gratefully, "we have a number of documents, but even without them we would consider ourselves entitled to bring charges on the basis of the statements and declarations of the defendants and witnesses and, if you like, on circumstantial evidence."

Meager, thought Radek, meager. But it got even more meager. "To distinguish true from false in court, the judge's experience usually suffices, and any judge who has more than a dozen trials behind him knows when the defendant has told the truth and when he has not. Then in your deliberation room, Comrade Judge, you will analyze the testimonies that have been presented here and ask the question about the motives behind this or that testimony. In any case, the circumstances of our criminal case, which, as you know, have been examined with all due care, convincingly confirm what the defendants have testified before this court. There is no reason to suppose that Pyatakov had not belonged to the Center, that Radek had not been present at diplomatic receptions and had not spoken to Mr. K. and Mr. H. and other gentlemen, or to suppose that he had not, together with Bukharin, served scrambled eggs and sausage to any unofficial persons who had arrived at his house . . ."

Dabbing the sweat from his upper lip, the prosecutor concluded, "If there have been any shortcomings in this trial, they consist not in the fact that the evidence is based on the confessions of the defendants, but in the fact that these defendants have not fully admitted to us their offenses against the Soviet state after all."

Truly, Radek thought, the man would have done better to let him draw up his plea as well. Except for the one nasty bit where Vyshinsky held up to him his, Radek's, stab at Zinoviev and Kamenev, it had been a pretty poor piece of prose—and even that cursing of the sinful pair had, after all, originally come from his pen.

✱

Tea had been brought, for the defendants as well, and Radek sat there, drained after this, the last day of the trial, and drank in small sips, letting the text of the charge, which Vyshinsky now read out, wash over him.

"I charge the members of the Anti-Soviet Trotskyist Parallel Center Pyatakov, Radek, Sokolnikov, Serebryakov, and and and with crimes under the following articles of the Criminal Code: 58-1a, treason against the fatherland; 58-6, espionage; 58-8, terror; 58-9, diversion; 58-11, founding secret criminal organizations. However, Comrade Judge, the main charge in this trial is treason against the fatherland. The law imposes the heaviest punishment on those who have committed this crime against the state, which our great Stalin's constitution rightly calls the gravest misdeed. The law demands that, if proven guilty, the criminals be sentenced to death by firing squad."

The tea-glass was emptied; Radek set it down and admired the equanimity with which he took note of the announcement of his own death: his heart had probably long since become familiar with the thought.

"You will have to decide, Comrade Judge," said the Prosecutor General, "whether you will find circumstances which will permit you to mitigate the punishment in the case of the individuals accused. I myself see no such circumstances. And it is not I alone who accuses. I accuse together with all our people, and I accuse criminals of the lowest kind who deserve only one sentence—death."

But then, Radek did not know why, Vyshinsky's words suddenly penetrated into the deeper layers of his consciousness, and he thought he felt the slight pressure of the pistol's muzzle that they would put into his neck, and he shuddered.

★

"I give the floor to the defendant Radek," announced the chairman.

In the brief pause before that, Vyshinsky had come to him again to warn, "You know, Radek, everything depends on what you say now and how you say it."

And Radek knew Vyshinsky was afraid: afraid that in a few

short sentences, spoken before the guards in the hall had silenced him with brute force, he might undo the effect of the whole long trial and all the previous trials, along with their countless testimonies and confessions; but none of the defendants before him had ever attempted such a thing, nor would those with him on this bench attempt it; they had been conditioned, in long hard work, to total docility, and what he, Radek, was able to do, a word here, a word there, to lay the tracks for those to come, that he had done and would now accomplish in this, his final word.

"Citizen Judges!" he began. "Having pleaded guilty to treason against the fatherland, any defense is out of the question. I can lay even less claim to extenuating circumstances. A person who has stood in the labor movement for three and a half decades, having pleaded guilty to treason against the fatherland, cannot mitigate that guilt by any circumstances whatsoever. Nor can I even claim that Trotsky seduced me. When I met Trotsky for the first time, I was already an adult person with established views. And however great Trotsky's role in all sorts of counterrevolutionary groups, for me his authority was minimal from the moment I myself took up the struggle against the Stalinist direction in the Party."

That was clear enough, he thought, they would believe him, those today, and those in the future, for whom he was really speaking. "I joined Trotsky's organization," he went on, "not for the sake of his theories, the feebleness of which I had understood during my first exile, but because there was no other group on which I could lean for the goals I had set myself. And I voluntarily stayed with this group, based on my own assessment of the situation. I bear full, exclusive responsibility for that."

And thought: now, after the political confession, the exposure of the whole thing, the proof of the most meager construction, which he had already provided once in the dialogue with Vyshinsky, and said, "And with that I could finish the last word, which is mine. But I consider it necessary to object to the light in which the prosecutor has made part of this trial appear. I have admitted my guilt, bitter as it was to me, because I believe in the benefits that the truth can bring to people. But if, in return, I have to hear from the mouth of the public prosecutor that there are simply bandits and spies in the dock here, I object to that—and not in order to defend myself, but for the sake of the evidence in this whole trial, in which the public prosecutor should care even more than I do—he wants to show that the Trotskyist organization has become an agency of those forces which are preparing a new world war."

He threw himself on the barrier that separated him from the judge and observers and prosecutor, and half spoke to the audience. "What proof do you have of this fact? The testimony of only two men: mine, that I received directives and letters from Trotsky—unfortunately I burned these papers—and Pyatakov's testimony that he had spoken to Trotsky personally. All other statements of all other defendants, they are based on both of our statements. So if on this bench there are only criminals and informers, on what will you base your assertions that what we have testified is the truth, the unshakable truth?"

There; Vyshinsky now hung in the net of his own logic; Radek saw him chewing his lip fiercely, and he resolved to advance still further, and more boldly, along the path once taken.

"Even if," he continued, "in view of my confessions I am not entitled to appear as a repentant Communist, my thirty-five years in the labor movement nevertheless entitle me—for all the mistakes with which they ended—to claim confidence on one point: that the masses of the people, by whose side I stood at all times, mean something to me. That is also why I deny the assertion that we are simply criminals who have lost all human traits. I am not fighting for my honor—that is lost—I am fighting so that the piece of truth that is in my statements is recognized here in this hall, and not only here in the hall, but also outside with the many people who do not understand how I could sink so low. It is important to me that these people are convinced from beginning to end and realize why I have made my statements . . ."

His tone had become solemn, and he knew that this was

his testament, and anything else he might say, though important enough, would be a swan song: the summary of what had happened, and, where it could be done, interspersed with it a few subtle corrections to Vyshinsky's version, pointing out its primitiveness.

"...and what kind of picture did I have in front of me? The first stage: Kirov was murdered. Years of terrorist preparation, dozens of prowling squads just waiting for the moment when they could kill a Party leader and the results of the terror, for me personally and in general: the loss of a human life, without any serious change in the political conditions. In order to carry out acts of terror against whole groups of government representatives, we could not get the necessary people to Moscow; that indicated the lack of forces of the organization. And on the other hand, I was too close to the government to imagine that it was possible to overthrow Soviet power by terror alone.... but since, as Trotsky asserts, socialism is impossible in a single country, now, in order to give proof of his theory, the revolution and socialism in this single country were to be destroyed by terror and treachery. Only, and this is conceded by the prosecutor himself, not even a cadre of a hundred men could be brought together with this platform. And Trotsky himself already felt his inner impotence and put his faith in Hitler..."

Vyshinsky, Radek noted, was getting more and more restless; he could not decide: was all his work being destroyed, or was someone building him up? In any case, Radek continued his political account of the conspiracy, which was quite unable to work, until he reached the point where it became serious again, bitterly serious: to his arrest, and his months of silence, which he had to explain so that Vyshinsky's, that is, Stalin's, version of the story would retain its internal coherence.

He had a fresh glass of tea handed to him and drank, slowly, several sips. Then he began, "Was I aware before my arrest that the matter would come down to this? Of course I had been aware of that. So why didn't I go straight to the Party, to the authorities, or at least make a full confession immediately after my arrest? The reason is simple: I was one of the leaders of this Center. I had to give the other members of the organization the time to separate from it and the possibility to confess their guilt to the government as well . . ."

Vyshinsky nodded with satisfaction. This was exactly the argument he himself had suggested to Radek, and Radek had indicated to him that he thought it was a little too simplistic; but now he used it after all.

"And then when I was interrogated," Radek reported further, "the head of the preliminary investigation also understood at once why I did not speak. He told me, you are not a little child after all; there are fifteen statements against you here, you can't wriggle out of it; if you nevertheless remain silent, it is only because you want to gain time and insight; please, check everything yourself."

And thought, grinning inwardly, oh, what a lovely picture of the nature of the NKVD and its behavior! And then, quite the experienced narrator, said, "For two and a half months I tormented the investigating judge. If the question arose here whether we were tortured during the preliminary investigation, I must say that it was not the investigating judge who tortured me, but I tortured the investigating judge by forcing him for two and a half months to hold the statements of the other defendants before me and to discover for me who had confessed and who had not confessed and who had confessed what. After that, he finally came before me and said, 'You are already the last one; why are you wasting your time and ours; why don't you tell us what you have wanted to tell us for a long time?' And I said, 'All right; tomorrow I will begin.' "

Vyshinsky looked directly proud. What a great defendant, he seemed to think, and for what a great trial!

But Radek turned to Ulrich, "And now for the conclusion, Citizen Judge. According to all the rigors of Soviet law, we will bear the responsibility in the conviction that your verdict, whatever it may be, will be a just one. We know that we have no right to speak to the masses; we are not teachers of the people. We, myself included, cannot demand any leniency, we have no right to it, what has been precludes any leniency, and life in the next five or ten years could turn out in such a way that leniency would only become torture. We have understood what historical forces we served as tools. It is unfortunate that, in spite of all our experiences, we have understood this so late; but may our insight be of use to anyone."

It was already late in the evening. Radek hoped that the man behind the lighted window high above the Moskva River, who he so often cursed, would soon hear his concluding words—as would the rest of the world.

The court had retired for deliberation.

There was nothing to do but wait. This, Radek thought, might be his last or, if the executioner took his time, penultimate night, according to Stalin's twenty-four-hour time limit between sentence and execution, and he found it somehow degrading that he had to spend it squatting on such uncomfortable furniture; but they were all sitting here so uncomfortably, waiting for things to happen: the seventeen defendants, like birds on a perch; behind them, separated from them by a barrier, the press representatives; Kotzov, he saw, nodding at him; then the diplomats, first of all Ambassador Davies, the new man from Washington; and behind them, again, the rest of the audience, all privileged people in one way or another, the most prominent among them probably the German novelist Feuchtwanger, whose face, it suddenly struck Radek, bore a strange resemblance to his own.

The hands of the large clock on the wall pointed to shortly before four in the morning, when suddenly life came into the dully dozing courtroom; guards trotted over and brought tea and a piece of bread for the defendants; those among the audience who had stretched their feet at the buffet in the vestibule returned, Vyshinsky and his assistants arrived, freshly shaved and joyfully excited; the scribes cleaned their pens; and at four o'clock sharp the door in the front wall opened, and through the parting dark red curtain the court entered its platform.

All rose and froze in awe, while the presiding judge, Ulrich, and his two associate judges sank into their ornamental armchairs; only Radek put his arm, tenderly almost, around the shoulder of Pyatakov, who was standing to his right, and whispered, "And it was not in vain after all."

Ulrich let the solemn mood take effect: history was being made here. Then he adjusted his red flat beret and began, "Judgment on behalf of the Union of Soviet Socialist Republics."

Pause.

And again, significantly, "The Military Collegium of the Supreme Court of the Union of Soviet Socialist Republics heard in open court in the city of Moscow from January 23 to 30, 1937, the criminal case against . . ."

Then, in an effort at a dispassionate tone, the names. Radek listened; his was, after Pyatakov's and Sokolnikov's, the third: "Radek, Karl Bernhardovich, born in 1885, journalist." And so on and so forth the others, in order of their bureaucratic importance; even here, Radek thought, in the world of political felons, there was a rank order established by Party officials, and he didn't know whether he should feel honored about his relatively high position in it or not.

Then Ulrich read out the register of sins of each of the defendants; there was terror and subversion and treason against the state, malicious activity and thwarting of state plans, arsons and assassinations, up to and including the overturning of Comrade Molotov's car into a rural ditch. Not an accident in the country, not a disaster, not a major catastrophe of the last few years, which could not be attributed to at least one of the defendants here; and the longer the list, the more indignant the tone and the hoarser the voice of the judge; only his, Radek's, mention was kept in strangely general terms, as if they had not been able to find anything specific against him.

Could it be, he asked himself. Would Stalin, who hardly ever fulfilled a promise, and even one so fleetingly hinted at, stick to the one he had made to the author of the Great Architect, of all those with whom he had had conflicts? And hadn't Vyshinsky just now, in his plea, announced that someone like Radek could not count on extenuating circumstances, no, never ever?

"On the basis of the foregoing," Judge Ulrich now read out, "and in accordance with Articles 319 and 320 of the Criminal Procedure Code, the Military Collegium of the Supreme Court of the Union of Soviet Socialist Republics has sentenced Pyatakov, Yuri Leonidovich, and Serebryakov, Leonid Petrovich, who, as members of the Anti-Soviet Trotskyist Center, organized and directly directed the treasonable espionage, diversion, sabotage and terrorist activities, to the maximum sentence: to be shot. Sokolnikov, Grigory Yakovlevich, and Radek, Karl Bernhardovich, who as members of the Anti-Soviet Trotskyist Center were responsible for its criminal activity, but did not directly participate in organizing and carrying out acts of diversion, piracy, espionage and terror, to ten years in prison each . . ."

The rest, the verdicts against the other defendants, he already no longer heard. His full consciousness—and with it the knowledge of the shock he had probably suffered—returned only when the guard in the green, tightened blouse stepped up to him, took him by the elbow, and led him, as the first of the long row of defendants, across the silent courtroom to the exit.

In the doorway, he turned, released himself from the man's grip, and once again sought a familiar glance in the hall, Pyatakov's or anyone else's, with whom he had spent the last few days. Then he raised his hand a little, hinting at a greeting, gave a barely noticeable shrug, and smiled.

Some said his smile was ironic. But in truth it was full of sadness.

✱

No one knows who murdered him, and when, and in which camp, and on whose orders.

Only I, who knew him better than most, can report that at the moment of his death he heard his mother's voice, "Lolek, dear," she cried, "come to me. With me you are safe."

Or had it been Larissa's voice? Or even that of his wife, Rosa? And he went to her.

Thanks to Wolfgang Lubitz, who made his material
on Radek available to me.

—STEFAN HEYM